2011
PUSHCART
PRIZE XXXV
BEST OF THE
SMALL PRESSES

EDITED BY BILL HENDERSON
WITH THE PUSHCART PRIZE EDITORS

Note: nominations for this series are invited from any small, independent, literary book press or magazine in the world, print or online. Up to six nominations—tear sheets or copies, selected from work published, or about to be published, in the calendar year—are accepted by our December 1 deadline each year. Write to Pushcart Fellowships, P.O. Box 380, Wainscott, N.Y. 11975 for more information or consult our websites www.pushcartprize.com. or pushcart press.org.

Acknowledgments

Selections for The Pushcart Prize are reprinted with the permission of authors and presses cited. Copyright reverts to authors and presses immediately after publication.

Distributed by W. W. Norton & Co.
500 Fifth Ave., New York, N.Y. 10110

Library of Congress Card Number: 76–58675
ISBN (hardcover): 978-1-888889-59-8
ISBN (paperback): 978-1-888889-60-4
ISSN: 0149–7863

For Elizabeth Richebourg Rea

INTRODUCTION

THIRTY-FIVE YEARS AGO, from a studio apartment in Yonkers, NY, the Pushcart Prize editors announced their first edition. Then, as now, lots of people helped—among them Paul Bowles, Ralph Ellison, Anaïs Nin, Joyce Carol Oates and Reynolds Price. Then, as now, publishing was in crisis. Conglomerates were snapping up publishers hoping to milk print for a profit. Now, our busy money folks don't even recognize print—fake books (Kindle), and fake publishers (vanity) abound.

My first taste of this contempt for literary culture was as a junior editor at Doubleday, then the world's largest book publisher—over 700 titles a year. I had my own cubicle, my own secretary and my own expense account that I was commanded to spend at lunches regaling literary agents on the glories of Doubleday. We occupied two floors of a Park Avenue office building, owned our printing plant, plus a big jet plane. I flew in that plane once to consult an important author—the only son of a hero President. The plane was supposed to impress the son but when we flew it the mere 60 miles to Valley Forge we discovered no place to land it. So we plunked the jet down far away from our author at the nearest Pennsylvania airport where we rented a Chevy and drove to Valley Forge. Impressive. Back we flew to New York the next day through a horrendous thunderstorm and were met by the company limo. An expensive rendezvous. But what did we care. We had money to squander.

About this time Marshall McLuhan declared, "the medium is the message" and for some reason all the Doubleday executives collapsed in worhip of McLuhan. Books were dead, the execs shuddered. They shredded all the company stationery which identified us as a book publisher and printed new letterheads revealing that we were now a "multi-media corporation"—TV, radio, etc., and, oh yes, books if anybody still cared.

For me at this point Doubleday died. I developed a core mistrust of the bottom line boys and girls. I busied myself with boozing at corporate parties and coaching the company softball team, which I founded as a challenge to *Esquire's* Captain Fiction, Gordon Lish. Our team was more a Central Park picnic than an athletic endeavor. *Esquire* beat us badly. ("It's OK to lose at a ballgame now and then just so you don't lose at the game of life" one Doubleday suit advised me—just before I was fired.)

I started Pushcart Press full time shortly thereafter and over the years witnessed a steady decline of the Doubleday colossus as it was bought and sold over and over and now exists as a mere shell in an odd shotgun marriage with Knopf. I never did find out what happened to the jet plane.

Pushcart, with no jet, but with lots of help from 220 plus volunteer Contributing Editors, nominations from 652 small presses and the earnest, unpaid efforts of our fiction readers and minimally reimbursed poetry co-editors (this year Julie Sheehan and Tom Sleigh) thrives. I have no longing for the Park Avenue cubicle. This backyard shack feels just fine. Plus I can still believe in words for their own sake—that they are sacred—and not be laughed at by those who imagine nothing is holy, especially words.

Thirty-five years—and what an edition this is! Brilliant work from 52 presses (itself a record)—69 stories, memoirs, poems and essays, many from presses never before included here—and so much more brilliance in the Special Mention section, as editor Tom Sleigh notes in his contribution to this introduction.

Our Pushcart Prize thrives (as does our employee owned distributor W.W. Norton) because we've remained independent of any institution and rely only on the support of our readers and the generous gifts of our endowment donors. No corporate or academic folk tromp around here. No politics. It's all very simple. Just words on paper.

o o o

A few years ago we featured the *Bellevue Literary Magazine*—new to us at the time—and this year I was thrilled to learn that a first novel published by Bellevue, *Tinkers* by Paul Harding, won the 2010 Pulitzer Prize.

For 42-year-old Harding it was a surprise culmination of a long hard slog and years of rejection slips (typically—"nobody wants to read a slow, comtemplative, meditative, quiet book") and years while the manuscript languished in a desk drawer.

The story of *Tinkers'* triumph, as reported in the *New York Times*, includes many heroes. First: Erika Goldman, editorial direction of Bellevue, "a deeply and empathetic reader," said Harding. Next, Lisa Solomon, a sales rep for independent press distributor Consortium, passionately flogged the novel to independent bookstores, who in turn took up the cause with their customers and brought it to the attention of Rebecca Pepper Sinkler, Chair of the Pulitzer fiction jury. "I think that sentence for sentence it was the most beautifully written and made the most gorgeous use of language of any of the books we looked at," said Ms. Sinkler.

From passionate small press editor to spirited independent book-sellers to the Pulitzer Prize—none of this could have happened that way in the big, big money world that happily watches independent stores sink under the weight of online giants and chains and purveyors of instant fake books.

❖   ❖   ❖

Speaking of fake, I recently received a semi-literate letter from an ex-ecutive at Northwestern University Press gleefully announcing that 45-year-old *TriQuarterly* was going under. He of course didn't put it quite that way, something about "expanding electronic dissemination and public access to the wonderful literature and essays that are pub-lished in *TriQuarterly*." First of all, I don't get the difference between "literature and essays." Next, I don't know why the beautiful print edi-tion of *TriQuarterly* is being killed for an exclusive online presence. It's simply not the same thing.

The reaction to this gleeful slaughter (as reported in the *Chronicle of Higher Education*) was swift: Jeffrey Lependorf, Executive Direc-tor of the Council of Literary Magazines and Presses, said, "this doesn't feel like the passing of the torch, it feels like the extinguishing of the flame."

Edward Hirsch, President of the Guggenheim Foundation, noted: "I think it's a catastrophe. It's just a terrible idea, and somewhat disgraceful, to take an imaginative, exciting journal . . . and turn it into a student-run, vaporous magazine on the web. Why take some-thing with the prestige and reputation of *TriQuarterly* and basically destroy it."

All this strikes me very close to home. In 1964, the late Charles Newman, a founding editor of the Pushcart Prize series, reinvigorated the early *TriQuarterly* into a national publication. He was succeeded by Elliot Anderson and then by Reginald Gibbons and Susan Hahn. In 1978, Elliot and Mary Kinzie edited TQ's *The Little Magazine in America: A Modern Documentary History*, detailing the history of dozens of 20th century presses with copious photos and illustrations. I was privileged to co-publish *The Little Magazine In America* as a cloth bound edition with *TriQuarterly*.

As I write this, that gorgeous volume sits in a place of honor on my bookshelf, a reminder of the spirit of those days. Rave reviews everywhere. Small press editors flew in for the big celebration night—two parties in one Manhattan evening. First at the Gotham Book Mart and next at George Plimpton's home and *Paris Review* office. George, a friend to Pushcart and all little presses was stuck overhead in a plane and couldn't land because of a rainstorm. Down below we waited for him. At one a.m. the TQ staff, Pushcart's editor and a gaggle of stalwarts, some of us a bit in our cups, greeted the bedraggled, wet George at his front door. And the party continued. There has never been such a little magazine history and probably never such a party night either.

Now it appears that for *TriQuarterly* the party is over. I hope not but I get the feeling as do Lependorf and Hirsch that to pass gas on the internet implies that words are vapor, not worthy of the beautiful *TriQuarterly*/Pushcart volume I now look at on the shelf which has not evaporated; it's there, it's real, I can touch it, admire the binding, the printing and the editors who contributed and I can remember the night we greeted George Plimpton at his front door barring his way with our joy.

❊   ❊   ❊

This book you hold in your hands, this PPXXXV, is there because of the generosity of a dear friend who died last year—Barbara Thompson Davis. In 2001, it seemed we could not survive. Printing costs had soared and in the wake of 9/11 sales had declined. We decided to start an endowment to save the Prize. We announced our goals, sure of a response from two dozen well-heeled prospects, and were shocked to our sneakers when nobody replied except Barbara. Gloom was thick in those days. If Barbara hadn't come through in a big way and reassured us that our endowment goals were indeed possible, I don't think the Prize would have reached its 35th birthday. Barbara herself was a two-time winner of the Pushcart Prize—for her stories "Tattoo" (PPVII) and "Crossing" (PPIX), and a constant cheerful friend and neighbor. We are here because she was there when we needed her.

⁂ ⁂ ⁂

Every year I ask our guest poetry editors to report to our readers on the experience of sifting through thousands of poems. This year Julie Sheehan and Tom Sleigh did the impossible.

Julie Sheehan's three poetry collections are *Bar Book: Poems & Otherwise*, *Orient Point* and *Thaw*. Her honors include a Whiting Writers' Award, the Elizabeth Matchett Stover Award from *Southwest Review*, the Robert H. Winner prize from Poetry Society of America, the Barnard Women Poets Prize and, from *Paris Review*, the Bernard F. Conners Prize.

Julie reports:

"Having read an estimated 1,800 poems nominated for a Pushcart Prize (a mere half of the nominees), I'm happy to report that the state of the art is very good indeed. I found a rich range of sensibilities treating an equally rich range of subjects—war, history, economics, art, death, love, God, the weather—with imagination and verve. And not always in the first person. And not always in long raggedy lines, or tight fisted lines, or received form, or improvised ones. And not always in narrative or meditative or dramatic or lyric modes. I found music and thought. I found excellent journals I'd never heard of publishing excellent work. We live among many voices asserting themselves in elegant language. Ignore the whiners who complain that post-modernism is destroying readers, that poems are too difficult or too accessible, that MFA programs are producing cookie cutter poets, or that too much poetry is being published. Bring it on! My only regret is that I had to choose a handful from this embarrassment of riches, an impossible albeit joyful task. I had wanted to choose 'D) all of the above,' but, alas, it was not on the test."

Tom Sleigh's most recent book of poetry *Space Walk*, won the Kingsley Tufts Award. His new book, *Army Cats*, is forthcoming in spring of 2011 from Graywolf. He has won many awards, including the Keats-

Shelley Prize, and grants from the Lila Wallace Fund, the American Academy of Arts and Letters, American Academy in Berlin, the Guggenheim Foundation and the National Endowment for the Arts.

Tom reports:

"Most polemics about American poetry collapse before the actual experience of reading it. So when Bill asked me to edit this edition with Julie Sheehan, I was curious to see what I'd find. Of course, there's a period style that comes out of Ashbery, the New York School, and the casualness of the blogosphere. And there's a period style based on personal recollection that comes out of Lowell, Bishop, and reality TV. The differences between these two modes have been discussed to death, particularly in the academy, so that any poet reading this book will know the basic drift: a language self or a personal self? Poetry as a cultural construct or the product of a daemon?

"But the actual experience of reading it, what happened to me as I read, revealed two basic facts: the polemics may be polarized, but the poets I selected for this volume know better: autobiographical lyric and conventions of fragmentation seem to have melded together. All the bloviation about personal narrative being obsolete, or breastbeating about the death of the self/author, have been transfigured to a more sophisticated understanding of both positions. Conventions of fragmentation can't be reduced to a set of quirky moves. A lyric self better be a language self first.

"As to the poems I included in this Pushcart, they need no explanation. But I do want to call attention to the Special Mentions, since only a dedicated reader will set out to find the poems on their own: Janice Harrington and Margaret Reges write description as a form of revelation, but without forsaking the physical. Jeffrey Harrison, Edward Field, and Philip Dacey are pitch perfect at reproducing what feels like actual speech, other people's as well as their own. Adam Day, Mary Leader, Pimone Triplett, and Jacqueline Osherow make complex hybrids of personal narrative and historical fact. Beth Bachmann and Mary Ruefle write off-center lyrics that nonetheless find their own path to lyric closure. Stephen Burt, Rebecca Seiferle, and Susan Holahan write a form of satire that includes lyric, polemic, and compassionate humor."

❖ ❖ ❖

As Julie's and Tom's statements indicate, an immense amount of energy went into the making of this 35th edition. That energy began of course with the thousands of poets and writers nominated, many of them in writing courses, many of them on their own in any number of places and occupations. Thank you.

To our readers, as every year, I say thank you. To the teachers of writing, such as Fred Leebron at Gettysburg College, who use the PP as a text, (Fred comments "Pushcart is must reading . . . an indispensable teaching tool,") I repeat my thank you.

To the hundreds of editors, and the donors to our endowment who make this book happen each year, all I can say is that I am very grateful.

It's not about speed, or money, or glory. It's all from the heart.

BH

11

THE PEOPLE WHO HELPED

FOUNDING EDITORS—Anaïs Nin (1903–1977), Buckminster Fuller (1895–1983), Charles Newman (1938–2006), Daniel Halpern, Gordon Lish, Harry Smith, Hugh Fox, Ishmael Reed, Joyce Carol Oates, Len Fulton, Leonard Randolph, Leslie Fiedler (1917–2003), Nona Balakian (1918–1991), Paul Bowles (1910–1999), Paul Engle (1908–1991), Ralph Ellison (1914–1994), Reynolds Price, Rhoda Schwartz, Richard Morris, Ted Wilentz (1915–2001), Tom Montag, William Phillips (1907–2002). Poetry editor: H. L. Van Brunt

CONTRIBUTING EDITORS FOR THIS EDITION—*Kim Addonizio, Dan Albergotti, Carolyn Alessio, Dick Allen, John Allman, Daniel Anderson, Idris Anderson, Antler, Philip Appleman, Tony Ardizzone, Renee Ashley, David Baker, Kim Barnes, Tony Barnstone, Ellen Bass, Claire Bateman, Bruce Beasley, Marvin Bell, Karen E. Bender, Pinckney Benedict, Ciaran Berry, Marie-Helene Bertino, Linda Bierds, Diann Blakely, Marianne Boruch, Michael Bowden, Betsy Boyd, John Bradley, Geoffrey Brock, Fleda Brown, Rosellen Brown, Michael Dennis Browne, Christopher Buckley, Andrea Hollander Budy, E. S. Bumas, Richard Burgin, Shannon Cain, Kathy J. Callaway, Kim Chinquee, Suzanne Cleary, Michael Collier, Jeremy Collins, Martha Collins, Robert Cording, Stephen Corey, Michael Czyzniejewski, Phil Dacey, Claire Davis, Chard deNiord, Ted Deppe, Sharon Dilworth, Matt Donovan, Rita Dove, Jack Driscoll, John Drury, Karl Elder, Angie Estes, Peter Everwine, Kathy Fagan, Ed Falco, Tom Filer, Gary Fincke, Chris Forhan, Ben Fountain, H. E. Francis, John Fulton, Richard Garcia, Scott Geiger, Reginald Gibbons, Gary Gildner, Marilyn Hacker, Susan Hahn, Mark Halliday, Jeffrey*

Hammond, James Harms, Jeffrey Harrison, Michael Heffernan, Daniel L. Henry, William Heyen, Bob Hicok, Kathleen Hill, Jane Hirshfield, Ted Hoagland, Christie Hodgen, Daniel Hoffman, Helen H. Houghton, Christopher Howell, Joe Hurka, Colette Inez, Mark Irwin, David Jauss, Jeff P. Jones, Laura Kasischke, Deborah Keenan, George Keithley, Brigit Pegeen Kelly, Thomas E. Kennedy, Kristin King, David Kirby, John Kistner, Judith Kitchen, Richard Kostelanetz, Maxine Kumin, Mary Kuryla, Wally Lamb, Dorianne Laux, Fred Leebron, Dana Levin, Philip Levine, E. J. Levy, Daniel S. Libman, Gerald Locklin, Rachel Loden, William Lychack, Amos Magliocco, Greil Marcus, Kathryn Maris, Clancy Martin, Michael Martone, Dan Masterson, Alice Mattison, Tracy Mayor, Robert McBrearty, Nancy McCabe, Rebecca McClanahan, Erin McGraw, Elizabeth McKenzie, Charles McLeod, Wesley McNair, Joseph Millar, Jim Moore, Joan Murray, Kirk Nesset, Aimee Nezhukumatathil, Joyce Carol Oates, Lance Olsen, Dzvinia Orlowsky, Peter Orner, Alan Michael Parker, Edith Pearlman, Lydia Peelle, Ben Percy, Lucia Perillo, Donald Platt, Andrew Porter, Joe Ashby Porter, C. E. Poverman, Sara Pritchard, Kevin Prufer, Lia Purpura, James Reiss, Paisley Rekdal, Donald Revell, Nancy Richard, Atsuro Riley, Katrina Roberts, Jessica Roeder, Gibbons Ruark, Vern Rutsala, Kay Ryan, Maxine Scates, Alice Schell, Brandon R. Schrand, Grace Schulman, Philip Schultz, Lloyd Schwartz, Salvatore Scibona, Maureen Seaton, Gerald Shapiro, Gary Short, Floyd Skloot, Arthur Smith, R. T. Smith, Debra Spark, Elizabeth Spires, David St. John, Maura Stanton, Maureen Stanton, Patricia Staton, Gerald Stern, Pamela Stewart, Terese Svoboda, Janet Sylvester, Ron Tanner, Katherine Taylor, Lysley Tenorio, Susan Terris, Robert Thomas, Jean Thompson, Melanie Rae Thon, Pauls Toutonghi, Alison Townsend, Lee Upton, Laura van den Berg, Dennis Vannatta, G. C. Waldrep, Sylvia Watanabe, Don Waters, Mary Yukari Waters, Michael Waters, Charles Harper Webb, Roger Weingarten, William Wenthe, Philip White, Dara Wier, Diane Williams, Naomi J. Williams, Eleanor Wilner, S. L. Wisenberg, Mark Wisniewski, David Wojahn, Carolyne Wright, Robert Wrigley, David Yezzi, Matt Yurdana, Christina Zawadiwsky, Paul Zimmer

PAST POETRY EDITORS—H.L. Van Brunt, Naomi Lazard, Lynne Spaulding, Herb Leibowitz, Jon Galassi, Grace Schulman, Carolyn Forché, Gerald Stern, Stanley Plumly, William Stafford, Philip Levine, David Wojahn, Jorie Graham, Robert Hass, Philip Booth, Jay Meek,

CONTENTS

THE RIVER NEMUNAS

fiction by ANTHONY DOERR

from TIN HOUSE

I'm fifteen years old. My parents are dead. I have a poodle named Mishap in a pet carrier between my ankles and a biography of Emily Dickinson in my lap. The flight attendant keeps refilling my apple juice. I'm thirty-six thousand feet over the Atlantic Ocean. Out my little smudgy window the whole world has turned to water.

I'm moving to Lithuania. Lithuania is in the upper right corner of Europe. Over by Russia. On the world map at school, Lithuania is pink.

Grandpa Z is waiting for me outside baggage claim. His belly looks big enough to fit a baby inside. He hugs me for a long time. Then he lifts Mishap out of his carrier and hugs Mishap, too.

Lithuania doesn't look pink. More like gray. Grandpa Z's little Peugeot is green and smells like rock dust. The sky sits low over the highway. We drive for a long time, past hundreds of half-finished concrete apartment buildings that look like they've been set here by the retreat of a huge flood. There are big Nokia signs and bigger Aquafresh signs.

Grandpa Z says, Aquafresh is good toothpaste. You have Aquafresh in Kansas?

I tell him we used Colgate.

He says, I find you Colgate.

We merge onto a four-lane divided highway. The land on both sides is broken into pastures that look awfully muddy for early July. It starts to rain. The Peugeot has no windshield wipers. Mishap dozes in my lap. Lithuania turns a steamy green. Grandpa Z drives with his head out the window.

Eventually we stop at a house with a peaked wooden roof and a central chimney. It looks exactly like the twenty other houses crowded in around it.

Home, says Grandpa Z, and Mishap jumps out.

The house is long and narrow, like a train car. Grandpa Z has three rooms: a kitchen in front, a bedroom in the middle, and a bathroom in the back. Outside there's a shed. He unfolds a card table. He brings me a little stack of Pringles on a plate. Then a steak. No green beans, no dinner rolls, nothing like that. We sit on the edge of his bed to eat. Grandpa Z doesn't say grace so I whisper it to myself. Bless us O Lord and these thy gifts. Mishap sniffs around skeptically between my feet.

Halfway through his steak Grandpa Z looks up at me and there are tears on his cheeks.

It's okay, I say. I've been saying it's okay a lot lately. I've said it to church ladies and flight attendants and counselors. I say, I'm fine, it's okay. I don't know if I'm fine or if it's okay, or if saying it makes anyone feel better. Mostly it's just something to say.

o   o   o

It was cancer. In case you were wondering. First they found it in Mom and she got her breasts cut off and her ovaries cut out but it was still in her, and then Dad got tested and it was in his lungs. I imagined cancer as a tree: a big, black, leafless tree inside Mom and another inside Dad. Mom's tree killed her in May. Dad's killed him three weeks later.

I'm an only child and have no other relatives so the lawyers sent me to live with Grandpa Z. The Z is for Zydrunas.

Grandpa Z's bed is in the kitchen because he's giving me the bedroom. The walls are bare plaster and the bed groans and the sheets smell like dust on a hot bulb. There's no shade on the window. On the dresser is a brand-new pink panda, which is sort of for babies, but also sort of cute. A price tag is still pinned to its ear: 39.99 L. The L is for Litas. I don't know if 39.99 is a lot or a little.

After I turn off the lamp, all I see is black. Something goes tap tap tap against the ceiling. I can hear Mishap panting at the foot of the bed. My three duffel bags, stacked against the wall, contain everything I own in the world.

Do I sound faraway? Do I sound lost? Probably I am. I whisper: Dear God, please watch over Mom in Heaven and please watch over

Dad in heaven and please watch over me in Lithuania. And please watch over Mishap, too. And Grandpa Z.

And then I feel the Big Sadness coming on, like there's a shiny and sharp ax blade buried inside my chest. The only way I can stay alive is to remain absolutely motionless so instead of whispering Dear God how could you do this to me, I only whisper Amen which Pastor Jenks back home told me means I believe, and I lay with my eyelids closed clutching Mishap and inhaling his smell, which always smells to me like corn chips, and practice breathing in light and breathing out a color—light, green, light, yellow—like the counselor told me to do when the panic comes.

*　*　*

At 4 a.m. the sun is already up. I sit in a lawn chair beside Grandpa's shed and watch Mishap sniff around in Lithuania. The sky is silver and big scarves of mist drag through the fields. A hundred little black birds land on the roof of Grandpa's shed, then take off again.

Each house in Grandpa Z's little cluster of houses has lace curtains in the windows. The houses are all the same but the lace is different in each one. One has a floral pattern, one a linear pattern, and another has circles butted up against each other. As I look, an old woman pushes aside a zig-zag-patterned curtain in one of the windows. She puts on a pair of huge glasses and waves me over and I can see there are tubes hooked through her nose.

Her house is twenty feet away from Grandpa Z's and it's full of Virgin Mary statues and herbs and smells like carrot peels. A man in a track suit in the back room is asleep on a bed. The old lady unhooks herself from a machine that looks like two scuba tanks hung on a wheeled rack, and she pats the couch and says a bunch of words to me in Russian. Her mouth is full of gold. She has a marble-sized mole under her right eye. Her calves are like bowling pins and her toes look beaten and crushed.

She nods at something I don't say and turns on a massive flat-screen television propped up on two cinderblocks, and together we watch a pastor give mass on TV. The colors are skewed and the audio is garbled. In his church there are maybe twenty-five people in folding chairs. When I was a baby mom talked to me in Lithuanian so I can understand some of the pastor's sermon. There's something about his daddy falling off his roof. He says this means that just because you

21

can't see something doesn't mean you shouldn't believe in it. I can't tell if he means Jesus or gravity.

Afterward the old lady brings me a big hot stuffed potato covered with bacon bits. She watches me eat through her huge, steamy eyeglasses.

Thanks, I say in Lithuanian, which sounds like achoo. She stares off into oblivion.

When I get back to Grandpa Z's house he has a magazine open in his lap with space diagrams in it.

You are at Mrs. Sabo's?

I was. Past tense, Grandpa.

Grandpa Z circles a finger beside his ear. Mrs. Sabo no more remember things, he says. You understand?

I nod.

I read here, Grandpa Z says, clearing his throat, that Earth has three moons. He bites his lower lip, thinking through the English. No, it used to has three moons. Earth used to has three moons. Long time ago. What do you think of this?

◦ ◦ ◦

You want to know? What it's like? To prop up the dam? To keep your fingers plugged in its cracks? To feel like every single breath that passes is another betrayal, another step farther away from what you were and where you were and who you were, another step deeper into the darkness?

Grandpa Z came to Kansas twice this spring. He sat in the rooms and smelled the smells. Now he leans forward till I can see the little red lightning bolts of veins in his eyes. You want to speak?

No thanks, Grandpa Z.

I mean talk, he says. Talk, Allie?

No. Thanks.

No? But to talk is good, no?

Grandpa Z makes gravestones. Gravestones in Lithuania aren't quite like the ones in America. They're glossy and smooth and made of granite, but most of them are etched with likenesses of the people buried underneath them. They're like black-and-white photos carved right into the stones. They're expensive and everyone spends money on them. Poor people, Grandpa Z says, spend the most. Some times he etches faces while other times he does the deceased's whole body, like a tall man standing in a leather jacket, life-size, very realistic, buttons on the cuffs and freckles on the cheeks. Grandpa Z shows me a Polaroid of a tombstone he made of a famous mobster. The stone is seven feet tall and has a life-size portrait of a suited man with his hands in his pockets sitting on the hood of a Mercedes. He says the family paid extra to have a halo added around the man's head.

Monday morning Grandpa Z goes to his workshop and school doesn't start for two months so I'm left alone in the house. By noon I've looked through all of Grandpa Z's drawers and his one closet. In the shed I find two fishing rods and an old aluminum boat under a tarp and eight jars of Lithuanian pennies and thousands of mouse-chewed British magazines: *Popular Science* and *Science Now* and *British Association for the Advancement of Physics*. There are magazines on polar bears and Mayan calendars and cell biology and lots of things I don't understand. Inside are faded cosmonauts and gorillas hooked up to machines and cartoon cars driving around on Mars.

Then Mrs. Sabo shows up. She shouts something in her derelict Russian and goes over to a chest of drawers and pulls open a cigarette box and inside are photographs.

Motina, she says, and points to me.

I say, I thought you couldn't remember things.

But she is sticking the photos under my nose like she has just remembered something and wants to get it out before she forgets it. Motina means Mom. All of the photos contain Mom when she was a girl. Here she is in a polar bear costume and here she is frowning over what might be an upturned lawnmower and here she is tramping barefoot through mud.

Mrs. Sabo and I lay out the pictures in a grid on Grandpa Z's card table. There are sixty-eight of them. Five-year-old Mom scowls in front of a rusted-out Soviet tank. Six-year-old Mom peels an orange. Nine-year-old Mom stands in the weeds. Looking at the photos starts a feeling in my gut like maybe I want to dig a shallow hole in the yard and lie down in it.

I separate out twelve of the pictures. In each of them, my mom—my Subaru-driving, cashew-eating, Barry-Manilow-listening, Lithuanian-immigrant, dead-because-of-cancer mom—is either standing in murky water or leaning over the side of a junky-looking boat, helping to hold up some part of a creepy and gigantic shark.

Erketas, Mrs. Sabo says, and nods gravely. Then she coughs for about two minutes straight.

Erketas?

23

But by now the coughing has shaken all the comprehension out of her. The man in the track suit comes over and says something and Mrs. Sabo stares at the lower part of his face for a while and eventually the man coaxes her back to her house. Grandpa Z comes home from his job at 2:31.

Grandpa, I say, your toilet paper might as well be made out of gravel.

He nods thoughtfully.

And is this my mom, I ask, with all these great whites?

Grandpa looks at the pictures and blinks and puts a knuckle between his teeth. For maybe thirty seconds he doesn't answer. He looks like he's standing outside an elevator waiting for the doors to open.

Finally he says, Erketas. He goes to a book in a box on the floor and opens it and pages through it and looks up and looks back down and says, Sturgeon.

Sturgeon. Erketas means sturgeon?

River fish. From the river.

We eat sausage for dinner. No bread, no salad. All through the meal the photos of Mom stare up at us.

I rinse the dishes. Grandpa Z says, You walk with me, Allie?

He leads me and Mishap across the field behind the colony of houses. There are neat little vegetable gardens and goats staked here and there. Grasshoppers skitter out in front of us. We clamber over a fence and pick our way around cow dung and nettles. The little trail heads toward some willows and on the other side of the willows is a river: quiet and brown, surprisingly far across. At first the river looks motionless, like a lake, but the more I look, the more I see it's moving very slowly.

Mishap sneezes. I don't think he's ever seen a river before. A line of cows saunters along on the far bank.

Grandpa Z says, Fishing. Is where your mother goes. Used to go. Past tense. He laughs an unsmiling laugh. Sometimes with her grandpa. Sometimes with Mrs. Sabo.

What's it called?

The River Nemunas. It is called the River Nemunas.

◦ ◦ ◦

Every hour the thought floats to the surface: If we're all going to end up happy together in Heaven then why does anyone wait? Every hour the Big Sadness hangs behind my ribs, sharp and gleaming, and it's all I can do to keep breathing.

Mrs. Sabo, Grandpa Z says, is either ninety years old or ninety-four years old. Not even her son knows for sure. She has lived through the first Lithuanian independence and the second one, too. She fought with the Russians the first time, against them the second time. Back when all these houses were a communal farm under the Soviets, she used to take a rowboat every day for thirty-five years and row six miles up the river to work in a chemical plant. She went fishing when no women went fishing, he says.

Nowadays Mrs. Sabo has to be hooked up to her oxygen machine every night. She doesn't seem to mind if I come over to watch TV. We turn the volume up really high to hear over the wheezing and banging of her pump. Sometimes we watch the Lithuanian pastor, sometimes we watch cartoons. Sometimes it's so late we only watch a channel that shows a satellite map of the world, rotating forever across the screen.

* * *

I've been in Lithuania two weeks when Counselor Mike calls on Grandpa Z's cell phone. Counselor Mike, a lawyer who chews bubblegum and wears basketball shorts. It's two in the morning in Kansas. He asks how I'm adjusting. Hearing his wide-open American voice calls up for me, in a sudden rush, summertime Kansas. It's like it's right there on the other end of the phone, the air silky, the last porch lights switched off, a fog of gnats hovering above Brown's pond, the moon coming to earth through sheets and layers and curtains of moisture, streetlights sending soft columns of light onto grocery store parking lots. And somewhere in that sleepy darkness Counselor Mike sits at his clunky kitchen table in his socks and asks an orphan in Lithuania how she's adjusting.

It takes me a full ten seconds to say, I'm fine, it's okay.

He says he needs to talk to Grandpa. We got an offer on the house, he says. Grown-up stuff.

Is the offer good?

Any offer is good.

I don't know what to say to that. I can hear music coming from his end, faraway and full of static. What does Counselor Mike listen to, deep in the Kansas night?

We're praying for you, Allie, he says.

25

Who's we?

Us at the office. And at church. Everyone. Everyone is praying for you.

Grandpa's at work, I say.

Then I walk Mishap across the field and over the fence and through the rocks to the river. The cows are still on the far side, eating whatever cows eat and whipping their tails back and forth.

Five thousand miles away Counselor Mike is staying up late to plan the sale of the orange plastic tiles Dad glues to the basement floor and the dent I put in the dining room wall and the raspberry bushes Mom planted in the backyard. He's going to sell our warped baking sheets and half-used shampoos and the six Jedi drinking glasses we got from Pizza Hut that Dad said we could keep only after asking our pastor if Star Wars would have been "endorsed by Jesus." Everything, all of it, our junk, our detritus, our memories. And I've got the family poodle and three duffel bags of too-small clothes and four photo albums, but no one left who can flesh out any of the photos. I'm five thousand miles and four weeks away and every minute that ratchets past is another minute that the world has kept on turning without Mom and Dad in it. And I'm supposed to live with Grandpa Z in Lithuania, what, for the rest of my life?

Thinking about the house sitting there empty back in Kansas starts the Big Sadness swinging in my chest like a pendulum and soon a blue nothingness is creeping around the edges of my vision. It comes on fast this time and the ax blade is slicing up organs willy-nilly and all of the sudden it feels like I'm looking into a very blue bag and someone's yanking the drawstring closed. I fall over into the willows.

I lie there for who knows how long. Up in the sky I see Dad emptying his pockets after work, dumping coins and breath mints and business cards onto the kitchen counter. I see mom cutting a fried chicken breast into tiny white triangles and dunking each piece in ketchup. I see the Virgin Mary walk out onto a little balcony between the clouds and look around and take ahold of French doors, one on either side of her, and slam them shut.

I can hear Mishap sniffing around nearby. I can hear the river sliding past and grasshoppers chewing the leaves and the sad, dreamy clanking of faraway cowbells. The sun is tiny and flame-blue. When I finally sit up, Mrs. Sabo is standing beside me. I didn't know she could walk so far. Little white butterflies are looping through the willows. The river glides past. She says something in machine-gun Russian and

26

I sit up and she sets her frozen hand on my forehead. Then we watch the river, Mrs. Sabo and Mishap and me, in the grass in the sun. And as we watch the water, and breathe, and I come back into myself—I swear—a fish as big as a nuclear missile leaps out of the river. Its belly is spotless white and its back is gray and it curls up in mid-air and flaps its tail and stretches like it's thinking. This time gravity will let me go.

When it comes back down, water explodes far enough across the river that some drops land on my feet.

Mishap raises his ears, cocks his head. The river heals itself over. Mrs. Sabo looks at me from behind her huge eyeglasses and blinks her milky eyes a dozen times.

Did you see that? Please tell me you saw that.

Mrs. Sabo only blinks.

Grandpa Z gets home at 3:29.

I bought you a surprise, he says. He opens the hatchback of the Peugeot and inside is a crate of American toilet paper.

Grandpa, I say. I want to go fishing.

*   *   *

Dad used to say God made the world and everything in it and Grandpa Z would say if God made the world and everything in it, then why isn't everything perfect? Why do we get backaches and why do beautiful healthy daughters get cancer? Then Dad would say well, God was a mystery and Grandpa Z would say God was a, what's the word, a security blanket for babies, and Dad would stomp off and Mom would throw down her napkin and blast some Lithuanian words at Grandpa and go jogging after Dad and I'd look at the plates on the table.

Grandpa Z crossed the ocean twice this spring to watch his daughter and son-in-law die. Did God have explanations for that? Now I stand in Grandpa Z's kitchen and listen to him say that there aren't any sturgeon anymore in the River Nemunas. There might be some left in the Baltic Sea, he says, but there aren't any in the river. He says his dad used to take Mom sturgeon fishing every Sunday for years and Mrs. Sabo probably caught a few in the old days but then there was overfishing and pesticides and the Kaunas dam and black-market caviar and his dad died and the last sturgeon died and the Soviet Union broke up and Mom grew up and went to university in the United States and married a creationist and no one has caught a sturgeon in the Nemunas River for twenty-five years.

27

Grandpa, I say, Mrs. Sabo and I saw a sturgeon. Today. Right over there. And I point out the window across the field to the line of willows.

It is photos, he says. You see the photos of your mother.

I saw a sturgeon, I say. Not in a picture. In the river.

Grandpa Z closes his eyelids and opens them. Then he holds me by the shoulders and looks me in the eyes and says, We see things. Sometimes they there. Sometimes they not there. We see them the same either way. You understand?

*　*　*

I saw a sturgeon. So did Mrs. Sabo. I go to bed and wake up mad. I throw the stuffed panda against the wall and stomp around on the porch and kick gravel in the driveway. Mishap barks at me.

In the morning I watch Grandpa Z drive off to work, big and pot-bellied and confused, and I can hear Mrs. Sabo's machine whirring and thunking in her house next door and I think: I should have told Grandpa Z to trust me. I should have told him about the pastor's old daddy and the stepladder and Jesus and gravity and how just because you don't see something doesn't mean you shouldn't believe in it.

Instead I wade into Grandpa Z's shed and start pulling out boxes and granite samples and chisels and rock saws and it takes me a half hour to clear a path and another half hour to drag the old aluminum boat into the driveway. It's flat-bottomed and has three bench seats and there are maybe a thousand spiders living beneath each one. I blast them out with a hose. I find a bottle of some toxic Lithuanian cleaner and I pour it all over the hull.

After a while Mrs. Sabo comes tottering out in her big eyeglasses and her little arms and looks at me like a praying mantis. She lets off a chain of coughs. Her son comes out in his track suit with a cigarette between his lips and he watches me work for ten minutes or so and then he leads his mother back inside.

Grandpa Z gets home at 3:27. There are boxes and hoses and rakes and tools all over the driveway. The bottle of solvent has left bright, silver streaks across the hull of the boat. I say, Mrs. Sabo and I saw a sturgeon in the river yesterday, Grandpa.

Grandpa Z blinks at me. He looks like maybe he's looking into the past at something he thought had ended a long time ago.

He says, No more sturgeon in the Nemunas.

I say, I want to try to catch one.

28

They not here, Grandpa Z says. They endangered species. It means—

I know what it means.

He looks from me to the boat to Mishap to me. He takes off his hat and drags his hand through his hair and puts his hat back on. Then he nudges the boat with the toe of his sneaker and shakes his head and Mishap wags his tail and a cloud blows out of the way. Sunlight explodes off of everything.

❋ ❋ ❋

I use an ancient, flat-tired dolly to drag the boat through the field and over the fence to the river. It takes me three hours. Then I lug the oars and fishing poles down. Then I walk back and tell Mrs. Sabo's son I'm taking her out on the river and guide Mrs. Sabo by the arm and lead her across the field and sit her in the bow of the boat. In the sunlight her skin looks like old candle wax.

We fish with blunt, seven-foot rods and ancient hooks that are as big as my hand. We use worms. Mrs. Sabo's face stays completely expressionless. The current is very slow and it's easy to paddle once in a while and keep the boat in the center of the river.

Mishap sits on the bench beside Mrs. Sabo and shivers with excitement. The river slips along. We see a whole herd of feral cats sleeping on a boulder in the sun. We see a deer twitching its ears in the shallows. Black and gray and green walls of trees slide past.

In the late afternoon I pull onto what turns out to be an island and Mrs. Sabo steps out of the boat and lifts up her housedress and has a long pee in the willows. I open a can of Pringles and we share it.

Did you know my mother? I ask Mrs. Sabo but she only glances over at me and gives me a dreamy look. As if she knows everything but I wouldn't understand. Her eyes are a thousand miles away. I like to think she's remembering other trips down the river, other afternoons in the sun. I read to her from one of Grandpa Z's nature magazines. I tell her a bald eagle's feathers weigh twice as much as its bones. I tell her aardvarks drink their water by eating cucumbers. I tell her that male emperor moths can smell female emperor moths flapping along six miles away.

It takes me a couple of hours of rowing to get back home. We watch big pivot sprinklers spray rainbows over a field of potatoes and we watch a thousand boxcars go rattling along behind a train. It's beautiful out here, I say.

Mrs. Sabo looks up. Remember? she asks in Lithuanian. But she doesn't say anything else.

We don't catch any fish. Mishap falls asleep. Mrs. Sabo's knees get sunburned.

❖ ❖ ❖

That one day is all it takes. Every morning Grandpa Z leaves to go carve dead people's faces into granite, and as soon as he's gone I take Mrs. Sabo out in the boat. An old-timer six houses down tells me I should be using rotten hamburger meat, not worms, and that I should stuff it inside the toes of pantyhose and tie the pantyhose to the hooks with elastic thread. So I get some hamburger and put it in a bucket in the sun until it smells like hell, but the pantyhose won't stay on the hook, and a lady at the convenience story in Mažeikiai says she hasn't seen a sturgeon in fifty years but when there were sturgeon they didn't want rotten food, they wanted fresh sand shrimp on big hooks.

I try deep holes behind rapids and eddies beside fields of bright yellow flowers and big, blue, shadowy troughs. I try clams and night crawlers and—once—frozen chicken thighs. I keep thinking Mrs. Sabo will pipe up, will remember, will tell me how it's done. But mostly she sits there with that long-gone look on her face. My brain gradually becomes like a map of the river bottom: gravel bars, two sunken cars with their rust-chewed rooftops just below the surface, long stretches of still water seething with trash. You'd think the surface of a river would be steady but it isn't. There are all these churnings and swirls and eddies, bubblings and blossomings, submerged stumps and plastic bags and spinning crowns of light down there, and when the sun is right sometimes you can see forty feet down.

We don't catch a sturgeon. We don't even see any. I begin to think maybe Grandpa Z is right, maybe sometimes the things we think we see aren't really what we see. But here's the surprising thing: It doesn't bother me. I like being out there with Mrs. Sabo. She seems okay with it, her son seems okay with it, and maybe I'm okay with it, too. Maybe it feels as if the wretchedness in my gut might be getting a little smaller.

When I was five I got an infection and Dr. Nasser put some drops in my eyes. Pretty soon all I could see were blurs and colors. Dad was a fog and Mom was a smudge and the world looked like it does when your eyes are completely full of tears. Four hours later, right around when Dr. Nasser said it would, my eyesight came back. I was riding in the backseat of Mom's Subaru and the world started coming back into focus. I was myself again and the trees were trees again, only the trees looked more alive than I'd ever seen them: the branches above our street were interlaced beneath an ocean of leaves, thousands and thousands of leaves scrolling past, dark on the tops and pale on the undersides, every individual leaf moving independently but still in concert with the others.

Going out on the Nemunas is sort of like that. You come down the path and step through the willows and it's like seeing the lights in the world come back on.

* * *

Even when there's not much of a person left, you can still learn things about her. I learn that Mrs. Sabo likes the smell of cinnamon. I learn she perks up any time we round this one particular bend in the river. Even with her little gold-capped teeth she chews food slowly and delicately, and I think maybe her mom must have been strict about that, like, Sit up straight, Chew carefully, Watch your manners. Emily Dickinson's mom was like that. Of course Emily Dickinson ended up terrified of death and wore only white clothes and would only talk to visitors through the closed door of her room.

Mid-August arrives and the nights are hot and damp. Grandpa Z keeps the windows open. I can hear Mrs. Sabo's oxygen machine wheezing and murmuring all night. In half-dreams it's a sound like the churning of the world through the universe.

Yellow, green, red runs the flag flapping in front of the post office. Sun up to, Grandpa Z says, land in the middle, blood down below. Lithuania: doormat of a thousand wars.

I miss Kansas. I miss the redbud trees, the rainstorms, how the college kids all wear purple on football Saturdays. I miss Mom walking into the grocery story and pushing her sunglasses up on her forehead, or Dad pedaling up a hill on his bicycle, me a little person in a bike trailer behind him, his maroon backpack bobbing up and down.

One day late in August Mrs. Sabo and I are drifting downstream, our lines trailing in the river, when Mrs. Sabo starts talking in Lithuanian. I've known her forty days and not heard her say so much in all of them combined. She tells me that the afterworld is a garden. She says it's on a big mountain on the other side of an ocean. This garden is always warm and there are no winters there and that's where the birds go in the fall. She waits a few minutes and then says that

31

death is a woman named Giltine. Giltine is tall, skinny, blind, and always really, really hungry. Mrs. Sabo says when Giltine walks past, mirrors splinter, beekeepers find coffin-shaped honeycombs in the hives, and people dream of teeth being pulled. Anytime you have a dream about the dentist, she says, that means death walked past you in the night.

One of Grandpa Z's magazines says that when a young albatross first takes wing, it can stay in the air without touching the ground for fifteen years. I think when I die I'd like to be tied to ten thousand balloons, so I could go floating into the clouds, and get blown off somewhere above the cities, and then the mountains, and then the ocean, just miles and miles of blue ocean, my corpse sailing above it all.

Maybe I could last fifteen years up there. Maybe an albatross could land on me and use me for a little resting perch. Maybe that's silly. But it makes as much sense, I think, as watching my Mom and Dad get buried in boxes in the mud.

❖   ❖   ❖

At nights Mrs. Sabo and I start watching a show called Boy Meets Grill on Mrs. Sabo's big TV. I try cooking zucchini crisps and Pepsi-basted eggplant. I try cooking asparagus Francis and broccoli Diane. Grandpa Z screws up his eyebrows sometimes when he comes in the door but he sits through my Bless Us O Lord and he eats everything I cook and washes it all down with Juozo beer. And some weekends he drives me up the road to little towns with names like Panemunė and Pagėgiai and we buy ice cream sandwiches from Lukoil stations, and Mishap sleeps in the hatchback and at dusk the sky goes from blue to purple and purple to black.

Almost every day in August Mrs. Sabo and I fish for sturgeon. I row upriver and drift us home, dropping our cinderblock anchor now and then to fish the deep holes. I sit in the bow and Mrs. Sabo sits in the stern and Mishap sleeps under the middle bench, and I wonder about how memories can be here one minute and then gone the next. I wonder about how the sky can be a huge, blue nothingness and at the same time it can also feel like a shelter.

❖   ❖   ❖

It's the last dawn in August. We are fishing a mile upstream from the house when Mrs. Sabo sits up and says something in Russian. The boat starts rocking back and forth. Then her reel starts screaming.

32

Mishap starts barking. Mrs. Sabo jams her heels against the hull and jabs the butt of her rod into her belly and holds on. The reel yowls.

Whatever is on the other end takes a lot of line. Mrs. Sabo clings to it and doesn't let go and a strange, fierce determination flows into her face. Her glasses slide down her nose. A splotch of sweat shaped like Australia blooms on the back of her blouse. She mutters to herself in Russian. Her little baggy arms quiver. Her rod is bent into an upside-down U.

What do I do? There's nobody there to answer so I say, Pray, and I pray. Mrs. Sabo's line disappears at a diagonal into the river and I can see it bending away through the water, dissolving into a coffee-colored darkness. The boat seems like it might actually be moving upriver and Mrs. Sabo's reel squeaks and it feels like what the Sunday school teacher used to tell us during choir practice when she'd say we were tapping into something larger than ourselves.

Slowly the line makes a full circuit of the boat. Mrs. Sabo pulls up on her rod and cranks her reel, gaining ground, inch by inch, little by little. Then she gets a bit of slack so she starts reeling like mad, taking in yards of line, and whatever it is on the other end tries to make a run.

Bubbles rise to the surface. The swivel and weight on Mrs. Sabo's line become visible. It holds there a minute, just below the surface of the water, as if we are about to see whatever is just below the leader, whatever is struggling there just beneath the surface, when, with a sound like a firecracker, Mrs. Sabo's line pops and the swivel and the broken leader fly up over our heads.

Mrs. Sabo staggers backward and nearly falls out of the boat. She drops the rod. Her glasses fall off. She says something like, Holy, holy, holy, holy.

Little ripples spread across the face of the river and are pulled downstream. Then there's nothing. The current laps quietly against the hull. We resume our quiet slide downriver. Mishap licks Mrs. Sabo's hands. And Mrs. Sabo gives me a little gold-toothed smile as if whatever was on the other end of her fishing line has just pulled her back into the present for a minute and in the silence I feel she's here, together with me, under the Lithuanian sunrise, both of us with decades left to live.

✳   ✳   ✳

Grandpa Z doesn't believe me. He sits on the edge of his bed, elbows on the card table, a mildly-renowned Lithuanian tombstone maker, with droopy eyes and broken blood vessels in his cheeks, a plate of half-eaten cauliflower parmesan in front of him, and wipes his eyes and tells me I need to start thinking about school clothes. He says maybe we caught a carp or an old tire but that for us to catch a sturgeon would be pretty much like catching a dinosaur, about as likely as dredging a big hundred-million-year-old Triceratops up out of the river muck.

Mrs. Sabo hooked one, I say.

Okay. Grandpa Z says. But he doesn't even look at me.

❊   ❊   ❊

Mažeikiai Senamiesecio Secondary School is made of sand-colored bricks. The windows are all black. A boy in the parking lot throws a tennis ball onto the roof and waits for the ball to roll down and catches it and does this over and over.

It looks like every other school, I say.

It looks nice, Grandpa Z says.

It starts to rain. He says, You are nervous, and I say, How come you don't believe me about the fish? He looks at me and looks back at the parking lot and rolls down the window and swipes raindrops from the windshield with his palm.

There are sturgeon in the river. Or there's one. There's at least one.

They all gone, Allie, he says. You only break your heart more with this fishing. You only make yourself more lonely, more sad.

So what, Grandpa, you don't believe in anything you can't see? You believe we don't have souls? You put a cross on every headstone you make, but you think the only thing that happens to us when we die is that we turn into mud?

For a while we watch the kid throw and catch his tennis ball. He never misses. Grandpa Z says, I come to Kansas. I ride airplane. I see tops of all clouds. No people up there. No gates, no Jesus. Your mother and father are in the sky sitting on the clouds? You think this?

I look back at Mishap, who's curled up in the hatchback against the rain. Maybe, I say. Maybe I think something like that.

❊   ❊   ❊

I make friends with a girl named Laima and another girl named Asta. They watch Boy Meets Grill, too. Their parents are not dead. Their

34

mothers yell at them for shaving their legs and tell them things like, I really wish you wouldn't chew your hangnails like that, Laima, or, Your skirt is way too short, Asta.

At night I lie in bed with Grandpa Z's unpainted plaster slowly cracking all around me and no shade on the window and Mrs. Sabo's machine wheezing next door and stars creeping imperceptibly across the windowpane and reread the part in my Emily Dickinson biography when she says, "To live is so startling it leaves little time for anything else." People still remember Emily Dickinson said that but when I try to remember a sentence Mom or Dad said I can't remember a single one. They probably said a million sentences to me before they died but tonight it seems all I have are prayers and clichés. When I shut my eyes I can see Mom and Dad at church, Mom holding a little maroon church songbook, Dad's little yachting belt and penny loafers. He leans over to whisper something to me—a little girl standing in the pew beside him. But when his mouth opens, no sound comes out.

∗ ∗ ∗

The willows along the river turn yellow. Our history teacher takes us on a field trip to the KGB musum in Vilnius. The KGB used to cram five or six prisoners into a room the size of a phone booth. They also had cells where prisoners had to stand for days in three inches of water with no place to sit or lie down. Did you know the arms of straightjackets used to be twelve or fourteen feet long? They'd knot them behind your back.

Late one night Mrs. Sabo and I watch a program about a tribe in South America. It shows a naked old guy roasting a yam on a stick. Then it shows a young guy in corduroys riding a moped. The young guy, the narrator lady tells us, is the old guy's grandson. No one wants to do the traditional tribe stuff anymore, the narrator lady says. The old people sit around on their haunches looking gloomy and the youngsters ride buses and move to the cities and listen to cassette tapes. None of the young people want to speak the original language, the narrator lady says, and no one bothers to teach it to their babies. The village used to have 150 people. All but six have moved away and are speaking Spanish now.

At the end the narrator says the tribe's old language has a word for standing in the rain looking at the back of a person you love. She says it has another word for shooting an arrow into a animal poorly, so that

35

it hurts the animal more than is necessary. To call a person this word, in the old language, the lady says, is the worst sort of curse you could imagine.

Fog swirls outside the windows. Mrs. Sabo stands and disconnects herself from the machine and takes a bottle of Juozo beer from the refrigerator. Then she goes out the front door and walks into the yard and stands at the far edge of the porch light and pours some beer into her cupped hand. She holds it out for a long time, and I'm wondering if Mrs. Sabo has finally drifted off the edge until out of the mist comes a white horse and it drinks the beer right out of her cupped hand and then Mrs. Sabo presses her forehead against the horse's big face and the two of them stay like that for a long time.

◦   ◦   ◦

That night I dream my molars come loose. My mouth fills with teeth. I know before I open my eyes that Mrs. Sabo is dead. People come over all day long. Her son leaves the windows and doors open for three days so that her soul can escape. At night I walk over to her house and sit with him and he smoke cigarettes and I watch cooking shows.

The River Nemunas, he says in Lithuanian, two nights after she's gone. He doesn't say anything else.

Two weeks later Grandpa drives me home from school and looks at me a long time and tells me he wants to go fishing.

Really? I say.

Yes, he says. He walks across the field with me; he lets me bait his hook. For three straight afternoons we fish together. He tells me that the chemical plant where Mrs. Sabo worked used to make cement and fertilizer and sulfuric acid, and under the Soviets some days the river would turn mustard yellow. He tells me that under the Soviets the farms here were collective farms, where many families worked a large area, and that's why the houses out here are in clusters and not spread out, each to its own plot, like farmhouses in Kansas.

On the fourth day, I'm fishing with a chicken carcass when my line goes tight. I count to three and try to yank my rod up. It doesn't budge. It's a feeling like I've hooked into the river bottom itself, like I'm trying to pull up the bedrock of Lithuania.

Grandpa Z looks over at my line and then at me. Snagged? he says. My arms feel like they're going to tear off. The current pulls the boat slowly downstream and soon the line is so tight drops are sizzling off it. Every once in a while a little line cranks off the reel. That's all that happens. If I were to let go of my rod, it would shoot upriver.

I consider cutting the line. Something pulls at me and the boat pulls at it and we stay like that for a long time, locked in a tug-of-war, my little fishing line holding the entire boat and me and Mishap and Grandpa Z steady against the current, as if I've hooked into a big, impossible plug of sadness resting on the bottom of the river.

You pull, I whisper to myself. Then you crank. Like Mrs. Sabo did. Pull, crank, pull, crank.

I try. My arms feel like they're disappearing. The boat rocks. Mishap pants. A bright silver wind comes down the river. It smells like wet pine trees. I close my eyes. I think about Mom's raspberry bushes, Dad's filing cabinet, the new family that's moving into our house, some new Mom hanging her clothes in Mom's closet, some new Dad calling to her from Dad's office, some teenage son tacking posters to my walls. I think about how Grandpa Z says the sky is blue because it's dusty and octopuses can unscrew the tops off jars and starfish have one foot and three mouths. I think: No matter what happens, no matter how wretched and gloomy everything can get, at least Mrs. Sabo got to feel this.

It's as if I'm going to separate at the waist. But gradually, eventually, I start to gain some ground. The boat rocks as I pull it a yard upstream. I heave the rod up, crank in a couple turns of line.

Pull, then crank. Pull, then crank. We skid another yard upstream. Grandpa Z's little eyes seem about to bulge out of their sockets.

It's not a fish. I know it's not a fish. It's just a big piece of trash at the bottom of the Nemunas River. I say a prayer Dad taught me about God being in the light and the water and the rocks, about God's mercy enduring forever. I say it quickly to myself, hissing it out through my lips, and pull then crank, pull then crank, God is in the light, God is in the water, God is in the rocks, and I can feel Mishap scrabbling around the boat with his little claws and I can even feel his heart beating in his chest, a little bright fist opening and closing, and I can feel the river pulling past the boat, its tributaries like fingernails dragging through the entire country, all of Lithuania draining into this one artery, five hundred sliding miles of water, all the way to the Baltic, which Grandpa Z says is the coldest sea in Europe, and something occurs to me that will probably seem obvious to you but that I never

37

thought about before: a river never stops. Wherever you are, whatever you're doing, forgetting, sleeping, mourning, dying—the rivers are still running.

Grandpa Z shouts. I open my eyes. Something is surfacing twenty feet away from the boat. It comes up slowly, like a submarine, as if from a dream: huge, breathtakingly huge, the size of a desk. It's a fish.

I can see four barbells under his snout, like snakes. I see his fog-colored belly. I see the big hook stuck through his jaw. He moves slowly, and eases his head back and forth, like a horse shaking off a wasp.

He is huge. He is tremendous. He is ten feet long.

Erketas, says Grandpa Z.

I can't hold it anymore, I say.

Grandpa Z says, You can.

Pull, crank. Breathe in light, breathe out color. The sturgeon comes to us upside down. His mouth sucks and opens, sucks and opens. His back is covered with armor. He looks fifty thousand years old.

For a full minute the fish floats beside the boat like a soft white railroad tie, the boat rocking gently, no Mrs. Sabo, no Mom and Dad, no tape measures or hanging scales, no photographs, my arms ablaze with pain and Mishap barking and Grandpa Z looking down as if he's been asked to witness a resurrection. The sturgeon's gills open and close. The flesh inside the gills is a brilliant, impossible crimson.

I hold him there for maybe ten more seconds. Who else sees him? The cows? The trees? Then Grandpa Z leans over, unfolds his pocketknife, and cuts the line. The fish floats beside the boat for a few seconds, stunned and sleepy. He doesn't flick his tail, doesn't flex his huge body. He simply sinks out of sight.

Mishap goes quiet. The boat wobbles and starts downriver. The river pours on and on. I think of those photos of Mom, as tall and thin as a blade of grass, a bike rider, a swimmer, a stranger, a suntanned sixthgrader who might still come pedaling up the driveway of her father's house some afternoon with a jump rope over her shoulder. I think of Mrs. Sabo, how her memories slipped away one by one into the twilight and left her here in a house in a field in the middle of Lithuania waiting for skinny, ravenous Giltine to carry her to a garden on the other side of the sky.

I feel the tiniest lightening. Like one pound out of a thousand has been lifted off my shoulders. Grandpa Z slowly dips his hands in the water and rubs them together. I can see each drop of water falling off his fingertips. I can see them dropping in perfect spheres and merging with the river.

* * *

We hardly ever talk about the fish. It's there between us, something we share. Maybe we feel like talking about it will ruin it. Grandpa Z spends his evenings etching Mrs. Sabo's face into her tombstone. Her son has offered several times to pay but Grandpa does it for free. He puts her on the granite without her glasses and her eyes look small and naked and girlish. He draws a lace-collared dress up tight around her throat and pearls around that, and he renders her hair in cotton-candy loops. It really is a very good job. It rains on the day they put it over her grave.

In November our whole school takes a bus to Plokštinė, an abandoned underground Soviet missile base where the Russians used to keep nukes. It looks like a grassy field, hemmed with birch, with an oversized pitcher's mound in each corner. There are no admission fees, no tourists, just a few signs in English and Lithuanian and a single strand of barbed wire—all that remains of seven layers of alarms, electric fences, razor cable, Dobermans, searchlights, and machine gun emplacements.

We go down a staircase in the center of the field. Electric bulbs dangle from cracked ceilings. The walls are cramped and rusty. I pass a tiny bunk room and a pair of generators with their guts torn out. Then a dripping black corridor, clotted with puddles. Eventually I reach a railing. The ceiling is belled out: one of the pitcher's mounds must be directly above me. I shine my flashlight ninety feet down. The bottom of the silo is all rust and shadows and echoes.

Here, not so long ago, they kept a thermonuclear ballistic missile as big as a tractor trailer. The iron collar around the rim of the hole has the 360 degrees of a compass painted around its circumference. Easier, I suppose, to aim for a compass heading than for Frankfurt.

The urge to know scrapes against the inability to know. What was Mrs. Sabo's life like? What was my mother's? We peer at the past through murky water; all we can see are shapes and figures. How much is real? And how much is merely threads and tombstones?

On the way home Lithuanian kids jostle in the seats around me, smelling of body odor. A stork flaps across a field in the last of the daylight. The boy beside me tells me to keep my eyes out the window, that to see a white horse at dusk is the best possible kind of luck.

39

* * *

Don't tell me how to grieve. Don't tell me ghosts fade away eventually, like they do in movies, waving goodbye with see-through hands. Lots of things fade away but ghosts like these don't, heartbreak like this doesn't. The ax blade is still as sharp and real inside me as it was six months ago.

I do my homework and feed my dog and say my prayers. Grandpa Z learns a little more English, I learn a little more Lithuanian, and soon both of us can talk in the past tense. And when I start to feel the Big Sadness cutting me up inside I try to remember Mrs. Sabo and the garden that is the afterworld and I watch the birds fly south in their flocks.

The sturgeon we caught was pale and armored and beautiful, splotched all over with age and lice. He was a big soft-boned hermit living at the bottom of a deep hole in a river that pours on and on like a green ghost through the fields of Lithuania. Is he an orphan like me? Does he spend all day every day searching for someone else he recognizes? And yet, wasn't he so gentle when I got him close to the boat? Wasn't he just as patient as a horse? Wasn't he just about as noble as anything?

Jesus, Dad used to say, is a golden boat on a long, dark river. That's one thing I can remember him saying.

It's quiet in Lithuania in November, and awful dark. I lie on my grandfather's bed and clutch Mishap and breathe in light and breathe out color. The house groans. I pray for Mom and Dad and Mrs. Sabo and Grandpa Z. I pray for those South American tribespeople on the television and their vanishing language. I pray for the lonely sturgeon, a monster, a lunker, last elder of a dying nation, drowsing in the bluest, deepest chambers of the River Nemunas.

Out the window it starts to snow.

Nominated by Tin House

TURNING YOURSELF INTO A WORK OF ART

by STEPHEN DUNN

from SHENANDOAH

If you find your left hand gesturing, involuntarily,
in the direction of the moon, it may be time
to handcuff your right to something cast iron,
impossible to move. Balance is everything,

or almost everything, if you want to be
a work of art. All too soon you'll be old,
and no amount of wisdom
will compensate for that wobble and drool.

You taste like a grape, a woman once said,
after she spit out something essentially yours.
Whether a detail like that should be included
in an attempt to turn yourself into a work of art

        is questionable.

But you'd like to think it a formal issue,
the way the straps of a purse, that memorable slash,
accentuated the breasts of that same woman,
guiding your eyes in a manner she intended.

    A work of art

always is in danger of wanting more
than it can give itself permission to have.
All your life, haven't you reached
for what hasn't yet been offered? Before you die

you think you must risk some falling apart
of whoever you are, your heart loose
and banging against its rib cage—
another formal issue. You have in mind a painting

in which a solitary green shoe in the forefront
exists only because that dagger with a jade handle
on the night table needed an aesthetic companion.
In other words, you wish to be an arrangement,

                    and you wish to be the arranger.

Can there ever be enough distance from yourself
to get yourself right? It's hard, and should be,
to become a work of art. Maybe the trick is
to avert your gaze, look a little sideways

            as an astronomer does.

That's how a faint star becomes visible—
just a glimpse at first, then the long adventure
of saying what exactly it is that shines
behind so much of its own smoke and gas.

Nominated by Jane Hirshfield, David Jauss, Jeremy Collins, Mark Irwin, Shenandoah

FROST MOUNTAIN PICNIC MASSACRE

fiction by SETH FRIED

from ONE STORY

Last year, the people in charge of the picnic blew us up. Every year it gets worse. That is, more people die. The Frost Mountain Picnic has always been a matter of uncertainty in our town and the massacre is the worst part. Even the people whose picnic blankets were not laid out directly upon the bombline were knocked unconscious by the airborne limbs of their neighbors, or at least had the black earth at the foot of Frost Mountain driven under their eyelids and fingernails and up into their sinuses. The apple dumpling carts and cotton candy stands and guess-your-weight booths that were not obliterated in the initial blasts leaned slowly into the newly-formed craters, each settling with a limp, hollow crumple. The few people along the bombline who survived the blast were at the very least blown into the trees.

The year before that, the boom of the polka band had obscured the scattered reports of far-off rifles. A grown man about to bite a caramel apple suddenly spun around wildly, as if propelled by the thin spray of blood from his neck. An old woman, holding her stomach, stumbled into a group of laughing teenagers. Someone fell forward into his funnel cake, and all day long we walked around as if we weren't aware of what was happening.

One year, the muskets of the Revolutionary War Reenactment Society were somehow packed with live ammunition. Another year, all the children who played in the picnic's Bouncy Castle died of radiation poisoning. Yet another year, it was discovered halfway through the picnic that a third of the port-a-potties contained poisonous snakes. The year we were offered free hot air balloon rides, none of the balloons that left—containing people laughing and waving from the baskets, snapping pictures as they ascended—ever returned.

Nevertheless, every year we still turn out in the hundreds to the quaint river quay in our marina district to await the boats that will take us to Frost Mountain. In a hilltop parking lot, we apply sunscreen to the noses of our children. We rifle through large canvas carryalls, taking inventory of fruit snacks, extra jelly sandals, Band-Aids, and juice boxes, trying to anticipate our children's inevitable needs and restlessness in the twenty minutes that they will have to wait for the boats to be readied. Anxious to claim our place in line, we head down the hill in a rush toward the massive white boats aloft in the water.

We wait in a long, roped queue that doubles back on itself countless times before reaching the loading platform with its blue vinyl awning. Once it's time to depart, the line will move forward, leading us to the platform, where the deckhands will divide us up evenly between the various boats. From there, we will be moved upriver, to the north of our city, where Frost Mountain looms. From the decks, we will eventually see a lush, green field interrupted by brightly colored tents and flashing carnival rides, the whole scene contained by the incredible height of Frost Mountain, reaching into the sky with its cold, blue splendor.

The sight of the picnic at the foot of Frost Mountain is so appealing that most of us will, once again, convince ourselves that this year will be different, that all we have in store for us is a day full of leisure and amusements—but sooner or later, one of the rides will collapse, or a truck of propane will explode near one of the food tents, killing dozens.

Of course, every year more people say they won't come. Every year, there are town meetings during which we all condemn the Frost Mountain Picnic. We meet in the empty tennis courts of the Constituent Metro Park where we vow to forsake the free bags of peanuts, the free baked butternut squashes, the free beer, the free tractor rides and firework expositions.

We grow red in the face, swearing our eternal alignment against all the various committees, public offices, and obscure private interests in charge of organizing the picnic. Every year, there are more people at the meetings who are walking on crutches and wearing eye patches from the injuries they sustained the previous year. Every year, there are more people holding up pictures of dead loved ones and beating their chests. Every year, there are more people getting angry, interrupting one another, and asking the gathered crowd if they might be allowed to speak first. Every year, loyalty oaths are signed. Every year, pledges to abstain from the Frost Mountain Picnic are given and received freely and every single year, without exception, everyone ends up going to the picnic anyway.

Often, the people who are the most vocally opposed to the picnic are also the most eager to get there, the people most likely to cut in line for the boats, the people most disdainful toward the half-dozen zealots picketing in the parking lot.

Waiting in line for the boats, our children rub their chins in the dirt and push their foreheads against our feet. They roll around on the ground and shout obscenities, then run in circles, screaming nonsense, while we play with the car keys in our pockets and gawk passively at the massive boats. Typically, we don't allow our children to misbehave this way. However, we do our best to understand. Their faces are in pain.

Our children's cheeks begin to ache as they wait in line for the boats, and continue to ache until their faces are painted at the Frost Mountain Picnic. We've come to understand that all children are born with phantom cat whiskers. All children are born with phantom dog faces. All children are born with phantom American flag foreheads, rainbow-patterned jawbones and deep, curving pirate scars, the absence of which haunts them throughout their youth. We understand that all children are born with searing and trivial images hidden in their faces, the absence of which causes them a great deal of discomfort. It is a pain that only the brush of a face painter can alleviate, each stroke revealing the cryptic pictures in our children's faces. Any good parent knows this.

Ten years ago, the massacre came in the form of twenty-five silverback gorillas set loose at the height of the picnic. Among the fatalities, a young girl by the name of Louise Morris was torn to pieces. Perhaps it was Louise's performance as Mary in the Christmas pageant of the preceding winter, or perhaps it was the grim look on the faces of the three silverback gorillas that tugged her arms and legs in opposite directions, or perhaps it was just that she was so much prettier and more well-behaved than the other children who were killed that day—but whatever the case, Louise Morris's death had a profound impact on the community.

That year, the town meetings grew into full-blown rallies. Louise Morris's picture ran on the front page of local newspapers every day for a month. We wore yellow ribbons to church and a local novelty shop began selling Remember Louise T-shirts, which were quickly fashionable. Under extreme pressure from the city council, the local zoo was forced to rid itself of its prized gorilla family, Gigi, Taffy and their newborn baby Jo-Jo, who were sold to the St. Louis Zoo, Calgary Zoo and Cleveland Zoo, respectively.

The school board added a three-day weekend to the district calendar in memoriam of Louise and successfully carried out a protest campaign against a school two districts away, demanding that they change their mascot from the Brightonville Gorillas to the Brightonville Lightning Bolts. Without any formal action from the school board, the opposition to teaching evolution in public schools began to enjoy a sudden, regional popularity. Without any written mandate, with only the collective moral outcry of the community to guide them, teachers slowly began removing from their classrooms the laminated posters that pictured our supposed, all-too-gorilla-like ancestors as they lumbered their way across the primordial landscape.

The community's reaction to Louise's death was so strong that, in time, it was hard to keep track of all the changes it had engendered. It was difficult to know where one change ended and another began. Perhaps it was our hatred of gorillas that eventually gave way to our distrust of large men with bad posture, which led to the impeachment of Mayor Castlebach. Perhaps our general fear of distant countries, the forests of which were either known or suspected to support gorilla populations, had more to do with the deportation of those four Kenyan exchange students than any of us cared to admit. With all the changes connected to Louise's death, there were many ins and outs, many complexities and half-attitudes, which made it difficult to calculate. In fact, the only thing that seemed at all the same was the Frost Mountain Picnic.

When the public meetings die down, we begin to see advertisements for next year's picnic. Naturally, the initial reaction is always more outrage. But after the advertisements persist for months and months, after we see them on more billboards and on the sides of buses, after we hear the radio jingles and watch the fluff pieces about the impending picnic on the local news, our attitudes invariably begin to soften. Though no one ever comes out and says it, the collective assumption seems to be that if the picnic can be advertised with so little reservation, then the problems surrounding it must have been solved. If such a pleasant jingle can be written for it, if the news anchor can discuss it with the meteorologist so vapidly, the picnic must be harmless. Our oaths against the impending picnic become difficult to maintain. Through the sheer optimism of those advertisements, the unfortunate events of the previous year are exorcized.

Those few citizens holding onto their anger are inevitably viewed as people who refuse to move on, people who thrive on discord. When they canvass neighborhoods and approach others on the streets with brochures containing facts about previous massacres, they are called conspiracy theorists and cranks. They're accused of remembering events creatively, of cherry-picking facts in order to accommodate their paranoid fantasies. Or else, it might be said of them that they have some valid points, which would bear consideration, if only their methods weren't so obnoxious, if only they didn't insist on holding up signs at street corners and putting fliers under our windshield wipers, if only they didn't look so self-righteous and affirmed in their opinions. Ultimately, the only thing that these dissenters ever manage to convince us is that to not attend the picnic is to exist outside of what is normal.

Waiting in line for the boats, we wear our Remember Louise T-shirts. We busily anticipate the free corndogs, the free ice cream cones, and the free party hats. Our children bark and grab at the passing legs of the deckhands as they move through the line in their crisp uniforms. Pale-blue pants neatly pressed, matching ties tucked into short-sleeve button-downs, the men acknowledge our children with exaggerated smiles. A deckhand drops to one knee and places his flat, white cap on a child's head. When the child screams, takes off the cap, and tries to tear it in half, the deckhand begins to laugh, as if the child has just said something delightful.

The charm of the deckhands is made all the more unbelievable by our children's outrageous behavior. Desperate to have their faces painted, our children writhe on the ground and moan after the deckhands as they make their way to the loading platform. Once they reach their place beneath the awning, the deckhands occasionally look back at the long line and flash those same exaggerated smiles. They wave excitedly, a gesture that sends our children into a revitalized frenzy.

On various occasions, it has been suggested that perhaps the trouble with our children's faces is only that we indulge them in it, that perhaps what they feel is not actually a physical discomfort, but an emotional discomfort similar to that of any child whose whims might be occasionally frustrated. It has been suggested that perhaps, as a rule, it may be better to do without face painting or, for that matter, anything that would cause them to act so wildly in its absence. It has been suggested that perhaps it would give our children more character if we were to let them suffer under the burden of the hidden images in their faces, forcing them to bring those images out gradually through the development of personal interests and pleasant dispositions, rather than having them crudely painted on.

Though, in the end, it's difficult for any of us to see it that way. After all, when the children wear their painted faces to school the next day, already smudged and fading, none of us wants our children to be the ones whose faces are bare. None of us wants our children to be the ones excluded or ridiculed. As good parents, we want our children to be successful, even if only in the most superficial way, as such small successes, we hope, might eventually lead to deeper, more meaningful ones. None of us wants our children to be accused of something arbitrary and most likely untrue due to the lack of some item of social significance. None of us has the confidence in our children to endure that type of thing.

None of us wants our children to become outcasts. None of us wants our children to become criminals or perverts. None of us wants our children to begin smoking marijuana or masturbating excessively. None of us wants our children to become homeless or adopt strange fetishes, driving away perfectly good mates who simply don't want to be peed on or tied down or have cigarettes put out on their backsides. None of us wants our children to begin hanging around public parks in order to steal people's dogs for some dark, unimaginable purpose. None of us wants our children to wait around outside churches after morning mass in black trench coats in order to flash the departing congregation their bruised, over-sexed genitals, genitals which were once tiny and adorable to us, genitals which we had once tucked lovingly into cloth diapers. None of us wants our children dispersing crowds of elderly churchgoers with their newly-wretched privates, sending those churchgoers screaming, groaning in disgust, fumbling with the keys to their Cadillacs, shielding their eyes in vain.

It isn't a judgment against people who have produced such children. It just isn't something we would want for our own. Even the parents who are less involved in their children's well-being are sick of paying the hospital bills when their unpainted children are pushed off the jungle gym or have their heads shoved into their jacket cubbies. Even those parents are sick of their kids getting nicknames like paintless, bare-face, and faggy-faggy-no-paint. Even those parents, for the most part, seem to understand.

Though the organizations and public offices in charge of the picnic remain vague and mysterious to us, it should be said that we are never directly denied information. It's simply a matter of our not knowing the right questions to ask or where to ask them.

One year, after twenty young couples were electrocuted to death in the Tunnel of Love, many of us showed up to public and private offices in groups and demanded explanations. But in each instance, we were simply informed by a disinterested clerk that the office in question had nothing to do with the picnic, and so could offer no information. Or else we were told that it had played such a small part that the only document on hand was a form reserving the park site for that particular date or a carbon copy of the event's temporary liquor license or some other trivial article.

When one of us asked where we could obtain more information or which office bore the most responsibility, the clerks offered us only a helpless look, as if to suggest that we were being unreasonable. And, truly, once we began to realize the gigantic apparatus of which each office was apparently only an incredibly small part, we had to admit that we were being unreasonable. It became clear that we were not dealing with an errant official or an ineffective ordinance, but an intersection between local government and private interests so complex that it was as if it was none of our business.

At the very most, a clerk referenced some huge, multi-national corporation said to be the primary orchestrator of the picnic. But what could be done with such information? Like that other apparatus, only on a much larger scale, such entities were too big to be properly held accountable for anything. The power of the people in charge of them was so far-reaching that by the time any one of their decisions had run its course, it was like trying to blame them for the weather. Also, because we already sensed ourselves to be a nuisance, we were reminded—a clerk pinching the bridge of his nose, and then replacing his glasses—that the walls of communication were built high around such people, and for good reason.

We wandered out of those offices in silence, our anger abated by our own embarrassment. Suddenly, we were afraid that the clerks had mistaken us for more conspiracy theorists and cranks. Mortified, we returned to those offices to apologize.

Truth be told, as compelled as each of us is to attend the Frost Mountain Picnic, for our own sake as much as for our children's, few of us ever really end up enjoying the aspects of the picnic which originally drew us there.

The craft tables, the petting zoos, the scores of musicians and wandering performers in their festively colored jerkins—once obtained, all the much-anticipated amusements tend to seem a little trite. Even a thing as difficult to disapprove of as free food doesn't usually satisfy any of us as much as we might pretend. The fried ice creams and elephant ears are all inevitably set aside by those of us who find ourselves feeling suddenly queasy, those of us who, while waiting in line for the boats, had only recently bragged of our hunger.

On the old, wilting merry-go-round, large groups of us sit with our tongues in our cheeks and almost before the ride starts, we wish for it to be over. Even the ironic enjoyment of a child's ride seems belabored and fake. On the merry-go-round, we look to our fellow horsemen and strain forward, feigning attempts to pull ahead. Leaning dramatically from our horses, we clap hands, cheer and force out laughter so awkward and shapeless that it makes our throats ache, so high-toned and weak that it makes our eyes water.

We understand that the amusements of the Frost Mountain Picnic are supposed to entertain us. We understand that when we talk about the picnic's amusements with others, we pretend as if they do. Around water coolers and in restaurants, we repeat stories about unfinished tins of caramel corn and slow, creaking rides on the witch's wheel as if they are deeply cherished memories.

In anticipation of the free such and such, and the free such and such, we manage to convince ourselves that we are indeed looking forward to the picnic. In our minds, we falsely attach value to the items that will be given so generously. Or else, we attempt to see our partic-

50

ipation as paying homage to something long past and romantic, a matter of heritage.

Among the difficulties we face in attempting to extricate ourselves from the Frost Mountain Picnic, a problem which is never fully addressed at the town meetings is the fact that—just as all those offices throughout the city perform simple tasks for the picnic, but then can claim no real knowledge or responsibility—most of us are involved with the picnic on many different levels, some of which might not even be completely known to us.

Any number of local businesses, social clubs, volunteer groups, local radio stations, television stations and departments of municipal utility are either sponsored or underwritten or provided endowments by those in charge of the Frost Mountain Picnic. If we were to buy a bag of oranges from a local grocer, if we were to drop a quarter into the milk jug of the young boy standing by the automatic doors in his soccer uniform, if we were to listen to the Top 40 radio droning from the store's speakers, if we were to flip on a light switch in our own home or flush a toilet, we would be contributing in one fashion or another to the Frost Mountain Picnic. Our role is not limited to our attendance, but extends to include our inclination to drink tap water, eat fresh fruit and go to the bathroom.

Moreover, even if we could deny ourselves these things, everywhere there are peculiar inconsistencies and non sequiturs, which, taken together, are ominous. Periodic bank errors are reported on our checking statements next to the letters FMP and, every week, strange, superfluous deductions are made from our paychecks by an unknown entity.

A rotary club, attempting to raise money for childhood leukemia, will later check its records only to find that a majority of the proceeds were somehow accidentally sent to a cotton candy distributor in New Jersey. When the Highway Patrol calls two weeks before the picnic to ask us if we'd care to donate to the Officers' Widows Fund, the call, routed through Philadelphia, Mexico City and Anchorage, appears on our phone bills as a 17-dollar charge.

We might volunteer to take part in a committee to discuss the repair of potholes throughout the city only to wind up somehow duped into preparing large mailings in the basements of public buildings, mailings which have nothing to do with potholes, but which include brochures in foreign languages with pictures of families laughing, eating corndogs and playing carnival games next to large, boldly colored words like *lustig* and *glücklich*.

Several times a year, men in dark blue suits flood the city. Without notice, without any noticeable regularity in their visits, they turn up everywhere. They drive slowly across town in large motorcades of black sedans with tinted windows. Dozens of them stand in line at the post office, mailing identical packages wrapped neatly in brown paper and fixed with small blue address labels. They stand outside office buildings and talk into the sleeves of their suit coats. Large groups of them sit in restaurants amid clouds of hushed laughter and cigarette smoke. The men are mostly older, but well-groomed and tan, with magnificently white teeth and expensive watches. They sit three to a bench in public parks and are seen hunched over surveyor's levels outside churches and hospitals and elementary schools. The men walk in and out of every imaginable type of building at every imaginable hour for days. Then, with even less warning than their arrival, they disappear.

One hardly knows what to do with such subtleties, such phenomena. One hardly knows how to combine them or how to separate them or how to consider them in relation to one another. But whatever their sum or difference, such occurrences tend to intensify the sensation that the Frost Mountain Picnic is, in fact, unavoidable. Though it's never expressly stated, the general consensus seems to be that there's nothing we can do which would ever come to any final good, which would ever change the picnic or the massacre or whatever machinations lie beneath either.

While we ourselves feel powerless to avoid it, many of us often hope that our children might eventually outgrow the picnic. After the town meetings, most of us are already well aware that we will betray our own pledges and loyalty oaths. We leave the meetings, feeling sheepish and impotent. Though, some of us do take the opportunity to stop and talk quietly with one another about the possibility that the next generation might eventually rise up and break the pattern of our complacency.

On the way home from the picnic, with the ring of mortar fire still in our ears or the stink of gorillas or gun powder in our noses, we steal glances at our sleeping children in the back seats of our station wagons and minivans. Typically, we are bandaged from some close brush with the massacre, our arms in slings improvised out of our torn and battered Remember Louise T-shirts. Our lips split, our noses bloodied, our palms sweaty on the steering wheel, we recall the first moments of the massacre, the first explosion, the first gunshot, the first creeping hum of the planes, the earth moving beneath our feet. We watch our children sleeping in the rear-view, moonlight passing over their peaceful faces. Through the unsightly globs of paint, we catch a glimpse of how our children were before the picnic endowed them with such an eager, selfish spirit.

When it comes time to leave the highway, as we drift slowly toward our exit, we are tempted to jerk the wheel in the other direction and speed off to some distant city, a place untouched by picnics. We know our husbands and wives wouldn't say a word, wouldn't ask for an explanation, wouldn't even turn their heads to watch our exit as it passes, but would keep their eyes forward, like ours, a look of exhilaration on their faces.

However, these fantasies are as appealing as they are unlikely, and so our hope remains tied into our children. Our children, who took their first steps while waiting in line for the boats, who muttered their first words to the face painters and jugglers, who lost their first teeth in the picnic's salt water taffy and red-rope licorice. Our children, who, as they grow older, begin to explain the picnic to us as if we don't understand it. Our children, who have begun to scorn and mock us if we so much as mention Frost Mountain, snap their gum and laugh with their friends, as if our old age and presumed irrelevance threatens the very existence of the picnic.

A horn sounds, signaling the line to move forward. No matter how long we wait for the boats, or how eager we might seem, there is always a slight pause between the sounding of the horn and the eventual lurching forward of the crowd. It is a moment in which we recall the year some of the boats sank as they left the picnic, how everyone aboard trusted the surprisingly bulky life jackets and sank to the bottom of the river like stones. It is a moment of looking from side to side, a moment of coughing and shrugging.

On the opposite shore, a small orchestra of men in dark suits begins to play the second movement of Beethoven's *Eroica*. Assembled under a large carnival tent, the men play expertly, ploddingly. Those whose parts have not yet come stand perfectly still or adjust the dark glasses on the bridge of their noses or speak slowly into the sleeves of their suit coats. The music sounds strange over the noise of the river and weighs heavily in the air.

It is a moment of clarity and anxiety, in which we hope that something will deliver us from our sense of obligation toward the picnic, the sense of embarrassment that would proceed from removing our children from the line, evoking tantrums so fierce as to be completely unimaginable. It is a moment in which we wait for some old emotion to well up in us, some passion our forefathers possessed that made them unafraid of change, no matter how radical or how dangerous or—the deckhands gesturing for us to move forward, their faces suddenly angry and impatient—how impossible.

Nominated by Michael Czyzniejewski, Marie-Helene Bertino, One Story

THE OPENING

by PHILIP SCHULTZ

from FIVE POINTS and PER CONTRA

For Connie Fox and William King

Everyone arrives later than everyone else,
taller than expected, the gossip anthropological
in nature, turning clockwise. Stubborn,
the art doesn't seem to mind being the center
of its own attention. Death remains in fashion,
while delight appears to be making a comeback.
Art, the conversation claims, is: "an assault on time,"
"a currency of doubt and opportunity," "a cease-fire
with calamity." Uninvited, it keeps on coming,
its mouth filled with intuition, such lovely feathers.
Ah, the white fluorescent walls, the landscapes grateful
to have survived their own stillness. Everyone seems
to want something, dogma, truth, a context, politics
is not out of the question, but passion twists the ephemeral
into perception, urges the phenomenal to confront
the merely mysterious. You know what I mean—all that
endless standing, stepping back, squinting, sighing, doing
and undoing, the middle torn out of its own beginning,
the pleading to be finished, finally, the fiery binge and hoist
of the impossible ingested, flattened to nothing, the honed figure
walking out the door, alone under the night's vast umbrella,
the hat complaining to the rectangle about its lack of grammar,
the hilarious despair of the square, the aluminum shiver longing

for the simplicity of the lowly nut and bolt, canvas stretched
across infinity, the disappointments, unbearable happiness,
beckoning for the feast to begin.

Nominated by Grace Schulman, Five Points

POEM

by GAIL MAZUR

from LITERARY IMAGINATION

They said the mind is an ocean,
but sometimes my mind is a pond
circular, shady,

obscure and surrounding the pond,
scrub oak, poison ivy, inedible
low hanging berries,

and twined with the berries, catbrier;
pond where I once swam to a raft
and climbed on, sun drying,

warming my young skin, boys—
that century.
They said the mind or they said something else—

another metaphor: metaphor,
the very liquid glue that helped the worlds—
tangible, solid and, oh, metaphysical—make sense;

and now, fearsome beings in the thick dark water,
but what?—snapping turtles, leeches,
creatures that sting . . .

Who were *they* to say such a thing?
—Or do I have that wrong?
The mind an ocean glorious infinite salty

teeming with syllables,
their tendrils filtered by greeny light?
They don't always get it *right*, do they?

No, it is an unenchanting thing,
the mind: unmusical, small
a dangerous hole, and stagnant,

murk and leaf-muck at the bottom,
mind an idea of idea-making,
idea of place, place to swim home to—

No, to swim away from, to drown, no, to float—

Nominated by Martha Collins, Lloyd Schwartz, Mark Halliday.

DOUBLE HAPPINESS

fiction by MARY-BETH HUGHES

from A PUBLIC SPACE

The outer office was much the same as she remembered it. The thick neat oak desk of Mrs. Lanahan, a manageable stack of buff folders in the far right corner. A small boy in a blazer likely to be his older brother's knocked unhappy heels against the chair leg. He'd been waiting for a while, a tear path nearly dry on his freckled cheek. Wide gray eyes skimmed Ann McCleary then let her go, no help. Someone's grandmother dispatched to pick up a sick child, nothing positive. Nothing that could distract or cajole Sister Mary Arthur to leniency.

Ann McCleary had boys of her own, long grown, boys she'd left to stew in that very chair. Her line: If you got yourself there, you'd done something to deserve it. She'd made a single exception with Terry, age seven, when a polished oxford lace-up went skidding under the desks to catch the attention of a girl he favored. Even younger, even in nursery school, Terry had some tiny thing stilled to contemplation, to watching him. She smiled to think of him, not the handsomest of her boys, but the one, the one who lit up the room.

Terry and his flying shoe, his father just in the grave a month, and he was making trouble. She'd come down to this very office, to Sister Mary Arthur nearly a girl then herself, a young woman with large responsibilities. Ann McCleary had appreciated the good qualities from the start, the kindness, the steely discipline of self that made her a deft judge of the foibles of others. Terry still as a stone, not kicking the edges of the chair leg, face turned down, the brown eye that wandered inward when he was upset wandered now, and Ann gave him the look, then retracted it. She remembered that like something physical, pulling back and seeing the situation for what it was. Dear heart, she'd said, just out of Mrs. Lanahan's hearing, Let me speak to Sister.

And Mary Arthur needed little enlightenment, they understood each other without much conversation. Just this once, Ann McCleary took one of her children, five in all, the last born only months before she lost her beloved Dan, just this once she'd intervened between cause and effect. Off to the Dairy Queen, then home where he watched *One Life To Live* while she ironed, and then *Dark Shadows* with his brothers when they came home from school themselves. His sister, Kathleen, demanded an explanation. Hands on her hips, already the litigator, always fierce for justice. He's sad, explained Ann to her only daughter.

We're all sad, said Kathleen.

Give me a kiss, Ann set the iron on its trivet, reached both hands to smooth back the bangs, grown out too long, that blocked her daughter's blue eyes. What did you hear about your grand project, is it to be Argentina or Brazil?

Mrs. Lanahan never fooled with false color in her hair, like so many of them in Holy Cross parish with frosted bobs, We're all becoming beach blanket blonds, said Ann McCleary on more than one occasion, but Mrs. Lanahan had given up. Even the nuns, the young ones especially, what young ones there were, did better. And Mary Arthur had always been elegant, her lovely hair, cut by an expensive hand. She was the public face of Holy Cross and no one begrudged her the care, the handsome suits or the good shoes, not the way they did Father's vintage Karmann Ghia, a disgrace, and an embarrassment.

But not an indecent man, really, and a fancy car was a small thing after all, he knew when to hide it away. And he'd backed her up when she'd said she wanted a funeral, no waiting. I can't wait, she'd said. And Father Jim Rielly understood, and two Saturdays later pulled down the garage door in the early morning and went in the side porch to the sacristy to make sure his best purple vestments were ready, and of course they were. Monmouth County was especially hard-hit, New Jersey struck almost as if the towers had stood on its side of the river. But only two from Rumson, it turned out, and this was about affluence and influence some said, who with any pull would take an office there. But Terry hadn't felt that way at all. So Ann McCleary knew influence and affluence were part of the endless chatter that said nothing to her. He came down for Sunday supper, a rare appearance, not like the oth-

60

ers with towheads and pregnant wives, girls who'd been so ambitious but now trailed toddlers through her beds and borders, breast-fed on the screened-in porch as if the neighbors were blind and dumb. Terry busy with business and still unsure about settling down, a favorite with his nieces and nephews, gave each a card with his new office address, just moved in. Views to Kansas, he said, to California, even, astonishing. They would all go visit, he said they must, and from his desk survey the world.

The Rumson police, the Little Silver police, the Middletown police especially insisted, they'd already had funerals of their own and knew what to expect. The roads were cordoned off from the Sea Bright Bridge to the Avenue of Two Rivers and cars parked for a mile all the way down Rumson Road, women in black sling-backs climbing the rutted grass along the road, made the shortcut through the tennis club across the school yard to the gray shingle church, capacity four hundred, someone said a thousand stood inside and out to hear Father Jim say no words could gather the force he needed to say his prayer, they would all join him in silence. Kathleen in the choir loft, alone, sang "Danny Boy" for her brother, for her father, and the thousand beyond prayer, beyond tears, shook and trembled now.

Her mother had said, No, not that, meaning the dress of black chiffon. It's not a cocktail party. At the house, just before, they were all biting each other's heads off. The toddlers weeping and throwing tantrums on the screened-in porch, before all the figuring out of which car who could manage, and who would drive Mom. In the end she'd ridden with Kathleen, who knew when to be still, unlike the boys, hugging her too hard, clutching at her hand. Boys were the bigger saps, she'd always known. Kathleen could drive without talking and she knew how to get through a police barrier without making the well-intentioned feel like fools.

Sister Mary Arthur must have been there, must have been crucial and efficient, and would have come to the club later, all were invited, encouraged to gather by the water where the boats rocked in the small cove, and cleats on sails knocked a beautiful music across the treetops, last of their dusty green. Early October, soon the leaves would be down and the boats in dry dock, she couldn't have waited another moment. She wore black, none of this nonsense of color for her. Though many in yellows even, and blues. Sister Mary Arthur would know to wear mourning, but Ann McCleary had no memory of her at all that day. None whatsoever. She saw Kathleen in her cocktail dress, which suited her, truth be told, bare-legged and barefoot in a dinghy with one of the Henderson boys, the one who saw it all, he claimed, from the Staten Island ferry. Long ride, said Ann. Excuse me, Mrs. McCleary? You saw it all, it must have been a very long ride. She was a stickler for exact speech. She was toggled far from sense with grief. Both versions arrived on dinner tables sooner or later. All admired her for going ahead, for deciding to acknowledge the loss when so many were waiting, and for what?

Her daughter Kathleen was thirty-five years old the day her brother likely died. At first they thought if anyone could survive, it would be Terry. They pictured him and the several others he'd no doubt been able to rally, rushing out of the falling ash, rowing to safety. They said it out loud, lifted up with the knowledge of his character, what would surely keep him, and anyone fortunate enough to be in his vicinity, safe. Kathleen had combed the city for the first sign. Not giving up. Even when her mother said, Come home, dear heart. Please. A little girl when she lost her father, Terry nearly seven and never to be a father himself, or a husband. Never had the chance, she'd overheard near the water, over the clang of the boats, the same wine glass still in her hand—Eat something, Mom—she caught the sob. Never wanted to be either, said Ann, he had no example to follow. And whose fault was that. Only her own. Only mine, she said, when asked.

Ann McCleary, said Sister Mary Arthur, smiling, stepping out of her sunny office, arms open by the hips, chest lifted, an unconscious mimicry of the gentle open arms of the Virgin. Come in, I've been looking forward to this all day. She gave an even glance to the miscreant in the chair, sighed, Come in, Mrs. McCleary, Ann, please.

She had a job in mind, and Sister heard her out. Didn't make the old joke about dislodging poor Mrs. Lanahan: Where will we find the solvent to melt that glue, I ask you? No, never her style, her way. She listened and nodded and said, Let me think about this a bit?

Of course, yes, said Ann McCleary, standing. This was quick, and now in her mortification, knew it wasn't what she was expecting. She'd grown used to a certain deference, people let her ahead of them in any line. And all the rest she didn't like to believe she noticed, because for so long she hadn't. Now to perceive her privilege was to have survived, and that was unthinkable.

You were lovely to take the time, she said, nodding.

Please, said Sister Mary Arthur, with the composure to stand quite still, to not glance at her desk or lean toward the side door, toward her next task, Please, she said, let's speak soon.

What did that mean? Ann McCleary who understood everything, who never needed any human utterance interpreted or explained, was baffled. On her way out, she looked down at the little redhead knocking his heels and thought, at least he knows what he's doing here.

So she wasn't waiting for the call that evening. Not a bit. She was nursing a glass of red wine for her heart, and a scrap of cheese on a Triscuit, when the phone rang and it was Sister Mary Arthur explaining her need for a lower school library. A vision, she said. One I've harbored for years.

A terrible thought went through Ann McCleary's mind: Even Sister Mary Arthur was after her imagined millions. And they were imaginary, though the papers went on about them. That, and everything else, the construction nonsense, the bullhorn the president picked up and to her mind never put down and for what. She tuned it all out. She went with Kathleen and the boys, but not their wives or their children, to stand in the frightening pit, to walk through cordons of police and to look up into the empty sky, and she waited. Waited for someone to say something she could listen to. Someone had mentioned the smell. Was it one of her boys? But she couldn't sense a thing. She was waiting to hear someone who wouldn't lie to her. But she knew the cost of that kind of speech because she'd seen it happen, once. But first, they'd stood in line at the Armory on Lexington to give up his hairbrush and the business card Terry had been so proud to hand to the babies, who chewed on them, Don't worry, Mom, they're engraved! Feel.

They'd gone down into the dark stone underground and waited as the lists were turned again and again, empty pages from the city examiner, from the morgue. Who thought to place them here in the cold stone room, airless. Kathleen unwrapped a protein bar from the checkered basket of a volunteer, Eat, Mom, please.

On the third day, Terry's company set up a center for the families at a midtown hotel. Black slick elevators coursed up the high tower to the rooms dim lit, a false lemon fragrance in the air. The internet. The phone banks. The food, constantly refreshed, pancakes, steaks, any kind of eggs. Like Easter, said Ann. And Kathleen said, Maybe we should go home. But she wanted to hear what the CEO had to say. So they went with the others, over a hundred, maybe two hundred, who could count. And they sat in a tiered room, round tables with blue tablecloths, pads, and pens. The microphones were difficult to adjust. Men in suits skipped up the sidelines and back and whispered to clumps of other suited men with heads down, hands in pockets.

They'd heard bits and pieces. They all knew about the stairwells now. They all had maps of the area, and diagrams of the buildings, they knew which elevators stopped on which segment and which went to the top. They had a sense of timing and possibility. They'd been tracking these things for days. Two days now. And on the third, the microphone settled finally into a stand, a man grayer than the rest broke free and said, after running a thumb across the mesh and hearing the purr, the crackle, he said, I'm the Chief Executive Officer and I'd like to tell you what I know. He said, Anyone who arrived at work on Tuesday—

Already the hands were in the air, how could they know? How could they know, was there a list somewhere, an attendance list perhaps? Something that could be distributed?

He said, and first he coughed, he said that he would try to find something like that, but this is what they knew so far, that no one, not a single person who arrived at work, who made it above the 72nd floor, who made the change and climbed into the second elevator, not a single person who arrived at work that day had survived. Not one. If they came to work, if they arrived. No one. Not a single one. Not anyone.

All around the ballroom hands shot up, what about Staircase A? And what about the walls that were only Sheetrock, easily penetrated, easily torn through. The man at the microphone pushed down the large black bulb at his mouth and sobbed. And the hands stayed in the air, some polite, all waiting for his composure to reassert itself. She was the only person in the room that believed him. She watched him for another minute. Let's go, she said to Kathleen. Outside the ballroom she waited, opening her purse to see that she still had her wallet, she'd been so forgetful lately. She waited while Kathleen called the boys who would be in Rumson already, looking for pots and pans. She waited another week then called Father Rielly, and he said, Of course, Ann, of course. She was grateful that he hadn't felt the least impulse to offer his counsel.

It was a miracle Sister Mary Arthur got through at all, Kathleen monopolized the phone so. Set up in her old bedroom, taking her time to sort out her next move. She'd left the perfectly good law firm behind to think about NGOs. She told her mother, There's so much I could be doing! So far, the doing involved tying up her mother's telephone lines and flirting with the Henderson boy. Whose wife everyone knew was a grave disappointment, according to Kathleen. Who says, Ann Mc-Cleary asked, what's to be disappointed about these days? Everything preset, pre-known. No surprises. And her daughter gave her the look she'd grown weary of in herself, the no-point-explaining look. There it is, the family crest, said Ann. She put a hand to her daughter's cheek, We must learn some new tricks. You and I. And that's why she'd gone to see Sister Mary Arthur. She needed to expand, she needed new experience or she'd die. Not that dying had been out of the question, she'd realized, after a long while, her own proclivity to slip away. And that understanding might have had something to do with Kathleen and the lovely suits piled up on the twin bed, and the job search that went nowhere.

First the fall, the kind of slip anyone might take, a spill off a high wet slate step. But she'd hit her head and her chest, a bruise spreading over her left side, blue as a sign from God. Something holy. Advil helped and was all she agreed to take, along with a bit of wine past five. That was the first winter. In spring she walked out to pick a flower, a daffodil and was bit by something nearly malarial. High fevers and her gait grew rigid from the inflammation. But she didn't understand herself until an early frost that third October put down a black ice unexpectedly in the night, and she drove to early Mass, and hit the brakes fast on a curve at the shake of something in her peripheral vision. Her rear wheels froze. She spun out and off the road and raced down the Kittrees' handsome hill to the decorative pond and sank. Passenger side aimed like an arrow to the muck that held the lilies tight at the bottom. She saw the water rise at her feet, and watched as calm as she might a faucet filling a pitcher. She knew she'd want to go home now, once she stepped out of the car, she'd have to miss Mass this one morning. The water was at her knees when she detached her house key from the ring, when she pushed open with a force she didn't know she had, the water just beginning to skim up the tipped driver's side. She jumped then waded, making havoc of Margaret Kittree's dormant flowers, making a mess, she told Kathleen, how will I ever apologize? That kind of thing takes years to develop and there I am, a lunatic out of nowhere. God forgive me. Everyone forgave her, and suggested Valium, Wellbutrin, Prozac, a grief group. But who could she possibly sit with who might look her in the eye and smile and say, I know you. Besides she had no time for groups, never had.

But then she'd had the idea, and maybe, if she was honest, it came from Kathleen and her endless chatter about doing good for the children in Africa. This was the substitute for romance with the Henderson boy. Or maybe no substitute, what could she really know these days. But why Africa, she thought, why not just here? There was one family in Rumson who'd lost a father. Ann McCleary invited the widow to tea. She used all her kindness, and spoke as she would, as she already had, to any one of her own children. When she left, a pretty girl with a dark bob, whose eyes, Ann hoped, would be less dark in time, when she backed away down the drive with a sweet wave, good-bye, called Ann. Good-bye.

But what about Holy Cross. She knew everything there was to know about children and many times she'd served as chaperone, as helper, someone as agile and as knowledgeable as herself, some use could surely be found.

A library? she said to Sister Mary Arthur. She had no wish to disguise her detachment, detachment was her best friend. Are you thinking of building something then? Maybe take over Father's precious garage.

No, no, not a bit, Ann, no, not in the least. I thought of something roving. Something that floats a bit, she laughed, and Ann always appreciated that laugh, and wondered how in these years it hadn't lost its light touch. Ann was listening, waiting to hear the laugh again: that's how she does it. I know all your tricks, Sister, she said.

It will be a bit of trick and I need a conjurer, a magician, will you help me?

It was a graceless thing, her cart. The wheels squeaked and the wire mesh caught at the pages and grilled them, engraved them with a crisscross. But this was the library Sister had in mind. Ann McCleary could choose her beneficiaries at will, one kindergarten, two first grades, two second grades. Why not Tuesdays, Sister said, Tuesday mornings nine-to-noon, Mrs. Lanahan will keep us in literature, and keep the cart locked safely in the supply closet. And here was her first battle. Mrs. Lanahan thought literature for small first readers involved saints and martyrs. Lurid paintings, the wounds especially crimson, even in her day the illustrations weren't so gruesome. No, she wouldn't read them, wouldn't even carry them. Ann McCleary held her ground and soon had tucked in books of her own, things she'd found on bookshelves kept for the towheads. And she wandered when she didn't mean to, just popping into the A&P for some radishes, but there she was next-door in Sally Hetzler's bookstore, who gave her a discount, for the library, and she became a regular customer.

The children weren't much interested. They had grandmothers of their own, and even Holy Cross had computers in the kindergarten. She never spoke about this to Mary Arthur, never said she wasn't quite as welcome as she'd hoped. And once when the blank faces greeted her as a stranger, even the teacher couldn't make her out, she'd wheeled her awkward cart all the way out to Father's garage and wept beside the Karmann Ghia where no one would think to look for her. She was not a quitter. But now she wondered why that mattered any more, that quality. She'd already held a high head, but maybe life shifted. Maybe the things that sustained you just wore out and new things, new people, needed other qualities, and yours just went to sleep. Sometimes a life just finished, unexpectedly, and it was the ones still wandering around in foolish stiff bodies after they were already done who were the sorry ones. She cried and cried and no one came to comfort her because who could.

Ann McCleary told her children when they were small, when things were hard, if they were sick, or especially for the older ones, for Terry, when their father died and they were too little to lose him, she told them that one day they would realize they were better, and that they'd been better for a while. They hadn't noticed the shift, it came so quietly and that was God's grace, she believed it, and she told them it was true. Only Terry gave her a hard time. He dove off the high dive two summers after his father's death, and by a wicked chance made the inward arc just to the spot where his chin cracked the tile edge. Blood bloomed out into the deep end and she caught him first, unconscious, the concussion a sure thing, and forty stitches in two layers, and black eyes, both, and bruises on the shoulders, a mess, a terrible mess, and she was forced to revise her theory, her theology. Sometimes the pain needs to reverberate for a long time, for longer than even you or anyone else might think necessary or fair. Sometimes that's how it goes, and God may or may not be a part of that, probably is, she told her boy. But it's anyone's guess, she said, surprising herself in the admittance. And later she remembered a smile in him, a long time later, too long she thought, when the others had bounced back, to her credit everyone said, they admired her, everyone did, to her credit her children thrived. And one day, Terry smiled a smile she recognized in her deepest self. He pulled a bit of onion grass out by the root, she just happened to spot him through her kitchen window, he was almost nine, now, and not so tall, beautiful hands, like his father's, long, someone made for a piano, up came the grass, roots and blades, and he examined it all closely, the whole package clutched in his hand and he smiled at the shape and the sharp stink of the roots, he put his face close then wrenched back and laughed, his face so happy, and then happy to be happy, the double happiness smile she called it, so hard-won, and it never left him after that, it became the way he smiled, the way he lit every room he ever walked into.

There were Tuesdays and more Tuesdays and they got used to her, and didn't stare when she pushed her squeaky cart into the classroom, and took her time lowering herself into the armchair Sister Mary Arthur had suffered the already over-furnished rooms to accommodate for this purpose, her floating library. More like a falling library, they said, our reader falls asleep! And so she did every once in a while on those warm spring mornings. When the five-year-olds laid out their mats and curled on the floor like kittens, she dozed too, the sound of her own voice putting her to sleep, sometimes first of all. She knew they complained about her. What part of a progressive curriculum did she serve? But Sister Mary Arthur was adamant, and Mrs. Lanahan whispered it was one of her *conceptions*. It's a charity case, said Mrs. Kelly, who taught the brighter first grade. It's fortunate I didn't quite hear that, Mrs. Kelly. Sister Mary Arthur's door was open, and even Mrs. Lanahan froze. But nothing more was said about it after that. And Ann McCleary became part of the landscape, along with the candy sales and the beanies worn to Mass.

There was a little boy of course, after a year or two, in the kinder-garten, who didn't entirely dislike a story read out loud. His parents were nostalgic that way, and she let him chew on the covers of the books she wasn't reading. Still teething are we? A big boy like you? And he smiled at her, and then a sly film of a second smile came too, he had to pull the thick cardboard cover away to accommodate his own full delight. Look at you, she laughed, a double happiness. He dropped the book and tumbled off. His attention snapped away in an instant. But a few weeks later it happened again, though now she knew to watch and wait was death. She'd only catch it by the very qui-etest chance, she told Kathleen. And only now and then.

Nominated by A Public Space

VICTORY

by TONY HOAGLAND

from LAKE EFFECT

In the old days the enemy's head would have been displayed
on the edge of the table at the press conference;

the sightless eyes staring, the blood crusted
around the tattered skin of the neck where the

top had been separated from the rest of him; the head
of state no longer a figure of speech,

but on the other hand no longer attached
to the nation of flesh, no longer attached

to anything at all. In the old days
victorious Tribal Chieftan A would have seized a handful

of the thick hair of Warlord B and lifted that fifteen pounds
of bone and meat high in the air and shaken it

for a roomful of patriots and suckers-up, some of them
already rehearsing the story they would tell that night

over their pots of gruel and beer,
and the people in the front row would be able to smell

the flesh starting to turn
and might in their quiet nausea imagine

how the head had been transported two days' ride from the battlefield
in a sack tied to the back of a horse

galloping over unmarked mountain roads,
battered against the saddle,

also kicked occasionally by the anxious rider,
a young lieutenant frightened

at being so clearly in the middle of history
that he feels sometimes like a small word

inside a very long sentence,
whose meaning he has no way to understand

except to continue riding
with this strange cargo bouncing behind him

and his orders to push forward
towards the city rising ahead, a place

where the citizens are ravenous for sensation
and the leaders severed from reason.

Nominated by Marianne Boruch, Jane Hirshfield, Charles Harper Webb,
Ellen Bass, Jim Moore, Lake Effect.

THE CASE FOR FREE WILL

by PATTY SEYBURN

from ARROYO LITERARY REVIEW

i.

When I was little, I thought the moon was Europe.
Or was like Europe.
Or would be like Europe, by the time I grew up.
Exotic, and far, but not impossibly far—we would go there
on vacation, once or twice, and learn about other cultures,
those that spawned ours—some of which died like
19th century mothers in childbirth.
By that time we would have found culture on the moon
and the moon's culture would be something like Europe's:
many museums with familiar paintings and sculptures,
canals and vast churches, old stone edifices,
gaudy commercials, bitter coffee and crusts of bread
and couture and whores in the windows
with Yma Sumac piped in.

ii.

It's early enough in the day to pursue
other interests, like bass fishing and shopping for overpriced objects.
Or, you could get a cup of coffee and brood as to why
joy eludes you at every turn, and you turn
quite a bit.
Consider how limitless the world seemed
when Armstrong landed his prodigious foot in that weird

powder and bounced along from there.
Houston, the Eagle has landed.
Let's take a dip in Tranquility Bay.
The astronauts, like gods, didn't comment on their feelings
or suggest a course of action. They were too busy
collecting rocks after uttering a scripted sentence missing an article
and pushing that symbol into terra incognita.

iii.

I was awake but not too aware back then.
Vietnam in my living room
but I missed the casualties.
I missed my father's heart attack, recovery.
I missed the Shelby Mustang, and the drumroll of assassinations.
Bound to leave my home, and not return.
Have you seen the pictures of the Saturn 5 separating?
Stage from stage, until the lunar module and lunar lander
are completely
on their own.
Get me out of this atmosphere!
Having done their part, they are dispensable.
If you think that happiness is a matter
of expectations fulfilled, think again.
That's the only bad habit I ever picked up.

iv.

And still there's the moon: half-dark, half-light,
never making us more welcome than on that first visit.
How does it expect to be like Europe?
People want to feel wanted and there is competition:
that hotbed, Mars.
Saturn, with those more than cocktail-party-distance rings.
And Venus, who seems close, beckons
but gives not an inch: tease and tart of the cosmos.
The planets cannot help what they are, locked
in orbit. Can we?
Before age five, I had free will.
William James said: *My first act of free will shall be to believe
in free will.*

After, destiny took over, and everything I decided
in the most labored fashion, was already
coded in the stars.

v.

Poor stars.
Rich stars.

Nominated by Arroyo Literary Review

MUNRO COUNTRY

by CHERYL STRAYED

from THE MISSOURI REVIEW

One afternoon when I was twenty-five, I opened the lid of the black metal mailbox that was bolted to the front of the house where I lived and found a plain white envelope addressed to me in a grandmotherly scrawl from an address in British Columbia. It was January in Minneapolis and cold—really cold—but I pulled my gloves off anyway and tore the envelope open and stood on the frozen wooden stairs to read the letter inside. *Dear Cheryl*, it began in the same hand that had addressed the envelope:

> Your letter and story were forwarded to me here in B.C. where I am staying until April—near to 2 of my daughters and my one grandchild. I want to say that I was moved and delighted by the Horse and Blue Canoe. It's a wonderful, unexpected kind of story and I wouldn't change a hair on its head. (That's what my favorite editor always says to me before he proposes about 50 changes.) You are quite right to stay out of academic life if you can. Are you eligible for any grants? If you were in Canada I'd certainly urge you to apply for one from the Canada Council. You must continue writing but you do have lots of time. You're two years younger than my youngest daughter. I wasn't writing nearly so well at your age.
>
> With great good wishes—Alice Munro

A shaky, sickening glee washed through me and then drained away almost immediately, replaced by a daffy disbelief: Alice Munro had written to me. *Alice! Munro!* Those two words were a kind of Holy Grail to me then: the lilting rise and fall of *Alice*, the double-barreled thunk of *Munro*. Together they seemed less like a name than an object I could hold in my hands—a stoneware bowl, perhaps, or a pewter platter, equal parts generous and unforgiving. They bore the weight of everything I loved, admired and understood about the art and craft of fiction, everything I ached to master myself.

She wasn't the only writer I loved, of course. Raymond Carver, Edna O'Brien, William Faulkner, Mary Gaitskill and Flannery O'Connor had each been profoundly important to me. From them and many others, I learned how to write. I studied their stories and novels, their sentences and scenes, excavated their plots and characters and descriptions and then attempted to do what they did all by myself on the page. From a purely craft standpoint, Alice Munro was at the lead of that pack in my mind, a virtuoso among virtuosos, but it wasn't her virtuosity that made her different from the others to me. Not her dazzling narrative authority or her gorgeously unvarnished prose, not her telescopic density or her breathtakingly intricate descriptions of the way her characters thought and lived and behaved. What made her different to me was another thing entirely, and it wasn't about style but subject and, even more precisely, it was about Alice Munro herself. It didn't matter that she was Canadian and thirty-seven years older than I and that her life was, in dozens of particular ways *not* like my own. When I read her stories, I felt like she'd lived my life.

The fictional world that she has spun in a fair portion of these stories has a name: Munro Country. It's the real-life Huron County, in southwestern Ontario, where Munro spent her girlhood and returned to live in middle age. In stories she's written for what's approaching fifty years, Munro evokes this hardscrabble place with searing specificity: its ramshackle farms and rutted roads, its small towns and social institutions and the complicated and contradictory, proud and humiliated, vain and self-effacing people who populate it.

I got my first taste of Munro Country when I read *Dance of the Happy Shades*, her first book, which was published in 1968, the year I was born. I'd found it on a sale table at a used bookstore near the University of Minnesota in Minneapolis, where I was a student. I bought it because it looked interesting and it was marked down to something like two dollars and because I was twenty and consumed at that age by a kind of roving, voracious hunger to shuck off the sunny, small-town beauty queen that I seemed to be and to become instead the earnest writer that I knew lived inside me. I felt instinctively that reading just about any work of serious fiction I could get my hands on would help me make that transformation. I didn't know anything about Alice Munro when I paid my two dollars and shoved her book into my bag. Didn't know that by then she'd published six books and was well on her way to being celebrated as "our Chekhov"—a comparison made first by the writer Cynthia Ozick but immediately embraced by her peers. Didn't know she'd won numerous major awards and appeared regularly in the *New Yorker* because I didn't, at that time, read the *New Yorker*. I didn't even know the *New Yorker* was a publication that anyone beyond the city limits of New York City would have an interest in reading. I only knew this, once I sat down to read the stories in *Dance of the Happy Shades:* those stories *knew me.*

They knew my mother too. And my stepfather and sister and brother. They even knew our two dogs, our one-horned goat named Katrina and the hens and the horses that lived in our yard. They knew the odd, picked-on boy who drowned in a lake one summer evening outside the town where I grew up and the flamboyantly feminist counselor who came from the Twin Cities to work at my school and only lasted one year. They knew the fundamentalist Christians who lived in falling-down houses and rusted-out trailers who wouldn't let their kids listen to music and the friendly old veteran who owned a rock shop and pushed himself around in a wheelchair after he lost both of his legs in the war. They knew, it seemed, the whole of Aitkin County, Minnesota, where I came of age. Its three tiny towns and dozens of far-flung townships, its long, lonesome roads and endless swamps, bogs, woods and lakes, its bars and businesses and wild and domesticated beasts, its farms and fishing holes, its corn feeds, county fairs and city councils, its deer hunters and demolition derbies, its tractor pulls and taciturn old-timers, its Finns and Ojibwes and back-to-the-land hippies, its hot, mosquito-ridden summers and brutally cold winters. But most of all, those stories knew me, the eager, curious, grandiose girl who grew up in the midst of this and wanted out as fiercely as she wanted to hold on to it forever.

I'd never felt known in quite that way by fiction—by anything, perhaps. I'd identified with characters and situations, of course; had plenty of moments, as a reader, of revelation and understanding and connection. But what I felt about Alice Munro after reading her stories went far beyond those things: I recognized her. Felt pinned and pierced by her, burned and branded by the truth and beauty of her words. *I love Alice Munro*, I took to saying, the way I did about any number of people I didn't know whose writing I admired—meaning, of course, that I loved her books. And I did. I devoured each of them after my chance discovery of *Dance of the Happy Shades*, my love intensifying with each volume. But I loved *her* too, in a way that felt slightly ridiculous even to me. It wasn't an obsessive stalker's love, though it did make me ache a little when I thought about it too much. It wasn't that I wanted anything from Alice Munro. I didn't expect her to love me back. It was that I longed to express my love for her. To explain, somehow, all the layers of things we had in common—the small towns and the corduroy roads, the experience of being the prodigal daughter in a place where daughters were not raised to be prodigal—and make her understand what her work had meant to me.

What I felt for Alice Munro was not something I was used to; I'd never been much of a fan. As a girl, I didn't cover my walls with posters or pictures of idols, the way most of my friends did. I'd never written a letter to a stranger I admired. And writing to Alice Munro seemed impossible anyway. Where would I send the letter? How could I find the words to express myself in full? Time passed, she published another book and I went on silently loving her, studying her stories, trying to write my own in imitation of her. She was scheduled to read at a museum in Minneapolis, and I bought a ticket, but she canceled at the last minute. And then, when I was twenty-two, my mother died and everything I felt for Alice Munro darkened, deepened.

Her mother had died young too, and she haunts the pages of Munro's stories the way my own mother began to haunt mine. I read Munro through my sorrow, rereading certain stories and scenes over and over again, memorizing particular sentences. Class and culture and cold country climates had bound me to Munro, but they had nothing on dead mothers. Ours had died differently—hers around sixty, after a long illness with Parkinson's disease, mine at forty-five, of lung cancer, only seven weeks after she was diagnosed—but I sensed viscerally that the losses Munro and I had suffered had gouged us in the same way. The fictional motherless daughters in her stories told me so. The sad, subtle ways they turned their heads, the glitteringly sharp laughter that tamped down the memories of the mothers they didn't have, the way they could never be free, never released, never shucked clean of the mothers who were loved or unloved, who had been wrong or almost always right, who lived on and on no matter how many years passed without them. And I understood more deeply the living mothers in Munro's fictions too. So often they seemed to be the same one, in story after story. The same enterprising, intellectually striving, socially thwarted, subtly unconventional and mildly whimsical woman, who, in spite of everything, had no choice but to get dinner on the table or the cows milked at dawn, and, always, there'd be wash to do.

Which was, to put it plainly, the story of my own mother's life.

I tried to write that story, the one of my mother's life and my own, mimicking Munro. Of course I failed, so I wrote whatever I could get down on the page. I wrote and wrote, read some more. I read and I wrote. At twenty-four, I finished a story that I thought was perhaps good enough to be published, so I sent it to a contest in England, and months later I got a phone call from a man in London, telling me that it had won. The prize, the man explained, was a Parker pen, a check that amounted to twenty-two hundred U.S. dollars and two copies of the book in which my story would be published. "One for you," he said with his British accent, "and one for your mum."

I hung up the phone and cried my heart out. I was happy about the prize. I was grateful for the money. I wasn't crying because of those things. I was crying because I didn't have a mother, or a father, for that matter. Because I didn't know what to do with the second copy of the book that contained my first published story.

"She writes about *me!*" my mother had once proudly proclaimed to her own mother about my first efforts as a writer—stories I'd written in college and had let her read. The three of us were riding in the car, driving to Duluth, where my mother would die in a month.

"I do *not*," I'd scoffed bitterly. I was twenty-two, past the stage where it seemed that every cell in my body longed to push my mother away, but her giddy insistence that my budding literary career bore any relation to her riled the old teenager in me back to life. I was furious and humiliated, regardless of her cancer. "I write about all kinds of things, not just you," I hissed, though it wasn't true. Each of the stories I'd written had, in fact, a thinly fictionalized version of my mother at its center.

"Okay, honey," she said soothingly, unperturbed.

That exchange played itself out horribly in my mind for years—one of the few regrets I have about what happened between the two of us in my mother's last days—and it played itself out again as I wept in my living room on the afternoon I heard my story had won a prize.

The story is called "The House with the Horse and the Blue Canoe," a barely fictionalized account of a hard and beautiful time in my girlhood, when my family lived in a dilapidated farmhouse that adjoined a pasture that enclosed our horse, Lady, and her makeshift water trough. The trough was a blue canoe my family had smashed up one winter using it as a toboggan on the big hill nearby that went down to a lake named Grace. The house was on the side of a well-traveled highway, so when people asked where we lived, all we had to say was "the house with the horse and the blue canoe," and everyone knew where we were talking about. In the story I wrote about the things that happened the year I was ten: how my stepfather fell from a roof and broke his back and how this led to us eventually having to move out of the farmhouse because we couldn't afford the rent. How in his months-long convalescence my stepfather carved and then painted an entire village of wooden figurines to populate the miniature log cabin that my mother put out each Christmas and how my mother sang "O Tannenbaum" to us as she lit the Christmas lights. It's not so much a story as a gathering of reminiscences, an elegy for the family I used to have, the one that died with my mother. And there was only one person on earth I wanted to read it: Alice Munro.

When I received my two copies of the book a few months later, I drafted the letter. It's lost to time, but I remember sitting at my computer for hours, composing each sentence, questioning each word, crafting the letter as painstakingly as I did my stories, trying to tell her everything but also rein myself in, to express my fervor without scaring her off. I included the copy of the book that was meant for my mother. I told her that I knew it was highly unlikely she had time to waste on reading my story, which, by the way, began on page 121, but if she was interested—*she might be interested*—well, then she should just go ahead and read it. I did not expect her to write me back. I knew she was far too busy to write me back. I was sure she received a deluge of letters from the likes of me, and how could she possibly write us all back, what with the demands of her actual writing, but if she would *like* to write me back, she should feel free to do so.

On the envelope I wrote her name above only the words "Clinton, Ontario, Canada." Having grown up in the country, where letters are sometimes addressed with the confidence of an absurd insularity— "Joe, who lives past the dump," say—I gambled that anyone who worked at the post office in Clinton would know where to find the now world-famous author. I mailed my letter and story to her on December 20th.

On January 18th her reply appeared in my mailbox.

I stood on the porch reading it and then I went inside and read it some more. I was leaving the next day for a writing residency at the Ucross Foundation in Wyoming, and I took the letter with me, neatly folded and in the envelope it had come in. I propped it on my desk in my studio and gazed at it for long stretches. It never occurred to me to write Munro back, to keep in touch, to attempt to parlay our exchange into something more. To do so seemed to me a violation of the gift she'd given me in her reply; it would be taking a mile when all I really needed was an inch. Her letter traveled with me, in me, for years as I wrote and tried to write, the best lines from it—*I wouldn't change a hair on its head* and *it's a wonderful, unexpected kind of story* and *I wasn't writing nearly so well at your age*—humming inside of me like an ancient gong.

By the time I turned thirty I'd begun publishing stories and essays, but I still hadn't managed to finish the novel I'd claimed to be writing for years. So I did what I'd told Alice Munro in my letter I would not do—I applied to graduate school to get my MFA in fiction writing, despite her agreement that I was "quite right to stay out of academic life" if I could. I couldn't. I'd been working mostly as a waitress for more than a decade, writing on the side. I'd won grants and gone to writing residencies every chance I got, but those things hadn't allowed me the shelter I needed to complete a book.

I went to Syracuse University and was mentored by a string of stunning writers and good souls—George Saunders, Mary Caponegro, Arthur Flowers and, in my final semester, Mary Gaitskill, who'd been a shining star in my constellation of literary influence. Each of them, along with my talented classmates, helped me further down the path, told me things that I needed to know, and still there was always Alice Munro, teaching me by the frank force of her fiction—how she moved her characters in and out of a room, how she conveyed an emotion or a moment just so. She was my most important mentor, though I'd never laid eyes on her until finally, at the end of my first year of graduate school, I got my chance.

She was participating in the New Yorker Festival in Manhattan, appearing in a double-header with Richard Ford. I took the train to see her on an uncharacteristically hot day in early May, traveling five and a half hours from Syracuse to Penn Station. Then the subway to the Lower East Side and a short, painful walk to the Angel Orensanz Foundation, the sandals I hadn't worn since the summer before raising blisters on my tender heels. The Angel Orensanz Foundation is a stylishly dilapidated former synagogue that dates back to the nineteenth century. I handed over my ticket just outside its gaping neogothic doors and walked inside, feeling silent and solemn amid the din of a hundred conversations all around me. I found a seat to the side of the stage, a few rows back. The room was cavernous and packed. Tickets had sold out months before. "Sarah Jessica Parker married Matthew Broderick here," the woman next to me said as I scanned the faces near the low stage, trying to spot Munro. And then the lights dimmed and the crowd hushed.

Richard Ford came on first. I watched him in profile, handsome and lean in a purple blazer and white shirt. He read "Reunion" by John Cheever and then his own story called "Reunion." I listened raptly, almost forgetting Alice Munro. I'd always admired Richard Ford too; his book *Rock Springs* was among those I'd read again and again. When he finished, Alice Munro walked elegantly onto the stage, her smile shy and bright, her hair soft and white. She wore dangling black stone earrings and a matching black stone necklace that sat close to her throat. Her cream-colored dress flowed bride-like to the floor, topped by an equally long black vest that closed with one button at her chest.

The sight of her knocked me sideways, the way so many of her stories had. At the sound of her voice, I wept. I'd not expected this. Futilely, I searched my purse for a tissue, as unobtrusively as I could, mortified by my tiny gasps and copious tears. I gave up and wiped my face with my bare hands and tried to concentrate on her words. She was reading a story called "Nettles," the crowd breathing with one breath. I weaved in and out of listening and quietly weeping, the tears seeping ridiculously out of me, despite my inner pleadings that I get a grip. Later I'd laugh when I told this story. I'd say that when I saw Alice Munro, I understood for the first time all those screaming, inconsolable girls in old footage of the Beatles in the '60s. And yet that wasn't what was happening at all. I wasn't crying for joy or excitement or because I was overcome with emotion to see someone I loved from afar. I was crying because something had come to an end. I knew it only in glimmers—it would take years until I fully understood—that a spell cast long before had been broken the moment Alice Munro walked onto the stage.

Of all the lines she'd written in her letter to me, of all the phrases that had repeated and hummed like a gong in my head, there was one that hummed more persistently than the rest: *You're two years younger than my youngest daughter.* Such a neutral statement, and yet I couldn't keep myself from coloring in the lines. In the country called Munro, I'd subconsciously staked a fantastical claim. *I could be her daughter,* I'd sometimes think, remembering those words she'd written about how close I was in age to her youngest. I'd have been the final one, kindred and kept and adored.

I didn't *really* think I was Alice Munro's daughter, of course. I'm not talking about delusion. I'm talking about longing and instinct and the eternal ache of a girl who lost her mom. About the way life, like a Munro story, unfurls and then turns back on itself in the most unpredictable, inexplicable ways, ambiguous and overlapping, perpetually at odds with itself. About how I loved Alice Munro more excruciatingly than I ever had in that moment she walked onto the stage and also how, in that very same moment, I began, finally, to let her go. Not Munro, the great writer, whom I continue to learn from and admire, but Munro the maternal mentor, from whom I simply had to move on. Munro Country had been my motherland for years, but by then, at thirty-two, hip-deep at last in my own novel, I understood that in order to write my book, I had to set out into territory that was all my own.

These realizations didn't come to me in great, lucid waves as I sat listening to "Nettles" while scrambling for something with which to blow my nose. They were not an epiphany. Instead they were ephemeral and shadowy, as if a bird had darted in and then disappeared into a dark corner of that cavernous room. At the sight of her, I only knew that I knew things I could not yet say. If you'd asked me why I was crying, I'd have told you the story about the girls and the Beatles in the '60s.

When she finished reading, she sat in a chair on the stage to receive her admirers. I hung back, dry-eyed and chastened, lingering toward the end of a long line. As I waited, I rehearsed what I would say when it was my turn. *I love your work! Your books have meant so much to me—to my development as a writer. Actually, you probably don't remember, but you wrote me a letter. You read a story of mine. You said you wouldn't change a hair on its head!* I swapped the words and phrases around in my mind, the same way I do when I'm writing—expanding and deleting, trying to craft an opening sentence that would draw her in and make her want to stay. But as the line inched forward, I could feel the words crumbling inside me, becoming more inane with each step in her direction. Should I even mention the letter? I wondered. Surely she wouldn't remember the letter. And doesn't *everyone* say they love her work? I tried to think of a single thing to say that she hadn't likely heard a thousand times before and came up with nothing. No matter what I said, I believed, my words wouldn't stick. I could feel them falling already, leaden and clichéd, straight from my mouth to the floor.

One person approached her and then left and another and another, until at last the person who stood in front of me stepped forward. It was my turn next, I realized, with a fluttering in my gut, and a minute or two later, Alice Munro's eyes met mine. She gazed at me with the same bland, agreeable and guardedly receptive expression as she had all the others, and in the flash of a second, I knew I wouldn't speak to her. There had been so many words between us already. Entire sentences she'd written that I'd etched into my brain. Gestures conveyed just so on the page. Those girls who laughed glitteringly. Women who turned their heads in sad and subtle ways. They were hers. They were mine. About the savage love I felt for them, there was both too much and nothing to say.

I gave her a small wave and then shifted my eyes and walked away.

Nominated by The Missouri Review

LABRADOR TEA

by ARTHUR SZE

from THE GINKGO LIGHT (Copper Canyon)

Labrador leaves in a jar with a kerchief lid
release an arctic aroma when simmered on a stove.

Yesterday when fire broke out in the bosque,
the air had the stench of cauliflower in a steamer

when water evaporates and the pot scalds.
Although Apache plume, along with clusters of

western peppergrass, makes fragrant the wash,
owls that frequent the hole high up the arroyo's

bank have already come and gone. Yesterday,
though honey locust leaves shimmered

in a gust, no wasp nest had yet formed
under the porch. Repotting a *Spathiphyllum*,

then uncoiling a hose, I suddenly hear surf
through open slats of a door. Sprinklers come on

in the dark; a yellow slug crawls on a rain-
slicked banana leaf; as the mind flits, imbibes,

84

leaves clothed underneath with rusty hairs
suffuse a boreal light glistening on tidal pools.

Nominated by Jim Moore, Copper Canyon Press

I AM MYSELF THREE SELVES AT LEAST

by JENNIFER K. SWEENEY

from ELEVEN ELEVEN

I am myself three selves at least,
the one who sweeps the brittle
bees, who saves the broken plates

and bowls, who counts to ten,
who tends the shoals,
who steeps the morning's Assam leaves

and when day is wrung
tightens clock springs.
And yes, the one who sat through youth

quiet as a tea stain, whose hand
went up and knees went down,
whose party dresses soaked with rain,

who dug up bones
of snakes and mice
and stashed them inside baby jars—

who did not eat,
but did not starve.
And the self who twists the fallen

dogwood sticks into her hair,
who knows the trick of grief
is there is nothing such as sin

and neither good to part
the air, whom autumn claims
skin by skin.

Nominated by Mark Irwin, Michael Waters, Eleven Eleven

THE COUSINS

fiction by CHARLES BAXTER

from TIN HOUSE

My cousin Brantford was named for our grandfather, who had made a fortune from a device used in aircraft navigation. I suppose it saved lives. A bad-tempered man with a scar above his cheekbone, my grandfather believed that the rich were rewarded for their merits and the poor deserved what they got. He did not care for his own grandchildren and referred to my cousin as "the little prince." In all fairness, he didn't like me either.

Brantford had roared through his college fund so rapidly that by the age of twenty-three he was down to pocket change. One bright spring day when I was visiting New York City and had called him up, he insisted on taking me to lunch at a midtown restaurant where the cost of the entrees was so high that a respectful noonday hush hung over its skeletal postmodern interior. Muttering oligarchs with monogrammed shirt cuffs gazed at entering patrons with a languid alertness. The maître d' wore one of those dark blue restaurant suits, and the wine list had been printed on velvety pages set in a stainless-steel three-ring binder.

By the time my cousin arrived, I had read the menu four times. He was late. You had to know Brantford to get used to him. A friend of mine said that my cousin looked like the mayor of a ruined city. Appearances mattered a great deal to Brantford, but his own were on a gradual slide. His face had a permanent alcoholic flush. His brownish-blond hair was parted on the right side and was too long by a few millimeters, trailing over his collar. Although he dressed well in flannel trousers and cordovan shoes, you could see the telltale food stains on his shirt, and the expression underneath his blond mustache had something subtly wrong with it—he smiled with a strangely discouraged and stale affability.

"Bunny," he said to me, sitting down with an audible expunging of air. He still used my childhood name. No one else did. He didn't give me a hug because we don't do that. "I see you've gotten started. You're having a martini?"

I nodded. "Morning tune-up," I said.

"Brave choice," Brantford grinned, simultaneously waving down the server. "Waitress," he said, pointing at my drink, "I'll have one of those. Very dry, please, no olive." The server nodded before giving Brantford a thin professional smile and gliding over to the bar.

We had a kind of solidarity, Brantford and I. I had two decades on him, but we were oddly similar, more like brothers than cousins. I had always seen in him some better qualities than those I actually possessed. For example, he was one of those people who always make you happier the moment you see them.

Before his drink arrived, we caught ourselves up. Brantford's mother, Aunt Margaret, had by that time been married to several different husbands, including a three-star Army general, and she currently resided in a small apartment cluttered with knickknacks near the corner of 92nd and Broadway.

Having spent herself in a wild youth and and at all times been given to manias, Brantford's mother had started taking a new medication called Elysium Max, which seemed to be keeping her on a steady course where life was concerned. Brantford instructed me to please phone her while I was in town, and I said I would. As for Brantford's two half-sisters, they were doing fine.

With this information out of the way, I asked Brantford how he was.

"I don't know. It's strange. Sometimes at night I have the feeling that I've murdered somebody." He stopped and glanced down at the tableware. "Someone's dead. Only I don't know who or what, or when I did it. I must've killed somebody. I'm sure of it. Thank you," he said with his first real smile of the day, as the server placed a martini in front of him.

"Well, that's just crazy," I said. "You haven't killed anyone."

"Doesn't matter if I have or haven't," he said, "if it feels that way. Maybe I should take a vacation."

"Brantford," I said. "You can't take a vacation. You don't work." I waited for a moment. "Do you?"

"Well," he said, "I'd like to. Besides, I work, in my way," he claimed, taking a sip of the martini. "And don't forget that I can be anything I want to be." This sentence was enunciated carefully and with precise despair, as if it had served as one of those lifelong mottoes that he no longer believed in.

What year was this? 1994? When someone begins to carry on as my cousin did, I'm never sure what to say. Tact is required. As a teenager, Brantford had told me that he aspired to be a concert pianist, and I was the one who had to remind him that he wasn't a musician and didn't play the piano. But Brantford had seen a fiery angel somewhere in the sky and thought it might descend on him. I hate those angels. I haven't always behaved well when people open their hearts to me.

"Well, what about the animals?" I asked. Brantford was always caring for damaged animals and had done so from the time he was a boy. He found them in streets and alleys and nursed them back to health and then let them go. But they tended to fall in with him and to get crushes on him. In whatever apartment or house he lived in, you would find recovering cats, mutts, and sparrows barking and chirping and mewling in response to him.

"No, not that," he said. "I would never make a living off those critters," he said. "That's a sideline. I love them too much."

"Veterinary school?" I asked.

"No, I couldn't. Absolutely not. I don't want to practice that kind of medicine with them," he said, as if he were speaking of family members. "If I made money off those little guys, I'd lose the gift. Besides, I don't have the discipline to get through another school. Willpower is not my strong suit. The world runs on willpower," he said, as if perplexed. He put his head back into his hands. "Willpower! Anyhow, would you please explain to me why it feels as if I've committed a murder?"

*　*　*

When I had first come to New York in the 1970s as an aspiring actor, I rode the subways everywhere, particularly the number 6, which in those days was still the Lexington IRT line. Sitting on that train one afternoon, squeezed between my fellow passengers as I helped one of them, a school-boy, with a nosebleed, I felt pleased with myself. I had assimilated. Having come to New York from the Midwest, I was anticipating my big break and meanwhile waited tables at a little bistro near Astor Place. Mine was a familiar story, one of those drabby little tales of ideals and artistic high-mindedness that wouldn't bear repeating if it weren't for the woman with whom I was then involved.

She had a quietly insubstantial quality. When you looked away from her, you couldn't be sure that she'd still be there when you looked back again. She knew how to vanish quickly from scenes she didn't like. Her ability to dematerialize was purposeful and was complicated by her appearance: day and night, she wore dark glasses. She had a sensitivity to light, a photophobia, which she had acquired as a result of a corneal infection. In those days, her casual friends thought that the dark glasses constituted a praiseworthy affectation. "She looks very cool," they would say.

Even her name—Giulietta, spelled in the Italian manner—seemed like an affectation. But Giulietta it was, the name with which, as a Catholic, she had been baptized. We'd met at the bistro where I carried menus and trays laden with food back and forth. Dining alone, cornered under a light fixture, she was reading a book by Bruno Bettelheim, and I deliberately served her a risotto entree that she hadn't ordered. I wanted to provoke her to conversation, even if it was hostile. I couldn't see her eyes behind those dark glasses, but I wanted to. Self-possession in any form attracts me, especially at night, in cities. Anyway, my studied incompetence as a waiter amused her. Eventually she gave me her phone number.

She worked in Brooklyn at a special school for mildly autistic and emotionally impaired little kids. The first time we slept together we had to move the teddy bears and the copies of the *New Yorker* off her bed. Sophistication and a certain childlike guilelessness lived side-by-side in her behavior. On Sunday morning she watched cartoons and *Meet the Press*, and in the afternoon she listened to the Bartók quartets while smoking marijuana, which she claimed was good for her eyesight. In her bathtub was a rubber duck, and in the living room a copy of *Anna Karenina*, which she had read three times.

We were inventive and energetic in our lovemaking, Giulietta and I, but her eyes stayed hidden no matter how dark it was. From her, I knew nothing of the look of recognition a woman can give to a man. All the same, I was beginning to love her. She comforted me and sustained me by attaching me to ordinary things: reading the Sunday paper in bed, making bad jokes—the rewards of plain everyday life.

One night I took her uptown for a party, near Columbia, at the apartment of another actor—Freddy Avery, who also happened to be a poet. Like many actors, Freddy enjoyed performing and was good at mimicry, and his parties tended to be raucous. You could easily commit an error in tone at those parties. You'd expose yourself as a hayseed if you were too sincere about anything. There was an Iron Law of Irony at Freddy's parties, so I was worried that if Giulietta and I arrived too early, we'd be mocked. No one was ever prompt at Freddy's parties (they always began at their midpoint, if I could put it that way), so we ducked into a bar to waste a bit of time before going up.

Under a leaded-glass, greenish lamp hanging down over our booth, Giulietta took my hand. "We don't have to go to this . . . thing," she said. "We could just escape to a movie and then head home."

"No," I said. "We have to do this. Anyway, all the movies have started."

"What's the big deal with this party, Benjamin?" she asked me. I couldn't see her eyes behind her dark glasses, but I knew they were trained on me. She wore a dark blue blouse, and her hair had been pinned back with a rainbow-colored barrette. The fingers of her hands, now on the table, had a long, aristocratic delicacy, but she bit her nails; the tips of her fingers had a raggedy appearance.

"Oh, interesting people will be there," I said. "Other actors. And literary types, you know, and dancers. They'll make you laugh."

"No," she said. "They'll make *you* laugh." She took a sip of her beer. She lit up a cigarette and blew the smoke toward the ceiling. "Dancers can't converse anyway. They're all autoerotic. If we go to this, I'm only doing it because of you. I want you to know that."

"Thank you," I said. "Listen, could you do me a favor?"

"Anything," she nodded.

"Well, it's one of those parties where the guests . . ."

"What?"

"It's like this. Those people are clever. You know, it's one of those uptown crowds. So what I'm asking is . . . do you think you could be clever tonight, please? As a favor to me? I know you can be like that. You can be funny; I know you, Giulietta. I've seen you sparkle. So could you be amusing? That's really all I ask."

This was years ago. Men were still asking women—or telling them—how to behave in public. I flinch, now, thinking about that request, but it didn't seem like much of anything to me back then. Giulietta leaned back and took her hand away from mine. Then she cleared her throat.

"You are so funny." She wasn't smiling. She seemed to be evaluating me. "Yes," she said. "Yes, all right." She dug her right index fingernail into the wood of the table, as if making a calculation. "I can be clever if you want me to be."

◦ ◦ ◦

After buzzing us up, Freddy Avery met us at the door of his apartment with an expression of jovial melancholy. "Hey hey hey," he said, ushering us in. "Ah. And this is Giulietta," he continued, staring at her dark glasses and her rainbow barrette. "Howdy do. You look like that character in the movie where the flowers started singing. Wasn't that sort of freaky and great?" He didn't wait for our answer. "It was a special effect. Flowers don't actually know how to sing. So it was sentimental. Well," he said, "now that you're both here, you brave kids should get something to drink. Help yourselves. Welcome, like I said." Even Freddy's bad grammar was between quotation marks.

Giulietta drifted away from me, and I found myself near the refrigerator listening to a tall, strikingly attractive brunette. She didn't introduce herself. With a vaguely French accent, she launched into a little speech. "I have something you must explain," she said. "I can't make good sense of who I am now. And so, what am I? First I am a candidate for one me, and then I am another. I am blown about. Just a little leaf—that is my self. What do you think I will be?" She didn't wait for me to answer. "I ask, 'Who am I, Renée?' I cannot sleep, wondering. Is life like this, in America? Full of such puzzles? Do you believe it is like this?"

I nodded. I said, "That's a very good accent you have there." She began to forage around in her purse as if she hadn't heard me. I hurried toward the living room and found myself in a corner next to another guest, the famous Pulitzer-Prize winning poet Burroughs Hammond, who was sitting in the only available chair. Freddy had befriended him, I had heard, at a literary gathering, and had taught the poet how to modulate his voice during readings. At the present moment, Burroughs Hammond was gripping a bottle of ginger ale and smoking an unfiltered mentholated cigarette. No one seemed to be engaging him in conversation. Apparently, he had intimidated the other guests, all of whom had wandered away from his corner.

I knew who he was. Everyone did. He was built like a linebacker— he had played high school football in Ohio—but he had a perpetually over-sensitive expression on his wide face. "The hothouse flower inside the Mack Truck" was one phrase I had heard to describe him. He had survived bouts of alcoholism and two broken marriages, had lost custody of his children, and had finally moved to New York, where he had sobered up. His poems, some of which I knew by heart, typically dealt with the sudden explosion of the inner life in the midst of an almost fatal loneliness. I particularly liked the concluding lines of "Poem with Several Birds," about a moment of resigned spiritual radiance:

> *Some god or other must be tracing, now,*
> *its way, this way, and the blossoms*
> *like the god are suspended in midair,*
> *and seeing shivers in the face of all this brilliance.*

I had repeated those lines to myself as I waited tables and took orders for salads. The fierce delicacy of Burroughs Hammond's poetry! On those nights when I had despaired and had waited for a god, any one of them, to arrive, his poetry had kept me sane. So when I spotted him at Freddy Avery's, I introduced myself and told him that I knew his poems and loved them. Gazing up at me through his thick horn-rim glasses, he asked politely what I did for a living. I said I waited tables, was an unemployed actor, and was working on a screenplay. He asked me what my screenplay was about and what it was called. I told him that it was a horror film and was entitled *Planet of Bugs*.

My screenplay had little chance of intriguing the poet, and at that moment I remembered something that Lorca had once said to Neruda. I thought it might get Burroughs Hammond's attention. " 'The greatest poet of the age,' " I said, "to quote Lorca, 'is Mickey Mouse.' So my ambition is to get great poetry up on the screen, just as Walt Disney did. Comic poetry. And horror poetry, too. Horror has a kind of poetry up on the screen. But I think most poets just don't get it. But you do. I mean, Yeats didn't understand. He couldn't even write a single play with actual human speech in it. His Irish peasants—! And T. S. Eliot's plays! All those Christian zombies. Zombie poetry written for other zombies. They were both such rotten playwrights—they thought they knew the vernacular, but they didn't. That's a real failing. Their time is past. You're a better poet, and when critics in the future start to evaluate—"

"—You," he said. He lifted his right arm and pointed at me. Suddenly I felt that I was in the presence of an Old Testament prophet who wasn't kidding and had never been kidding about anything. "You are the scum of the Earth," he said calmly. I backed away from him.

He continued to point at me. "You are the scum of the Earth," he repeated.

Everyone was looking at him, and when that job had been completed, everyone was looking at me. Some Charles Mingus riffs thudded out of the record player. Then the other guests started laughing at my embarrassment. I glanced around to see where Giulietta had gone to, because I needed to make a rapid escape from that party and I needed her to help me demonstrate a certain mindfulness. But she wasn't anywhere now that I needed her, not in the living room, not in the kitchen, or the hallway, or the bathroom. After searching for her, I descended the stairs from the apartment as quickly as I could and found myself back out on the street.

* * *

Now, years later, I no longer remember which one of the nearest subway stops I found that night. I can remember the consoling smell of New York City air, the feeling that perhaps anonymity might provide me with some relief. I shouted at a light pole. I walked a few blocks, brushed against several pedestrians, descended another set of stairs, reached into my pocket, and pulled out a subway token. In my right hand, I discovered that I was still holding on to a plastic cup with beer in it.

Only one other man stood on the subway platform that night. The express came speeding through on the middle tracks. The trains were all spray-painted with graffiti in those days, and they'd rattle into the stations looking like giant multicolored mechanical caterpillars—amusement park rides scrawled over with beautifully creepy hieroglyphs, preceded by a tornado-like racket and a blast of salty fetid air.

The other man standing on the platform looked like the winos that Burroughs Hammond had written about in his fragmentary hymns to life following those nights he had spent in the drunk tank. *No other life could be as precious to me/as this one,* he had written. If only I could experience some kindly feeling for a stranger, I thought, possibly I might find myself redeemed by the fates who were quietly ordering my humiliations, one after the other.

Therefore, I did what you never do on a subway platform. I exchanged a glance with the other man.

He approached me. On his face there appeared for a moment an expression of the deepest lucidity. He raised his eyelids as if flabbergasted by my very existence. I noticed that he was wearing over his torn shirt a leather vest stained with dark red blotches—blood or wine, I suppose now. He wore no socks. For the second time that evening, someone pointed at me. "That's a beer you have," he said, his voice burbling up as if through clogged plumbing. "Is there extra?"

I handed over the plastic cup to him. He took a swig. Then, his eyes deep in mad concentration, he yanked down his trouser's zipper and urinated into the beer. He handed the cup back to me.

I took the cup out of this poor madman's grasp and put it down on the subway platform, and then I hauled back and slugged him in the face. He fell immediately. My knuckles stung. He began to crawl toward the subway tracks, and I heard distantly the local train rumbling toward the station, approaching us. With the studied calm of an accomplished actor who has had one or two early successes, I left that subway station and ascended the stairs two at a time to the street. Then, conscience-crippled and heartsick, I went back. I couldn't see the man I had hit. Finally I returned to the street and flagged down a taxi and returned to my apartment.

For the next few days, I checked the newspapers for reports of an accidental death in the subway of a drunk who had crawled into the path of a train, and when I didn't find any such story, I began to feel as if I had dreamed up the entire evening from start to finish, or, rather, that someone else had dreamed it up for me and put me as the lead actor into it—this cautionary tale whose moral was that I had no gift for the life I'd been leading. I took to bed the way you do when you have to think something out. My identity having overtaken me, I called in sick to the restaurant and didn't manage to get to an audition I had scheduled. A lethargy thrummed through me, and I dreamed that someone pointed at my body stretched out on the floor and said, "It's dead." What frightened me was not my death, but that pronoun: "I" had become an "it."

There's no profit in dwelling on the foolishness of one's youth. Everyone's past is a mess. And I wouldn't have thought of my days as an actor if it weren't for my cousin Brantford's having told me twenty years later over lunch in an expensive restaurant that he felt as if he had killed someone, and if my cousin and I hadn't had a kind of solidarity. By that time, Giulietta and I had children of our own, two boys, Elijah and Jacob, and the guttering seediness of New York in the 1970s was distant history, and I only came to the city to visit my cousin and my aunt. By then, I was a visitor from Minnesota, where we had moved and where I was a partner in the firm of Wilwersheid and Lampe. I was no longer an inhabitant of New York. I had become a family man and a tourist.

Do I need to prove that I love my wife and children, or that my existence has become terribly precious to me? They hold me to this earth. Once, back then in my twenties, all I wanted to do was to throw my life away. But then, somehow, usually by accident, you experience joy. And the problem with joy is that it binds you to life; it makes you greedy for more happiness. You experience avarice. You hope your life will go on forever.

* * *

A day or so after having lunch with Brantford, I went up to visit Aunt Margaret. She had started to bend over from the osteoporosis that would cripple her, or maybe it was the calcium-reducing effects of her antidepressant and the diet of Kung Pao chicken, vodka, and cigarettes she lived on. She was terrifyingly lucid, as always. The vodka merely seemed to have sharpened her wits. She was so unblurred, I hoped she wasn't about to go into one of her tailspins. Copies of *Foreign Affairs* lay around her apartment near the porcelain figurines. NPR drifted in from a radio on the windowsill. She had been reading Tacitus, she told me. "*The Annals of Imperial Rome.* Have you ever read it, Benjamin?"

"No," I said. I sank back on the sofa, irritating one of the cats, who leaped up away from me before taking up a position on the windowsill.

"You should. I can't read the Latin anymore, but I can read it in English. Frighteningly relevant. During the reign of Tiberius, Sejanus's daughter is arrested and led away. 'What did I do? Where are you taking me? I won't do it again,' this girl says. My God. Think of all the thousands who have said those very words in this century. I've said them myself. I used to say them to my father."

"Your father?"

"Of course. He could be cruel. He would lead me away, and he punished me. He probably had his reasons. He knew me. Well, I was a terrible girl," she said dreamily. "I was willful. Always getting into situations. I was . . . forward. *There's* an antiquated adjective. Well. These days, if I were young again, I could come into my own, no one would even be paying the slightest attention to me. I'd go from boy to boy like a bee sampling flowers, but in those days, they called us 'wild' and they hid us away. Thank god for progress. Have you seen Brantford, by the way?"

I told her I'd had lunch with him and that he'd said he felt as if he had killed somebody.

"Really. I wonder what he's thinking. He must be all worn out. Is he still drinking? Did he tell you about his girlfriend? That child of his?"

"What child? No, he didn't tell me. Who's this?"

"Funny that he didn't tell you." She stood up and went over to a miniature grandfather clock, only eight inches high, on the mantel. "Heavens," she said, "where are my manners? I should offer you some tea. Or maybe a sandwich." This customary politeness sounded odd coming from her.

"No, thank you." I shook my head. "Aunt Margaret, what child are you talking about?"

"It's not a baby, not yet. Don't misunderstand me. They haven't had a baby, those two. But Brantford's found a girlfriend, and she might as well be a baby, she's so young. Eighteen years old, for heaven's sake. He discovered her in a department store, selling clothes behind the counter. Shirts and things. She's another one of his strays. And of course he doesn't have a dime to his name anymore, and he takes her everywhere on his credit cards when he's not living off of her, and he still doesn't have a clue what to do with himself. Animals all over the place, but no job. He spends all day teaching dogs how to walk and birds how to fly. I suppose it's my fault. They'll blame me. They blame me for everything."

"What's her name? This girl?" I asked. "He didn't mention her to me."

"Camille," Aunt Margaret told me. "And of course she's beautiful— they all are, at that age—but so what? A nineteenth-century name and a beautiful face and figure and no personality at all and no money. They think love is everything, and they get sentimental, but love really isn't much. Just a little girl, this Camille. She likes the animals, of course, but she doesn't know what she's getting into with him." She looked at me slyly. "Do you still envy him? You mustn't envy or pity him, you know. And how is Giulietta?" Aunt Margaret had never approved of Giulietta and thought my marriage to her had been ill-advised. "And your darling children? Those boys? How are they, Benjamin?"

Aunt Margaret turned out to be wrong about Camille, who was not a sentimentalist after all. I met her for the first time at the memorial service five years after she and my cousin Brantford had become a couple. By then, she and Brantford had had a son, Robert, and my cousin had ended his life by stepping out into an intersection into the path of an oncoming taxi at the corner of Park Avenue and 82nd Street. If he couldn't live in that neighborhood, he could at least die there. He suffered a ruptured spleen, and his heart stopped before they admitted him to the ER. He had entered that intersection against a red light—it was unclear whether he had been careless or suicidal, but it was midday, and my cousin was accustomed to city traffic. Well. You always want to reserve judgment, but the blood analysis showed that he had been sober. I wish he had been drunk. We could have blamed it on that, and it would have been a kind of consolation, and we would have thought better of him.

One witness reported that Brantford had rushed onto Park Avenue to rescue a dog that had been running south. Maybe that was it.

In the months before his death, he had found a job working in the produce department at a grocery. When he couldn't manage the tasks that he considered beneath him—stacking the pears and lining up the tomatoes—he took a position as a clerk behind the counter at a pet food store on Avenue B. A name tag dangled from his shirt. He told me by telephone he hated that anyone coming into the store could find out his first name and then use it. It offended him. But he loved the store and could have worked there forever if it hadn't gone out of business. After that, he worked briefly at a collection agency making phone calls to deadbeats. He edited one issue of a humorous Web literary magazine entitled the *Potboiler*. What Brantford had expected from life and what it had actually given him must have been so distinct and so dissonant that he probably felt his dignity dropping away little by little until he simply wasn't himself anymore. He didn't seem to be anybody and he had no resources of humility to help turn that nothingness into a refuge. He and Camille lived in a cluttered little walkup in Brooklyn. I think he must have felt quietly panic-stricken, him and his animals. Time was going to run out on all of them. There would be no more fixes.

I wanted to help him—he was almost a model for me, but not quite—but I didn't know how to exercise compassion with him, or how to express the pity that Aunt Margaret said I shouldn't feel. I think my example sometimes goaded him into despair, as did his furred and feathered patients, who couldn't stand life without him.

At the memorial service, Camille carried the baby in a front pack, and she walked through the doors of the church in a blast of sunlight that seemed to cascade around her and then to advance before her as she proceeded up the aisle. Sunlight from the stained glass windows caught her in momentary droplets and parallelograms of blues and reds. When she reached the first pew, she projected the tender, brave dignity of a woman on whom too many burdens have been placed too quickly.

Afterwards, following the eulogies and the hymns, Camille and I stood out on the lawn. Aunt Margaret, with whom I had been sitting, had gone back to her apartment in a hired car. Camille had seemed surprised by me and had given me an astonished look when I approached her, my hand out.

"Ah, it's you," she said. "The cousin. I wondered if you'd come."

I gave her a hug.

"Sorry," she said, tearfully grinning. "You startled me. You're family, and your face is a little like Branty's. You have the same cheerful scowl, you two." She lifted baby Robert, who had been crying, out of the front pack, opened her blouse, drew back her bra and set the baby there to nurse. "Why didn't you ever come to see us?" she asked me, fixing me with a steady expression of wonderment as she nursed the baby. "He loved you. He said so. He called you 'Bunny.' Just like one of his animals."

"Yes. I didn't think . . . I don't think that Brantford wanted me to see him," I said. "And it was always like a zoo, wherever he was."

"That's unkind. We had to give the animals away, back to the official rescuers. It was *not* like a zoo. Zoos are noisy. The inmates don't want to be there. Brantford's creatures loved him and kept still if he wanted them to be. Why'd you say that? I'm sure he invited you over whenever you were in town."

She looked at me with an expression of honesty, solemn and accusing. I said, "Isn't it a beautiful day?"

"Yes. It's always a beautiful day. That's not the subject."

I had the feeling that I would never have a normal conversation with this woman. "You were so *good* for him," I blurted out, and her expression did not change. "But you should have seen through him. He must have wanted to keep you for himself and his birds and cats and dogs. You were his last precious possession. And, no, he really *didn't* invite me to meet you. Something happened to him," I said, a bit manically. "He turned into something he hadn't been. Maybe that was it. Being poor."

"Oh," she said, after turning back toward me and sizing me up, "*poor*. Well. We liked being poor. It was sort of Buddhist. It was harder for him than for me. We lived as a family, I'll say that. And I loved him. He was a sweetie, and very devoted to me and Robert and his animals." She hoisted the baby and burped him. "He had a very old soul. He wasn't a suicide, if that's what you're thinking. Are you all right?"

"Why?"

"You look like you're going to faint."

"Oh, I'm managing," I said. In truth, my head felt as if the late-afternoon sunlight were going right through the skull bones with ease, soaking the gray matter with photons. "Listen," I asked her, "do you want to go for a drink?"

"I can't drink," she said. "I'm nursing. And you're married, and you have children." How old-fashioned she was! I decided to press forward anyway.

"All right, then," I said. "Let's have coffee."

❊   ❊   ❊

There is a peculiar lull that takes over New York in early afternoon, around two-thirty. In the neighborhood coffee shops, the city's initial morning energy drains out and a pleasant tedium, a trance, holds sway for a few minutes. In any other civilized urban setting, the people would be taking siestas. Here, voices grow subdued and gestures remain incomplete. You lean back in your chair to watch the vapor trails aimed toward LaGuardia or Newark, and for once no one calls you, there is nothing to do. Radios are tuned to baseball, and conversations stop as you drift off to imagine the runner on second, edging toward third. Camille and I went into a little greasy spoon called Here to Eat and sat down at a table near the front window. The cook stared out at the blurring sidewalk, his eyelids heavy. He seemed massively indifferent to our presence and our general needs. The server barely noticed that we were there. She sat at one of the counter stools working on a crossword. No one even looked up.

Eventually the server brought us two cups of stale, burned coffee.

"At last," I said. "I thought it'd never come."

The baby was asleep in the crook of Camille's right arm. After a few minutes of pleasantries, Camille asked me, "So. Why are you here?"

"Why am I here? I'm here because of Brantford. For his memory. We were always close."

"You were?" she said.

"I thought so," I replied.

Her face, I now noticed, had the roundedness that women's faces acquire after childbirth. Errant bangs fell over her forehead, and she blew a stream of air upward toward them. She gave me a straight look. "He talked about you as his long-lost brother, the one who never came to see him."

"Please. I—"

She wasn't finished "You look alike," she said, "but that doesn't mean that you were alike. You could have been his identical twin and you wouldn't have been any closer to him than you are now. Anyway, what was I asking? Oh, yes. Why are you here? With me? Now."

"For coffee. To talk. To get to know you." I straightened my necktie. "After all, he was my cousin." I thought for a moment. "I loved him. He was better than me. I need to talk about him, and you didn't plan a reception. Isn't that unusual?"

"No, it isn't. You wanted to get to know me?" She leaned back and licked her chapped lips.

"Yes."

"Kind of belated, isn't it?" She sipped the hot coffee and then set it down.

"Belated?"

"Given the circumstances?" She gazed out the window, then lifted the baby to her shoulder again. "For the personal intimacies? For the details?" Her sudden modulation in tone was very pure. So was her irony. She had a kind of emotional Puritanism that despised the parade of shadows on the wall, of which I was the current one.

"Okay. Why do you think I'm here?" I asked her, taken aback by her behavior. The inside of my mouth had turned to cotton; rudeness does that to me.

"You're here to exercise your compassion," she said quickly. "And to serve up some awful belated charity. And, finally, to patronize me." She smiled at me. "*La belle pauvre*. How's that? Think that sounds about right?"

"You're a tough one," I said. "I wasn't going to patronize you at all."

She squirmed in the booth as if her physical discomfort could be shed from her skin and dropped on the floor. "Well, you probably weren't planning on it, I'll give you credit for that." She poured more cream into her coffee. My heart was thumping away in my chest. "Look at you," she said. "Goddamn it, you have a crush on me. I can tell. I can always tell about things like that." She started humming "In a Sentimental Mood." After a moment, she said, "You men. You're really something, you guys." She bit at a fingernail. "At least Branty had his animals. They'll escort him into heaven."

"I don't know why you're talking this way to me," I said. "You're being unnecessarily cruel."

"It's my generation," she said. "We get to the point. But I went a bit too far. It's been a hard day. I was crying all morning. I can't think straight. My apologies."

"Actually," I said. "I don't get you at all." This wasn't quite true.

"Good. At last."

We sat there for a while.

"You're a lawyer, aren't you?"

"Yes," I said. She stirred her coffee. Her spoon clicked against the cup.

"Big firm?"

"Yeah." Outside the diner, traffic passed on Lexington. The moon was visible in the sky. I could see it.

"Well, do me a favor, all right? Don't ask me about Brantford's debts." She settled back in the booth, while the server came and poured more burned coffee into her cup. "I don't need any professional advice just now."

I stared at her.

"Actually," she said, "I could use some money. To tide me over, et cetera. Your Aunt Margaret said that you would generously donate something for the cause." She gave me a vague look. " 'Benjamin will come to your aid,' she said. And, yes, I can see that you will." She smiled. "Think of me as a wounded bird."

"How much do you need?" I asked.

"You really love this, don't you?" She gave me another careless smile. "You're in your element."

"No," I said. "I'm not sure I've ever had a conversation like this before."

"Well, you've had it now. Okay," she said. "I'll tell you what. You have my address. Send me a check. You'll enjoy sending the check, and then more checks after that. So that's your assignment. You're one of those guys who loves to exercise his pity, his empathy. You're one of those rare, sensitive men with a big bank account. Just send that check."

"And in return?"

"In return," she said, "I'll like you. I'll have a nice meal with you whenever you're in town. I'll give you a grateful little kiss on the cheek." She began to cry and then, abruptly, stopped. She pulled out a handkerchief from her purse and blew her nose.

"No, you won't. Why on earth do you say that?"

"You're absolutely right, I won't. I wanted to see how you'd react. I thought I'd rattle your cage. I'm grief-stricken. And I'm giddy." She laughed merrily, and the baby startled and lifted his little hands. "Poor guy, you'll never figure out any of this."

"Exactly right," I said. "You think I'm oblivious to things, don't you?"

"I have no idea, but if I do think so," she said thoughtfully, "I'll let you know. I didn't fifteen minutes ago."

"It seems," I said, "that you want to keep me in a posture of perpetual contrition." I was suddenly proud of that phrase. It summed everything up.

"Ha. 'Perpetual contrition.' Well, that'd be a start. You really don't know what Brantford thought of you, do you? Look: call your wife. Tell her about me. It'd be good for you, good for you both. Because you're . . ."

I reached out and took her hand before she could pronounce the condemning adjective or the noun she had picked out. It was a preemptive move. It was either that or slapping her. "That's quite enough," I said. I held on to her hand for dear life. The skin was warm and damp, and she didn't pull it away. For five minutes we sat there holding hands in silence. Then I dropped some money on the table for the coffee. Her baby began to cry. I identified with that sound. As I stood up, she said, "You shouldn't have been afraid."

She was capable of therapeutic misrepresentation. I knew I would indeed start sending her those checks before very long—thousands of dollars, every year. It would go on and on. I would be paying this particular bill forever. I owed them that.

"I'm a storm at sea," she said. "A basket case. Who knows? We might become friends after all." She laughed again, inappropriately (I thought), and I saw on her arm a tattoo of a chickadee, and on the other arm, a tattoo of a smiling dog.

104

Back in the hotel, I called Giulietta, and I told her everything that Camille had ordered me to say.

° ° °

That night, I walked down a few blocks to a small neighborhood market, where I stole a Gala apple—I put it into my jacket pocket—and a bunch of flowers, which I carried out onto the street, holding them ostentatiously in front of me. If you have the right expression on your face, you can shoplift anything. I had learned that from my acting classes. More than enough money resided in my wallet for purchases, but shoplifting apparently was called for. It was an emotional necessity. I packed the apple in my suitcase and took the flowers into the hotel bathroom and put them into the sink before filling the sink with water. But I realized belatedly that there was no way I would be able to get them back home before they wilted.

So after I had arrived in the Minneapolis airport the next day, I bought another spray of flowers from one of those airport florists. Out on the street, I found a cab.

The driver smiled at the flowers I was carrying. "Very nice. You are surely a gentleman," he said, with a clear, clipped accent. I asked him where he was from, and he said he was Ethiopian. I told him that at first I had thought perhaps he was a Somali, since so many cabdrivers in Minneapolis were from there.

He made an odd guttural noise. "Oh, no, not Somali," he said. "Extremely not. I am Ethiopian . . . very different," he said. "We do not look the same, either," he said crossly.

I complimented him on his excellent English. "Yes, yes," he said impatiently, wanting to get back to the subject of Ethiopians and Somalis. "We Ethiopians went into their country, you know. Americans do not always realize this. The Somalis should have been grateful to us, but they were not. They never are. We made an effort to stop their civil war. But they like war, the Somalis. And they do not respect the law, so it is all war, to them. A Somali does not respect the law. He does not have it in him."

I said I didn't know that.

"For who are those flowers?" he asked. "Your wife?"

"Yes," I told him.

"They are pretty except for the lilies." He drove onto the entry ramp of the freeway. The turn signal in the cab sounded like a heart monitor. "Myself, I do not care for lilies. Do you know what we say

105

about Somalis, what we Ethiopians say? We say, 'The Somali has nine hearts.' This means: a Somali will not reveal his heart to you. He will reveal a false heart, not his true one. But you get past that, in time, and you get to the second heart. This heart is also and once again false. In repetition you will be shown and told the thing which is not. You will never get to the ninth heart, which is the true one, the door to the soul. The Somali keeps that heart to himself."

"The thing which is not?" I asked him. Outside, the sun had set.

"You do not understand this?" He looked at me in the rearview mirror. "This very important matter?"

"Well, maybe I do," I said. "You know, my wife works with Somali children."

The cab driver did not say anything, but he tugged at his ear.

"Somali children in Minneapolis have a very high rate of autism," I said. "It's strange. No one seems to knows why. Some say it's the diet, some say that they don't get enough sunlight. Anyway, my wife works with Somali children."

"Trying to make them normal?" the cab driver asked. "Oh, well. You are a good man, to give her flowers." He gazed out at the night. "Look at this dark air," he said. "It will snow soon."

o   o   o

With my suitcase, my apple, and my flowers, I stood waiting on the front porch of our house. Instead of unlocking the door as I normally would have, I thought I would ring the bell just as a stranger might, as someone who hopes to be welcomed. I always enjoyed surprising Giulietta and the boys whenever I returned from trips, and with that male pride in homecoming from a battle, large or small, I was eager to tell them tales about where I had been and what I had done and whom I had defeated and the trophies with which I had returned. Standing on the welcome mat, I looked inside through the windows into the entryway and beyond into the living room, and I saw my son Jacob lying on the floor reading from his history textbook. His class had been studying the American Revolution. He ran his hand through his hair. He needed a haircut. He had a sweet, studious look on his face, and I felt proud of him beyond measure. I rang the bell. They would all rush to greet me.

The bell apparently wasn't working, and Jacob didn't move from his settled position. I would have to fix that bell. I released my grip on the suitcase and headed toward the side door, where we had another doorbell. Again I rang and again no one answered. If it had made a noise, I couldn't hear it. So I went around to the back, brushing past the hateful peonies, stepping over a broken sidewalk stone, and I took up a spot in the grassy yard, still carrying my spray of flowers. Behind me, I could smell a skunk, and I heard a car alarm in the distance. If I had been Brantford, all the yard animals would have approached me. But if I had been Brantford, I wouldn't be living in this house. I wouldn't be here.

Giulietta sat in the back den. I could see her through the windows. She was home-tutoring a little Somali girl, guiding her along a balance beam a few inches off the floor, and when that task was finished, they began to toss a beanbag back and forth to each other, practicing midline exercises. Her parents sat on two chairs by the wall, watching her, the mother dressed in a flowing robe.

I felt the presence of my cousin next to me out there in the yard, and in that contagious silence I was reminded of my beautiful wife and children who were stubbornly not coming to the door in response to my little joke with the doorbell. So I rapped on the window expecting to startle Giulietta, but when she looked up, I could not see through her dark glasses to where she was looking, nor could I tell whether she really intended to let me into the house ever again.

I have loved this life so much. I was prepared to wait out there forever.

Nominated by Marianne Boruch, Bill Lychack, Tin House

THE DECISION

by TIMOTHY LIU

from THE YALE REVIEW

When I removed

the ring I had
been wearing for

a decade, a ghost

ring remained
underneath—the skin

slightly paler

where the gold
had been—my finger

cinched where it

had been constricted
as I prepared to

step into the night—

Nominated by Bruce Beasley, Maura Stanton

LORES OF LAST UNICORNS

by JEN HIRT

from THE GETTYSBURG REVIEW

When I was a young girl, I collected unicorns.

I received them for birthdays and Christmas and Easter and straight-A report cards. Glass, ceramic, stone, brass, wooden, pewter, plastic, plush, necklaces, T-shirts, bedspreads, pillow shams, and wallpaper. I owned snow-globe unicorn music boxes, a tinkling chorus of "Born Free." For my first slumber party, my dad rented a new device called a VCR, and I selected the animated feature *The Last Unicorn*. The party, the VCR, the movie—I was thrice cool and showered with unicorn gifts.

At some point, I linked the action of collecting to the fervor of believing. I collected unicorns for study, preparing to separate the charlatans from the real deal. At school, I cultivated this aspect of my personality, haughty and armed with esoteric knowledge at the prime age of nine. For example, I called the unicorn's horn by its correct name, *alicorn*. My first foray into creative writing, for the annual Young Author's Conference, was a short story called "A Quest in Alicorn Forest." With my cousin's white Arabian stallion as a model, I illustrated the capricious adventure of three unicorns who had to save their herd from fuzzy pink things. My ten-page book was displayed on the fourth-grade fiction table.

My belief got a boost when my grandparents gave me Odell Shepard's dense history, *The Lore of the Unicorn*. They were wishful. I was too young to read anything more complex than *The Black Stallion* series. Undaunted, I studied the historical illustrations for hours. So many variations to consider—would I believe in the unicorn with the lion's tail and cloven hooves? The bearded unicorn? Or the ones like deer? I favored the unicorns that looked like Arabian horses, but these, I realized, were the offspring of whimsical T-shirts and the horses I learned to ride on at Valleywood Farm. Reconciling my imaginary unicorn with the historical ones was my first lesson in compromise. I still resist Shepard's book.

No one gift or illustration sparked my bullheaded devotion to believing. I constructed a circular logic: I believed in unicorns because they were real, and unicorns would be more real the more people believed in them. I was a little girl for whom biological evidence was incomprehensible. My world was simple magic. A reputation followed me, and small towns don't let you shake your past. Here is proof: my brother gave me a porcelain unicorn for my twenty-seventh birthday.

A couple years ago, when I was moving for the sixth time in as many years, lugging a box of carefully wrapped glass unicorns from my childhood, I started to wonder why I had ever gotten into unicorns.

On the subconscious level, I must have believed in unicorns because adults did not. I was a well-off child who had everything except grounds for defiance. What better animal for covering that ground than a unicorn, an incredible creature discredited by the practical world of moms and dads? It is as if I were saying, "You think you can give me everything, but you cannot give me a unicorn."

In 1983, renowed photographer Robert Vavra published *Unicorns I Have Known*. The bestseller was an oversized photo collection of what appeared to be real unicorns in real locations. When I received the book, probably in '84 or '85, it quickly trumped the black-and-white illustrations of *The Lore of the Unicorn* as my primary resource. My favorite photo is on page eighty-five. A lone unicorn canters along the edge of a barren woodland in winter. Vavra snapped the shot just as the unicorn's tremendous mane blew back. There are so many shades of white—sky, snowfield, hide, horn, mane, tail. To the left of the picture, Vavra reprinted a claim by Dr. Olfert Dapper. In 1673, he had seen unicorns running along the border, two legs in Canada, two in America. "They live in the loneliest wilderness and are so shy," Dapper wrote. Vavra appended epigraphs to each picture, but this one is notable. He had all but located Dapper's unicorn, just three hundred years later. I was enamored. I thought this was real.

The back pages of the book offer Vavra's written narrative as he traipsed around the globe, slung with cameras, lucking again and again into unicorns. Each picture has an imaginative endnote. If one is wondering why there is a picture of a peacock on page nine, the endnote explains: "This peacock, practically hidden in deep foliage, had just screamed to warn a unicorn of my presence in the forest of southern Nepal." Vavra adds enticing bits of discovery to his pictorial descriptions. A friend in Sudan had seen three unicorns. Vavra himself had translated a secret unicorn document at the Archives of India in Spain, a document then mysteriously stolen. And, of course, there was the acquisition of a bizarre journal, found in a Madrid flea market and conveniently written in perfect English, purporting to be the only true account of all things unicorn. To these cryptic rumors, Vavra adds pseudo-scientific claims, such as the one positing that unicorns communicate by a crude language of lines and dots scraped into bark. I turned the pages of that book so many times that they eased from their binding. The gold-embossed title wore away to *Unicorns I Have*.

The 1988 sequel, titled *The Unicorn of Kilimanjaro*, was equally satisfying. I studied Vavra's claim that Hemingway knew of the solitary unicorn who roamed Africa's famous mountain. I looked long and hard at the photo where Vavra, leaving his camera in the hands of a trail guide, bowed his head and stepped to the tolerant unicorn, so close, so there. So connected.

Describing the beauty of the unicorns is difficult, even now. They are uncanny, clearly horselike, but endowed with voluminous manes, huge eyes, and self-awareness, as if they know they are being photographed for the first time. On one page, a unicorn lowers his horn and charges the camera. A single damning eye—milky blue like that of a husky—glares through the lavish forelock swept aside by the force of the charge.

In 1995, when I was twenty years old and considering writing about unicorn lore for a college class, I browsed my Vavra books. On page sixty-six, I saw something that changed everything: the Kilimanjaro unicorn was shod with the faint metal curve of horseshoes. It was the first time, in seven years of meticulously perusing the book, that I had noticed. My past disconnected.

In the photo, the unicorn, which Vavra refers to as a stag because it is male, is cornered against a red cliff. His hind legs are planted firmly, front hooves raised, muscles tensed. The horseshoes are obvious on the front feet. Vavra wrote in his endnotes:

First African unicorn! . . . Slowly pick up camera with 500-
millimeter lens. Side of mountain is very dark. Hopefully,
with 400 ASA film and white unicorn, will be enough light.

During the sighting, he was aware of the "sharp smacking of stag's
hooves against red rock." I bet.

Reconsidering *Unicorns I Have Known*, I was suddenly aware that
the unicorns looked suspiciously like the Spanish Andalusian horses
from Vavra's renowed book, *Equus Reined*. Andalusians, an ancient
breed, can be nearly white with tremendous manes and tails. They are
smart horses, easily trained, the foundation stock for the Lipizzaner
stallions. The "unicorns" I was looking at were Andalusians. What I
was seeing was no longer evidence of existence; I was seeing, carefully
obscured in all the other pictures, evidence of the human need to pro-
mulgate legend, to proclaim from the heights of deception that yes,
the unicorn could be real, not because the world was once a blank
slate of possibilities, but because the definition of *real* is as blurry as
Vavra's first photo of a unicorn, a shot of a vaguely equine tornado of
white mane spotted in the Tamazunchale jungle of Mexico in the
spring of 1968.

In the moments after noticing the horseshoes, I felt startled, then
annoyed, then silly. Ridiculous, this belief. Here I was, a student at a
private liberal arts college, surrounded by scholars, and I was still lost
in unicorn books. I closed my book, slid my fingers over the cover
shot—the unicorn's head turned toward the reader with an inquiring
eye, the savanna sun lighting a soft evening background. So air-
brushed. I opened the book and started at page one. I became a Sher-
lock Holmes, in search of horseshoes and halter marks.

By the end, page sixty-six was my only evidence, albeit incontro-
vertible. I surfaced from the undertow with a realization. Maybe I had
been looking for those horseshoes all along. What made me finally see
them?

I caught myself daydreaming on a hike along the Appalachian Trail
near my home in Pennsylvania. I could almost see that slip of white
equine through the vines and brush, could almost hear the startled
thunder if I were to happen upon a few unicorns around the next
bend. It was absurd. But I wasn't the first. So many before me, from
Pliny the Elder to Marco Polo to Robert Vavra, had wished into near

reality these vivid imaginings. Greeting cards would have me believe that wishing is all sweet surprise and happiness. But I know that in every wish lives a fiction, often a dark fiction.

In 1577, a cadre of European explorers poking around the Arctic for the Northwest Passage found a dead "sea unicorn." Captain Martin Frobisher ordered the company to pause to consider the fishlike creature "which had in its nose a horn straight and torquet." One of Frobisher's assistants, a man named Dionise Settle, later wrote about what he heard secondhand. The sea unicorn's horn tip had been broken some time ago, and the men could peer into the space of the spiral. Well-steeped in the lore of the purifying powers of a unicorn horn (be it from sea or land), and giddy over the price such a find would bring at the feet of the queen, ambitious seamen put the horn to the test. They scuttled spiders into the hollow horn, and the spiders died. The sailors declared the horn authentic and gave it to Queen Elizabeth. Today, it is on display at the British Museum.

The acquisition of the alicorn was the single bright spot in Frobisher's northern adventures. Not a stellar navigator, he wasted time getting lost in northern bays and inlets. One of his ships deserted. He brought back chunks of black topsoil supposedly speckled with gold; when experts proved him wrong, authorities threatened him with jail. Settle—the writer of the spider account—did little to promote international harmony when he advanced his belief that the Inuit were savage cannibals who had obviously eaten five men missing from an earlier expedition.

I don't know what to think of the unicorn story in light of Frobisher's mistakes and misconceptions. I have to agree with Odell Shepard, who analyzed the story this way: Surely what the men found was a decomposing narwhal. The males have a wayward tooth, not a tusk or horn, which grows through the head. Narwhals, which are white, were hunted to near extinction in the sixteenth and seventeenth centuries, and many historians agree that the fabled alicorns presented to royalty were actually narwhal tusks. The legend was that an alicorn chalice neutralized poisoned wine, because another legend claimed that unicorns dipped their horns into rivers to purify the water for the woodland creatures. Meanwhile, I recently read that all of Britain's drinking water contains molecules of Prozac. This could mean Britain has no unicorns. It could also mean Britain's unicorns are hard at work.

I don't doubt that the spiders died that chilly day in the wild North. Consider the context: medieval explanations of the animal kingdom held that it was split between the pure and the impure, and that in a just and godly world, the pure animals would reign victorious over the impure. It was a rehearsal for Armageddon. Here is what I think happened: the spiders died because they were overcome by a horn saturated in sea salt and the detritus from a rotting whale head. Or they froze.

I did not see the Living Unicorn at the Ringling Brothers and Barnum & Bailey Circus in the mid-eighties. The controversy I remember well—was Lancelot the Living Unicorn a surgically altered goat, or was he the unicorn of myth and legend? The circus debuted the animal in New York City to much fanfare, embracing the crowd-drawing debate. Starry photos were leaked to the media. The animal had a delicate head, cascades of curly fur, and an undeniably huge and single horn on his forehead. At the request of animal rights activists, the USDA made an appearance and proclaimed the beast to be a male Angora goat whose horn buds had been spliced together when he was a kid and then shaped into a ten-inch horn as he matured—not a *natural* unicorn, but *technically* a unicorn. The circus responded with a full-page ad in the *New York Times*, suggesting that the government was out to destroy the fantasies of childhood. The ad was a ringmaster of propaganda, urging parents to bring their children to the circus before government officials ruined everyone's Sunday afternoon.

The second controversy—where did Lancelot come from? A handful of publications tentatively provided the peculiar answer. Morning Glory Ravenheart and Oberon Zell Ravenheart were his owners. The Ravenhearts are part of a polyamorous and pagan organization living in California, whose members go about their peaceful, randy ways while awaiting the next great event in the Age of Aquarius. Oberon is the patriarch of the Church of All Worlds, a religion he invented after reading the sci-fi novel *Stranger in a Strange Land*. Oberon also conceived of a "handfasting" ceremony that allowed Ravenhearts to marry multiple Ravenhearts. Morning Glory, however, has been his main soul mate since the sixties, when they met at a New Age conference.

No news media gave the Ravenhearts more than fifty words of print, and a single obscure Web site published this rebuttal to the USDA: Lancelot was not a surgically altered goat. He was a unicorn

114

created with "appropriate magical rites" involving spirits, a waxing moon, and chunks of quartz.

Controversy helps all, however. The Ravenhearts hired a lawyer and secured the patent to the technique for creating one horn from two, even though they weren't the first to splice the horns of goats or sheep or cattle. The Prince of Wales received a gift of one-horned rams in 1906, and in 1933, Dr. Franklin Dove spliced the horns on an Ayrshire calf at his farm near Orono, Maine. I have read teasing fragments of the prince's gift, but I have seen actual photos of Dr. Dove's creation. In the most famous photo, the mature Ayrshire stands at attention, a front leg slightly forward, in the traditional pose for bovines led around state fair arenas. He is all white except for a black spot around his eye and jowl. He is almost neckless. His body, such a rectangle of meat cuts, cannot be graceful. The background offers no context, invites no speculation. His horn, which appears black in the colorless photo, looks like an obelisk. It doesn't come from his forehead—it angles from the lumpy poll between the ears, almost like an extension of the spine. This, a unicorn? Dove published his findings in *Scientific Monthly*, making the bizarre claim that the calf was "conscious of peculiar power; . . . his ability to inherit the earth gives him the virtue of meekness." Dove, I think, did not know the difference between meekness and dullness.

Thankfully, the Ravenhearts didn't indulge in the pretense that their Living Unicorn would inherit the earth—its ability to siphon circus profit would do. They licensed Living Unicorns to the Ringling Circus from 1984 to 1988. When not fulfilling his duties as a mystic lover, or to augment those duties, Oberon trailored the animals to participate in Renaissance fairs. Nothing woos a girl like a unicorn. With the substantial revenue, the Ravenhearts hired a film crew and struck out for New Guinea to solve the mystery of mermaid sightings. Soon broke, they claimed they had solved the mermystery but had no finances for finishing the film. The footage remains unseen. Morning Glory and Oberon now run Mythic Images out of Sonoma County, selling New Age statuary and accoutrements. According to one Web site, they are hoping to breed a phoenix.

I was ten or eleven at the time of the circus unicorn controversy, in possession of *Unicorns I Have Known*, and I remember turning a very cold shoulder, as cold as the icy waters around a dead narwhal. I had no desire to be part of a crowd looking down at a unicorn on display. News photos were enough—Lancelot was sparkling white, displayed on a rolling stage with a beautiful woman at his side, always in the spotlight. He looked fat under all those long Angora curls, like a house cat, and he was, without doubt, a goat. The horn looked too thick, heavy, and vaguely obscene because it was dark and marbled and smooth, not delicate and ivory and spiraled.

When I would finally see my unicorn, I wanted to be the *only* one to see it. I wanted it to be wild. I wanted to be Robert Vavra, my eyes the gateway to something never seen, my camera and film the book of a new bible.

The circus unicorn was too easy. Buy a ticket, go to the show. Unlike the tigers and elephants and ponies, the circus unicorn didn't have to earn its keep. It could just *be* while other animals mastered their tricks. The Living Unicorn was a human trick mastered by Morning Glory and Oberon. I would not go to a circus to see the results of a trick.

Despite my disdain, I had no problem lingering over Vavra's photos for more than a decade, themselves another result of another trick. How come? The isolation of those unicorns drew my allegiance and my sympathy. I was romanced by the idea that something so enchanting was destined to a life of solitude. I imagined that the unicorns accepted their fate as loners, yet desired companionship. I didn't know much about the complexities of desire when I was twelve, lost in Vavra's books. Now I know that often we desire most intensely what we cannot have. For me, the unicorns have been the best breed of desire—reliably eternal because it is perpetually unfulfilled.

The lonesome unicorn is as solid an archetype as the noble unicorn. In a famous moment from Tennessee Williams's *The Glass Menagerie*, John notices that all of Laura's glass animals have real counterparts, except for the unicorn. John comments, "Poor little fellow, he must feel sort of lonesome." The line resonates with anyone who feels different, who knows they are one sidestep from the pack, two shadows from the sun. Another example: in *The Last Unicorn* by Peter Beagle, a solitary unicorn befriends an outcast magician and a hard-nosed barmaid. The three learn the secret of the vanished unicorns. A lonely old king used a demonic red bull to drive the unicorns into the ocean where, with the unicorns captured in the waves and undertow, the king could peer down at them from his tower whenever he wanted. It is not the only tale about unicorns, water, and loneliness. Shel Silverstein wrote a rollicking poem about how Noah could not convince the unicorn pair to board the ark. Frisky play in the rising waters turned into a desolate demise, and that is why, according to Silverstein, there are no more unicorns. Another biblical story claims that Adam named the unicorn first, before even looking at all the other animals, and thus it was forever set apart—set alone.

I grew up on unicorn mythology. At the same time, I was being indoctrinated into the group activity of public school, a place where you couldn't even go to the bathroom alone. Naturally, I resisted. I remember trying to play alone at free time. The teacher would ask if I was sick. I would say no. Then why wasn't I playing with the other kids? I never had a satisfying answer.

Did I sense that the unicorn's mystique was a halo around privilege and solitude? Public school in northeast Ohio offered little in the way of privilege or solitude. If I aligned myself with unicorns out of a rebellious need for defiance in a stable life, it makes sense that my belief in unicorns was just an analogy for my belief that young people could benefit from solitude, that we didn't all have to be running around in adult-approved groups.

Maybe, when I was twenty, I saw the horseshoes on the Kilimanjaro unicorn because I was finally an adult. At college I was learning to see, and more importantly, to see *through*, to think critically. For the first time in my educational history, tests were not about memorization, success not about practical applications, and if I wanted to research unicorns, I could, and *I could do it alone*. When Alice met the unicorn in Wonderland, they struck a deal. "Now that we have seen each other,' said the unicorn, 'if you'll believe in me, I'll believe in you. Is that a bargain?' " As a child, I had an irrational fear that no one would believe in me, that no one would notice me in the group. Chalk it up to being the shortest girl, relegated to the end of the line or the vulnerable front row on class-picture day. Believing in unicorns was part of a secret and altruistic exchange. I would notice them so they would notice me.

By the time I was on scholarship at that small private college, trying to decide whether or not to write about unicorns, I was long over the fear of not being noticed. My deal with the unicorns was done. I could see them for what they were.

Humans have a history of not being able to see things for what they are. Sight is the sense we rely on the most, so one might suppose that it would be the most acute sense. Yet wild claims pockmark history,

117

supported always by the power of witness. We all know the cliché "seeing is believing." The unicorn is hardly an egregious example of something made more real after the seven-word testimony of "I saw it with my own eyes." Consider, for instance, the vegetable lamb.

The vegetable lamb is the least sexy of the mythical beasts. They are so obscure they rarely make the cut in books about dragons and centaurs. Nonetheless, someone claimed to have seen one, and the myth lingers.

The story is that vegetable lambs birth themselves from deep flowers, such as the orange canal of the trumpet vine flower. Wet with pollen and bleating bees, they shiver on the grass, bound to the throat of the flower by a vine in place of an umbilical cord. Eventually, a vegetable lamb will eat all the grass within reach of the vine. Days later, it dies from hunger—it refuses to eat the trumpet vine, because that would be eating itself.

What if Vavra had created seventy photos sequencing the struggle of vegetable lambs? What if, in his endnotes, he referred to a fourteenth-century monk named Brother Oderich? He was the first to document vegetable lambs, writing, "There groweth a manner of Fruyt that men fynden with inne a lytlle Best, in Flessche, in Bone and Blode." Oderich ate the first vegetable lamb he saw. He noted that the entire event, from discovery to lunch, was a marvel. "Of that fruit I have eten," he wrote. He was on a fifteen-year vacation to the Far East. The vegetable lamb was something to write home about.

So what the hell were vegetable lambs? They were a folktale about cotton, that peculiar plant whose pods burst open with white fluff, which, for lack of a better comparison, early farmers held up against wool. Cotton was like wool, wool grew on lambs, but cotton came from plants, so maybe there was a lamb inside the plant.

I don't know what Brother Oderich ate in the fourteenth century. I think he was ripped on opium. Regardless, I want to paginate the book of the vegetable lamb's life because narratives don't belong exclusively to the beautiful, the mystical, the long lived. Enough with the shampooed hides of circus ponies. The vegetable lamb was white too.

I imagine Robert Vavra would not be interested in the dire plight of vegetable lambs. I blame him and I don't. There is something helplessly placental about vegetable lambs, as if we would all be better off the quicker they died. But unicorns are not all sugar and pillows either, and while some of Vavra's unicorns are clearly aggressive, ready to pummel the next groom who approaches with a comb for those impractical manes, none are so aggressive as the unicorn in Albrecht Dürer's 1516 etching *The Rape of Persephone*.

In the etching, Pluto is riding a unicorn as he kidnaps a buxom Persephone. Pluto gropes Persephone's naked hips, clutching her to his side. He is mounted on the unicorn, bracing Persephone against his right thigh. Pluto leans back to balance—the powerful animal and the resistance of the captive frustrate him. His free hand clutches a wisp of mane. Persephone's arms are thrown back in futility. One hand points to the edge of the unicorn's eye, wide as a hole, wide as lust, as if Persephone's pointing is an accusation—"You witness. You are complicit." The unicorn's horn curves down—a scythe. It lacks the spiral detail. His horn looks shaggy, made of bark or hide. His chin is tucked to his neck, and his mouth swallows Persephone's scream. His mane tangles her hair. He is a Clydesdale of a unicorn, ready to crush fairies and piss on rainbows. He probably put Pluto up to this. The unicorn wears no saddle, doesn't fight a bit and bridle. He is wild but obedient to the scent of cunt.

A merging of myth and mythology, it is one of the few works on paper outside of the fantasy genre that shows someone riding a unicorn. It is also one of the few depictions of the unicorn that not only breaks from the status quo, but tramples it. This is no virgin subduing a unicorn in the woods behind King Arthur's castle, no tapestry pet wearing a collar, no coat-of-arms insignia. This is virile, violent. No unicorn-as-metaphor-for-Christ for miles around. The unicorn is a mad mix—muscle bound as a bull, hooves cloven like an old ox, eyes wide as a gator's, a mouth like a raptor. And he has thick hair in all the wrong places, on his hindquarters and where his front legs meet his belly. Odell Shepard says that Dürer was evoking a tradition attributed to Zoroastrian artists, who represented "not any single species of animal but a combination of several species which they regarded as the leaders of the pure creation." This leader of a pure creation is brutal, not the white of heaven but the cold wet whites of the eyes that can't believe what they are seeing.

Last year, I rented the special edition DVD of the 1986 movie *Legend*. Directed by Ridley Scott of *Alien* fame and starring a young Tom

Cruise, *Legend* was a mostly forgettable live-action fantasy using the worn conflict of good versus evil. Highlights included two live unicorns filmed in the blurry sun of slow motion. Forest Dweller Jack (Cruise) introduces the lovely but naive Princess Lily (Mia Sara) to the unicorns. He explains one rule: never touch them. Naturally, she pets one a split second later, and all of creation is thrown out of whack. The black-horned devil named Darkness (Tim Curry) sends his minions to find the unicorns (made mortal by the touch of a mortal). He wants to cut off their horns and squander everything good in the world. Jack and Lily team up with an oddball club of gnomes and sprites as they try to save the unicorns, or in more blatant terms, as they try to restore the ivory-horned metaphor for harmony, love, and respect.

I rented the DVD for the special feature. It was titled "The Fastest Steeds." While footage of the unicorn pair plays, Ridley Scott narrates in a voice-over about how he obtained the unicorns. He sent a producer to Seville, Spain, location of the renowned Andalusians—the same place Vavra pointed his camera just a few years earlier. The producer returned to Britain with six white Andalusians and a trainer named Jorge.

Most of the feature shows the horses on set as unicorns, and Scott's narration is unfocused and not worth remembering. Except for one sequence—one of the more fascinating events I have ever seen.

Grainy footage shows a white mare held by two men, one on each side. She tosses her head against the halter, which is slanted against her eye because the handler on the right, who is not paying attention, is pulling the halter down at the wrong angle. The man on the left lifts a prosthetic horn and twists it onto what appears to be a screw-centered patch of fur glued to the mare's forehead. The handlers chuckle and converse with someone out of frame, but there is no sound for this, just Scott blathering on in voice-over about something other than unicorns.

As the handler secures the horn, the mare lowers her head obediently. The handler on the right still pulls her halter. He is not paying attention, will not ease up now that she has obeyed. He is smoking, and he never takes the cigarette from his mouth. The long ash hangs in the space between man and beast. It hangs perilously, making me nervous. The ash is going to fall into the mare's eye.

In the narrative voice-over, the producer laughs about the travails of getting the horses to the soundstage during a storm. Then it ends, and the next feature is about how the soundstage (and entire set) burned down in the middle of filming.

I watched again. I paused it, forwarded it frame by frame. Here is the horse. Here is the horn. Here is the unicorn. The resistance, the obedience, the curve of ash, and the black eyes of the mare. I was reminded of other unfortunate footage—a state fair's diving donkeys, or Edison electrocuting an elephant. Routine, unique. Justified in context, bizarre when out.

And singular. Seeing a horn screwed to a horse's head was as rare an event as seeing a unicorn. As a child, I had hoped to see a unicorn but also understood I probably wouldn't. At the same time, I had never even thought about the possibility of seeing a horn screwed onto a forehead. I had finally seen *something* in the two minutes of footage—but *what*?

It is the long ash on the cigarette that remains the important detail. White horse, fake horn, gray ash. Sacred, profane, and simultaneous. Sometimes, the unicorn is a prop to be assembled. In the moment between horse and unicorn, there is a fabulous disappearance.

Legend claims unicorns can disappear at will. Vavra capitalized on this attribute by claiming that unicorns could also disappear from photos. In *Unicorns I Have Known*, he included landscapes of red poppies, no unicorn in sight. The endnotes explain that the unicorn disappeared sometime between the aperture smacking shut and the print dripping dry on a clothesline in a darkroom. Following that line of logic, I might open the book one day to find on every page a simple landscape.

But I don't anticipate a mass vanishing. Unicorns disappear only when it matters. The book is out of print—a compromise? What about the special feature from *Legend*? I used to think those unicorns were real. I wrestled with uneasiness—why didn't all the unicorns disappear? What was the magic that let them be seen?

I am on my way to an answer. I will become a magician yet. Where once I saw the unicorns, I can't stop seeing the long ash of the cigarette and how the halter rubs the wrong way, like an unwitting hand on the genie's lamp.

Unicorns don't exist. But something does. I can't stop seeing the unicorn disappear. I have no strength to look away. What am I collecting? Collect because you believe—I thought that was how it worked, back before I saw the horseshoes. Now I doubt because I desire, and desire because I doubt. If Pluto and his mad unicorn run me down, I might like it. But I am also the mare on the movie set, caught between halter and horn. She and I have learned something. We blink our eyes a heartbeat before the ash falls.

Nominated by Jeff P. Jones, Gettysburg Review

THE EVICTION

by RODNEY JONES

from FIVE POINTS

My privilege to have witnessed this, so late in the middle
        of the 20th Century
that already it seemed historical, almost like having seen
        Erasmus or Thucydides:
a shack at the end of a field road, an eczema of garden,
        domineckers on the porch—
the whole place stank of sweat, coal oil, and excrement,
        and under it, the ghosts
of things rotted and desiccated so far past the organic
        there remained only
the stark elemental testimony of sulfur and ammonia.

Why were we there? Because the wife, the principle filth,
        big-man-big
and raccoon-mean, had been bootlegging and pimping
        the grown daughters,
and the husband, the little cross-eyed gimp, with the chaw-
        mark like a burn-scar
down the neck-creases, who might have been the father
        of seven or eight
of the fourteen living children, liked to lay up drunk
        while the udders
of the jerseys wilted and Johnson grass choked the cotton.

What else? Feuds, wrecks, debts, petty thieveries, arm-
        twistings, and beatings—
When my grandfather, at the behest of my grandmother,
        told the woman to get out,
she had sulled up, there had been a quarrel, a death threat
        he had taken out a warrant,
and now that the thirty days of the warrant had expired,
        and he might
physically evict them, move their belongings out of the house,
        and set them on the road,
with what care they loaded these things onto the wagon.

First, the brown sofa, with the springs working out of it,
        then the cable spool table,
cane chairs nailed together or bound with baling twine,
        fruit jars, kettles, and pots—
A straining and grunting with eyes—but the girl Sheila—
        she was my friend—
and Paul—he would go to college and become something—
        an architect?, an engineer?—
With what omissions do I lard memory? By what secret
        jurisprudence
do my inner committees invent logic and a sentence?

Almost half a century, what does it matter that the terrible
        mother of sharecroppers
who prayed to Bacchus to become anything other than rows
        of cotton
has turned into a stand of pines and risen into a paper factory?
        The shack is gone.
One night three drunk volunteer firemen came and set a fire
        to practice putting it out.
I know the man who puts his neighbor out in the road
        is a cold son of a bitch,
yet I am no sweeter than my grandfather. I study the ground.

Nominated by Pinckney Benedict, R. T. Smith, Five Points

FEM CARE

fiction by ELLIOTT HOLT

from KENYON REVIEW ONLINE

Halfway through the first day of our annual Beauty Summit in Miami, the facilitator says it's time to take a break from our ideation session and have a team experience. We all close our laptops and look up at the giant screens at the front of the hotel ballroom. We've already seen a series of inspirational videos put together by the ad agency. We've seen children running on beaches, reeds blowing in the wind, interracial dance troupes. We're prepared for more.

But then this wiry pipe cleaner of a man who definitely doesn't work for the company goes to the podium. He's wearing a grey business suit and a red and yellow jester's hat. "Hullo," he says. "I am German and I am part of za World Laughter Federation."

"Is Germany funny?" says Eileen Callahan from R&D. She's working with the cosmetic division to develop a foundation that works at the cellular level.

The cosmetic team is at the table on our right; the hair care team is at the table on our left. I'm with fem care. Anti-dandruff is at the table behind us. The fine fragrance group is across the room. They're all in from the Paris office and think they're too sophisticated to sit with the rest of us.

"Now wiz the hands up in the air," says the German in the jester hat. "HO. HO. HA HA HA."

We all repeat after him: "HO. HO. HA HA HA." It doesn't feel like laughter. It feels like something more sinister.

"What are we supposed to *feel* here?" says Luis Gonzalez, who is an assistant brand manager on fem care. After two years of marketing natural fiber maxi-pads to Latin American women, he's learned to look for emotion in everything.

"I bet you didn't think you could spend a whole day talking about the menstrual cycle," he said to me earlier.

"Luis, I'm a woman," I said. "Menstruation is actually a pretty familiar topic."

"Und now, we are at a cocktail party and we shake the martini and laugh." The German roams around the room, approaching each table with his imaginary cocktail shaker. He moves with the jumpy, staccato rhythm of a silent film star.

"HO. HO. Hee hee hee," we say, and shake up our own invisible drinks.

"Mine's a mojito!" says Luis. He's wearing a Hawaiian print shirt.

Forced joviality makes me nervous. It's the reason I never liked summer camp.

"Okay," says the German jester. "Now the scolding laugh." He wags a finger at our table, as if he needs to make an example of fem care, as if we're not already treated like the ugly stepchildren.

"HO. HO. HEH HEH HEH," we repeat. He moves on to chastise the others into participation.

I like my job. I really do. I am good at market research. I get to know my consumers as I analyze data about their lives. I know how much money they make and what they do for a living and how many children they have and how many computers they own and what magazines they read. And even without the names—because I almost never know their names—I have a strong sense of what matters to these women. I know what kind of food they're making for dinner. I imagine them preparing tacos with the Old El Paso kit, and then tucking their children in and reading *Goodnight Moon*. I imagine them waking up in the middle of the night because they are so worried that they'll oversleep. They're lying there, frozen with anxiety, counting the minutes until their alarm clocks go off and they have to pack lunches. Tiny cups of applesauce and pre-wrapped crackers with cheese and carrot sticks that will end up in the trash can with every other kid's vegetables. All that miniature food is enough to make anyone crazy. They're tired of taking care of everyone and of trying to do so many things at once. And so it means something to know that our products improve their lives in some small way. That, thanks to us, their skin feels softer, their armpits are dry, their hair is shiny, and their maxi-pads don't leak. And that thanks to our double-digit growth, I just got a raise.

Luis is wagging a finger at Barb Lawson. Barb spends her life scolding the rest of us, so it does feel pretty good to give her a taste of her own medicine. If Barb is overly combative, it's because she is the kind of woman who never wears the right thing, and she knows it. She's got nothing but her patented anti-dandruff technology to make her feel special.

"HO. HO. HEH HEH HEH," we say, and there's nothing light-hearted about it.

I keep waiting for the moment when the fake laughs inspire real ones. I figure that's the point of this exercise. But as I look around, it seems like we're in the saddest place on Earth. It's like all the hopelessness we've ever felt is concentrated in this enormous room right now. I can feel all the unanswered letters, all the lost dogs, the mateless mittens lying alone in snowdrifts. These laughing exercises make me want to kill myself. And I know how I'd do it too. It would be an homage to Sylvia Plath and her oven, just to subvert everyone's expectations.

"Annie from CRD? Who knew she liked poetry?" they'd say.

I have to get out of this conference room. I feel like I've been trapped in here for a week already. I spend most of my days alone in my office and all these group sessions are wearing me out.

"Luis," I say, "I need to go find a tampon."

Despite his posturing, proximity to an actual menstruating woman still makes Luis squeamish. I can see it in his face. I slip out the back of the ballroom. The hallway is over-air-conditioned, and the carpet has a garish pattern in gold and brown. I want to get as far from the conference as possible, so I head for the elevators and ride to the sixth floor, where the gym and outdoor pool are located. When I get to the pool, there's no one else there. It's just me and fifty lounge chairs with blue and white striped cushions. There are cabanas draped in flowing white fabric and a border of orange trees around the perimeter of the deck. It's impossibly glamorous.

I still get a kick out of staying in nice hotels. I always feel like I am impersonating a grown-up when I go on business trips. I check into my room and wonder if there is a hidden camera ready to record behavior that is less than adult. Is someone watching while I extract blackheads from my nose and smear them on the mirror? What do my colleagues do alone in their rooms while I am scrutinizing my pores and waiting to be found out?

I cross the pool deck to the ladies' lounge on the other side. And it's only when I've hoisted up my dress and made myself comfortable on one of the toilets that I hear a muffled whine from the stall next to mine. I lean my head over and peer under the divider and see a pair of black stilettos.

"Are you okay?" I say after a moment. I think the woman has a right to know I'm here. I wouldn't want her to think I'm eavesdropping.

She hesitates when she hears my voice and then she starts crying the way children do, in loud and furious spurts. I give her a minute or two to get it out of her system while I exit my stall to wash my hands. The soap is a soy and pomegranate concoction that's very on trend— everyone is doing naturals and organics these days.

I hear a break in the sobs and clear my throat. "Can I do anything?"

"I don't know. Are you a dry cleaner?" The voice is raspy and sure of itself.

"Pardon?" I say.

"I have blood all over my fucking dress," the woman says.

"Oh, God," I say. "I hate that."

I can hear her rotating the toilet paper roll on its spindle.

"Do you need a tampon?" I say and can't help but be excited to find a research subject when I wasn't even looking. You never know when you'll unearth a good consumer insight.

"I don't think a tampon can soak up this mess," she says.

"Or I could get you a pad," I say. "There's nothing more degrading than walking around with a wad of toilet paper in your pants. Trust me, I've been there."

"It's not my period," she says.

"Oh," I say. "How long has the bleeding been going on?"

"Two days." She blows her nose. "If you must know, I had an abortion the day before yesterday."

"Well," I say.

I hear her tearing more toilet paper off the roll and adopt my most reassuring moderator voice. "The bleeding is normal. But it must be uncomfortable. Do you need some ibuprofen?"

I've always been a person that people confide in. I think it's because people think I'm too square to have my own secrets. I look innocent and trustworthy and ready to listen. I was a peer counselor in college.

128

It was my job to coax the girls with bulimia to stop sticking their fingers down their throats, to convince the date rape victims to press charges against their attackers. They told me their stories because they thought they'd never see me again. It's a powerful feeling to be privy to something that others aren't. I understand why people can't keep secrets. They spill them because they can't resist showing off the authority they were granted.

"He doesn't even know I was pregnant," she says from inside the stall. "He has grown children. In college. He always complains about the tuition." She starts to laugh as if it's the funniest thing she's ever heard. But then she stops laughing as suddenly as she started and emits a sound that's somewhere between a snort and a cough.

"Do you have kids?" I ask. I'm still about ten years away from menopause, but I know my eggs are like dying stars; they'll burn through their fuel and go dark eventually.

"I planned to," she says.

I'm trying to decide how to tell her that the first two weeks are the hardest and that it really does get better after that. But then I hear the toilet flush.

The woman emerges from the stall. She is willowy with shiny black hair and chic even with red teary streaks on her cheeks. She looks like the kind of woman who has never succumbed to the urge to eat a second donut. She's a little older than I am, probably in her early forties, but I don't see a wedding ring. I try to imagine her when she was in ninth grade. It's a game I play, looking through the lens of adolescent angst to see who would have been a friend in the days when they were hard to come by. This woman, with groomed eyebrows and the effortless elegance I associate with French actresses, was probably recruited to pose for advanced drawing. She probably skipped classes to smoke cigarettes with the boys in some rock band. Or dated a college guy who picked her up from school and took her back to his dorm to have sex before his roommate returned from class.

"Look at this," she says, turning around to show me a kidney-shaped bloodstain on the back of her green print dress. "Diane von Furstenberg. Ruined."

"Maybe not," I say. "It will probably come out."

She says she has to give a presentation in about five minutes. That she doesn't have time to walk all the way to the elevator bank and go up to her room on the twenty-first floor. And so I make the offer before I can second-guess my Pollyanna instincts. "You can borrow my dress," I say. "We could trade. You wear mine, I wear yours." I do have time to go to my room and change.

She scrutinizes my black dress for a minute and her eyes linger on my hips. "*I'm* a size six," she says. "Sometimes I'm a four."

I crane my head around to see the tag inside my dress. It's an eight. "It's a wrap dress, so you can just belt it tighter." I yank it over my head.

"What the hell," the woman says, and shimmies out of her own dress. She's wearing a black lace bra and control top pantyhose stuffed with tissue. I'm wearing no bra—because I'm so flat that I don't really need one—and a threadbare pair of white Hanes that I vowed to throw out a long time ago. I always wear old, stained underwear when I have my period. Plus there is an embarrassing streak of orange—an unsightly souvenir from an experiment with self-tanner—on my thigh. Now I find myself crossing my left hand over my bare breasts while I hold out the dress with my right hand.

That's when she notices my wrist.

"You're with the conference?" she says. She stares at my bracelet in horror.

We all have to wear these red rubber bracelets to identify us as official participants who have signed confidentiality agreements. God forbid someone from L'Oreal should sneak into the ballroom. The woman reluctantly holds up her right wrist. She's wearing a red bracelet too. I didn't notice it under her sleeves when she was dressed.

"I'm Annie, Global CRD, fem care," I say, holding my dress against my body.

"Based at Bear Valley?" She tosses her soiled dress onto the bathroom counter.

I nod.

She exhales very slowly, as if blowing smoke rings. "Quite a run you've had in Mexico. With *Nature's Mother,* I mean."

"It should be a billion dollar brand by 2015."

"So I hear. These days I'm focused on upstream skin care projects. You know, Neptune, Panacea."

It figures that she's in skin care marketing. The skin care people are the big men on campus, the homecoming queens. And project Panacea is very high priority. I don't know much about it, but there's been chatter. It could be the next big breakthrough in anti-aging.

130

She reaches inside her discarded dress and pulls out the lanyard with her nametag. It reads, "Susan Graves."

"You're Susan Graves?"

"That's me." She begins to massage her temples.

I've seen her picture on the annual report, but she looks different here. Softer, younger. Naked. Almost naked, anyway. She's the first woman to head the beauty care division. She's in charge of about fifty brands around the world. They say she's in line to be CEO, if Samuels ever steps down.

Susan Graves takes my dress out of my hand and slips it over her head.

"Are you sure you're okay?" I say. I don't want her to leave.

She belts the dress into place. It looks better on her than it does on me.

"Sometimes this business really gets to me. Sometimes I think I should just pack it in and move to Lake Tahoe or something. Get out while I'm still young enough to remember how to live."

"I know what you mean," I say, but I don't really. I'd miss my consumers. I'd miss their stories. When I drink my coffee in the morning, I think about the forty-two-year-old executive assistant in Seattle who gets migraines every month and finds that acupuncture and a latte are the only things that ease her pain. When I'm driving to work, I think about the twenty-seven-year-old teacher in Quito who stays in bed for two days because her cramps are so debilitating. Or the thirty-four-year-old caterer in Atlanta whose pad leaked all over her jeans on a first date. I'd be lost without those women. These days, they're all I've got.

Susan Graves looks at me as if I'm a room she'd like to makeover. "I have to run," she says. "They're waiting for me."

* *

Back in the ballroom, Luis wants to know where I've been. He doesn't even notice that I have changed into trousers.

"I had to get the concierge to get me a box of tampons," I say. "It was an emergency."

The group has already started the next ideation session. They're brainstorming about relevant emotional benefits for *Nature's Mother*. We're supposed to come up with category-specific emotions and Luis is taking notes.

"You're on your period, Annie," says Luis. He stands at the easel,

131

ready to record my thoughts on our giant notepad. "How do you feel? How do you wish you felt?"

Allegra, who works in marketing with Luis, says women at this time of the month want to be free, unfettered, full of hope and possibility. "They want their beauty to be in bloom."

Luis writes this down. "Beauty in bloom" will probably end up as a commercial tagline; it's just the kind of ball the agency in Chicago would run with. I wonder how it will translate into Spanish.

I can see Susan Graves across the room at the skin care table. She's a commanding presence, gesturing as the others in her group watch.

"I think that women want their days to feel like any other day of the month," Allegra is saying.

"I think women want to be empowered by their own femininity, their fertility. Menstruation is a drag, but it's what separates the women from the boys," I say and almost believe it.

"This is good," says Luis. "This is really good."

° °

R&D and CRD rarely get included in conferences like this. This is painfully obvious at the group dinner by the pool that evening. It's a buffet and we can sit wherever we want. The marketing people recognize one another like fraternity brothers with a secret handshake. They are based in different countries and work on different brands, but they gravitate toward the same four tables in the center of the patio. They wear expensive shoes and talk about wine. Even Luis has been welcomed into the mix. The rest of us are left to mingle awkwardly, having high school cafeteria flashbacks as we try to find empty seats at the peripheral tables. I find myself next to Barb Lawson and I know it's going to be a long evening.

"Look at them," says Barb, gesturing at the marketing people. "Full of ideas that we can't support technically. They want to talk about channeling moisture to the parts of the scalp that need it most. They expect me to support a targeted hydra-delivery system. I told them I can't support that."

I see Susan Graves in the buffet line, daintily serving herself salad. She's an anomaly because, despite the fact that we're a beauty company, we don't have very many beautiful people working for us. Some of us are attractive, yes, but not beautiful. She looks up for a moment and I wave at her. She's a mere ten feet from our table but pretends that she doesn't see me. She looks right through my raised arm, as if I'm totally invisible, as if I'm just another researcher hidden behind a two-way mirror at focus groups, and then turns her gaze to the basket of bread on the buffet table. She's trying to decide between a sourdough roll and a French boule. My hand lingers in the air until my flickering fingers finally burn out and I let them fall into my lap and hope that no one saw my unrequited wave.

"I'm a scientist, not a magician," Barb is saying.

Another R&D guy named Charlie pipes up. "Yeah, they think they're all that."

"Good chicken," I say.

Barb rolls her eyes as if I can't possibly understand the cross she has to bear. "Marketing is all fluff, Annie," she says. "These people are getting all the credit for selling our products. Why do they sell well? Because they work well. Why do they work well? Because I made them work well."

"Barb," I say. "It's hard for them too. Susan Graves was crying this afternoon. I saw her weeping hysterically in the bathroom."

As soon as I say it, I know I've gone too far. Barb is eager for ammunition and I realize that Susan Graves is a big gun. I try to backpedal, but it's too late. There are ten people around me who want to know what she was crying about.

"Maybe they should transfer Susan Graves to pharma; she could market antidepressants," someone says.

"It could have been hay fever," I say, but the damage has been done.

I stay with my half-eaten chicken while Barb Lawson slips off to another table, whispers something to another R&D woman. There's a giddy energy that sweeps around the edge of the patio. They've got something on Susan Graves and they're not afraid to use it. I'd like to warn Susan somehow, pull her aside and let her know that the attack is coming. But she's in the middle of a serious conversation with a bald man. She's wearing a black dress with a gold belt. It's a dress with no room for a baby.

"I think I'm going up to bed," I say to no one in particular.

In my hotel room, I break into the mini-bar even though it's against company policy. I eat a can of Pringles and a bag of Peanut M&Ms. I'm halfway through a jar of cashews when I drift off. I dream of babies in jester hats, floating in a pool. There are babies everywhere, forming circles like synchronized swimmers, kicking their dimpled pink legs in the air, in unison, until the image divides, cleaving like a zygote, and then subdivides and subdivides again, creating a kaleidoscope of plump baby limbs against the chlorinated blue.

I am woken by a knock at my door. Housekeeping has already been there to turn down my bed, it's almost two in the morning, but I open the door anyway. It's Susan Graves. She's swept her hair up and her eyes are a little puffy, but she's still alarmingly beautiful. "I have your garment," she says, as she brushes past me into my room.

I follow her. She tosses my wadded up dress onto the desk and sits down in the armchair by the window while I make a hasty attempt to brush the potato chip crumbs out of my sheets. I'm wearing my hotel robe and feel like a hausfrau. I can't believe that Susan Graves is in my room.

"I'm sorry you had to witness that little sob fest today."

I sit down on the bed, facing her. I would like to be her friend. We could make spa appointments together. We would read fashion magazines while we got pedicures. She'd help me choose a polish color. I'd gravitate toward a neutral pink, but she'd push me to try something a little more vibrant. A cherry red maybe. That would really be something.

"It's important that my team not question my decision making ability," she says.

"Sure."

"And if they think I'm having a meltdown . . ."

"You're not having a meltdown."

"But if the perception is that I am having a meltdown . . ."

"Yes."

"Or if they think I'm some kind of floozy . . ."

"Yes."

"Then that's a problem," she says. "A problem you can fix."

"Oh, anything. Tell me what I can do to help."

This is the moment, I think, when she confides in me about all the causes of her unhappiness. An affair with a married man, maybe. A sister with leukemia. An Eastern European product launch gone awry. I'm ready for anything. I picture her legs in the stirrups, waiting for the OB/GYN. If she'd give me an opening, I'd tell her what it feels like to have sex for the first time after an abortion. How tentative I was, how desperate I felt to be fucked especially hard as some kind of punishment for being less than vigilant with birth control.

134

"They'll eventually give up trying to get to the bottom of my mystery," she says. "As long as you don't say anything."

"I just mentioned that you were crying," I say. "I didn't tell them why. I didn't say anything about your procedure."

Susan Graves folds her arms across her abdomen as if she's in pain. As if she's got cramps. If only Luis were here to see this. The emotion that a lot of women experience when they get their period every month is relief. Thank God I'm not pregnant, they think. They remember the nights when the condom broke, when the condom wasn't used at all, when the rhythm method seemed more than adequate, when it just felt good to be wanted. Thank you, God; I'll never take another chance again.

"I didn't tell them," I say again. "Not that."

She studies me carefully, trying to decipher whether I'm telling the truth, and I get the feeling she's never had women friends. She's the type who would order her steak rare just to prove she can keep up with the boys. Our company may market products to women, but they're not ready for real women's issues.

"Maybe you should take some time off and rest," I say. "You've been through a lot. You've probably got plenty of vacation days."

"I don't need time off."

"You said that sometimes you just can't take this business."

"Is that what you heard?"

"That's what you said."

"No, I said sometimes I just can't take the *people* in this business. There are people who just don't belong here. It's up to me to decide who those people are."

I think of the quarterly emails that are sent to all of us in beauty care. Words of inspiration, straight from the desk of Susan Graves. *"Think of the consumer as a friend,"* read one. *"If you could take her out for coffee, what would she have to say? Isn't it time you let her voice be heard?"*

"When is your next performance review?" She sits back in her armchair and crosses her legs. She has great legs for a woman her age. No spider veins crawling across her calves, no dimpled flesh around the knee.

"Not for five months."

"Maybe we should accelerate that timeline," she says. "I think it's time to review your performance, don't you?" She lets her hair down and shakes it out. She has mastered the nonchalant flip of our shampoo commercials.

I am not much of a drinker, but I go to the mini-bar and pull out one of the tiny bottles of vodka.

"I'll take one of those," she says.

I hand her a bottle. She unscrews the lid and takes a swig without puckering her lips the way most people do when they swallow something that harsh.

"I used to be in CRD. Did you know that?" she says.

I shake my head. Susan Graves seems like she vaulted straight from business school into the glossy world of marketing. It's hard to imagine her toiling away in the unglamorous world of the Consumer Research Division. It's hard to imagine her working her way up from anywhere.

"It's true. CRD in AP/DO. We never got any respect."

The antiperspirant and deodorant divisions still don't get any respect. It's as bad as fem care. Sweat and blood are not much fun.

"And there were so few women then. It was horrible. We girls have to take care of each other, don't you think?" She smiles at me. One, of her incisors is especially pointed; a snaggletooth that would be a flaw on anyone else. I suspect that her lovers have run their tongues over the sharp edge of that tooth and known they were in the presence of someone special. "A word from the right person and you could be promoted ahead of schedule. Perhaps you're ready to run a division of CRD. You might have a future in management."

"I didn't tell them," I say.

"Then we're in business," says Susan Graves. She raises her bottle, as if to make a toast.

"Cheers," I say.

"I'll be watching you," she says.

◦ ◦

Our goal in CRD is to build relationships, to engender loyalty by making consumers feel like our brands understand them. Equity scans tell us which brands are "for someone like me." We test our advertisements for engagingness, persuasiveness and recall, and then peruse the consumer verbatims to see what their statements reveal. We put demographic and psychographic boxes around people, reducing them to their key attributes to fit them on our market map.

Nature's Mother has captured a huge share of developing markets, especially Catholic countries where women don't believe in tampons. Before launch, it was my research that showed that consumers in those countries were afraid of synthetic materials. That's why our pads—at least for this particular brand—are made with natural fibers and chamomile. Our marketing campaign is called "Absorbing Life." We have other fem care brands too, including the best-selling tampon in the United States. But *Nature's Mother* is helping us build the business in Latin America and Eastern Europe. We're going into China next year. It's a white space launch that could make my career.

After Susan Graves leaves my room, I can't fall asleep. I lie on my back, then on my stomach, then on my back again. I tell myself I should brush my teeth, but I just stare at the ceiling and wonder what I would do if I actually got promoted. Will I end up sending inspirational emails to everyone in beauty care? *Don't forget that the consumer has the same hopes and fears as we do. Don't forget that there are things about her that no test can tell us. Consumers cry too.*

I can't stay in bed any longer, so at four-fifteen in the morning, I pull on a pair of jeans and a T-shirt, slip on my sneakers and leave my room. The hotel is eerily quiet at this hour—even the cynical laughter of late-night talk shows has long been put to bed—and I hear nothing from the guest rooms on my hall. In the elevator, I hardly recognize myself in the mirrored walls: my image is watery and diluted. I'm sinking deeper. Down on the fourth floor, the conference room is empty. Our summit doesn't resume until eight o'clock, and without any body heat, it's shockingly cold. I prop the doors open to let in some of the light from the lobby and survey the scene. In the semi-darkness, the easels look like abandoned playground equipment. There are dozens of pages of ideas—the eager scribbling of various brand managers—posted haphazardly on the walls. I find my way to the fem care table and turn our easel pad toward the light. Luis has written: "Beauty in bloom—Empowered by fertility???"

My pregnancy, all seven weeks of it, occurred when I was a senior in high school. My boyfriend lived around the corner from me and we used to walk our dogs together late at night, letting the leashes tangle up while we kissed. He was an abstract painter and a varsity tennis player, a shambling presence with a ponytail and a penchant for post-punk music. I feel like a butcher sometimes, slicing thinner and thinner until no one is recognizable. He was all those things, but he was also unbearably sad, and honest about his sadness in a way that people can be at seventeen, and our sadness attracted each other like depressed magnets, and for a while, the mere fact of one another's presence was enough of a buoy to keep us afloat, to crystallize our moods into an exquisite kind of melancholy, and sometimes to make us bubbly in a way we didn't remember we knew how to be. We were kissing regularly under streetlights, in the rain even, giggling while our poor golden retrievers were knotted together. I miss feeling that connected to another person. His name was Paul. But then there was the pregnancy test I couldn't bring myself to tell him about and the appointment I made without his knowledge. Eventually, I started timing my dog walks so that I wouldn't run into him.

In just three hours, Luis and the others will be back down here, ready to ideate. I could pretend that none of this ever happened and hope that management really is in my future. Susan Graves and I don't work in the same building. Once we're back in Bear Valley, I probably won't see her at all. And yet, her name will still be invoked in meetings; her emails will circulate like commandments. She'll still be watching me. Luis's handwriting is slanting and insistent. I pick up one of the markers from our table and turn over a fresh page on the easel pad. Emotional benefits. I just need to figure out what I feel.

I used to watch Paul from behind the curtains of my bedroom window as he walked slowly past my house, dawdling in case I came outside. He always looked up at my window as if identifying constellations, as if he saw something eternal and bright about us. Now, nearly twenty years later, he probably wouldn't recognize me if I passed him on the street.

I've been with the company for ten years. I'm one hundred percent vested. I'm signed up for the fem care softball team. I try to imagine what else I'd be good at, if I left and had to find another job. Interviews were never my strong suit. *Give me an example of a challenge you faced and describe how you handled that challenge.* I wonder if Susan Graves is sleeping. If she's wearing a silk eye mask over her hydrating night treatment. If certainty is reasserting itself inside her as she dreams. Or if, in the morning, she will wake to a murkiness that can't be washed and exfoliated away. *What would you say are your greatest weaknesses? What might you do differently, if you could?*

Nominated by Laura van den Berg

OCULAR

by ROSANNA WARREN

from THE AMERICAN SCHOLAR

So damp the pages of novels curl up like vine leaves,
the stories smear. In the Métro this morning
a man was scraping a poster from the wall:

all the promised felicity hung in shreds.
My eye is swollen, purple. I can't read, near
or far. My childhood is far.

I slept on a naked mattress the pit bull ripped;
it reeked of smoke, needles littered the floor.
I starved myself, I admired my delicate ribs,

the leaves of a petrified prehistoric fern.
I was prehistoric, my eye teeth turned to fangs.
Day marched in carrying night on his shoulders,

a wizened old man. I preferred night.
Come to me, I said, I'll kiss you anyway,
even if you're ancient and I'm blind and bruised,

we'll laugh, we'll be the Book of Revelations,
I'll wear lingerie from the crypt and we'll eat at the Loveless Café
where biscuits steam and no one spits in the jam.

That was years ago. Night's tired now,
we've worn each other out. We hardly meet.
But I still have one good eye, and when I squint,

you wouldn't believe what I see.

Nominated by The American Scholar

ANALPHABET

by MARTIN MORAN

from PLOUGHSHARES

Siba keeps shaking his head as if pushing a vision away. His chest is heaving, tears are spilling down his cheeks, but he is silent, choking back any sound. We are walking west on East Eighty-sixth Street, the leafless trees of Central Park a few blocks ahead. We move under a green awning and past a doorman in a long coat studded with golden buttons. For the briefest moment I raise my right hand and place it against Siba's back, between his shoulder blades. Then I dig in my jacket pocket, come up with a crumpled napkin. He takes it, presses it to his nose, wipes at his eyes.

"*Respire,*" I say to him in his native tongue, French. Breathe.

I don't know what else to say.

It's only the second time we've met. The first was two days before when he gripped my hand in greeting outside the clinic on the second floor of Saint Luke's Hospital. He was there to tell a physician, a volunteer with Doctors of the World, all he remembered of what happened back in Africa, so that the doctor could examine him and write an affidavit on behalf of Siba's request for asylum. I was there to interpret—nervous about doing a good job, about meeting a survivor of torture. As he took my hand he emanated joy. His beauty, the flash of his teeth, his bright eyes, startled me. I was, I think, expecting someone broken.

"*Si je n'arrête pas . . .*" he pauses, shakes his head, chokes the tears. "*Si je n'arrête pas de pleurer, je deviens aveugle.*" If I don't stop crying, I will go blind.

"*Ce n'est pas vrai,*" I tell him. "It's not true. Crying won't make you

141

blind. Tears are OK, tears are . . . are good." I hear my awkward French drift off into the cold. I wonder who might have told him such a thing, if he means it as literally as it seems he does. What can it feel like to know that how well you tell your story, how convincingly, might be the difference between sanctuary and deportation, between liberty and death? I am aware of how busily I am trying to draw lines between him and me, wanting so keenly (why?) to find connections in our earthly experience.

Siba and I have just spent nearly three hours with a psychologist. His second of two required medical interviews. She broke her questions down into three categories. First: Tell me about your childhood, your family, your life growing up. Second: Tell me about your arrest and torture. And third, the most difficult for Siba to grasp: What do you feel are the consequences of what happened to you? Siba kept shaking his head, it seemed he didn't understand the notion of consequences. It was too abstract, perhaps, or the narrative of cause and effect too pat. Too simple. Too American? Or maybe my translation was inadequate. She was trying to quantify, to record specifics of Posttraumatic Stress Disorder. Concrete things the asylum judge might want to read. "Are you frightened when you hear loud noises? Is it hard to concentrate? Do you sleep? Tell me how your life is different now." Siba's response was to look silently past the large bookcase to a window facing the Chrysler Building poking up in the distance, above the sea of East Side apartments. She waited, then asked a few more things about his health, made some notes and said, "I will write the best report I can for you. You are a brave young man." Here, against all rules of being the unobtrusive interpreter, I began to cry. "The United States would be lucky to have you as a citizen," she said, and he cried too as he thanked her and expressed his dream to gain citizenship, to find and bring his family here. The mention of his wife, his child, undid him. She turned to me and pointed to her watch. I hustled Siba out of the room. "Où se trouve la douche?" he whispered. Where is the shower? I knew he meant toilet. I found a key; let him into the men's room where he remained for a long time.

Both of us are dazed to find ourselves on a sunny sidewalk passing regally dressed doormen. The February day is frigid. Siba is ill dressed against the cold, winter is still a surprise for him, as are most things here. He wears a slim windbreaker, no hat, no gloves. I don't want to just deposit him at the PATH train for his trip back to New Jersey as I was instructed to do. Instead, we just walk. I keep glancing up at him. He's tall. Though barely twenty-three, he seems to me infinitely older—husband, father, refugee. His wife and child and parents all in hiding back in Sudan or Chad, if they're alive. There is no way of knowing, trying to make contact would only imperil them. He speaks again, words rough and swollen with the story.

"If I don't stop crying, I will lose my vision."

"*Non*," I say. But what do I know of his vision, his home, his beliefs?

We pause at the corner of Park Avenue. The midday crowd is weaving swiftly around us, all suits and purpose. I ask if I can buy him lunch. He says he can't eat, but we cross the street and sit at the bar at Demarchalier—a neighborhood restaurant, French. He sips orange juice. I eat a bowl of potato soup. Above the shelves of liquor, CNN is on—scenes of American life, of Hillary and Obama. Siba is transfixed. Two ladies enjoy pâté and white wine in the window. Siba points to where the ladies sit, to the curtains framing them, and suddenly he brightens.

"That's what I did at home!" he tells me. "When I moved to the city. I made curtains for people's houses." He asks me for a pen, grabs a napkin and draws picture after picture of windows and drapes. He stops to show me each kind of curtain, the different ways they billow and hang. His smile knocks me out. His laughter. I ask him if I can keep the drawings, if he will sign the napkin. He laughs again and signs with a great flourish—three names chock full of vowels. He turns to me. "I will do this work again someday. In America." The light from his dark eyes is incandescent.

In the past year, I have come to find myself in rooms with survivors of torture. Why?

A) Because I want to put all these years of studying French to use?

B) Because I want to explore if and how people forgive?

C) Because I want to understand survival of trauma?

D) Because I wish to be saved by doing good works?

E) All of the above?

The place I call home sits on the high ground of Northern Manhattan on a narrow stretch of Cabrini Boulevard. It is named for Saint Frances Xavier Cabrini, the first American Saint, canonized in 1946. I pass her corpse (minus her head which is somewhere in Italy) nearly every day. It is encased in glass in a church just across from where you catch the A train. Her full title: Virgin Foundress of the Institute of the Missionary Sisters of the Sacred Heart. An immigrant herself, she was devoted to immigrants, to the poor. She founded sixty-seven schools, hospitals and orphanages across the U.S. and beyond. Mostly, mind you, by horse and buggy. I wonder at her purpose-driven life.

Nearing fifty, I've mislaid what I once thought was fierce ambition. Purpose. I've lost my way. For three decades, I've made my living as an actor, spending much of the last couple of years galloping around at the Shubert Theater playing Sir Robin, the Monty Python knight who poops his pants at the least sign of danger. One of the warriors of King Arthur's Round Table on a quest to find the Holy Grail: the miraculous cup, the answer to the meaning of life.

Oh we're off to war, because we're not yet dead,
We will all enlist as the Knights that Arthur led!

It's a dream job, singing on Broadway, eight times a week. But I felt a terrible restlessness. A deep sense that there was something else I was meant to be doing. Somewhere out there in the world. One day, I read a plea posted by the renowned organization, Doctors Without Borders. They were looking for French-speaking support staff to come and work for at least six to nine months at a refugee camp. I heard this call as my answer, and filled out the application. "I have come to feel in recent months a yearning to give back in some way. To be of use in parts of the world where poverty and strife are real and part of everyday life."

One sunny afternoon, between a matinee and an evening performance, I went to Doctors Without Borders headquarters in Chelsea for my interview. I wore a fresh-pressed, button-down shirt and sat at a large conference table across from a very serious woman with cropped, gray hair. She was, I felt sure, an ex-nun. She tested my French. That went OK. She grilled me: "Do you have experience managing groups of people?" I was president of the Catholic Youth Organization. I directed *The Sound of Music.* She had me view a video on the gritty realities of life in a refugee camp. I watched knowing how lucky they'd be to have capable, sunshiny me. She put a twelve-page, multiple-choice test in front of me and left the room. I stared at it for a very long time: Questions on purchase orders, the shelf life of canned fruit, metric conversions, the rights and wrongs of installing software. I couldn't deduce a single answer. Finally, like a delinquent sixth grader, I quickly colored in all the little dots at random. When she returned she looked over my work briefly. "Mr. Moran, have you ever labored in close quarters with others over a long period of time with the threat of death all around you?"

"Well," I responded, "have you ever worked out of town in a troubled new musical headed for Broadway?" She squinted at me then stared at her Birkenstocks. A letter came two weeks later thanking me and politely expressing concern that I lacked third world experience.

A month or so after receiving my rejection, I mentioned the disappointment to Sara, an old friend. "Hey," she said. "You don't need to go to the Ivory Coast to be of help. Have you *looked* around our city?" She's a therapist. It turned out that one of the groups she works with, The International Institute, which was founded in Jersey City in 1917 to assist refugees from all over the globe, was in constant need of volunteers.

The downtown A train is packed, morning commuters huddled over headlines printed in Polish, English, Spanish, Chinese. I find a seat between a young man in beige corduroys who wears a yarmulke and a brown-skinned schoolgirl studying geometry. A sign across from me features a chubby-faced, balding man with a tight-lipped, trust-me look. *Deportation? Green Card? Immigration Questions?* He's an expert, a lawyer. In large print across the center of the ad it says: *Call 1-800-Immigration or 1-800-Innocence.*

In my lap, I hold notes on Siba's reasons for fleeing his country, his request to remain here. It is part of an I-589. A Department of Homeland Security U.S. Citizenship and Immigration Services Application for Asylum and for "Withholding of Removal." I study the text, flip through my French-English Dictionary, look up Chad in the back of my leather-bound calendar. Chad is orange, just below Libya, touching Sudan and green Cameroon. The little map makes Africa look like a children's jigsaw puzzle.

The doctor is an older man, soft-spoken, retired, I think. He moves with a kind of unhurried gentleness. He takes Siba's hand, welcomes him. He asks me if I've done this before and I tell him it's my first time. "Well," he says, "we'll go easy, we'll stop when need be, OK? Tell Siba we're in no rush here." He smiles and gestures for us to sit.

I arrange the folding chairs (as taught in my "Introduction to Interpreting" course) so that client and doctor face one another. I am slightly off to the side. "It's best when you disappear," said our instructor, a Russian émigré. "You are a shared tongue, nothing more. A conduit for communication."

"How are you feeling today?" The doctor asks.

"OK, *merci. J'ai mal à la tête.*" I have a headache.

"Just today, or often?"

"Often."

One small window allows a swath of warm light into the stark room: a desk; a narrow counter with jars of long Q-tips and tongue depressors; an exam table; our three folding chairs and two trashcans, one marked "Biohazard." I feel my heart against my ribs and smile at Siba, who seems calm. The doctor looks up.

"Tell me what happened."

He explains quietly, his supple, dark wrists in constant motion.

He was in his native village for a visit. A meeting at a friend's house. They discussed the need for clean water, for schools. The situation was desperate. Sick children, no education, men arbitrarily arrested, accused of being anti-government rebels. In the midst of the meeting, soldiers burst in, killed some, arrested others, Siba among them. Siba was cuffed, blindfolded, thrown in the back of a truck. Two days later, he was locked away in a filthy cell. Why? A story of violent tribal rivalry.

He becomes most anguished not when describing the physical abuse but when he recounts the *not being believed.* When he talks of his countrymen calling him a liar. "They won't *listen.* They are so angry. I've done nothing. *I am not a rebel soldier,* I tell them. They don't *believe* me."

An hour later Siba has taken his shirt and pants off and sits, slump-shouldered, with his legs stretched before him on the exam table. Sunlight falls across his face. The doctor holds a yellow measuring tape across Siba's back, between his shoulder blades, as if fitting him for a new suit. Determining, then documenting, the length and depth of each of Siba's scars. Sometimes the doctor touches a particular mark and asks: Is this from the wooden club, or was this from the broken glass? I translate, thinking: this is unfolding one block from the Metropolitan Opera House.

"They put the glass in the crooks of your arms, your knees?" The doctor points to the back of his own knees, trying to get a handle on this particular method of extracting information. Siba nods and describes how the glass was shaped, how they bent and bound his limbs.

146

"They tightened the ropes, they kept yelling questions, beating me about the head and back until I passed out."

"This happened how many times?"

"Four."

"Did you always lose consciousness?"

"Yes. I woke up back in my cell."

I walk him the long way around, past Lincoln Center, to the subway station. Like a tour guide, I point out the Met, Alice Tully Hall, Christopher Columbus. He asks me what "Opera" means.

"Love stories, tragedies, told with singing." He looks confused. I open wide and belt out a few measures of Puccini. His laugh is long and wonderful.

In the station I write my number on the page of a notebook, rip it out and hand it to him. "If you need anything." He nods. I stare down at the floor. I want to say something about how honored I am, how amazing to have met. "Three stops to Thirty-fourth, then look for PATH," I say, pointing out the sign for the D train.

"Oui, merci." He takes my hand. His grip, his eyes, surprise me to tears. We move toward one another and embrace.

I've long wanted to travel to Africa. I got to visit once, though far south of where Siba lived. Johannesburg and Cape Town. I'd been invited because my one-man play was being performed by a South African actor and the troupe asked if I would come and help with promotion, join a panel at the University on the subject of reconciliation.

"We'd like to discuss, among other things, the question: How do you forgive the unforgivable?"

"Oh," I remember saying into the phone to the polite British-sounding man. "Really? I'm no expert."

The play, an eighty-minute monologue that I've often performed, is based upon my memoir: the story of what I think happened when I was twelve and tumbled into sex with a counselor many years my senior at a Catholic boy's camp. I spent a long time composing simple sentences about the complexity of this, about the everlasting search for peace.

"Well, we think your play," the man said, "speaks to the complications of reconciling ourselves to the past. We thought this could be a valuable cultural exchange."

"I'm honored," I said, feeling a strange but familiar sorrow, an em-

147

barrassment that I'd somehow become the go-to guy on the subject of sex abuse and forgiveness. What I once meant by forgiveness comes and goes, sneaks away.

When, a few years ago, I tracked down and faced the now old man who wronged me, it came to me so clearly how he was beside the point. Forgiveness was a choice, a gift I would give to myself. Liberty. But these days I have been haunted by the thought that I skipped some important manly step, that I did not *make him pay*. That I remain broken and weak in some essential way. That I would be someone better, somewhere else, if *it* hadn't happened.

Anger moves in and obliterates the view.

Sometimes I hear the voice of my theatrical agent Steve, the man who gets me work. He's a dad of three. A tough, wonderful guy whom I love and admire. I hear his voice saying to me, right after he saw my play for the first time: "So, you had a tape recorder in your pocket when you went to confront that guy? Jeez. I would have had a fucking gun."

"Have you heard about the Truth and Reconciliation Committee?" the man from South Africa asked.

"Kind of," I said.

"It offered a space in which victims could make their stories heard. Amnesty would be provided for those who had violated human rights if they were truthful, took responsibility. Restorative justice rather than retributive justice. It's a continuing debate whether this has worked, you know?"

Restorative.

Retributive.

So there's more than one kind of justice?

Siba and I are seated on a wooden bench where Wall Street stops to meet the East River. He has a job nearby washing dishes at a sandwich shop. There's a large dock to our right where a fleet of fat boats, bright yellow trimmed with black, are coming and going busily.

"Taxis?" Siba asks.

"Water taxis," I say.

It's October, clear as can be. The late afternoon sun is blazing at our backs, poised perfectly above the cluster of skyscrapers to scatter its light all across the surface of the river. It looks as though the boats, rather than floating on the water, are gliding through liquid sun. *"C'est génial ici,"* says Siba.

"Brilliant," I agree, nudging him toward English. I point to my mouth. "Brilliant."

"Brilliant," he repeats with his elegant version of an American *r*.

It's eight months now that I've known him. We don't meet often but he has a cell and, when it works, when he's able to pay for the minutes, we check in by phone. Every conversation begins the exact same way. He asks:

How is your Mother?

Fine.

And your brother?

Good.

His health?

Better.

I'm happy to hear that. And your sisters?

He remembers, it seems, anything I happen to share about my family. I want to ask him about his, of course, but I dare not. If he had news, he'd tell me. I always ask about his case. It's worrisome. Since the Patriot Act was passed in 2001, the quota for refugees has dropped dramatically, the process for asylum seekers becomes much more difficult. Even hostile. There are many months of waiting. Thankfully, Siba has a good lawyer.

Today, we sip our drinks and watch the boats. We are each holding cranberry-flavored Vitamin Waters. We got them in the fancy deli across the street. He wondered what was in it. I tried to explain about electrolytes and vitamins. "But how could water cost three dollars a bottle, why would anyone buy it?" he had asked.

"Siba?"

"Yes?"

"Are you angry? I mean about what happened to you?"

"No."

"Really?"

We're silent awhile. Then he looks at me and says,

"It's like it was an accident. That's how I think of it. An accident. I was there in that place and that time and it happened and . . ."

"And?"

He looks out at the blazing water. "This is life."

We're silent for a time. Then he says, "They, they are *analphabète*."

I repeat the word. I've never heard it. (I look up the French later that night: *Illiterate. Without alphabet.*)

"Most of them," he continues, "those soldiers, they grew up with

149

nothing. The army recruits them. I got to go to the city, get an education. They . . . they don't know what they are doing." He says this with a kind of grace, sadness. "My country is, it is trouble and trouble."

"Your whole life has changed because of what happened."

"Yes."

He takes a sip of water, the color of thin blood.

"What if the accident hadn't happened?" I ask.

"What if? That's a silly question."

"You must think about your family all the time."

"I carry them with me, but I cannot think about them all the time. I need to live. If I grieve all the time, I will . . ."

He goes silent.

"I must live," he says. "Here. In front of me. Then we will see what will happen. You are lucky to be born here," he says. "Here you have *justice*."

The way he says the word, so reverent. It's as if I've never heard it, taken it and so much for granted. The boats keep coming and going. It's nearing rush hour.

"Where is the Statue of Liberty from here?" he asks.

I point behind us. "She's over, the other side of all these buildings."

"I'd like to go one day. Take a picture there," he says.

We head down Wall Street. He points up to a huge, black skyscraper. "On Saturdays, I get to deliver sandwiches here," he says, grinning. "They come down to meet me, or sometimes I go in and all the way up to the offices! The people are very nice." He describes the secretary he met on the thirtieth floor, how they shake hands and how she teaches him a word or two of English. I wonder what she would think if she knew the story of the young man from a Sudanese village who delivers her lunch.

We pass Trinity Church and then the cemetery where a piece of one of the towers, on the morning they collapsed, came down like a spear, stuck in the ground amidst the old graves. I tell Siba the story. We walk on past the giant cranes at work in the midst of the great empty space and join the many moving toward the PATH. We pause at the entrance.

"Call me, OK?"

"I will, Martin. Please, tell your family hello from me."

Nominated by Ploughshares

LORD GOD BIRD

by COLIN CHENEY

from NOTRE DAME REVIEW

> *. . . and other possible sources of this pale blur include the pale head markings of a pileated woodpecker, light reflecting off the bird's back, or video processing artifacts.*
>
> —David A. Sibley, *Science*, 17 March 2006

Po, ninety, marks his canvas with charcoal
taped to a length of bamboo,
says he paints for the rare moment
when he is moved by someone outside himself. Ghosts:
a father dead of TB, an island of murdered friends.

And now he is sketching a Siberian tiger
machine-gunned fifty-years-ago
that just yesterday startled a daydreaming G.I.
who glimpsed it running through the pencil & ironbark
orchids of the Korean DMZ, of the minefield.
But this orchid he roughs in now
he dug from the peak of Huayna Picchu
& carried home on the plane in a damp paper bag.
Its flowers small & spotted as with Pollack's brush.

In Camcorder footage, following the wing's ventral
surface, Sibley must have, for a moment,
known he was watching spirit
photographs, not the Civil War forgeries, but the real ghosts.

I would have lied too, I would have
said it was a common thing, accounted for, not the terror
of what the bird's apparition would then have to mean.

I love the Arkansas of the American mind
where, in some quantum trick in cells of the brain,
the lost things flare back
for a few months only to disappear again.
The Greeks had a name for this empty frame in the Camcorder
left filming in the swamp: *Aornos*, meaning *birdless*.

Looking hard at the barest outline of wing,
I hear the old chaos of the songbirds
Po gave away one by one to make room for Sylvia's memories
in their emptied cages,
Sylvia who yesterday he found asleep
beneath her sculptures—clay over chicken wire, feathers
from the birds—wearing her best jewelry & a nightgown.

Nominated by Dan Albergotti, Ciaran Berry, Phil Dacey, Maxine Scates, G. C. Waldrep

STEAL SMALL

fiction by CAITLIN HORROCKS

from PRAIRIE SCHOONER

I live in a good house now, with an attic where the roof makes a triangle and the heat collects. You can stand up there and see out back to the barbed wire where our property meets the neighbor's, and past that the highway. The neighbor still farms, soy planted right up against the fence. We haven't planted anything, unless you count the animals. That's what Leo does, what he grows. From the attic you can see the kennels, laid out in a half circle in the backyard, all figured so the mean ones don't fight, the sweet ones calm the fussy ones down, and the bitches can't get puppies. Leo can hold them all in his head, who needs what and eats what and is looking sick and should probably be sold on before it looks any sicker. He's got a good mind for organization. I've got a good mind for keeping stuff tidy, which is important in a house like this, which is big and decent and full of what a person needs but has fifteen dogs caged up in the back. Fifteen give or take. In a good month, take.

Leo got a real nasty scratch about a month ago, spiraling from the back of his hand down the inside of his arm. I had him sit on the bathroom counter while I got alcohol and cotton balls out of the cupboard. I dabbed my way down his arm. "Second time this week," I said. "You should watch yourself better."

"It wasn't the Rottie," he said, looking up, and I couldn't tell whether or not he liked what I'd done to the ceiling. It's light blue now, with clouds. I did the clouds with a can of white paint and more cotton balls, more dabbing.

"If it wasn't the Rottie—"

"One of the cage doors. I need to go back out with the wire cutters."

"You need one of those shots?"

"Tetanus? I'm fine," he said, but there's no way of knowing with Leo if he meant fine because he'd had one or fine because fine's what you are when you don't think too much about yourself, about how you're really doing and what you really need. We're both of us fine most of the time.

I was long done with the alcohol but I was standing between Leo's legs and he'd put his feet together behind me, up against the backs of my thighs. I still had his left hand in mine. I brushed the backs of his knuckles. "The gangrene's back," he said, which it was, but he doesn't need to warn me like he thinks he does. He doesn't really have gangrene, just some weird skin thing that makes him itch so bad he scratches even in his sleep, until the skin breaks open and starts oozing, sometimes blood and sometimes something clear and sometimes both together, so his skin shines in the light like a pink glaze, like glass or pastry. He always warns me, before I uncover an elbow, or the back of a knee, or lift his shirt to find a patch on his belly. I kissed the back of his hand, a clear part, close to his wrist. His legs dropped down and he let me go, his heels kicking the cupboard doors.

"I'll go start dinner," I said.

"I'll be back in soon," he said, and hopped down off the counter. He's much taller than me, long like a noodle and skinny in his jeans. His hair's long but not too long, tied back and never greasy. He's got a Cheshire cat inked on his left front forearm. The tattoo seems to keep away the gangrene, and he jokes that he's going to save up, become the Illustrated Man, stop selling dogs at the Pick n' Trades and just sell tickets for people to see him in his shorts.

For dinner I broiled some frozen fish, microwaved some frozen peas, baked a couple of potatoes. The window over the sink faces the back, and Leo had the dunk tank out. I guess you're supposed to spray flea stuff around the kennels, air them out with no dogs inside, but we're almost full up until the Pick n' Trade in Joplin, and there's nowhere to move the dogs to. So he took them one by one out of the kennels and dumped them in the tank, pyrethrum insecticide mixed with water, strong enough to keep the fleas off them until market. It's bad for their eyes and skin, worse for their tempers, but Class B dealers don't mind with temperament. Leo had gloves on, a pair he stole from the outfitter's offices at the slaughterhouse, but the Rottweiler might have gotten him anyway. We've had her here for a month, since Leo found her in the Lamar classifieds and went to pick her up. I think she's homesick.

The fish didn't taste like much but Leo's always gracious. "Where'd you learn this one?" he asks. "How'd you make that?" I sewed two buttons back onto a shirt of his the other day, which doesn't take more than a needle and a pair of eyes, but he acted like he'd seen a miracle. Did my mother sew, he asked, had she taught me, and I wanted to laugh but then he'd ask what was funny. It wasn't something my mom would care about, the way other people looked in their clothes. When Mouse got boobs I was the one who had to tell her that she needed a bra. The elastic had gone out of my old ones, but I could drive by then so we went to Wal-Mart and charged some things. It was a nice afternoon, doing that together.

Mouse lives in St. Louis now. She's going to college, studying biology. She sends me postcards, always of the Arch, the Mississippi River, things I already know how they look like. I'd like to see her campus, the streets where she lives, but she's never volunteered. She says she has a boyfriend who's studying business, and I thought about writing back how Leo has a business, too, but then she'd ask selling what. *Lyssa*, she writes. *Mango of my eye and possum of my heart. How goes it? I took summer term classes so I've got more finals already. I don't think I'll be able to make it for a visit. How's what's-his-face? It's cold and rainy in St. Louis. Hope the weather's better in Neosho. Love and Squalor, Mouse.* She always signs the postcards *Love and Squalor*, and I know it's a joke but I don't get what's funny.

Leo only bunches part-time. He works days over at National Beef. He's one of the top guys there who's not management, a twelve-dollar-an-hour man. He started off down the chain, but now he's a knocker. He stands up on the catwalk with a bolt gun and lets the cows have it as they come down the chute. "Pow, right between the eyes," he told me. He talks big but I don't think he enjoys it all that much. He stands eight hours in his rubber coverall, goggles, his hair tied back and stuffed under a net. The slaughterhouse has been losing money so steady they've got the line sped up to a cow every nine seconds, trying to do in volume what they can't do in beef prices. Down the chute and up by the ankles; Leo's quick hand on the bolt gun is the only thing saving the cows from being butchered alive. "Goddamn angel of mercy," Leo says. "What kind of a life does a cow have, anyway?" He says top line speed is 400 an hour, which means Leo can kill 3,200 animals in a day, minus his breaks, two fifteen-minute ones, and a half hour for lunch.

I work twenty hours a week at the Goodwill, mostly sorting donations. I'd work more if they had the hours for me. It's nasty work in lots of little ways, but since Leo's work is what it is, I can't complain to him. We have to keep the stuffed toys wrapped in plastic for two weeks in the back, to suffocate any lice that might be on them. We have to check the clothes for stains, like old blood the color of sweet potatoes on the insides of women's pants. If the clothes are stained too bad to sell, they're shipped out in big bundles to somewhere else, somewhere in Africa or South America or something.

Leo ate his potato last, scooping out the halves and then rolling the skins up into tubes with salt and pepper inside. He ate the tubes with his hands, like brown paper hot dogs. I got out ice cream bowls, a half gallon of vanilla and the kind of chocolate sauce that hardens on top of the ice cream. "I'm glad it wasn't the Rottie," I said. "Who scratched you. She's a pretty one."

"Pretty ugly. She's a dog."

"All your pretty uglies."

"You too, Miss Lyss. You can be my favorite. My prettiest ugly."

I tapped my spoon against the hard chocolate. Underneath the shell my ice cream was already melting.

"I'm just kidding," Leo said.

"Stop messing with the gangrene. You'll make it worse." He was rubbing his knuckles up and down on the edge of the table. When he's itching bad he'll rub his fingers against stuff without even realizing and the skin breaks open right away. There are little smears of blood all over the house, on the prickly surfaces that feel best when he's itching—the rough carpet in the rec room, the weave of the couch, the furry cover on the toilet. I could track him through the house like that, like a hurt animal, something leaking and in pain.

"Maybe it *is* worse this time. Maybe I have leprosy. My nose'll fall off. Then I'll be *your* pretty ugly."

"If your nose falls off you're not going to be my anything," I said, which sounded kind of mean, and I thought about telling him the truth, which is that he'd be my lovely ugly even if his nose did fall off, and then that seemed pathetic and I thought perhaps I shouldn't say anything at all so I didn't.

"If you're not working tomorrow, can you come with me?" he asked.

"Carthage?"

"Webb City."

"You got a paper?"

"We can pick one up there. Look through it over some breakfast. We'll go to the Denny's off 71."

"Sure," I said, and hoped he didn't think the Denny's was what swayed me. I don't do what I do for Leo so he'll buy me breakfast.

In bed that night I was careful of the gangrene. Leo fell asleep right after but it took me awhile. It had been dark for hours but the weather wasn't cooling. We had the ceiling fan going and the windows open. The crickets were chirping the way they did all summer, a long low buzz like power lines, and the dogs were suffering in the heat. I bet Leo'd never find anyone else who can listen to dogs cry the way I can. They call out and I can turn over and not hear them, not even a bit. I don't need the radio, or the TV. I just need my own two ears and then I don't hear a thing. I dreamed good dreams but I don't remember what they were.

At Denny's, Leo got the Grand Slam and I got waffles. He took the classifieds from the *Webb City Gazette* and let me have everything else. I read about a meth lab bust and a church swap sale on the front page while Leo circled ads with a red pen. I grew up in Webb City, but with Mouse in St. Louis, there's not much to bring me back. I don't know where my mom's got to these days.

"Anything promising?"

"Loads. Some purebreds, too. Or so they're claiming. I thought we'd try and hit those first."

"Sounds fine." I went to check my hair and makeup in the bathroom while Leo settled up. I was wearing a flowered dress and sandals, my hair down, a little liner for my eyes and color for my lips, not too much. Like a Sunday School teacher, Leo said, and it was strange to hear something like that come out of him as a compliment. Leo was wearing khaki pants and a long-sleeved shirt that covered his tattoo but was too hot for the weather. He already had sweat stains under his arms. We sat in the van with the air conditioning on while Leo started calling houses on his cell phone. Beagles are good finds. Hounds, Labs, retrievers, too, either purebred or close enough so you can tell the breed without squinting. It's because they're mid-sized dogs with large chest cavities, the way Leo explains it. I don't quite know why that's important but I guess it makes them easy to work with.

Before I moved in with Leo the biggest thing I'd ever stolen was a stick of butter. Not even a package, a single stick. Mouse and I had decided we wanted to make chocolate chip cookies. We found a recipe on an index card in the kitchen but none of the ingredients. All we needed was a teaspoon of this, a half-teaspoon of that, and we didn't have anything. One eighth of a teaspoon baking soda. We looked at the tiny bowl of the measuring spoon, the size of the nail on Mouse's pinky finger. We found a chain of little plastic snap-off paint tubs that had come with a paint-by-number set, and cleaned them out and put them in Mouse's pink vinyl purse. At the grocery store we took baking soda and baking powder off the shelf, looked both ways for clerks, opened the containers, and tapped out a few spoonfuls into the tubs. We were doing the same thing with a tin of cinnamon in the spice aisle when a woman confronted us, a lady with a cart full of food like kids would eat, fruit snacks and Hi-C. "What do you girls think you're doing?" she asked.

"We want to make cookies," Mouse said.

"Are you going to pay for that?"

"We can't. So we're only taking a little," I said, and Mouse nodded solemnly, because Mouse was already an expert in solemn truths.

The woman looked at us in our old shorts and stained T-shirts and you could watch her feeling sorry for us, deciding to let us keep right on stealing. I let Mouse put two eggs and the stick of butter in her purse after she promised to be careful with them. At the check out we paid for flour and sugar and chocolate chips and asked for two plastic bags. I put them on the handlebars of my bike, one on each side, because I figured Mouse had enough to worry about with the eggs in her purse.

The next morning, Mouse and I were eating some of our cookies for breakfast when Mom came home. "Where'd you get cookies?" she asked, and we told her, because we figured she either wouldn't care or would think we were resourceful. She put some bread in the toaster and opened the fridge. "Where's the butter?" she asked.

"There isn't any."

"You don't put four sticks of butter in a batch of cookies."

"That's why we only took one," Mouse said.

"Lyssa and Mouse. You steal, you steal something worth taking. Then I'd at least have butter for the damn toast."

That's one of the only pieces of advice Mouse and I can remember getting from her, and I didn't even take it. I still steal small. Not things other people want, or things that are worth a lot. I just take what I need.

158

The first house we went to in Webb City was in my old neighborhood, a street that had been kept up a little better than the one I grew up on. The house was a nice little ranch, painted white with geraniums in the window boxes. Leo rang the doorbell and then stepped back so we were standing side by side. The woman who came to the door had an armful of brown cardboard boxes, so Leo kept it short. "Mrs. Sidore?" he said. "I called a few minutes ago. About the dog. Leo Tillet."

We were shown to the couch in the living room, which was full of boxes labeled Estate Sale, and Rubbish, and Keep, and Kids Might Want??? I could feel Leo smile. Death lingers on a dog. Families want rid of it. Leo's a quick appraiser, and I knew he was looking over Mrs. Sidore and the dog she brought in, which even I could tell was a poodle, purebred or pretty close, a little gray around the muzzle but spry enough. "You're quick off the mark. The first call we've had."

"My wife and I wanted to get the jump on the Sunday ads. We've been looking for a dog and we were interested in poodles, so when we saw your ad—"

"She's purebred, from a breeder near Kansas City. I've got the American Kennel Association papers. She's been taken good care of. Shots, and spayed, although I think she's past puppies by now."

"What's her name?" Leo asked, scratching around the dog's ears until she started to wag so hard her whole butt waggled. Leo's awfully good with dogs. Good with people, too; he asked all the right questions, about health conditions, about how much exercise old Muffy needed, whether she could be let off a leash. "We have a nice piece," he said. "In the country outside of Neosho. She'd have room to run around."

"It sounds lovely," Mrs. Sidore said. "Honestly I was worried, with the dog being old, that she'd be hard to place. I don't suppose families with kids would want her, knowing she'll die and having to explain it."

"It's just my wife and me right now," Leo said. "And we don't have time to train a puppy."

"Well, Mr. Tillet, the ad was Free to a Good Home and you seem a good home and she's still free. I'll grab her papers, if you're decided, and a box of her things."

Our house is full of dog bowls, and Muffy wouldn't need toys, but Leo let Mrs. Sidore get them. I held the dog on my lap as we drove away. On the next block we stopped and Leo unlocked the back of the van. He has kennel space for six dogs back there. We locked Muffy

159

into a cage with a dish of water and one of the toys from her box, and Leo checked the next house on his list against his map.

Leo's lucky we've got a good neighbor, by which I mean we never see each other, and never give each other any trouble. His house is on the far end of his property, and even on a clear night the sound from our yard doesn't travel. If we actually wanted to let Muffy roam free, he wouldn't say boo about it. Mouse and I, our neighbor growing up was Mr. Martin, who had a house just like ours except that ours was yellow and his was green. One summer he decided to have a big yard sale and got all his buddies to bring over every piece of old furniture they could find, either on consignment or just to save them a trip to the dump. Offer the customers a wide selection, he kept saying, lining couches up along his driveway and across his front yard until his entire property was covered over like a furniture store, chairs in one corner, desks in another, big appliances, like an old fridge with a bright chrome handle, back by his garage. He seemed to do okay. People came and hauled some stuff away, or shook on something and promised to be back later for it. The next weekend, though, he still had half a Goodwill store spread out over his lawn. That weekend it rained, and in the morning all the furniture was soaking. Mouse and I balanced on the backs of the couches, knocking each other off onto the cushions and listening to the squelch. Pools of water rose up in perfect footprints where we stepped, and the beginning of a smell, damp and lush, was just beginning to curl up from the upholstery. Mr. Martin chased us off that morning and stood for a while on his lawn, reaching his right arm up over his head to scratch at the back of his neck. Mouse and I stared at the hair growing in his armpit and wondered what he'd do.

Of course, the easiest thing to do with a yard full of soaking furniture is nothing at all, and for years that's what Mr. Martin seemed settled on doing. He gave up trying to run us off, and in winter we made snow forts out of the sofas, pelted each other with secret stores of snowballs hidden under chairs and in desk drawers. After the first winter's snow melted, the smell had taken hold. The furniture was wet and moldering, the wood splitting with rot, the cushions mildewing. A pair of raccoons had started a den underneath a loveseat, and a skunk had a nest of babies under a recliner. Mouse and I would jump onto the loveseat, both together, on the count of three. When our feet pounded the springs the raccoons would shriek and shoot out. We played hide and seek, and once Mouse accidentally locked herself in the old fridge, but I found her and let her out.

One family Leo and I visited that Sunday had already placed their dog. A few more were playing coy, taking our information and giving us the third degree. The fat guy with the Akita had a long list of names on a yellow legal pad, but the lady with the bichon frise just wrote Leo's name and number at the top of a blank page. "I've had a few people show some interest. I'll let you know," she said, and you could tell she hadn't, but she was mighty suspicious of why a guy like Leo would want a dog like a bichon. We picked up a chocolate Labrador from a couple who was moving to a one-bedroom apartment in Kansas City in a week. An English terrier from an old woman whose family was putting her in a nursing home. She tried to serve us tea and tiny little short-bread cookies, but she dropped the cookies into the tea and didn't seem to notice. The tea was in white china cups, and you could look down inside and see the cookie dissolving, settling in a thick layer across the bottom. The dog was skinny, with long nails, like the woman couldn't remember how to take care of it. She kissed Leo on the cheek when he took the terrier into his arms.

The summer Mouse locked herself in the fridge was the summer Mr. Martin started locking himself out of his garage. The first time it happened, Mouse was alone, playing at Boat, trying to hop as far across his yard as she could without touching the ground, which was really water and full of sharks. She'd asked me to play and I'd refused, just because I was five years older and I could, even though when we stood on chairs and rocked back and forth we moved in rhythm, without even trying, because we could feel the same waves.

"Hey Mouse," Mr. Martin said. "I seem to have a problem." The neighborhood was quiet and I was on our front porch, reading, so I could hear as he explained how he'd locked himself out of his garage, and how there was a small window, tiny, around the back, that he didn't think he'd fit through, but Mouse surely would, and I remember hearing her agree, and it follows that I must have heard the garage door grind open and then fall shut again, but I don't remember noticing. I remember that she was gone a long time, and that I got impatient because I'd decided I wanted to play Boat after all, and I wanted to hear what Mr. Martin's garage looked like on the inside, and then I remember being annoyed because when Mouse finally came back to our house she wouldn't play Boat, and she wouldn't tell me about Mr.

161

Martin's garage. She wouldn't tell me anything. She just shrugged and went to her room, and it was a long time before I could make her come out.

It was late afternoon, and we thought people might be sitting down to Sunday dinner, so Leo swung by the Neosho County Animal Impoundment Facility. It's not a real pound, like in an old cartoon, but where the cops put the dogs who've been seized or taken from abusive homes, or the really messed up strays. Nobody cares what happens to them anymore; the cops aren't like the Humane Society, checking you out to see if you can provide your Time and Love and A Little Piece of Yourself to every adoptee. The cops just want the crazy dogs out of their hair, so they don't ask too many questions. Leo pulled the van right up to the gates, the back outfitted with his cages and kennels, the poodle and the Lab and terrier in there already yelping at each other. Should have raised everybody's eyebrows, and instead they're all like, how convenient. You came prepared. Leo picked out two, a boxer mix and a pinscher mix. The cops had already had the dogs' toenails cut down, and Leo was wearing gloves, so he got them muzzled and in the back all right. Once the van started up, though, the new dogs howled and barked and rattled around. "Listen to that racket back there," Leo said. "Good riddance, am I right?"

The summer Mouse locked herself in the fridge I'd find her with popsicles, the kind that pull apart, and I'd ask her for halves, but she'd refuse to share. I spied on her and found out that she got them from Mr. Martin as thanks for unlocking his garage door from the inside, which she seemed to have to do a lot those days, and I wondered if Mr. Martin was much older than he looked and was getting to be the forgetful kind of crazy that old people got to be. I asked her if the next time Mr. Martin locked himself out I could open the door for him and get a popsicle, and when she looked at me and shook her head, I called her selfish.

We were driving back through Webb City to get on the highway, heading home for the day, when I saw the Found Dog sign. We were stopped at a red light and I put my finger on the car window where the sign was, so if you squinted my index finger was petting the Dalmatian's head. "That's a gorgeous dog," I said. "The owner must be freaking out."

Leo looked over where I was pointing, and instead of going straight on green he turned right, pulled over, hopped out, and tore the flyer off the pole. "Truman Street," he said. "You know where that is?"

162

"I can look at the map," I said, and I did, without even asking him why he wanted to know. I didn't think we'd go there; that's how dumb I am, sometimes.

"What do you think?" Leo asked. "Should we give it a shot?"

"Give what a shot?"

He held the flyer up next to his face, like he was asking if I thought there was a resemblance.

"It's not for taking," I said. "They're just looking for the owner."

"They been looking for a while," Leo said, shaking the paper. The flyer was stiff and rumpled, like it had gotten rained on and had time to dry.

"It rained yesterday. We don't know how long that's been up."

"Let me just find out then. Let me call and see if they've still got the dog."

I didn't see the harm in that, maybe because I don't see a lot of things I ought to. The dog hadn't been picked up, and when Leo made a sound in his throat like joy, like relief, when he thanked the person on the phone for making up those flyers, I knew we were locked into going.

"You don't even know the dog's name," I said on the way over, trying to protest and navigate at the same time, which didn't work out so well because the whole time I was giving reasons not to go, I was interrupting myself with the turns he had to make to get there.

"I can do this," he said.

"The dog belongs to someone. It probably ran away and some poor family is tearing their hair out looking for it."

"Since when do you care about that?"

"Since always. You bunch unwanted dogs. This is a Wanted Dog."

"I want it."

"It's Wanted by someone who isn't just going to sell it on in a week for a little cash."

"Not a little. A lot of cash. Jorgen told me at the market in Lamar that Parke-Davis needs Dalmatians. They want to test an eye medication. Something to do with all the genetic blindness in the breed. They're paying top dollar."

"To Jorgen. Not to you."

"He'll give a fair cut."

I studied the picture on the flyer. "I don't think this one's blind."

"Doesn't need to be. They want sighted ones, too. Controls, or maybe they drug them and then blind them or something."

163

"You're a jerk," I said, but Leo didn't think I meant it.

When I found Mouse in the fridge I called her stupid. "Stupid stupid stupid," I said. "You stuck yourself in a refrigerator." I pronounced all five syllables of the word because maybe I didn't get to open garage doors and eat double-sized popsicles, but I was her big sister and Mouse had better learn it.

"I'm *hiding*," Mouse said, and I noticed that she'd been crying but didn't seem scared, not of running out of air or being trapped forever with her feet in a crisper drawer.

"Fine," I said, because I'd expected her to be grateful to me for finding her and letting her out, and instead I was learning that she wasn't scared of any of the things I'd be scared of, and I didn't understand anymore what did scare her. "Hide, then." I shut the door on her, and when I finally opened it she tried to bolt past me, like the raccoons when we startled them, but she was all folded up from being squeezed in the fridge and she fell out on her knees. I laughed at her as she picked herself up and walked across the yard into our house. She felt very far away then, and I followed to catch up, but even when we were in the same room after that the feeling stayed, like I'd stretched one of her hair ties too far and made it useless as a string, all the elastic gone out of it.

Leo went up the front walk of 1206 Truman Street with a leash slung over his shoulder, a pink nylon collar dangling down his back. The flyer had said "she," so Leo took the collar off Muffy, the dead woman's poodle, and attached a lead. He left Muffy's tags in the driver's side drink holder.

He rang the door bell, which set a dog to barking somewhere inside. The man who answered the door was bald on top, round about the middle, with a polo shirt and a nice smile. Leo was still shaking his hand, saying "Hello, Mr. Minton. Dale, if that's all right," when the Dalmatian came up behind the man and pressed its head between his legs, barking at Leo. Not aggressive, but curious, just checking out what's what. Leo knelt down and caught the dog's collar, leaning over her so all Dale Minton could see was the top of Leo's head, his shiny hair, pulled back neat. I could see Leo reaching for the collar, catching the tags between his fingers for a quick glance. "Perdita," he said. "Oh, honey. I've been worried sick."

"Perdita. Like the Disney movie," I said. *"The 101 Dalmatians."*

Leo glared, because I wasn't helping.

"Yeah," Dale said. "My kids loved the name. They have the movie on video."

"Is that right?" Leo said, admiringly.

"So this is your dog, then?"

"Sure is. Where'd you find her?"

"Out in the street. We worried she'd get hit."

"My wife thinks she left the gate open, and Perdita's got a wandering streak." Leo let his hands roam over Perdita's head, behind her flapping ears, under them, down her neck and under her muzzle. He reached for her belly and stroked her sides. He found a place on her stomach that made her sigh, and pulled back to let Dale see. "She always seems to have an itch right about here," Leo said, and drove his fingers in until the dog whuffed and turned her head up to lick Leo's face. "Bit tricky to find, but scratch it and she's yours forever."

"Is there a Pongo?"

"Like the movie? We'd like to, someday. A Pongo and some puppies, Rolly and Dopey and Dancer and Vixen, or whatever they were."

"Dopey's a dwarf," I said. "And the other two were reindeer."

"Then I'll let you do the naming, honey," Leo said, and the voice he used with me was a lot sharper than the one he used with the dog.

After that things went fast. Leo was gearing up for more questions, where we lived, how long we'd had the dog, but Dale seemed satisfied. Perdita was in heaven, and Leo looked in love, bending his face down so her long, flat tongue could lick his cheek. Dale called the kids into the front hall to say their goodbyes, and Leo offered him some reward money. Dale shook his head. He seemed like an upstanding kind of guy. When we pulled away I had Perdita in my lap. I assumed Leo would pull over in a couple of streets to move her to the back, but he never did. We drove the 45 minutes home that way, with the dog cradled in my lap, her head out the window, tongue hanging out, drooling for joy.

At home Leo got the dogs settled in the kennels out back. It was a good haul, he said, all hale and healthy, serum dogs for sure. That's not saying all that much. A dog only needs to look like it'll last seven days to be a serum dog. After that it's a question of degree. Acute dogs look likely to drop dead in twenty-four hours or less. The laboratories don't have much use for them. They're sold lot rate, in bulk, like coffee beans at the supermarket. Leo doesn't have the USDA license to sell direct, but Jorgen does. There are lots of regulars, all Class B dealer licensed. They show up at the Pick n' Trades, the flea markets, all over Neosho County. After the dogs are out of Leo's hands, they're on their way to a lab. Pharmaceuticals, or cosmetics, biology departments, or medical schools. Leo bunches regular and knows what he's doing: good breeds, good animals, healthy enough to bring serum price. He'll come home with as much in his pocket as a week at National Beef.

The first night Perdita was caged out back she howled for hours. The moon was almost full, soft and yellow like an egg yolk. I tried to sleep, pressed my head down into the pillow, into the curve of Leo's shoulder, which is bony but still nice to sleep on. I tried to wedge my hands against my ears, but I couldn't not-hear the way I'm used to. I got out of bed and went outside. Some of the dogs were sleeping, the old hands, the slow-breathing inmates who didn't pay Perdita any mind. The dogs from today, the poodle, the terrier, the chocolate Lab, the boxer, and the pinscher, were all anxious. Perdita stopped howling for a moment to look at me, and then just tilted her head back up and screamed. The moon was bright and her white coat glowed, with the spots standing out like little patches of night, spreading, eating away at her like Leo's gangrene, until there'd be no glowing left. Her teeth were shiny and the light made her eyes look bright and flat. There was a breeze that whipped between my knees and under the long T-shirt I wear to bed, but there was no one to be modest for except the dogs. I stepped closer to the kennels, and the grass under my feet went to dirt, packed hard and scrabbled by dog toes. I put my hand on the latch to Perdita's cage. I stood there, just like that, thinking about all the useless things that might happen if I let her go. The way she might be hit by a truck on the highway trying to scent her way cross-county, or how Leo'd be angry but mostly just confused at why I'd do a thing like that, take money out of his pocket and bread off our table. How Leo'd always been decent to me, but I'd seen the unkindness in him, and I didn't want to see it again pointed in my direction. How if Perdita had managed to get lost in Webb City, she'd probably never find home from way out here. How if I let her out, not much good would come of it for anyone. She'd stopped howling while I stood there, looking at me with eyes that were probably supposed to be pleading but in the night were flat and fierce and reflective. "Sorry, honey," I said, and stepped away from the cage, and the dog started up again, piercing and pathetic. She howled every night for the week before Joplin, until Leo came home without her and I slept a little better.

The summer Mouse locked herself in a fridge, and Mr. Martin locked himself out of his own garage, over and over, the only thing I ever noticed was how Mouse had popsicles and wouldn't share. I was angry at her and for a long time that was all I remembered about that summer. I couldn't even tell you when she stopped having popsicles, or when Mr. Martin finally had the rotting furniture hauled away, or when I realized that I had never been able to protect her, not ever, and that whatever's good about her life now is in spite of me just like it's in spite of Mom and Mr. Martin and everybody else, and that if I had the opportunity to steal again for her, I'd steal big. Something better than butter, better than a dog, because I let her go away from me and into a garage again and again, and whatever I'm doing now is nothing compared to that.

Joplin was a month ago, so the Rottie's probably dead by now, and the poodle, the terrier, the Lab. I assume Perdita's dead, too. It seems dangerous to think otherwise. If she isn't, I should probably be wishing for her that she was, but mostly I've got enough on my own plate without worrying about the dogs. Mouse still sends me the same dumb postcards. The Goodwill still pays six an hour. Leo's still elbow deep in cow brains. His skin thing is getting worse. He's got patches so bad they're swampy with fluid, where his shirts stick and scabs won't form. He's always been hourly at National Beef so there's no insurance. It's like he's molting into something new and horrible, and all I want to do is hold his skin closed, press the seams of him together, so he won't fall apart and nothing in our lives will change because I figure I'm about as happy as I'm going to get the way things are. So I refuse to wish Leo nice, or the dogs free, or my sister happy, or myself forgiven, or much of anything all that much different than it's likely to get. I just won't wish them, and then when they all don't happen, it won't mean a thing to me. If this is what I get in this world, I'll take it. Love and squalor, but mostly love. I'll take it and I'll take it and I will not be sorry.

Nominated by Laura van den Berg, Prairie Schooner

THE BEES OF DEIR KIFA

by MICHAEL COLLIER

from VIRGINIA QUARTERLY REVIEW

The sun going down is lost in the gorge to the south,
lost in the rows of olive trees, light in the webs of their limbs.

This is the time when the thousands and thousands come home.
It is not the time for the keeper's veil and gloves,

not the time for stoking the smoker with pine needles.
It would be better to do that at midday, under a hot sun,

when the precincts are quieter; it would be better to disturb
few rather than many. At noon, the hives are like villages,

gates opened toward the sun or like small countries
carved from empires to keep the peace, each with its habits—

some ruled better by better queens, some frantic and uncertain,
some with drifting populations, others busy with robbing,

and even the wasps and hornets, the fierce invaders who have settled
among the natives, are involved in the ancient trades.

But now with the sun gone, the blue summer twilight
tinged with thyme and the silver underside of olive leaves

calm in the furrowed groves, darkening the white chunks
of limestone exposed in the tillage, the keeper in his vestments

squeezes the bellows of the smoker, blows a thin blue stream
into an entrance, loosens the top, like a box lid, and delivers more.

For a while, the hive cannot understand what it says to itself.
Now a single Babel presides in the alleys and passageways

and as block by block, the keeper takes his census,
he could go ungloved, unveiled, if it weren't for the un-pacified,

the unconfused, returning, mouths gorged with nectar,
legs orange with pollen, landing, amassing, alerting the lulled

to scale their wax trellis or find the glove's worn thumb, the hood's
broken zipper and plant the eviscerating stinger.

For Zein and Bilal El-Amine

Nominated by C. E. Poverman, Elizabeth Spires, Grace Schulman, Virginia Quarterly Review

MY FATHER'S HATS

by JEFFREY HAMMOND

from SHENANDOAH

When I was little, my father's life could be read in his hats. Two relics of his early years as a pipeline worker and utility lineman hung on pegs in the back porch: a silver hard hat stamped "Ohio Oil Company" and an electrician's helmet in yellow, non-conducting plastic. A duffle bag stored in a closet contained the white "Dixie cup" and blue watch cap from his Navy days. After he took correspondence courses and joined Ohio Oil's accounting department, a snappy gray fedora appeared on a hook in the same closet. The next hook held a straw boater that he wore when he sang in barbershop quartets.

My father was a hat man—which is to say, he was a man of his times. In 1950s photographs of city streets, nearly every male is hatted: soft caps for blue-collar workers, porkpies and fedoras for white-collar. Pictures of crowds from half a century earlier tell the same story, except that we see straw hats and bowlers. Not long after Dad exchanged his hard hat for a fedora, however, the prominence of the man's hat in America came to an end. The bare-headed Jack Kennedy signaled the arrival of what the Romans once called a *novus homo*—and this "new man" was hatless and bold. The formality of the hatted gentleman was out; the vigor of the hatless go-getter was in.

Although male headwear returned in the 1980s with the arrival of the ubiquitous baseball cap, hats never reclaimed their place in standard business attire. The baseball cap, softer and rounder than its Victorian, kepi-like predecessor, cut across class lines. On the blue-collar side, it subsumed and replaced a variety of working hats: carpenters, plumbers, electricians and farm workers all embraced its one-hat-fits-

170

all appeal. On the white-collar side, Yuppies borrowed it from Gen-Xers as the visual proclamation of successful men at leisure.

My father remained a hat man to the end, though he never succumbed to wearing a baseball cap. Here it was the absence of a hat that made his story readable: having played semi-pro ball in his teens and twenties, he eschewed baseball caps because he no longer played the game. In his view, any non-ballplayer who wore one was a phony, a man in an unearned hat.

This put Dad in a dilemma when he retired. Baseball caps were out of the question, but for someone who agreed with Oliver Wendell Holmes that "The hat is the *ultimum moriens* of respectability," facing the world bare-headed was like leaving the house naked. He eventually settled on a solution common among American males of his generation: those small-brimmed, Scottish-looking hats associated with old-timey golfers, variously called "flat caps," "golf caps," "cabbie caps" or "Windsor caps." Often sporting boldly checked patterns, these hats were Dad's sole extravagance. Though I'm tempted to call them "dapper," he would have rejected the characterization as vaguely British—an apt word for David Niven, perhaps, but not for him. He would have been right: "dapper" seems ironic in reference to anything having to do with my father. A broody man given to occasional depression, he wore his golf caps as catalysts for putting on his best face, for looking self-contained and placid rather than worried or sad. He abandoned these caps only on the coldest winter days, for a Russian fur hat that made him resemble a man lost on the tundra—a better match, actually, with the dour expression of his face in repose.

Although a sense of propriety was clearly at work in my father's conviction that a civilized man always wears a hat in public, there was no vanity. At five-feet-seven, he may have appreciated the enhanced sense of presence that hats gave him. I suspect, however, that their appeal had a darker side. An intensely private man, he preferred his hats loose-fitting, which let him wear them low in the front, nearly covering his eyes. Dad's golf caps kept a manageable roof on the world, a sense of limits and boundaries—not least on himself. A man in a dapper hat will be less likely to appear worried or sad. And if such a man is also shy and wants to go about his business unseen, he can simply pull down his hat-brim a bit—as my father often did.

WHEN I WAS growing up, hat racks and hat hooks were everywhere: restaurants, school lobbies, libraries and barber shops. Convinced that hats marked their wearers as adults, I was certain that as a grownup I'd be wearing one all the time, like my father. Nineteenth-century British poet and essayist Leigh Hunt once claimed that children develop "an educated antipathy to the hat" because they go hatless at school. In my case the effect was just the opposite: I couldn't wait to get my grown-up hat.

Winter hats did not count in this calculus of maturation, because all Midwestern males understand the necessity of a winter hat for man and boy alike. Indeed, I grew up thinking that the absence of a hat on a grown-up man, especially in winter, was a sign of either unemployment or unmanly hair-pride. This education in winter hats began immediately: my first extant picture shows a baby in a knitted beret being hoisted in the air against a backdrop of bare trees. In later pictures I'm wearing a stocking cap; still later, one of those furlined hats with ear flaps that can be buckled atop the head when not in use. We kids were constantly being warned that eighty-five percent of our body heat was lost through our heads. Whenever I heard this, I visualized a boy with steam—maybe his very soul—wafting up from his bare crown. We took such warnings to heart: mittens and gloves vanished by the dozen, but I don't recall anyone ever losing a winter hat.

With the coming of spring, the hat assumed its usual role for children: an item of imaginative play, a vehicle for trying on an adult self for size. My father's hats saw frequent duty in these games, except for the fedora, which I was forbidden to touch. This was no great loss: I wouldn't have known how to play "accountant" anyway. My favorite was his magnificent hard hat, which made me the object of envy during neighborhood games of war: with my head encased in its springy webbing, dirt clods bounced harmlessly off its surface. I also owned two actual, made-for-kids playhats: a green cowboy hat that eventually lost its shape and ended with the brim drooping all around, like a fisherman's cap; and a Davy Crockett "coonskin cap," which wasn't really made from a dead raccoon but smelled as if it were when wet.

These were exceptions in a non-winter world where kids went hatless, as we were fated to do as post-JFK adults. Only one playmate routinely wore a hat: a man in his thirties whose mental age was around ten and who often joined in our games. "Big Larry," as we called him, was rarely without his white sea captain's hat, a "peaked cap" with a shiny black brim and a gold anchor on the front. The nearest body of water was Lake Erie, fifty miles away, but Big Larry's hat did not seem at all strange. Even though he played with us like a regular kid, we knew that he was really a grownup: hadn't he earned his right to a permanent, everyday hat?

IN THE BEGINNING, of course, all hats were "winter hats"—functional defenses against cold, wind, rain and scorching sun. In colder climates, our Paleolithic forebears wore close-fitting caps stitched together from animal skins. Where it was warmer, the fit was generally looser and the material was woven fabric. In the West the functional hat remained essentially unchanged for centuries. The close-fitting felt cap (Greek *pilos*, Latin *pileus*) was the everyday worker's hat—the classical equivalent, I suppose, to the baseball cap. Other functional hats were designed for fighting or traveling. The Greeks called the war helmet a *pilos chalkous* or bronze cap; the Roman helmet was a *cassis* in metal and a *galea* in leather. Greeks and Romans shared a word for the traveler's hat: the *petasos* or *petasus*. This is Mercury's famous hat, and as its broad brim suggests, ancient tourists were not big on vacation tans. The *pileus*-like Phrygian cap of late antiquity, named for its alleged origins in central Turkey, remained the standard hat of non-elite European males into the Middle Ages. This is the pointy, stocking-like cap that we see in pictures of Dante and Chaucer. Except for materials and workmanship, the hats of our two greatest Medieval poets were first cousins to the sewn-hide caps found on some of the Bog people.

Ancient "playhats"—that is, hats with social significance—came in the Fertile Crescent with the rise of urban cultures and specialized roles and occupations. In contrast to the sameness of functional hats, playhats assumed as many forms as the social elites that they distinguished: priests, wealthy merchants, members of the ruling family and especially the headman of that family, the king himself. The pure but blunt symbolism of the crown made it the ultimate playhat: the big man got to wear the big hat. The crown also anticipated the transformative magic of the 1950s child's playhat: it invested whoever wore it with the very power that it signified. If you wanted to change the king, you removed his hat; if you wanted to change the kingdom, you changed the hat itself. Upper and Lower Egypt could not be unified until someone thought to combine the southern crown and the northern crown into a double crown—two playhats in one—so that nobody would feel left out. In the city-states of Mesopotamia, where rulers wore conical caps that echoed warrior's helmets, the king deferred only to those whose hats were bigger than his: the gods. Carved at the top of the Code of Hammurabi is an image of the Babylonian king receiving the laws from the sun god Shamash. Like brothers dressed for church in the 1950s, they are wearing matching hats, except that the god's hat is stacked three layers higher.

The Greek elites, with their ostensibly democratic bent and their proto-JFK taste for the natural look, generally went hatless unless they were fighting or traveling—and in this, as in most things, the Romans followed suit. But classical headgear, when it appeared, still carried social and occupational significance. A headband marked the Olympic athlete and the charioteer; a laurel wreath the poet or orator. The magnificent toga, which was forbidden by law to be worn by anyone but the wealthy, had a status-marking "hat" built into it: its ample folds could be pulled up, hood-like, to shield aristocratic heads from the elements and, of course, from the prying eyes of the *hoi polloi*—a winter hat and a playhat rolled into one.

THE ANCIENT NEAR EASTERN crown leapfrogged Greece and Rome to reassert itself in Medieval Europe. In its broad sweep, Medieval history was a tug-of-war between quasi-centralized kingdoms and semi-autonomous fiefdoms: a struggle over not only who got to wear the big hat, but how many people could wear big hats at once. Medieval noblemen did not shy from elaborate playhats: asserting their status as petty rulers, they wore conical contraptions that resembled personal Towers of Babel. This movement toward bigger hats for more people extended into the Renaissance. With the rise of the merchant class, technical improvements in fabric-stiffening and tanning and the increasing complexity of social niceties in town and at court, the luxury hat came into its own.

Thus began the Golden Age of the man's hat in Europe. The sixteenth-century hat of choice, often called the German *barett*, was a large soft hat with a turned-up brim, which eventually widened into a "halo" brim that was often pinned up, or "cocked." As the century progressed, the hat crown stiffened and rose—a none-too-subtle emblem of the Renaissance Male feeling his oats. The rising crown culminated in the *capotain*, the basic "Pilgrim hat" that we remember from grade-school Thanksgivings. Seventeenth-century Puritans generally kept their *capotains* dark and narrow-brimmed, but Cavaliers let the brims spread out like manta rays until the man's hat became a work of baroque art, often with colorful feathers. The young John Donne positioned himself between Puritan and Cavalier extremes when he posed for his portrait in an immense *capotain*: although its insanely wide brim is tipped at a jaunty angle, the hat itself is a somber black.

The Age of Reason had trouble rationalizing the fancy hat, and many early eighteenth-century gentlemen exchanged hats for wigs. When the hat returned later in the century, it was in the chastened form of the serviceable "three-cornered" hat: George Washington's tricorne. This hat was further simplified into the bicorne: Napoleon's hat. This simplifying of men's hats culminated with the French Revolution, which brought the return of the original people's hat: the old Phrygian cap. Given its revolutionary symbolism, the Phrygian cap might be called a winter hat that became a playhat, a hat with significance. The Republicans' motto could have been Liberty, Equality and No Big Hats—and as the saying goes, heavy was the head that wore the biggest one. Louis XVI lost hat and head in one fell swoop.

Burgeoning commerce in the late eighteenth and early nineteenth centuries led to a further democratizing of luxury menswear, and playhats once again began to look like playhats. It was at this point that the gentleman's hat became a fashion statement, a volatile index of shifting tastes. My Davy Crockett cap was by no means the first hat to generate a frenzy: by the end of the eighteenth century nearly every hat began as a fad. In the 1790s, Beau Brummell's London saw the "dandy's" hat, with its flat top, narrow brim and wide and often flared crown: think of Lewis Carroll's Mad Hatter. This hat quickly rose and narrowed into the classic top hat or "stovepipe," destined to become the archetypal formal hat but originally an everyday item. Now it was not kings or aristocrats who wore the big hat, but capitalists. If Eustace Tilley could speak from those *New Yorker* covers, he would insist that a big man in shipping or banking deserved an imposing hat no less than a big man in politics or war. The top hat became so big as to be unwieldy, a troublesome burden when carried; in 1812 a French hatter named Antoine Gibus obligingly invented a collapsible model.

At mid-century came a popular hat first manufactured by a pair of brothers from London named Bowler; in America this hat was called a derby. Soon afterward came the homburg, a sporting hat with a soft, deeply indented crown. During this period Italy became famous for its hats, as improvements in the industrial production of felt, developed chiefly in Turin and Monza, made the luxury hat even more affordable. Another Italian hat, the straw boater from Tuscany featured in Renoir's light-drenched boating party, became a summer-time rage throughout Europe and America. In 1906 Teddy Roosevelt created another "peak" in hat history by dedicating the Panama Canal in what instantly became known as the "Panama" hat. With the introduction of the flat-topped porkpie and the round-topped fedora in the early 1900s, the man's hat finally stabilized. Porkpies and fedoras would still be appropriate in a small-town Ohio accounting department half a century later.

IN DEFIANCE OF the post-Renaissance hat as a reflection of fashion trends, one kind of hat has always symbolized the opposite of change. I'm talking, of course, about religious hats. The sacred hat, which typically preserves a particular historical moment in the development of a religious tradition, has replaced the crown as the quintessential playhat: once you don one, you become what it stands for. According to an old rabbinical saying, the Jewish yarmulka is a reminder that "There is always something above you." As outward piety grows, so does the hat: from the simple *kippah* to the Hasidic *shtreimel* or *kolpik*. Catholic hats mark out a pious hierarchy by individuals rather than groups. The priest traditionally wears either the tufted *biretta* or the simpler skullcap or *zucchetto*, also called a *pileolus* after its ancient origins. A Catholic bishop wears a mitre, pointed if he is Roman and bulbous if he is Orthodox. In addition to the bishop's mitre, a cardinal gets "the red hat," a scarlet *zucchetto*. And until fairly recently, the pope got the biggest hat of all: the three-layered papal tiara that replicated, in gold and silver, the High Priest's headdress of ancient Israel.

Anti-hierarchical dissenters who embraced Luther's "priesthood of all believers" stood the sacred hat on its head, so to speak. Quaker George Fox articulated the Reformers' view that no man's hat was holier than another's. "When the Lord sent me forth into the world," Fox declared, "He forbade me to put off my hat for any, high or low." The old-order Amish continue to find piety in the everyday hat as a tangible rejection of ecclesiastical, political and military authority; in keeping with the conservatism of holy hats, Amish men wear the everyday Alsatian farmer's hat of the eighteenth century. The Protestant disdain for fancy hats wound up influencing Roman Catholicism: after Vatican II, Pope Paul VI reasserted papal humility by laying the tiara aside. No pope has worn it since.

By their hats ye shall know them. As the sacred hat makes especially clear, however, throughout most of history this wasn't a matter of being known in a personal way: people haven't always been autonomous "individuals" in the sense that we moderns are. This held true until the Renaissance, when humanistic philosophies began to chip away at the social person to expose what we might call the "inner" self. Although this increasing stress on private selfhood produced some extravagant men's hats along the way, it didn't reach its logical conclusion until the countercultural Sixties. Because the past two centuries had offered fewer expressive options in men's clothing than in women's, the call to do one's own thing seemed to bode well for the man's hat. If there ever was a time for men to don self-expressive hats, it was the Summer of Love.

We missed our chance, of course. There was no "hippie hat," unless you count the headband or bandanna. A few "heads" went for the *Whole Earth Catalog* look with floppy woodsman's hats, and some opted for vaguely nautical caps—the Jim Seals or early John Lennon look. There was also John Phillips of The Mamas and the Papas in that ridiculous fur hat. But if Phillips was trying to start something, nobody followed him. You couldn't very well celebrate the age of "hair, long beautiful hair," by covering yours with what had recently become the second most potent symbol of male subservience and constraint, surpassed only by the necktie. The result was a moment of special irony in the history of American male fashion: a mere decade after JFK took our hats away, we could have worn any hat that struck our fancy, convention be damned. For better or worse, an alternative history was lost. If we had done our own thing hat-wise, imagine what might have appeared in subsequent years: investment bankers sporting huge purple fezzes, driving instructors in wide-brimmed Zorro hats, maybe even a retired accountant in a shiny top hat—all calmly going about their business, observing and being observed with the splendid ease of men effecting infinite self-actualizations through their hats.

So much for all the hats that might have been. My childhood assumption about grownups and headwear has been overturned. Nowadays only kids wear hats, a custom reinforced every spring when college graduates toss their mortar-boards into the air. This reversal requires new Scripture: When I was a child I thought and spake and wore hats like a child, but now that I am become a man, I have put aside childish hats. The 1980s Canadian pop band Men Without Hats had a good run but a short one, most likely because their name was too banal. Except for those pesky baseball caps, aren't we all men without hats?

THERE WAS A time when a gentleman's choice of a hat reflected a deep commitment. Leigh Hunt observed that "we are not fond of a new hat" because we get too attached to that "true friend," our old hat. John Clare, the half-mad "Peasant Poet of Northamptonshire" and Hunt's contemporary, adored his floppy bucket hat, claiming it was a gift from Gypsies and writing his poems on it. The new hat demanded nearly as much allegiance, not as a friend or fetish but as a pricy bauble—the equivalent of a new car losing half its value when it leaves the lot. Hunt, pondering the new hat the day after its purchase, described its inevitable fall in Miltonic terms: "How altered! How dejected!"

That's a lot of emotional investment in a hat: maybe JFK did us all a favor by giving us one less thing to worry about. Besides, can't a man get so attached to a hat that he gets trapped in it? Hunt alluded to hats as agents of self-fossilizing when he observed the military veterans of his day clinging to their old bicornes despite the popularity of round hats with brims. These aging warriors, he observed, "could not willingly part with their habitual dignity": indeed, an old military hat might well be kept "in memory of its victories when young," like wearing one's service record on one's head.

History shows that the decision to stick with a particular hat cannot be made lightly. Once a hat becomes personally iconic, it's yours for good. Henceforth and forever, you will be a one-hat man. The young Walt Whitman chose wisely: his rakish slouch hat in the frontispiece portrait of *Leaves of Grass* was perfect for this free-and-easy speaker. The young Jack Donne chose less wisely, unaware that Dean Donne of St. Paul's would someday have to live that mammoth *capotain* down. I feel for him: who knows what monstrosity I might have selected in the late Sixties had I been given the option?

Shakespeare, too crafty to get trapped in a particular hat, trusted bravely to his balding head, but not everyone had his foresight. Think of Washington, doomed forever to hold—rarely wear—that blue tricorne; or Napoleon with his ever-present bicorne; or Charles De Gaulle, hawk-like and haughty in his kepi. Would we even recognize Honest Abe without his stovepipe, Sherlock Holmes without his plaid "deerstalker" or Roy Rogers without his white Stetson? Indeed, the iconic hat can overpower the face beneath it. Set a porkpie atop a nondescript face and you've got Buster Keaton. Replace the porkpie with a *toque* and you've got Wolfgang Puck. Replace the *toque* with a horned helmet and you've got Erik the Red. Trade the helmet for a green cap with a feather, and the man becomes Robin Hood. Trade the feathered cap for a khaki garrison cap and he's Eisenhower on V-E Day. If our imaginary hat-model were to don my father's sub-zero hat, he'd be Ike's old adversary Khrushchev—unless he had a goatee, in which case he'd be Lenin.

WITH THE DECLINE in the actual wearing of hats, their symbolic power has increased, though not necessarily their legibility. Every hat nowadays is a playhat, a prop for projecting an identity that may or may not be genuine. This trend is summed up in that Texas saying about a man being "all hat and no cattle": by their hats ye shall know not necessarily them, but who they're trying to be. To be sure, classic Westerns relied on white hats and black hats to define the moral landscape, with Roy Rogers on one side and Yul Brynner in *The Magnificent Seven* on the other. But the symbolic reliability even of iconic hats has been compromised. Didn't the black-hatted Brynner turn good guy by training townsfolk to defend themselves? Didn't Richard Boone's Paladin wear a black hat? And good-guy Garth Brooks?

Despite this interpretive confusion, some of us still cover our heads with objects that we hope will be read in certain ways. Although the Romans claimed that clothes make the man, a carefully chosen hat offers an even quicker take on the man whom it makes. These playhat-enhanced dramas are going on all around us. A factory worker from Cleveland who dreams of country music stardom will not go onstage at that club in the Flats without his cowboy hat. A young man in St. Louis clutches a sheaf of poems as he shuffles toward a microphone in a black beret that signals, if only for tonight, a working poet and not a refugee from a shorthorn ranch who has enrolled in an MFA program. A tourist who finds himself in a sketchy Brooklyn neighborhood at night instinctively turns his baseball cap around so that he resembles either a hip-hop performer or a baseball catcher without his mask: either way, he feels safer than he did a second ago.

The man's hat has become less a physical object than a piece of visual shorthand that is sometimes legible and sometimes not. Although a movie or cartoon explorer without his pith helmet is just a guy in a jungle, most hats have become impossible to read. The only place to see a crown nowadays is in Burger King commercials: has the crown come to mean char-broiled? Lincoln's top hat no longer connotes dignity, but has instead been consigned to chimney-sweep ads in the Yellow Pages and middle-school magicians; professional magicians have long since abandoned it for the David Copperfield, regular-guy look. The beret has been rent into antithetical meanings: if green it signals the toughest of the tough, the Special Forces; but if black it signals the jazz musician—or our young poet—trying to prolong those beatnik days. Even the baseball cap has become schizophrenic. Peak forward, it graces every living head at Tru-Value, Walmart or Best Buy on a Saturday afternoon. But as our Brooklyn tourist knows, when worn backwards it conveys street-smart disgust toward everything for which Tru-Value, Walmart and Best Buy stand. Wear the cap forward as you fill your cart; now turn the bill around and leave all that middle-class crap behind with a sneer.

The man's hat is like a gong reverberating long after it has been struck. We still "know" hats, but we know them in the same way that we know potters' wheels, shoe-trees and typewriters. The hats we remember best, the famous media hats, have all gone to the pop-culture museum: Ralph Kramden's busman's cap and Ed Norton's sewer-worker's porkpie; Abbot's slick fedora and Costello's eloquent derby; Laurel and Hardy's black bowlers, less headwear than visual props; the floppy bucket hat worn by Gilligan on his island; the mammoth turban of Johnny Carson's Carnac the Magnificent. The raggedy hat of the cartoon bum, its torn crown hanging in a flap, shares exhibit space with the shabby stovepipe of Dr. Seuss's *Cat in the Hat* and the "old slouch hat" that Dean Martin extolled, with Whitman, as perfect for "just bummin' around." Martin's insouciant hat, however, is an exception in popular songs, where the hat usually suggests going first-class for a change: "Puttin' on my top hat" with Fred Astaire for an escape echoed in the call to "grab your coat and get your hat" en route to "the sunny side of the street."

As late as 1983, ZZ Top included a top hat among the essential props of the "sharp dressed man" who gets all the ladies. A fancy hat, however imaginary, might even get you an otherwise unattainable lady, as the fictional Thomas Parke D'Invilliers suggests in Fitzgerald's motto for *The Great Gatsby*:

> Then wear the gold hat, if that will move her;
> If you can bounce high, bounce high for her too,
> Till she cry "Lover, gold-hatted, high-bouncing lover,
> I must have you!"

Fitzgerald's frantic suitor wouldn't be wearing that gold hat if he didn't want the woman: clearly, he's trying way too hard. But suppose he wins her: sooner or later he'll have to take off that hat—and then what?

If hats can be deployed this cynically, it's hard to take them seriously. And yet, a lack of faith in our own hats might be prompting us to take other people's hats *too* seriously. There's precedent for this in the various outsider hats of American history: Indian headdresses, African masks and the "coolie" hats of Asian immigrants, the latter replaced with the Mao caps of Asian Communists. Given the recent political climate, the sombrero would be demonized were it not for the fact that the first thing an illegal immigrant acquires in this country is a proper American hat: a baseball cap. Nowadays, of course, the most potent icons of otherness include the *keffiyeh*, the more elaborately wrapped *cheche*, the *Jinnah* cap, and that bewildering diversity of wrapped headwear which Americans lump together as the "turban." Although these head-borne symbols of Not Us prompt discomfort whenever they turn up at airports, they shouldn't. The poet Alexander Pope wore a fashionable turban in early eighteenth-century London and never once, so far as we know, blew anything up. And Charles Manson must have worn a baseball cap at some point in his life: Manson was Not Us with a vengeance, but if we ran every time we saw a baseball cap, we'd have nowhere to go.

THAT THE HAT was once indispensable is underscored by the basic nature of the relevant etymologies. The Anglo-Saxon "Haet" is cognate with the Old German, Old Norse and Old Teutonic words for "hood." "Cap" is even older, stemming from the proto-Indo European word for "head," the origin of both the Latin *caput* and the German *Kopf*. Now, of course, the man's hat is going the way of the "petard": we know that it's bad to get hoisted on one, but we don't know what it is.

Someday we won't remember what men's hats were—the inevitable outcome of the hat's gradual transformation into a metaphor. The once-literal custom of tipping our hats as a sign of respect has already fossilized into an imagined gesture: today we "tip our hats," often begrudgingly but never actually, to someone who has bested us at something. Baseball players say this all the time about the team that has just defeated them, but they're about the only men left who could act on their words, which they never do. When ballplayers concede, more darkly, that "we got our hats handed to us," they're also telling what could still be a truth.

Colloquial speech preserves other verbal traces of that fabricky thing which men used to wear and which used to have so intimate a relationship to its wearer. A memory of this intimacy recurs in such phrases as "wherever I hang my hat is home," though home has no peg for the nonexistent object that supposedly defines it. The male politician will continue to announce that he's "throwing his hat into the ring" even though he wears no hat for fear of matting his leonine, Kennedyesque hair. When our politician needs funding, he will approach potential donors with "hat in hand" and ask them to "pass the hat," thereby using the same archaism for both his heart and the money that keeps it pumping. Sometimes a hat symbolizes the head rather than the heart. A discreet man keeps a confidence in his head, or "under his hat," and when he is about to blab, he warns us to "hold onto your hat." If he seems too proud of his insider's knowledge, we might tell him to check his long-forgotten hat-size.

A dim memory of the versatility of hats survives whenever we complain about having to "wear many hats" at work, where our performance hinges on whether we don our "thinking caps" or forget to, and thus wear the "dunce cap." If we've done a really smart thing on the job, we've pulled a nonexistent rabbit out of our nonexistent hat; if we do it three times, the boss might acknowledge our "hat-trick" with a raise. If we're dull but opinionated, co-workers might accuse us of talking through our hats. Our uninformed pronouncements might even make them mad as hatters.

UNLIKE MY FATHER, I have no scruple against baseball caps, which I began wearing in my mid-forties. This was not entirely due to vanity. While attending an academic conference in San Diego, I spent a hatless June afternoon walking the beach at La Jolla with three equally clueless English professors from the East and Midwest. Surprised that night by my peeling head, I bought a cheap baseball cap the next day. Several months later, when a small literary magazine sent me a baseball cap as payment for an essay, I took it as an omen.

I'm less brave than Shakespeare: matted hat-hair seems a small price to pay for concealing the monkish bald spot on my crown, a precise echo of my father's pattern. I'll also concede that I feel younger and hipper in a baseball cap. Deep down, though, I'm enough of my father's son to appreciate the defining limits of a peak above my eyes, a chaos-reducing frame through which to view the world. As Dad knew, a hatted head feels more protected than a bare one, even if what threatens it is psychological rather than meterological. While my father's hats made him feel more upbeat, mine make me feel more tranquil: it's easier to avoid being a hot-head under the regulating containment of a baseball cap.

I now live just outside of Washington, D. C., where winters are mild by Midwestern standards. My winter hat—a thick stocking cap—is necessary only around ten days a year. The rest of the time, unless I bravely decide to leave the house hatless and thus naked, I'll choose one of three baseball caps: one plain, one featuring the logo of that literary magazine and one with the logo of a local Ford dealership. Hanging in my office at the college where I teach is a hard hat, the relic of a summer job at an Illinois tank farm and, I hope, an effective comic prop for defusing difficult student conferences. Although these hats might not tell my story as legibly as my father's hats once told his, they'll have to do. A member of a hatless generation has to start somewhere.

At the moment indoors and hatless, I am studying photographs of my father in his various hats. Here's Dad on the pipeline in his hard hat; in the next shot he wears a pipeliner's soft hat, like a striped engineer's cap with the brim turned up. Here's the sailor, his white Dixie cup cocked at a jaunty angle. And here's the accountant on a business trip to, of all places, my current city, where he strides down Pennsylvania Avenue in a wool coat and a pulled-down fedora. A series of declining-father pictures follows, more of these because there were more cameras around, and in every outside shot Dad is wearing one of those Scottish golf caps. These pictures form a partly animated flip-movie: the face ages from picture to picture, but except for color and pattern, the hat stays the same.

The last of my father's golf caps was more subdued than most. A Christmas present from my mother, who always had better taste, it was solid gray. When Dad died last year at the age of eighty-nine, I asked my mother if I could have it. Still smelling of his hair, this was the hat that got him to the end—a fitting memento, along with three sweaters and his company pin, for me to bring back from Ohio.

This hat, now hanging with my baseball caps near the front door, seems destined for future use. The day will come—if it hasn't already and I just don't realize it—when baseball caps will start looking silly on me. On that day I'll realize that these caps no longer convey midlife male ease, but instead make me look like a man who is trying too hard, like Fitzgerald's gold-hatted bouncer. I've noticed, though, that among men only a decade or so older than I am now, golf caps are still in fashion. Although this is an alarming recognition, it's oddly comforting to know that I'm pretty much set, hat-wise. As a child I waited patiently for my grown-up hat. Now I realize that this hat is waiting for me.

Nominated by R. T. Smith, Shenandoah

CAPRICCIO IN E MINOR FOR BLOWFLY AND STRINGS

by PAUL MULDOON

from SUGAR HOUSE REVIEW

for John Ashbery

Sometimes a wind is content to wrap itself in the flag
where it was once inclined to raise
the roof by, albeit discreetly, loosening a ridge tile
here and there. This was before discretion became the better part
of the fire-resistant velour of modern car upholstery. Not even the
    burning of a tire
around a woman's neck may effect as much change

as a flaying Swift witnessed near the Bristol Corn Exchange.
Now all vessels intending to proceed through the bridge must show a
    flag
by day and at night a white light. It seems all youthful rebels tire
of their youthful spirits, spirits we used to raise
with the art-house title-sequence. Once Swift himself took the part
of a lyric ode's ability to slate, a catch to tile,

against Vanbrugh's blockbuster of modern wit and style
and exposed it to the elements. Sometimes maggots will fling their
    loose change
into the hat of a woman by the side of the road, a fiddler whose part
is notated here and there by a little flag
to remind her to try to raise

the emotional stakes. Sometimes a wind betokens the fact we never tire

of describing Swift as a master of satire
while leaving him for the most part unread. That Swift may have had a tile
loose is a topic no one much cares to raise
in this era of live and let loaf. Sometimes change for the sake of change
might not be the worst flag
under which to sail as when maggots, for their part,

are content to be in a crowd-scene from which they'll nonetheless depart
about as gracefully as Swift would retire
from a debate on the slave trade. It seems all youthful spirits flag
where they were once so volatile.
Gone are the days when a wind would call for change
in an art-house way, hoping to raise

the level of debate above the producer-paraphrase
to which we've now succumbed. Sometimes a maggot doesn't want a speaking part
like an animal "of largest size." Everything will change
for Troy as for Tyre
when it's doused in gasoline, like a woman dumped on a flame-retardant tile
by two carjackers who would flag

her down while pretending to change a tire.
Sometimes it's not enough for a wind to play its part and meekly take its turn in the turnstile.
Sometimes raising a flag isn't enough to raise a red flag.

Nominated by Sugar House Review

MEMORIES OF THE DECADENCE

fiction by HARI KUNZRU

from PEN AMERICA

At the beginning of the Decadence it was easy. Although we were bored, and though everything had been done before, we were seized with a peculiar sense of potential. Our anomie had something optimistic to it. This was the golden age of our decline.

During the Decadence we went for promenades in the poorer quarters of the city, pausing to examine choice deformities, examples of disease or dementia. Soon we began to imitate them, at first only in mannerisms, later using makeup, drugs, prosthetics, or surgery. At length it became impossible to tell the fashionable from the afflicted. We thought this a salutary moral lesson, and took delight in ignoring it.

During the Decadence we ate and drank to excess, until a point came when excess went out of fashion. Mathematicians told us the attractor governing our consumption was a simple period which, though occasionally disrupted by shifts elsewhere in the libidinal economy, was reasonably easy to map. Manufacturers of luxury foods and the proprietors of health farms, spas, and colonic irrigation parlors learned to track the so-called Bulimia Cycle, and for a time such businesses became extremely profitable. Soon, however, activity became so intense that the pattern was disrupted and our predictions went awry, setting in motion a wave of bankruptcies, suicides, and social ostracisms.

During the Decadence we gave up sexual intercourse, substituting

187

for it various kinds of fetishism. We refined our tastes, narrowing their range and fantastically increasing their complexity. Certain people became interested in abstraction, concentrating perhaps on household objects or patterns of light and shade. Such citizens were known to climax spontaneously at the sight of a safety pin or a line of red-tail lights stretching forward along a dual carriageway.

During the erotic phase of the Decadence, combinations of time, place, mood, and the presence of physical objects became ever more specific. An increasing percentage of resources was dedicated to sexual research and organization. Orgasms began to require corporate sponsorship, a trend which reached its apogee in the meticulously planned bacchanals at Nuremberg, Jonestown, and Hyde Park. The latter, in which an estimated two hundred thousand people participated in a ritual designed solely to produce the little death in a middle-aged software billionaire, was considered the high point of the movement. A cluster of massively parallel processors were connected to a variety of front-end delivery devices. When triggered, they instantiated patented pleasure-algorithms in the crowd, causing runaway positive feedback which was gathered into a series of giant cells, amusingly styled to represent luminous linga and yoni. When the charge had accumulated to a sufficient degree it was fed back via a fiber-optic core to the Park Lane hotel suite where the entrepreneur lay, bathed in the glow of his hi-res monitors. The crowd themselves, devotees of the influential cult of autoerotic consumption, financed the event through ticket sales and the purchase of various items of merchandising. The energy generated by their activity produced a small quantity of almost-clear seminal fluid on the raw silk sheets of the billionaire's bed, and augmented his bank balance by an estimated twelve and a half million pounds. It was thus considered a success, and plans for a two-hundred-date world tour were drawn up, only to be scotched by his premature death from skin cancer in a Hawaii tanning dome. Soon afterwards, a fashion for feverish masturbatory interiority gained favor, inaugurating a rage for Keats, broom closets, and antique printed pornography. Boarding schools were set up throughout the country. The days of the megabacchanals drew temporarily to a close.

The involvement of large numbers of people in organized sexual experimentation necessitated the development of information networks, directories, and algebraic search engines dedicated to matching those of compatible tastes. Nymphets were put in touch with elderly professors, cyborg freaks with the manufacturers of Japanese industrial robots, those interested in coercion with those who wanted to be coerced. This last category caused some problems among purist dominants, for whom the desire to be coerced disqualified some candidates from consideration as slaves, concentration camp inmates, or members of religious orders. A standard disclaimer form was quickly developed. Willingness to sign meant automatic barring as an involuntary submissive. These questions of consent were handled by the Society of Sadean Solicitors (SSS), whose obsessive fascination with the Byzantine complexities of this area of law never once led them to waive their exorbitant fees.

During the Decadence, eroticism itself was only a passing fad. The information network which enabled efficient sexual contact itself became the object of our interests. Connoisseurs of classifications, indices, and filing systems paid astronomical sums for rare databases. We became collectors of objects, not from any particular interest in the things themselves, but simply for the opportunities they presented us for cataloguing. Some citizens rejected computer automation altogether, taking pride in feats of card-indexing. Cross-referencing by hand became an art as much appreciated as sculpture or the programming of combat games.

We soon developed an acute awareness of taxonomy. Classification according to phylum, genus, and species became de rigueur, not just for biological material, but in many other fields as well. Televised public debates were held over the correct designation of common phenomena. They were conducted along the lines of medieval theological disputations, and took place in a studio mocked up to represent the cloisters of the twelfth-century University of Bologna. The only anachronism was the pair of bikini-clad girls who operated the digital scoreboard.

We engaged in a passionate love affair with hierarchies, all the more intense for our awareness that they were meaningless, even ridiculous as tools for understanding our distributed, networked world. As the ebbs and flows of our frenzied culture became more extreme, we turned to the verities of dead, static systems to comfort ourselves, soothing the ache of the data pumping faster through our bruised, red-raw flesh. We relearned Abulafia's Kaballah and studied the circular taxonomies of the Catalan, Ramón Lull. We rejected Watson and Crick for Paracelsus and John Dee, embraced Galen and the four humors, studied the Tree of Knowledge, the Body Politic, the Great

Chain of Being, and the angelology of the Scholastics. We wept at the beauty of the Metaphysical Grammarians, and yearned to know the true Hebrew that God spoke to Adam before the flood.

Eventually the cult of learning collapsed altogether and with it, the preoccupation with self-definition which had driven the entire early period of the Decadence. Citizens no longer cared to record or understand the minutiae of their personal experience. They left themselves unexplored. After the collapse of all extant systems of knowledge, a feature of the early decadent period, subjective experience had become the only reference point for establishing meaning or value. Ceasing even to ask what one wanted thus became considered the most advanced form of transgression. Embracing this, we conducted the pursuit of pleasure in a lackluster, half-hearted way. If we stumbled on something we liked, it was purely by chance. Maybe we would return to it. More often than not we would limp off somewhere else. There were many casualties. Service industries suffered dreadfully. Aesthetics collapsed as a discipline.

During this critical period of the Decadence, we did whatever we could to avoid the act of choice. We chose our political leaders via a lottery, and organized our social lives by an ingenious system of random number generation. Many citizens abandoned even their most basic bodily functions to chance. Gambling disappeared as a pastime, since none of us were interested in beating the odds.

Pure randomness soon fell into decline. Some definition returned, though our codes were still fuzzy, unclear, and imprecise. The vague vogue, as it became known, lasted some time, though the inexact measuring systems in use during this phase render impossible any accurate statement of its length, impact, or intensity. It was a time of rumor, myth, superstition, and nameless fear. Certain revisionist scholars have accordingly refused to recognize it as a historical entity, since it seems in so many ways continuous with the rest of our troubled, fluid times.

Having exhausted the most arcane possibilities of body and mind, having become bored with boredom itself, we began to adopt postures of total commitment. Ideologies were formed, wars fought, and causes died for, all in a spirit of absolute hedonism. We believed because it pleased us to believe. Our crusades and jihads were as bloody as any in history. We performed breathtaking acts of self-sacrifice and exacted violent retribution on our enemies. Bizarre monotheisms arose, whose fiery ill-worded theologies afforded ample opportunity for schisms, heresies, and apostasy. There were public crucifixions. Young men with faraway eyes held their hands in flame rather than sign documents of recantation. Soon totalitarianism swept through our cities, bringing tanks and napalm in its wake. We covered the earth in ashes. The devastation ushered in a period of mourning, during which we wept rivers of tears, planted trees, and erected monuments whose poignancy matched the vastness of our remorse. Joy followed hard on the heels of our mourning. Lassitude followed joy. Our prophets and scientists ran simulations to predict the next lurch of our communal whims, but each time their code was outdated as soon as it was compiled. The cycle ran faster, cults and movements swarming like flies on a carcass, paradigms blooming and withering like exotic cancers. Soon there was only speed, a sensation of pure intensity.

Then one day the Decadence ended. We began to be moderate in all things. Our decisions were considered, the product of sound judgment. Our institutions stabilized and prepared themselves for steady growth. We quoted maxims to each other. "A little and often." "Mens sana in corpore sano." Now our economists have quelled the speculators, advocating cooperation and a sound industrial base. We believe in the family, in community, and an undefined spirituality, though if you asked us we could not tell you why. Debating is of no interest anymore. We want a quiet life. "All to the good," as we often say to our neighbors. We are content. And yet . . . And yet there is something stale in the air. Citizens whisper in the social clubs. They say that it cannot last.

Nominated by PEN America

TO THE FURIES WHO VISITED ME IN THE BASEMENT OF DUANE READE

by SHARON DOLIN

from 5 A.M.

I bow and give thanks—not as moth to the flame
but as the singeing flame   You made me quake as I stood
    with my dog waiting behind the line to get to the counter.
                                        Stuck

as if struck with palsy between the painkillers and
the glasses for close reading   I spied there   waiting at the Drop-Off
    line—or was it the Pick-Up line—the two of them   fluttering eyes

at each other in their blind love-bubble: she—whom I had never
seen before   now   in profile   with her serpentine
    graying hair   gazing up at him   who had   twelve years

before   almost to the day   gazed in and given me a ring
                                  and who still
wore the ring I had given him   *I am my Beloved's*
    inscribed within.   Now which Beloved was *that*?

O Eumenides, You swelled my head and heart with seething African
                                                bees
(inside Apollo whispered, "You can just leave, walk back
        upstairs.")   But You steaming, stunned me, voices

of Medea, of Clytemnestra, of Dido, of Circe, of Judith,
of Tamar, of Ariadne, of Electra, of Agave You all buzzed
        all clamored as I watched them

for the longest five minutes of my life: as initimate
as the yolk and white inside an uncracked egg—they could
        have been in bed

until   after a century   he turned from the counter
to encounter my gaze and without a flicker of . . .
        with no nod to me who was still his wife—as though he foresaw

what was coming—as unavoidable and elastic as seconds before a
                                           crash—
as though he could shield her from the blowtorch of our collective
                                        rage
        took her shoulder—the as-yet blind, limping one

the weak woman as I had once been (before You possessed me)—the
                                        one
who had not seen me—who had never seen me—to guide her
        down another aisle:

YOU FUCKING BITCH!   with death-heat blast   shrieked out
Alecto   Tisiphone   Megaera
        so she had to run—look up at me   look

at all the women betrayed by other women—
at first blank-faced as though blindsided by a stranger
        then a shutter of recognition so she veered

away as though I were radioactive   rabid
and might bite her.   I bow and give thanks
        O Dirae   for giving me daggermouth

and the scornful heart that no longer cares
what he thinks of me when I cared for too long.
    And I let Your fury seizure through me

like the first pain-shiver of labor   or some earth-tremor.
Abandoned wife but not unsexed.
    Come, You winged goddesses in Your short kid skirts

and huntress boots: Re-sex me here. Not suppliant
but with my one-headed dog ready to take down
    to Hell any man or woman who dares deceive and kill

my love. Let me rise into the moonlight—shake frenzied breasts
                                    arms
ass   in a belly dance with Your Maenads and piping goatmen.

Nominated by John Allman, Judith Vollmer, 5 A.M

CHILDREN ARE THE ONLY ONES WHO BLUSH

fiction by JOE MENO

from ONE STORY

Art school is where I'd meet my sister each Wednesday, and then, the two of us would travel, by cab, to couple's counseling. Although Jane and I were twins, by the age of nineteen, she was already two years ahead of me in school, and because both of our parents were psychiatrists, and because I had been diagnosed with a rare social disorder, a disorder of my parent's own invention, Jane and I were forced to undergo couple's therapy every Wednesday afternoon. The counseling sessions were ninety minutes long and held in a dentist's office. As both of my parents were well-known in their field, they had a difficult time finding a colleague to analyze their children, and so they were forced to settle on a dentist named Dr. Dank, a former psychiatrist who had turned his talents to dentistry. He was an incredibly hairy man who smoked while my sister and I reclined in twin gray dental chairs. Dr. Dank did all he could to convince me that I was angry at my twin sister for being smarter and also that I was gay.

Once I had made the mistake of mentioning to my sister that the doorman of our building was "handsome"—to me, he looked like a comic book hero with a slim mustache. She frequently brought this remark up in our sessions as evidence of my latent homosexual desires. She would leave various kinds of gay pornography for me on my bed. I would come from school and find a magazine or videotape lying there and stare at it—at the faces of the oiled, suntanned men and their arching, shaven genitals—then return the magazine to my pillow,

195

and back out of my room like a thief. Jane was nineteen and a sculpture major in art school. She was also taking a minor in psychology through correspondence courses in the mail. Technically, I was still a senior in high school. My sister's sophistication, her worldliness and intelligence were absolutely terrifying to me.

In the taxi on the way to our counseling appointments, I would stare across the backseat at her, studying her profile. Jane had short black hair; she was skinny and there was a field of freckles on her nose which made her seem a lot younger than she actually was. When she wasn't looking, that's where I'd always stare, at the freckles on the bridge of her nose.

"Jack, what's happening with your gym class?" she asked me. One of the reasons my sister was two years ahead of me in school was because I failed gym, year after year. As part of my social disorder, I was paralyzed by a fear of stranger's bodily fluids, their blood, sweat, spit, urine, even their tears. If someone sneezed near me, I would begin to convulse violently. I was unable to participate in any gym activity where bodily fluids were involved. Because of this, and because my disorder was unrecognized anywhere outside our household, I had failed gym every semester for the last three years and had yet to finish high school.

"Dad told me you have a new gym teacher this year," Jane said. "Is he nice?"

"His name is Mr. Trask. He asked me why I don't participate and I told him I had a medical condition and then he told me to go sit in the bleachers. I'm supposed to meet with him tomorrow to talk about it."

"Did you give any more thought to what we talked about in therapy last week?"

"What? That the reason I'm failing gym is because I won't admit I'm gay?"

"Dr. Dank completely agreed with me, Jack. You're queer. You're living a lie. The sooner you admit it, the happier we'll all be."

I decided then, watching the Chicago Avenue traffic drizzling past, not to argue with her. For all I knew I was queer. I had never kissed a girl. Also, I had a poster from the musical *Miss Saigon* hanging in my room, a gift from Mr. Brice, my marching band instructor, the only teacher at my school who had made accommodations for my fictional disorder. Jane might be right. It was entirely possible that I was gay.

A day later I met with Mr. Trask, who was a tousled-haired, thoroughly-bearded man. He sat across from me in a swivel chair, his running shorts riding up his broad hairy thighs. If I glanced long enough, I could see the dark cavity of his crotch. As disgusting as it was, it was hard not to stare.

"Why do you keep failing gym?" he asked.

"I'm afraid of bodily fluids."

"Well, they're not going to let you graduate unless you pass gym class."

"I know. I've already accepted that I won't graduate from high school. It doesn't bother me."

"Hold on," he said, leaning back in the chair, the running shorts inching even higher. "Here's what we're going to do. Your parents are shrinks right?"

"Yes."

"You get me some valium and I'll make sure you'll graduate."

After class, I called my father. A day or so later, I gave Mr. Trask what he had asked for. From then on, I spent gym class watching the other boys my age sword-fighting with upturned tennis rackets and knew I was missing nothing.

The next week, I met my sister Jane for our counseling appointment in front of her art school, where a number of young men and women gathered to smoke cigarettes, looking purposeful and shabby. Jane marched up to me, said hello, and then pointed at a gawky-looking young man who was leaning against the wall, lighting a clove cigarette.

"Look? How about him? Go tell him you'd like to give him a blowjob."

I looked away, shaking my head, and said something like, "I don't think so."

"You need to grow up. Part of being an adult is dealing with adult feelings. Do you want to end up an old dirty queer getting teenage boys to suck you off in bathrooms or something? Because that's what will happen, Jack. You have to deal with this openly before you sublimate it."

I had no idea how I was supposed to answer.

Just then a girl named Jill Thirby came up to us and said, "My name is Jill Thirby. My father and mother are both famous artists. You may have heard of them." Jill Thirby had a yellow dress on and long brown hair. She also had black-framed glasses and these dangly yellow earrings. "I'm working on this really intense project right now and I was wondering if you guys would like to help."

197

"What is it?" I asked, staring at her long yellow scarf.

"Basically, I'm trying to make things fly."

"What does that mean?" Jane asked tersely.

"I'm attaching hundreds of balloons to different things to see what'll fly and what won't."

"Wow. That sounds cool," I said.

"That sounds fucking stupid," Jane cursed. "That's exactly what the world needs. More childish, performance-art bullshit. Why don't you do something meaningful? Like confront what's happening in the Middle East?"

Jill Thirby looked ashamed all of a sudden, her yellow eye-shadow going red. "You don't have to talk to me like that. I was just trying to be . . . I'm just trying to do something nice."

"Well, why don't you do something nice somewhere else?" Jane asked.

Jill Thirby nodded, still shocked, and walked away. I looked over at Jane and asked her, "What's your problem?"

"She is my problem. I can't believe how many girls there are like her. Their fathers don't love them enough and so they go to art school and everything they make is this twee, meaningless bullshit. They don't ever deal with anything serious, you know. Like I bet that girl never even heard of the Situationists. I bet she has no idea what's going on in Palestine right now."

"What?"

"Forget it. We're late for Dr. Dank. Let's go," she said and then, unfortunately, we did.

That afternoon in therapy, Jane suggested that the real reason I was afraid of bodily fluids was because I was in denial of my own sexuality. I did not argue with her. The whole next week during gym class, I watched the other boys in class doing windsprints, their bodies virulent with overripe sweat. It was the intimacy I did not like, I wanted to tell her. The idea of sharing something vital with someone I did not know or understand.

Outside of the sculpture building the next Wednesday, while I was waiting on my sister, I ran into Jill Thirby again. She was still dressed in yellow, this time with a yellow stocking hat, with a yellow ball on the end. She had yellow mittens on and was chewing what appeared to be yellow gum.

"Hey," I said. "I wanted to say I'm sorry. You know, about my sister, the other day."

"I don't get why some people have to be so negative. She's really, really mean."

"Have you gotten anything to fly yet?"

"Not yet," she said, itching her nose. "I've tried a chair, a pineapple, and a bowling ball. None of them even got off the ground."

"Well, if you ever need any help, I'd be happy to give you a hand."

"What are you doing right now?" she asked.

"Nothing," I said, glancing around, seeing my sister was late once again.

"Do you want to help me then? I was going to try and float a bird-cage."

A few moments later, we climbed up the fire escape to the roof of the student dorm and stood looking out over the city. Jill Thirby had about fifty red helium balloons with her, which she promptly tied to an empty birdcage. "Okay, here we go," she said, and we both stepped away. The birdcage did not move, though the balloons fluttered back and forth in the wind, dancing ferociously.

"Maybe you need something smaller," I said.

Jill Thirby kneeled beside the birdcage, inspecting it, and said, "Or more balloons possibly." I thought about leaning over and trying to kiss her. She saw me looking at her in a funny way and said, "What is it? Is there something in my teeth? It's this weird problem I have. My teeth are too far apart. I always have food stuck in them. My dad's constantly reminding me to brush them."

"No. I was just . . . it's nothing."

"Do you want to try and float something else tomorrow?"

"Okay," I said, and took her hand as she stepped back onto the fire escape.

Jane was waiting outside the sculpture building swearing to herself when I found her. She squinted at me angrily when I said hello.

"Do you know what time it is? Where the fuck were you? Mom and dad pay by the hour if you didn't happen to notice."

"I was helping out that girl Jill Thirby."

"What? Why were you hanging out with her?"

"I don't know. She seems nice. I like her glasses and everything."

"Why are you in such denial? Jesus, Jack, everyone's trying to help you but you're not even trying."

"What did I do?"

199

"Just when we're getting somewhere with your therapy, you decide to ditch your appointment to go 'hang' with a 'girl.' That's textbook denial. Seriously."

"I just wanted to see if she could make something float."

"I guess we should just stop worrying about your severe emotional issues because, all of a sudden, you like some Jewish girl."

"What? She's not Jewish."

"She's definitely Jewish."

"So what? Mom's Jewish," I said.

"You are so completely clueless. Why don't you screw this girl and get it over with? And maybe then you'll be ready to admit what your problem really is."

"I don't want to screw anyone."

"Bullshit. You want to screw her in her little Jew butt."

"I'm going to walk home by myself now," I said and then, for once, I did.

The following week I did not wait for Jane to go to couple's counseling. Instead I met Jill Thirby outside the sculpture building and we walked up and down the street looking for things in the trash that we could try and make fly. We were sorting through some garbage cans when she found a small gray cat. It was undernourished and hiding under a moldy cardboard box. Jill Thirby held it to her chest and decided to take it back to her dorm, where we washed it in the common bathroom sink, and then fed it black licorice from the vending machine. "I have the perfect name for it," Jill Thirby said. "Blah-blah."

"That's good," I said. Jill Thirby leaned over and held the cat to her chest, burying her face in the animal's wet gray fur.

"Do you want to spend the night here?" she asked me suddenly. "I don't have intercourse with anyone I don't know intimately, but you can sleep here if you want."

I told her okay. Later that evening, as we were lying in bed together, Jill Thirby began to cry. I did not know what was happening at first. I laid there, holding my breath, pretending to be asleep. Her shoulders were shaking, her back trembling before me. She was holding the cat to her chest and the cat was meowing, trying to get free. I thought about putting my hand on her arm or saying something out loud but I was afraid of what would happen if she knew I wasn't asleep. Finally, I asked her what was wrong, and she said, "I'm sick of being related to my father and mother." Then she sniffled and said, "But I miss them both a lot," and then turned away from me, the cat leaping off the bed. In the darkness, Jill Thirby became quiet and it seemed like she had momentarily disappeared.

The next day I was late for school. I hurried into gym class and took my spot on the wood bleachers and watched the other poor saps running laps. Mr. Trask saw me and climbed the bleachers, and then took a seat beside me, staring off into the distance at something that I don't think existed. He turned and looked at me and said, "How old are you, Jack?"

"Nineteen."

"Nineteen. Jesus. You should have finished school a year ago."

"I know."

"Don't you want to get out of here?"

"Not really. I don't have any idea what's supposed to happen next."

Mr. Trask nodded, then fumbled through his extremely tight shorts for a pack of cigarettes. He offered me one. I shook my head, feeling pretty uncomfortable all of a sudden. He inhaled deeply and then started to cough, his rasps sounding exactly like a gym whistle, high and tinny. "I'll tell you something: I don't think anybody knows what the hell comes next. I mean I see these kids, and some of them walk around like they got it all figured out—they're going to this college or that college or what, I dunno. I'll let you in on a little secret: if someone comes up to you and tells you they got anything figured out, you can be sure of one thing. They're full of it. Because the thing is, as soon as you figure one thing out, you see there's a whole other world of shit you don't understand. The people who think they know it all, those are the ones to beware of. And that's all I got to say about that."

I nodded, seeing two pale sophomores—in the middle of the track—begin to collapse from exhaustion.

"Do you think your dad could get me some barbiturates? I think I need something stronger. I'm having a heck of a time sorting out my thoughts this week."

"I'll look into it."

"Great." Mr. Trask nodded and then stood. He held his hands in front of his face like a megaphone and shouted, "Okay, ladies, bring it in."

After class, I waited around the art school campus all afternoon, hoping to find Jill Thirby again. It was getting dark when I saw her sneaking across the student pavilion with what looked to be several hundred red balloons. I followed her from a distance, watched her as she climbed up the fire escape, back to the roof of the dorm. Halfway up, she heard me climbing beneath her and looked down, then smiled a wide, goofy smile, holding the balloons with one hand, and her yellow stocking cap with the other.

"What are you doing?" I asked.

"Today I got a brilliant idea: I decided to try and float myself."

"That doesn't sound so good."

"I did some calculations." She scrambled into her pocket with her free hand and handed me a piece of graph paper on which was the most incomprehensible drawing I had ever seen: there were numbers and arrows and what appeared to be a cloud of some kind.

"Maybe you should practice first."

"With what?"

"I don't know. Something not too high."

"That's something my dad would probably tell me," Jill Thirby said. "I guess we could try it from my dorm room. I live on the second floor so if I fell, it wouldn't be so bad."

"Okay, that sounds good," I said but as soon as we got to her room, we started to kiss instead, and then Jill was pulling down her long yellow tights, and she had pale yellow underwear on, and then those were off, and I could see her thighs, the plains of her hips, the entire dark world between, and she was saying, "I usually don't have sex with people I don't know for at least three months," but then we did it anyway. For some reason, for the first time in as long as I could remember, I did not think about the danger of bodily fluids. Things were passed between us but it did not bother me. A few minutes later, we were lying in bed, and she still had her yellow stocking hat on with the yellow ball at the end, and I don't know why but I suddenly blurted out, "Jill Thirby, do you want to be my girlfriend?"

Jill Thirby's face went blank just then. "I thought you were gay. That's what your sister told me."

"I know, that's what everyone keeps telling me." I looked her in the face, her lips smudged with yellow lipstick, and asked her again. "Do you want to be my girlfriend anyway?"

She smiled at me softly, blinked once, and then said: "Thanks but no thanks."

I sat in bed and watched her dress quickly. "You should probably go," she said. The cat we had found, Blah-blah, seemed to look at me anxiously, too, and so I put my clothes on fast and left in a hurry.

When I got home, my parents and sister were there waiting for me. So was Dr. Dank. For the next two hours I sat in the gray armchair while my sister and Dr. Dank tried to get me to admit I was incredibly unhappy. I told them I had never been happier.

"Jack, how can you be happy?" my sister asked, arms folded, standing over me. Her silver hairpin looked like a threat, pointing down at me. "Look at you. You spend all your time alone. You're completely disinterested in dating. You're failing high school. You have no intellectual curiosity. It's not normal, Jack. It's not even abnormal. It's subnormal or something like that."

Dr. Dank puffed out two nostrils full of smoke and said, "I couldn't agree more. It is subnormal. And also, he hasn't been flossing. He's becoming a prime candidate for gum disease."

"Why don't you just admit you're gay so we can all just move on?" my sister groaned.

I stared at my parents, who hadn't spoken a word since I walked in. My father looked exhausted. My mother looked bored. She had a notepad in her lap, taking notes, though I think she was actually finishing a crossword puzzle. It was pretty obvious, even in their professional detachment, who they were siding with. I sat in the armchair, facing them all, my father pulling off his glasses to clean them. He did this whenever he thought a patient was lying. I knew this because he had told me several times before that psychiatry was as much performance as it was science. Taking off his glasses and cleaning them was one of his signature moves. I tried to look at my mother but she was busy scribbling down the answer to 15 across. Neither one of them would dare to look me in the eye. So I glanced over at my sister, who was still standing above me, arms crossed, her dark eyebrows looking like they had not been groomed in some time. I understood right then that, no matter what, she would always be smarter than me, more sophisticated, as would the rest of my family. I thought maybe this was the reason all of them were, on their own, pretty miserable. I decided right then to just give in and agree and try to make them all happy.

"You're right," I said, looking down at my gray plaid socks. "It's true. I'm gay. I'm really gay."

Jane grinned, tears coming to her eyes. She slid her arms around

203

my neck and hugged me savagely, saying, "Doesn't it feel like an incredible weight has been lifted, Jack?" and I nodded because it was true in a way. She was hugging me and my father was patting me on the back and Dr. Dank was celebrating by lighting my mother's cigarette. It did feel good to have Jane feel proud of me, even for a moment, even for the absolute wrong reasons. I told everyone I loved them then and that I needed to get some sleep. Before I closed the door, I heard Dr. Dank announce that couple's counseling for my sister and I would resume the very next day, and now that everything was in the open, our sessions were going to have to be bumped up to twice a week.

I did not hear from Jill Thirby for almost a month, not until she called to say that the cat we had found in the trash was dying. She asked me to come over and help her take it to the vet. I didn't have any reason to say no. When I got to her room, Jill Thirby was standing in the door with a small cardboard box: inside the cat was curled up, mewling. Its eyes were barely open and its entire body seemed to shudder.

"He looks bad," I said.

"I know. He keeps crying. I don't know what to do."

"Why did you call me?" I asked.

"Because I don't want to go by myself."

Jill Thirby had looked in the phone book and found an animal shelter in midtown. We called and made an appointment and then waited at the bus stop. Twice I thought the cat was dead, its rheumy eyes gazing up at us without any kind of life, but then it started to cry again, the sound of which made my hands feel shaky.

After we got to the shelter, after we were led down the hall to a tiny examination room, after the vet looked at the cat's scrawny stomach and weak legs and failing kidneys, he suggested Jill Thirby have it put to sleep. Jill Thirby immediately started sobbing. I had never seen anyone crying before like that. She was trying to say something but she was crying too hard and so I took her hand. She had yellow mittens on and I felt the stitches there against my palm and said, "It's okay," and Jill Thirby nodded and then the vet disappeared, taking the cat with him, and we stood alone in the tiny white room, like we were on the set of some soap opera, and Jill Thirby was still crying, and then we were waiting at the bus stop, and then we were getting on the bus, and the whole time we were sitting there, she was still holding the empty cardboard box, and we sat beside each other, watching the buildings go past in a blur, riding past my stop, past the stop for her school, past the part of the city we knew, at that moment wondering who we were, what was going to happen to us, waiting, like everybody else, for someone to tell us what to do.

Nominated by Andrew Porter, One Story

ROME

by BRIGIT PEGEEN KELLY

from PLOUGHSHARES

I saw once, in a rose garden, a remarkable statue of the Roman she-wolf and her twins, a reproduction of an ancient statue—not the famous bronze statue, so often copied, in which the wolf's blunt head swings forward toward the viewer like a sad battering ram, but an even older statue, of provenance less clear. The wolf had been cut out of black stone, made blacker by the garden's shadows, and she stood in profile, her elegant head pointed toward something far beyond her, her long unmarked body and legs—narrower and more finely-boned than the body and legs of wolves as we know them—possessed, it seemed, of a great stillness, like the saturated stillness of the roses, but tightly-nerved, set, on the instant, to move. Under her belly, stood the boys, under her black breasts, not babes, as one might expect, but two lean boys, cut from the same shadowed stone as the wolf, but disproportionately small, grown boys no bigger than starlings, though still, like the wolf, oddly fine of face and limb, one boy pressing four fingers against one long breast, his other hand cupped beneath it to catch the falling milk, the second boy wrapping both arms around another breast, as if to carry it off, neither boy suckling, both instead turned toward you, dreamy, sweetly sly, as if to chide you for interrupting their feeding, or as if they were plotting a good trick . . . Beautiful, those boys among the roses. Beautiful, the black wolf. But it was the breasts that held the eye, a double row of four black breasts, eight smooth breasts, each narrowing to a strict point, piercing sharp, exactly the shape of the ivory tooth of the shark.

Nominated by Ted Deppe, Marianne Boruch, Dan Masterson, Maxine Scates

ON COMING BACK
AS A BUZZARD

by LIA PURPURA

from ORION

I know, coming back as a crow is a lot more attractive. If crows and buzzards do the same rough job—picking, tearing, and cleaning up—who wouldn't rather return as a shiny blue crow with a mind for locks and puzzles? A strong voice, and poem-struck. Sleek, familial, omen-bearing. Full of mourning and ardor and talk. Buzzards are nothing like this, but something other, complicated by strangeness and ugliness. They intensify my thinking. They look prehistoric, pieced together, concerned. I might simply say I feel closer to them—always have—and proceed. Because, really, as I turn it over, the problem I'm working on here, coming back as a buzzard, has not so much to do with buzzards after all.

A buzzard is *expected* at the table. The rush would be over by the time I got there and I, my lateness sanctioned, might rightfully slip in. I wouldn't saunter, nor would I blow in dramatically—*flounce*, as my grandmother would say. The road would be the dinner table (just as the dinner table, with its veering discussions, is always a road somewhere) and others' distraction would resolve—well, I would resolve it—into a clean plate.

I would be missed if I were not there. Not at first, not in the frenzy, but later.

Without me, no outlines, no profiles come clear. The very idea of scaffolding is diminished.

"The smaller scraps are tastier" would have no defender. "Close to the bone" would fall out of use as a measure of sharply felt truth.

Without a chance to walk away from abundance, thus proving their wealth, none of the first eaters would be content with their portion. I make their bestowing upon the least of us possible.

With me around, mishaps—side of the highway, over a cliff, more slowly dispensed by poison—do not have to be turned to a higher purpose. I step in. I make use of.

And here, I'm whittling away at the problem.

As a buzzard, I'd know the end of a thing is precisely not that. Things go on, in their way. My presence making the end a beginning, reinterpreting the idea of abundance, allowing for the ever-giving nature of Nature—I'd know these not as religious thoughts. It's rather that, apportioned rightly, there's always enough, more than enough. "Nothing but gifts on this poor, poor earth," says Milosz, who understood perfectly the resemblance between dissolve and increase. Rain scours and sun burns away excesses of form. And rain also seeds, and sun urges forth fuses of green.

I'd love best the movement of stages and increments, to repeat "this bank and shoal of time" while below me banks and shoals of a body went on welling/receding, rising and dropping. I'd be perched on a wire, waiting, ticking off not the meat reducing, but how what's left, like a dune, shifts and reconstitutes. Yes, it *looks* like I hover, and the hovering, I know, suggests a discomfiting eagerness. Malevolence. Why is that? I haven't killed a thing. If the waiting seems untoward, it may be confirming something too real, too true: all the parts that slip from sight, can't be easily had, collapse in on themselves and require digging, all the parts that promise small, intense bursts of sweetness unnerve us—while the easily abundant, the spans, the expanses (thick haunch, round belly and shoulder), all that lifts easily to another's lips, and retains its form till the end—seems pure. Right and deserved. Proper and lawful. Thus butchers have their neat diagrams. One knows to call for *chop, loin, shank, rump.*

I'd get to be one who, when passed the plate, seeks first the succulent eye. This would mark me: *foreigner.* Stubborn lover of scraps and dark meat. Base. Trained on want and come to love piecemeal offerings—the shreds and overlooked tenderness too small for a meal, but carefully, singularly gathered—like brief moments that burst: isolate beams of sun in truck fumes, underside of wrist against wrist, sudden cool from a sewer grate rising. I incline toward the tucked and folded parts (the old country can't be bred out of me), the internals with names that lack correspondence, the sweetbreads and umbles, bungs, hoods, liver-and-lights. If the road is a plate, then the outskirts of fields and settlements where piles are heaped are plates, too. And the gullies, the ditches, the alleys—all plates. I'd get to reorder your thoughts about troves, to prove the spilled and shoveled-aside to be treasure. To reconfer notions of milk and honey, and how to approach the unbidden.

I resemble, as I suppose we all do, the things I consume: bent to those raw flaps of meat, red, torn, cast aside, my head also looks like a leftover thing, chewed. I have my ways of avoiding attention: vomit to turn away predators. Shit, like the elegant stork, on my legs to cool off, to disinfect the swarming microbes I tread daily. I am gentle. And cautious. I ride the thermals and flap very little (conserve, conserve) and locate food by smell. I'm a black V in air. A group of us on the ground is a *venue*. In the air we're a *kettle*.

I reuse even the language.

A simple word, *aftermath*, structures my day. Sometimes I think *epic*—doesn't everyone apply to their journey a story? Then *flyblown, feculent, scavenge* come—how it must seem to others—and the frame of my story's reduced. Things are made daily again. The first eaters are furiously driven—by hunger, and brute need releasing trap doors in the brain. Such push and ambition! I hold things in pantry spots in my body and take out and eat what I've saved when I need it, and so am never furious. On my plate, choice reduces. I take what I come upon, and the work of a breeze cools the bowl's steaming contents. There's a beauty in this singularity: consider bringing to each occasion your one perfect bowl, one neat fork/spoon/knife set. That when the chance comes, you're given to draw the tine-curves between lips, pull, lick, tap clean the spoon's curvature—and for these sensations, there's ample time. Time pinned open, like the core of a long summer afternoon.

Am I happy? Yes, in momentary ways. Which I think is a good way to feel about things that come when they will, and not when you will them. While I'm waiting, I get to be with the light as it shifts off the wet phone wire, catches low sun, holds, pearls and unpearls drops of water. If I bounce just a little, they shiver and fall, and my weight calls more pearls to me. There's light over the blood-matted rib-fur, and higher up, translucing on the still-unripped ear of the fox. Light through drops of fresh resin on pine limbs, light on ditchwater never-minding the murk. I get fixed by spoors of light, silver shine on silks and tassels, light choosing the lowliest, palest blue gristle for lavishing. I wait at a height and from afar, with what looks like a hunch-shouldered burden. Below, the red coils of spilled guts gather dust on the ground. Such a red and its steam in the cold gets to be *shock*—and *riches*. Any red interruption on asphalt, on hillside, at dune's edge—*shock*, and not a strewn thing, not waste. Not a mess. Plump entrails crusting with sage and dirt tighten in sun: piercing *that* is an undersung moment, filled with a tender resistance, a sweetness, slick curves and tangles to dip into, tear, stretch, snap, and swallow.

The problem with coming back as a buzzard is the notion of *coming back*.

I can't believe in the coming-back.

Sure, I play the dinnertime game, everyone identifying their animal-soul, the one they choose to reveal their best depth, the one, when the time comes, they hope fate will award them: strong eagle! smart dolphin! joyful golden retriever! But there's the issue of where I'd have to go first, in order to make a return. And the idea of things I did or failed to do in a lifetime fixing the terms of my return—and the keeping of records, and just who's totting it up. As soon as I imagine returning anew (brave-stallion reward, dung-beetle reproach) I lose heart. It's too easy.

Anyway, I already think like a buzzard.

The times I forget my child, most powerfully marked by the moments that follow, in which I abruptly remember him again, with sharp breath, disturbed at the oversight—those times are evidence enough of my fall into reverie, into all that is set, unbidden, before me: inclinations gone to full folds, bone-shaded hollows, easings and slouchings, taut ridges, matched dips, cupped small of the back, back of the neck, the ever-giving body—yes, I take what's set before me. So much feels hosted—and fleet. I chew a little koan: all things go / always more where that came from.

That the world calls me to hissing and grunting, that I am given a nose for decay's weird sweetness, that I am arranged in a broken-winged pose to dry feathers and bake off mites in the sun, that I love the wait, that I have my turn, that no one wants my job so I go on being needed—I have my human equivalences for these.

Nominated by Fleda Brown, Orion

MODEL PRISON MODEL

by TERRANCE HAYES

from RATTLE

Here in this small expertly crafted model
you can see the layout of the prison I will erect:
the 17,500 six-by-eight cells, the wards
for dreamers reduced to beggars to my right,

the wards for strangers who might be or become
enemies to my left. It has taken years of research
and perspiration to design and assemble
this miniature, but with your support

it should only take 12 to 18 months to build
it to functioning size. You may note the words
(*Prison is for the unindoctrinated*) painted
on the tiny sign at the main gate are still wet.

I finished them while waiting for you to arrive.
They are the smell of civilization in the air.
Let me direct your attentions to the barbed wire
which thickens to a virtual cyclone of fangs

above the prison. With a good fence
to draw upon I was able to create
a terrific somberness and then lie down
and look through it at the prisoners

and officers inside. I feel like this is a good time
to tell you my father, mother and closest cousin
have worked decades as correctional officers
for the State. Nonetheless when I, a black poet,

was asked to participate in the construction
of this vision, I was surprised.
During those first uninspired years I smoked
so much I would have set myself on fire

had I not been weeping most of the time.
I am told the first time my uncle was an inmate,
my father would find him cowering
in his cell like a folded rag. Between jail

he works Saturdays helping out a man
at a flea market fruit stand, my uncle Junior.
You will note the imposing guard towers
at each corner of the prison. In the yard

below them I will loose vicious, obedient dogs.
Whether you consider dogs symbols
of security or symbols of danger depends
upon whether you're inside or outside

the fence. In our current positions
around the model you and I represent
the mulling picketers: the just and vengeful,
the holy and grief-stricken citizens.

Standing along the corridor
leading to the preliminary de-dressing area,
several savage and savaged widows will insult
the new inmates. Even a slur is a form

of welcome. I plan to have the vocalists
among the prisoners sing for the old men
who die there. Perhaps their song will soften
the picketers. The prison of the picketer,

let me remark, is a landscape of dry riverbeds,
canyons and caves. During the uninspired hours
I imagined that land as the color of brick
set to flame. Everything gets tender in fire.

I imagined the melancholy stone of the prison
with a sort of geological desire. I imagined
the rehabilitated before the parole board
spilling brightly lit jive, alive with the indecipherable,

indecipherably alive. Everything is excited
by freedom. But I don't know. I feel like no matter how
large we build this prison, it isn't going to save us.
Please permit me to end my presentation for now.

We might get so caught up imagining the future,
we'll never find our way. Come. Bend over and try
moving forward while looking between your legs
to get a sense of what it feels like trying to escape.

Nominated by Joan Murray, Lucia Perillo, Rattle

GOD

by AMY LEACH

from THE MASSACHUSETTS REVIEW

The hoopoe and the bat do not say this word. Neither do the eagles or the vultures or the black vultures. The hyena and the wild goat and the night creatures refrain from using it, too. I have found stoats busy in the gutters, doing what they wish, but never uttering this word. A ferret may slip off one's lap, stalk away along the floorboard with a bend in his back, crush under the back door and leave. Outside in the dark, nobody knows for certain what escaped ferrets do, but they've never been heard saying the word, or even forming it silently with their mouths.

People say the word repeatedly, and the more they repeat it, the less I can understand it: listening to words I do not understand is like swallowing stones. With each repetition of the word it is like I am given another stone to swallow. I can't keep up, for it is hard to swallow stones. I have stones filling my mouth and stones in my lap, and stones falling out of my pockets, and the stones keep coming heavy and hard.

The word refers to someone no one has ever seen. Perhaps this is why people say it over and over, as if repetition of a word can make up for the absence of its referent. They say it pleases him, to say his name incessantly—they sing it in songs and chant it together and broadcast it loudly on the radio, on signs. Perhaps it pleases him. I do not know. It does not please me.

Some evenings as I sit there with all these stony words piling up on me, I get so overwhelmed that I become indifferent, and I spit the stones out and let the heap on my lap fall to the floor, and I walk away and go out the back door. The escaped ferrets are out there. The hoopoe and the bat are out there, and I listen to them, and I drop into the pond and swim with the black eels, and I listen to the eels. I listen to the jackrabbits and the javelinas and the sandhill cranes, for they are all out there. And so is he to whom the over-uttered word refers. He is there because his words are there.

His words do not rain down like rocks on those he speaks to, but they mount up with wings or leap through brambles or swim blackly in ponds. They sleep hanging from trees, stomachs full of hunted insects, or grow tall and imperious and leafy in the forest. Many, if not most, of his words hope never to be heard—rooting blindly through their dirt-homes or proliferating on the tops of mountains, they are dismayed when they are discovered, and rush away. His words are not repetitive: the only thing his words have in common with each other is that they are strange and they are themselves—they move on their own, through gutters and caves and swamps and the sky, and some of his words, when they get tired of hearing his name over and over, and wish to hear him speak, escape out the back door, like ferrets, like me.

Nominated by Lia Purpura, Massachusetts Review

CHECHNYA

fiction by ANTHONY MARRA

from NARRATIVE

After her sister, Natasha, died, Sonja began sleeping in the hospital. She returned home to wash her clothes a few days a month, but those days became fewer and fewer. No reason to return, no need to wash her clothes. She only wears hospital scrubs anyway.

She wakes on a cot in the trauma unit. She sleeps there intentionally, in anticipation of the next critical patient. Some days roused by the shuffle of footsteps, the cries of family members, she stands and a body takes her place on the cot and she works on resuscitation, knowing she is awake because she could dream nothing like this.

"A man is waiting here to see you," a nurse says. Sonja, still on the cot, rubs the weariness from her eyes.

"About what?"

The nurse hesitates. "He's right out here."

A minute later in the hallway the man introduces himself. "My name is Akhmed." He speaks Russian without an accent, but by now Sonja feels more comfortable conversing in Chechen. A short beard descends from Akhmed's face. For a moment she thinks he's a religious man, then remembers that most men have grown their beards out. Few have shaving cream, fewer have mirrors. The war has made the country's cheeks and chins devout.

He gestures to a small girl, no older than eight, standing beside him. "My wife and I cannot care for her," Akhmed says. "You must take her."

"This isn't an orphanage."

"There are no orphanages."

The request is not uncommon. The hospital receives humanitarian aid, has food and clean water. Most important, it tends to the injured regardless of ethnicity or military affiliation, making the hospital one of the few larger buildings left untargeted by either side in the war. Newly injured arrive each day, too many to care for. Sonja shakes her head. Too many dying; she cannot be expected to care for the living as well.

"Her father was taken by the rebels on Saturday. On Sunday the army came and took her mother."

Sonja looks at the wall calendar, as if a date could make sense of the times. "Today is Monday," she says.

Akhmed glowers. Sonja often sees defiance from rebels and occasionally from soldiers, but rarely from civilians.

"I can't," she says, but her voice falters, her justification failing.

"I was a medical student before the war," Akhmed says, switching to Chechen. "In my final year. I will work here until a home is found for the girl."

Sonja surveys the corridor: a handful of patients, no doctors. Those with money, with advanced degrees and the foresight to flee the country, have done so.

"Parents decide which of their children they can afford to feed on which days. No one will take this girl," Sonja says.

"Then I will keep working."

"Does she speak?" Sonja looks to the girl. "What's your name?"

"Havaa," Akhmed answers.

Six months earlier Sonja's sister, Natasha, was repatriated from Italy. When Sonja heard the knock and opened the door, she couldn't believe how healthy her sister looked. She hugged her sister, joked about the padding on her hips. Whatever horrors Natasha had experienced in the West, she'd put fat around her waist.

"I am home," Natasha said, holding the hug longer than Sonja thought necessary. They ate dinner before the sun went down, potatoes boiled over the furnace. The army had cut the electric lines four years earlier. They had never been repaired. Sonja showed her sister to the spare room by candlelight, gestured to the bed. "This is the place you sleep, Natasha."

They spent the week in a state of heightened civility. No prying questions. All talk was small. What Sonja noticed, she did not comment on. A bottle of Ribavirin antiviral pills on the bathroom sink.

Cigarette burns on Natasha's shoulders. Sonja worked on surgeries, and Natasha worked on sleeping. Sonja brought food home from the hospital, and Natasha ate it. Sonja started the fire in the morning, and Natasha slept. There were mornings, and there were nights. This is life, Sonja thought.

Akhmed is true to his word. Five minutes after Sonja accepts the girl, he is washed and suited in scrubs. Sonja takes him on a tour of the hospital. All but two wings are closed for lack of staff. She shows him the cardiology, internal medicine, and endocrinology wards. A layer of dust covers the floors, their footprints leaving a trail. Sonja thinks of the moon landing, how she saw the footage for the first time when she arrived in London.

"Where is everything?" Akhmed asks. Beds, sheets, hypodermics, disposable gowns, surgical tape, film dressing, thermometers, IV bags, forceps—any item of practical medical use is gone. Empty cabinets, open drawers, locked rooms, closed blinds, taped-over windowpanes, the stale air remain.

"The trauma and maternity wards. And we're struggling to keep them both open."

Akhmed runs his fingers through his beard. "Trauma, that's obvious. You have to keep trauma open. But maternity?"

Sonja's laugh rings down the empty hall. "I know. It's funny, isn't it? Everyone is either fucking or dying."

"No." Akhmed shakes his head, and Sonja wonders if he's offended by her profanity. "They are coming into the world, and they are leaving the world and it's happening here."

Sonja nods, wonders if Akhmed is religious after all.

Ten years earlier, on the morning of December 11, 1994, the day the Russian army crossed into Chechnya, Sonja woke in the London City College graduate dormitory. She ate a quick breakfast of instant coffee and a day-old scone, the latter by now her favorite British food. Gray clouds lined the horizon as she climbed the escalator at Holborn and walked across Lincoln's Inn Field to the Royal College of Surgeons. She attended a lecture by a nationally renowned neurosurgeon and took pride in her ability to follow the snaking sentences of foreign academia. Attached to the Royal College was a museum dedicated to the history of anatomy and pathology. After thanking the lecturer and pausing in the atrium for a cigarette, she walked through the mu-

218

seum's curious exhibitions. A display detailing the history of non-Egyptian mummification. An alcove dedicated entirely to the tibia. One room remained stuck in her memory, or her memory in it. The room exhibited a collection of the 1,474 skulls collected by nineteenth-century physician Joseph Barnard Davis. A fractured skull of a Roman woman found in the ruins of Pompeii. The skulls of five stillborns, each collapsed just above the temple. The skulls of nine Chinese pirates hanged in Ningpo. Aborigines from Tasmania. Congolese from Leopold's rubber mines. But the skull that Sonja remembered was that of a Bengali cannibal. Fully intact, the mandible still locked against the temporal, the twenty-two bones that constitute the human skull all accounted for. The eight bones forming the neurocranial brain case bathed in halogenated light. From the size of the plates, the prominence of certain supraorbital ridges and temporal lines, and overall size and solidity of the skull, Sonja could tell it belonged to a man. The skull looked no different from those of the Chinese pirates, the Tasmanian Aborigines. The nose and eyes, which once gave the man physical distinction, were dark cavities. She read the placard, written by a Victorian phrenologist. *There are no characteristics to distinguish the cranium of a cannibal from that of an ordinary man.*

Sonja shows Akhmed the new maternity ward, reconstructed in the oncology division after a stray shell leveled the original maternity ward five months earlier. A doctor and several nurses tend to two postpartum mothers. One holds her child, his head a bald bulb protruding from surgical gown swaddling. The other mother is unconscious. Her infant lies in an incubator, looking more like a crushed bird than a human.

"Poor nutrition in utero?" Akhmed asks.

"No nutrition in utero. In the past few years, we've had only a dozen women healthy enough to give birth to healthy children."

"And I imagine their husbands are not civilians."

It takes Akhmed more than two hours to reach the hamlet at the edge of the mountain. He rides a rusty three-speed, the gears whistling against the wind. A kilometer before every checkpoint, he hoists the bike frame over his shoulder and walks through the woods, circumnavigating the platoons of young Russian soldiers. It is as dark when he arrives home as it was sixteen hours earlier, when he left with Havaa.

His wife lies in bed, beads of perspiration stippling her forehead despite the cold. He kisses her cheek and empties the bedpan. She has only a few months left.

"Where were you?" she asks.

"Just checking the mail," he says in explanation of his absence.

"Oh, has my sister written?"

"No, not today."

In the kitchen Akhmed starts a fire in the wooden stove, brings a saucer of water to boil. He divides the cup of rationed rice into two uneven servings, the larger for his wife. She has difficulty sitting upright. Akhmed takes off his coat and folds it into a cushion for her head.

"Has anyone visited today?" he asks, knowing she wouldn't remember anyway.

"Oh, no," she says. "I've kept to myself."

"You're sure no one came by? Not Ramzan?" Before the war Akhmed spent Saturday afternoons playing chess with his neighbors Ramzan and Dokka, Havaa's father. Ramzan had been a trader, a middleman carrying goods from the city to the mountains. The gratuities he awarded himself from every shipment provided their Saturday afternoons with otherwise unaffordable luxuries. They ate and played chess in their hamlet at the edge of the mountain, far from the trail of tank treads. Then the war came, and Akhmed no longer trusted his neighbor. Ramzan peddled information now, a far more precious commodity than goat cheese and plum wine.

Akhmed waits for his wife to respond. The silence becomes an answer itself. He sits on the bed beside his wife and feeds her rice. For years they tried to have children, with no success. Akhmed believed their marriage to be cursed. As he brushes the crumbs from his wife's lips and pulls the blanket to her chin, he thinks of just how wrong he was.

After Akhmed leaves, Sonja returns to the waiting room. The girl sits on a folding chair, slouching against the metal back. Already Sonja has forgotten her name. She hands the girl a doll from the maternity ward. "What's this?" the girl asks.

"A doll."

The girl turns it over, not knowing what to do with it.

"Are you hungry? Eat this," Sonja says. She hands the girl an energy bar designed for marathon runners, a new addition to the humanitarian aid drops. The girl bends the bar, unsure what to do with it. "What is it?"

"Let's go to sleep." Sonja shows the girl to a cot in the trauma ward, then unfolds the sheets and spreads them across the mat. "Are you comfortable?" Sonja asks.

Lying across the cot, the girl shakes her head. "The pillow is lumpy."

Natasha slept for sixteen hours a day after returning from Italy. Sonja worried about her and didn't need a medical degree to know something was wrong. Natasha had been home for fourteen days and had spent ten of those asleep.

"You must do something, go somewhere," Sonja said at breakfast. They never discussed Natasha's time abroad.

"There is nothing to do, nowhere to go."

"Go for a walk, then."

"There's a war going on."

"There has always been a war. That shouldn't get in the way of daily exercise."

Sonja spent the day in surgery. Two children came in after stepping on a land mine. They didn't have legs, and they didn't survive the surgery.

Natasha's eyes were red when Sonja arrived home.

"Why are you crying?" she asked.

"I went for a walk and saw Sulim in the street. He looked at me and laughed."

Sonja slapped her sister across the face. How could she shed tears for the past? Natasha stopped crying and didn't seem surprised. As they ate in silence, the bruise on her cheek grew to a crimson swell.

A constellation of vital phenomena, Sonja thought. Tomorrow it would look worse, but Natasha would live. Sonja couldn't pity the living.

Before she went to bed she broke an icicle from the roof, crushed it in a plastic bag, and placed it outside her sister's door. Sonja knocked and before the door opened went back to her room.

Natasha never forgot the admiration with which her sister had spoken of the West. Natasha applied to the same universities as Sonja, but without Sonja's superior test scores. After completing secondary school, Natasha had a job bagging groceries, a steady boyfriend, Friday nights at the cinema or the dance club, Europop on the radio. Then came war and the siege of the city, five hundred thousand land mines, massacres in distant Russian schools and theaters. What remained was Natasha herself. When she had enough to eat, she was beautiful. Sonja may have once been the most promising medical student in all of Chechnya, but no one had ever turned to watch her as she walked down the street. Natasha reminded herself of this, used it to countervail her envy. Sonja was in London, and Natasha knew she wouldn't return. They hadn't spoken in years, not since the day in December 1994 when Sonja called home after the army crossed the border. The next day shelling severed the city's central telephone server, making transcontinental communication impossible. But Natasha tried not to think of her sister. Her ugly sister with her big brain. No one was paid per IQ point when buildings fell. The war made everything physical: survival, retaliation, even comfort. Avenues existed for women who could make themselves attractive without the benefit of a mirror or running water.

His name was Sulim. Two years above her at school and rumored to have a cousin in the *obshchina*, the Chechen mafia. He had compressed features, as if as a child he'd been hit in the face with a frying pan. She sat with him in a bar that served nothing. The owner was disappeared. The bar had no door, liquor, or employees, but the regulars still returned each afternoon. Their lips were blue from drinking windshield wiper fluid. The city had no electricity, no plumbing, no food, no cars. But there was no shortage of windshield wiper fluid.

"You want to get out. Who doesn't?" he said.

"I know I can be successful in the West."

Sulim pursed his lips. "Anyone can be successful when they are not dodging bullets." He pulled a plastic soda bottle from his jacket pocket and scanned the room before taking a quick sip. "Real vodka."

"I will work off the debt."

"Will you?"

"I know there are trafficking routes, ways of getting people from here to there."

Sulim shook his head. "Those are for pretty girls in poor countries, not pretty girls in war countries. It used to be that a woman who disappeared needed to reappear on the other side of the world to make money. Now, they just disappear. Reappearance has too high an overhead. Kidnapping, abduction, this is our national industry."

Natasha stood to leave. Money paled against the desire to simply leave this country. She didn't care if a pot of gold sat at the other side. She just wanted to get over the rainbow. "Wait," Sulim said. He paused to light a cigarette. At this stage in the war, Kazakh tobacco was considered a luxury. "You are a friend. We went to school together, no? Where do you want to go?"

"London," Natasha responded.

"Then in London you will be an au pair. Do you know what that is?" Natasha shook her head.

"It's a French word. It means you watch the children while the parents are at work."

"So I will be a grandmother?"

Sulim smiled. "Yes, something like a grandmother."

It was Sulim's smile, more than his words, that Natasha mistrusted. "I'm not my sister, but I'm not a fool."

"There may be other things. Dancing. Entertaining. Being, what's the word, enticing."

Natasha knew it meant prostitution. Some repatriated women called it slavery. Even if it's true, Natasha thought, so what? Does he think I am afraid of *it*?

"Okay," she said. "Make me au pair. Make me reappear."

An associate of Sulim's cousin transported Natasha with five other women to the Georgia border. From there they crossed the Black Sea, arriving to port sixty kilometers south of Odessa as local fishing trawlers caught the morning's breeze. Two of the women stayed with the Chechen handler. Natasha and the three others went with two Ukrainian men in a transport truck. The back door slammed shut. When it opened again, they were in Serbia. She spent the first night in a stone cellar with ten other women, half still girls, the youngest no older than twelve. "Where am I?" she asked the closest one. The woman responded in Bulgarian. Natasha had difficulty comprehending the distant Slavic tongue. "The breaking grounds," the woman said. Natasha didn't understand. What ground was to be broken? They were in a cellar, already underground. She looked at her dirty clothes, the soil rubbed against her palms, and understood. She was the ground.

When there's work to do, Sonja takes amphetamines to stave off sleep. There's always work to do. A man is carried in, a piece of shrapnel

223

lodged in his chest. He's dead before reaching the surgery table, but Sonja still treats the wound. She undresses him, pulling the shard of aluminum casing from between his ribs, then cleans and bandages the gash. The man's right elbow is calloused from hours spent lying on the ground, pointing a rifle. His chest and shoulder are bruised from the kickback. Sonja knows by the size and location of the bruises that this man was a sniper. A tumor protrudes from the man's thigh. Benign, a buildup of fatty tissue, but it's unsightly. She cuts out the lump, four stitches to close the incision.

"You must return in ten days so I can remove the stitches," Sonja says aloud. "If you see any pus, any sign of infection, you must return at once."

She examines the ankles, shakes powder on the toes to alleviate his athlete's foot. "You must wear sandals when you go to the *banya*. You must not wear other people's shoes. If you do, you risk becoming the victim of foot fungus."

She works her way back up the body, pausing at the torso to ask the man's weight, quizzing him on his diet. She cradles the man's cheeks between her palms and speaks to his deadened eyes. "There are no characteristics to distinguish the cranium of a cannibal from that of an ordinary man," she says. "But from the length of the supraorbital ridge, I can ascertain that you are most certainly an asshole."

Two hands on her shoulders gently pull her away from the corpse.

"Come," Akhmed says. His breath is warm against her neck, his flesh a few degrees warmer than the dead sniper's. "Rest for a moment."

Akhmed takes her to the waiting room, pushing her into a chair when she resists.

"You must rest," he commands.

"Don't tell me what to do. I'm not tired. You have worked here for three days. Who do you think you are?"

"I think I am someone who slept last night." He goes to the book closet, scans the disordered stack, and picks a thick volume. "Read this if you need help falling asleep," he says, handing her a medical dictionary.

Alone in the waiting room, Sonja lifts the dictionary. The binding creaks like rusty hinges as she opens the cover. The book closet is rarely opened, and she's surprised Akhmed even knows of its existence. Surgeons don't consult the medical textbooks. They learn their craft as a glasscutter learns his. Most lessons from medical school have

224

proven irrelevant. Lectures at the Royal College didn't cover car bombs.

Five months earlier, a stray shell fell on the old maternity ward. Fortunately, no expectant mothers or newborns were present, and only one person died. The water pipes burst, flooding the entire first floor. After the fire exits had all been opened to drain the water, a centimeter of water remained. A doctor slipped, dislocating his shoulder. Sonja directed a nurse to carpet the hallways with towels and then with paper when the towels ran out. "There is none," a nurse said.

"None?"

"None," the nurse replied.

Looking back, Sonja wonders if the nurse was in shock. Sonja wonders if she was in shock herself, because she thought nothing peculiar of the absence of paper in the hospital. "Then go to the textbook closet, tear out the pages."

"Which books?"

Sonja was exasperated but too tired for anger. "All of them. Wait," she called after the nurse. "Not the medical dictionary."

The medical dictionary was one of the few texts to survive the day intact. Sonja flips through it: the names of internal arteries, the average length of a human rib, the definition of a foot. Then halfway through the book, at the bottom of a page, there's a word followed by a one-sentence explanation. *Life: noun; a constellation of vital phenomena—organization, irritability, movement, growth, reproduction, adaptation.*

Sonja dozes off with the dictionary open on her lap. The sleep isn't real, isn't slumber, only a fitfulness exacerbated by the comedown from amphetamines. Dehydration, exhaustion, poor nutrition, a depletion of serotonin. She knows the symptoms but can't explain them in her dreams.

Sonja wakes up to an amphetamine hangover: headache, dry mouth, accelerated heart rate. She goes out for a smoke, pulling a white filtered Marlboro from the pack. She received a carton as largesse from a warlord's wife, whose child she delivered. A few deep inhalations, the carbon soaking into her capillaries. Cancer is not a concern. Akhmed walks out a few minutes later, his hands wrapped around a cup of tea.

"I overheard you on the satellite phone earlier," he says. "You were speaking English."

"A Scottish friend of mine. He said Chechnya was in the British news today." Sonja smiles. "Al-Qaeda has come to our mountains. Now the West pays attention."

"How is it you know someone from Scotland?"

"I went to medical school in London. I stayed for six years."

"In London." Akhmed seems impressed. "And you came back?"

Sonja nods. "I had left my sister here. She was sixteen when I left. I spoke to her on the day the army crossed the border but couldn't reach her after that. I didn't know if she was alive or dead. It was like she had been disappeared. But she hadn't. I was the one who had disappeared. So I came back."

"Family is a good thing, an important thing to come back to."

"She wasn't here when I returned."

"I'm sorry."

"She reappeared, eventually."

"She's one of the lucky ones."

"Was," Sonja corrects him.

An army convoy rumbles over the asphalt, personnel carriers and armored trucks. Ten minutes later an elderly woman passes down the street in the opposite direction. She pushes a cart of tin scraps, pausing every few meters to massage her wrists. Sonja lights another cigarette, gives it to Akhmed.

"Tolstoy once traveled here," Akhmed says. "He wrote a book about us."

"What did he have to say?"

Akhmed shrugs. "I don't know. I never read it."

"I don't even think about it ending."

Akhmed shrugs again. "When Tolstoy came to the Caucasus, the war was already fifty years old."

"It won't end."

"Let me tell you a story," Akhmed says, flourishing his cigarette like a baton. "It is more beautiful than anything Tolstoy ever wrote because it is true. It is a story about an imam and a mosque."

When Akhmed reaches home, Ramzan is waiting.

"Good evening, friend," he says as Akhmed chains his bicycle to a tree trunk. "It is tragic what happened to Dokka."

Akhmed nods.

"First Dokka, then his wife. And I'm told that even Havaa has disappeared?"

226

War did not change Ramzan, Akhmed notices. It merely changed what he traded.

"By soldiers or insurgents?" Akhmed asks.

"Neither. She's been disappeared by someone else entirely." Ramzan studies Akhmed, without pretense of friendship. "Though I hear both are eager to speak with her."

"Why? She's only a girl."

"Who knows." Ramzan shrugs. "Perhaps she saw something, heard something, or they just think she did. It doesn't matter why."

Ramzan muses, pulls a Marlboro from his pocket, and lights it against the wind. "I heard you walked out of town with her the other morning."

"I don't know where she is."

"Don't be stupid," Ramzan warns, but Akhmed is already walking away. He locks the door behind him and goes to the bedroom. He kisses his wife on the cheek, and she stirs but sleeps on. From his coat pocket he takes a hypodermic syringe and a bottle of morphine, stolen from the hospital trauma unit, and places them under the bed.

The morning after Sonja hit her sister, she made excessive noise while brewing tea. She banged pots into each other, dropped one pan then another. She wanted to make sure Natasha was awake before she knocked.

"Natasha," Sonja called quietly through the cracked door. "You must wake up."

Natasha's face had swollen overnight, a patch of deep purple stitched to her cheekbone. She didn't meet Sonja's eyes.

"You must come to the hospital," Sonja said. "There is a little open wound by your eye, and this flat has enough dust to infect a paper cut."

"I am not afraid of dust."

"You should be."

Natasha glared. For a moment Sonja worried Natasha would invoke the past. The brothels, the pimps, the beatings. And to be struck by her own sister. Was Sonja no better? She dismissed the question as soon as she asked it. There was no question. She returned from London, leaving a second-year residency, a Scottish fiancé, and a land unbroken by war. She left that all to return to her sister. And why? She dismissed the question. Because blood is thicker than water, and guilt is thickest of all.

"Fine," Natasha said. "Let's go."

At the hospital Sonja dressed the wound with antiseptic ointment. She softly rubbed the cream across the flesh, blowing it dry. That was her apology. A few patients waited for treatment, but nothing urgent. A case of the common cold. A sprained ankle. Sonja had heard no gunfire, no explosions all morning. It was a good day. She decided to take Natasha on a brief tour of the hospital. They walked through the ghost wards, the empty hallways and deserted laboratories. "This was once one of the foremost oncology departments in the entire USSR," Sonja said as they passed through rooms stripped of all purpose and function. "Party officials from as far away as Vladivostok came for treatment." They paused at a hulking MRI machine. "It is a shame we can't use this, but it requires too much electricity. Our generator would shut off, or at least shut off the lights, if we tried to scan." The tour ended at the maternity ward. A woman had given birth the previous night. Her child was born with a collapsed lung, but the doctor on call acted quickly and the child lived. The mother held the infant to her breast. She beamed as Natasha and Sonja approached.

"She will live," the mother said, shaking her head with disbelief. She looked at Natasha, taking her for a nurse. "I'm so glad you are here."

Natasha glanced at Sonja. "I am just walking through."

"Nonsense," the mother said. "You save lives."

Natasha smiled. The baby finished suckling and looked upward.

"Do you want to hold her?" the mother asked.

"No."

"Nonsense," the mother said. "Of course you want to hold her."

"I must go, but you stay here," Sonja whispered as Natasha took the infant in her arms. "There is a common cold in need of my urgent attention."

After she was broken, the handlers sold Natasha to a brothel just outside Kosovo, which catered to the UN peacekeeping forces stationed nearby. *Breaking*—the hypodermic of heroin, the gang rape, the auction block.

A month passed, and an Albanian purchased her with three others, took them south through the cinder-block city of Tirana, then across the Adriatic by speedboat. Natasha's passport traveled with her, but never in her possession. It was her deed, carried by whoever owed her. She was sold three more times, but certain things remained constant. Each morning she was injected with heroin. By afternoon she was itching. By evening she was willing to perform as required to ensure a shot later that night. She knew: she would be killed if she fled, she would be arrested if she went to the police, she would be found by Sulim's cousin if she went home. She did not know where she was, what language was spoken, where to get money, how to get her passport back, how to get home.

It felt like autumn, but maybe it was spring. She once saw ancient ruins, great stone pillars, walls without roofs. Days passed without distinction. Time was marked not by minutes but by men. Eight one night, eleven the next. Each felt like a porcupine between her legs. Men from Rome, Naples, and Palermo. Men from Scotland, Luxembourg, and Germany. American men. Australian men. They called her Natasha, and she didn't understand how they knew her name. Then another woman told her: *That's what any girl from Eastern Europe is called. We're all Natashas.* An average day consisted of ten men, three cheeseburgers, four glasses of tap water, and two shots. A toothbrush, no toothpaste. Weeks without tasting fresh air. The repatriated women had been right. Modern-day slavery, but there was nothing modern about it. The days passed, but they were all nights. The fifteenth floor of an apartment high-rise, locked doors and windows. Eight Natashas in total. Four bunk beds crammed into the bedroom. Fucked on a king-sized bed, falling asleep on a lower bunk. One Natasha died. Seven Natashas left. A new Natasha arrived to fill in the eighth bunk. They were all interchangeable. All replaceable and all disposable. The pimp was Russian, said his brother had lost his legs in the siege of Grozny. The belt around the bicep, the two taps on the syringe, the blood pulled into the barrel, the push of the plunger, the moment of peace. The threat of being beaten with electrical wires. The meals from Burger King and KFC, the slices of pizza. The junkie dreams crowding into daylight.

Three women fight over a loaf of bread found lying on the street. Before any of them can reach the loaf, they are clawing at each other's hair, drawing blood and screaming imprecations. One of the women slips through, sprinting to the bread. She lifts the loaf, triggering the land mine beneath it. She loses her arms and dies of blood loss on the way to the hospital. The two other women still bring her in.

"It's like they think we are magicians," Sonja tells Akhmed. They share a cigarette in the evening air.

"Medical miracles are the only miracles most of us will ever see." He strokes his beard as he speaks, a nervous tic that gives him the appearance of a man in great thought and trouble.

"Did you have the beard between the wars?"

Akhmed shakes his head.

Darkness shrouds the distant rubble, the fields where buildings once stood. The hospital generator produces the only electricity for miles, and the two doctors stand in the island of floodlight. Sonja looks at her fingers. Calluses, bitten nails. She blushes and drops them, but Akhmed catches her hands in his own.

"These belong to a lumberjack," he laughs. "Big, strong woodsman hands."

His hands are warm. She doesn't know what the morning will bring.

His hands move to her forearms. He has a delicate touch, a surgeon's sensitivity and patience.

"I keep thinking in Latin," she says. "The names of bones. Radius. Ulna."

"This is your arm," Akhmed says. "This is your shoulder." He touches her chin, her cheeks. "And lips," he says and leans to her. "Our lips."

A moment and she pulls away. She understands transgressions of the flesh. A kiss, a falling embrace, these are not transgressions. Akhmed has a wife, but touch that does not cause pain is a small violation.

Later that night when Sonja returns to the waiting room the girl says, "You disappeared."

"But I came back."

They eat energy bars, drink lukewarm tea. The girl has developed a taste for the chocolate flavor. Sonja wipes the crumbs from the girl's cheeks, tells her to brush her teeth. They go to the trauma ward to sleep. All but one hospital cot is still wet with the blood of the day. Sonja pulls the curtain around the cot, and the girl doesn't see what surrounds her.

"We must share a bed tonight, okay?"

The girl nods, takes off her shoes, and climbs in. The sheets feel clean against Sonja's skin. The girl wraps her arms around Sonja's neck.

"I forgot your name," Sonja says, not a question but a point of fact.

"I'm Havaa."

"Havaa. That name is nice." They lie together on the cot, Sonja's breaths shallower than the girl's. She thinks of Akhmed.

"I want to go home."

"A home is nothing more than the place you sleep."

This quiets the girl for a moment. Then she speaks again. "I'm not tired. Tell me a story."

Sonja yawns, tries to think of a story that will give the girl pleasant dreams.

"This is a story of an imam and a mosque," she begins.

Ramzan again approaches Akhmed as he chains his bicycle to the tree trunk. Again he questions Akhmed, and again Akhmed claims ignorance.

Ramzan shakes his head. "You disappoint me, friend. I know you took the girl away. You're a doctor, think logically. You have a sick wife to think about. Your silence is reckless."

"I don't have anything to tell you."

"We're in the wilderness," Ramzan says, patting the trunk with his gloved hand. "A wilderness without Moses, without prophets or angels to guide us. We are a forest at the edge of the earth. But you don't see this. You only see this particular tree."

"A forest is what," asks Akhmed, "if not a collection of particular trees?"

Later that night Akhmed lies awake beside his wife as the wind carries the murmur of approaching trucks. He's fully dressed. He's prepared. When the trucks pull up to his house, he has already loaded the syringe with enough morphine to stop the heart of a healthy man. Some men are cannibals and some are angels, he thinks, but most are merely men. His wife remains asleep, unaware of any reality beyond her dreams. He takes the time to disinfect her forearm before piercing the skin. A sigh as the drug hits her bloodstream, her eyelids flashing open, her heart rate slowing to silence. The men outside pound on the front door, but the sound of fists on wood reveals neither ethnicity nor allegiance. Akhmed puts a small bandage on the pulseless vein, then draws his palm across her face, closing her eyes. The pounding against the door grows louder as the men outside switch from fists to feet. There's innocence in the world, Akhmed believes, and it is possessed not only by the young and naive. When the men break through the door, Akhmed is on his knees. He prays for his wife, that Allah may welcome her in paradise. He prays for Havaa, that she might live to have a natural death. But when the men start beating him, when they throw him into the back of the waiting truck, Akhmed prays only for himself.

Natasha went with Sonja to the hospital each morning. She worked in the maternity ward. The head of pediatrics gladly put her to work. She fed newborns and disinfected instruments. She scrubbed bedpans, washed sheets. When a birth coincided with a bombing, the nurses all rushed to the trauma ward, and Natasha alone assisted the doctor with the delivery. She slept less and began keeping the same schedule as Sonja. During downtime, Sonja dropped by the maternity ward and always found Natasha busy. She could not sit still, could not not be working. When she completed everything asked of her, she asked to do more. Sonja didn't know if Natasha could bear children, if she could ever again let a man touch her. But she could do this, Sonja thought, peeking through the door as Natasha hushed a newborn to sleep. The infant in her arms would learn to live in this world, and so too would Natasha. Sonja believed this, and she shut the door and returned to the trauma ward.

Two days later Sonja was smoking a cigarette outside when a shell crashed into the hospital's east wing. A whistle in the afternoon air, then the detonation. She ran inside as others ran out. The ceiling fixtures went dark. Blue light flashing from fire alarms. No fires, only water spreading across the floor. She ran. She slipped and fell. She ran. Nurses wheeled the bedridden into the hallways, toward the emergency exits. The hopeless cases were left to die. A passing doctor grabbed Sonja by the collar, tried to drag her with him. "We're under attack," he cried. She shook him off and kept running. She ran against the water, against the bewildered infirm.

In the maternity ward she stumbled over the rubble. Water pipes had turned to cataracts. Cotton ball islands and sheet gauze archipelagoes floated across the flood. Daylight fell through the open walls. Sonja dropped to her knees. She felt through the water. A piece of brick. Broken cinder. When she had returned from London, she did everything she could; she met with officers in both army and insurgency; she asked in Russian and Chechen *where is* and *do you know* and *how can I.*

232

Later, Sonja stands over her sister's body in the trauma ward. On Natasha's cheek a hint of bruising remains.

The Italian vice police shut down the brothel, arresting everyone who spoke Russian, as if a common language made them complicit. Natasha spent a week in jail on prostitution and indecency charges before being transferred to a clinic specializing in victims of human trafficking.

The woman psychiatrist sat behind a desk and spoke Russian in a lilting Italian accent. Her syllables seemed in danger of fluttering away. The questions she asked sounded simple but could not be answered.

"What happened?"

"How did you get here?"

"Are you okay?"

Natasha tried to respond but kept stumbling over her words.

"It's fine. Everything is fine," the Italian woman said. "Just start at the beginning."

"The beginning?" Natasha laughed. There was no beginning. "My sister won a scholarship to study in London, and everyone was so fucking proud of her."

Within two months Natasha had finished her program of methadone maintenance treatment. She still took Ribavirin antiviral, still needed it for another thirty-six weeks to wipe out the hepatitis-C. She hadn't opened the envelope containing the results of the HIV test. Her request for refugee status was denied. The only refugees from the conflict given amnesty had names like Nurbiika, Nurishat, and Nazha, not Natasha. She was ethnic Russian, and even though she had never been north of the Chechen border, though the land shelled by the Red Army belonged to her as much as Nurbiika, Nurishat, and Nazha, she was not the war's refugee. The psychiatrist said she would speak with the immigration officials and would give a strong recommendation for amnesty, but in the end all she could secure for Natasha was a six-month supply of Ribavirin.

On the way to the airport, Natasha clutched her passport. She didn't let go of it when asked by the customs official. Her arm stretched across the kiosk, her fingers pinching the corner of the passport as the official stamped and scanned the document. She had no luggage. The planes looked like big metal birds. Graceful creatures incapable of harm. She had never been on a plane, never seen a plane that did not drop bombs.

A voice came over the intercom in a language she didn't understand. The cabin doors shut and the plane taxied to the runway, the hum of the turbines going to a growl. The landscape smeared across the window, then liftoff. She watched the ground. The plane gained altitude, and the men on the streets below shrank to pinpricks, then they were gone altogether. She exhaled. The earth fell away. She was free.

On Friday Sonja spends the day in surgery and doesn't see Akhmed. She has only one surgery on Saturday, none on Sunday, but she does not see him. On Monday she asks one of the nurses.

"I heard he disappeared, was disappeared." the nurse says. "Three men came to his house on Thursday night."

Sonja nods and turns away. She does not need to hear the rest, whether the three men were soldiers or insurgents, what they wanted, what they would do.

That evening Sonja sees the girl curled up on the sofa. Sonja holds her palm to the girl's forehead, her index and middle fingers to the girl's wrist.

"Am I sick?" the girl asks.

"No. You are in perfect health." And after she says the words, it seems like a small miracle. A person with perfect health, a body physically capable of living. "I have an idea," Sonja says. "You said that pillow is lumpy, didn't you?"

The girl nods.

An hour later they are walking to Sonja's flat. Block after block, the only change is the location of craters, the dispersion of brick. Sonja tries to remember what the street used to look like. She gives up after a block. This is what it is. Scorch marks fanned out across the concrete. Clouds gathered on the horizon. Her hand. The girl's hand. This is what it is.

Sonja unlocks the door. "I have not been here in a few months," she says.

They eat dinner before the sun goes down, potatoes boiled over the furnace. Later, Sonja shows the girl down the hall by candlelight. She opens the door to Natasha's room and gestures to the bed. "This is where you sleep."

A story circulated throughout the city during the war. Somewhere in the city center, a mosque remained standing. No one knew with certainty the name of the mosque, the name of the street or neighborhood. The siege had remapped the city, obliterating all prior designations. Months of continual shelling had leveled the rest of the block, but the mosque remained standing. Ruins all around. But still standing, four untouched spires and a turquoise dome. Each morning the imam stood at the entrance and sang the call to prayer. Some said the hand of God shielded the mosque. Sonja knew the story was apocryphal, but even after the city's last mosque collapsed, she continued to tell it.

Nominated by Narrative

THE DARK RIDES

by CHASE TWICHELL

from NEW ENGLAND REVIEW

The girl who likes to get high
wonders if her flower will ever unfurl,
or will there be a tight not-fully-formed
green part that chars before blooming?
Can something pinch an infant bud
so there's a missing branch forever?

Dark attractions was another
name for the dark rides:
the Gold Mine with candy wrappers
stapled to a fence for the loot,
the Black Swans "love tunnel,"
where couples whimpered
and squealed. In her underworld,
just below this one, not an inch away,
there's always a Midway strung
with garish lights, and a small paddock
of saddled ponies circling nose to tail.

To explain her own childhood, she studies
the childhood of the girl who was eventually
returned to her family unharmed,
though her bad luck dates from that time,
as well as the illusion of looking through glass.
There are lessons she's learned and unlearned

ten thousand times, caught in the drag
of one pole or another, the need to know
the wordless truth of what she is,
and the equally fierce and endless denials,
the pure-hearted questions answered by lies,
the prayers subsumed by smoke or thinned
to nothing in the fumes of alcohol.
She longs to know whatever it is
she keeps herself from knowing. Or rather,
the knowledge comes to her but she loses it
again among the small herd of centaurs
she keeps on her desk, of which only one
is female—bronze, late nineteenth century,
grapevine crown, anatomy explicit (though tiny).
The horse's maneless neck becomes
the maiden's torso, the two bodies one.
You have to fuck the horse to fuck the girl.

Nominated by Joan Murray

REMEMBERING
SAMUEL BECKETT

by BARNEY ROSSET

from CONJUNCTIONS

Sylvia Beach wrote to me in New York, asking for an appointment. For many years she had been the famous proprietor of Shakespeare and Company, the leading and legendary English-language bookstore in Paris. She had been the close friend and publisher of James Joyce. She had also known Sam Beckett for many years. During our meeting she spoke about Beckett in the warmest terms as a writer of great importance whose day would surely come.

Sylvia Beach's words sounded a magical note.

When I had read Beckett's pieces in *Transition Workshop*, edited by Eugene Jolas in Paris, I was still a student at the New School. Jolas had Beckett listed under the category of "paramyths." Other writers listed in the same genre included Kay Boyle, Ernest Hemingway, James Joyce, Franz Kafka, Katherine Anne Porter, Gertrude Stein, and Dylan Thomas. And of course there was also Henry Miller, represented by pieces from *The Cosmological Eye* and *Tropic of Cancer*—the very books I had written a term paper about as a freshman at Swarthmore College in 1940–41.

One day in 1953, I saw a small item in, I believe, *The New York Times*. It told of the opening in Paris on January 5th of that year of a play by Samuel Beckett. It was called *Waiting for Godot*. I somehow got a copy of *Godot*—it had only been published in French, the language in which Beckett had written it—and read it. My immediate response was, here was a kind of human insight that I had never experienced before. I wanted to publish it. I set about finding Beckett's New York agent, Marian Saunders, and made one of the earliest Grove Press contracts. The contract itself was with Beckett's French publisher, Éditions de Minuit, the first of many I was to sign with them. It called for an advance of $1,000 against royalties, which might become due not only on *Godot* but also on Sam's novels, *Molloy*, *Malone Dies*, and *The Unnamable*.

About this time, after I had read *Godot*, I asked Wallace Fowlie, a specialist in French literature who had been one of my professors as well as my friend at the New School, to give me his opinion of it. I believed him to be a far more conservative reader than I. But he more than confirmed what Sylvia Beach had said to me and what I myself had concluded. He said, "Beckett will come to be known as one of the greatest writers of the twentieth century."

I had the same sort of feeling about two more "French" writers we contracted for in that same year: Eugène Ionesco and Jean Genet.

*　*　*

June 18, 1953
New York

Dear Mr. Beckett,

It is about time that I write a letter to you—now that agents, publishers, friends, etc., have all acted as go-betweens. A copy of our Grove Press catalogue has already been mailed to you, so you will be able to see what kind of a publisher you have been latched onto. I hope that you won't be too disappointed.

We are very happy to have the contract back from Minuit, and believe me, we will do what we can to make your work known in this country.

For me, the first order of the day would appear to be the translation. I have just sent off a letter to *Merlin* editor Alex Trocchi telling him that the difficulties did not seem as ominous from here as they evidently do from there, to him at least.

If you would accept my first choice as translator the whole thing would be easily settled. That choice of course, being you. That already apparently is a satisfactory solution insofar as the play is concerned.

As for translation of the novels, I am waiting first, to hear

239

from you, what you advise, and whether or not you will tackle them yourself. If your decision is no, and I do hope that it won't be, we can discuss between us the likely people to do it.

Sylvia Beach is certainly the one you must blame for your future appearance on the Grove Press list. After she talked of you in beautiful words I immediately decided that what Grove Press needed most in the world was Samuel Beckett. I told her that, and then she suggested that I make a specific offer. I certainly had not thought of that up to the very moment she took out a piece of paper and pencil and prepared to write down the terms.

A second person was also very important—Wallace Fowlie. At my request he read the play and the two novels with great care, and came back with the urgent plea for me to take on your work. Fowlie is also on our list. His new translation of Rimbaud's *Illuminations*, and a long study of them, is just now coming out. This would seem to be an already indecently long letter, so I will close. If you would give me your own address we might be able to communicate directly in the future.

Sincerely,
Barney Rosset

∗ ∗ ∗

June 25, 1953
Paris

Dear Mr. Rosset,

Thank you for your letter of June 18. Above my private address, confidentially. For serious matters write to me here, for business to Lindon, Ed. de Minuit, please.

Re: translations. I shall send you to-day or to-morrow my first version of *Godot*.

This translation has been rushed, but I do not think the final version will differ from it very much. With regard to the novels my position is that I should greatly prefer not to undertake the job myself, while having the right to revise whatever translation is made. But I know from experience how much more difficult it is to revise a bad translation than to do the thing oneself. I translated myself some years ago two very brief fragments for Georges Duthuit's *Transition*. If I can get hold of the number in which they appeared I shall send it to you.

With regard to my work in general I hope you realize what you are letting yourself in for. I do not mean the heart of the matter, which is unlikely to disturb anybody, but certain obscenities of form which may not have struck you in French as they will in English, and which frankly (it is better you should know this before we get going) I am not at all disposed to mitigate. I do not of course realize what is possible in America from this point of view and what is not. Certainly as far as I know such passages, faithfully translated, would not be tolerated in England.

Sylvia Beach said very nice things about the Grove Press and that you might be over here in the late summer. I hope you will.

Thanking you for taking this chance with my work and wishing us a fair wind, I am

Yours sincerely,
Samuel Beckett

* * *

July 13, 1953
New York

Dear Mr. Beckett,

It was nice to receive your letter of June 25 and then your letter of July 5.

First I must tell you that I have not received your translation of *Godot*. I am most anxious to see it. I would like to plan on publication of the play for 1954, either in the first or second half of the year, depending entirely upon completion date of the translation. I would think the ideal thing would be to coincide publication with performance, but that is ideal only and I would not think it wise to indefinitely postpone publication while waiting for the performance.

As to the translation of the novels, I am naturally disappointed to hear that you prefer not to undertake translation yourself. I can well see your point, however, and it would seem a little sad to attempt to take off that much time to go back over your own books but I hope that you will change your mind.

As to the obscenities within the books, my suggestion is that we do not worry about that until it becomes necessary. Sometimes things like that have a way of solving themselves.

I do hope you locate a copy of *Transition* with the fragments translated by yourself.

I do plan on going to Europe in the fall, and I will certainly look forward to meeting you then.

Yours sincerely,
Barney Rosset

✿ ✿ ✿

July 18, 1953
Paris 15me

Dear Mr. Rosset,

In raising the question of the obscenities I simply wished to make it clear from the outset that the only modifications of them that I am prepared to accept are of a kind with those which hold for the text as a whole, i.e. made necessary by the change from one language to another. The problem therefore is no more complicated than this: Are you prepared to print the result? I am convinced you will agree with me that a clear understanding on this matter before we set to work is equally indispensable for you, the translator and myself.

Herewith *Transition* with my translation of fragments from *Molloy* and *Malone*.

Yours sincerely,
Samuel Beckett

✿ ✿ ✿

July 31, 1953
New York

Dear Mr. Beckett,

Your translation of *Godot* did finally arrive. I like it very much, and it seems to me that you have done a fine job. The long speech by Lucky is particularly good and the whole play reads extremely well.

If I were to make any criticism it would be that one can tell that the translation was done by a person more used to "English" speech than American. Thus the use of words such as "bloody"—and a few others—might lead an audience to think the play was originally done by an Englishman in English. This is a small point, but in a few places a neutralization of the speech away from the specifically English flavor might have the result of enhancing the French origins for an American reader. Beyond that technical point I have little to say, excepting that I am now extremely desirous of seeing the play on a stage—in any language.

I read the fragments by you in *Transition*, and again I must say that I liked them very much, leading to the continuance of my belief that you would be the best possible translator for the novels. I really do not see how anybody else can get the sound quality, to name one thing, but I am willing to be convinced.

By all means, the translation should be done with only those modifications required by the change from one language to another. If an insurmountable obstacle is to appear, let it first appear.

I will look forward to hearing about progress towards a translation.

Yours sincerely,
Barney Rosset

❊   ❊   ❊

August 4, 1953
New York

Dear Mr. Beckett,

I am putting aside *Watt*, which I received this morning, to write this letter. Fifty pages poured over me and I will inundate myself again as soon as possible. After the sample of *Godot* went back to you, the first part of *Molloy* arrived and I was most favorably impressed with it. I remember Bowles's story in the second issue of *Merlin* and it does seem that he has a real sympathy for your writing. If you feel satisfied, and find it convenient to work with him, then my opinion would be to tell you to go ahead. Short of your doing the work yourself the best would be to be able to really guide someone else along—and that situation you seem to have found.

Again a mention of words. Those such as "skivvy" and "cutty" are unknown here, and when used they give the writing a most definite British stamp. That is perfectly all right if it is the effect you desire. If you are desirous of a little more vagueness as to where the scene is set it would be better to use substitutes which are of common usage both here and in Britain.

I am happy to be reading *Watt* and I hope to see more of *Molloy* soon.

With best regards,
Barney Rosset

o   o   o

September 1, 1953
Paris 15me

Dear Mr. Rosset,

Thank you for your letters of August 4th and July 31st both received yesterday only.

It is good news that my translation of *Godot* meets with your approval. It was done in great haste to facilitate the negotiations of Mr. Oram and I do not myself regard it as very satisfactory. But I have not yet had the courage to revise it.

I understand your point about the Anglicisms and shall be glad to consider whatever suggestions you have to make in this connection. But the problem involved here is a far-reaching one. Bowles's text as revised by me is bound to be quite un-American in rhythm and atmosphere and the mere substitution here and there of the American for the English term is hardly likely to improve matters, on the contrary. We can of course avoid those words which are incomprehensible to the American reader, such as "skivvy" and "cutty," and it will be a help to have them pointed out to us. In *Godot* I tried to retain the French atmosphere as much as possible and you may have noticed the use of English and

American place-names is confined to Lucky whose own name might seem to justify them.

Yours sincerely,
Samuel Beckett

✧ ✧ ✧

Shortly after this exchange of letters, my wife Loly and I went to Paris for the first of many meetings with Sam Beckett. Loly and I were married at New York City Hall on September 15, 1953, and the next day we embarked for Europe on the small but elegant French liner *Le Flandre*. I was seasick before we got out of New York Harbor.

Our first meeting took place at the bar of the Pont Royale Hotel on Rue Montalembert, almost next door to France's largest literary publisher, Gallimard. Beckett came in, tall, trench coated, and taciturn, on his way to another appointment. He said he had only time for one quick one. "He arrived late," Loly remembered. "He looked most uncomfortable and never said a word except that he had to leave soon. I was pained by his shyness, which matched Barney's, and, in desperation, I told him how much I had enjoyed reading *Godot*. At that, we clicked, and he became warm and fun."

The other appointment forgotten, the three of us went to dinner and to various bars, ending up at Sam's old hangout, La Coupole, on Boulevard Montparnasse at three in the morning, with Beckett ordering champagne.

✧ ✧ ✧

14/12/Paris
15me
(1953)

Dear Barney and Loly,

Sorry for the no to design you seem to like. It was good of you to consult me. Don't think of me as a nietman. The idea is all right. But I think the variety of symbols is a bad mistake. They make a hideous column and destroy the cohesion of the page. And I don't like the suggestion and the attempt to express it of a hierarchy of characters. A la rigueur, if you wish, simple capitals, E. for Estragon, V. for Vladimir, etc., since no confusion is possible, and perhaps no heavier in type than those of the text. But I prefer the full name. Their repetition, even when corresponding speech amounts to no more than a syllable, has its function in the sense that it reinforces the repetitive text. The symbols are variety and the whole affair is monotony. Another possibility is to set the names in the middle of the page and text beneath, thus:

ESTRAGON
I'd rather he'd dance, it'd be more fun.
POZZO
Not necessarily.
ESTRAGON
Wouldn't it, Didi, be more fun?
VLADIMIR
I'd like well to hear him think.
ESTRAGON
Perhaps he could dance first and think afterwards,
if it isn't too much to ask him.

But personally I prefer the Minuit composition. The same is used by Gallimard for Adamov's theatre (1st vol. just out). But if you prefer the simple capitals it will be all right with me. Could you not possibly postpone setting of galleys until 1st week in January, by which time you will have received the definitive text? I have made a fair number of changes, particularly in Lucky's tirade, and a lot of correcting would be avoided if you could delay things for a few weeks.

The tour of Babylone *Godot* mostly in Germany (including the Grundgens theatre in Düsseldorf), but also as far as the Milan Piccolo, seems to have been successful. Marvellous photos, unposed, much superior to the French, were taken in Krefeld during actual performance. One in particular is fantastic (end of Act 1, Vladimir drawing Estragon towards wings, with moon and tree). It is the play and would make a remarkable cover for your book. I shall call at the theatre this afternoon before posting this and add address of photographer in case you are interested in purchasing the set.

Best wishes for Xmas and the New Year,
Sam

246

That was the same Beckett who a year later would write me: "It's hard to go on with everything loathed and repudiated as soon as formulated, and in the act of formulation, and before formulation . . . I'm horribly tired and stupefied, but not yet tired and stupefied enough. To write is impossible, but not yet impossible enough."

It was the same lovely, courtly Beckett who had written:

ESTRAGON: I can't go on.
VLADIMIR: That's what you think.

The problem of who was going to translate *Godot* into English was a thorny one. Perhaps when Beckett wrote in French, no one looked over his shoulder, and he could achieve a more dispassionate purity. Perhaps he was also angry at the British for failing him as publishers. His novel *Murphy* and a short-story collection, *More Pricks Than Kicks*, had achieved little notice in England. Perhaps Beckett felt he was too lyrical in English. He was always striving to take away as many of his writer's tools as possible before having to cease writing—taking away tools as you'd take away a shovel from a person who wants to dig.

Beckett had never been truly satisfied with any of his English translators, and I constantly tried to persuade him to do the translation job himself. I think he always wanted to go back to writing in English, which he did, mostly, from then on. But I felt he needed to be encouraged. Sam finally came to the only possible conclusion. He did the translation of *Godot* himself. The novels trailed behind.

"It's so nice where we are—snowed-in, quiet, and sootless, that I think you might like it," I wrote my new author in January 1954 from our East Hampton bunkerlike Quonset-hut home. The letter concerned the page proofs of *Waiting for Godot*, the work that would change the course of modern theater.

Our correspondence, formal at first, warmed quickly. Sometimes Beckett typed, at my rather brash request, and sometimes letters were written in his almost indecipherable script. "You know, Barney, I think my writing days are over," Beckett wrote in 1954. And later: "I'm sick of all this old vomit and despair more and more of even being able to puke again. . . . Perhaps I can feel a little bit of what you are going through." In a world where writers switch publishers at the first shake of a martini pitcher, our transatlantic communications seemed to float on a sea of tranquility and trust.

Grove published *Waiting for Godot* in 1954 and Genet's *The Maids* and *Deathwatch* as well.

* * *

Suzanne Deschevaux-Dumesnil, who finally became Sam's wife in 1961, had been his strongest supporter for many years. She was his manager and practical organizer, tending to his every need, protecting him from the world, and vigorously promoting his career. Tall, handsome, and austere, she was even more reclusive than he, never, as far as I know, learning English, and walling herself off from his friends. I remembered her making an attempt to study English at Berlitz when we first met, but it seemed to go against her grain, and I never actually heard her speak anything but French.

During the German occupation of Paris, Sam and Suzanne, who were part of the Resistance and were in danger of arrest by the Gestapo, went to the South of France and hid out on an isolated farm near Roussillon, in the Vaucluse, to which Beckett specifically refers in *Godot* as well as mentioning one of the local farmers by name. There in the Vaucluse the emptiness and monotony of the days stretched on until it must have seemed like an eternity to Beckett.

For three years in the Vaucluse, Beckett and Suzanne were mostly alone, and I get the feeling of their being bored with each other, and not knowing how to pass the time, and wondering what they were doing there and when the hell they were going to get out, and not wanting ever to see each other again, and yet not being able to leave one another. The heart of *Godot* must be inextricably intertwined with all of this. In one exchange between the protagonists Estragon has gone off and is beaten up. Upon his return there is this exchange:

VLADIMIR: You again! . . . Come here till embrace you . . . Where did you spend the night?

ESTRAGON: Don't touch me! Don't question me! Don't speak to me! Stay with me!

VLADIMIR: Did I ever leave you?

ESTRAGON: You let me go.

While Beckett clearly indicates an all-male cast for *Godot*, and refused permission to two top American actresses, Estelle Parsons and Shelley Winters, to perform it in 1969, writing Ms. Parsons that "theater sex is not interchangeable," I believe he'd taken that very real situation—he and Suzanne on a farm, waiting—and converted it into an eternal predicament, a universal myth. I thought the latent sexuality became much clearer in the New York 1988 Lincoln Center production of *Godot* with Robin Williams as Estragon and Steve Martin as Vladimir. They pushed forward the male/female sides of their characters.

Beckett's life with Suzanne seemed to have had the despairing yet persevering, separate yet joined quality of many of his other plays as well. In *Endgame*:

HAMM: Why do you stay with me?

CLOV: Why do you keep me?

HAMM: There's no one else.

CLOV: There's nowhere else.

Beckett was extremely precise about his stage directions, including the look and size of the sets, and I believe that the configuration of his and Suzanne's two Paris apartments reflected their deepening impasse as graphically as did his instructions for the settings of his plays.

Their first apartment, at 6 Rue des Favorites, was in a fairly lively neighborhood. It was a tiny duplex, two small rooms, one above the other, the lower one sparsely furnished with just enough chairs for a few people to sit down, and a couple of paintings. It had a claustrophobic feeling, but at least it was close to friendly restaurants and bars once you got outside. I never saw the upstairs bedroom, but cannot imagine it to have been particularly sybaritic. When Sam and Suzanne fled Paris to escape from the Nazis, the latter did them an accidental favor. Their apartment was locked up and left that way so that after the war they were able to reoccupy it without anything having been changed.

One night when they still lived there, Sam and I spent an evening together. I was driving and I remember that the dawn was just coming up as we got to Rue Fremicourt. Then something happened. All the streetlights went out. It was not because dawn was breaking. An electricity strike had just started. In Paris, at least at that time, you got into your house by pushing a button, on the outside, to get your door to open. Without this *minuterie* functioning you could not get in or even warn somebody inside that you were there.

So Sam and I drove to my hotel, Le Pont Royal. There the front door was open but the elevator was not working. We trudged up seven floors to my isolated room at the top, briefly looked at the sun rising over Paris, and then climbed into bed, a nice big double one. Now I could say that I had been to bed with Samuel Beckett.

When Sam and Suzanne moved, it was to an even more appropriate setting for Beckett. It was right across from the Santé prison, with a view down into the exercise yard. Sam had a deep identification with prisoners, so this flat was made to order. The neighborhood, near the outskirts of Paris where the Metro emerges from the underground to run down the middle of Boulevard St. Jacques (he lived at No. 38), was grim, impersonal, as bleak as any Beckett setting. It's hard to find a place like that in Paris, a *banlieu* where there are hardly any bars or restaurants or little shops or people in the streets. The building in which Beckett lived had several floors, a cramped entryway, and the usual tiny French elevator. On his landing, small in itself, were two doors leading to two separate apartments. To reach Sam's, you turned right, and he let you in. To the left you would find Suzanne. There were two rooms in Sam's part, a small study with a lot of books and papers very neatly arranged, and a bedroom with a skinny cot and an ordinary bureau. Then there was a narrow little kitchen placed horizontally in the rear. It was rather like a corridor that connected the two apartments from the rear. So the living spaces were connected but you could close them off, with doors placed at each end of the kitchen. Her friends could come and go to her place, and his friends could visit his place, but they didn't have to see one another if they didn't feel like it. It was a unique, chilly arrangement, and I never saw Suzanne again after the move. Of course, that might have been because I fell asleep at the Paris opening of *Endgame* sitting beside her. I'd just flown in from New York and was half dead of jet lag—I heard she never forgave me for that. Later I understand that she became ill, and increasingly difficult and withdrawn, and perhaps saw no one. Sam and she were in Tunisia, the land of her birth, when it was announced that he had won the Nobel Prize in Literature.

Beckett had at least one close woman friend I know of during this lifetime with Suzanne. She was an English woman, Barbara Bray, a translator who had worked for the BBC in London. Previously married, with two children, Barbara was nearly thirty years younger than Beckett. She moved to France in the early 1950s, and has lived there ever since. She was very attractive, slim, dark haired, as I remember, and pretty in an English way. She was extremely intelligent and quite similar to Beckett: laid-back, and concerned with accuracy in translation. She was very close to him, and she may well have been one of the strongest attachments during the period I knew him. I remember several instances when he and I had been out drinking and it was late, but not so late for us—only about three in the morning. I'd offer to walk him home, and he would say something like: "No, I'm going to stop by and see Barbara."

During this period Beckett continued to live with Suzanne. When he finally married her in Folkestone, England, in 1961, he was fifty-four, she sixty-one.

Barbara's close friendship with Beckett continued. I remember one evening in particular in 1965 when Harold Pinter was in Paris for the opening of the French production of his plays *The Collection* and *The Lover*. Barbara, Harold, Sam, my girlfriend at the time, Nicole Tessier, and I were at a bar right off Boulevard Montparnasse where Beckett liked to go. It was called the Falstaff and featured beer. To me, except for the name, it was as French as anyplace else.

We occupied a narrow table that butted up against a wall, Barbara and Harold seated opposite each other, then Sam and my girlfriend next to each other, with me at the end. I began to notice that Barbara and Harold were discussing Sam, very admiringly, but sort of as if he were a sacred object they were having an academic chat about, not involving him in the conversation at all. I could see that he was getting increasingly irritated, and finally Sam took his stein and banged it on the table hard enough to spill some beer. Then he got up and walked across the room in the ungainly gait he had before his cataract operation, which gave people the impression that he was drunk when he was just having difficulty seeing. I watched him slowly climb the narrow stairs to the men's room and disappear. A hush fell over our table. Then he reappeared and seemed to be making his way back to us when he stopped about twenty feet away and sat down at another table with two people whom I slowly realized were total strangers to him. He stared at us for a few minutes, then rejoined us without comment or excuse. That was one of his rare shows of anger. Perhaps a touch of jealousy could enter the head of even a great psychoanalyst.

Similar moments of passion appear here and there in the emotional texture of Beckett's work, sudden oases of piercingly romantic fulfillment and loss in which the prose becomes suffused with sensuality and then with tears. I felt this most in *Krapp's Last Tape*, my favorite Beckett play, a monologue written in English in 1958. In it, a ruined old man plays and replays tapes from his younger days, trying to find some meaning in his life. One passage is excruciatingly passionate. The affair between Krapp and his lover has now been destroyed beyond retrieval.

> *We drifted in among the flags and stuck. The way they went down, sighing, before the stem!* (Pause.) *I lay down across her with my face in her breasts and my hand on her. We lay there without moving. But under us all moved, and moved us, gently, up and down, and from side to side.*
>
> *Then:* . . . *Scalded the eyes out of me reading Effie again, a page a day, with tears again. Effie* . . . (Pause.) *Could have been happy with her, up there on the Baltic, and the pines, and the dunes.*
>
> *Then the previous tape is replayed.*

Led to it by Beckett, I searched for the nineteenth-century German novelist Theodor Fontane's *Effi Briest* for clues to this passage. Finally Beckett revealed to me that it related to a summer with his cousin Peggy Sinclair in 1929 at a small resort on the Baltic Sea, where Peggy was engrossed in Fontane's novel about a young girl's calamitous life that ended with her death from tuberculosis. Although Beckett was only twenty-three at the time, his feeling for Peggy Sinclair, and the memory of their being together, survived her engagement to another man and her death in 1933, ironically also of tuberculosis.

The story struck an incredibly strong chord in me. It reopened my suffering of the loss of a young love, my Nancy Ashenhurst. I still grieve for Nancy, and have dreams about her. This bond of early bereavement led me to find other references to Peggy Sinclair in Beckett's later works, particularly in *Ohio Impromptu*, a short play of extraordinary lyricism that was published by Grove in 1981 in a collection called *Rockaby*. In *Ohio Impromptu* the protagonist seeks relief from the memory of "the dear face" by moving to an unfamiliar place, "back to where nothing ever shared." However, there is no relief until a man sent by "the dear name" comes to comfort him by reading and rereading "a sad tale from a worn volume." Finally the messenger says he has had word from "the dear name" that he (the messenger) shall not come again:

> So the sad tale, they stayed on as though turned to stone . . .
> what thoughts who knows. Thoughts, no, not thoughts. Pro-
> founds of mind. Buried in who knows what profounds of
> mind.

Beckett often sat "as though turned to stone" during his long silences. I remember him "buried in who knows what *profounds* of mind."

His friendship with Barbara Bray, I think, may well have given inspiration for a short, extremely bitter 1963 work called *Play* in which a husband, wife, and mistress, encased up to their necks in urns, are trapped in an eternal triangle, condemned endlessly to repeat the details of the husband and mistress's affair under the glare of a harsh, inquisitorial spotlight.

Shortly after completing *Play*, which Alan Schneider directed at the Cherry Lane Theatre in Greenwich Village, Beckett made his only trip to the United States. It was in the summer of 1964, and he came to be here for the shooting in New York of his motion picture *Film*, which I had commissioned him to write.

* * *

In 1962 I had started a new unit to produce films outside of Grove Press—called Evergreen Productions—but with Grove people, specifically Fred Jordan and Dick Seaver, and one outsider who was by then a close friend, Alan Schneider, whom I had come to know because of Sam Beckett.

Very ambitiously, I made a list of writers—with the help of my associates—whom we asked to write scripts for us to produce. Those writers were, first and foremost, Samuel Beckett, as well as Harold Pinter, Eugène Ionesco, Marguerite Duras, and Alain Robbe-Grillet. They all said yes to our request and all of them wrote their scripts. Duras and Robbe-Grillet both wrote full-length scenarios for us. We envisaged the Beckett, Ionesco, and Pinter scripts as constituting a trilogy.

These five were all Grove Press authors. I invited three more authors to contribute. Another Grove author, Jean Genet, was asked. Fred Jordan and I went to London to make the request, but he said no. (Strangely, years later we bought the rights and became the U.S. distributor of the one film he wrote and directed himself—a wonderful silent black-and-white film, *Un Chant d'Amour.*)

The last two authors we asked to write scripts for us (they were not Grove Press authors) were Ingeborg Bachmann and Günter Grass. I trailed Bachmann to Zurich (I think) to get her no, and I went to Berlin to see Grass. He lived in what I recall as being a sort of bombed-out area, in a precarious, small building. You reached its second floor if he wanted you to, via a ladder that he extended down to you in lieu of a staircase. Grass was completely charming and friendly, but the outcome was the same as with Bachmann.

Out of the five scripts we did get, we were able only to produce Samuel Beckett's *Film.*

I set out to create a production team to turn Beckett's script into a motion picture. The most important member of that team was Sam himself. He wrote, he guided, and he kept the ship afloat. Alan Schneider had had no previous film experience but had done a great deal of successful theater directing, including plays by Pinter, Albee, and especially Beckett. There was no doubt in my mind that we could overcome that problem. The other top two people on the team were Sidney Meyers and Boris Kaufman.

Sidney Meyers was an acclaimed veteran filmmaker. In 1960 he had been awarded the Flaherty Documentary Award for *Savage Eye* (which he shared with Joseph Strick and Ben Maddow). Haskell Wexler and Helen Levitt were the cinematographers. Meyers was nominated for both the Venice Film Festival Golden Lion Award in 1949 and for an Academy Award for *The Quiet One* in 1950.

He was also a consummate musician, a self-effacing, literate, and intelligent man, and he got along beautifully with Sam. And, not incidentally, he had helped me in a very important and selfless way at the end of the production work on an earlier film project of mine, *Strange Victory.*

And then there was Boris Kaufman. He was the brother of the famous Soviet directors Dziga Vertov and Mikhail Kaufman. Also, unbeknownst to me, he had won the Academy Award in 1954 for *On the Waterfront.* But it was very important for me that he was the cinematographer on Jean Vigo's great films *L'Atalante* (1934), *Zéro de*

Conduite (1933), and À *Propos de Nice* (1930). These were perhaps my favorite films above all others. The filmmaker I had felt most akin to was Vigo.

Amos Vogel, in his book *Film as a Subversive Art*, said about Vigo's *Zéro de Conduite*: "In this anarchist masterpiece—a poetic, surreal portrayal of revolt in a boys' school—Vigo also summarizes the suffocating atmosphere of French petty bourgeoisie life, seen, as the rest of the film, through a child's eyes: the *pater familias* who never emerges from his papers, the kitsch décor, the girl, her underwear showing: though the hero is blindfolded, we know he sees it all."

Our crew was now complete.

Judith Schmidt, my invaluable assistant, retyped the script after conferences held and audiotaped in East Hampton. We had brought Beckett to stay there when he first arrived from Paris. He arrived at night at the little East Hampton airport. It was a very dramatic landing—they had thrown on some searchlights and it all reminded me of *Casablanca*. Several days later, we went back to New York City to shoot *Film*.

Alan Schneider had suggested Buster Keaton for the lead role in *Film* and Sam liked the idea. So Alan flew out to Hollywood to attempt to sign up Buster. There he found the great silent star living in extremely modest circumstances. On arrival, Alan had to wait in a separate room while Keaton finished up an imaginary (perhaps drunk) poker game with, among others, the legendary but long-dead Hollywood moguls Louis B. Mayer and Irving Thalberg. Keaton took the job. He would die a year and half after completing the shooting of *Film*.

Sometime after *Film* was finished and being shown, Kenneth Brownlow, a Keaton/Chaplin scholar, interviewed Beckett about working with Keaton. Beckett had said, "Buster Keaton was inaccessible. He had a poker mind as well as a poker face. I doubt if he ever read the text—I don't think he approved of it or liked it. But he agreed to do it and he was very competent. He was not our first choice. It was Schneider's idea to use Keaton, who was available. . . . He had great endurance, he was very tough, and, yes, reliable. And when you saw that face at the end—oh." He smiled. "At last."

When Brownlow asked Beckett if he had ever told Keaton what the film was about, Sam said:

> I never did, no. I had very little to do with him. He sat in his dressing room, playing cards . . . until he was needed. The

only time he came alive was when he described what happened when they were making films in the old days. That was very enjoyable. I remember him saying that they started with a beginning and an end and improvised the rest as they went along. Of course, he tried to suggest gags of his own. . . . His movement was excellent—covering up the mirror, putting out the animals—all that was very well done. To cover the mirror, he took his big coat off and he asked me what he was wearing underneath. I hadn't thought of that. I said, "The same coat." He liked that. The only gag he approved of was the scene where he tries to get rid of the animals—he puts out the cat and the dog comes back, and he puts out the dog and the cat comes back—that was really the only scene he enjoyed doing.

Brownlow asked Sam what the film meant, what it was about, and he replied, "It's about a man trying to escape from perception of all kinds—from all perceivers, even divine perceivers. There is a picture which he pulls down. But he can't escape from self-perception. It is an idea from Bishop Berkeley, the Irish philosopher and idealist. 'To be is to be perceived'—*'Esse est percipi.'* The man who desires to cease to be must cease to be perceived. If being is being perceived, to cease being is to cease to be perceived."

Beckett went on to say that distinguishing between the modes of being perceived was a major technical roadblock: "There was one big problem we couldn't solve—the two perceptions—the extraneous perception and his own acute perception. The eye that follows sees him and his own hazy, reluctant perception of various objects. Boris Kaufman devised a way of distinguishing between them. The extraneous perception was all right, but we didn't solve his own. He tried to use a filter—his view being hazy and ill defined. This worked at a certain distance but for close-ups it was no good. Otherwise it was a good job."

Besides the problem of capturing the two perceptions there was another technical problem. It was when we attempted to use "deep focus" in the film. Originally, *Film* was meant to run nearly thirty minutes. Eight of those minutes were to have been used in one very long shot in which a number of actors would make their only appearance. The shot was based on a technique developed by Samuel Goldwyn and his great cameraman Greg Toland to achieve deep focus. A little later it was used to stunning effect by Orson Welles, with Toland as cameraman, in *Citizen Kane*. Even when panning their camera, deep focus allowed objects from as close as a few feet to as far as several hundred feet to be seen in the same shot with equal clarity. Toland's work was so important to Welles that he gave his cameraman equal billing. Sad to say, our deep focus work in *Film* was unsuccessful. Despite the abundant expertise of our group, the extremely difficult shot was ruined by a stroboscopic effect that caused the images to jump around.

We went on without that shot. Beckett averted this incipient disaster by removing the scene from the script.

In his book *Entrances* Alan Schneider says, "Sidney [Meyers] proceeded to do a very quick, very rough cut for Sam to look at before taking off for Paris. And that first cut turned out to be not far off from what we finally used. The editing was painstaking—and painful, Sidney always gently trying to break the mold we had set in the shooting, and Sam and I in our different ways always gently holding him to it. There was no question of sparring over who had the legal first cut or final cut or whatever. We talked, argued, tried various ways, from Moviola to screen and back again, to make it come out as much the film that Sam had first envisioned as we could."

In New York, Sam and Alan stayed with me and my new wife, Cristina, in our house on Houston Street in Greenwich Village. When the shooting stopped, all Beckett wanted to do was get back to France as soon as possible so we booked an early morning flight, set our alarm, and I promised to wake him at 7:30 a.m. in time to get to the airport. At 9:00 a.m. Cristina and I woke up, horrified to find that we had overslept, and we were appalled to stumble over Beckett sitting outside our bedroom door, wearing his overcoat even though it was July. He had his packed bag on the floor next to him and was sound asleep. It never occurred to him to knock on our door. I made another airline reservation for 5:00 p.m., and the three of us spent the day at the New York World's Fair in Flushing Meadows, wandering among the exhibits. We somehow managed to lose our homesick writer along the way. After a frantic search we found him, on a bench, sound asleep again. We revived him enough for him to buy two knitted Greek purses—one for Cristina and one for Suzanne—whereupon we escorted him to an air-conditioned bar at what was then Idlewild Airport for drinks until departure time. "This is somehow not the right country for me," Sam said at the bar. "The people are too

257

strange." Then he said, "God bless," got on the plane, and was gone, never to return again.

❋ ❋ ❋

Once Sam was back in Paris, things went on as before—I continued to visit him there. Since both he and I had been deeply involved in school athletic competition, I as co-captain of my high school football team and Beckett the leader of his school cricket squad, we found a common ground in sports. I tried my hand at Beckett's favorite pastimes, chess and billiards, but found them too maddeningly demanding of precision. Beckett, for his part, enjoyed playing my more slapdash table tennis. As a spectator sport we settled on tennis, which we both had once played, and now we often attended matches at Roland Garros stadium outside Paris. I remember one time in particular, a match between the great American Pancho Gonzales and Lew Hoad, the Australian champion of the time. The referee was a Basque and an admirer of Beckett's. As he mounted his tall chair courtside, he waved enthusiastically at Sam. A couple of sets later, before a booing crowd, the referee was ejected at Gonzales's request after making a number of quite legitimate calls against him. He paused to chat for a moment in the midst of his forced exit.

Usually, however, Sam the writer and I the publisher just went out eating and drinking and talking. Beckett always had very set ideas about where to go and what to eat. At first his tastes were quite broad, but as the years went by they narrowed down, exactly like his writing, and the choices got fewer and fewer. In the beginning Beckett favored the Closerie des Lilas on Boulevard Montparnasse, where Hemingway had liked to go, and where names of famous writers were embossed on the tables. There was also the grandiose La Coupole, a small bar called Rosebud, and the allegedly English pub Falstaff. But especially congenial was a seafood brasserie in a tough, nightlife neighborhood nearby called Ile des Marquises where *le patron* revered Beckett and had a photograph of him on the wall along with huge glossies of Marcel Cerdan (the Algerian boxer and world middleweight champion killed in a transatlantic crash), the great American boxer Sugar Ray Robinson, and other assorted personalities. Beckett's photo was between the two fighters.

One New Year's Eve, probably in the early seventies, Cristina, her mother, and our children—my daughter, Tansey, and son, Beckett, a namesake—were in Paris with me. Beckett was vacationing in Morocco with Suzanne. That night the phone rang in our hotel room. It was Matthew Josephson, the famed Hollywood agent, calling to say he was representing Steve McQueen, who desperately wanted to make a film of *Waiting for Godot*. Money was no object, Beckett could have complete control and any other actors he chose: Laurence Olivier, Peter O'Toole, and Marlon Brando—who was then about to do *Apocalypse Now*—were mentioned. After I ascertained that the agent was very much for real, and that the top price for a film property seemed to be $500,000, then a princely sum, I wrote to him and stipulated that amount. Josephson replied that the offer was $350,000, and it was absolutely firm and put in writing. The matter was dropped until I saw Beckett again on St. Patrick's Day for dinner at the Ile des Marquises. Anxious to secure some money for Sam, I told him of the offer for the proposed film, playing up Steve McQueen and, for some reason, Brando. Beckett asked what this McQueen looked like and I, grasping at straws, summoned up an image of James Garner. "He's a tall, husky, good-looking guy," I winged it. And Marlon Brando? "Even bigger, a huge, heavy-set fellow." Sam thought for a while and then said, "No. It will never work. My characters are shadows."

Near the end, Beckett refused to go to his old haunts, and it all narrowed down to an ersatz bistro called Le Petit Café in a monstrosity of a new hotel near his apartment. Originally the hotel was called the PLM, later changed to Pullman St. Jacques. It had a garish, undersized, Vegas-like marquee, and I thought of its lobby as resembling a souped-up railway station at rush hour with busloads of German and Japanese tourists swarming up and down its long escalators. All it needed was a bank of slot machines. Visiting athletes were also a specialty, and I remember the Scottish rugby team, brawny men in tams and kilts, all drunk as lords, horsing around in the lobby to the astonishment of a tour group of early-teenage Japanese girls. I also recall a boxing ring being set up in the lobby, and a loudspeaker announcing: "Will the Australian trampoline team please report to the fourth floor." Beckett stayed oblivious to it, totally out of place and impassive in the midst of all this international action.

I, after intricate maneuvering, brought Beckett and photographer Richard Avedon together in April 1979 at Le Petit Café, in one of the most awkward and enigmatic encounters of my life. The celebrated photographer said his technique of using a white sheet as a backdrop was philosophically derived from Beckett. He also said to me that he'd shot everybody he wanted to with the exception of Greta Garbo and

259

Beckett. I made arrangements for Avedon and Beckett to meet, stressing to Avedon that there was no guarantee Beckett would actually agree to pose and it would not be an easy task to convince him.

Avedon came from Tokyo and I from New York with my fourth wife, Lisa, Tansey, and my son, Beckett, now ten years old. Sam Beckett was his usual self, silent but listening. Lisa and my kids did the same, while Avedon, who seemed nervous, talked nonstop for about an hour until finally he said: "OK, let's take the pictures." He asked Samuel Beckett and my Beckett to go with him, and the three of them crossed the street and, for about half an hour, disappeared into a passageway through the Metro overpass. When they returned, nobody described what had happened, but I assumed the pictures had been taken.

I heard nothing further for a couple of months until one day I received two superb, very moving photos of my son with Samuel Beckett, beautifully mounted and framed and signed by Avedon. About a month later Sam himself, who had never before shown the slightest interest in such matters, asked what had happened to the photos. I wrote Avedon and received what I thought was a very peculiar response to the effect that Avedon had not taken any pictures of Samuel Beckett alone that day because the writer had seemed "unhappy," but that, because I had gone to so much trouble, he had taken a few shots of the two Becketts together.

My son, Beckett, said that after crossing under the Metro overpass they'd come to a wall where a white sheet had been tacked up and an assistant waited for them in a car. There was a large camera fastened to a tripod. He described Avedon setting up the shot, then focusing his camera with a black cloth over his head, then stepping out and squeezing the bulb a few times for the two Becketts and then for Sam Beckett alone. The missing Beckett photos supposedly appeared in the French magazine *Egoiste*. I have never seen them, but a portrait of Sam alone was in Avedon's retrospective at the Metropolitan Museum of Art in New York in 2005.

o   o   o

A later, thornier encounter at Le Petit Café involved Beckett and Peter Getty, son of the famously wealthy Ann Getty, who, with Lord Weidenfeld, had bought Grove from me in 1985. After Getty and Weidenfeld promised to keep me as CEO, they ousted me without ceremony the following year. Smart and young, Peter Getty, who often borrowed subway fare from Grove employees to get uptown to his

Fifth Avenue apartment, had learned I was meeting Beckett in Paris soon after my ouster, and asked to be introduced. I agreed, and Getty flew over, checked into a suite at the Ritz, and taxied out to Beckett's unlikely hangout, Le Petit Café, with a book he wanted autographed.

This was the only time Sam was not friendly to someone I introduced him to. It was a short, tense meeting. After autographing the book, he glared at Peter and asked: "How could you do this to Barney, and what do you plan to do about it?" Peter was very embarrassed, and mumbled something about consulting with his mother. Later, I heard that Beckett had told another suppliant from Grove, "You will get no more blood out of this stone," and he never allowed them to publish anything new of his again.

To me and a group of others assembled in his honor at La Coupole he said, "There is only one thing an author can do for his publisher and that is write something for him." And he did exactly that. It was the little book called *Stirrings Still*. It was to be his last prose work, and he dedicated it to me.

Stirrings Still is the meditations of an old man contemplating death. It brought back to me an ether dream I had had as a little boy. I had an out-of-body experience, seeing myself as an object rocketing into space, zooming through a black void until I was transformed into a "knob of blackness." I knew I was experiencing the terror of my own death. Still, now, unable to sleep in a totally darkened room, I am hounded by that dream. When he wrote *Stirrings Still*, I don't know how much Sam was actually thinking of me, but I think I know why he wrote it. He was facing his own dream of death, which was fast approaching, and which, possibly, he finally made bearable by acceptance of that approaching darkness.

> Such and much more such the hubbub in his mind so-called till nothing left from deep within but only ever fainter oh to end. No matter how no matter where. Time and grief and self so-called. Oh all to end.

*   *   *

Beckett's health was clearly failing, although I couldn't admit this to myself. We now met exclusively at Le Petit Café, which had become his "club," and where he was totally ignored by outsiders. I took to actually staying at the Pullman St. Jacques, the hotel where the café was located, in order to be near him, and sometimes I ate meals alone in the fast-food café off the hotel's lobby. At breakfast they gave you a set of plastic-coated photographs, not unlike a deck of cards. One card had an egg on it, another card two eggs, another card a strip of bacon, and so on. To order, you went to the cashier and handed her the cards you'd selected. In a funny way, it was pure Beckett. They'd done away with the menu entirely, eliminating the need for words or translations of words; you could choose a meal in total silence. In the same vein, Beckett had made increasing use of the stage directions "pause" and "silence" in his work, and had pared down his vocabulary to fewer and fewer words.

At some point, Sam began having dizzy spells and falling in his apartment; apparently not enough blood was circulating to his brain. After brief stays in several hospitals he was moved to a nursing home only a few blocks from where he lived. The desire to go on had lessened even more. He was unsteady on his feet and even thinner, if that were possible, and therefore seemed taller and more and more like a figure done by his friend Alberto Giacometti, who had given Sam a drawing of a thin, striding man. Sam gave it to Cristina and me as a wedding present, and we later used it on the cover of a reprint of Sam's novel *Molloy*. Now he was just a ghost of even that drawing.

The nursing home was on a side street, and looked like the other small buildings on the block with only a discreet plaque announcing its institutional function. You entered a sparsely furnished sitting room in which a number of old women, some with walkers, watched a couple of ancient TV sets. Then you went through a little dining room out into a tiny courtyard with a walkway and some grass. There were a few rooms looking out onto it. Beckett was in the first room, a cubicle with space enough only for a bed, a table, and two wooden chairs, with a small bath off it.

I visited Sam there a number of times. I found it cell-like and depressing and, along with his British publisher, John Calder, tried to devise ways to move him to more comfortable quarters. But it wasn't easy to do Beckett a favor.

He also seemed to resist attempts to make his life more pleasant, in his perverse fashion managing to get a phone on which he could not make overseas calls, declining to have a TV set or stereo equipment (although he loved music) or a bookcase or even a typewriter. He wrote things down in a little notebook in his small, intricate handwriting, kept his engagement records meticulously, and he did always seem to have a bottle of Irish whiskey handy.

With Beckett it was a mistake to suppose that problems readily lent themselves to solutions, or that one thing necessarily led to another. Sam had started to go for walks, and sort of boasted to me—if you could ever say that about Beckett—that he could walk farther than where his own apartment was, five blocks away. One day he had told me he needed some papers from his apartment, so I asked why he didn't go home and pick them up and I would go with him. Beckett threw up his hands. First roadblock: There was too much traffic on his boulevard; it made him dizzy. Well, let's go in a car, I said, pressing on. Beckett replied that he didn't have a car. Not to worry, I said, I'll get the car. Let's drive there. I was greeted with stony silence, and that was the end of that.

Perhaps a major factor was that Suzanne was still at the apartment and Beckett was ambivalent about the idea of seeing her. It was such an archetypical Beckett situation. It was *Endgame* again. Now they were Nagg and Nell in their garbage cans, unable to reach each other. She was ill, dying actually, although I didn't know that, and he was ill. They were separated by only five blocks, yet they couldn't see each other. He needed papers from his apartment, yet he couldn't go there—all the entrances and exits were blocked.

The last time I visited Beckett I brought along an American TV set I had kept in Paris just for possible use with Sam, and a videotape of *Godot* being performed by the inmates of San Quentin Prison. I had previously carted all this heavy equipment—the set, a transformer, and a VCR—in a huge shopping bag through customs to the Pullman St. Jacques, where Beckett used to actually come to my room. Now I lugged it all to the nursing home.

Sam was visibly moved by the tape; the inmates had understood his play. So I thought, now I've got something going that he can enjoy in this arid place—we can have a correspondence utilizing videotapes. As I left, I casually asked Beckett if he would store the set for future viewings. "Oh no, no, no," Sam answered, "I have no use for it." And the subject was closed.

As I struggled out with my shopping bag, he said: "Oh, Barney, that's too heavy for you. You shouldn't carry that." Then he walked over, lifted it, turned to me, and said, "No, it's all right. You can." Again: You can't go on, you'll go on.

It was clear that the prospect of the introduction of ease or entertainment into his life distracted Beckett from the larger endgame already embarked on in his mind. A few months later he was *Not I*, as in the title of one of his plays. There was, at last, an *Act Without Words*.

Sam died on December 22, 1989. He was buried next to Suzanne, who had died six months earlier, in the famous Cimetière du Montparnasse.

I was told that Barbara Bray was one of the few mourners at the secretive funeral. I received a letter from her that began:

Dear Barney,
What can I say? We are all huddled together in our loss.

Nominated by Conjunctions

A SLIP OF PAPER

by LOUISE GLÜCK

from THE THREEPENNY REVIEW

Today I went to the doctor—
the doctor said I was dying,
not in those words, but when I said it
she didn't deny it—

What have you done to your body, her silence says.
We gave it to you and look what you did to it,
how you abused it.
I'm not talking only of cigarettes, she says,
but also of poor diet, of drink.

She's a young woman; the stiff white coat disguises her body.
Her hair's pulled back, the little female wisps
suppressed by a dark band. She's not at ease here,

behind her desk, with her diploma over her head,
reading a list of numbers in columns,
some flagged for her attention.
Her spine's straight also, showing no feeling.

No one taught me how to care for my body.
You grow up watched by your mother or grandmother.
Once you're free of them, your wife takes over, but she's nervous,
she doesn't go too far. So this body I have,

that the doctor blames me for—it's always been supervised by women,
and let me tell you, they left a lot out.

The doctor looks at me—
between us, a stack of books and folders.
Except for us, the clinic's empty.

There's a trap-door here, and through that door,
the country of the dead. And the living push you through,
they want you there first, ahead of them.

The doctor knows this. She has her books,
I have my cigarettes. Finally
she writes something on a slip of paper.
This will help your blood pressure, she says.

And I pocket it, a sign to go.
And once I'm outside, I tear it up, like a ticket to the other world.

She was crazy to come here,
a place where she knows no one.
She's alone; she has no wedding ring.
She goes home alone, to her place outside the village.
And she has her one glass of wine a day,
her dinner that isn't a dinner.

And she takes off that white coat:
between that coat and her body,
there's just a thin layer of cotton.
And at some point, that comes off too.

To get born, your body makes a pact with death,
and from that moment, all it tries to do is cheat—

You get into bed alone. Maybe you sleep, maybe you never wake up.
But for a long time you hear every sound.
It's a night like any summer night; the dark never comes.

Nominated by Threepenny Review

MR. TALL

fiction by TONY EARLEY

from THE SOUTHERN REVIEW

On the first Saturday in January 1931, when she was sixteen years old, Plutina Scroggs married Charlie Shires in her father's house beside the railroad track in Dillsboro, North Carolina. That morning she bathed her mother and wrestled her into a white nightgown trimmed with lace, bought specially for the occasion. (A stroke had rendered Mrs. Scroggs mute, bedridden, and, so far as anyone could tell, senseless as a pillow when Plutina was eleven years old.) Both her older sister Henrietta and her father believed Plutina to be betraying them—not necessarily by marrying Charlie Shires but by moving away from Dillsboro, leaving them shorthanded with an invalid to care for—and quietly but pointedly made their displeasure known. Her father refused to speak to Charlie that morning and despite the bitter weather sat alone on the front porch without a coat until the preacher called him in for the ceremony. At the last minute Henrietta decided that their mother couldn't be left alone for the fifteen minutes it would take Charlie and Plutina to say their vows and eat a piece of cake and chose instead to sit at Mrs. Scrogg's bedside, melodramatically stroking her hand.

Before Plutina left she went into her parents' bedroom and kissed her mother, but not Henrietta, good-bye. Plutina's thoughtless relegation of Henrietta to a life of servitude (Henrietta's view) and Henrietta's unforgivably bad manners on the happiest day of Plutina's life (Plutina's version) provided yeast for the grievances and recriminations and snits that would intermittently bubble up between the sisters for the better part of the next seventy years.

As Charlie and Plutina were leaving the house, Plutina heard the window of the front room slide open a crack. Out of sight behind the winter curtains Henrietta began to wail. Her father looked at Plutina and said, "I hope you're happy."

"I am," Plutina said, perhaps a little more haughtily than she would have liked, considering the solemn nature of the occasion. At that moment her most troubling secret was that she loved her father more than she loved Charlie Shires.

To Charlie, her father said, "All sales are final, son. Don't try bringing her back."

Charlie nodded curtly and said, "Don't come looking for her, neither." Then he picked up her suitcase and they made their way along the duckboards down the muddy street to the train station.

Plutina's father worked for the railroad as a switchman, and she had grown up riding the train (as far as Asheville to the east and Murphy to the west) but she had never before ridden it as a married woman. Charlie took off his coat and placed it between them so that they could hold hands underneath it. She was too embarrassed to look at him for very long at a time, so she put on her glasses and stared out the window at the river and the muddy fields and the houses and barns tucked up against the gray mountains. Each time the train passed a farmstead, she thought with some degree of wonder, Married people live in that house, and married people live in that house, and married people live in *that* house. She felt as if she had been granted admission into some benevolent secret society to which almost everyone belonged but of which hardly anyone ever spoke.

The flag wasn't out at Whittier so the train didn't stop until Bryson City, where it took on coal and water for the run up to Topton. Plutina had never thought much of Bryson City as a town (as a native of Jackson County she patriotically preferred Sylva, which in her opinion had the nicer courthouse), but when she stepped off of the train the shop windows of the town seemed brighter, its sidewalks more crowded, the errands of its inhabitants more urgent than any place she had ever been, including Asheville. A taxicab honked at them when they tried to cross the street. Charlie pointed at a brick hotel with a revolving door and grinned and jabbed her in the ribs with his elbow. She shook her head because she honestly didn't know what he meant. (And when he said, "If the train was going to be here awhile me and you could check in," she still didn't know what he meant.) He led her instead to a noisy diner filled with men who kept their hats on inside, where the two of them sat at the counter beneath a blue cloud of cigarette smoke and splurged on lunches of egg salad sandwiches and fried potatoes and Coca-Cola floats, a meal that Plutina would cite to the end of her days as the best one she ever put in her mouth.

They didn't talk much going through the gorge, but then nobody else in the car did, either. Something about the gorge always made people hush. To Plutina's eye the cleft between the mountains west of Bryson had never looked wide enough to contain both the railroad and the thunderous, pitching river that roiled along beside the tracks. Most of the scary stories she knew were set there—tales about robbers and train wrecks and hangings and feuds and Indian war parties and men you encountered walking along the road in the moonlight who vanished as you approached them. Conversation in the car didn't pick up again until the train huffed over the grade at Topton and started down the other side. Ordinarily the exhilaration she felt on leaving the gorge behind would have set Plutina talking as well, but when her ears popped at the top of the grade she suddenly understood, with the clarity of revelation, that for the first time in her life she would not be turning around in Murphy and heading back to Dillsboro. She had thoroughly and permanently *left home*.

Much to her surprise, she found that she not only missed Henrietta but felt awful about abandoning her. Truth be told, Henrietta was long-waisted and flat-chested and hard to get along with, and wouldn't have had an easy time finding a husband worth having under the best of circumstances. But now, because Plutina had allowed the only boy ever to chase her to actually catch her, and had bolted without a second thought from underneath their shared responsibilities, Henrietta was pretty much damned to the spinsterhood to which everyone had always feared she was fated—unless, of course, Mrs. Scroggs drastically picked up the pace of her dying, which, five years into the process, didn't seem likely. As the train descended toward the valley floor—a valley cut by a river whose name she didn't even know— Plutina became convinced that if she traveled one mile farther away from Dillsboro she would start crying and never stop. How could she have left her family behind so callously? Oh, Plutina, she thought, removing her glasses, the world on this side of the gorge suddenly too hard and ugly to contemplate, you *are* a hussy—which is exactly what Henrietta had called her when she announced that she was marrying Charlie Shires and leaving home.

When they arrived at Argyle in the middle of the afternoon, few people were about and the handful of stores and businesses huddled along Main Street already seemed to be closing down for the evening. At that particular moment the deadness of the place suited Plutina fine. Charlie didn't own a car (yet, but he had promised) and she hadn't been looking forward to having strangers see her ride a mule through the middle of town like some common hillbilly. (The roads, Charlie had explained several times, were too bad for him to bring the wagon.) She walked with him to the livery stable where he had boarded the mule the night before. The livery stable also doubled as a Dodge dealership, a fact that gave Plutina the impression, which she never quite got over, that the town of Argyle was a place where things could go either way. Charlie saddled the mule and lifted her onto its broad back, where she primly sat sidesaddle. She tried to look regal and unconcerned as he led her out of town toward the looming mountains, despite the fact that she was terrified of the mule. Her father had always owned a car, and as a town girl, she had ridden horseback very little—certainly never anything as big and dangerous-looking as Charlie's beast of a mule. She would've straddled the animal and held on to the saddle horn for dear life but didn't want the first impression she made in Hayes County to be parading down Main Street with her dress hiked halfway up to her tail and her legs hanging out for everyone to see.

Charlie's people came from the high ridges above Bryson City, where the government had recently flushed them from their perches when it bought (or illegally seized, depending on your point of view) most of the land in Swain County for the park, a scattering from which the Shires as a clan never quite regrouped. There weren't many of them to begin with, and when they left Swain they flew every which way. Charlie had borrowed enough money from an uncle to buy eighty-three acres of land and set up housekeeping in the deep mountains ten miles outside of town. (Charlie's property had figured heavily in her calculations as she considered his proposal—calculations she silently adjusted once she understood that the majority of that property approached the vertical in pitch.) She had almost gotten used to riding the mule, and was beginning to sleepily pretend that she and Charlie were Mary and Joseph on the way to Bethlehem, when Charlie climbed on behind her and wrapped the arm not holding her suitcase around her in such a way that his forearm casually but noticeably pressed into her breasts. (Unlike Henrietta, *she* was not flat-chested.)

The forwardness and broad-daylight nature of this affection struck her as a little common, but she was glad to have both the warmth he provided as well someone to keep her from falling off the mule in case she dozed.

The road away from town climbed up and up and—each time it no longer seemed possible—up some more. She tried to remember the way back to Argyle as they rode along, but was soon lost beyond finding. They weaved in and out and around the ridges the way a child might have found her way through a drawing room packed with adults. More than once they seemed on the verge of dead-ending into the face of a mountain, only to veer at the last minute into some previously hidden pass; in the passes the road picked its way along the courses of narrow, white creeks that bounded down from the high country. Because Dillsboro lay on a riverbank in a wide, fertile valley, the mountains Plutina had grown up knowing stood politely some distance away from where she had viewed them. These new peaks, however, pressed in on her like rude strangers. They seemed haphazardly piled on top of each other, like toys in a box or apples in a bowl, and left little room between them for anything so pleasant as a valley, let alone one with bottomland enough for a farm. She didn't know where Charlie was taking her, but she began to think that it couldn't be any place good.

An hour and a half into their journey the road tunneled through a hollow so thick with balsam and rhododendron that they could see neither the sky above their heads nor the rushing stream whose echo hissed in the leaves all around them. Once they climbed out of the hollow Plutina noticed that the woods continued to hiss even though they had moved out of earshot of the creek. It had begun to sleet. The small, flat hat that she wore with her wedding suit was mostly ornamental, and within minutes her hair began to freeze. Plutina's hair had never once froze before she married Charlie Shires and set off on a mule into the wilderness, so she pushed his forearm away from her breasts. Back in Dillsboro, Henrietta would be cooking supper, probably chicken. Henrietta was good with chicken. Their father would be reading and rattling the Asheville paper, which came without fail every afternoon on the train. He was more than likely grumbling about Herbert Hoover to anybody who would listen. Now Henrietta was the only possibility. With the hand she wasn't using to hold on to the mule, she reached up and patted her stiff hair. Plutina found the state of the world too much to think about with frozen hair, so she decided to go ahead and cry. If Charlie noticed her sobbing he never let on.

Just when she began to consider the possibility that Charlie was taking her off into the mountains to die, they rounded a bend and he pointed off to the right and said, "There's our house." It was small and white and occupied the top of a small knob that sprouted at the base of App Mountain. Already more than a hundred years old, it had begun life as a dogtrot cabin constructed out of chestnut logs by some pioneer whose name had been forgotten. Later occupants had enclosed the dogtrot and covered the logs, outside and in, with weatherboarding and plaster. Miraculously, the house overlooked a narrow but perfectly flat creek valley.

He helped Plutina down off the mule and they ran onto the porch as if they had been caught in a sudden shower only moments before, and were not already soaked through and half frozen. When he picked her up to carry her across the threshold she felt ice breaking on her coat. He put her down in the dark, largely empty center room and set her suitcase on the floor beside her. "That way's the kitchen," he said, pointing to the left, "and that way's the bedroom. I've got to put the mule up." Then he was gone. He hadn't even lit a lamp. Plutina sat down on top of her suitcase, facing the front door. Although her teeth were chattering, and had been for a while, she couldn't be sure if the rest of her was shivering from the cold or because she was so mad. She made up her mind that when Charlie Shires opened that door again she was going to call him everything but the son of a righteous God and demand that he take her back to Argyle that instant and put her on the next train to Dillsboro. Her daddy would take her in no matter what he had told Charlie. Luckily, the barn was behind the house and Charlie returned through the back door with a handful of eggs from the chicken coop and set to building a fire in the stove. Charlie banged around in the kitchen for a few minutes before she decided to join him. I'm only going, she told herself, because that's where the fire is.

Plutina awoke early the next morning, before first light, and one by one reconsidered the surprises of the night before. Her nightgown was still pushed above her waist, and Charlie was spooned up against her, which didn't feel that different than Henrietta being spooned up against her, except that she didn't have on any underwear and Charlie was naked as the day he was born and clutching one of her breasts like it was something that would blow up if he dropped it.

The sheets, she figured, and probably her best nightgown, had to be a sight. If it hadn't snowed she was going to find out first light where Charlie kept the washtub, then build a fire and give everything a good scrubbing. (She could only hope they hadn't gotten any blood on the quilts; blood was nearly impossible to get out of a quilt.) As for the sex itself, well, that had hurt worse than she had thought it would—which was saying something because after Plutina started going out with Charlie Shires, Henrietta had been explicit in her speculation about the pain girls experienced when they lost their virginity. "It's like getting shot with a gun. It's like being crucified. It's like getting branded." Henrietta had only been trying to scare her, of course, but her speculations hadn't been that far off the mark.

Still, awful as the sex had been, she sensed glimmering off in the distance the faint possibility that she might somehow be able to find pleasure of her own in it. The thought troubled her a little. She had occasionally sneaked and read parts of Song of Solomon when she was supposed to be memorizing Bible verses for Sunday school, but she hadn't been able to make heads or tails out of it, all that talk about young stags and mountains and spices and pomegranates. Because of her mother's stroke Plutina would never find out just what, if anything, Mrs. Scroggs would have had to say; the one time she had shown a passage to Henrietta, Henrietta had slapped her face and ran into their room and slammed the door.

That afternoon, Plutina sat wrapped up on the back steps and watched Charlie chop wood. He grew so warm with the labor that he took off his coat, then his shirt, before finally wiggling out of the top part of his union suit and letting it dangle down behind him as he worked. His bare skin steamed in the cold. Despite the lingering soreness, Plutina felt warm and blurry *down there*. (*Down there*. She hated that phrase. It made her private parts sound like South Carolina.) When Charlie glanced over at her she blushed so exorbitantly that he grinned. She couldn't look at him just then so she picked at a loose thread on one of her coat buttons until she almost worked the button off the coat. She could feel him watching her. Her nipples puckered up the way they did when she ate a pickle. Female place. Down there. Vagina. South Carolina. She twisted impatiently on the step. Now she knew why babies got mad and cried when they wanted

273

to tell you something. They didn't know the right words. Charlie drove the ax into the chopping block. The echo clapping off the mountainside made her jump.

"What's the matter with you?" he asked.

"Nothing's the matter with me."

"Well, you look like something's the matter with you."

"Well, there ain't." She finally forced herself to glance up at him. Tallywhacker, she thought. Dick. Peter. Charlie. "It's cold out here," she said. "You interested in going inside?"

In the spring of 1933 Charlie took a job working on the new road through the Smokies. They had eaten well enough in 1931 and 1932 but made only enough money farming to cover the fertilizer bills. Charlie left home Sunday afternoons after dinner and walked over the mountains to the work camp near Bryson. He walked back home Fridays after he got off, arriving at the farm by 2:00 AM. Plutina would have preferred to stay with her family while Charlie was gone, but the farm work fell to her. That spring and early summer she not only kept up her vegetable garden, but she fed the animals and hoed and fertilized the cotton and the corn and the watermelons. Most days she had to work from can to can't just to stay close to even with all she had to do. The work seemed to her a hateful thing she chased but never once caught. She just tried to keep it in sight, and in the process developed the mannish calluses of a field hand. (Charlie did the cultivating when he came home on weekends. Sometimes he had to work Sunday mornings to get it all done.) Plutina took Friday afternoons off to straighten up the house so it would be clean when Charlie got home. Before she went to bed she drew enough water from the well to fill the washtub. When Charlie stomped onto the back porch she lit a lamp and went out and sat with him while he bathed. If the night was chilly she lit a fire in the kitchen and boiled a kettle of water to pour into the tub. Charlie always washed himself with his back turned to her but whenever he turned around his thing pointed at her like a weather vane. They had both thinned down to gristle and skeleton, and when he climbed on top of her each of them complained about the other's rough hands and boniness.

Before Charlie went to work on the road crew Plutina had never spent a night alone. She had, in fact, spent precious few nights in a bed by herself. She wasn't particularly scared during the daylight hours because she had so much to do, but she suffered through the nights. She was afraid that when word got out that a young girl stayed by herself in the middle of nowhere men from three counties would line up to rape her. Whenever she dozed off their faces peered in the window. Panthers leapt into her bedroom and landed almost silently on the floor. Ghosts of the old settlers creaked through the rooms. Haints formed in the mist that rose from the creek and floated on the night breeze toward the mountainside. Large animals ran through the woods and the leaves said, *shhhhhhhhhh*. The cicadas and whippoorwills chanted, *run away run away run away*. The mountain itself leaned over the house and watched her. When it breathed in it sucked the curtains tight against the window frame. Once Charlie learned how frightened she was he brought home a dog that had been hanging around the work camp, but it was a skulky, mistrustful creature who spent most of the two weeks it stayed there cowering under the house. One morning she tossed a biscuit toward it while it wasn't looking and it lit out down the road and never came back. She began sleeping with the head of the ax resting on Charlie's pillow. She kept a butcher knife underneath her side of the mattress, its handle poking out where she could grab it. Charlie's shotgun leaned loaded in the corner, but she was almost as afraid of shooting it as she was of the things she imagined coming through the window.

But she stayed. Word surely got out about the Shires girl who spent the week by herself up App valley, but nobody came to rape her. She never stopped being afraid, but learned to go to sleep anyway. Over time fewer faces appeared at the window and the panthers stopped coming entirely. She missed one period and then she missed another. Charlie had the week of the Fourth of July off and they laid by the crops. She didn't tell him. When he returned to work she found herself facing the prospect of several weeks by herself with relatively little to do. What surprised her most during the lull was how lonely she was. She tried taking naps after dinner to pass the time but the house was too hot, the air too still. She always wound up crying. She sat on the front steps and stared down the road and imagined someone coming around the bend—a neighbor girl her own age who lived just over the hill and had a lot of fun about her and loved to play games and sing and sit beside her and lean close and whisper about the boys she knew. But when that girl never materialized (Plutina knew that in reality nobody at all lived over that hill or that hill or that hill or that hill almost all the way to Argyle), she dragged herself up to milk the cow and feed Charlie's hateful mule. When she tried singing alone she found her voice too loud for the valley, the mountain too close and too big, the echo it shot back at her sharp as a scold. The nearest church was four miles away but they were Holy Roller Jesus jumpers who spoke in unknown tongues. The nearest Baptist church was all the way in town. Sometimes she got mad at the silence and went into the yard and worked up her courage and made herself holler out of spite. One moonlit night she dreamed she saw her mother walking through the vegetable garden and woke up heartbroken because she hadn't come in to talk. Sometimes she waded in the creek and caught crawdads and looked into their foreign faces and let them go.

The only neighbor near enough to honestly be called one was Mr. William Tolliver, who lived a mile or so beyond the Shires at the end of the road on the only other farm in the valley. (Beyond Tolliver's place the mountains became impassable to anything other than a creature willing to crawl through the laurel straight up and straight down.) Tolliver was known to everyone who knew him or knew about him as Mr. Tall, because he stood somewhere north of six and a half feet. Although Mr. Tall's front door lay within an easy stroll of her own, Plutina had never laid eyes on him, or even his farm. Charlie had told her never to walk in that direction, and she hadn't. Mr. Tall was a hermit. All she knew about him she had learned from storekeepers and the women in the churchyard the few times Charlie had taken her to town. ("Oh," people always said, a little startled, when she told them that she lived up App Valley, "that's out by Mr. Tall's.")

A long time before, Mr. Tall's young wife and baby daughter had drowned in the gorge. The three of them had been to Bryson City and were riding home on the train. A tree had fallen across the track, and while Tolliver and the rest of the men tried to move the tree, the women and children got out to walk around. When Mrs. Tolliver put the baby down it ran straight to the river and fell in. Mrs. Tolliver jumped in after the baby. The rapids washed both of them up under a rock, where they drowned. Mr. Tall was never quite right again. He came to town less and less and eventually stopped coming entirely. Now everybody said he would shoot you if you set foot on his place. Of course, people also said that he had reasons other than not being right for wanting to be left alone. He had an apple orchard that his ancestors had planted when they came to the valley. He used the apples to make brandy. Twice a year, Three Scott, who ran a mercantile in Argyle, hauled a load of supplies out to Tolliver's and supposedly hauled a load of apple brandy back to town. (Plutina had seen Scott's wagon go by and knew at least the hauling supplies part of the story to be true. The brandy part people only whispered about.) Nobody else ever saw Mr. Tall. All Three Scott would say about him was, "If I was you I wouldn't go up in there."

One afternoon Plutina was sitting on the front step staring down the road when, for no reason she could think of, she turned and stared up the road instead. She said, out loud, "Why, Mr. Tall," as if he had walked up behind her on the street to say hello. She couldn't see his place, of course, because the flank of App Mountain buttressed into the valley between their two farms, but she imagined him coming around the foot of the ridge. He was walking. He was riding a horse. He was carrying a gun. He wasn't carrying a gun. He smelled awful because he never bathed. He smelled good because Scott brought him soap and bay rum and he was the kind of hermit who was overly particular and washed himself every day. She imagined what she would do when she saw him. She would run in the house and bolt the door. She would fly up the mountain and hide in the woods. He would chase her. He would go on by. She would say howdy when he drew abreast of the house. He would howdy back, or he would stare straight ahead and pretend he didn't hear her. They would talk about how the garden could use some rain and how the watermelons were getting ripe, or they wouldn't. She began to tap the step with her foot. Mr. Tall was more fun to think about than the neighbor girl she knew would never come. It was almost like having a new friend. (She was getting a little tired of the neighbor girl, anyway; all she ever wanted to talk about was herself.) Soon Plutina's attention settled on the wooded, tapering ridge that blocked her view to the end of the valley. She figured that if she climbed it and looked over the top she might be able to see through to Mr. Tall's farm. She bet the place was overgrown and falling in, the fields waist deep in briars and hardwood bushes and cedar trees, the roofs of the outbuildings collapsed in on themselves. (She reconsidered and put roofs back on the barn and the chicken house. She knew that Mr. Tall kept at least a few animals because some mornings, when the wind blew just right, she could hear his rooster crowing and his cow lowing to be milked, and he had to keep them somewhere. She had never heard a dog bark, though.) Mr. Tall supposedly lived in a big house, a fine house, but Plutina imagined the yard full of trash, that Mr. Tall just opened the door and pitched it out. The windows were blocked by the boxwoods that his wife had planted and he hadn't cut back since she died. Poison oak

277

grew up the outside walls and turned bloody red in the fall. Inside the house was lamp-lighting dark. It smelled like piss and old man. Mr. Tall stayed drunk all the time. He sat in a horsehair chair in the parlor and watched dust float in the single, scrawny sunbeam that sneaked in past the boxwoods. There was a clock on the mantel but he never wound it. He had dribbled canned soup and tobacco juice down the front of his shirt but he didn't care. Cats jumped in through the windows and ate out of the nasty pans on the stove. Mice nested in the stuffing of the cushions on the love seat. His sheets hadn't been changed in years. Upstairs behind a closed door was a room with a crib in it. Mr. Tall never opened that door. Plutina didn't have a crib yet. (She knew she needed to tell Charlie she was having a baby, but for some reason enjoyed the secret, her knowing and his not knowing.) She wondered if it was bad luck to put your baby in a dead baby's crib. *Mr. Tall*, she imagined asking him, *what would you take for that crib upstairs?* He looked up miserably from the horsehair chair. He waved his hand. The dust swirled. *Go ahead and take it,* he said. *I don't need it no more.* Plutina put her hand over her mouth and giggled. "Lord," she whispered, "Charlie would have a fit if he knew what I was thinking about."

The next day she had to crawl through the laurel to get to the top of the ridge, and once there, couldn't see a thing. When she made her way down the other side she found her view blocked by a cornfield. She stomped her foot. She didn't know how wide the field was, nor how close she would be to Mr. Tall's house when she came out the other side, so she just went home, where she pouted but did not enjoy it because there was nobody there to notice. The day after that she took a deep breath and plowed into the corn. The middles of Mr. Tall's corn rows were cleaner than the middles of her corn rows, which stung her a little, but the stalks themselves didn't seem to be any higher, or the ears any further along. She was as afraid as she had been on any of her first nights alone, but unlike the fear she had experienced then, this new fear somehow felt good around its edges, almost like a sex feeling. Her heart thrummed painfully in her chest, but she had to clamp her hand tightly over her mouth to keep from laughing out loud. She suddenly had to pee and squatted in the middle of the field to keep from wetting herself. She bit on her knuckle and sniggered the whole time. As she approached the end of the corn row she dropped to her hands and knees and crawled the last several yards. When she peeked out she discovered a small pasture bisected by a small, muddy branch. A Guernsey cow and a slick, black mule cropped at the grass. Beyond the pasture lay a barn and a chicken coop—both as sound as she had imagined they would be—and a pig-pen and a corncrib and a smokehouse and a shed covering a wagon and several other small buildings she couldn't identify, all of them up-right and square, their roofs intact. (Even Mr. Tall's toilet looked solid.) Across the farmyard stood a two-story log house, as fine as any in Dillsboro, with long windows and whitewashed window frames and a covered porch wrapping around the three sides she could see. The lower slope of App Mountain swept away from the backyard, and the orchard she had heard about rose in terraced avenues for some dis-tance up the mountainside. The trees were neatly pruned, their limbs drooping and heavy with apples just beginning to color. Plutina dropped back onto her heels and shook her head with wonder. "Oh, Mr. Tall," she whispered. "You have a *beautiful* farm."

For the next couple of weeks she rushed through her work in the mornings so she could spend at least part of the afternoon peeking out of the corn at Mr. Tall's immaculate farm. (When Charlie came home weekends she now had two secrets she didn't tell him.) The yard of the house, she noted approvingly, was swept clean; not one piece of stickweed sprouted in the pasture, even along the branch; no morning glories clung to the fence posts. Nothing about the place suggested tragedy or despair or even strangeness. The only remotely odd thing was that in days and days of watching she never once caught sight of Mr. Tall. She might have become worried about him, except that from her hiding place she could tell that in the hours she wasn't watching somebody was milking the cow and slopping the hog and strewing corn for the chickens. One day the orchard rows were empty and the next day bushel baskets were stacked at intervals all the way to the top of the terraces; one day the two bean rows in the garden were thick with beans, and the next the staked-up vines had been stripped. Plutina became exasperated with Mr. Tall, as if he had made a series of appointments with her but failed to keep any of them. She began to doubt she would ever catch a glimpse of him, but did not want to stop her spying just in case he appeared. She memorized every detail of his farm and found that at suppertime she did not want to return to her own, which had started to seem small and scruffy and unprosperous by comparison. (*Charlie* had started to seem small and scruffy and un-prosperous by comparison.) She began curling up on the sun-warmed dirt at the edge of the field and allowing herself to doze. When the air stirred the corn leaves whispered secrets she could almost make out. Every so often she opened her eyes and sat up and gazed across the pasture and said, "Mr. Tall?" but he was never there.

On the third Monday of her vigil, Plutina rose from her hiding place at the edge of the field and in a crouch hurried along the fence toward the mountain. To her left Mr. Tall's house was visible only intermittently between the outbuildings. When she reached the corner of the pasture she looked down the fence row and gauged the distance to the barn, which was maybe fifty yards away. She drew a deep breath, whispered, "Go!" and sprinted toward it. The cow raised its head and looked at her as she ran. The mule honked in alarm and trotted halfway across the pasture, its ears and tail erect, shitting as it went. When she reached the barn she tagged the wall and turned around and raced back to where she had started. She dropped to her knees and watched the house intently. Nothing happened. She couldn't remember ever feeling happier than she did right then. She hadn't felt nearly so exhilarated when she said, "I do."

The next day she stopped at the barn with her back pressed to the wall. She stole a look around the corner, then pulled her skirt up over her calves and dashed down through the farmyard from building to building to building toward Mr. Tall's house. The chickens flapped up in a ruckus. The mule brayed and galloped away, this time toward the cornfield. When she reached the smokehouse and stopped, she knew she couldn't be more than thirty or forty yards away from the house. She whispered, "I'm going to tag your house, Mr. Tall," but she couldn't make her legs move. She counted to ten several times but remained rooted in place. Eventually she felt a cold point of courage flare in her chest, rise into her throat, and emerge from her mouth as a grunt. Then she was off, her right hand extended toward Mr. Tall's house. She had taken no more than five steps when a stocky brown dog with a white face and pale eyes and an immense, square head shot from under the back porch and made straight for her, running so hard its belly almost dragged the ground. In a panic she turned and sprinted back the way she had come, but hadn't even cleared the smokehouse when she realized she had no chance of getting away. The dog was almost on her already. She pushed up the latch of the corncrib, jumped inside and pulled the door closed just as the dog skidded to a stop outside. It barked and snarled and snapped and bit at the corner of the door. With her fingernails she clung to the wire nailed to the inside of the door and struggled to hold it closed. She could see the dog through the slats, could feel its spitty breath on her legs. It leapt up and shoved with its front paws against the building with such force that it landed on its back. Plutina felt the heavy, wooden outside latch drop back into place with a thunk.

Once the latch fell, the dog stopped lunging, as if locking Plutina inside the corncrib had been its plan all along. It remained posted just outside the door, however, growling almost silently, its head cocked, staring at the point where she had vanished. Every so often it turned its head and barked sharply toward the house. Plutina tried to shush it, but when she did the dog leapt snapping at the door. She backed away and looked around wildly. The slats nailed to the outside would have been easy enough to kick out, but the inside of the crib was a cage of tightly woven wire mesh stapled every few inches to the studs and the floor, even the roof joists, to keep rats from getting into the corn. It was constructed so soundly that the door didn't even have a hole for a latch string. A few bushels of last year's corn lay spilling from the corners, but that was all. There was nothing she could use to pull up the wire. She could *see* out, but she couldn't *get* out. She closed her eyes and whispered, "Oh Jesus, I need Charlie to come get me right this instant."

Behind her a screen door slammed, and she whirled toward the house. Coming down the back steps was the tallest man Plutina had ever laid eyes on. His legs were so long she thought at first they were stilts. He wore overalls of unimaginable length; eight or more inches of wrist poked out from beneath his buttoned shirt sleeves. *Mr. Tall.* He had a long, white beard. He dropped a straw hat onto his longish white hair as he stepped into the yard. She couldn't see his eyes for the shadow of the hat brim. She slowly backed against the wire at the front of the crib, but leapt away when the dog managed to insert its snout between two of the slats near the floor and bite at the wire just behind her ankle. She stood in the middle of the floor and through the slats watched Mr. Tall stride slowly toward her. Hot piss ran down her leg. "Noggin!" Mr. Tall said in a gruff voice as he approached. "What you got in there?"

Mr. Tall squinted in through the slats and immediately jumped backward. He slapped his shirt sleeves and the front of his overalls as if yellow jackets were swarming on him. "Good . . . who . . . shit," he said. When he stopped whacking himself he rapidly shook his head. He cautiously stepped back toward the building and leaned forward to stare in at her.

"Who are you?" he said.

Plutina opened her mouth to speak but found that her breath had left and taken her name with it. Her own hands waved uselessly around her face.

"I said, Who. Are. You."

Her face contorted and scrunched. A string of snot swung from her nose and she wiped it on the back of her arm. "Please don't kill me, Mr. Tall," she managed to say. "I promise I didn't know you had a dog and I didn't mean to get all locked up in your corncrib like this and make you come outside. I promise I didn't. I swear."

Mr. Tall closed his eyes and grabbed hold of his ears. He stomped his foot. "Who are you! Who are you! Who are you!" he said.

"I was just playing a game and yesterday I came out of the corn and ran and tagged your barn and today I didn't know you were home and after I got to the barn again I decided to run down and tag your house but your dog came out from under the porch and—"

He stopped her by raising his hand. "For the love of God in heaven before he calls me home," he said, "will you shut up for one solitary minute and tell me your goddamned name?"

"Scroggs," she said. "I'm Plutina Scroggs."

"Scroggs? There ain't no Scroggs live within thirty miles of here."

"Shires, I meant. Plutina Shires. I was Plutina Scroggs before I got married. My daddy's Parcell Scroggs from over in Dillsboro, he works for the railroad, but then I got married to Charlie Shires three years ago this January and now my name is Plutina Shires. I don't know why I said Scroggs."

"So you live other side of the ridge then."

"Yes, sir."

"And you came sneaking around over here to steal something because you didn't think I was home and you didn't know I had a dog."

"Oh, no, sir. I was just playing a game because I was lonesome and I've been hiding in the corn to see what you looked like but I didn't never see you and then I decided to tag your house because I didn't know you had a dog."

"You were going to tag my house."

"Yes, sir."

"Because you were playing a game."

"Yes, sir."

"And you're sure you weren't trying to steal something? Because I *got* a dog."

"No, sir."

"And I'll turn him loose on you, too, I don't care if you are a girl, if I catch you trying to carry something off."

"Oh, no, sir," she said. "I'm going to have a baby."

Mr. Tall blinked slowly.

"What did you just say?"

"I said I'm going to have a baby. I don't know why I just told you that. I ain't told nobody. I ain't even told Charlie yet. I don't know why I ain't told him but I ain't." She watched him look down at her feet. She looked down at the puddle she was standing in.

"Is that your water broke?" he asked.

"No, sir," she said, suddenly aware of her wet dress clinging to her legs. "I accidentally peed on your floor but if you got a rag somewhere I'll be glad to clean it up."

Mr. Tall took off his hat with his left hand and clapped his right hand onto the top of his head. He closed his eyes. "Good Lord," he said.

"I'm real sorry about the floor. I just think I was afraid of your dog, is all."

He put his hat back on. "How old are you?"

"I'm almost nineteen."

"And you're sure that ain't your water broke."

"No, sir. I mean, yes, sir. I mean, it's just pee."

Mr. Tall sighed and lifted the latch and opened the door. "Come out of there," he said.

Plutina glanced down at the dog. The dog stared up at her. It had blue eyes, of all things. "Is that dog going to bite me?" she asked.

"Noggin," Mr. Tall said. "Get under the house." Instantly, the dog turned and trotted around the corner of the crib. "Come out of there," he repeated.

Plutina's legs wobbled as she moved forward. For a second the floor wavered and she thought she might vomit. She tried to hold her dress away from her legs without pulling it up as she stepped from the crib.

Mr. Tall walked a few steps away from the crib and turned around in a slow circle, his hands on his hips, as if trying to remember where he had put something. "Son of a bitch," he mumbled.

"Can I please go home now?" she asked.

Mr. Tall looked at her appraisingly. "You don't look too good."

"I'm sorry. I promise I am."

"Come on," Mr. Tall said. He started toward the house.

Plutina followed him unsteadily across the yard, watching the line of shadow underneath the porch. Her legs shook so badly that even if he let her go she didn't think she would be able to make it around the ridge.

"Mr. Tall," she said. "Please stop."

He turned toward her.

"Are you going to sic that dog on me?"

"What the hell kind of question is that?"

"I just need to know if you are, is all. Because if you are I think I'm about to fall down."

"Just come on. Don't worry about the dog."

When they reached the porch he pointed at the steps. "You sit there," he said.

Plutina sat down. Mr. Tall climbed past her and disappeared into the house. She smelled awful. She didn't know where the dog was. She didn't know if she would ever see her mama again. She pressed the heels of her palms into her eyes. She heard the screen door open and close and Mr. Tall cross the porch. She felt the steps give as he came down the stairs. She tried to stop crying, but it was too late.

"Drink this," he said, extending a glass toward her.

"I just want to go home," she said.

"Drink it. I churned it this morning."

Plutina had never cared for buttermilk, but figured if she didn't drink it he would never let her go. The buttermilk *was* fresh, and it was cool enough, and the glass didn't stink, and she thought she might be able to keep it down if she took small sips. But then she imagined a bunch of cats with their heads stuck down inside a milk bucket and felt everything in her stomach rush up into the back of her throat. She closed her eyes and swallowed and waited until the sick feeling slid back toward her stomach.

"Mmm," she said. "This is good."

He nodded. He walked a few feet away and sat down on the edge of the porch. "I'll sit over here," he said. "Till you finish that." He put his hands on his knees and stared out toward the orchard.

Plutina looked down into the glass. She didn't see how in the world she could drink another swallow.

Mr. Tall jumped up so suddenly that he startled her. He hurried up the steps past her and pointed at what looked like the butt end of a metal spike sticking out of one of the logs up high near the door frame.

"I'll bet you ain't never seen anything like that, have you?" he said.

"No, sir," she said. "What is it?"

"Bullet," he answered, his eyebrows raised expectantly.

"Who shot it?" she asked.

Mr. Tall shrugged. "Don't know. Indians, I reckon. Home guard, maybe. Tories. I just don't know." He stepped close to the wall and squinted up at the bullet. "It's always been here."

"Do you have a cat?" she asked.

"What?"

"Do you have a cat?"

"Nah. I hate a damn cat."

"I ain't got a cat, neither," she said. "I ain't even got a dog. We had a dog that Charlie brought home but I threw a biscuit at it and it ran away."

"You don't like buttermilk, do you?"

"No, sir."

"Then you want some water?"

"No, sir. Thank you, though."

"That's all I got to drink. Water and buttermilk."

"I'm fine, really."

"I don't care for sweet milk."

"Do I have to finish this?"

"Nah," he said, giving the bullet a last squint. "You best be getting on."

Plutina jumped up. The world tilted suddenly and she discovered that her right cheek was resting on the dirt. She wondered how it got there. Mr. Tall hovered over her, his hands wheeling through the air like swallows.

"Shit," he said. "Damn, damn, damn."

She pushed herself on to her hands and knees, made sure her dress wasn't hiked up, then crawled back to the steps, where she sat down beside the buttermilk glass. "I guess I need to try that again," she said. "I didn't do so good."

"The baby," Mr. Tall sputtered. "Is something the matter with you? You've got to go back to your house right now. Ain't nobody here can take you to town if you need to go."

Plutina started to cry again. "I'm just scared, is all, Mr. Tall. That dog scared me and you scared me and I can't stand buttermilk and I'm embarrassed because I peed on my dress and my legs won't work. If I need to go to town I'll ride Charlie's damn mule and take my own self.

As soon as I can walk I'll go back to my house and leave you alone and you won't never see me no more, I can promise you that."

Mr. Tall's mouth opened but he didn't say anything. He stalked away from her without a word and disappeared around the corner of the house. After a few moments Plutina began to worry about the dog and eased two steps closer to the back door. If that dog came out from under the porch she was going inside, no matter what. She would run upstairs to the room with the crib in it and slam the door. Mr. Tall soon reappeared on the other side of the house and kept going, his face bright red, striding rapidly toward the farmyard. Before he reached the corncrib he stopped and pointed an incredibly long finger at her.

"How the hell was I supposed to know you don't like buttermilk? Nobody asked you to come over here."

Plutina didn't know what to say to that, so she didn't say anything.

"That's just what I figured," he said.

He came back a few minutes later leading the black mule, which he positioned parallel to the edge of the porch. He nodded at Plutina.

"Climb on," he said.

Mr. Tall's mule was even bigger than Charlie's mule. She already knew it to be easily spooked. She watched it shiver a fly off its glossy back. "But my dress is wet," she said. "I don't want to get pee on your mule."

"It's a mule," Mr. Tall said. "He smells like shit anyway."

Mr. Tall dropped Plutina off at her house and led the mule away without saying a word. When she called after him he waved without turning around. She went inside and washed herself and changed her dress. She lay down and closed her eyes and pitched instantly into sleep. When she awoke it was black dark. The cow was hoarse from complaining to be milked and Charlie's mule rhythmically kicked the side of the barn. She could hear the pig snuffling in its empty trough. Plutina lit the lantern and went out and fed the mule and slopped the pig and milked the cow without knowing if it was nine thirty in the evening or the last of the dark before daylight.

When Charlie came home that weekend she didn't tell him about her adventure at Mr. Tall's but she did tell him she was going to have a baby. He was bathing on the porch when she told him, his back to her. Moths drew streaks around the lantern and ticked against the glass; from the mountainside fell the shrill scree of tree frogs. Charlie didn't say anything. She watched his shoulders go up and down once.

286

When he turned around she saw that he was smiling a little, but in the lantern light she couldn't read his eyes.

"Well, what do you think about that?" she asked.

"I reckon it was bound to happen, the way me and you go at it."

"I reckon."

"I'm surprised it took this long," he said. "I thought we'd have had half a houseful by now."

Something inside her dried up and hardened into stone. Mr. Tall had been nicer about it while she was locked in his corncrib standing in a puddle of piss. "I'm going inside," she said. Wouldn't nobody be putting up the mule on the Shires place before morning, if then.

That Sunday night, after Charlie went back to Bryson, Plutina found she couldn't stop thinking about Mr. Tall. She lay awake and tried to remember everything he had said to her. He had been mostly kind, she decided—gruffer than her father, but still nicer; worse tempered than Charlie, but more thoughtful. If Mr. Tall had been her daddy he wouldn't have said to Charlie what her daddy had said about not bringing her back. If he had been her husband he would have had more to say about her being pregnant than what took you so long. As she slid into sleep their conversation extended from what they had actually said to each other into reams of talk about everything under the sun. She told him something extremely important that took her a long time to say, but when she woke up she couldn't remember what it was.

Monday while she worked she wondered why Mr. Tall hadn't jumped in after his wife and baby. She pictured him running down the railroad embankment toward the river. Women on the riverbank were screaming and crying and pointing into the rapids. Maybe he did jump, she thought, he just didn't drown. Maybe somebody stopped him from jumping. Plutina placed herself on the riverbank between Mr. Tall and the water. She wore a long, black skirt and a high-collared blouse, a cameo pin—she was a woman in an old photograph. Mr. Tall's eyes were wild as he ran down the hill. He threw down his hat. He was going to jump. She stepped in front of him and wrapped her arms around him at the water's edge. He tottered dangerously at the edge of the rapids. He wanted to go in, although she could see in his eyes he knew there was no use. The river roared at her back and covered them both with spray. If he went in he would take her with him. She would drown underneath the same rock as Mrs. Tall. *No, Mr. Tall, no!* she shouted into his ear. *There's nothing you can do. They're with Jesus now.* Eventually she felt his arms wrap around her waist. He stumbled back from the river's edge and began to sob. She had saved him. *There, there, Mr. Tall*, she said. *There, there.* She helped him back to the train.

A few weeks later she heard a soft footstep on the front porch and ran and jerked open the door, thinking Charlie had quit his job and come home to surprise her. Instead she saw Mr. Tall hurrying across the yard toward the road. Beside the door sat a peck basket of ripe apples.

"Mr. Tall!" she called. "Mr. Tall, wait."

He stopped and turned slowly toward the house.

"Thank you for the apples," she said.

"They're sour," he said. "They're not fit to eat but they cook good." He waved and started to turn away.

"Wait," she said again. "Wait. Do you like pie? Let me make you a pie. Come back tomorrow evening and I'll have an apple pie for you. You can eat it with your supper."

She watched his mouth work rapidly, trying to make an excuse.

"I won't ask you to come in," she said. "I'll just hand you the pie when you come and you can take it home and eat it. You can leave the pan down in the yard when you're done. You don't even have to wash it. I make a good pie. You like apple pie, don't you?"

Mr. Tall nodded, but he looked miserable.

"Will you come back tomorrow?"

"I . . ." he said. "We'll see."

Plutina waved. "See you tomorrow," she said, closing the door before he changed his mind.

The next morning at first light she sat on the back porch peeling apples. She wanted to get her baking done before the heat of the day. It was a Wednesday. She had enough sugar to make three pies, but barely enough cinnamon for one. She didn't have a sign of a clove. Mr. Tall's pie would be fair enough, but it wouldn't be her best. The other two would only be adequate. She planned to eat them both herself anyway. If she gave Charlie a piece of apple pie, he would naturally want to know where the apples came from, since they didn't have a tree. Plutina didn't see how she could tell Charlie Mr. Tall gave her the apples without also telling him about the spying and the dog and her being locked in the corncrib and peeing on the floor and gagging on the buttermilk and Mr. Tall having to carry her home on the mule. And while she didn't want Charlie to know specifically that she had gotten into trouble at Mr. Tall's, she also didn't want him to know about Mr. Tall generally—although she tried to keep that part of her secret pushed out of the way so she didn't have to consider the implications of keeping such a secret from her husband. She simply decided that Mr. Tall was her friend and she would keep him for herself. She was going to make her friend an apple pie—nothing wrong with that, just being neighborly—and she would eat the other two herself. Nothing wrong with that, either. She was going to have a baby. She ought to be able to eat as many apple pies as she wanted. She would give the apple peels to the pig and the rest of the apples to the mule. That struck her as a waste—giving perfectly good apples to a mule— but there was nothing she could do about it.

When Mr. Tall stepped onto the porch the next afternoon, Plutina pulled open the door and extended the pie toward him so suddenly that he flinched a little. "Slow down, now," he said.

"Here's your pie," she said. "I didn't have a clove, but I did have a little cinnamon in the kitchen. I hope it's fit to eat."

Mr. Tall took the pie from her and stared down at it a long time. With one hand he touched the bib pocket of his overalls. "What do I owe you?" he asked.

"Mr. *Tall*," she said. "Don't be silly. You don't owe me a thing."

He looked down at the pie again. "Well, I thank you."

"You're very welcome."

"All right. I best get on, then."

"Don't rush off," she said.

"I got to get back."

"Well, come see us."

He touched the brim of his hat with his finger. Plutina watched him start across the yard. "Mr. Tall," she called after him, feeling as she spoke, yet unable to keep herself from speaking, that she was about to misstep in the dark and fall a long way. "I'm sorry about your wife and little baby."

Mr. Tall stopped and stiffened in his tracks. His shoulders widened. He stood up straighter. He seemed to grow several inches before he whirled on her. "What did you just say?" he asked.

"Mr. Tall, I—"

"What did you just say?"

"Please don't be mad."

"Who the hell do you think you are?"

"I don't think I'm nobody, Mr. Tall, I swear I don't."

"Don't you *ever* talk to me like that again."

289

"I'm sorry, Mr. Tall. I didn't mean to. I just wanted to make you feel better, is all."

He gaped at her. "Feel better?" he said. He stepped toward her. "You say you want to make me *feel* better?"

Plutina covered her mouth with her hands.

"May God *damn* you," he said. He closed his eyes and threw the pie against the side of the house. "How about that? You think that makes me feel better?"

"Mr. Tall, don't."

He took another step.

"Please stop, Mr. Tall."

"Let me look at your titties."

"What?"

"You heard me. That ought to make me feel better. Show me them ripe little titties you got."

"Oh, no, Mr. Tall. Please no."

"You know how long it's been since I *seen* a titty?"

"Mr. Tall, I think I'm going to be sick."

"You trying to be my *wife* now? Is that it? You going to come over to my house and fuck me in my bed? Is that what you want?"

Plutina stepped to the edge of the porch and vomited half an apple pie into the yard. She dropped to her knees and held on to a post and retched.

"I hope your baby *dies*," he said. "I hope it dies right now."

She rolled onto her side and curled up with her back to the yard and closed her eyes. If Mr. Tall wanted to kill her, well, that would be all right. She lay there and listened to him pant in the yard. Then she listened to him walk away.

Nominated by Kirk Nesset, The Southern Review

HITHER & YON

by L.S. ASEKOFF

from PLOUGHSHARES

Presto!
Vortices that spin off birds
from a passing shadow to a developing storm.
As soon as light hits the water, they're in the zone,
low in the shallows, waiting out the night,
the paralysis of the icy laws of fact.
Amphibian between being, non-being,
who does not know the number of his fingers?
Or as the Sumerians say, *Where did you go? Nowhere? Then why are
    you so late?*
Leafing through the green catalogue
you see the white iris dug up for the animal grave,
the heavens unscrolling ripe figs of stars,
& the four goosemen let loose in the land.
Blockhead! Ironist! Merchant! Traveler!
All this calculating on lines with quills
the fall of light, pricing of goods, a cheetah's turn of speed,
the shape of a wing, a leaf, a mountain torrent,
crosshatches on the sunflower's crown,
all this doubling back & going on
strands you once more across the borders,
traveling by wordless relations & signs.
Where is the center? Our lilac midnights, our blazing meridians?
The dot of a different zero?

Old Blue Ball, Erasable You,
always arriving, you will go everywhere.
"Sire, I have rubbed in my hand the first experimental model
   universe,
a soft India rubber bag."

Nominated by Kathleen Hill, Ploughshares

FREAKY BEASTS: REVELATIONS OF A ONE-TIME BODYBUILDER

by WILLIAM GIRALDI

from THE KENYON REVIEW

Now, my tongue, the mystery telling
Of the glorious Body sing
—Thomas Aquinas, *Pange Lingua Gloriosi*

We walked the earth as gods, heroes, monsters, true anomalies who existed in an underground culture of iron and anabolic drugs, of mammoth protein dishes and a shared understanding that we were *Übermenschen*, superior to the unmuscled rabble of the world. Our ways were alien, extreme, unholy, hellbent. We puked and bled and broke laws in search of massive, striated muscle, in search of stares and whistles from strangers. I see now that we shunned the wimpy Christian ideal that places a beautiful soul above the perfection of physical form. Instead, we were magnificent Greeks, idolizing male beauty and believing that the exterior was a reflection or embodiment of the interior. Achilles, Adonis, Atlas, Hercules: look at them. And, my Lord, we were arrogant, solipsistic bastards. We were New Jersey bodybuilders, and, for a brief time, singing the body electric, I lived in triumph.

But before immersing myself in the clandestine madness of belonging to this club for gods, I was a naïve sixteen-year-old whose first-ever serious girlfriend had chewed up his heart and spat it on the pavement. My uncle Tony had been a weightlifter and bodybuilder in his early twenties and, missing the iron, had recently set up a no-nonsense, professional-grade gym in one half of his basement: dumbbell set from 10 to 100, squat rack, pulley machine, preacher bench, and the scores of Olympic plates held in various racks under the mirrors. My uncle lived across the street from my grandmother, and since my father was struggling to raise three kids by himself, besieged by a revolting mortgage, we ate dinner every night at my grandmother's house.

One late afternoon before dinner, stultified by grief and boredom, I went into the basement to visit my uncle, absentmindedly picked up a barbell to squeeze out a set of bicep curls, and found a passion I didn't know I needed. Part of my motive became to alter my pathetic, emaciated physique into a monument worthy of my estranged girlfriend's lust, and another part was an (unconscious) attempt to meet my family's outrageous, Homeric standards of manliness; their conception of the masculine was divided into the heroic and the cowardly, with no room for gradation. But the largest part of my motive was simply to stave off the aimlessness I felt bearing down on me. And I didn't become just another body in my uncle's basement gym every weekday from 3:30 to 5:00; I became his trusted partner, and together we set out on a mission of manliness.

Those first results I noticed in the mirror produced euphoria, infective and addictive. After only a few weeks of high calorie force-feeding—enormous piles of pasta for dinner each evening, a quart of protein shake before bed each night—and not a single missed day of training, my deltoids and pectorals began to mushroom, my biceps balloon, my back thicken and widen, my traps swell out from my neck, my quads sweep out from my waist. Each week I packed on more pounds, and my strength increased steadily; more and more plates were added to my bench press, my squat, my straight-bar and preacher-bar curls. In that fluorescent end of my uncle's basement, with the primal howls of AC/DC blaring through a pair of speakers, with the scent of dampness and rust hanging in that stagnant air, with posters of Bruce Lee and bodybuilder Tom Platz looking on (Platz was a steroid-ballooned aberration with the legs of a rhinoceros), I witnessed that teenage boy transform in the mirror before me, and the transformation proved all-empowering. I could move boulders, topple buildings. And already I had been thinking about achieving an outrageous freakiness with anabolic steroids in my own blood, but at this early stage I knew very little about drugs. That would change.

In the seminal documentary *Pumping Iron* (1977), Arnold Schwartzenegger—still the monarch of all things bodybuilding—likened a good workout pump to an orgasm. Despite the ecstasy of those pumps, I cared more for what was permanent, for what I could carry through the day with me: the body armor that announced the arrival of a formidable opponent, a disciplined warrior . . . a man. Because, after all, being a man is the chief concern of any adolescent male, whether he recognizes it or not. In my family the concern was amplified: Giraldi men were burly, stoic, hard-working carpenters, and I needed to make my place among them. I had the formula—I had it right there, bulging out in luscious roundness from beneath my T-shirt. In *War and Peace* Tolstoy likens the body to a machine, and so what I sought was the best possible machine, the mightiest machine, perhaps believing that it would make life's certain travails more endurable, much the way a luxury car makes highway traffic less nightmarish. And "machine" is the perfect word, because the grotesque bodybuilders I admired and aspired to join looked more mechanical than human.

I trained all that summer like a Spartan, and when I returned to school in September, as a junior at Hillsborough High, some people had trouble recognizing me. Friends and enemies both appeared befuddled, and my ex-girlfriend eyed me with fascination from distant recesses of the hallway. My math teacher, Mr. Roba—former Marine and star athlete—blessed me with what remains perhaps the greatest compliment I've ever received. He said, "It looks good on you, kid." In June they had beheld a 115-pound waif with longish hair and a blanched, pimply complexion. What stood before them now was something altogether different—it didn't seem plausible: 145 pounds of lean muscle beneath a bronze sheath. The awe-struck reaction I prompted is the sole reason any person desires the physical conversion I had achieved, never mind what he tells you about the health benefits. Compliments and admiration are what fuel the addiction to the iron, to the mirror. And I did manage to win back my estranged girlfriend, though the reunion was a laughable failure and lasted only a few months.

Milan Kundera has named youth "the lyrical age" because, like the lyric poet, the youth is "focused almost exclusively on himself, is unable to see, to comprehend, to judge clearly the world around him." Give to this same youth the self-worship that bodybuilding fosters and what you get is a Narcissus so detached from the normality of others that his ego threatens to turn him into a loathsome sociopath, one who sees himself as walking poetry. But I had no qualms about my new life: it was indeed an addiction—one that would soon take me into some seedy, steroid-infested corners—but it also allowed me strength, poise, surety of character, and respite from a brutish melancholy. And so I intensified my training, since 145 pounds was still a munchkin; I needed another fifty pounds of lean mass, and it looked like anabolic drugs were the only route. If someone had told me then that in just over a year I would waltz across a stage in a frenzied bodybuilding competition, wearing only a blue bikini bottom, tanned an unnatural bronze, and mushroomed on three different anabolic drugs, I would have doubted it. My only focus at this juncture was to look like a genetically enhanced Atlas, to be the strongest eighteen-year-old guy in town. Formal competition seemed an impossibility.

Each day I devoured muscle magazines and took intricate notes on specialized diets and new training methods; these notes filled my composition pads alongside rudimentary observations on *The Great Gatsby*, *The Sun Also Rises*, and *The Catcher in the Rye*—the three novels that would play the most instrumental role in my pursuit of literature. Then, in my senior year of high school, after eighteen months of steadfast training, my uncle began to go wayward, lose interest, get more involved in work and his children. But he had taught me every trick I needed in order to forge ahead without him: what to eat, how much, and at what times (eating was still my biggest issue—I hated to force-feed myself every night before bed, wolfing down a thick turkey sandwich); how to increase mass and strength (high weight, low reps); how to sculpt that mass (low weight, high reps); how to alter a workout routine in order to overcome a plateau, that dreaded wasteland of making no gains; how to target a lagging body part (pectorals in my case); how to get inspired for two unforgiving exercises known to defeat even the most austere bodybuilder, squats and dead-lifts. "Squats and deads are what separate the men from the boys," my uncle would say.

My uncle had come from the Draconian gyms of New Jersey, Apollo Gym and Diamond Gym, hardcore dungeons for freaky beasts, elite training fields that eschewed the pencil-neck businessman and the middle-aged housewife. These gyms were bastions of unapologetic masculinity, of men preparing for the most pretigious bodybuilding competitions in Jersey, and my uncle cut his teeth there among the cracked mirrors, leaky pipes, and bloodstained floors. Some men carried buckets from exercise to exercise because they trained to the point of puking. To walk through those gyms was to be among single-minded giants, dedicated champions injecting themselves with the finest drugs science could muster. My uncle himself was always too honorable for drugs—for him the only glory came in doing it naturally, and he never had the slightest urge to step onstage. I didn't either.

As in gorilla or chimpanzee troops, reverence and fear dominated those gyms; if a larger, more animalistic specimen needed a machine or dumbbell, you humbly surrendered it. And you always kept yourself covered in a sweatshirt and sweatpants: to flaunt your own hard-won muscle in the presence of even greater muscle was blasphemous, hubristic, a cause for shame. This same hubris damns Pentheus in *The Bacchae* of Euripides: the young ruler tries to flex his muscle in the presence of the god Dionysus, but the god possesses superior muscle, and so Pentheus dies a gruesome death. The play is a masterpiece of eroticism, which was exactly how we bodybuilders viewed ourselves and each other: as muscled Casanovas. I didn't realize till long after I had left that odd world that, despite all the female attention and sex with women, the eroticism was chiefly homoerotic. We were more Greek than we realized (about which more later).

So my uncle imparted to me that Draconian workout ethic. When he retired from the iron, he allowed me to bring over my own training partners—since the kind of heavy lifting we executed made training without a partner or spotter deadly—and I in turn attempted to impart the same view to the friends who tried to join me. My long-time comrade Russ Brit began coming to my uncle's dungeon, and to my surprise he possessed the blood-and-guts warrior credo. Then, in a comical twist I couldn't have foreseen, my enemy Jimmy Ruh asked me to train him. Jimmy was the football player and class president who had snagged my girlfriend away from me eighteen months earlier. We were supposed to brawl in the parking lot a number of times but, thankfully, those brawls never came to fruition—I would have been savaged and humiliated. Now, thinking me a mighty Proteus, Jimmy wanted me to transform him the way I had transformed myself. And we attempted to undergo such tutelage, but Jimmy didn't have the necessary genetics for muscle mass, or the even-more-necessary barbarian gumption to wrestle with iron five days a week. The psychological benefits of witnessing another man get crushed by the fierce training regimen and severe diet were in themselves almost worth the hours of sweat-drenched agony.

This severe diet, the bane of many, was for me not so severe because, like my uncle, I had a rapid metabolism: gaining and keeping weight was my problem. I could eat hefty portions of whatever I wanted (as long as I consumed the requisite grams of protein) and, as long as I kept training, the pounds adhered to the proper places, filled out my deltoids, quadriceps, pectorals, and biceps. I was doubly lucky because my waist was only twenty-nine inches, which allowed me the much-sought-after V-shape. Also, in addition to having full muscle bellies, I had narrow joints, which meant that I always appeared more muscular than was actually the case. For the competitive bodybuilder, aesthetics matter more than strength. I would discover that when you're on stage nobody cares about how much you bench press.

A precontest diet exacts cruel punishment, but at this point in my development I was able to eat anything, as long as I ate. And I did, nearly every two hours: I carried Tupperware containers to school, containers over-stuffed with tuna fish and wheat bread, and I sat in the hallway between classes and forced down the food. Fellow students glared at me as they passed by holding their noses. The smell of tuna fish was another way for me to garner attention, to announce my distinction, my discipline, my godliness. But still, I hated it—all those mounds of protein piled before me several times a day. It was exhausting to eat that much. A bodybuilder spends half his time thinking about the iron, and the other half thinking about food. If he ever gives himself a break from thoughts of iron and food, he thinks about drugs.

My first real attempt to score a cache of steroids came about through my boyhood chum Russ Brit, who was still training with me in my uncle's basement. Russ knew someone who frequented the pizzeria where he worked part-time, someone who had promised him a shipment of anabolics from a hardcore gym in New York. Youth is brazen—or, as Disraeli has it, "Youth is a blunder"—and so, after discovering the location of this guy's apartment, I rode my twelve-speed bicycle there and knocked on his door. After telling him who I was, I tried to hand him a fistful of cash in exchange for the ampoules and needles. This nervous young man told me that the shipment hadn't arrived yet but that it would within a week, and then he asked me not to show up at his apartment anymore. I rode home without feeling even the slightest bit of blunder in me, certain that I was one step closer to procuring the drugs I needed to realize my ideal physical form. I never once considered steroids a weaker man's short-cut; the kind of freakiness I desired just wasn't possible without them.

Of course we never heard from that fellow again, but sometime during my senior year of high school some pals and I were able to score—through vigilant negotiations with other bodybuilders and weight lifters who belonged to various gyms in the area—a potent oral anabolic called Anadrol. Designed for anemics, Anadrol was the most sought after bodybuilding drug on the black market, a badass chemical invention that increased size and strength as nothing else could. Anadrol was so attractive, not only because of its supreme effectiveness, but because it wasn't an injectable steroid: many of my companions had a fear of needles, a paranoia about addiction and disease, and weren't capable of plunging one into their buttocks.

The irony is that injectable steroids are much healthier because, unlike pills, they get directly assimilated by the body without having to pass through the liver. Anadrol, on the other hand, was so potent it unleashed hell upon the liver—sometimes I could feel mine aching. But the stuff was sweet magic: I inflated from 155 pounds to 165 pounds in just two weeks, and this for someone who could go months on end without gaining a single pound. Never mind the high blood pressure that caused me constant, beleaguering headaches: the granite roundness of my deltoids and biceps, the added body mass I felt in each step, the way my quads shook under my sweatpants, how my lats (latissimus dorsi) propped up my arms—it was so intoxicating I could think nothing of the possibility that I had begun inflicting damage on my vital organs with black market chemicals.

Nearly everyone in my orbit noticed the added mass, the increased irritability and aggression, my complaints of headaches. My pal Mark Holden one afternoon ransacked my locker in hope of finding my pills; he said I looked like a cartoon character and was damned impossible to be around. I bickered incessantly with my new girlfriend Monique. Testosterone is the Yahweh hormone: too much turns a man into a hostile, unreasonable despot eager to flex his brawn. One day in the hallway I literally ripped a door off its hinges when it wouldn't open properly, and for some reason this felt good to me, much the way I imagine Yahweh grinning as he smites Gomorrah to ash. My uncle noticed the change in me, as well. At a picnic, a family member asked me, "How are you doing?" to which my uncle countered, "*What* are you doing?" He meant, What kind of poison are you pushing into your body? He of all people knew what a drug physique looked like, and he didn't approve, although he never mentioned it to me again.

* *

At around the time of my high school graduation my uncle's basement ceased to be enough for me. I had up till this point avoided joining a real gym because I feared I was not muscular enough to hold my own—this despite the fact that I was now 165 pounds at five feet eight inches, had only three percent body fat, was pumped full of Anadrol, and was lifting my highest numbers ever: 225 bench press for five reps, 315 squat for eight, 400 dead-lift for three, 125 barbell curl for ten. Some boyhood friends from my hometown had recently joined the weightlifting and bodybuilding cult and were training at a gym a few towns over called the Physical Edge. Set back in an industrial park, off an ordinary road with patches of forest, the Edge was a sprawling facility with modern equipment, and it catered to both the overweight housewife and the dogged bodybuilder. I have seldom known the brand of excitement I experienced upon joining that gym and becoming a key member of its core. I was eighteen years old, fresh from high school, postponing college, living at home rent-free, loving a girlfriend who modeled in Manhattan: these are the formative circumstances old men miss.

Within only a week of joining I paired up with Pauly, a short Italian with diamond thighs, monstrous arms, and an unforgiving case of acne from anabolic steroids. His partner had just suffered a hernia lifting too much weight, and so Pauly had been hunting for a serious, skilled replacement. His choosing me was confirmation that my rigorous training had impressed him, that I had achieved the kind of muscularity that wins admiration. We trained like animals: grumbled and groaned, spat and sweat, cursed and yelled. Our weight was heavy, our focus undeterred. And Pauly wasn't the only one impressed by my attitude and physique: the manager and head trainer of the Edge offered me a job working the morning shift from five to twelve, which meant that I was now an Edge representative. I had been there less than a month and was already the go-to guy, beginning friendships with gargantuan freaks of nature, guys who were so consumed by drugs and the bodybuilding lifestyle that they could scarcely hold a two-minute conversation with anybody who wasn't.

The fact that these champions considered me worthy of their

friendship loaded me with a pride and honor that I have not felt since. What did they look like? You've seen them on the cover of magazines: the vascularity, thick cords coursing over dense, lean muscle; the complexion, a mixture of bronze, orange, and red; the outfits, skimpy and skintight; the facial expressions, determined and of singular purpose. And the women there who flocked to us: they, too, were fitness maniacs, all of them obsessed with physical perfection. We inspired each other immensely, helped each other with the weights and machines— skin against skin, sweat against sweat, the sexual grunts and groans coming from us as the iron rose and fell, as our strong blood surged through muscle tissue. The women spent hours there training, stretching, and talking with us, wanting to bathe in the expert light we radiated. This was our army, and part of the pleasure of belonging resulted from the secrecy, the illegality, the shunning of normal people and their normal ways.

It got to the point where most of us could not associate with anyone who wasn't a member of that army. Although none of us drank alcohol we would sometimes go to a popular bar and delight in how the whole place would part for us to pass through, this band of mechanical mammals. But we lived mostly for the charged environment of the Edge, looking forward to it when we weren't there and savoring every minute we were. We could not imagine how ordinary people walked through this life without muscle. And for me this was especially true: I literally could not imagine what that felt like, much the way any given person can never accurately fathom having the genitalia of the opposite sex.

Imagine us there in the locker room of the Physical Edge: a clan of hairless, nearly naked men harpooning each other's buttocks with needles, massaging the painful cramps out of each other's deltoids and quads, positioning each other into poses before the mirror, lying naked in the tanning bed, showering each other with compliments on muscle shape and density. . . . Didn't this strike any of us as extremely gay? As a love affair with the muscled male form? If a sexologist had shown up and pointed this out to us, we would have insisted that he just didn't understand—the passion, the code, the discipline, the masculinity *in extremis* . . . right before slapping him senseless. We would have insisted that a portion of our esoteric zeal resulted from wanting to astonish women, to bed as many as possible. After all, procreative dominance is the main benefit of being alpha male in a chimpanzee or gorilla troop—those noble cousins of ours who would have felt quite

301

at home in our gym. Or pick up Darwin's masterpiece and reread the chapter "Selection in Relation to Sex" to see how eerily similar a bodybuilder is to a bird: flashy plumage influences sexual success.

But the real aim of our esoteric zeal—so hidden from us then—was to astonish each other, to gain the unadulterated affection and admiration of other elite men. As in Hemingway's universe of men relying on men for survival, of disdaining the female and her interfering ways, we too responded only to male influence and praise. The irony, of course, is that we had ourselves turned into females: we sought the esteem and approval of men, shaved and tanned our bodies, wore scant clothing, were food-obsessed beyond reason. We had undergone sex changes and behaved exactly as prototypical women, constantly fretting over our fragile images and self-worth and control or lack of it— it was straight from the pages of an anorexia handbook. Pauly's hideous case of acne brought on by steroids was a tolerable consequence of his trying to be beautiful, much the way anorexic women become skeletal and hirsute and hideous in their quest to be stunning.

So the male bodybuilder and the female anorexic are separate though equal manifestations of the same social pressure placed upon both genders: women must be rail thin, men superhero muscular, and damn everything else. You can blame prime-time TV and the magazine rack at the grocery store, but the real culprit is a modern malaise dictating that nothing is ever good enough: your job, your car, your spouse, your body. And so we dive into dangerous extremes to achieve an unattainable perfection, forgetting that the goal is to be attractive and healthy and loved. This is the American Dream of our bodies, as fallacious and silly as the American Dream that sells us all a ruse of guaranteed economic success (with a splash of fame). We different genders are more equivalent than we get credit for, and nowhere is this more obvious than in the gym.

So what did the Homeric patriarchs of my family think about my turning into a woman, my father and grandfather and the uncles I was desperate to impress? They didn't see it that way because I looked like a magazine's dream of masculinity, all marble brawn. And the truth is that they remained mostly ignorant to what happened at the Edge; they never saw my shaved body (except for my arms in the summer), didn't know that I pined after the acceptance of other men, considered my food obsession a necessary sign of election, and didn't witness us there in the locker room like a band of adoring femmes.

Of course I didn't see it that way either, because I was too young and too busy harvesting the benefits of my physique. But, oddly, the most titillating erotic affair I experienced during my time at the Edge was not the result of the body I had so obsessively sculpted, but of F. Scott Fitzgerald. I had been keeping my pursuit of literature a secret from my family and bodybuilding comrades because reading Goethe and writing stories were considered effeminate, anathema, a high-minded waste of time that could in no way aid one's muscle mass. Erika came to the Edge every morning just after I opened the doors at 5:00 a.m., and she would sit at the counter for a while, chatting with me as she sipped on the protein shake I had blended for her. When one morning she pulled out of her duffel bag a copy of *The Beautiful and Damned*, I said, "Anthony and Gloria Patch. Miserable, aren't they?" I had finished the novel three weeks earlier, and Erika looked across the counter at me as if I had just conjured the dead. She said, "You read?" I said, "Yes." She said, "Books?" I said, "Yes." She said, "*Literary* books?" And I said, "Yes, I think so." My relationship with Monique was dying; she had gone off to Rutgers and buried me in the farthest reaches of her gray heart. So for the next few weeks I went to Erika's apartment in the middle of the night, and as she ground fanatically in my lap with her wild blonde hair flitting around her head, she'd say, "Call me Daisy!" and this I would do, right before the eager ejaculatory bliss that only youth and anabolic steroids can inspire.

The drugs were necessary now—and not merely a tool for my vanity—because an inevitability had occurred: my fellow enthusiasts had talked me into competing in a popular bodybuilding show called the Muscle Beach, held in Point Pleasant, New Jersey. I wasn't surprised by my allowing them to convince me of this; being around so many competitive bodybuilders at the Edge had begun to make me curious about my own potential on stage. It seemed the natural next step: from my uncle's basement to the Edge to competing on stage. Was I petrified of having to strut almost naked in front of several thousand people, all of whom would be scrutinizing my every millimeter? Someone this deep in the bodybuilding headspace doesn't blink at dancing in a bikini bottom; in fact, that's the point: to show the cosmos what you created. I viewed my readiness for the stage as another signal of my worthiness as a man, never mind the fact that the competitive bodybuilder is more femmy than his noncompetitive brethren: a

303

guy in a bikini wearing self-tanning bronzer and performing a little dance routine.

If I intensified my training, altered my diet slightly, and became even more of a single-minded beast, I could place high in the teenage division. Pauly and I and some others had been driving around Jersey each Saturday to watch different competitions, and at one of these shows we all became convinced that I could excel onstage if I wanted to. But I would have to wean myself from the Sustanon 250 I was injecting every week because this mass-building, oil-based anabolic caused water retention, and water retention blurred vascularity and muscle striation. It made one look strong, yes, but also puffy, and puffy was not the desired aesthetic on stage; rather, one wanted to look "ripped" or "shredded"—diaphanous skin with no water beneath the surface so that the thin lines of muscle composite were visible.

I had begun accumulating boxes of steroids for my own use; the drugs would come into the gym from our key sources—two fellow freaks we trusted—and I bought up whatever I could, even if I wasn't just then using that particular blend of testosterone. Word of one's drug stash passed quickly through an incestuous gym such as ours, and when a fellow soldier needed an anabolic for his battle, you happily sold it to him. This hoarding and selling became rather chimerical once when a pal named Tom stopped by my place to pick up a thousand dollars worth of Dianabol, a magical anabolic difficult to come by. Tom was a gigantic cop, six feet seven inches tall and well over three hundred pounds, and he arrived at my apartment that day in his police cruiser and police uniform. So I sold a uniformed cop a bag of anabolic steroids in my sunlit kitchen. Through the window above the sink I watched him leave, and I remember saying aloud to myself, "What on earth am I doing?" But I didn't give it much thought after that moment, because this was the reality of the world we inhabited. None of us experienced even a second of shame over our drug use— shame was for everyday people, and we were champions who relished the secrecy and law breaking.

My precontest training spanned several weeks; the most taxing part was the purified diet: chicken breast, cup of brown rice, cup of steamed broccoli—all of it plain, seven times a day. My dreams were detailed collages of chocolate, cake, and candy. When I stopped the heavy anabolic drugs, I lost some of my mass, but this was necessary: each day I got leaner, more striated, more vascular. This effect was helped along by a drug called Winstrol-V, a water-based steroid designed to make horses run faster—it burned as it went in. Each evening after my workout I sat on the exercise bike for fifty minutes and tried not to let anyone see that I was holding Goethe's novel *The Sorrows of Young Werther*. I practiced my contest routine in the aerobics room under the guidance of some contest veterans who wanted me to win, to represent the Edge in the teenage division.

Sometimes the image in the mirror startled me: that chiseled bronze statue had my eyes. When I shopped in the supermarket at night I could see the other shoppers pointing and whispering, and some of them not in admiration, but mockery. As I rappelled deeper into a contest mentality, I had mostly forgotten to think about the patriarchs of my family, about whether or not they were proud of what I had accomplished. If they wanted a real man (albeit one who had turned into a woman), there I stood. But the solipsistic bastard doesn't have the space to consider his family; he's too consumed with his own lovely vision of himself. And was I a real man now, or just an image of one?

Scores of supporters and family members trekked down to Point Pleasant for my competition; the air inside that auditorium felt radioactive. Backstage, Pauly and some other pals from the gym covered me in a final coat of bronze paint—skin must be as dark as possible in order for muscle definition to be visible under the strong lights, otherwise your cuts get washed out. The distinct coppery smell of this body paint nearly overwhelmed me—every man backstage was drenched in the stuff. And there we stood in our bikini bottoms, eighty misunderstood warriors from each weight division, gently pumping up with the dumbbells, our eyeballs glowing against our newly blackened hides. Stage fright did not occur to me, and failure did not occur to me, even though I was smaller and weaker than I had been before the new diet. I spotted other teenagers who were larger than I was, but Pauly and the guys kept making the point: "You're shredded, bro. That dude ain't ripped like you. You're nails, got veins everywhere. Don't sweat him. You're *nails*." Of course it was a monumental task not to sweat because I was wearing an extra layer of bronze skin and the temperature backstage rose to ninety degrees.

My song began and I strutted onstage to the eruption of shouts and hollers. The hot lights distorted my vision of the crowd; I could make out only a few faces; the rest was a bleary canvas of color. I performed my muscle-showing, semidance routine just as I had practiced it for weeks, and after a minute and forty seconds I was done, walking off into the wings, my hand held high in appreciation, exhilaration, joy. After every man had his chance to perform individually, all ten of us in the teenage division stood in queue on stage for the group competition, during which the judges called for various poses: front double bi, back lat spread, etc. Because my physique was harder and more symmetrical than the larger guys, I won second place that night. I carried offstage a two-foot sculpture trophy that weighed forty pounds, and as I walked behind the curtain and out into the fluorescent hallway that led to my seat in the auditorium, I became flooded by bliss. There's no other word for it. Bliss. I haven't felt that way since.

* *

Things began to unravel after that. The Edge went bankrupt and chained its doors closed; our group scattered to various other gyms in central Jersey. My relationship with Monique crumbled for good, my father sold my boyhood home, and a ruthless melancholy clobbered me into oblivion. Pauly and I remained training partners—I planned to compete in another bodybuilding show in just five months—but without the camaraderie and compassion at the Edge, the training and drugs and lifestyle began to lose their meaning for me. Pauly and I were driving long distances to try out various gyms in Jersey, but none of them ever came close to promising the happiness we experienced at the Edge. At this time of suicidal blackness my physique never looked better: I was fifteen pounds heavier than my previous contest weight, harder and more symmetrical, and this because I got the drug cocktail right. But still: I suffered through each workout with Pauly and through each forced meal (depression annihilated my appetite). I missed the Edge, regretted my estrangement from Monique, and read Raymond Carver's doleful stories every night and morning, wanting to shift my life from the gym to the library . . . wanting to write. I was nineteen years old and felt the jadedness of someone twice my age.

When it was time to step on stage again, I didn't even care: I fell asleep in my car in the parking lot before the show. That day and the day before I had screwed up my diet in a way I could not rectify—if you don't have the proper ratio of carbohydrates, potassium, and water in your muscle tissue before you step onstage, all your cuts vanish. Pauly said he couldn't spot a single abdominal muscle from his seat in the audience. It didn't matter. I took fourth place and walked offstage.

The depression would get a lot worse before I could begin to see my way out of it; the old crowd from the Edge—all those men and women I cared so much about and shared so much with—promised to keep in touch, but it never happened. Without the Edge as our mother ship we were unconnected orphans. If I thought that bodybuilders lived a bizarre, esoteric life, I was soon to find out that the life of a writer can be every bit as solitary and obsessive. People ask me all the time now if I miss those glory days, if I miss having that physique, that mind-set, those dangerous methods. How could someone miss so much vanity, so much narcissistic pride and drug use? And why did I walk away so suddenly? The truth is that I had simply outgrown the iron, that fixation on my physique. I couldn't reconcile being a bodybuilder with wanting to be a student of Homer, Milton, Hopkins. And let's face it: a grown man looks rather silly flexing his biceps in the mirror, especially if he's holding *The Iliad* in one hand. I had found another way of being a man, one that involved imagination, knowledge, compassion. If the men of my family and my former gym friends couldn't buy that, I couldn't help them.

But I do miss those days terribly. And who wouldn't miss them? Didn't you see us?

Nominated by Joyce Carol Oates, The Kenyon Review

WEAR

by JAY ROGOFF

from THE JOURNAL

The birds wear air
and the fish wear water.
Once we knew
the soul wore matter
but now, no matter,
the soul wears down.
The duckling's down
lets it wear water
in wearying weather.
The weather wears
the sun's fire
that warms the earth
in its wrap of air.
Earth wears the moon
and the moon wears water,
pulling the tides
from their coastal harbor
and wearing them down
upon the sand
where the tides wear land,
where we wore each other
like winter clothing.
We watched our breath
and into the ground
we wore each other,

honeymooners
on a train
squabbling over
the lower berth.
Christ, how can you
lie, my darling,
naked under
cover in the winter,
wearing earth?

Nominated by Daniel Hoffman

THEY SAY

by LAURA KASISCHKE

from NEW ENGLAND REVIEW

one-twelfth of our lives is wasted
standing in a line.

The sacred path of that.

Ahead of me, a man in black, his broad back.
Behind me, a woman like me
unwinding her white veils.

And beyond us all, the ticket-taker, or the old
lady with our change, or

the officials with our food, our stamps, our unsigned papers, our
gas masks, our inoculations.

It hasn't happened yet.
It hasn't begun or ended.
It hasn't granted us its bliss
or exploded in our faces.
The baby watches the ceiling from its cradle.
The cat stares at the crack in the foundation.
The grandfather flies the sick child's kite higher
and higher. I set

my husband's silverware on the table.
I place a napkin beside
my son's plate.

Soon enough,
but not tonight.
Ahead of us, that man's black back.
Behind us, her white veils.

Ahead of us, the nakedness, the gate.

Behind us, the serene errand-boy, the cigarette, the wink-and-nod,
   the waiting.

Beyond that, too late.

Nominated by Pinckney Benedict, James Harms, Mark Irwin

SHEEP MAY SAFELY GRAZE

fiction by JESS ROW

from THE THREEPENNY REVIEW

It was a tiny leak, no more than a pinprick, and a few eyedroppers' full of gas that killed my youngest daughter, Jolie, at summer camp when she was eight years old. She was in a motorboat on a lake, Lake St. Clair, learning to waterski. The fuel line ruptured; gas leaked into the bilge, and when the driver started the engine the boat exploded. The two other girls next to her on the rear seat, in lifejackets, also died. The driver, who should have checked the fuel tanks, who should have smelled the gas—a nineteen-year-old, named Rick Paradisi—suffered third-degree burns over most of his body and survived for three months in a coma.

The story was in the newspapers all up and down the East Coast that July. In our neighborhood, at the supermarket, at the filling station, we were briefly famous. Nobody would take our money. The front hallway was lined with flowers. Strangers mowed the lawn and picked up our dry cleaning.

Then something else happened. It may have been the McDonald's massacre, or the Democratic convention where Mondale was nominated. It was the summer of 1984: the world was full of unexpected calamities. Mercifully, we were forgotten. The film footage of my life, which records this event in the glare and jagged shadows of midsummer, dims, grows grainy, goes dark.

I can offer only commonplaces.

A certain stony afternoon light in the sky outside my office window. The aftertaste of a thousand watery cups of coffee. My hands and feet

312

were always cold; I wore gloves and wool socks in May. At night I turned on every light in the house: I hated the look of a shadowy corner.

Wherever I was alone, in the car, on the Metro, in my study, I had to have music playing. I went out and bought a Sony Walkman expressly for this purpose. Rossini, Stravinsky, Gounod, Telemann: it didn't matter. At work my secretary slid papers under my elbow with little notes attached: *Sign here. This is due next Monday. Call Evans at the GAO.* It was as if, by degrees, without noticing, I'd become deaf, and everyone around me was too polite to point it out.

In those days—before I took early retirement, did some desultory computer consulting, and finally stopped working for good, in 2002— I ran the small inhouse publishing office at the National Security Agency. This was an administrative post, and I was a civilian, not an agent. Nonetheless, for obvious reasons, I had a very high security clearance. All twelve of us did: copyeditors, designers, secretaries, technicians. A jammed page pulled out of a Xerox machine in that office might be worth a hundred thousand dollars. I published our most sensitive materials: the reports that went to the Joint Chiefs of Staff. No one else was allowed to see them. I stood in front of the printer myself, and carried them in a plain manila envelope to the rear entrance of the Old Executive Office Building.

On the rare occasions when someone asks about my career, I offer a standard, canned response: I have nothing to add to the historical record. I suppose this makes me look like the proverbial cog in the wheel, the faceless bureaucrat. (I should know: Rachel and I were German majors in college; we read *Der Prozess* in the same seminar.) But I have to accept that silent—almost imperceptible—humiliation, because the more unpleasant truth is that I paid very little attention to the content of the materials we published. I had trouble remembering specifics even from day to day. It wasn't necessary, and it would have been distracting. I was an editor, a proofreader. Innocent people, civilians, can die, *have* died, over a misplaced comma in a sensitive document, let alone a badly chosen word, like *friendly* or *unfortunate*. In intelligence you come to appreciate that behind every word on a sheet of paper is a vulnerable human body. My counterpart at the CIA once showed me a file of examples, with photographs. For years I kept a typed quotation from Wittgenstein on the bulletin board above my desk: *Whereof one cannot speak, thereof one must be silent.*

* * *

313

I had a therapist, of course, assigned by my doctor. At each session he tried to explain to me what stage of the grieving process I was experiencing. I couldn't help myself: I kept insisting that he give me an exact definition of each word he used, what function it served, what could be considered X and not Y. This last point particularly bothered me. If I had a bad day at work, and missed my stop, and then barked at the cab driver for running a red light and refused to tip him, was that grief? If I found myself unexpectedly tearing up during the final scene of *Un Ballo en Maschera*, having to grope in Rachel's handbag for a tissue, was that, too, grief? And why should I victimize myself by reliving these feelings, by groping to find equivalents for them in words? Wasn't it enough to have had the feelings in the first place?

The advantage of this calamity, I told him, was that it was utterly arbitrary: a clean break, a window opened and closed. There was no way Rachel and I could blame ourselves, no way we could associate ourselves with it at all. Jolie had existed and one day had ceased to exist. We had no interest in lawsuits or safety campaigns or any of the other desiderata of grieving parents. Our mourning, I said, was purely and simply that. A clean wound. One day it would be healed.

He said he found it interesting that I thought the same rules that applied to everyone else wouldn't apply to me.

I lost my temper. I told him I thought it was a sham, these systems, these lists, these processes he kept proposing. An emotion, I said, isn't an abstraction, isn't an object, can't be verified, and therefore can't be categorized. I told him he should stop playing God.

He laughed, and said I should read Wittgenstein. That was the end of therapy for me.

Of Rachel during all that time I have only one memory: perched on the edge of Alex's bed, still in her librarian's brown mules, drying her hands on a towel, and telling a story, whispering it, into the darkened room where both children slept. Whether she made the stories up beforehand or improvised on the spot I have no idea, but she spoke without hesitation, without a text, for half an hour or forty-five minutes at a time. One day it was a romance between two hedgehogs in Scotland and the next a unicorn searching for her mother in the Himalayas. It was her unshakeable confidence in the happy outcomes of her stories, I like to think, that saved Alex and Merrill some of the pain of the randomness of this one.

In my own way I too was an undistracted parent. I could wait an hour in the pickup line at school, or sit through a Parents' Association meeting, or spend an entire morning at a swim meet, without once checking my watch, without wishing I had brought the paper. Reagan was re-elected. It was hard to summon up the expected outrage.

I should say—by way of disclaimer? of apology?—that I've never held particularly strong political beliefs. In this I take after my father, the postmaster of Sheffield, Connecticut, who sometimes would come out onto the post office floor and collect mail from waiting customers just for the pleasure of canceling it at his desk by hand. I shared with him a special appreciation for the beauty of the impersonal gesture. An old woman in Topeka receives her Social Security check every month not because anyone loves her or even remembers her name. The crossing guard stopping traffic in front of the elementary school need not recognize a single child that scampers past. One's human inadequacies are not the point. Efficiency, permanence, and careful design, I would have said, are the basis of real human charity and kindness.

If it was grief that I was feeling—and I still hate to use the word—it was this sense of the implacable nature of these structures that I wrapped around myself, like a blanket, or a cocoon. The momentary life of sensations, feelings, opinions, went right through me. Just existing, for the time being, was enough. I paid the mortgage, I bought groceries, I balanced the checkbook. I slept deeply and dreamlessly in the arms of a beautiful machine. It was a not entirely unpleasant existence.

In November of 1985, during an early cold snap, a homeless man named Jevon Morris froze to death on a grate downtown, in front of the National Archives. He stayed there, frozen, through the morning rush hour, with hundreds passing by on their way to work or to the Mall and the museums. They walked past a heap of rags, a motionless form wrapped in an oily blanket, unable to tell whether it—he, she—was alive or dead. Finally, around noon, the smell of putrefaction was so strong that a passing policeman noticed it.

I read the story in the newspaper sitting at our kitchen table after work, drinking tea, listening to WGMS. It was Rachel's day to pick up the children. When I finished I found I couldn't lift my arms from the table. I sat paralyzed, my elbows resting on the outspread paper, my eyes locked on the windowsill, where, I noticed, someone or something had knocked a knuckle-sized crater in the wood. The sill jutted out a few inches from the wall; it had an old-fashioned fleur-de-lis carved molding underneath, and had been painted over probably twenty times in the sixty years of the house's life, so that the original edges and fine detail had long since disappeared. I myself had applied the most recent coat, seven years before. Whatever it was had been sharp enough to dig through that quarter-inch skin of paint and gouge into the bare wood, leaving a few tiny splinters sticking out. It was, in all likelihood, Alex's fault. He sat nearest the windowsill at dinnertime, and he was the kind of careless child who wasn't above putting his soccer cleats on in the front hall, or idly swinging something hard and heavy—a pair of scissors, say—enough to chip paint, or break glass.

The radio, at that moment, was playing the third movement of Charles Ives's first string quartet, *adagio cantabile*, with its odd, stately movement between simple major triads and dissonant flatted fifths. Its inability to stay on one track seemed to mock me. As I stared at it, that little divot of raw wood grew larger and larger; I felt that I could look into it and through it, that I might be swallowed up inside it, and that in there, from the other side, came screams of ceaseless pain. Without seeing it, precisely, I knew what was there: a human face, a black man's face, pressed up against the other side of the wall, not three feet away from my own. And behind him were other faces, other bodies, packed in tight. In the space between the interior latex paint of that wall and the cedar shingles outside, I felt certain, were countless bodies, unable to move.

I know it sounds absurd. In my entire life, my thoroughly ordinary existence in a leafy, mostly peaceful, sheltered corner of the planet, I've never again experienced anything like it. If I were given to hyperbole I might say that I had looked through a window into the world's wounded soul.

I came out of the daydream, went to the sink, poured out my tea, and quickly took a swig of Rachel's double-strength coffee, cold, straight from the carafe. The sudden shock of the caffeine would do it, I thought, would wake me up, finally, from the months of stupor, from my collapsing will, now turning into midday hallucinations, bizarre narcissistic fantasies. Either this, I thought, or a doctor for real, a psychiatrist, someone with a prescription pad and admitting privileges.

That didn't happen. Instead, almost unwillingly, I began to think about procedures, systems, chains of command. Whose job it was, for example, to write the rules that dictated to the Capitol Police when they should and should not patrol the streets for the sleeping homeless. I never doubted that there was such a policy. We are extremely good at writing policies in this city. And we are also good at understanding the difference between an empty rule and an enforceable one.

The radio announcer that day had a strange sense of humor. Immediately after the Ives came the Eugene Ormandy recording of Bach's "Sheep May Safely Graze," its treacly melody like a jingle from an old commercial. Ordinarily I would have risen and turned it off. But the chiming chords had the strangest, most inexplicable effect on me. I began to think of his childhood, of Jevon Morris's childhood. I saw him in his kindergarten class, on a threadbare carpet, kneeling, separate from the others. The teacher, I knew, had just shouted at him, had humiliated him, for something he hadn't done. Someone had wadded up a little ball of white bread and thrown it at him, and it was still there, stuck to his collar. He was blushing fiercely, even to the tips of his ears, and throttling back a sob.

As the music shifted into minor chords I found my eyes pooling with tears.

Someone is responsible, I thought. Someone knows why this has happened, and I will punish him.

On Wednesday of the week before Thanksgiving I took our office's box of donated canned goods to a shelter inside an abandoned school on P Street. It was all very organized; a girl not much older than Merrill took the box and started systematically unpacking it, putting each can and box into a different marked bin, one for each food group. I stared at her for a moment, at the extraordinary quickness of her slim, pale arms, and the way she methodically brushed her sandy hair out of her eyes every time she bent down. Her expressionless competence. Someone had told her that the world could be saved this way. I turned and walked up the stairs, past the sign marked *Paid Shelter Staff Only*, and knocked on the director's door.

Her name was Jenny Parker; she was about thirty-five, in jeans and a hooded sweatshirt and ripped sneakers. The ashtray on her desk was full. It wasn't an office, of course, but an old classroom, with chairs piled up against one wall. One of the windows had a pane missing; someone had tried to cover it with a piece of cardboard and Scotch tape, which had, of course, flapped away. It would be polite to say that she looked like she hadn't slept for a number of days. The circles under her eyes were as dark as bruises.

Listen, I said, I'm not here to take up your time. But I'm just wondering, as a citizen, if there's anything we can do on a bigger level. On a national level. I mean, this is an emergency. People are dying in the streets.

I could tell, in the moment that it took her to respond, that she was trying hard to stop herself from saying something derisive, that it took an effort for her to control the muscles that wanted to twist her lips into a bleak and skeletal grin.

Well, she said, we appreciate whatever you can give us here. We need all the grassroots support we can get. Right now we can only keep the heat on in the building for twelve hours of the day. Six at night to six in the morning. I haven't been paid in a month and a half.

I can write you a check right now.

Well, fine, she said. We appreciate that. But there is a bill, actually, if you're interested. It's in the Senate right now, in committee. To introduce a line item for homeless services into the HUD budget for the first time. It's a lost cause, but you're welcome to write a letter if you like. You work for the government, don't you?

Why is it a lost cause?

Oh, she said, the secretary doesn't support it. Frank Murphy. He's your typical Republican troglodyte from Idaho. He doesn't understand why a Vietnam vet in a wheelchair, on disability for twenty years, missing all but three teeth, can't get a job. Sorry if I'm offending you.

No, I said, I'm not an appointee. Civil service for fifteen years.

Yeah. She looked at her watch and began checking things off on a clipboard. I'd bet you work out at Langley, she said. That would be my first guess.

Why do you say that?

Because of your eyes, she said, without looking up. I grew up here. I should know.

I did my research. I read the reports in *Congressional Quarterly* and the *National Journal* and the Hill newsletters. What she had said was true, broadly speaking. Murphy had used his allies in the House to cut off discussion of the line item in committee before the Democrats had had a chance to pounce on it. He'd been unsuccessful. There had been three days of hearings, a whole stream of activists and homeless people and lobbyists of all shapes and sizes. Hardly any of it made the news, of course, because it was all doomed in advance: an item never makes it into a department's budget without the Secretary's support. Humiliation, in this case, hadn't done a bit of good. The final vote on the bill had been delayed until January, a last-ditch attempt by the Democrats to put pressure on the White House over the Christmas holiday. Politically speaking, that year, it was one lost cause among many.

Next to one article—"Homeless Abandoned a Second Time"— I found a small, grainy photograph: a middle-aged, fair-haired man, with a long jaw and a pronounced V-shaped wrinkle in his forehead— a perpetually pained look, a man who hated to have his picture taken. He had made a small fortune consolidating stockyards; he'd chaired the Idaho Chamber of Commerce and the state GOP. There was more, but I brought out my nail scissors and cut out the picture, leaving the rest in the wastebasket. Fearing the newsprint would rub off, I slid it carefully into a nylon holder in my wallet, next to my library card, just opposite a family picture, taken in our backyard the week after Jolie was born.

The gun came from Tim's Hunting Supply, far out on Rockville Pike, near Gaithersburg. It was a .38 Police Special, and it cost $150, including the Maryland registration and license. I used a false address in Bethesda I'd gotten out of the phone book. When I told the man behind the counter I'd never fired a pistol before, hoping he would at least show me how to load it, he shook his head and handed me a Gun Safety pamphlet.

On my way back into the District I pulled off Georgia Avenue into a disused parking lot behind a dry cleaner's and took the pistol out of its box. In the store, on a flannel mat on the counter beside three other guns, it had seemed small, thin-barrelled, pedestrian. A sensible starter gun, the man had said, you can get the ammo anywhere, it's foolproof, never jams. He looked like he wished he had somewhere else to be.

In my hand, now, it felt heavy enough to pull my hand to the floor.

Am I capable of this, I wondered, am I capable of murder? A month had elapsed, now, since Jevon Morris's death. It was early December; the children had two weeks left until winter vacation. The next weekend we would caravan out to Turkey Run Farm with two other fami-

319

lies to pick our own Christmas trees, an old tradition by now. And I had grown used to the memory of that afternoon, that strange vision, a gnawing stomachache of an obligation unmet. It wouldn't let me rest. I was afflicted with compassion, I thought. I was carrying it around me like tuberculosis.

I wrapped my left hand around my right, holding the pistol in a position of prayer. The longer I held it, the heavier it became, until I felt—I swear—that it could carry my whole body with it, that it would lead me wherever it wanted.

Frank Murphy's house was a small white-brick Cape Cod on Ellicott Street, near New Mexico Avenue and the Russian embassy, on the boundary of Rock Creek Park. The houses on Ellicott are built high on the slope, high enough to look out over the treetops across the park and see the Washington Monument and the Capitol dome. Many of them have garages built into the hill at street level, but Murphy's, as it happened, did not. He would park his car—or walk the long downhill slope from the Metro—and approach the stone steps up to his house on foot.

In December in Washington the light begins to fail at quarter of four; by four-thirty it is completely dark. I knew his face only from photographs. In order to make sure it was him I would have to be no more than ten feet away.

I left work as soon as I could, and parked in front of the house next door at five after five. Rachel had promised the children macaroni and cheese with cut-up hot dogs for dinner, and I had promised I would bring home ice cream after the meeting, by eight at the latest. Neapolitan ice cream, Merrill was particular about that, a brick of it, from the High's dairy store at Connecticut and Woodley Road.

When he approached, I thought, I would get out of the car, walk as close as possible, shoot once, at his chest, get back into the car and drive away. At the corner I would pause, momentarily, roll down the passenger side window, and throw the gun over the rail into the woods. That was all. If I was followed, if I was caught, I would not resist, I would not plead innocence. That was all I knew. As soon as I switched off the car an extraordinary calm descended over me; I could feel, or imagined I could feel, not just my heartbeat, but the tidal push-pull of blood traveling from my heart to the tiniest capillaries of my fingers and toes, and receding back again.

The car I drove in those years was a 1982 Toyota Tercel station

320

wagon, dark blue, with vinyl upholstery. It was the first new car Rachel and I had owned. I can describe it in intimate detail: the four-speed automatic transmission that lasted ten years, the parking brake that tended to stick on cold winter nights, the oil light blinking at random. By that December it had accumulated the dents and stains of three years' hard use in a family with young children. There was, for example, a tear in the ceiling fabric where someone had jammed a loose tent pole on a camping trip two summers back. I was in the habit of carrying coffee to work in a thermos that once had leaked on the passenger seat, and that particular odor always lingered, no matter how many times we used shampoo and hung air fresheners off the dashboard.

It had no cassette player, of course, and I didn't trust the radio at that hour, didn't want to hear traffic reports and news bulletins, the bustle of a city tidying up its day. So I had brought with me my Walkman, that delightful invention, and looped its headphones around my neck, so that the music would play *sotto voce*, underneath the sound of cars swishing by, doors slamming, leather soles clacking on the sidewalk. The cassette I had selected—need I even say this? should I have to explain everything?—was the Eroica Symphony, Leonard Bernstein conducting.

At quarter of seven I heard the unmistakable chugging of a car downshifting, and the white glare of headlights came up over my shoulders and raked across the dashboard. A tan Mercury sedan slowed three car lengths ahead of me, and backed, at a creep, into an open spot. The driver had to correct his turn twice; even so, he left the rear of the car sticking out six inches too far from the curb, at an almost insouciant angle.

I disentangled the headphones from my neck and opened the door as quietly as I could. The gun was in my right hand. I had on a pair of thin green cotton gloves, and as I moved out into the cold I realized sweat had soaked through the palms and fingers. It was as if I'd dipped my hands in ice water. Instinctively I shoved the gun into the waistband of my pants and dug my hands into the pockets of my jacket, balling them into fists. I was afraid they might become numb.

It shouldn't have surprised me, that the man who stood up out of his car looked quite different from his photograph. He had gained weight, recently; his jacket flapped open on either side of his belly, too tight to button, and his pants looked as if they had been cinched at the waist. As he came up the sidewalk he transferred his briefcase from one hand to the other and ran his fingers through his hair, which was badly, unmistakably dyed, several shades darker than his natural color.

I've spent my life surrounded by federal bureaucrats and the unlucky outsiders, the appointees, who oversee them. I've seen the former executives dashing around with charts and graphs, with turquoise bracelets and onyx pinky rings; the buzzcut ex-Marines who want to take you out for barbeque and Jack and Cokes, the holy-eyed Mormons with the crates of Pepsi and the LDS Christmas cards. Over time—if they last long enough—all of them are defeated by Washington. They exchange their monogrammed briefcases for navy-blue duffel bags; they enroll in wine-tasting classes and buy subscriptions to the Kennedy Center. They learn the unhurried pace of their secretaries, and the names of all the security guards and the janitors. Their faces take on a certain placid softness that is easy to confuse with mere slack disappointment.

Never have I seen one as undone as Frank Murphy. Whatever pallid and insubstantial comforts he took from the world in his former life were now gone. He walked with a slight rolling motion, from side to side, as if buffeted by winds only he could feel. Everything about him seemed to express a certain muted panic, a wild grasping for reassurance.

I wouldn't call it pity, this feeling I had. Pity is far too weak a word. I was gripped with a terrible feeling that this stranger, this contemptible specimen, was someone I had known all my life. I was enmeshed; I was caught. But I had already stood up out of the car, and he could see me; it was too late to drive away. I had to complete the plan. I walked toward him, crossing the sidewalk at a slight angle, keeping my hands in my pockets, out of sight.

I lost my dog, I said. He ran off with his leash. It's never happened before.

He stopped walking and stared at me, holding his briefcase with both hands, protectively, at crotch level. His eyes seemed to rotate in their sockets, as if straining to establish parallax, to see me from the proper angle. His nose twitched. He gave a little ghostly cough, a whispery expulsion of breath.

Haven't seen him, he said. Sure he came up this way? He'll be in the park by now. That's what they all do. Run toward the park.

His breath stank of the kind of cheap red wine served with Triscuits and blocks of white cheese. He had been at a retirement party. I knew

322

it immediately. It was what they served at a secretary's retirement party, alongside candied almonds and white layer cake.

You ought to yell for him, he said. Shouldn't you? What's his name?

Her name, I said. Trixie.

Trixie, he shouted, in a high, reedy, strangling voice. He clasped his briefcase between his knees and cupped his hands around his mouth. I had to join in. *Trixie*, we both shouted, and listened to the reverberations dying away, and the faint hiss of traffic on the Parkway, invisible in the dark below.

Well, keep walking, then, he said. It's the only thing to do.

He stuck out his hand. I recognized it; an instinctive gesture, a habit you pick up around politicians. Shake hands at the least opportunity. I loosened my right fist from the pocket of my jacket, where the edge of the glove had gotten stuck on something, a loose stitch, a hidden zipper. And in my clumsiness I butted the heel of my hand against the butt of the pistol, and it fell out of my waistband and clattered onto the sidewalk.

He looked down at it, slowly, and even more slowly raised his head and stared at me. His eyes had turned blood-black, like obsidian beads.

Where I come from, he said, his head weaving slightly, we don't carry one of those around unless we intend to use it.

I remembered a line of poetry, unable to place the author: *intimate as a dog's imploring glance, and yet again, forever, turned away.*

His mouth was a crumpled tissue of misery. Kill me, he was saying, and I won't tell, and no one will suspect you. Another random murder on a dark Washington street, a botched robbery, a man bleeding to death on the sidewalk steps outside his house.

I must have looked at him with something like horror, because his eyes widened, and he took a step back. Easy now, he said. No offense. Go on, pick it up. Get it out of here. They're illegal in this town, you know. You must not be from Washington.

As I stooped down I noticed one of his shoelaces was untied. I had a strange protective urge to reach out and tie it for him. Instead, saying nothing, I covered the pistol with my palm and scooped it up and into my pocket in one smooth motion, as if I'd been doing this kind of thing for years.

Go on, he said. Go find your dog. As if he'd just remembered why I was there.

323

I walked away from him; I turned, to be precise, and walked back to my car, in full view of my formerly intended victim. Without so much as looking back to see if his eyes followed me or if he was lurching up the steps as if I had never existed. It was eight-fifteen, I saw, as soon as I turned over the engine. I drove away feeling, for the first time, defeated, and relieved, by the world's sheer unrelenting ugliness.

It's possible, when you've been married for twenty-five or thirty years, when your children have grown up and moved away, to keep coming across the tail ends of conversations you started in a different decade, and to realize that whole areas of existence have lain dormant all that time, like seeds in an envelope. There's nothing unusual in that.

Or, to put it another way: when one becomes a parent, when you are charged with the care of tiny, shivering, vulnerable creatures—I picture them, all three of them, just out of the swimming pool, wrapped in towels, shuddering, their fatless bodies unable to protect them from the faintest breeze—you lose the capacity to see beyond the immediate visible world. Losing a child, of course, only makes this worse. Abstractions, including the abstraction which is romantic love, lose their lustre. You and your spouse become more like partners in a business enterprise. I'm trafficking here in pure clichés, of course. But one can't avoid them. I accepted that long ago. We are who we are.

Rachel's career and mine have had opposite trajectories. When I was at the NSA she toiled away for years as an art librarian in the city system; once Alex and Merrill went to college she returned to school and finished her PhD on Klimt and Schiele at Johns Hopkins; and now she's much in demand as a museum consultant, a specialist in securing government funding for immense and unpopular projects. A few years ago we tore down the wall between Alex and Merrill's old bedrooms and replaced the windows with a glass curtain wall, and now half the second floor is her office: a beautiful room, if I may say so, a sunlit gallery with floor-to-ceiling white bookshelves, antique barnwood flooring, and a replica George Nakashima desk. I think I enjoy it more than she does. I go in there to dust and vacuum and stare through the window through the branches of the enormous white oak that dominates our backyard.

Last Wednesday—the fourteenth of October, 2004—she called me from a hotel in Berlin. They have her there for three weeks, helping to prepare plans for the Unification Museum. It was midnight in Central Europe; five o'clock in the evening on the East Coast.

I was walking through the Alexanderplatz, she said, after the meeting, full of coffee and pastry, and I was headed back to the hotel, wrapped up in my gray wool cape, you know the one I mean, and I felt very *European*. Jürgen and Peter and the rest of them were so quiet and respectful, they complimented me on my German, they wanted to know if I was being properly cared for, if I had a ride to the airport. I was floating on a cloud of gentleness and propriety. I was halfway across the square, and then, apropos of nothing, I thought, *Sobibor*. And I burst into tears. There were people all around me, but they were too polite to notice. Maybe it happens all the time here. Maybe Berliners are used to seeing strangers sobbing on street corners.

And then I got back to the hotel, she said, and I cleaned myself up. I was brave about it. Peter picked me up at seven and took me to an Indian restaurant, somewhere out in the suburbs. It was quite a drive. He didn't say much while we were in the car. Maybe he sensed that something had happened.

Well? *Had* something happened?

I don't know, she said. Yes. I mean, I began thinking, I'm too old for this shit. I wondered whether I took too many of those new blood pressure pills. But it's not that. I just felt that—I just didn't understand how they do it, how they can look around and not feel everything just *steeped* in blood. I know, I know. It's melodramatic. And hypocritical.

Don't be so hard on yourself, I said. Things like that happen when you're traveling.

Well, she said, I was an idiot, I was feeling fragile, I don't know, but I brought it up at the restaurant. Talk about tactless and crude. I've never seen such a long silence, I think, at a dinner table. Everybody got very interested in their food.

And then finally Jürgen said to me: Let me tell you a little story.

She was quiet for long enough that I noticed a faint fizzing over the phone line, like a can of soda just opened: the only indication that she was not next door, but five thousand miles away. My heart quaked.

And? What was the story?

Give me a minute, she said. I have to stretch out my legs. I don't want to paraphrase. All right. You ready? This is what he said.

When I was young, he said, I would go to visit my grandparents in Koblenz, in the Rhine Gorge. They lived a little way outside of town on a large property that originally belonged to my great-grandfather. On one side of the property was the main house, where they stayed, and around the other side, there was a large pond, and then a little stucco house on the opposite side of that. In that stucco house lived my uncle Willem. He was blind in one eye, and he was very fat, and he lived alone, never leaving the grounds. He mowed the lawns and collected apples from the apple trees and so on. And he loved to see me whenever I would come. He loved chocolate bars, and I always brought him a whole box of them. My parents gave me the money. I was the only person in the family he would talk to.

She let out a long sigh, cracked the seal on a bottle of water, and took a swig; I heard, or imagined I could hear, the plastic knocking against her teeth. It was then, strangely, with that sound, that I understood what she was doing: relaxing into the role, into the extemporaneous pleasures of the story. She had never needed notes, only an audience. An occasion.

I don't remember when I realized that he had been in the Waffen SS, that he had been a *Lagerkommandant* at Treblinka. He certainly didn't keep it a secret. He had his uniform hanging up in a closet in his house, covered with medals. But I remember very clearly that there was a year when I fully came to realize what that meant. I watched a program, in English class, as it happens, a documentary on the Nuremberg trials. And then I had to go back to my grandparents' house the next summer and decide what I was going to do about Uncle Willem.

Would I still talk to him? Would I visit him, as I had before, and drink the very sweet cider that he made himself, in barrels, in the back of his house? Should I punish him by having nothing to do with him, like the rest of the family? I thought for a time that I should push him into the pond and make it look like an accident.

And what happened? I asked her. What did he say?

He died. He had a heart attack, that same year, in the springtime. And this is what Jürgen said: I've never in my life felt more relieved. For once in my life I was spared having to stand in judgment over what no single human being can judge. I sometimes wonder, he said, what it would be like to have no one in my own family whose crimes I could point to. I imagine it must be like being in a balloon with no ballast, nothing tethering me to the earth. My own children, of course, are in that position. Their grandparents are all long dead. It's a terrible thing, to think of yourself always as innocent. Because you see the world, as it were, from the air. You can't help it. There are the innocent like you, and then there are the others, the terribly, terribly guilty.

It's late, I said. You ought to get some rest. It's another long day for you tomorrow, and then you have to catch an early flight the next morning. Christ, you're not thirty-five anymore, Rachel. Get to bed. He's a stranger. And a self-righteous jerk, if I may say so. He doesn't know anything about our lives.

Well, I started it, she said. I opened my stupid mouth. And he was polite enough not to mention any more *recent* events. Abu Ghraib. Guantánamo. I would say he showed remarkable restraint. And of course I never told him what *you* used to do for a living.

I had just opened the freezer, holding the phone in my left hand, wondering what I would eat for dinner that night. I stayed there, staring at a stack of Lean Cuisine entrees, in a cloud of cold mist. It isn't like me to get angry at her over the phone. When we argue, it's face to face, over some minor irritant: Who lost the water bill? Who threw away the grapefruit spoons? But lately, I've noticed, when she's tired, sleepy, or drunk, Rachel has a glib and reckless way of running down our lives. I don't know what it's about. I ought to be more solicitous, more concerned; instead I grow annoyed and dismissive. It's as if I've decided the era of discussions in our marriage is over. Wittgenstein, I thought, Wittgenstein, you have cursed me, with the crutch of principled silence.

Oh, come on, she said. You were up to your ears in it. El Salvador, Nicaragua, Angola. Just because we never really discussed it, does that make me an idiot? Listen, I'm not excusing myself. We all lived off that salary. I could have taken the kids and left. I enjoyed it a little. It was like being married to a secret agent without the risk.

You're still drunk, I said. Go to sleep, Rachel. Before you say something really stupid.

Innocent people commit the most terrible crimes, she said. Sometimes without even lifting a finger. Don't say you don't know what I mean. You know exactly what I mean.

Not for the first time it occurred to me, remembering Frank Murphy's swollen face, the desperate thrust of his outstretched hand, that if one more streetlight had been broken on Ellicott Street I might still be in prison. But given the right circumstances, I thought, in those same months, I could have done almost anything. Set off a car bomb. Worn a dynamite belt. I had been, in my own small way, a fanatic. Listening to her, I observed this about myself with a certain perverse satisfaction. It was the one aspect of my life that had evaded all suspicion.

Oh, Rachel, I said, with a half-pantomimed sigh, as if gathering up breath for some unspecified future purpose. You have no idea. It could have been much worse.

You mean it *is* much worse, she said. She had gotten into bed; I could see her, kicking off her shoes, lying back with the receiver tilted up in the air. Worse than the Age of Reagan, I mean. Who would have thought that was only the beginning? But eventually you would have resigned. I know you would have. Like Stu Rushfield and Parker and Bill Thorndike at the State Department. You would have made me proud.

Maybe I would have, in one way or another, I said. But I didn't, is that right? Isn't that what matters? I disappointed you.

No, she said. That's the worst of it. You're a good man. You stayed. You took care of us. At the time I don't think I would have minded if you were Eichmann. It breaks my heart, thinking back on it. I would have overlooked almost anything. I hope you don't mind my saying this. You can't argue with the truth, I suppose.

It occurred to me that this would be the moment to test her theory. A confession, if ever, was in order right then. But there was no way I was prepared to make one. It was too late in the day; I had already stuck a frozen pizza in the toaster oven and poured a half-measure of Dewars over ice. I wasn't in the mood for a marathon phone call, as if we were two teenagers. This was the converse of history, I thought, the secret unwritten history, of men yawning late at night, too ashamed to tell their wives who said what about the nuclear test or the planned assassination of the prime minister, and dying of a stroke the next day.

And yet otherwise I didn't deserve her forgiveness, or her love.

What I had been arguing for, silently, hoping for, working for, was to become a ghost, to disappear, like the others, into the walls of my own house. I didn't want to be replicated. I never wanted there to be another story like this one. If I could, I thought, I would stop this story, too. If it were a tape recorder, I would go back to the beginning and erase it, erase the sound of my own voice. The weight of years on these sagging vocal cords, the gravelly burr, the pretend wisdom. No one should be allowed to speak this way, I thought, even into the unknown, even to you. But I drank the drug of inertia long ago. I can't spit it out.

No, I said. You can't argue with the truth.

* * *

In our living room we have a framed photograph I took of Jolie at six, playing in the sprinkler in the backyard. She looks over her shoulder at the camera, her face crinkled up with pleasure, the water striking between her shoulder blades and spraying everywhere, dotting the lens with droplets.

She had enormous bottle-green eyes and very dark, very straight brown hair. And a dimpled chin, and fair skin, much paler than any of the rest of us. My mother was descended from an Anglo-Irish family, and I suppose a few of those genes made their way to her. She sunburned easily and freckled everywhere. A little slip of a girl, my God. Even by that summer she was just four feet tall.

Schafe können sicher weiden,
Sheep can safely graze
Wo ein guter Hirte wacht.
where a good shepherd watches over them.
Wo Regenten wohl regieren,
Where rulers are ruling well,
Kann man Ruh und Friede spüren
we may feel peace and rest
Und was Länder glücklich macht
and what makes countries happy.

At the kitchen table, I cut the brown paper backing with a razor blade; I remove the paperboard and the photograph and the mat, and carefully lift out the square pane of glass, so no one will be injured. I take what remains and wrap it in a plastic garbage bag, and carry it out to the curb. Pickup is tomorrow morning. I cut the brown paper backing with a razor blade; I expect it to hurt; I expect it to bleed. I expect the razor blade to stray across the palm of my outstretched hand. But that is never the way it is with me. In my life I have been the shepherd from the air, praying, don't look up, don't let me see your faces, for who knows what I'll do to the world if I lose you.

Nominated by Tom Filer, Jessica Roeder, Katherine Taylor, Threepenny Review

A DEAD MAN IN NASHVILLE

by AMANDA REA

from THE SUN

Our first night in Nashville, a man died right in front of us on Broadway. My father was at the wheel, my brother was in the seat beside him, and I was in back with the window rolled down, taking in the musty, fertile smell of the South. We'd just pulled a U-Haul full of my brother's ragged belongings eleven hundred miles from Colorado and had raised a beer or two in celebration of our arrival. Now we were headed for the honky-tonks, where we planned to listen to a few country covers, eat fried pickles, and watch cowboys strut around in boots that had never touched anything but concrete.

It was 10:30 on a Wednesday night, and we were tired but happy. Uncommonly so. It had been a long time since the three of us had been together, and our individual lives were looking up: I'd just finished my first year in graduate school; my father had remarried after thirteen years as a bachelor; and my brother had decided to leave the college town where he'd been veering toward alcoholism and relocate to Nashville, where, at the end of three days, my father and I would leave him to execute a vague plan of breaking into the music business. He hoped to find work at one of the publishing companies on Music Row in any capacity—as an intern or even a janitor—and work his way up to production or artist management. Once established, he intended to help our father realize a lifelong dream.

My father is a singer-songwriter. At fifty-four he was sharpening his stage presence, his guitar work, and his vocal range. He was teaching himself complicated chord progressions and thickening the calluses on his fingertips, working to finish his first studio album. He had always been a musician, but he had always been something else, too: a cattleman, a ditch digger, a pool player, a construction worker. Though his musical talent had emerged at a young age, his parents had not encouraged it. They were practical, hardworking ranchers, and they listened to his songs with an indifference that bordered on rebuke. My father grew up and established a ranch of his own, and when that venture failed, he built custom log homes for the wealthy. Every day for thirty years he laced up his work boots before dawn and came home after dusk, covered in mud or sawdust. He married my mother, divorced her, raised my brother and me, and ushered his parents through the ends of their lives, and all the while he wrote songs, scribbling lyrics down on whatever was handy, be it a yellow legal pad or a two-by-four.

When my brother and I were children, we learned to sleep through our father's jam sessions, regardless of how long they lasted or how loudly the music resounded through the trailer's walls. His songs, however sad or irreverent, became our lullabies. His friends, most of whom would die of drug overdoses, became like uncles to us. They ruffled our hair and laughed at our jokes: thin and bespectacled Guy, who cranked away on his harmonica; ponytailed, half-Navajo J.R., who closed his eyes when he sang harmony and tapped his cowboy boots on the orange carpet. They played while my father sang of women haunted by the men who had abused them as children, of old men trapped in bodies that would not die, of convicts ambling down from Greyhound buses to stare at a world they scarcely knew. His voice sounded a little bit like Leonard Cohen's, with a Dylanesque nasal edge, the latter owing to his many broken noses—first in car accidents and fistfights, then from the unexpected swing of a cow's head, and finally in an innocent wrestling match with my brother, whose hands shook for two days after he heard the snap of my father's cartilage against the wooden arm of the couch.

Our father's songs matched the roughness of his voice. Many had an apocalyptic quality, an end-of-civilization darkness, a defiance of authority, religion, and law. They were not ideal for dancing. Nor did they seem to entertain the elderly, sunburned tourists who sat slumped in the local bars. But sometimes—and my body sagged with relief when it happened—a crowd would go silent and listen, and then rise to their feet in whistling ovation. Once, I saw a woman wiping away tears. I saw men line up to shake my father's hand. I loved his songs and knew every word of them, even the ones he forgot. I loved the good nights, when strangers heard his lyrics and understood, and I dreaded the crowds of drunks who wouldn't listen, the smug producers who told my father that his songs weren't sentimental enough for housewives; who said, "We might have signed you twenty-five years ago, but now you're too late."

That success eluded our father only reinforced a resentment my brother and I had been cultivating for years, a chip on our shoulders that had grown every time a kid on our school bus referred to "that junky old trailer where nobody lives." Once, when a man introduced himself to my brother by saying, "Hi, I'm Rich," my brother said, "Yeah? Well, I'm poor. What's it to ya?" Poverty, we believed, was not our natural state. Our ascension was imminent. One day somebody with taste and influence would hear one of Dad's songs, and, by some mysterious process, we'd have a regular house: a house with heat that came from heating vents and not a secondhand wood stove; a house where the water in the toilet didn't freeze at night; a house where, when you took a crap in the bathroom, you couldn't then run to the living-room window and watch it shoot from the broken sewage pipe in the backyard. I sketched floor plans. I lost myself in *Better Homes and Gardens*. When we drove into town, I pressed my forehead against the passenger window of my father's old truck, staring with envy at the homes we passed, some of which were merely double-wides or rattletrap farmhouses. Though we'd never set foot in a church, I'd put my hands together, look vaguely upward, and think, *Please help Dad get to Nashville.*

And now we were finally here, in the city we'd invoked a thousand times. The night air felt heavy and warm as we passed through the suburbs toward the downtown skyline. Alongside the highway stood austere white churches, drive-through barbecue joints, billboards touting home-style biscuits, and a roadside undergrowth so impossibly thick I couldn't imagine anyone hacking through it. Everywhere was a low whir of insects and a damp, earthy smell that reminded me of my grandmother's basement.

At the intersection of Third Avenue and Broadway, we stopped at a red light. We were in the left-turn lane, a cream-colored Cadillac in front of us, its turn signal flashing.

"Brand-new," my father said, nodding at the Cadillac. Its plates were temporary tags issued that day.

When the light turned green, the Cadillac didn't move. My father let the truck roll forward slightly and honked. It was a polite honk, as honks go, meant only to get the driver's attention. Still the car didn't move.

The light turned red again. Though the Cadillac's windows were darkly tinted, we could see the outline of the driver's head, which moved slightly, as though he'd straightened himself in the seat. Then he was still.

The light turned green. Again the Cadillac didn't go. Its turn signal continued to flash. Horns sounded behind us. My father took a deep breath and kicked down the emergency brake. "I think the son of a bitch is dead."

As soon as he said it, I knew he was right.

Still, when Dad got out of the truck, I feared that the man inside the Cadillac was not dead but deranged, that he might gun my father down or leap from the car and butcher him with a knife. I wanted to call my father back, tell him to pull around the Cadillac, as more-sensible drivers had done. Getting involved seemed like something a rural person would do, and I'd spent much of my life trying not to behave like one.

But my father was not afraid of much. He'd grown up on a cattle ranch, seen death and administered it to livestock. He'd inhabited redneck bars and pool halls, spent nights under bridges when he couldn't afford a motel. He'd been struck by a rattlesnake and by lightning. He approached the Cadillac matter-of-factly. I held my breath as he leaned to look in the driver's-side window. He was still for a moment. Then he turned and gave us a grim nod.

My brother put on our hazard lights, and we got out of the truck. Other drivers honked at us, gawked, then swerved away in frustration. As a bus tried to pull around, my father jogged to the bus driver's window.

"Can you radio for an ambulance? This man up here is dead."

"If he's dead," the driver drawled, "then he don't need no ambulance." He wedged the nose of the bus into traffic and went on.

Remembering I had my cellphone, I pulled it out and dialed 911. I turned in a circle, looking for street signs, anything I could use to describe the intersection. The store windows were packed with cowboy hats and feather boas and towers of shiny postcards. While the phone rang, my brother slowly approached the Cadillac to look inside. He stood there for a moment, then put his hands in his pockets and moved away.

Then a police officer came rumbling around the corner on a motorcycle. Thinking he'd come to help us, I ended my call. But the officer did not seem to notice the traffic snarl or see my brother's waving arms. He'd have gone right past had my father not stepped into the street, where he could not be missed, and called, "Hey, we need some help here!"

The officer hit his siren, releasing a long wail. He maneuvered the motorcycle around and came to an abrupt stop in front of us. He was a short man with a round face and bulging, watery eyes, helmet sitting atop his head like half an eggshell. With a great show of irritation, he clambered off the motorcycle and stomped toward my father with his hand on his baton.

"Is there a problem here?" he asked.

"I believe this man up here is dead."

The officer looked around my father at the Cadillac, then at our truck parked behind it. He squinted at our out-of-state plates and pulled a notepad from his shirt pocket.

"Where are you-all from?" he asked.

We told him.

"And what brings you to downtown Nashville?"

"It's not us," my brother said, pointing. "This guy has something wrong with him."

The policeman wrote down our license number. "Have you-all been drinking tonight?"

My heart began to race. We'd had a couple of beers to christen my brother's new apartment, and my father had three prior DUIS. He'd paid the fines, taken the classes, spent the time in jail, but another arrest could have sent him away for years. I'd had only one beer, so when the officer asked who'd been driving, I said I had. He looked me over, eyebrows raised.

"Listen, God damn it," my father said. "The man in that car needs medical attention."

I reached for my cellphone and hit redial, cursing myself for having hung up in the first place. It still seemed to me that the man's death could be reversed, that his brain or heart might be restarted somehow, if only someone could help him. The motorcycle's red lights flashed across the pavement as the officer pulled up against our bumper, running our plates, glaring at my father. It was clear to me that the officer intended to arrest him, if not all of us.

That's when the dead man's car took off.

Perhaps rigor mortis had set in, causing his foot to stiffen and slip from the brake. Whatever the cause, the Cadillac began to roll forward down the hill, heading for two busy intersections and then the Cumberland River.

"Well," the officer said, "it looks like he's moving now."

"He's not moving!" I shouted. "He's fucking rolling!"

The officer whirled on me, eyes bulging. I froze. I have always refused to show respect to police officers, substitute teachers, and anyone else who demands my respect before earning it. For a grim moment I thought my reckoning had finally come. The officer stepped up to me, scowling, his chest inches from mine. But even as he tried to intimidate me, he cast fearful glances over my shoulder at the street. Perhaps he'd refused to approach the Cadillac not because he didn't understand that there was a dead man inside, but because he *did*. He'd shied from it like a horse from the scent of another horse's blood, hoping that someone else would intervene, someone who knew what to do, someone with initiative. He'd performed his duties the way I'd played high-school soccer—running in the same direction as everyone else but hanging back, keeping a teammate between me and the ball.

Soon the commotion behind me was too much to ignore, and the officer turned his attention to the street. The dead man's Cadillac had crossed Third Avenue and was sailing through two red lights. Cars honked and swerved. Men on the sidewalk pulled their wives and girlfriends to safety. Others dropped their bags and flattened themselves against buildings. The Cadillac rolled on, a silent white ship. It must have been going twenty miles an hour when it reached the end of the street, jumped the curb, and slammed into a thick oak overlooking the dark stripe of the river. There was the *whoosh* of exploding air bags, and the doors of the Cadillac flew open. The oak's branches swayed. The street was quiet for a moment. Then smoke began to roil from beneath the crumpled hood, and two men burst from the doors of Big River Brewery and ran to the dead man's aid.

The officer stood there, mouth open. Then he pointed at each of us in turn.

"Nobody moves! You hear me?"

He ran to his motorcycle and, for an uncomfortable moment, struggled to heave his leg over the seat. His siren wailed importantly as he sped away.

The keys were already coming toward me in the air when I turned to ask my father for them. I caught them and drove us through the wet nighttime streets. It had begun to drizzle, a soft, warm rain, unlike the pelting cold of a Colorado storm. We drove straight back to my brother's new, paint-smelling apartment, saying little.

For the next two days we stayed in. We played poker, made a pot of green chili, watched an old movie we'd already seen. My brother arranged his furniture and unpacked boxes, and the three of us resumed a quiet rhythm of cohabitation, living as we had before college had separated us, before my father had remarried and moved out of our trailer and into a respectable house in town. We reminisced about the trailer, about how tall the weeds had grown in the well-fertilized backyard, about the forgotten jug of apple cider that had exploded one night as we'd watched TV, splattering us in fermented juice and shards of glass. We remembered the pile of old Christmas trees that had accumulated in the driveway—the way the tinsel had clung to their branches long after the needles had browned and fallen away—and how one winter we'd had to burn them for firewood: first the old Christmas trees, then the doghouse, then the front steps. We laughed at the unlikelihood of our having been so happy. Even now I wake after a good night's sleep believing I'm in that trailer, warm beneath a smoke-smelling sleeping bag, with my father and brother just down the hall, all of us so close we can hear each other breathing.

But even as we reminisced, we thought of the dead man. We combed the Nashville newspapers but never found any mention of the runaway Cadillac, or its deceased driver. I realized that I'd never completed my second call to 911, though I couldn't remember hanging up.

We talked about what we might have done differently. We might have tried to get the car's door open. We might have attempted resuscitation (though, honestly, none of us knew how to perform it). We might have had the presence of mind to turn the Cadillac's engine off and pull the emergency brake.

I regretted that I'd never looked inside the Cadillac at the dead man's face. Even my brother, who is too squeamish to bait a fishhook, had looked. He described the driver as a broad-shouldered man, whose bald head gleamed in the light from the street and whose face was etched diagonally from ear to chin with a deep, jagged scar. He wore an expensive-looking white suit and sunglasses, though the sun had long since gone down. His ring-bedecked hands had slipped from the wheel into his lap.

Maybe he was a mobster, my brother said. Maybe he'd died of an aneurysm. Too much cocaine, my father said, and his heart had just stopped. The scar? A knife fight. A fall from a tire swing when he was four.

"He wasn't much to look at," my father told me. "And you'll have plenty of chances to look at dead people."

He was right, of course. I'd already seen dead loved ones, grandparents laid out in rosy makeup, casket lids open, hands carefully arranged. And on a dark street in Los Angeles I'd seen a wrecked motorcycle, its tires slowly spinning, and just beyond the reach of the streetlight a man so twisted he could not have been alive. The police were there, standing behind their squad car, arms crossed. I suppose it isn't unusual. There are people dying everywhere, of diseases and violence and age, lives blinking out all around us like house lights at night. We are dying as we sit here. Perhaps what is more surprising than seeing a dead stranger is how few of them we see.

Late that first night, after our encounter with the dead man, the rain began to fall in gray sheets. I couldn't see how we were going to leave my little brother there, in a town where people died at traffic lights, where cops made emergencies worse, where hunched figures dragged battered guitar cases down the streets. I could tell that my father was apprehensive too. He gave no more pep talks to my brother about how they'd revolutionize the Nashville sound. There was no more talk about how my brother's gregariousness could get him in any door. We knew he'd have to get a job in the next few days, something temporary to pay the bills until he got a foothold in the industry, but we did not know then how long these jobs would mire him: first selling used furniture, then selling high heels to Southern belles, then killing rats and spiders, then serving lunches at a chain restaurant, then cleaning the slave quarters on an old plantation, after which he'd start his own business and go broke. We could not foresee how he would work and try and go hungry, or how some nights he'd get drunk and cry from loneliness, which would last not months but years. But we'd begun to sense this disappointment, as if the dead man's appearance in our path had been an omen.

"Play us some of your old songs," my brother asked our father, and he did—one about a gambler, one about lost love, and one that we knew was about our mother, whom he'd loved deeply for many years before their bitter divorce. As he sang, his voice softened, and he got a faraway look that had scared me as a child. He'd always explained that he was only concentrating, but his eyes could go so cold and dead that his soul seemed gone from his body, and, unable to look at them, I'd focus on his fingers moving up and down the neck of the guitar. But I was older now, and I looked at him while I listened, following the lyrics down well-worn paths. I looked at the creases around his eyes and at his hair, which in recent years had turned entirely silver. I felt grief welling up in me, though I didn't know what for. I tried to distract myself by thinking of the next couple of days: We'd take a trip to the Grand Ole Opry, maybe, or try some Southern barbecue, just as soon as the rain let up. Perhaps my father and I could stay an extra day or two—there wasn't any reason to leave so soon. But there was no stopping it. I felt my face heating up, my throat constricting. I have always cried at the least provocation.

"Oh, no," my brother said and chuckled, scooting closer to put an arm around me.

My father smiled and shook his head. He moved quickly into a mock love song called "Old What's-Her-Face" that he always reserves for crowds who are losing heart.

Nominated by The Sun

THE PROBLEM OF WATER

by EMILY TODER

from SIXTH FINCH

The problem of water is that it's odorless
Water is not sensed until it is too late
You think you are all right and then water
It has been said water moves faster than horses
but it has not been said what kind of horses
Well water used to be the most popular and inane of
waters. Now water is domesticated and still popular
Water is not in a lot of desserts
I don't know how much water matters to babies
Room temperature is like a golden retriever to water
A room without water is not like a soul without water
It is perfectly all right
A running water is safer than a still one
The second problem of water
is that it is tempting for people
to give birth in it. The second problem of water is that
to speak of water one must also speak
of cohesion. Water does not travel alone
It is difficult speak about this
Surely there can be no birth without water
Water can pile up on a penny
What people forget is that water is very heavy
Water animals have no tastebuds
It's because water is odorless and colorless
They have no lungs

In water there is no weight. Water colors
are a human error. Water is often offered
after there has been a human problem
The second problem of water is that its origins
are cloudy. It is a chicken
and it is an egg. It is like a child
casting director. Water is made
out of three pieces like a nice suit
and like a nice trinity or tripod
The pieces are joined by bonds
Water fears nothing but oil
When you come to the water
you should fear nothing.

Nominated by Sixth Finch

SHELTER

fiction by SUSAN PERABO

from THE IOWA REVIEW

More often than not it happens like so: in the middle of the night I'm woken up by a car door slamming out front. Usually the car's idling and there's a little bit of radio playing and sometimes there's a whistle or tongue click or scuffle. Not often words. People come alone mostly, and people who do what they're doing aren't the kind of people who'd have words for a dog, though every so often someone'll say a *sorry* or a *see ya* before getting back into the car and driving away. When I can tell they're good and gone I pull out of bed and, unless it's winter, open up the front door in my nightie and bare feet and usually the dog's standing about where it was dropped, wagging its tail and looking up the road after the car, not getting the picture entirely, and I rattle my jar of milkbones and nine times out of ten the mutt'll turn and run right up to me, and I let it stay in the house until morning, so it doesn't have to go meet all the others out back in the kennel in the middle of the night. They're barking by now, of course—they bark all the time, once one starts they all gotta be heard—but the sound is familiar to me as crickets or trucks on the highway, so I hardly hear it anymore.

I've found families for somewhere near four hundred homeless dogs across the state of New Hampshire. For twenty-five years I answered the phone for Dr. Brick, the town vet, but when Doc retired I looked around and saw I was fifty-two and had lots of days left and no clear way to fill them. I was still living in the house I'd grown up in, the mortgage long since settled. And I had a little money saved, so I didn't need a job that would pay much, if anything. I'd seen lots of hard-luck dogs in my years with Dr. Brick, strays brought in by folks who'd found but couldn't keep them, healthy, good dogs taken down (sometimes by me, in the back of my station wagon) to the shelter where I knew damn well they'd be gassed in a matter of weeks. So it seemed like maybe this was a way I could fill those days.

I've been at it nearly a decade now, so a lot of people know I do what I do, and if all a person wants is a regular old dog—not one to show or train for some job or another—they might call me instead of going to a pet store or a puppy mill. Then what I do is I go out to the person's house, check things over to make sure they've got the right kind of space and the right reasons to be looking for a dog—that they're not the type to lose interest or change their minds after a week or two, landing the dog right back where it started—and then once they've signed the papers I let them come out to my place and take their pick from the lot. For the picking, the dogs line up against the kennel fence, slapping tails and nosing through the holes. A few hang back, some shy, others seeming not to care, scratching at a flea or stretching out in the sunshine, like they don't give a damn who wants them and never did.

Twenty dollars is all I ask as payment, enough to buy a couple more bags of the store-brand food for the ones left behind. Some people give me more. One time a lady from Hanover wrote me a check for five hundred dollars. She said I was doing the Lord's work. I thought to myself that maybe the Lord had more important things to worry about than a kennel full of slobbering dogs, but I wasn't about to say so, standing there with her check in my hand. The truth was, I didn't really know why I did what I did, and I didn't see any reason to spend a whole lot of time thinking about it. It was just the way it was.

I've gotten through a lot by not over-thinking things, by being able to keep certain matters out of my mind. You busy yourself with living, however it is you choose to busy yourself—dogs or kids or broken cars or numbers in a book—and you might well forget that after a year of anticipation your father decided not to move the family to Florida after all, or that the man you almost married had a change of heart at the last minute and traded you in for another. My sister, who lives down in Boston, thinks all the time about everything and as a result takes a half-dozen pills every morning. Last year I watched her suffer every detail of her daughter's wedding and I thought: *you can have it*. And so when I felt that thing while I was soaping in the shower, that thing like an acorn, I just put it right out of my mind. I went on tend-

342

ing to my dogs and making home visits and doing what I do and I went so far as to cancel my yearly check-up with Dr. Lands because I knew once I had on that paper gown there would be no more not thinking about it. And one day in October, when I was starting to feel a little weak walking from the house to the kennel and the acorn wasn't an acorn anymore but a walnut, I drove up to the top of my dirt drive and swung shut the rusty iron gate and put a sign on the bars that said CLOSED—DO NOT DROP DOGS. Because I had nineteen dogs in the kennel and I had to find homes for all of them before I was dead.

It was a week or so later, around about Halloween, that I got a call from a man named Jerry who said he'd read about my kennel in his local newspaper and wanted to get one of my dogs. A big dog, he said.

"Not tall and bony," he said over the telephone. "Stocky. Fat if you have one. Do you?"

"Sure," I said. "I got all kinds." They were barking out back as we spoke.

"I'd like to see them immediately." He talked swift and clipped like a military man, everything an order. "I'll be there at three o'clock."

I hesitated, but not for more than a breath or two. I needed to place the dogs in a hurry, sure, but I had to stick to the rules. What did the dogs care about a little lump? All they wanted was somebody who'd take them and keep them. So I told this Jerry I would have to make a home visit first, and if he passed he could come out and take his pick.

"I'll bring references," he said. "There's no need for—"

"This is the way it works," I said. "No home visit, no dog."

He didn't say anything for a minute, but I could tell he was still there. I could practically hear the spokes in his head creaking through the telephone line. Then he said, "Just you? Nobody else?"

"There is nobody else," I said.

And so he gave me directions to his house, up in Cornish, about forty miles from my town. We set a time for the following morning.

One day last year I did a home visit in New London and I was walking through the house and I saw an old man sitting in an easy chair and I knew right off he was dead. His hands were droopy in his lap in a way only dead hands droop. So I said to the woman walking me around— she wanted a little dog, one that would sit on her lap while she did the crossword—I said *ma'am is that man okay?* even though I knew full well he wasn't, but didn't know quite how to say it. And she says *oh*

343

Daddy always takes his nap around this time, and instead of telling her that her father was dead as a doornail I just said *oh, all right*. And I guess a little while after I left she must have figured it out. I don't know what exactly happened because she never did call me about getting a little dog.

Lying in bed that night before I went out to Jerry's, I started thinking of that old man and his droopy hands. I tried to imagine the way my body would relax when I went, which direction my head would nod to, where my eyes might be fixed before somebody had a chance to shut them. When my mother died, down at the hospital in Manchester, frail as a leaf, she gave a little gasp of surprise right before the end. I wondered if anything would surprise me, if I would think something different than I'd thought before.

Then I pushed all that garbage out of my mind and went to sleep.

There was a gate at Jerry's driveway, with a little box like at Wendy's. I poked the button and a crackly woman came on and I told her who I was and she sighed and said, "Come on up." And the gate swung open and I pulled through. And right then an idea started coming to me that these were people who could take three or four of my dogs. There must have been ten acres of grass and trees from what I could see and every bit of it fenced. The house was just shy of a mansion, two stories with tall windows and long white steps leading to a front porch that was empty but big enough to hold twenty rocking chairs. I parked my car at the foot of those stairs and saw Jerry was waiting for me up on the porch. He was older than he'd sounded on the phone. He looked eighty, though he also looked like he'd be okay with a few big dogs, tall and spry and with those muscled forearms you always find yourself looking at a moment too long. He had a head full of gray hair that was going in a hundred directions and a rectangle chin. There was no sign of the woman who'd sighed into the box.

"You got a lot of room for a dog to run," I called to him as I got out of the car.

"I don't want a dog to run," he said, crossing those arms as I climbed the steps toward him. "I want a dog to lie on my feet."

"Most dogs'll want to run every so often," I said, reaching the top. My words came out thin and wheezy. It was weary work, climbing, and I wasn't sure how many stairs I had left in me.

"Don't you have a fat, old dog?"

I gathered my breath. "Sure I do. I got a few of 'em in fact. But even fat, old dogs need to get up every so often."

He twisted his lips into a lopsided frown. He looked like a child when he did it, a young child experimenting in the bathroom mirror with what his own face could do, and I nearly busted out laughing.

"What is it you need to see?" he asked.

By now, frankly, I was more than a little curious. I'd been to a lot of houses, met a lot of people. And I know they say everyone's different, that we're just like snowflakes, no two alike and all that, but I think that's a load. I think most people are alike. I think most people go from the job to the TV to the pillow. In between are meals and a quick game of catch or checkers and a telephone call and one minute of looking out the window wondering what happened to someone.

But there was something about Jerry that wasn't like a person you met coming and going, something about the way he was old and young all at once. Plus, if I was going to talk him into taking more than one of my dogs (four was the number I had in my head right then), I was going to have to warm him up a little bit first.

"I need to look inside," I said. "I need to see where the dog'll be kept."

"The dog will be kept in the dungeon," he said. "And forced to wear a clown costume."

"Listen, you'd be surprised," I said. "I've had some real weirdos. Once I—"

"No need for stories," he said, opening the door.

I figured he must have been moving in. The first two rooms we entered—what might have been a living room and dining room—were empty of furniture, the walls peeling paint. Our footsteps on the wood floors echoed all the way to the high ceilings.

"Where you comin' from?" I asked. "Out of state?"

"Pardon?"

I gestured to the emptiness. "I'm guessin' you just bought the place?"

"I've lived here for fifty years," he said. "So it depends on your definition of *just*."

In the kitchen there was a breakfast nook-type area with a small circle table and two wood chairs. There was nothing on the counters, and I don't mean there were no plates or cups or cereal boxes. There was just *nothing*—no toaster or sugar bowl or roll of paper towels. The

345

only things in the whole room that would have moved in an earth-quake were two dog bowls in the corner by the fridge. One of the bowls was filled to the rim with water.

"You got a dog already?" I asked. "Lookin' for a pal?"

"No dog." He cleared his throat. "Just the bowls so far."

"A dog needs bowls, all right," I said.

"Then you're satisfied. I can—"

"Just one more thing," I said. "I need to see where the dog will sleep. Some people, they—"

He held up his hand. "No stories," he said.

He led me to a small room off the kitchen. If it hadn't been connected by wood and plaster you couldn't have convinced me it was part of the same house. First off, it was tiny compared to everything else—maybe it had been a laundry room or a mud porch. But now it was carpeted with thick brown shag and stuffed with furniture: a fat brown recliner, a rickety old tray table, and one of those big fancy TVs with cables and speakers and slots for movies and whatnot. *The Andy Griffith Show* was playing on the TV. There was an open jar of pickles and three cans of ginger ale on the tray table, and at least four or five socks flopped on the floor like dead fish.

"This is where it'll sleep?"

"I expect so," he said. "It's where I spend most of my time."

No kiddin', I thought. But instead I said, "Are there others in the household?"

"Possibly," he said, taking a small step away from me. "But they won't have anything to do with the dog. The dog will be my responsibility."

He said this like he was repeating something he'd been told a bunch of times, and I thought again that he was like a gray-haired boy. Here he stood, seventy-five, eighty years old, and I could imagine that crackly woman on the intercom saying to him, "I'm not feeding that dog, not walking that dog, not brushing that dog. You bring a dog into this house, you better be willing to take care of it, buster." And Jerry toeing the floor, like little Opie Taylor on TV, saying, "Oh yes ma'am, I'll take care of it, I promise."

"Here's the thing," I said. "There's paperwork you gotta fill out, and there's a form that needs signed by everyone in the household. I don't want a dog coming back to me because someone here doesn't want it."

"I won't return the dog," he said.

"I know you're thinking that's true," I said. "I know you—"

346

"I won't return the dog," he said angrily. "No matter what."

"You feel that way now," I said. "But you might change your mind if there's someone harping on you about it every time it makes a noise or sheds some fur. Everyone has to sign off on the form. Everyone. No form, no dog."

He scowled. "I'll be in touch," he said.

Here's a fact: nobody wants a dog in November. Spring's the best—no surprise there—and summer's fine and early fall calls to mind pictures of happy dogs playing in leaf piles, and even December brings out a few folks looking for a Christmas present. But nobody in the state of New Hampshire's thinking about dogs those first weeks of bitter cold leading up to Thanksgiving, when the threat of snow sits over every house big and small and it's only a matter of time before simple things—getting to work, picking up groceries—aren't so simple.

Not that I didn't knock myself out trying. I spent extra money for color ads in the local paper, taped signs in every store window, waived the $20 fee. This brought out a couple more people than usual, and after the home visits and the paperwork I was down to just under a dozen dogs by the middle of November. But I had to move faster. At this rate it would take well into the new year to find spots for them all, and I was pretty sure I didn't have that long.

My sister called, asking me to come down to Boston for Thanksgiving, but I told her I was too busy. I might have gone—there was something nice even thinking about it, a heavy meal and voices talking over each other and a football game on somewhere—but I was afraid if I went I would buckle and tell her about what was inside me, and I knew right where that would lead. By the time that turkey's bones were simmering for soup I'd be in some specialist's office and there'd be cousins and nieces and god knows who turning up with flowers.

"Some day I'm just gonna come up there and kidnap you," she said. "All alone in the old house with those dogs out back, it's not right. You come live near me and we'll go for lunch every day and play bridge with the other ladies on the block. Two sisters growing old together."

"What'll Joe think of that?"

"What Joe thinks of everything—that he should turn up the TV."

We'd thought, for almost a year when I was twenty-three and she was twenty-one, that her and I and the men we were fixing to marry would take vacations together, play shuffleboard on the deck of a cruise ship, ride donkeys down the Grand Canyon.

"I miss you," she said. "You might as well be a million miles away."

"I'll see you soon," I said. "Not now, but soon."

It was the next Friday, around lunchtime, when Jerry came out to my place. He drove a big pickup truck, shiny black and no more than a couple years old. He pulled past the dirt drive and onto the grass and on up to the kennel, which most people have the common courtesy not to do. He was already out of the truck and looking at the dogs by the time I'd gotten on my coat and gloves and made my way up there. He wasn't dressed for the weather—it was twenty-something degrees—and he had his hands tucked into the pits of his flannel shirt.

"Talked her into it, did ya?" I asked him.

He didn't look at me, just kept checking out the dogs. "Talked who into what?"

"The one who didn't want a dog. Promised her you'd take good care of it?"

He rubbed his hands together and then blew into them. "Are there any fatter ones?"

Most of the outright strays were skin and bones. But there were at least three overweight dogs—orphaned by divorce or allergy most likely—standing not ten feet from him when he said this.

"Look at that black one," I said. A bit of dizziness blew through my head and I took hold of the fence pole to steady myself. "You want fatter than that?"

"He a barker?"

"They're dogs," I said. "They bark. But no, he's not one that keeps you up nights. That one in the corner—he's a fatty, too, and quiet. The two get on well. You want 'em both, I'll charge you just for the one."

He shook his head. "I don't want two dogs," he said. He still hadn't looked at me.

"You got a big yard, all fenced up. Shame to let it go to waste."

Now he finally turned. In the cold his face was a little gray, his eyes watery. "It's not going to waste," he said.

"Well," I said. "Come on down to the house and we'll write it up."

I was stalling, really. The sky promised snow and probably no one else would come by today, and though being alone wasn't something that'd bothered me in many a year, the truth was in the early afternoons it was starting to get to me just a little bit. Plus maybe I could convince him if I gave him a cup of coffee. We walked down to the house. I hadn't been much for picking up in the last couple months, and there was a lot of mess around the living room, including a couple empty boxes that the bulk milkbones had come in that I'd just left lying near the front door.

"You want a coffee?" I asked him, a little embarrassed by the state of things.

"You're moving," he said, looking around the room.

"No," I said. "I just—"

"You are. You're moving. I saw the sign on the gate." He pointed a bony finger at me. "You don't want any more dogs because you're moving down to Florida to live in a condominium. You're going to get skinny and leathery and wear shorts with flowers on them."

I laughed a little. "All right," I said. "Have it your way. Do you want a coffee or not?"

"You're not going to like it down there," he said. He sat down at my kitchen table, which was covered in junk mail and paper napkins.

"Now how could you know that? You don't even know my name."

"You're not going to like it," he said. "This is your home. Look at this place. Nobody in Florida lives like this."

"Where's your paperwork?" I asked. "In the truck?"

"I don't have it," he said. "And I'm not going to have it. But you're going to give me that fat black dog anyway, because you're moving to Florida and you want to get rid of those mutts as soon as you can."

I thought about making a deal. I thought about saying, okay, mister smarty-pants, take two, the black one and his pal, and I'll take your word for it that you won't change your mind, that you'll keep them no matter what that crackly woman might say. I thought about it for five or six seconds, probably, which is likely the longest I've taken someone's word for it in thirty years. But then I remembered, and felt like a fool for forgetting: you never know what a person will do. They'll tell you one thing and five minutes later do something else. I'd seen it again and again.

"She needs to sign," I said, pushing back from the table. "I'll get you another copy if you—"

"What will you do down there?" he asked. "Bingo?"

"You really got me all figured out," I said.

He finished his coffee and set the cup down on some yellowed envelopes. "Do you know who I am?" he asked.

"Sure," I said. "You're a rich man with a fenced yard big enough for a half-dozen dogs who's afraid to ask a woman to sign a piece of paper."

He scoffed. "And you're too scared to give me a dog without a guarantee. What do you care? You'll be sunning yourself by the time the dog knows which door he goes out to pee."

"My dogs," I said. "My rules."

It's almost always something tiny that fouls things up, ruins your plans big or small. A couple days later I was at the grocery store and feeling a little woozy. I hadn't been eating very good, had been sick to my stomach if I put much more in there than a few cookies, so sometimes I swayed a bit on my feet and had to find a spot to sit. So I was pulling out a bag of dog food from the bottom shelf and I felt that wave wash over me and stood up and then all the colors came rushing at me at once and that's the last I remember.

"Ma'am," the nurse said. "Do you know where you are?"

Well, I thought, I'm looking at a gal in a nurse's uniform, so unless it's Halloween I guess I'm at the hospital. But I didn't say this, only nodded.

"You hit your head," she said. She was a black gal, cute, with the braids in her hair. "Do you remember?"

I nodded again. What I was trying to figure out was if they'd already given me the once-over. I was thinking, by the look on her face, that they probably had.

"The doctor will be back shortly," she said. "Just stay here and rest."

"The place is only two miles from my house," my sister said.

In the hospital room there were cards and flowers and bright balloons bobbing in the corners, all the things I'd been hoping I could be spared.

"I can come up every afternoon," she said. "It's the best care in Boston, which you know means the best care anywhere. There's a lake with ducks. And the big goldfish."

"I'm sure it's nice," I said. I was watching the local news, on the television way up high. I'd turned off the sound but I knew well enough what they were saying, and all in all it was better than anything coming out of my sister's mouth.

"A man came today while I was packing," she said.

I turned away from the news lady. "Did he take a dog?"

"He didn't come for a dog. He came for you. You got a boyfriend you didn't tell me about?"

"Who was it?"

"He didn't say. He brought you this." She handed me a beach towel. It had a flaky picture of a golden retriever on it. It was one of those towels you might get at K-Mart, rough to the touch, ready to fall apart the first time you put it in the washer.

"He said you could take it to Florida with you, to remember your dogs. I said you must be thinking of somebody else. My sister's not going anywhere. I said—"

"Don't," I said. I turned back to the TV. The weather map was bright blue with snow. "I don't want to know what you said."

"Well, I'm sorry if I talked out of turn. I didn't have a clue in the world who he was and why he was bringing you a present. It didn't occur to me until he was driving off that he might be your—"

"He was just a man who was thinking about a dog," I said.

"He seemed awfully sorry to hear about your trouble."

I kept my eyes on the TV. "That what he said?"

"No," she admitted. "He didn't say anything. He just *seemed*. Then he took his truck and left. But I guess he still wanted you to have this, even after I told him about . . ."

She held the towel out to me.

"Just pack it away with everything else," I said.

"Why don't I leave it for now?" she said, tucking it beside me. "I'll just leave it in case."

That night I wrote him a postcard. I still had his address from when I'd gone up to his house. I was thinking ten dogs was better than eleven. I was thinking all the guarantees in the world didn't mean anything. I'd had a life full of them, paperwork stepping stones from the time I was twenty-four all the way to this hospital bed. And now I could see the path in front of me, down to Boston, and then the end of it.

I had that rough towel across my cold knees.

"Jerry," I wrote on the card. "Take the black one. I trust you won't bring it back."

Yesterday my sister came to tell me the dogs had run off.

"I'm so sorry," she said. "When I got there the kennel gate was standing open and they were all gone, every one of them. I'm sorry, honey. I know—"

"It's all right," I said, patting her hand. "There's nothing you could do."

"I bet they'll get taken in," she said. "Some of them, at least. They're good dogs. They'll find homes on their own, honey. They'll find little boys who—"

"Shhhh," I said, because I could hear something in the distance, gravel crunching under tires, claws scraping on metal, a man cursing me. I smiled. I could see it now, clear as day: the gate hanging open, the dust kicking up, eleven dogs crowded in the bed of that black truck. Old Jerry was scowling. Where were they all gonna sleep? And what was he supposed to tell that woman? He was going to have to do some fast talking, that was for sure, but he'd work it out. He'd been living in that big empty house for fifty years. Once he was set on something, he wasn't the type to change his mind.

Nominated by The Iowa Review

A WALL IN NAPLES
AND NOTHING MORE

by PHILIP LEVINE

from FIELD

There *is* more, there's the perfect
blue of sky, there's a window, and hanging
from the sill what could be garments
of green cloth. Or perhaps they're rugs?
Where is everyone? you ask. Someone
must live in this house, for this wall
surely belongs to a house, why else
would there be washing on a day
of such perfect sky? You assume
that everyone is free to take in
the beach, to leisurely stroll the strand,
weather permitting, to leave shoes
and socks on a towel even here
in a city famous for petty crime.
For Thomas Jones, not the singer
the ladies threw knickers and room keys
at, but the Welsh painter, it was light
unblurring a surface until the light
became the object itself the way
these words or any others can't.
I'm doing my feeble best to entrance you
without a broad palette of the colors
which can make a thing like nothing

else, make it come alive with the grubby
texture all actual things possess
after the wind and weather batter them
the way all my years battered
my tongue and teeth until whatever
I say comes out sounding inaccurate,
wrong, ugly. Yes, ugly, the way a wall
becomes after whoever was meant
to be kept out or kept in has been
transformed perfectly into the light
and dust that collect constantly
on each object in a living world.

Nominated Christopher Buckley, Michael Collier, Dorianne Laux, David St. John,
Charles Harper Webb, Grace Schulman, Christina Zawadiwsky, Field

SONTAG'S RULES

by SIGRID NUNEZ

from TIN HOUSE

It was my first time ever going to a writers' colony, and, for some reason I no longer recall, I had to postpone the date on which I was supposed to arrive. I was concerned that arriving late would be frowned on. But Susan insisted this was not a bad thing. "It's always good to start off anything by breaking a rule." For her, arriving late *was* the rule. "The only time I worry about being late is for a plane or for the opera." When people complained about always having to wait for her, she was unapologetic. "I figure, if people aren't smart enough to bring along something to read . . ." (But when certain people wised up and she ended up having to wait for them, she was not pleased.) My own fastidious punctuality could get on her nerves. Out to lunch with her one day, realizing I was going to be late getting back to work, I jumped up from the table, and she scoffed. "Sit down! You don't have to be there on the dot. Don't be so servile." *Servile* was one of her favorite words.

Exceptionalism. Was it really a good idea for the three of us—Susan, her son, myself—to share the same household? Shouldn't David and I get a place of our own? She said she saw no reason why we couldn't all go on living together, even if David and I were to have a child. She'd gladly support us all if she had to, she said. And when I expressed doubts she said, "Don't be so conventional. Who says we have to live like everyone else?"

Once, on St. Mark's Place, she pointed out two eccentric-looking women, one middle-aged, the other elderly, both dressed like gypsies and with long, flowing gray hair: "Old bohemians." And she added, jokingly, "Us in thirty years."

More than thirty years have passed, and she is dead, and there is no bohemia anymore.

Why was I going to a writers' colony, anyway? She herself would never do that. If she was going to hole up and work for a spell, let it be in a hotel. She'd done that a couple of times and loved it, ordering sandwiches and coffee from room service and working feverishly. But to be secluded in some rural retreat just sounded grim. And what sort of inspiration was to be found in the country? Had I never read Plato? (Socrates to Phaedrus: "I'm a lover of learning, and trees and open country won't teach me anything.") I never knew anyone more appreciative than she was of the beautiful in art and in human physical appearance—"I'm a beauty freak" was something she said all the time—and yet I never knew anyone less moved by the beauties of nature. Why would anyone want to leave exciting Manhattan for a month in the woods? When I said I could easily imagine moving to the country, not then but when I was older, she was appalled. "That sounds like *retiring*." The very word made her ill.

From time to time, because her parents lived there, she'd have to fly to Hawaii. When I said I was dying to visit America's most beautiful state, she was baffled. "But it's totally boring." Curiosity was a supreme virtue in her book, and she herself was endlessly curious—but not about the natural world. Living on Riverside Drive, she sometimes spoke admiringly of the view, especially the fine sunsets, but I never knew her to cross the street to go to Riverside Park.

Once, I showed her a story I was working on in which a dragonfly appeared. "What's that? Something you made up?" When I started to describe what a dragonfly was, she cut me off. "Never mind." It wasn't important; it was boring.

Boring, like *servile*, was one of her favorite words. Another was *exemplary*. Also, *serious*. "You can tell how serious people are by looking at their books." She meant not only what books they had on their shelves, but how the books were arranged. At that time—the late seventies—she had about six thousand books, perhaps a third of the number she would eventually own. Because of her, I arranged my books by subject and in chronological rather than alphabetical order. I wanted to be serious.

356

"It *is* harder for a woman," she acknowledged. Meaning: to be serious, to take herself seriously, to get others to take her seriously. *She* had put her foot down while still a child. Let gender get in her way? Not on your life! But most women were too timid. Most women were afraid to assert themselves, afraid of looking too smart, too ambitious, too confident. They were afraid of being unladylike. They did not want to be seen as hard or cold or self-centered or arrogant. They were afraid of looking masculine. Rule number one was to get over all that.

Here is one of my favorite Susan Sontag stories.

It was sometime in the early sixties, when she'd just become a Farrar, Straus and Giroux author, and she was invited to a dinner party at her publisher's Upper-East-Side townhouse. Back then, it was the custom chez Straus for the guests to separate after dinner, the men repairing to one room, the women to another. For a moment Susan was puzzled. Then it hit her. Without a word to the hostess, she stalked off to join the men. Dorothea Straus told the story gleefully years later. "And that was that! Susan broke the tradition, and we never split up after dinner again."

She was certainly not afraid of looking masculine. And she was impatient with other women for not being more like her, for not being able to leave the women's room and go join the men.

She always wore pants (usually jeans) and low-heeled shoes (usually sneakers), and she refused to carry a purse. The attachment of women to purses perplexed her. She made fun of me for taking mine everywhere. Where had women gotten the idea they'd be lost without one? Men didn't carry purses, hadn't I noticed? Why did women *burden* themselves? Why not instead always wear clothes with pockets large enough to hold keys, wallet, and cigarettes, as men did?

She said, "Here's a big difference between you and me. You wear makeup and you dress in a certain way that's meant to draw attention and help people find you attractive. But I won't do anything to draw attention to my looks. If someone wants to, they can take a closer look and maybe they'll discover I'm attractive. But I'm not going to do anything to help them." Mine was the typical female way, hers was the way of most men.

* * *

No makeup, but she dyed her hair. And she wore cologne. Men's cologne: Dior Homme.

She was a great admirer of Elizabeth Hardwick's work, but she thought Hardwick was yet another woman fettered by her femininity ("I have always, all of my life, been looking for help from a man," Hardwick wrote), in this case a particularly pungent Southern brand of it. (On the other hand, in a conversation about women writers I once had with Hardwick, when I mentioned Susan she said, "She's not really a woman.")

She thought Virginia Woolf was a genius, but to hold her above all other literary idols as I did then struck Susan as callow; predictable. Besides, something about Woolf—something I think had everything to do with Woolf's mental and physical illnesses (her weaknesses, in other words)—made Susan squeamish. The first volume of Woolf's letters had recently come out, and Susan said she could not read them. She was put off by the many intimate letters to Woolf's beloved older friend, Violet Dickinson, the silly endearments and girlish prattle, and Woolf's habit of presenting herself as a cute little animal. Susan hated childish language of any kind and always boasted that she had never spoken baby talk with her son when he was little.

* * *

She was suspicious of women with menstrual complaints. She herself had always taken her periods in stride, and she thought that a lot of women must be exaggerating the inconveniences and discomforts of theirs. Or they were buying into old myths about the delicacy and vulnerability of the female body. In my case, diagnosis was simple: "You're neurasthenic." In fact, she suspected that many people exaggerated or overreacted to both physical and emotional pain, an attitude that no doubt owed much to her having had cancer and having stoically withstood radical surgery and chemotherapy.

Seeing me curled up in her son's lap, she fixed me with a cool I've-got-your-number look and lisped mockingly, "The little girl and her *big man.*"

She was a feminist, but she was often critical of her feminist sisters and of much of the rhetoric of feminism for being naive, sentimental, and anti-intellectual. And she could be hostile to those who complained about being underrepresented in the arts or banned from the canon, ungently reminding them that the canon (or art, or genius, or talent, or literature) was not an equal opportunity employer.

She was a feminist who found most women wanting. There was a certain friend she saw regularly, a brilliant man whom she loved to hear talk and whom, though he was married, she usually saw alone. Those times when his wife did come along were inevitably disappointing. With his wife there, Susan complained, the conversation of this brilliant and intellectually stimulating man somehow became boring.

She was exasperated to find that the company of even very intelligent women was usually not as interesting as that of intelligent men.

                                                        *   *   *

Over the years, I have met or learned about a surprising number of people who said it was reading Susan Sontag when they were young that had made them want to be writers. Although this was not true of me, her influence on how I think and write has been profound. By the time I got to know her I was already out of school, but I'd been a mostly indifferent, highly distracted student, and the gaps in my knowledge were huge. Though she hadn't grown up in New York, she was far more of a New Yorker than I, who'd always lived there, and to the city's cultural life you could have no better guide. Small wonder I considered meeting her one of the luckiest strokes of my life. It's quite possible that, in time, I'd have discovered on my own writers like John Berger and Walter Benjamin and E. M. Cioran and Simone Weil. But the fact remains, I learned about them first from her. Though I'm sure she was often dismayed to hear what I hadn't read, how much I didn't know, she did not make me feel ashamed. Among other things, she understood what it was like to come from a background where there were few books and no intellectual spirit or guidance; she had come from such a background herself. She said, "You and I didn't have what David's been able to take for granted from birth."

She was a natural mentor. You could not live with her and avoid being mentored, was the delightful truth of it. Even someone who met her only once was likely to go away with a reading list. She was naturally didactic and moralistic; she wanted to be an influence, a model, *exemplary*. She wanted to improve the minds and refine the tastes of other people, to tell people things they didn't know (in some cases, things they didn't even want to know but that she insisted they damn well ought to). But if educating others was an obligation, it was also loads of fun. She was the opposite of Thomas Bernhard's comic "possessive thinker," who feeds on the fantasy that every book or painting or piece of music he loves has been created solely for and belongs solely to him and whose "art selfishness" makes the thought of anyone else enjoying or appreciating the works of genius he reveres intolerable. She wanted her passions to be shared by all, and to respond with equal intensity to any work she loved was to give her one of her biggest pleasures.

Some of her enthusiasms mystified me. As we sat in the theater sharing a giant chocolate bar, I kept wondering why she'd wanted to see a double feature of old Katherine Hepburn movies, both of which she said she'd already seen more than twenty times. Of course, she was *besotted* (another favorite word) with moviegoing—in the way only someone who never watches television can be, perhaps. (We know this now: if one size screen doesn't addict you, another one will.) We went to the movies all the time. Ozu, Kurosawa, Godard, Bresson, Resnais—each of these names is linked in my mind with her own. It was with her that I first learned how much more exciting a movie is when watched from a seat close up to the screen. Because of her I still always sit in the front of the theater, I still resist watching any movie on television, and have never been able to bring myself to rent movie videos or DVDs.

Among living American writers, she admired, besides Hardwick, Donald Barthelme, William Gass, Leonard Michaels, Grace Paley. But she had no more use for most contemporary American fiction than she did for most contemporary American film. In her view, the last first-rate American novel had been *Light in August*, by Faulkner (a writer she respected but did not love). Of course Philip Roth and John Updike were good writers, but she could summon no enthusiasm for the things they wrote about. Later, she would not find the influence of Raymond Carver on American fiction something to cheer. It wasn't at all that she was against minimalism, she said; she just couldn't be thrilled about a writer "who writes the same way he talks."

What thrilled her instead was the work of certain Europeans, for example Italo Calvino, Bohumil Hrabal, Peter Handke, Stanislaw Lem. They, along with Latin American writers like Jorge Luis Borges and Julio Cortázar, were creating far more daring and original work than her less ambitious fellow Americans. She liked to describe all highly inventive, form- or genre-bending writing as science fiction, in contrast to banal contemporary American realism. It was this kind of literature she thought a fiction writer should aspire to, and that she believed would continue to matter.

She was a natural mentor . . . who hated teaching. Teach as little as possible, she said. Best not to teach at all. She said, "I saw the best writers of my generation destroyed by teaching." She said the life of the writer and the life of the academic would always be at odds. She liked to refer to herself as a self-defrocked academic. She was even prouder to call herself self-created. I never had a mentor, she said. Though she must have learned something while married to her University of Chicago professor, sociologist and cultural critic Philip Rieff, a marriage that began when she was a sophomore and he was twenty-eight and ended when she left him seven years later. And she'd had other professors, among them Leo Strauss and Kenneth Burke, whom she remembered as extraordinary teachers and for whom she had no end of praise. But however else these men might have inspired her, it was not to be a great teacher herself.

Like many other writers, she equated teaching with failure. Besides, she had never wanted to be anyone's employee. The worst part of teaching was that it was, inescapably, a job, and for her to take any job was humiliating. But then, she also found the idea of borrowing a book from the library instead of buying her own copy humiliating. Taking public transportation instead of a cab was deeply humiliating. Divaism? She seemed to think any self-respecting person would understand and feel as she did.

I found it strange that there was this one part of her life—the teaching she did, either before or after I met her—that she never talked about. About being a student, she talked a lot. In fact, I'd never known anyone to speak with such reverence about his or her own student days. It gave her a special glow to talk about that time, making me think it must have been the happiest of her life. She said the University of Chicago had made her the mind she was; it was there that she'd learned, if not how to write, how to read closely and how to think critically. She still cherished her course notebooks from those days.

Now it occurs to me that at least some of her resistance to teaching might have had to do with her passion for being a student. She had

361

the habits and the aura of a student all her life. She was also, all but physically, always young. People close to her often compared her to a child (her inability to be alone; her undiminishable capacity for wonder; her being without health insurance in her forties, when she got cancer, even though health insurance was easily affordable in those days). David and I joked that she was our enfant terrible. (Once, when she was struggling to finish an essay, angry that we weren't being supportive enough, she said, "If you won't do it for me, at least you could do it for Western culture.") My enduring image of her fits exactly that of a student, a fanatical one: staying up all night, surrounded by piles of books and papers, speeding, chain-smoking, reading, note taking, pounding the typewriter, driven, competitive. She would write that A-plus essay. She would go to the head of the class.

Even her apartment—strictly anti-bourgeois, unapologetically *ungemütlich*—evoked student life. Its main feature was the growing number of books, but they were mostly paperbacks, and the shelves were cheap pine board. Furniture was sparse, there were no curtains or rugs, and the kitchen had few supplies. No cooking was done there, unless it was by some visitor. No entertaining, not even on holidays. If there was a guest, he or she would be offered a cup of Café Bustelo (never any kind of alcohol) or might be invited to join us for a frozen dinner or a bowl of canned soup. People visiting for the first time were clearly surprised to find the celebrated middle-aged writer living like a grad student. (Everything changes. In her mid-fifties she would say: "I realized I was working just as hard, if not harder, than everyone I knew, and making less money than any of them." And so she transformed that part of her life. But the time I'm talking about was before—before the grand Chelsea penthouse, the enormous library, the rare editions, the art collection, the designer clothes, the country house, the personal assistant, the housekeeper, the personal chef. And one day when I was around the same age she had been when we met, she shook her head at me and said, "What are you planning to do, live like a grad student the rest of your life?")

Whenever some university made her an offer she knew she *shouldn't* refuse, she was torn. Often she turned it down even though she needed money, and then she would congratulate herself. She was amazed at those who made a much better living from writing than she did yet were still tempted by tenure. She was outraged to hear other writers complain, as many often did, about how their teaching made them miserable because it interfered with their writing. In general, she had contempt for people who didn't do what they truly wanted to do. She believed that most people, unless they are very poor, make their own lives, and, to her, security over freedom was a deplorable choice. It was servile.

She believed that, in our culture, at least, people were much freer than they thought they were and had more options than they seemed willing to acknowledge. She also believed that how other people treated you was, if not wholly, mostly within your control, and she was always after me to *take* that control. *Stop letting people bully you*, she would bully me.

Which brings me to another favorite story.

She said, "I know you won't believe this, but when I was your age I was a lot more like you than like I am today. And I can prove it!" It turned out the playwright Maria Irene Fornes was coming to visit that day. Fornes and Susan had been lovers almost twenty years earlier, after Susan had divorced her husband and moved to New York. When Fornes arrived, as soon as she'd introduced us, Susan said, "Tell Sigrid what I was like when you met me. Go on, go on!"

"She was an idiot," Fornes said.

When she'd stopped laughing Susan said to me, "The point I was trying to make is that there's hope for you, too."

*   *   *

When, recently, I see that Javier Marías has said that the worst thing a writer can do is to take himself or his work too seriously, I think I understand. I think I even agree with him. I think if I had thought this way myself when I was young, my life could have been happier. I might even have turned out to be a better writer. Nevertheless, I'm grateful to have had as an early model someone who held such an exalted, unironic view of the writer's vocation. ("And you must *think* of it as a vocation. Never as a career.")

Virginia Woolf lived as if literature were a religion and she one of its priests. Susan made me think of the antiquated hyperbole of Thomas Carlyle: the writer as hero. There could *be* no nobler pursuit, no greater adventure, no more rewarding quest. And she shared Woolf's worship of books, her idea of heaven as eternal reading.

She said, "Pay no attention to these writers who claim you can't be a serious writer and a voracious reader at the same time." (Two such writers, I recall, were V. S. Naipaul and Norman Mailer.) After all, what mattered was the life of the mind, and for that life to be lived fully, reading was *the* necessity. Aiming for a book a day was not too high (though something I myself could not achieve). Because of her, I began reading too fast.

Because of her I began writing my name in each new book I acquired. I began clipping articles from newspapers and magazines and filing them in various books. Like her, I always read with a pencil in hand (never a pen), for underlining.

In school, I had studied with Elizabeth Hardwick, and though she was at times encouraging I always got the feeling from her that if I gave myself over completely to the writer's life I would find more unhappiness than fulfillment. For years afterward, whenever I spoke to her I noticed she almost always asked about my writing only after she'd asked about my love life. ("Do you still have that nice young man?") She used to tell her Barnard students that you had to be really bored with life to become a writer. Somehow I don't believe she thought this was true for men.

On the other hand, with Susan, I felt as if I were being given permission to devote myself to these two vocations—reading and writing—that were so often difficult to justify. And it was clear that, no matter how hard or frustrating or daunting it was—and no matter how much like a long punishment writing a book could be—she would not have chosen any other way; she would not have wanted any other life than the life she had.

"You have to care about every comma."

"A writer's standards can't ever possibly be too high."

"Never worry about being obsessive. I like obsessive people. Obsessive people make great art."

To read a whole shelf of books to research one twenty-page essay, to spend months writing and rewriting, going through one entire ream of typing paper before those twenty pages could be called done—for the serious writer this was, of course, normal. Satisfaction? "I always think everything I write is shit," she said. But of course, you didn't do it to feel good about yourself. You didn't do it for your own enjoyment (unlike reading), or for catharsis, or to express yourself, or to please some particular audience. You did it for literature, she said. And there was nothing wrong with never being satisfied with what you did.

"The question you have to ask yourself is whether what you're writing is necessary." I didn't know about this. *Necessary?* That way, I thought, lies writer's block.

Because of her I resisted switching from typewriter to word processor. ("You want to *slow down*, not speed up. The last thing you want is something that's going to make writing *easier*.")

One way in which she considered herself a terrible model was in her work habits. She had no discipline, she said. She could not steel herself to write every day, as everyone knew was best. But it was not so much lack of discipline as a hunger to do many other things besides write. She wanted to travel a lot and go out every night—and to me the most fitting of all the things that were said upon her death was by Hardwick: "In the end, nothing is more touching to the emotions than to think of her own loss of evenings at 'happenings,' at dance recitals, the opera, movies."

Lincoln Center. For the rest of my life, I think, I will never hear the orchestra tuning up or watch the chandeliers rise toward the ceiling of the opera house without remembering her.

To get herself to work, she had to clear out big chunks of time during which she would do nothing else. She would take speed and work around the clock, never leaving the apartment, rarely leaving her desk. We'd go to sleep to the sound of her typing and wake up to the sound of her typing. This could go on for weeks. And though she often said she wished she could work in a less self-destructive way, she believed it was only after going at it full throttle for many hours that your mind really started to click and you'd come up with your best ideas.

She said a writer should never pay attention to reviews, good or bad. "In fact, you'll see, the good ones will often make you feel even worse than the bad ones." Besides, she said, people are sheep. If one person says something's good, the next person says it's good, and so on. "And if *I* say something's good, *everyone* says it's good."

She said, "Don't be afraid to steal. I steal from other writers all the time." And she could point to no few instances of writers stealing from her.

She said, "Beware of ghettoization. Resist the pressure to think of yourself as a woman writer." And, "Resist the temptation to think of yourself as a victim."

365

She was a natural mentor, but she was not maternal. Though she always said her biggest regret was not having had more children, I found it almost impossible to imagine her nursing, or tending to an infant or a small child. I could more easily imagine her digging ditches or break dancing or milking a cow. In fact, she told me she never really wanted her son to think of her as his mother. "I'd rather he see me as—oh, I don't know, his goofy big sister." From the time she knew she was pregnant till the day she went into labor, she never saw a doctor. "I didn't know you were supposed to." Endlessly curious; at least one book a day—but not one book about pregnancy or child care, she said. She was the opposite of women like Michelle Obama: she was a mother last.

She liked to tell a story about the time a group of other young mothers approached her to express concern about her parenting, suggesting she needed guidance. It wasn't that they were busybodies, she said. They were just unliberated fifties women stuck with conventional ideas of what a proper woman, wife, and mother should be. I asked her if they had made her feel guilty, and she replied emphatically *no*. She had never felt any guilt about the kind of mother she was. "Not one iota."

First I moved out, then David and I broke up, and not long after that David got a place of his own. Over the next few years, a period when she was often depressed, I had more contact with her than I had with him, though it never amounted to much. Always she complained of being lonely, of feeling rejected; abandoned. Sometimes she wept. She had gotten it into her head that everything she ever did in her life was first of all to win David's love and respect. As if he were the parent and she the child.

While I was still in school, at Columbia, I had taken a course in Modern British Literature with Edward Said. Whenever I mentioned him Susan would tease. "Sounds like you've got a crush." (Though Susan had probably met Said by this time, the two had not yet become friends.) There was truth to this. A lot of students were smitten with brilliant, handsome young Professor Said.

And then, somehow—I can't remember the details except that I had nothing to do with them—Professor Said was coming to visit!

I have never understood what happened that day. I remember that the four of us were in the living room, where there was only one comfortable chair. I remember that Said sat in that chair without taking off his coat and that he had brought an umbrella, which he placed on the floor beside the chair. And the whole time, he kept reaching down to pick up the umbrella and then immediately put it down on the floor again.

I didn't say anything, David didn't say anything, and though Susan did her best to engage him, Said didn't say much of anything, either. He sat there in his coat, nervously playing with the umbrella and not saying much, and when he did say something it was mumbled. He sat in the one comfortable chair, the only comfortable chair in the whole apartment, looking as uncomfortable as if he were sitting on nails, picking up the umbrella and putting it down again, nodding at whatever Susan said but obviously too distracted to be really listening. Of what was discussed all I can recall is who was and who wasn't still on the faculty at Columbia where, years before, Susan had taught, too. The entire visit, though it did not last long, was excruciating, and it was a great relief when he was gone.

And after he was gone Susan came to find me. "Are you all right?" I shrugged. "Look," she said. "I have no idea what that was all about, but I do know how you feel and I'm sorry." What was she talking about? "I know what it's like when you admire someone and then you see them in an unflattering light. I know it can be very painful."

We sat together for a while, smoking and talking. How many hours we used to spend like that, smoking and talking. To me it was unfathomable: the busiest, most productive person I knew, who somehow always had time for a long conversation.

"But that's what happens," she said. "You have to be prepared for that." It had happened to her a lot, she said. Once she started meeting writers and artists, it happened over and over. "I'd be so thrilled about meeting these people—my heroes! my idols!" And over and over she would feel let down or even betrayed. And she was so disillusioned that she'd end up regretting having met them, because now she couldn't worship them or their work anymore, at least not in the same pure way.

One of her favorite books was Balzac's *Lost Illusions*, which she insisted I must read at once.

One of her favorite films was *Tokyo Story*. "I try to go see it once a year." (And in those days, if you lived in Manhattan, this could be done.)

367

She was shocked when I didn't love it. (I am ashamed to say, that first time, I found Ozu's masterpiece too slow.)

"But didn't you get it? What about the part, after the mother's funeral"—and she recited an exchange that takes place between the youngest daughter and the daughter-in-law. "Oh my god!" She clutched her throat. "Didn't that make you *weep*?"

What a dumb clod I must have seemed to her. I thought of lying just to protect her. But then she waved her hand and said, "Oh, it's just because you're too young. Years from now you'll see it again, and then you'll understand." Confident.

Actually, it didn't take years. And I didn't have to see the movie again.

Kyoko: Isn't life disappointing?
Noriko: Yes, it is.

Nominated by C.E. Poverman

BLACKSTONE

by C.K. WILLIAMS

from THE THREEPENNY REVIEW

When Blackstone the magician cut a woman in half in the Branford
theater
near the famous Lincoln statue in already part way down the chute
Newark,

he used a gigantic buzz saw, and the woman let out a shriek that out-
shrieked
the whirling blade and drilled directly into the void of our little boy
crotches.

That must be when we learned that real men were supposed to hurt
women,
make them cry then leave them, because we saw the blade go in,
right in,

her waist was bare—look!—and so, in her silvery garlanded bra,
shining,
were her breasts, oh round, silvery garlanded tops of breasts shining.

Which must be when we went insane, and were sent to drive our
culture insane . . .
"Show me your breasts, please," "*Shame on you, hide your breasts—
shame.*"

Nothing else mattered, just silvery garlanded breasts, and still she
    shrieked,
the blade was still going in, under her breasts, and nothing else
    mattered.

Oh Branford theater, with your scabby plaster and threadbare scrim,
you didn't matter, and Newark, your tax-base oozing away to the
    suburbs,

you didn't matter, nor your government by corruption, nor swelling
    slums—
you were invisible now, those breasts had made you before our eyes
    vanish,

as Blackstone would make doves then a horse before our eyes vanish,
as at the end factories and businesses from our vanquished city
    would vanish.

Oh Blackstone, gesturing, conjuring, with your looming, piercing
    glare.
Oh gleaming, hurtling blade, oh drawn-out scream, oh perfect,
    thrilling arc of pain.

Nominated by Dick Allen, Joan Murray, Kay Ryan, Threepenny Review

BARTER

by RAVI SHANKAR

from AGNI

—for Catherine Barnett

Possessed of some rudimentary detection skills,
I can spot a Rothko or a liar at twenty paces.
Can panfry dosas, walk on rooftops, misplace bills

in the most obvious places, clutter open spaces
with dog-eared books or newspaper clippings.
I've been known to win at cards or in most races,

like upon the blacktop during recess, zipping
to snatch a chalk eraser. Can speak, if soused,
in decent French, & remain adept at equipping

friends for a camping trip. Have even roused
flame from flint & steel, still know my knots
from clove hitch to bowline, & when housed

by a friend, I know enough that dinner's bought
by me. Could, if pressed, construct metafiction,
elaborate fun house mirrors of prose that cannot

be turned into a movie. Have worked construction,
broken floors with a jackhammer. Sold knives
one summer to suburban housewives, using diction

of tang & rivet. Can dispense a kiss that survives
the lips, solve algebraic equations, & score goals
in soccer. Say I've taken the shape of many lives.

Nominated by Dick Allen

THINGS WE'LL NEED FOR THE COMING DIFFICULTIES

fiction by VALERIE VOGRIN

from AGNI

First

There were so many resources—had been since the 1960s: frugal living and self-sufficiency and survivalist guides in addition to solar power and alternative energy handbooks. In particular, the must-have lists provided by the survivalists seemed reassuringly complete, as if you could shop your way to utter preparedness for the unprecedented. It took awhile, studying these books over the years, becoming a bit obsessive perhaps, before you really grasped their limitations. While water purification tablets and a superbly well-stocked first aid kit might be applicable to many if not most emergency situations, the future was unknowable, after all.

Henceforth, as you continued your preparations, you became something of an amateur odds-maker, betting on the likelihood of one type of disaster over another. Finally, it became clear that you must come up with another list, not of the things you will need, but of the things that will allow you to live.

Mason's list

Plenty of writing paper, pencils, St. John's Wort, oomph, equanimity, playing cards, jigsaw puzzles, board games, hard cider, bird seed,

Joseph Campbell, Kierkegaard, Merton, Hafiz, Blake, coffee, guitar, replacement strings, good boots, better socks.

Shay's list
Olive and aloe soap, almond body butter, pumice stone, shell collection, running shoes, spare buttons and shoelaces, needle and thread, Chapstick, emery boards, unreasonable optimism, *The Complete Letters of Vincent van Gogh*, Neruda, Hass, Marquez, star charts, classical lullabies, Satie, chocolate, cocoa, yarn, knitting books.

~

Mason's abilities in carpentry, plumbing, and wiring had been exotic and attractive. Here was a guy who knew his way around the tool shed. He bought for quality. He measured twice and cut once. He laughed easily and loudly in an I-just-can't-help-myself way that made other people smile. He was sturdy.

Shay hadn't wanted to support another of the men who were usually drawn to her: overeducated, self-medicating, underemployed depressives. She was no longer interested in the shifty, neurotic love they offered. It would be a novelty, Shay had thought ten years ago, to spend some time living in Mason's funky, earth-sheltered, solar-powered house in the woods—quite like a fairytale dwelling. And Mason, something like the humble woodsman, sawdust in his hair and eyelashes.

useful skills she brought to the table
—pie making
—knitting, mending
—native proficiency in Spanish (maybe; though certainly less practical in the Midwest)

other skills, above average, currently irrelevant
—distinguished (full professional) proficiency in Catalan
—life master ranking, duplicate bridge
—ordering the best dish on the menu

what is meant by difficulties
—the calamities the "Chicken Littles" had long forecast, i.e. epidemic viruses, civil unrest, catastrophic weather incidents, terrorism, and even a plague of pesticide-resistant corn weevils.

—the kinds of things that had once made for wincingly funny jokes in late-night talk show hosts' monologues

—things that made you a bit ashamed you'd ever blithely used the phrase "when the shit hits the fan"

something they agree is worthy of concern

What would happen to their dog if something happened to them? Paisley was a terrific barker, a great raiser of alarm, but she was an arthritic old Irish wolfhound mix, never much of a biter or a fighter, and wasn't particularly good at distinguishing between actual danger and a stray cat or squirrel.

ongoing discussion about weapons

They spoke of guns in low voices in bed with the lights out; she was against them, of course.

According to Mason, Shay had a bizarre, non-animal lack of regard for self-preservation. He'd met many self-professed pacifists over the years and they were all phonies, well-meaning and otherwise, every one of them. Maybe they didn't eat meat, kill spiders, or wear leather shoes. Maybe they were against capital punishment and animal testing. Maybe they'd never fight as soldiers or join a militia. But when a knife was pressed to their throats, when something deadly crept up on a loved one, you'd see something else again: a pretty pitiful fight for life, unarmed and panicked. But Shay was a different matter, he had to admit.

"We're all going to die," Shay said. "That's what an animal doesn't know. That's how we can be different. By having some dignity."

He pressed his lips tight.

"What? Go ahead, say whatever it is you want to say."

What Mason wanted was to change her mind. Or have her pretend to change her mind, say she'd fight back. But the only way he could think to accomplish this was by scaring her and he wouldn't do that. He hoped he'd know when it was time to tell her about the guns and ammunition he'd hidden in his shop. He hoped she knew he had ignored her protests.

~

From the beginning Shay had thought that the house was a marvel—a Hobbit dwelling built right into the side of a hill. An expanse of south-facing floor-to-ceiling windows stretched the width of the house

375

and breathed in light. The domed ceiling of the main room, the rough-textured stuccoed walls, and the odd, earth-hugging silence made it a sacred, contemplative place. You felt contained rather than buried. It was a house that didn't favor one season over another, equally adept at sheltering its inhabitants from sun, wind, snow, and rain. Now she appreciated that it was something else again: concealed and defendable. Surrounded by woods, invisible from three sides, and nearly invisible behind a stand of bamboo from the fourth, it was as obscure and ingenious as its builder.

the things that have surprised her the most
—that right now she can't say that she is in love with him
—that the university was one of the first things to shut down
—that it happened in her lifetime
—that it all happened so fast

~

Once, they were cocktail party questions: How do you imagine the end of the world as we know it? Would you rather die of heat or cold? Which would be harder to give up, going to the movies or having pizza delivered, driving fast down the freeway or getting a pedicure?

Would people in the future understand it better than they did now? Just how far back would you have to stand in order to connect the dots between events of the early part of the century and these troubled late-middle years? As a younger woman, reading novels that imagined various post-industrial, post-apocalyptic worlds, she had found it hard to take them seriously. They seemed a bit hysterical. Yet she'd chosen a man with exactly the qualities that would be helpful if disaster did strike. She had known from their first date, hadn't she?—that here was a man who would be useful even when there were no more stock brokerages or think tanks or small claims courts.

things she regrets (synonymous in her mind with things Mason would consider ridiculous even to think about; but then he says regret is for sissies)
That she once cried as she said goodbye to the woman who had given her impeccable haircuts for over six years before quitting the business and moving to Florida. That she had chosen to maintain a relationship with a grim, impoverished sculptor over a long, humid summer rather than travel again to Catalonia. That she had made no great

376

mark on her profession. That she'd never ridden a horse. That she didn't play an instrument. That when she was eleven she'd made her little sister sad enough to run away; although Elise had made it no farther than the neighbor's garage, her red plastic suitcase had been heartbreakingly well packed. (She hoped Elise's practicality was serving her well now.)

things about which she is wrong
—him and regret (He puts up a good front, but he regrets far more of his life than he embraces. Truly and daily he is heavy with regret. He loves Shay foremost because she is his last chance for redemption. He will try to keep her safe.)
—that she thinks he doesn't wonder whether the effort to survive isn't pathetic
—that he's exaggerating or being dramatic when he tells her he had been a bad man

things he thinks she's wrong about
—that she was ever really in love with him (He figured it had been his best swindle, a real razzle-dazzle. He made her laugh, he built her bookshelves, he planted a redtwig dogwood in the front yard in her honor. He was the handy, practical guy who made her feel cared for.)

~

Mason worried that what he took to be Shay's listlessness would drag her down to some place he would be unable to reach. Surely she felt differently about her life—less content—now that she had very little choice in how it continued. Weather permitting, she took early morning runs in the woods, but she sat for many hours in the big chair reading. Her coffee grew cold but she didn't get up to reheat it. He could never sit still like that for so long. Sometimes the lopsided slant of her head told him that she was arguing with herself again.

"I mean, all along I had trouble convincing myself that what I did was important. So how can I convince myself now that translating another short story by a writer from Reus is in any way worthwhile?" In addition to teaching she had published several volumes of English translations of Catalan literature and edited an anthology.

There was no use hoping she didn't expect an answer. When she was upset her eyes went lizardy, barely blinking. "Maybe that's not the

377

right question," he said. Mason looked down at his hands, the curve of black beneath each fingernail.

"What do you mean?"

"It's your work, right? Translating?"

"I guess."

"No, it is, Shay. I know it is. And I think that's about all we can do right now—our work."

"You mean like keep on keepin' on?" She sneered slightly and he froze. But she got up and kissed him hard on the lips. "Thank you."

~

Mason gardened like he did everything else, doggedly. He was the only man she'd ever been with who ground his teeth while making love. The garden grew by rows, yards, quarter-acres. She enjoyed kneeling beside him in the dirt and helping him weed—an excuse to watch his fingers deftly separate the lacy fronds of the carrots from the thatched leaves of the weeds. This was his gift, she thought, knowing what belonged and what didn't.

After

And then one afternoon, after so many days had unfolded in so much the same way, Wayne arrived.

Paisley barked and barked. She never did relax when he was near.

~

Shay and Wayne had started graduate school at the same time and that first semester they took a course together, History of the Spanish Language, with Professor Sabina Torrijos-Garcia. Wayne claimed to have seduced Sabina, but he mocked her scholarship and her pointy-toed designer shoes. Wayne didn't like the women he slept with. Shay learned that the hard way. He cooked delicate omelettes for Shay's supper and read Neruda to her by candlelight while she took bubble baths, but he wouldn't spend the night at her apartment and never invited her to his. Wayne helped with her dissertation. He once arranged to get them into the National Gallery after hours because she had told him it was one of the things she dreamed of. She ran her finger very lightly over the horse's standing front hoof in El Greco's *St. Jerome and the Beggar*. He frequently called in the middle of the night to berate Shay for her immaturity, her laziness, her perfume, her inferior accent. The calls continued even after she stopped sleeping with him. He got her drunk on tequila and took her for long humid drives with the top down on his 1957 El Dorado convertible. The calls continued even after she earned her degree and moved away.

She had never mentioned him to Mason and she told him very little after Wayne arrived. How did you explain such a crooked thing?

what Wayne presented upon his arrival, as though offering up bounty
—a twenty-pound block of six-year aged raw-milk cheddar
—two dozen fresh eggs
—a bag of lemons
—three bottles of George Dickel No. 12
—a set of crystal-studded dominos
—heirloom tomato seeds
—a grain mill

~

It took less than a second, the sizing up, before Mason had an inkling of what Wayne had been to Shay. And in the next moment, sharp and quick, like a joint snapped back into its socket, he saw Wayne for what he was. And then another shock, the jolt of recognition coming right back from this man: *I see you, too.*

In that moment, Mason was a radiologist studying the X-ray of his own former self's soul: the epic selfishness, high pain threshold, and excess self-regard crossed with a thirst for admiration, recklessness, duplicity. And showing up like a grey tumor-shadow on the pale oval of the soul's lung: the willingness to inflict pain.

This was a man who might take everything from him, including all the ways he believed he had changed in the past fifteen years.

~

Wayne told them he'd traveled mostly at night, sticking to rural highways in disrepair. He professed to know little more than they did about the situation at large. He said he'd been holed up for most of the past year at an old commune-turned-compound in the Ozarks. "The men were a bit too enthused about their weaponry. They said they didn't want trouble but I didn't quite believe them. They had a very nice dairy operation, though. I'm going to miss the fresh milk."

"That's quite a ride you got there," Mason said. A clean, rust-free white van with newish tires and a shiny blue tarp strapped over some kind of cargo on the roof.

"I'm knackered," Wayne said. "Okay if I set up my tent up in your trees?"

Mason felt Shay studying his face. He forced his expression into carefree cordiality. "Absolutely," he said. "That stand over there will give you the best wind break. You want a hand?"

"Not necessary. I've got an ace tent, a breeze to put up."

"Once you've had a chance to rest, you'll come in for cocktails, yes? And dinner?" Shay asked.

"I'd be delighted." Wayne winked at Shay.

~

Mason slammed the door to his shop. He could have laughed like a maniac—could have thrashed his workshop, taken an axe to the table he'd been working on for Shay. He spun around in the center of the room, looking for something to pick up or hold onto that would calm him. But every polished tool, every cunning little wooden thing, only inspired the desire to crush, splinter, demolish. Oh what a hackneyed plot! Old boyfriend comes to town, stirs up trouble, tests the durability of the commitment. If you were the current boyfriend there were so many ways to suffer defeat. From lose the girl to make a jealous horse's ass of yourself to the painful disclosure of unwanted facts about: self, girl, relationship. And these days, you could only hope that this might be the worst of it. Fuck all.

~

"Quite a house," Wayne said.

"Except for pouring the concrete, Mason built it himself." Shay stretched her lips into a smile. She hated her tone, knew it sounded like she was bragging about a small child.

"This is an example of an elevational design plan, is that right?"

Mason's eyebrows didn't even raise, but she could see his jaw muscles working. "That's right."

"You've got what, four or five feet of land above?"

"Five."

"Sounds ideal." And yet his tone conveyed skepticism.

Mason made a wasps' nest humming sound in the back of his throat. The men were still standing in the middle of the room just below the skylight.

"This must be—what—almost twenty years old?" Wayne asked.

"Sixteen."

"Still, man, you were definitely ahead of the curve. So tell me, was building this house the act of a prescient man or of a good, old-fashioned tree hugger?"

"I think of myself as pragmatic."

"Yes, *pragmatic*," Wayne said, his inflection suggesting pragmatism was a venereal disease.

Shay could have screamed. Stop it!

"Has Shay told you about our road trip to Charleston?"

Mason snorted. "We could all hold our liquor better when we were younger, I gather."

Shay wasn't even sure they'd ever gone to Charleston. She remembered Atlantic City, Cooperstown, Philadelphia . . .

"Speaking of which," Mason continued, "why don't we try out some of that very fine Tennessee whiskey?"

"I'll get glasses and ice," Shay said. She felt unreasonably guilty, knowing that Wayne would take his straight up no ice and not knowing until this minute if Mason even drank whiskey, Tennessee or Irish or Canadian or Scotch, much less how. She and Mason had never been on a road trip. If they hit the road now they'd be running for their lives.

~

"Is that an *English* accent?" Mason asked when they were nestled in bed, Paisley a warm, dog-breathy mound between them.

"It's a nothing accent. He was born and raised in the Northwest. Puget Sound? Bremerton maybe? He's always talked like that." And she was talking too much.

"Of course the real question is where'd he get all that stuff?"

"Who knows?"

"You don't seem a bit surprised, though."

"He has a way of inspiring people to give him things." She felt her cheeks redden. Was she defending Wayne? She switched off the bedside lamp.

"*Give* him things?"

"That's right. Give him things."

"And you don't think that's strange?"

"They're gifts, Mason. Wonderful gifts. I'd almost forgotten what a lemon smelled like."

"I've never given or received gifts like this."

"I haven't seen him in twenty years," she said.

381

"A special occasion indeed."

"What about the rocking chair you gave Ellen? It's exquisite, worth fifty sets of dominos." Why couldn't she just shut up?

"I *made* the chair *for* Ellen. Wayne didn't lay those eggs."

A laugh sputtered in her throat. "Very funny," she said. "I'm not saying it's normal. He has strange powers of persuasion, okay?"

"I'm sure that's the case," he said. "What do you suppose he'll be persuading us to give to him?"

That was a very good question. "Are you mad at me?" she asked. There was something wrong and it was her fault.

"No!"

~

Only on the first night was Mason able to outlast him. It wasn't the drinking that did him in, but sheer weariness. Fifteen years ago, at the outset of his self-transformation, he'd decided to be the kind of man who rose with sun, and he signed a pact with his body that he was unwilling to break. So he turned in first and got up at dawn, whereas Wayne slept in, Wayne napped, and Wayne drowsed about, languid and yawning until cocktail hour. Only then did he come fully awake, perched like a wide-eyed owl, hungry for whatever they served him and ready for hours and hours of conversation.

Dear Shay tried to steer them away from memory lane. Wayne would oblige by talking about himself for some time: the thrill of being invited into the imam's quarters in a gypsy encampment in Bosnia, the only non-Muslim man ever allowed into that particular camp; learning how to make a perfect béchamel for moussaka while living briefly with a Greek heiress on Santos; playing harmonica for spare change in Trafalgar Square on Boxing Day after his pocket had been picked at the Tate. Stories from the old world. But then he'd swerve hard in the other direction. "Remember how drunk we got on Ouzo the day we rented that boat on Dundee Creek?" And there was nothing for Shay to do but answer. Wayne's voice, with its lulling faux-accent, just soft enough so that you had to lean in to hear, made Mason sleepy.

"Time for me to hit the hay." He refused to compete with this man; he refused to show his contempt.

"Sweet dreams. I'll be along soon."

"G'night, kind gentleman." Wayne's voice all oily satisfaction. "Another brilliant evening."

For not the last time, Mason thought he'd just as happily kill the man as invite him into his home. It had been a long while since he'd had such a thought.

The hard thing—the best thing, he convinced himself—was to wait and see.

~

"I'm pretty tuckered out, too," Shay said.

"All right, then, just one more for the road—in a manner of speaking." Wayne refilled their glasses. "So who are you still in touch with?"

"What do you mean? By smoke signal?"

"Don't be silly. I mean, last known whereabouts type of thing."

"Hard to say. Most of the people I stayed in touch with were affiliated with universities. Who knows where they've gotten to now."

"Anyone around here?"

"No."

"Well, who were you in touch with most recently?"

She felt his mind working on hers as if it were a fork in a telekinesis experiment. Her brain felt hot.

"Have you heard from Berman?" Berman had been involved in politics when they were in school. After graduation he'd gotten a job with the State Department.

"Really, Wayne, I've lost track. That was all a long time ago."

"Really, Wayne," he mocked. "It's none of your business. You're on your own, oldest friend of mine. Lovely."

Shay was surprised by the wave of shame that washed over her. Until this moment she'd believed she had severed the hold Wayne had on her when she had finally told him a decade ago to stop calling and he had. The shame was followed by anger. She caught a whiff of sulfur, as though a match had just been lit. She remembered that one of their fellow grad students had half-jokingly referred to Wayne as the dark lord.

She steadied her voice. "That's not what I meant. It's just that since I moved in here, and especially since I left the university, I've been cut off."

"Meaning what? Are you a prisoner here?"

"I cut *myself* off. Whenever I do hear from anyone, it's always bad news."

He smiled wickedly, as if to say *Gotcha!* "So who have you heard from?"

She yawned and lowered her eyes, signalling her intent to end the conversation and go to bed. And she truly was tired. She threw him a bone, told him about the months-old letter she'd received from her sister, delivered through acquaintances of Mason's in town a year before. Elise had settled into an agricultural "faith community" in Iowa. "We do what we can to ease the suffering of our neighbors," she had written. "The flu has hit this area hard and there is so much work to be done."

"It's hard to imagine Elise churning butter or applying poultices," Shay said. "In my mind she's always wearing a smart Ann Taylor suit." She didn't tell him how the earnestness of Elise's letter, which she had closed simply "God bless you," had made Shay feel unworthy and that she hadn't been able to work on her translations for months afterward. She didn't tell him that this letter from her sister, a former district attorney in Chicago, had frightened her—that *this* was the thing that had convinced her there would be no going back to the way things had been.

"I've always wondered what it would be like to be a person who wanted nothing more than to do good works," Wayne said. He grinned at her incredulous expression. "Well, *vaguely* wondered. I'd only do it if I thought I could be a celebrity—the thinking man's Mother Theresa." He swallowed the last of his drink and got up to leave. He brushed his lips against her cheek, whispered in her ear. "You're one of those women who becomes more beautiful with age."

What she felt at his touch, his compliment, she had no word for. Not in any of her languages.

~

They'd seen only what came *out* of the van to this point; it was sort of like a magician's hat designed to thrill an audience. Who knew what still lay hidden in the folds of its satin lining? A pony? A hot air balloon? Vials of anthrax? The ghost of fucking Pablo Neruda? Mason certainly didn't need permission to inspect the premises, yet he'd more or less snuck away while Shay was rolling out pie crusts and Paisley lay beneath the table, hoping for a scrap of dough to fall her way.

Wayne's dark green tent was a doozy, an expensive marvel of engineering, an artifact from the era when climbing and camping were pasttimes for folks with plenty of disposable income. This thing hadn't been constructed for Arkansas weather—this baby was for mountaineering. It'd hold up in a Himalayan gale. Mason admired how the system of panels that mapped the tent's main tension lines along the poles and down the side panels to the main guy points acted as a truss structure that held the poles in a stable arch.

Mason was a few feet away when he heard a squawk from inside the van. The side panel was ajar. He edged toward it. Now he could see that the blue tarp had been rolled up, exposing a double-looped antenna and a pair of solar panels. Mason focused his attention on the four-inch gap. He needed to get closer than he wanted to—close enough to get caught—in order to really see inside the van.

Wayne was crouched over a bulky stack of electronic components, an array of dials and switches and cords. This was something Mason knew little about, though it seemed like a good guess that the thing Wayne was attending to was some kind of shortwave radio. The slight movement of Wayne's right arm and an irregular but rhythmic clicking told him that Wayne was dispatching a message in Morse code.

Wayne swivelled at the exact moment Mason had known he would, the moment at which he himself would have become aware of being watched, so that just as Wayne began to turn Mason leapt sideways behind the van. As expected, the van door rolled open and Wayne probably looked out in all directions and cocked an ear, but he didn't step out—as Mason would have—didn't circle the van's perimeter. That was Mason's advantage: Wayne's certainty that he was too clever to be found out.

~

Mason held to his practice of going to bed early, though he didn't sleep. He was too aware of their ongoing discussions. Or rather he heard Wayne's tone—presumptuous, wheedling, breaking into Spanish—his voice audible *now*—and Shay's voice barely there. He tried to turn their voices into something else, the sound of a remembered dryer tumbling.

Had he thought that one day he would reenter the society of his fellow human beings? That this would signal the completion of his "rehabilitation"? Penman was the only friend he had hung onto—another man who had reinvented himself. Penman the quiet, once-upon-a-time Green Beret who had set up house with Ellen and now kept bees and bred dogs. Mason knew that doubting Shay shamed him. But why hadn't she been more surprised by Wayne's arrival?

When Shay came into the bedroom she turned off the light beside the bed first thing, denying his view of her undressing. And she felt different when she came to bed. She affectionately rubbed her feet against his, but let Paisley stay where she was between them. Shay told Mason she was too tired to talk—having used up her words on Wayne.

Was it this perceived, maybe imagined, withdrawal that made him keep his discovery to himself? Or was he waiting to figure out what Wayne's equipment meant?

"Has he said anything about his plans?"

She groaned, playing up her weariness. "I would tell you, I *will* tell you if he does. But he enjoys being mysterious."

"And you don't think that's because he has something to hide?"

"As opposed to the rest of us?"

He leaned across her, a bit roughly, and switched the lamp back on. But her expression was calm, even amused, as she watched him, waiting for his pronouncement.

"Shay. Listen. I need you to believe me. That man is a threat."

"This has nothing to do with believing you or not."

~

They heard the whine of engines as they shared their morning coffee. She hadn't felt up to a run, or perhaps she had sensed something amiss. Mason jumped up, his left hand already outstretched for the binoculars that hung on a nail by the window.

She joined him. It was six dirt bikes, crisscrossing the hills and valleys beyond their property. If she remembered right, kids from the university had used to come out here on their mountain bikes. *Screamin' terrain.*

She felt Mason calculating—the distance between the bikes and the house; how long it would take him to get the guns and ammunition from his top-secret cache in the shop and be ready to mount some sort of defense if the bikers approached; the likelihood of their approaching; the probabilities regarding the bikers' motives. He stayed where he was. After about ten minutes the bikes stopped on a grassy ridge. Mason grunted. He handed her the binoculars and went back to the table to fetch their coffee cups. What did he see that she couldn't see? The riders could have been men or women. They were trim and wearing camo and black helmets. She shivered, watching their binoculars tilted in her direction. Their gaze seemed to pass over the house—but maybe that was wishful thinking—and they trained their

386

binoculars several times on the big green tent and the white van. The men—she decided they were men—were making no effort to go unseen. She didn't need Mason to tell her that this was more threatening than if they'd been covert.

~

For another hour the motorcyclists tooled up and around the hills and surveilled, but came no closer. Wayne showed up less than an hour after they finally drove off.

Mason headed him off before he reached the door. "Good morning," he said. This was the first time Wayne had come to the house before late afternoon.

"Quite the tourist destination you've got here," Wayne said in the smarmy voice he'd used with hotel managers and maitre d's. How dare he talk to them that way?

"Besides you," Mason said, "those guys are the first people we've seen out here in almost a year."

"Is that so?"

"Quite a coincidence," Mason said.

"We got a bit of this in the Ozarks, too. Makeshift patrols, one militia group or other making sure nobody's infringing on their territory. Nothing to worry about, I'd say."

"Are there people looking for you?" Mason asked.

Why did the question surprise her? Wasn't this just as likely as Wayne having somehow called in these interlopers?

"Do you mean, am I a wanted man?" Wayne laughed heartily. "What a thought!"

Wayne was false. She'd always known he was false and she was reminding herself of this as he added, as if it had just occurred to him to ask, "Have any of those fellows stopped by?"

"We had a couple of them in for tea while you performed your morning toilette," Mason said.

"Ha! Good one."

~

Mason closed the door behind him and headed to the shop, dismissing Wayne, but he heard Wayne following.

Mason opened a can of dark stain and picked up his brush. The strips of sycamore were ready to be cut, but his hand was shaking too hard to use the wood knife. His design for the marquetry was ambitious. He liked to imagine how Shay would react when he unveiled the finished table.

"Shay was never my type," Wayne announced.

He glanced at Wayne, as if registering surprise that he was there. The intricate design was composed of intersecting chevrons.

"Physically, *sexually*, I mean."

"I'm not at all interested in discussing that."

Wayne stepped closer. "I don't want you to have the wrong idea about things."

What were the words that would make this man shut up and go away? How much of this was he supposed to listen to? "It's clear to me there's nothing between you now," Mason said. "That's all that matters to me."

Wayne nodded sagely. If he'd had a beard he would have stroked it. He picked up one of Mason's knives, then another, and felt their heft in his palm. He settled on a straight razor Mason kept throatslittingly sharpened on a ceramic stone.

Try me, Mason thought. *Go ahead.*

"That's an admirable stance to take," Wayne said.

A pistol sat beneath the chamois just to his left. "Spoken as a man who has worn out his welcome," Mason said. He and Penman had gone out to some abandoned corn fields for target practice a few months before.

Wayne held the razor just above a piece of veneer Mason had left unstained. It would constitute the lightest shade of his design. Wayne's hands did not shake.

"In that case, I'll leave you to your handiwork. Unless you have an objection, I think I'll trouble your sweetheart for a spot of tea." He snapped the razor closed, as if to pocket it, then, meeting Mason's eyes, flipped it onto the work table. "Ciao."

~

She saw Wayne leave the shop. He didn't knock and he didn't wipe his feet on the doormat and she watched his feet shedding sawdust as he walked across the room. Paisley sat up and cocked her head as if she, too, realized that this was the first time Shay and Wayne had been alone together in the house. Shay was glad for the rolling pin in her hand. She was glad she'd chosen to make peach pies, Mason's favorite.

"So Shay, my darling, tell me again—what in the world are you do-ing out here in the wilds?"

"You said yourself that I look good. I'm thriving 'out here,' Wayne. How many people can say that these days?"

"It's a pretty small life, don't you think? Are you sure you haven't been bewitched?"

"This is the life I yearned for when I was teaching—ample time and space and quiet."

"Ah yes, a bucolic paradise. You and your handyman."

She would not talk to him about Mason.

"It's not that I can't see the attraction," he said. "It is simply enchanting. And of course he does have you all to himself."

Such a menacing, sly man. She was shot through with the certainty that he intended to stay, to harm. "There's nothing for you here, Wayne." She knew her voice sounded ridiculous, melodramatic.

"I'm not sure I believe you," he said.

~

Yet he didn't show up for dinner and he was gone in the morning. Mason had been up first and presumably had noted the absence of the tent and van as he headed to the shop, if not before, but he left her to discover Wayne's departure for herself.

She wasn't exactly sure she remembered Mason getting up. Had it been dark? What if he wasn't in the shop? But there he was, striding toward the garden with a pair of wire cutters in his hand, before she could panic or develop further hypotheses.

She looked out at the flattened grass where Wayne's tent had stood, and felt relief mixed with something sour. She was glad that Mason would be happy.

Only he didn't seem happy. He was angry. When he returned to the house he paced back and forth, breathing hard, as though trying to expel something from his lungs.

~

"He didn't spoil anything," she told him.

Yet the house felt spoiled. As if everything—every spoon, chair, cup, and book—had been shifted a millimeter out of place. When had the fabric of the sofa faded? Why was that cupboard door sagging on its hinges? If not spoiled, then made wrong, as if this house was an earnest but imperfect replica of their home.

"Nothing's changed," she said.

Her naiveté was too much sometimes. Too heavy a burden. Wayne's

389

visit made clear that he'd let his guard down, succumbing to the temptation to ignore what existed beyond their immediate area. He feared they would pay for his lapse. He felt cheated out of a confrontation, though surely no good would have come of it. He had been ready to taste Wayne's blood. To dig Wayne's grave.

The man had left no clue, no note. There would be no answers about the radio or the riders. Where he'd gone, whether he'd return.

~

That afternoon Mason cycled off. "Don't expect me back tonight."

She would not say the wrong thing again. She would not cling.

"I promise to be home in the morning."

Be safe, she thought—words he would surely scoff at.

They were long hours, but she trusted that he was a man of his word. She turned things over in her mind. No matter what Mason thought, Wayne hadn't found them because of her. Except in the sense that she had once been something to him. She wished she hadn't told Wayne about her sister. Yet he could have found her through Elise.

Sure enough, around seven the next morning Mason and Penman trundled up in a prehistoric-looking bulldozer and spent the daylight hours erasing the driveway. There was more to it than that, but she understood that when they were through there would no longer be a sign of them from the road.

~

"Do you ever stop to think how awful it would be for me if someone hurt you? If they hurt you and made me watch? I can't let that happen."

"Is this about Wayne?"

"This is about our life. This is about the worst thing I can imagine."

He watched her face as she closed her eyes. He wondered what pictures flickered in her mind. He would never know what she imagined.

Her flesh was holy. It had always driven him crazy how careless she was in the kitchen. Her burns and cuts made him feel weak, powerless to prevent harm. What he imagined awake was worse than his nightmares. Knives flashed brighter, sharper, pressed against her skin. He would never know if Wayne had asked her to leave with him.

"I never claimed I wouldn't run," she said. She yanked on the shoelaces of her running shoes. "What do you think this is about?"

390

That was about as comforting as a cup of lukewarm tea, Mason thought. He knew Shay had been fast. She had run a half-dozen better-than-respectable marathons in her twenties and thirties, with one top-twenty finish in Los Angeles. But *fast* wouldn't save many people.

"Fast is better than nothing," she said, and he smiled, gladdened a bit by her knowing the way his mind worked.

~

They spoke gently. They nursed each other from the twin insults of intrusion and anti-climax. For some time they ate melted-cheese sandwiches and thick slices of cheese with fresh-baked bread; they drank lemonade, put slices of lemon in their water, and Shay buried her nose in each spent half-lemon; they drank the one remaining bottle of whiskey in two back-to-back drinking nights during which they made drunk talk and declarations of love and played a few dull games of dominoes, but it wasn't the game for them, they decided. They were gin-rummy and double-solitaire types. And eventually they began to dispose of what remained, though Mason couldn't make himself throw away seeds that might date back 150 years. He carefully planted them, just a few pinches in each #10 envelope labeled in Wayne's small calligraphic print. Mason smashed the empty whisky bottles and buried the shards away from the house. On a long run along a dried-up creek bed Shay dropped the dominoes one by one, a glittering path leading from no place to no place in particular. She pushed the grain mill to the very back of the most out-of-the-way cupboard in the kitchen.

The soles of her running shoes were losing their tread. She still had three new pairs of shoes but one day she wouldn't be able to run. Their resources were both plentiful and finite. She considered restarting their conversation about raising some animals—sheep for wool, goats, maybe, for milk. Creatures for comfort—the noises and smells of other living things. But it was another of those conversations that would circle around to the same unjoyful conclusion. Their safety—she did see that—depended on not drawing attention to themselves, and livestock and additional structures would make the property more evidently inhabited.

reminders of Wayne
—the absent driveway

391

—the rectangle of dirt his van had occupied; it was simply there, like the shadow of a geometric cloud; Mason watched Shay avoid it when she filled the bird feeders, veering around it like a sidewalk crack
—Shay's affection; if she didn't love him, exactly, she did love living with him in the house he'd built; she had stayed when she might have left
—splinters of eggshell in the compost
—the following summer, their white plates piled with lush, multicolored slices of tomatoes: Black Krim, Red Brandywine, Zapotec Pleated; mid-winter, mouth-watering fantasies of next year's tomatoes

what surprised them both

They were less lonely, though neither of them put those words to their feelings, or attributed them to Wayne's visit. Instead, they agreed it was the cool nights of early autumn that caused them to lie skin to skin, pressed together in the middle of their large bed. Mason started teaching Shay how to play guitar. He put his fingers over hers to direct them to the right spots on the frets. He hummed as she stretched her fingers to make the notes. She heard music in her head now, melodic folk songs.

The cool mornings meant sunrise was once again a blessing. Mason would set off on his bike at dawn, venturing to the outskirts of town to deposit bags of produce in drop boxes the locals had established over the past few years, and to hide others in the bushes beside rusting mailboxes and at the ends of alleys. You couldn't be sure who still lived where. If the food was gone on his next run he added that spot to his list.

They canned and canned and Mason built a bigger dehydrator. Several times Penman and Ellen came by with jugs of moonshine and chicken sausages and the two couples ate and sang the old songs together. In October they brought out a puppy, too, a small white terrier with a perfectly round brown spot on her side that Shay and Mason named Genius. Paisley seemed puzzled by Genius's arrival, but not altogether displeased. Shay and Mason put her gorgeous new desk next to the window. She loved how the inlaid pattern looked like a cross between argyle socks and an M.C. Escher drawing. In the afternoon sunlight she reread her favorite poems and began a new set of translations, often working through until dinner. Or she knit. Realizing they would need only so many scarves and mittens themselves, she started giving them to Mason, along with knitted washcloths and wool socks, to add to his anonymous care packages. And whereas before Shay had sat still for so many hours, thereafter she frequently went outside, throughout the day, taking a step or two toward Mason's shop or the garden, listening until she heard the scrape or clang of an implement that told her where he was.

Nominated by Agni

LIGHT OR DARK SPEECH

by WILLIAM OLSEN

from BLACKBIRD

Reading this word and that word takes you somewhere else, and no-body toasts November around here. Watching words swim in low chair light calls back worms punctuating our summer patio, out of their element, plucked up by a friend less squeamish than I, squirm-ing, tossed to the side—snapping in the air like hooked fish, then drooping over the pachysandra. This is to say, the words don't flood out, they crawl up, they go wherever they are flung, at least when I'm not thinking too hard about what I'm reading, sheltered in a cottage from winds that could tear the open book of the roof and throw it and its margins and its gutters across the street. Flashing backwards and forwards in blinking streetlights, that's as far-fetched as books fly. For all this I'm still only reading because reading is calm and dry enough. I could now fall back into the armchair of morbidity, which Browning said is worth the soul's study. I once told my mother in a dream you are dead and later Mary told me you are farther along than I am for I still have a feeling of respect for the dead. I am always telling my mother she is dead while she's always telling me off. Even when I'm reading she's reading me the riot act. Morbidity, worth the soul's study. And the least-peaceable kingdom. That salmon I touched with the tip of a stick charred by a beach fire, sand glazing it, dead, out of time, and always in season. Yet there is still ambition on its face, not even cessation is rest. I am sad because the Bluebird closes by No-vember. Because beer sounds are at least a company. Of many instant friends in many mirrors. Sadness is always human . . . sluggish head-lights in the rearview mirror, the past you just can't trust not to run

394

you off the road. I told my mother she was dead. And she told me *You know how bubbles creep up the side of a glass, Then, suddenly, pull off, start out, suspend on the surface then pop? What happens next I and they have escaped.* She never wrote me but a few letters. She spoke a lot, for, of, at, to, with me. Dark speech in the afternoons, light speech in the mornings. Now this wind—a consciousness upon a consciousness—this wind I was and am gets no good done. The time it takes to think to ask why passes. As for whether there should be a ceremony for her few lost letters, burn them once and for all and have the ashes scatter by hand, with hesitation, the way a feeling, before saying something, scrunches the face. I climb into bed with that face and read while the wind gets to its point, which is to make things move and tear things down without tipping its hand. I read and read until there is nothing but words, and the book falls to the floor like a roof to a house without floors or walls, a house of words, words that preceded me, words behind and ahead of me, before and after me, read in the light or spoken in the dark.

Nominated by Susan Hahn, David Wojahn, David Jauss

THE WATERMARK

by SUSAN McCALLUM-SMITH

from THE GETTYSBURG REVIEW

A year after my parents separated, I saw my father on the other side of a narrow street. He walked straight by without any gesture of greeting. No one else was around. It dawned on me, after a second or so, that he hadn't recognized me. I hadn't changed from a goose to a swan, or some such nonsense; I had simply had a haircut and stopped dressing like a boy. My first job had also nudged me from childhood into womanhood, making my walk more purposeful, less dancing, my expression less open and more reserved. I paused, aware that I felt nothing more than an aloof curiosity, and watched him walk away. If I were fanciful I would say that this was the moment I became a writer.

The archipelago of St. Kilda lies in the Outer Hebrides, three hours by boat off the northwest coast of Scotland. In the late seventeenth century, its residents worked its land and cliffs, paying rent to the MacLeod Clan of Skye with the meat, feathers, and oils they harvested from St. Kilda's abundant population of puffins, gannets, and fulmars. The Gaelic-speaking villagers converted early to the joyless tenets of the Free Church of Scotland, scuppering their natural bent for music and poetry. The harsh misery of their daily lives was matched only by the weather. By the turn of the twentieth century, the dwindling population had been riddled by poverty and inbreeding; a photograph in Edinburgh's public library reveals a row of school children with identical thin, pinched faces framed by flat dark hair. In 1930, the last St. Kildans, mostly women, asked to be evacuated to the mainland, exhausted by their isolation.

Over the centuries, the islanders had developed their own unique postal system. They threw their messages into the sea. They addressed their letters then rolled and corked them inside medicine bottles, which were placed in a small wooden box shaped like a boat. Buoyed by inflated sheep bladders, these "mail boats" were cast into the Atlantic to snag the upswing of the Gulf Stream, which swept them toward the fishing grounds and the East. A passing trawler would scoop them up and transport them to the mainland, or they would wash onto the shores or rocks of Skye or Shetland, Norway or Denmark. The St. Kildans held their breaths till the yearly delivery of supplies and return mail arrived from the mainland to discover if their voices had been heard.

Before 1900, a few pennies enclosed in the mail boat's hold would cover the postage, and the post office paid a reward to those who found it and sent the contents on. After 1900, the St. Kildans attached stamps to their letters. Not surprisingly, such stamps and letters are highly prized. My father is a stamp collector; he probably knew the lengths to which the St. Kildans went to communicate with the world around them, but he never told me.

Philately derives from the French, *philatélie*, which in turn has its roots in the Greek words *philo*, meaning "loving" and *atelia*, meaning "free" or "exempt from tax." My father was a passionate philatelist, who spent every spare moment collecting and collating, mounting and cataloging his tiny scraps of colored paper. He never shared the history of his hobby with me because we rarely talked to one another. I remember few complete conversations with him during the first seventeen years of my life, though I know some must have occurred since we lived in the same house. All I have are perforated snippets. Every evening at six thirty sharp, I called, "Dad!" when my mother put the dinner plates on the kitchen table. This was the extent of our daily exchange.

My parents had an unhappy marriage. When I was around five years old, my father became convinced that his four children had taken his wife's side in their feud. Therefore when he stopped talking to her, he stopped talking to all of us. When he was at work, or out cycling, or at a stamp fair, or had disappeared on his two-week summer holiday alone, our house prattled with laughter and conversation. When he was at home, it thrummed with silence. If addressed, he answered in monosyllables. He hated loud noises—door slamming and cutlery rattling—so we learned to tiptoe, eat our food quietly, pick our words carefully should we try to talk to one another over the dinner table, while he stared at his plate and ate. Television saved me some of the time—evenings were spent watching *Starsky & Hutch* or *Kojak*, making an absence of conversation appear natural—and books saved me the rest. I learned to pretend that life was normal, despite the mute father in the living room.

As the youngest of the four children, I kept chattering long after my siblings had shut up. Between the ages of five and ten, I assumed his taciturnity was symptomatic of the unfathomable nature of all adult behavior, and I would babble before him, like a persistent postman delivering unwanted letters that he refused to accept or open. By the time I entered my teens, however, his deliberate intent to cut all communication between us had succeeded. We spent whole days together in the same house, even in the same room, without sharing a word. Why didn't I simply talk to him? It is a fair question for which I have no satisfying answer. Every consecutive soundless minute, hour, day, month, and year extended the distance between us, until I felt that we lived on opposite shores of a hostile sea, and I would be unable to shout loud enough to be heard.

My mother left my father when I was seventeen, after twenty-eight years of marriage. We walked, my mother, one of my sisters, my brother, and I, the two miles or so back and forth to my grandmother's one-bedroom, high-rise flat, ferrying our clothes and essential belongings in plastic shopping bags. My mother filed for divorce and registered us with the local council as homeless. A few months later we moved out of my grandmother's house and into a flat of our own. The new flat was smaller than our old home, in a rougher part of Glasgow, and we had little furniture and no money. I secured part-time work, and by combining our wages, we managed to survive. I had never been happier.

The earliest known message-delivery system was devised by the Incas, who used runners to convey information from one end of their empire to the other. The Greeks devised an identical system, the basis of the Olympic sports of the marathon and the relay, later replacing the runners with riders on horseback, who rode between defined stages.

Shortly after uniting the kingdoms of Scotland and England in 1603, James I formed a monopoly for the carrying of letters under the British Post Master General, setting the standard for postal systems around the world. The original system, however, had a flaw that left it vulnerable to extortion and bribery: all letters were paid for by the addressee and not the sender. The addressee could refuse to receive and pay for any correspondence that failed to excite his interest, leaving the delivery of mail at the whim of those to whom it was addressed. Furthermore, British politicians were granted the right to transport documents free of charge around the kingdom, a right they exploited by selling their postal services for exorbitant fees. Some politicians earned a large chunk of their income from this lucrative sideline, and corruption was rife. Naturally, the British parliament vociferously opposed, though failed to stop, the Great Postal Reform of 1839–1840, which democratized communication and introduced the penny post. Under the new reforms, the sender paid the cost of delivering a letter—and proof of payment was attached to the document itself in the form of the Penny Black stamp.

The introduction of the Penny Black was a tremendous success, and the fame of this little black rectangle decorated with the profile of Queen Victoria extends outside the world of philately. Because so many were issued, the value of the Penny Black, with the exception of its first minting, is not as high as some may suppose. Nevertheless, perhaps my father would have accepted my childish babblings had they arrived appropriately franked.

My father never abused us or beat us. His feud with my mother was verbal, not physical. He smoked cigarettes (Benson & Hedges) every day and cigars (Hamlet) at Christmas, all lit with Swann Vestas matches, but he never drank, with the exception of my mother's homemade ginger wine, a brew so potent it once blew off the doors of an expensive quarter-sawn ash sideboard. As far as I know, he was never unfaithful to my mother.

He was not a monster—it is important to say that—yet I was terrified of him. His silence was impenetrable. Twenty years after we left, I still dream of being trapped in our old house, and awake kicking at the blankets, panic-stricken and claustrophobic. Nevertheless, a few memories muddy my attempt to dismiss all my childhood as "the bad old days."

I remember him putting ointment on my knees at the kitchen sink after I had fallen over in the garden, taking me to Glasgow's Mitchell library to help me find books for an art project, and being soothed on his lap after a nightmare. I am convinced that we listened to the 1969

399

moon landing on the radio together, though I would have been only three years old at the time. I know his favorite Beatles song was "The Fool on the Hill."

He loved Rogers & Hammerstein musicals and would sing along whenever they were on television. He could carry a tune, and sometimes I would join in, and we would harmonize through the chorus of "Getting to know you, getting to know all about you. Getting to like you, getting to hope you like me," until its end. Then he would clear his throat and light another cigarette, and I would refold my cramped legs.

My sister's dog greeted him enthusiastically at the end of every day and always lay by his chair when he was home, despite his stern disapproval of pets and his conviction that the dog, too, had taken his wife's side. When he thought no one was looking, he would reach out a hand and lay it gently on its head.

One Sunday when I was fifteen, a bout of hellish menstrual cramps reduced me to a curled lump on my bed. Neither my mother nor my sisters were home. The only thing that alleviated the pain was a hot-water bottle, but when I tried to move, I felt I would either faint or throw up. I sobbed quietly in the silence of the house for some time before I plucked up enough courage to call him. My first yells of "Dad!" were feeble, as if I were being forced, and unwilling, to punch through glass. Eventually I heard the living-room door creak open. Then, nothing. I yelled again. When he arrived at my bedroom, he looked bewildered, vulnerable. Either the sound of his name or the sight of his daughter wrestling with puberty had caught him off guard.

"Can you get me a hot-water bottle?" I said.

He never asked me what was wrong. A conversation about "women's problems" would have nudged this already rare exchange into the realm of the surreal. He disappeared and came back ten minutes later with the hot-water bottle. He paused a moment before leaving, then shut the door quietly behind him.

Such glimpses of this other side of his nature prove that he didn't lack empathy, only that he deliberately chose not to express it. I find these instances of tenderness almost unforgivable.

The authenticity of stamps is often determined by the paper on which they are printed. Skilled philatelists learn to differentiate between the cloudy tint of Silurian and the silken threads of Dickenson, between the sleek gloss of *emaille* and the *chinois* tang of *lignes brillantes*, between the wide pinstripe of *batonné* and the oniony slithers of *pelure*, between woven, laid, card, double, granite, safety, ribbed, chalky, and blue.

Each manufacturer embosses its distinctive paper with a watermark, a unique design embedded in the papermaking mold. The watermark of a stamp is of primary importance to the collector as it verifies its belonging to a particular sheet or family of stamps, its right to inclusion in the clan. It defines the time, date, and origin of its printing and prevents against fraud. The watermark is a stamp's DNA. Some watermarks are visible by simply holding the stamp up to the light, while others require bathing in the correct fluid, causing them to materialize on the surface of the paper like a skeleton. Watermarks remain long after the stamps' colors fade, like a fossil or an imprint. The watermark is the stamp's memory.

Children, according to my father's Victorian views, were to be seen and not heard. He severely disapproved of *Top of the Pops*, piercings, gambling, football (with its Glaswegian overtones of hooliganism and sectarianism), pubs, alcohol, bad language, slang, and couples living together without being married—of anything that could be construed as "common."

He greeted my natural left-handedness with horror, believing that left-handed penmanship was crass and inelegant. He would move my pencil from my left hand to my right whenever he could, until, after a while, I automatically swapped it over whenever he entered the room. By my teens, I was ambidextrous.

Though discussing politics was taboo, I suspect he admired Margaret Thatcher and voted Conservative, making him an anomaly in 1980s Scotland. He never gave us pocket money and, apart from some necklaces when I was very young (a Celtic cross, an Egyptian ankh), and a pen-and-pencil set on my twelfth birthday, never gave us gifts that I can remember, despite my mother's attempts to hide the fact by crediting both of them on all gift labels attached to gifts she bought and paid for herself.

He demanded frugality with household expenses and kept the heat turned down low and unnecessary lights turned off, and he perpetually closed open doors with a martyred sigh. Therefore, my childhood memories take place in settings both chilly and dark, and my calves still bear the scars of sitting on the hallway electric radiator. A hot bath once a week was allowed for personal hygiene, cold water sufficed the rest of the time. Reading alone in one's room wasted a healthy bulb. My sisters and I washed our hair after school, before he came home from work, to avoid lectures about the cost of hot water.

In fact it was money, the most hackneyed thorn in the side of marriage, that proved my parents' final undoing. My father was a hoarder, my mother, a spender. When my brother and sisters started to work and contributed a portion of their wages to the household, my father cut the amount he gave to my mother by an equal amount. So, although the family income was increasing as a whole, my mother's budget for food and bills remained exactly the same.

By my early teens, my mother decided to go back to work. My father severely disapproved, but she did it anyway, taking a job as a seamstress in a local factory making clothes for Marks & Spencer. In response to her audacity, he told her that he would no longer be giving her as much from his wages as she was now able to make up the difference from her own. I assume, though this is conjecture, that he spent the money he saved through the income from both my siblings and my mother on stamps. The number of his albums grew, filling one side of the living-room bookshelves in tall, leather-bound rows.

On one memorable occasion he called a family meeting. My three siblings and I headed for the living room, ready for the usual dictatorial pronouncement about crumbs on the Afghan or a chip in the Lalique, and lined up in order of our heights like a depleted legion of Von Trapps. Someone, he said, had been using too much toilet paper. That morning, before leaving for work, he had noticed a full roll in the bathroom, and yet, this evening on his return, mere tatters remained.

"Two sheets," he announced, with a convincing authority, "should be more than sufficient for any eventuality."

My siblings and I laugh over our collective memories of Life with Father. Our homes today are filled with music and noise and conversation and overheated rooms flooded with unnecessary light. If we had lived in a different country, in a different culture, his diatribe about toilet paper would provide fascinating fodder for analysts, but we were raised in Glasgow, where life was something you got over and got on with, without the mollycoddling of psychiatry. So we did, and we have moved on, or think we have, but has he? In his desire to enforce his authority over his mouthy, unruly wife, he sacrificed his relationship with his children and has no relationship at all with his grandchildren. It is as if he were determined to sever himself from our clan, to be a rarity, to stand alone, singular, to burn any ties that tethered him to a present, a past, or a future. When he looked at us, he saw only his adversaries; he recognized no part of himself.

The philatelist's Holy Grail is the rarity. The Mauritius Post Office issued two stamps in 1847 that are now considered the most valuable in the world. In 1929, Lundy Island issued Puffin Stamps, which are not only rare but attractive, and the desirable Flimsies from the 1930s are considered the most romantic, having been used for mail sent by carrier pigeons between New Zealand and the Great Barrier Reef.

In 1918, a postal worker in the United States inadvertently sold a sheet of airmail stamps on which the image of a biplane had been printed upside down. The United States Postal Service instantly withdrew from circulation the remaining stamps of this faulty batch, making the 1918 Airmail Invert the stamp most coveted by North American collectors. Perhaps the upside-down biplane confirmed the public's suspicion that these new-fangled contraptions were a bad idea.

In the mid-nineteen hundreds, the government of British Guiana in South America printed one-cent stamps for the mailing of newspapers. By the following century, it was widely believed that only one of these stamps remained, which was owned, with considerable pride, by an American millionaire named Hind. Suddenly, another collector came forward, professing to have a second Guiana stamp. Hind promptly bought it. After paying for it, he set it alight using the tip of his cigar. "Now," he is purported to have said while watching it burn, "there is only one one-cent Guiana stamp in the world."

My father was a man of meticulous habits: he polished his shoes every evening and shaved with a straight razor every morning. Only my mother was allowed to iron his shirts, as he was particular about his collars and cuffs. He had impeccable taste for antiques, china, and tweed. Once a week, he walked to the library to return his books and take out some chunky hardbacks by Frederick Forsyth or Harold Robbins. The Harold Robbins combined with his tolerance of *The Benny Hill Show* reveal a fondness for smut that bothers me now but seemed normal and prevalent in the 1970s.

On one evening every other week, he went out for reasons that remained a mystery until recently, when I discovered that he attended Masonic meetings. Given his misogynistic distaste for housework, it amuses me to imagine him with one trouser leg rolled up and wearing an apron during the silly Masonic rituals. Every Sunday he attended the Methodist Church with the rest of us in tow, all scoured faces and uncomfortable shoes, like the Scottish Cleavers. He oiled his way amongst the congregation, oozing charm, before returning home in silence. On Saturdays, if the weather was dry, he would go cycling to unknown destinations, returning sweaty and crackling with sunburn, or he might disappear on the train to Edinburgh to return late in the evening, clutching small grease-proof paper packets of new stamps. If the weather was wet, he would spread one of his leather portfolios on the dining-room table and catalog his collection.

Too big and grand for the room, our dining table had extra leaves that were only used for New Year's Eve dinners. This hulking piece of furniture was the physical manifestation of my father's middle-class aspirations. After all, we didn't actually *have* a dining room. Unknown to him, my mother had used wood glue to reattach an arm of one of its six matching carver chairs. It had broken off one afternoon after I had been swinging on it while spying, out our living-room window, on a boy I had a crush on. As a baby, I had also teethed against one of the table's legs, but mother-to-the-rescue had sanded down the rough edge and disguised the nibbles with shoe polish. She did the same again when our dog, too, discovered the soothing properties of mahogany. I wonder if my father has found those flaws yet.

I can see this table on a wet Sunday afternoon. A cloth extends two thirds up its length. Two photographic trays made of white enameled metal sit side by side filled with water, their lips outlined in black. Individual stamps float face down in one tray, like little corpses from a maritime disaster, the remnants of the envelopes they once franked peeling off their backs like loose clothing. In the second tray, the newly refreshed and naked stamps float face up. To the left and right of my father's hands lie a copy of the Stanley Gibbons reference catalog, a magnifying glass, a calligraphy pen and ink pot, sets of tweezers, and a perforation gauge to measure the distance between the little pie-crust edges of each stamp and confirm their authenticity. At the top of the table is a humidor, for sweating the backing from stamps too precious to risk dipping in water, and a pile of clean white blotting paper. In front of him sits the watermark bowl, my favorite thing of all, the size of a generous teacup with a jet black interior just large enough for a sheet of four. Sometimes I would stand behind him while he tested a stamp's lineage and watch as the watermark embossed into its flesh rose to the surface.

The only time my father was unable to resist a conversation was when I mentioned stamps. One damp Sunday, when I was around eight years old, I asked him to show me what he was doing. Thinking me converted after a long and somewhat technical lecture, he bought me a pack of starter mixed stamps the following weekend, with pictures of wild animals on the front, as animals were my current craze. However, I wanted to arrange the stamps in my favorite colors or species, not according to any logical format such as country of origin or face value or size. I also tended to pick them up with icky fingers and tried to swap them with my friends for paper dolls or chewing-gum cards. Sometimes the temptation to lick the back and slap them on stuff, including lampposts or the dog, proved too much. Before long, he gave up on me because of my lack of seriousness. Hobbies, he maintained, were *not* games. He failed to see I had reeled him in under false pretenses on that wet Sunday afternoon. I had simply wanted him to talk to me.

In nineteenth-century America, the desperation of families to communicate with one another was such that an amateur mailman with grit and a mule could make a fortune by carrying letters to loved ones in unmapped regions, in exchange for exorbitant amounts of gold, if and when the addressees were found. Approaching mail steamers triggered a bedlam of punch-ups and queue jumping at San Francisco's dock. A Dr. William McCollom wrote in 1850 that his description of such mayhem might seem fanciful to his readers but "falls short of giving an adequate idea of the immense amount of letters that the steamers bring to San Francisco, and of the throng that rush after them in their intense anxiety to hear from home."

Ten years later, at 2:45 AM, on April 4, 1860, William Hamilton left Sacramento on the West coast carrying sixty-nine letters, on the first ride east of the newly formed Pony Express. Meanwhile, Johnny Frey had left St. Joe on the opposite coast late the evening before, and the two riders passed one another somewhere outside Salt Lake City. The cross-country trip of approximately two thousand miles took ten days, and the cost of a letter was five dollars. The Pony Express blinked from reality to myth in less than a year because of the beginning of the Civil War and the advent of the telegraph.

My parents married in 1955. I have a photograph of each of them taken around this time. I study it, trying to fathom how straight-laced,

405

conservative William Brown McCallum ended up with sassy socialist Margaret Stewart Hamilton.

My mother turns coquettishly toward the camera, leading me to suspect my father was behind it. The expression on her face is a dare. She wears a checked tweed coat with princess sleeves, a beret, and fur gloves and holds a Grace Kelly bag. Her hair is cut like Doris Day's. She is tiny, just five feet tall, with an upturned nose. I believe her assertions that she was the most stylish girl ever to live in a one-room tenement flat, and the most successful sales associate in the gentleman's haberdashery department of the Co-Op Department Store in Glasgow. The only child of an atheist socialist campaigner and a former suffragette, she appears flirtatious, self-confident, ambitious.

My father was the youngest of three sons. A photograph of his father reveals a man wearing a starched clip-on collar, a watch chain, and razor-creased pinstripe trousers designed for standing at attention. His mother hardly ever sat down. At dinner, she served her husband and sons then ate the leftovers alone in the kitchen. According to family legend, she lived and died a skivvy.

In the photograph of my father, he walks purposefully down some unknown street, in a trilby and belted trench coat over a tweed suit with cuffed trousers. He is handsome in that fragile way of First World War poets, and not as tall as I once imagined, only around five feet nine inches. Stylish, with a fair complexion and ashy blond hair, he has a pensive expression, which hovers around his slim nose and thin, sensitive mouth. A regular Trevor Howard with something perpetually in his eye; I can understand my mother's attraction.

My parents met at the dance that took place every Wednesday and Saturday night in the Toledo Ballroom in Glasgow. Without fail my mother would miss the last tram home and have to walk back with her girlfriends, their stiletto heels stumbling over the tramlines, before falling into bed and getting up at five for work.

Their courtship had a dashing edge considering they were a working-class couple, generously funded by my father, who had just become an apprenticed timber clerk. He took her to the Rogano for oysters, still one of Glasgow's swankiest restaurants, and to the Theatre Royal to see a production of, ominously, *The King and I*. My maternal grandfather was skeptical about his daughter's choice, sensing his future son-in-law was a snob and a Sunday Christian. What must have surprised him more, though, was that she had chosen a man without a sense of humor. My grandfather never addressed my father as William or Bill, but nicknamed him Wullie, emphasizing its working-class pronunciation, which he sensed, correctly, would annoy my father intensely. My grandfather always took his daughter's part whenever my parents' marriage foundered, and my father sensed a rival for his wife's affection in the person of his charismatic father-in-law, whom she adored.

According to my mother (whose viewpoint is, naturally, skewed, though I trust her gist), everything changed after my parents married. William began laying down the law. He didn't believe that married women should work, especially in a men's clothing store, and she gave up her job at the Co-Op. That such an independently minded young woman would have abandoned her career so easily is proof of how besotted she must once have been. Or perhaps proof of her uncertainty in her own independence. He also believed that married women no longer needed friends; a husband and children should be sufficient company. He systematically severed her from everyone she knew by becoming moody and petulant if she spent time with anyone other than him. As though to seal the deal, three children were produced in quick succession.

My mother still smiles over her determination to name their first-born after her father, regardless of the sex of the child. My eldest sister, therefore, is called Billie, and my father probably believes to this day the fib his young wife told him, in a flush of faked wifely adoration, that they should name their daughter after him. But Billie was named for my grandfather, Willie Hamilton, who, in turn, coincidentally, shared the name of one of those first riders of the Pony Express, willing to travel over two thousand miles to satisfy the yearnings of prospectors and settlers for a few words from home.

My parents' photographs show a handsome couple with a singular stylishness, and hint at a strong sexual attraction. I like to believe this is true; I refuse to accept that love didn't play some part in this disparate union. "Those were the days," my mother says, ruefully, "the days before 'taste and try before you buy.' " The photographs also hint of a connection based on mutual ambition; they both dress and appear wealthier than they actually were. I suspect they shared a desire to move one rung up the social ladder, out of the working class and into the lower middle class. My father must have seemed quite a catch. He had the prospect of an exciting future in a white-collar job provided he worked hard and applied himself. Apprenticed to a lumber company in Glasgow, he would become a timber merchant, visiting the docks at Greenock and Grangemouth to inspect and grade the quality of woods that arrived from Africa, the Indies, and Scandinavia in sap-saturated, resin-scented crates.

However, he lacked drive; although they both had the appearance of ambition, only my mother had the fact of it. They spent the first eleven years of their married life raising their first three children in a one-room-and-kitchen tenement flat in the south side of Glasgow, sharing a bathroom on the communal landing and an outside cludgie at the end of the backgreen with the other five families in the close.

The year before I was born, they moved to a three-bedroom council flat, which my mother considered a palace as it had a separate kitchen and bathroom. My father, now a qualified timber merchant, began to fill it with over-large, expensive furniture made from, without question, ravishing cuts of wood, while my mother nagged him to spend his increased earnings on holidays beyond Scarborough and Whitley Bay, or on the installation of a telephone, or to learn to drive and buy a car.

Opportunities rose for his promotion in the world of forestry and wood importing, but my father refused them all. Overseas postings to Central Africa and Burma were considered, and at one time, a chance to emigrate from Scotland to Australia. My mother elbowed him to go, but he dithered too long over his decisions. He trusted the advice of his own father, who said that terrible things happened overseas and foreigners couldn't be trusted. My mother watched as my father's coworkers gained promotion and moved their families out of council accommodations and into houses they had bought themselves, in the hoity-toity suburbs of Giffnock or Newton Mearns, while she cooked, cleaned, baked, sewed, and struggled to balance the household bills, and my father bought furniture and stamps.

Still, our council flat and comprehensive schooling failed to convince him that we were no better than the "common" lot. He acted as if our family were somehow above our neighbors. A bus stop stood not ten yards from our close, yet he walked a mile every day, rain or shine, to the railway station to take the train to work, the *Glasgow Herald* tucked under one arm, the train being a classier form of transportation in his mind than a bus.

"He needed a bomb in his arse," my mother says, still baffled by what could possibly have held him back.

Fear held him back. He couldn't swim, and he couldn't drive, and he was terrified of water, flying, heights, elevators, dentists (he put three spoonfuls of sugar in his mug of tea and suffered agonies for years as his teeth disintegrated), illness, blood, his father-in-law, intelligent women (despite his crushes on Felicity Kendall and every female news anchor on the BBC), and his boss. He had a starstruck respect for people in positions of authority, like teachers or policemen, and for anyone whom he perceived to be above him in the class hierarchy. He tended to call men he wanted to impress "Sir."

Like many fearful people, he was a bully within his own home and changed his personality according to his audience. Above all, he feared my mother's words. During arguments she tended to get the better of him, stooping to satire and sarcasm, employing a pungent vocabulary learned from her days working in the factory. His only defense was silence. Perhaps it was natural and inevitable that he would barricade himself behind it and refuse to come out.

"Love is blind," my mother has said often in the intervening years. "God knows, I was taken in by that daft bugger."

My mother has reinvented her past since her divorce. She enjoys her life so much now that she can't tolerate the fact that she could have enjoyed it so much sooner. She is proud of her decision to step away from her marriage at age fifty, at how she managed to stand up to, and get the better of, William Brown McCallum. Still, I sometimes find myself thinking, she waited twenty-eight years to do it. And while she hesitated, we waited with her, at the bottom of that dark well of silence. There is no doubt the daft bugger took her in, but she took him in too.

I often rib my mum that my father isn't really my father, that I was, in fact, a love child from some illicit affair. But I know he is my father—we look alike, and over the years I have recognized parts of his personality in myself: my love of classical music, my need for solitude, my addiction to sugar, my ability to be comfortable for long periods of time on my own, a pathetic desire to please those in authority, a fear of what other people think of me, a snobbishness about furniture and words, an inability to finish projects that I have started, an appearance of ambition that far outstrips the fact of it. We are an accidental *tête-bèche*, he and I, two stamps joined together yet inverted in relation to one another.

Some of the rarest stamps in the world come from the smaller corners of the British Commonwealth and the British Overseas Territories.

409

The Cook Islands, the Pitcairn Islands, Mauritius, South Orkneys, the Maldives, the Solomon Islands, and Papua New Guinea are just some of the countries whose stamps my father collects. Unlike many of my school friends, I knew of the Falklands long before the infamous war of 1980, and I could locate the archipelago of Vanuatu, and the Christmas, Gilbert, and Ellice Islands on a map.

Despite this focus, he also snipped the stamps from every piece of mail, from letters to circulars to electricity bills, and regardless of the feud, everyone in our home would automatically place any envelopes we received by our father's ashtray.

I was often tempted when he was away from home to look through his albums. It was not the stamps themselves that interested me, but the exotic landscapes they stood for. I was desperate to run away, and some of these destinations sounded like they would be just about far away enough.

I last saw my father thirteen years ago, ten years after he passed me, unknowingly, in the street. By this time I was living with Arthur, then my fiancé, now my husband, in north London. My father telephoned one day, and at first I didn't recognize his voice. Somewhere in the midst of our stilted conversation, I discovered with shock that I had agreed he could stay with us for one night when he passed through on a cycling tour. I called Arthur at work. "Guess who's coming to dinner?" I said.

I plunged into a panic, determined to make no special effort yet driven to an orgy of cleaning. I polished our mismatched furniture collection of hand-me-downs and loaners from our landlord. I bought flowers and placed them on the upturned boxes masquerading as end tables under Laura Ashley fabric remnants; heaven knows, I may even have lit candles. Although my passion for books and opera is genuine, I succumbed to a pretentious urge to rearrange glossy hardbacks about interior decor and foreign travel to more prominent effect, and placed a CD of arias in the player. When Arthur asked about his future father-in-law, I told him to expect an intimidating blend of Trevor Howard and John Wayne.

When the day arrived, I answered the front door to find someone resembling the Birds Eye fisherman holding a rucksack and a set of bicycle clips. He was small and middle-aged with ruddy cheeks and a white beard, and wore a dirty yellow anorak and Lycra shorts with a chamois-leather bum. He was much shorter than I expected, and not simply because of my confidence-boosting three-inch heels, which I

410

insisted on wearing all evening. Arthur towered over us both at six feet two.

"Hello, Dad," I said, as if he had just popped out to the shops.

Our flat in Muswell Hill had been converted from two floors of a red-brick Edwardian terraced house. It reeked of middle-class Britishness—the upright, patriotic, bubble-and-squeak Britishness of coronations and Ealing comedies. It had a large bay window in the living room, where we had placed a dining table. Here we ate dinner, as the light faded to darkness, and the black railings of Alexandria Park speared above the garden hedge in the gloom. Arthur sat between us, and my father and I faced one another. From the neck up, our two profiles would have been visible to anyone who happened to pass by that evening, like a homely silhouette of conviviality, or heads of state on a first-class stamp.

I can't remember exactly what we ate, probably spaghetti Bolognese or chili con carne, the only two dishes I could make from scratch, anchored at one end with a salad and at the other with a Marks & Spencer cake. As the meal progressed, my stress morphed into a vindictive arrogance, as I plied us all with alcohol and made sure to remark that Arthur and I were living in sin, in the hope that my father would raise some moral objection and, at last, the fight could begin.

We talked about the present as though we had arrived at this moment, newborn. My siblings, his ex-wife, his grandchildren, the tiny diamond on my left hand—these subjects we avoided, though I sensed them crowding the shadowy corners of the room. And we talked of Hong Kong, where, in the early 1950s, my father passed his two years of National Service with the Royal Highland Fusiliers. He had traveled there by boat, a six-week journey via the Suez Canal and around the coast of India. His role, ostensibly, was that of a radio signalman supporting the troops in the conflict in Korea, but based on the photographs that have survived, he seemed to spend most of his time sightseeing and picking up girls. Young Chinese women in bathing costumes lean their childlike bodies away from the camera and into the burly Scotsmen at their sides, who grin from ear to ear in ill-fitting mufti.

Father's national service in Hong Kong had always had a mythical edge for me—no one else I knew had been somewhere so exotic—but by this point in my career as a fashion buyer, I had visited the Far East several times, including Hong Kong. I derived a malicious enjoyment from asking him if he had been to other parts of Asia such as Taiwan,

Japan, or South Korea, places I knew he hadn't visited but that I had. Arthur rolled his eyes at my intemperate bragging—I don't think I was ever more like my father than at this moment—and plugged gaps in our conversation with harmless asides and small talk.

My father ducked and dodged like a politician. Everything he ate was wonderful, the wine was wonderful, the flat was wonderful, and he addressed Arthur, a man less than half his age, as "Sir." He insisted on stepping into the garden whenever he wanted to smoke. When my favorite duet from *The Pearl Fishers* played on the CD, he accompanied it, and the wavering vibrato of his whistling jangled off the bones in my spine. By having barely secured a Bachelor's degree, and by living in a cramped flat in a borderline respectable middle-class area of London, and by working in a low-tier fashion job with a renowned but slowly going bankrupt company and drinking cheap red wine and listening to classical music with my meals, I had been transformed in his eyes from someone he could ignore, to the type of person whom he slavishly admired. My vain and needy preparations had succeeded; he was impressed. By the end of the evening, his cloying sycophancy made me want to slap him.

At last, at long last, he went to bed. Arthur and I tidied up the kitchen in silence; my father seemed to have brought it into the house with him. Undressing in our room before bed, Arthur whispered, trying not to laugh, "John Wayne? He looks more like a cross between Billy Whiz and Jimmy Johnston." He was right. My father did look like a blend of the cartoon character and the Celtic football player. Arthur's joke annoyed me, though, for it implied that this cauldron of fear and fury lodged in my gut since childhood was inconsequential flimflam that could now be easily poured away.

He got into bed beside me. "He seems pretty harmless," he said.

A few moments later Arthur was asleep. Lying in the dark, I heard my father clear his throat in the other room. The house seemed besieged with unsaid words; I imagined them smothering the windows and clogging the doorjambs like bats. Caffeinated adrenaline pumped through me, and I considered sneaking out of bed, getting dressed, and going to hide somewhere until my father had left. Where could I go? The tube station? The abandoned Alexandria Palace? To my friend Ellie's flat over in Highgate?

Arthur awoke at 5:00 AM to find me sitting up in bed. "Get him out of here," I said. "Get him out of here before I ask him who the fuck he thinks he is."

Foolishly, I had offered to wash my father's clothes the night before, but we didn't have a tumble dryer, so they were still damp. Arthur put the wet washing in a sports bag and tiptoed out the flat and down to the local Laundromat with a collection of fifty-pence pieces and spent an hour watching his future father-in-law's Y-fronts tumble dry. When my father awoke I gave him a mug of coffee and a neatly folded pile of warm laundry. After doddering about with his rucksack and bicycle clips for an agonizingly elongated half hour, he left.

In the late afternoon, the telephone rang. He thanked me for letting him stay. After an awkward pause, into which I gather I was supposed to say he was welcome anytime but didn't, he said, "I wanted to tell you I love you."

"Yes, I know." I hung up. I knew nothing of the sort. Three months later Arthur and I left the United Kingdom to live in Canada, and when we got married the following year, it was my mother who accompanied me down the aisle.

Rumors that the wife of the Lord Justice Clerk of Scotland had died proved to be greatly exaggerated. After James Erskine had arranged an ornate funeral for his dearly departed in Edinburgh in 1736, a letter corked in a whisky bottle floated ashore, in which she pleaded to be rescued from St. Kilda. Erskine had arranged for her abduction and imprisonment on the island, to stop her testifying about his Jacobite plotting. The odds that Mrs. Erskine's message in a bottle would be found are surprisingly high. Although there are no accurate records of the number of St. Kilda mail boats picked up versus those that were launched, it is estimated that roughly two thirds of the letters sent were received.

My father sometimes sends me a birthday card, and often a Christmas card. His choices are baffling—mushy and over scale, festooned with flowers and hearts addressed to "My darling daughter," the envelopes and messages crafted in his meticulous, childish calligraphy. I recognize the irony that our relationship should now be conducted by mail, and this long-distance conversation is the only way that I know he is still alive.

When friends ask me where my father is now, I am tempted to say, "I don't know," to avoid explanations. He has retired and lives in an apartment in Grangemouth, an unattractive town in Central Scotland on the banks of the Firth of Forth, whose skyline is punctuated by the spewing funnels of oil terminals and processing plants, which contribute to some of the highest instances of cancer in Europe. According to my brother, my father's flat is crowded with all the oversized furniture he took from our home, of which he had been so proud, and which I imagine now is old-fashioned and threadbare, the faded boot polish revealing the gnawing of children and dogs as starkly as on bone. The stamp collection is locked in vaults in a bank.

My eldest sister lives nearby, his purported namesake, and every now and then her good nature sends her checking to see if he is okay. This is not an easy task, given that he refuses to answer the telephone or the door. When she finally gets hold of him, she gives him a dressing-down on the issue of responsibility as if he were a naughty child. She lives in perpetual fear that he will die in that flat and his body will decay until discovered by horrified neighbors who will sell their story to the tabloids and cause us all to be slandered for cruelty and neglect.

Close friends are concerned by my unwillingness to pursue a relationship with him. One day he will need us, and my siblings and I will go, and until then the link between us will feel like held breath. Some things in life are meant to remain unresolved, I believe, an unfashionable view to hold in the United States where I now live, a country obsessed with a desire for closure, as though every experience, every thought, every relationship, must be buttoned, hooked and eyed. My reflections on my father are filled with wonder, not by his actions (or inactions), but at how he (and I) illustrate the ridiculous lengths to which a human being will go in order to make a point.

I send him a Christmas card and a letter every year and always let him know when I have changed address. I choose the stamp, pressing the postal clerk to offer more intriguing alternatives to the standard airmail selection, and position it at a sharp right angle one third of an inch or so in from the top right-hand corner of the envelope. I like to imagine that he snips it off carefully and holds it up to the light.

Nominated by Jeremy Collins, Alice Mattison, Gettysburg Review

STAGFLATION

by JOANNA FUHRMAN

from PAGEANT (Alice James Books)

When the rent went up, we shifted
all motion west, lifted the bottoms
of our pant legs as if crossing a creek.

No one cared that our poems were made
of torqued magnetic force or that our
hands could translate the language of light

into a million fractured dialects. We still
had to climb. Like every other army of bald
Rapunzels scaling the leaning tower of Babel.

When the rent doubled, we drew smiles
around our real smiles, curtsied our way
into the arms of identical semiotics experts

who changed our names to fit the texture
of the times, tucked in our billowing tunics,
whipped our hair into vertical configurations,

—blond Aqua-Netted beehives—tall enough
to pass through the school's cracked skylight,
to reach the blimps inching through the noise.

Nominated by Linda Bierds

TWO MIDNIGHTS IN A JUG

fiction by MARC WATKINS

from BOULEVARD

Follow any hollow in the Ozarks and it'll come to river or stream where soft clay the color of rust covers jagged limestone along the banks. Mountains cut by water dot the horizon, their peaks smoothed over millennia into knolls and greened with trees. In Eminence, MO, folks call trailer courts neighborhoods and hundred-year-old farm houses with acreage equal to a football field are mansions. There's one high school, and you'll get sidelong looks if you finish. People will talk, call you learnt, expect you to work at the mega hog farm as manager with an education. You'll need a wife, finding her's easy cause every household's got at least one daughter ready for marriage, and you won't meet her at a bar, there's only a few in town. More likely it'll be at a church, there's twenty inside city limits.

Here is where you're born and here is what you are.

Margret Jean lives in a single-wide trailer with her husband and son at the bottom of a hollow east of Eminence, just downwind of the mega hog farm. She rolls out of bed in her neon orange muumuu bought at the flea market. Her bare feet touch cold linoleum beneath her bed, some of the tile edges curl upwards till their ends make a knife of plastic. She walks to the kitchen, avoiding the painful tiles without looking, walking by memory to the kitchen, the trailer floor heaving and shaking all the while.

She sits at the foldout table next to office filing cabinets stained with grease. This is her pantry. Her husband Cordell made coffee before he left coon hunting and the pot simmers on the propane stove. The trailer was once an office for Pequod construction before Cordell bought it at auction when the bank took the house. Thirty-two feet long by eight feet wide. Margret Jean and Cordell sleep in what used to be the manager's office next to the one bathroom in the trailer, the plumbing unconnected but they still use the commode. A five gallon bucket sits beneath the trailer to catch waste, and they drop a handful of lime after each use to cut the smell, emptying the bucket at night. Margret Jean looks outside at the ash falling softly against the kitchen window from the manure fire at the mega hog farm smoldering since early June. She pours herself a cup of coffee and looks at the calendar tacked to the fridge. Three weeks now, gonna turn to four and fire's still burning.

She turns her nose to the bathroom. Smells like Abe didn't clean the shit bucket out. She walks to the far end of the trailer and searches for her son Abner. The main room has wood paneling from floor to ceiling with a sleeping bag in one corner of the floor for Abe, a plasma television hangs from the far wall. When she finds Abe gone, she walks to the trailer door and kicks the towel away at the foot of the threshold put there to keep ash coming through the void and filling the trailer with the smell of burnt hog shit while she slept.

Margret Jean opens the door and sticks her head outside. Beyond the far ridge of the hollow a cloud of ash from the hog fire rises skyward, just as it has done now for near on a month. A thin snow of ash falls steadily from the sky. Everything stopped growing because of the ash. Yard full of yellow fescue, the stalks brittle and short. The few acres of soybeans Cordell still owned and planted spread out in front of the trailer, the leaves of the soybeans a hue of dark green, growing white at the tips, and sagging under the weight of the ash until they touched the soil where they rot. Some of Cordell's hounds huddle beneath the trailer to keep out of the ash fall.

The smell from the ash lingers over everything, causing bile to rise in her throat. They were used to the smell of the hog farm, the wet heavy stink of processed hog waste left to dry in the open air till it becomes manure, but smelling it burnt was altogether different, like barbequed bacon simmered in rancid lard. Margret Jean looks over the dead grass and rotten fields of soybeans. So this is kingdom come.

Off to her right is her husband's seventy-six Chevrolet Nova, the tires long flat, and the lime green paint all but sandblasted off, replaced with gray primer a shade lighter than the ash covering its windows. She hollers for Abe when she doesn't see him in the yard or out in the field. The windshield wipers click on the Nova, the blades

417

screech against glass, brushing away the fine layer of ash on the windshield. Abe stares at her from behind the driver's seat, his fourteen year-old face pale, eyes narrow, brow furrowed in concentration, no doubt imagining how it would feel to take the Nova out on the highway.

"You, Abe." Margret Jean brings her hands to her hips. "Get your ass over to the shit bucket and dump it."

Abe puts his hands on the wheel and ignores his mother. Margret Jean shakes her head. Her son left school in the spring and wouldn't be returning come fall. His education was over, a job at the hog farm his likely future, but Cordell wouldn't have his only son work there while the fire still burned.

She cleans the satellite dish bolted on the skin of the trailer, wiping away the ash covering it. One of the hounds moans beneath the trailer. Margret Jean leans down and pets the dog named Trixie, one of Cordell's favorite bitches. Bandages cover the dog's hind end from where Cordell burned Trixie's ass with buckshot. Cordell aimed too low when he fired the shotgun, and instead of just busting the air above the dog's head and frightening her, some of the shot had rolled off her back, peeling away her fur and ripping her skin, and one of the pellets had penetrated and shattered the bone in her left hind leg. Trixie lost the leg. Now she hobbled under the trailer with three legs, howling and crying at all hours.

Margret Jean stops petting Trixie and looks at Abe. "Make sure and give Trixie her medicine."

She walks back inside, passing the Peqoud construction logo stenciled in six foot tall letters of garish red paint on the trailer's white aluminum siding. The living room is empty of furniture except a pair of recliners still covered in plastic Cordell bought to go along with the fifty-inch plasma television hanging on the opposite wall. Margret Jean sits down in the left chair and flips on the Weather Channel, her bright orange muumuu bunching around her knees as her ankles slide along the cold plastic, revealing a web of varicose veins on her feet. The only books in the trailer are a *TV Guide* and a Pentecostal bible. Margret Jean reaches for the *TV Guide*, hoping the channel lineup might offer relief.

Not long after this, Louvinia arrives at the trailer. She's in her late forties and goes to the same church as Margret Jean. The two women have known each other for years. Louvinia brushes ash from the crushed blue pant suit she wears for her job as a secretary out at the hog farm. "Fire gonna be smothered later today. Brung in bulldozers, Margret Jean, bulldozers. Would've been doused weeks ago if the damned EPA let us use hoses." She finishes brushing off the ash. "My," she says, staring at the television hanging from the wall. "When did you get that?"

Margret Jean doesn't move from her recliner. She turns to Louvinia. "Cordell bought it with money the church done raised for us on account of the fire."

Louvinia sits in the other recliner. "Supposed to use Christian charity for essentials." She lets her hands run along the plastic. "And these chairs, my word."

"Cordell says football's more important." Margret Jean bites her lip. "Did you bring it?"

Louvinia reaches into her purse made from fake alligator skin and pulls out a bottle of Cialis and sets it on the coffee table next to the bible. Margret Jean mutes the TV. Both women stare at the bottle.

Louvinia grasps Margret Jean's hand. "You didn't tell me Cordell suffered from the dysfunction."

Margret Jean straightens her posture, letting her large breasts sag in the muumuu. "I'm the one needing them pills, not Cordell."

Louvinia takes her hand away. "Now that's silly. These here pills won't work for a female."

"Don't matter who they're made for, I'm needing 'em something awful."

"Whatever for?"

Margret Jean shakes her head. "Cordell told me last time we had relations I was as dry as sandpaper."

Louvinia pats Margret Jean's arm, then rubs her shoulder. "Why you're just goin through the change is all."

"The hell you say. I'm only thirty-eight."

Louvinia presses her palm to her chest. "I wern't much older than you when it happened."

Margret Jean sighs, then folds her arms beneath her chest. "It's just a question of excitement is all."

Louvinia lets a grin spread across her face. "Is it excitement, or Cordell's technique?"

"Now hush. His technique's just fine. He hasn't changed it one bit in twenty years of marriage."

"Maybe that's the problem. You ever ask him to try new things?" Louvinia sticks out her tongue and waves it in the air.

Margret Jean's face turns red. "Cordell'll think I'm a prevert." Louvinia moves her tongue from side to side. Margret Jean rises out of her chair. "Now you stop that."

The blueticks huddled under the trailer sound long, plentiful howls. Margret Jean looks out the window and sees Cordell tromping out the woods with a coon flung over his shoulder. He stops at the trailer door, kicks off his brogans then hangs the coon carcass on the skin of the trailer to let the weather sweeten the meat for three or four days. Cordell quiets the hounds then steps inside the trailer.

"How do," Louvinia says.

Cordell ignores her. He unbuttons his flannel shirt and tosses it on the linoleum, revealing his bare chest to the women.

Margret Jean stamps across the room. "Can't you see we got company? Put your shirt back on."

"Lay off," Cordell says, flipping the television over to ESPN. "I'm tick bit and tired."

Margret Jean stares at the small deer ticks attached to Cordell's skin. She goes in the kitchen and gets the borax and vinegar needed to kill the ticks. She returns and kneels at his side. Louvinia pulls the recliner handle and stretches herself out and tells Cordell how the fire at the manure plant will soon be over. Cordell scratches at the ticks, and pretends to listen to what Louvinia is saying while Margret Jean mixes the borax and vinegar together.

Margret Jean finishes mixing the concoction and searches for ticks on her husband. Beginning with his arms, she uses her fingers to needle the coarse gray hairs that cover his forearm like fur, his muscles flexing beneath her touch. They never discussed sex and she knew that Cordell would never do such a thing as Louvinia suggested. He spent most of his time hunting since they lost the house, and when he wasn't hunting, he was sitting in front of the television.

She runs her palms along the insides of his arm pits, the damp hair smelling of sweat and dirt. Cordell nods his head dumbly at Louvinia's words, only focused on the television, ignoring even his wife's soft fingers. She can't remember the last time Cordell touched her, let his hands run over her body when they made love. She moves her fingers along his bicep then along his shoulders until they touch the base of his neck and the start of his wiry beard. She finds a deer tick among the whiskers, fat on blood. Cordell winces when she pulls the head of the tick out from his skin and tells her to go easy. The only time he ever pays attention to Margret Jean is when he's afraid of her.

420

Down along Cordell's chest and peppered round his navel are dozens of seed ticks, each no bigger than the head of a pencil. Margret Jean makes a bowl out of her hands and pours the mixture of borax and salt onto her husband's gut and watches it pool in his navel. Louvinia stops talking and goose flesh rises on Cordell's skin as they all watch the ticks drown in the sizzling mix of vinegar salt.

Margret Jean looks up and catches her husband's eye with her own, and she thinks she sees desire in his eyes. She covers his hand with her own and parts her lips. Cordell notices the little bottle on the table. He reaches for it, but Margret Jean snatches it away, rises and walks into the bedroom. Cordell follows his wife. Louvinia watches them leave then takes up the remote and begins searching the channels to see her afternoon stories.

Margret Jean sits on the bed, looking at the linoleum. Cordell hovers above her, vinegar salt dripping off his stomach.

"You sick?" he asks, reaching for the pills. Margret Jean loosens her grip and Cordell takes the bottle, reads the label, then furrows his brow. "Says these is for e-rectile dis-function."

Margret Jean rests her hands in her lap and shows her husband a calm face. "I bought'em and I aim to use'em."

"Not on me, you won't."

"They ain't for you, you big dummy" Margret Jean says, pressing a palm to her chest. "Them pills is for me."

Cordell shakes his head, and waves the bottle in front of his wife. "I'm as virile as ever."

Margret Jean rises from bed and closes the door. "Keep your voice down." Cordell walks to the other side of bed, dripping vinegar salt all over the floor. The two face one another with the bed between them. Margret Jean keeps her calm.

"Know you for a born liar if ever you claim I'm impotent."

"Now, hush. Cordell, I done told you them pills is for me and I want'em back."

"Bullshit." Cordell shoves the bottle in his pocket. "You think I can't satisfy you no more?"

Margret Jean's arms begin to shiver. There's a flyswatter on the nightstand she uses to smack insects that get in the trailer. She picks it up and looks at her husband as if he were a horse fly.

Cordell watches her raise the flyswatter above her shoulder. "Just what you gonna do with that?"

"Damn you Cordell Meacham Cochrane," she says. "If you don't gimme them pills—" Cordell side steps towards the door. Margret Jean moves her body and blocks him.

"By God," Cordell says. He grabs hold of the nightstand and lifts it in the air to use as a shield. The nightstand drawer opens, spilling papers and a bottle of perfume onto the floor. The bottle breaks when it hits the linoleum. The room fills with the smell of ripe strawberries. It's Margret Jean's favorite perfume. She wears it each day to keep the smell of hog shit off her skin and her clothes. Both of them stare at the broken bottle. Margret Jean's eyes begin to well up.

"You sonofabitch."

He sets the nightstand down. "Now, darling—"

"I've abided you my whole life, didn't say nothing when the bank took the house and kept my mouth shut when you dragged us to live in this sardine box, but I'll be damned if I'll let you go bout breaking my things." She lurches forward, swinging the flyswatter at her husband's head. Cordell ducks, but Margret Jean smacks his temple with the wire handle of the flyswatter. He covers his head. She takes a step back. "Now gimme them pills." Cordell reaches out with both arms and pushes his wife onto the bed and rushes out of the bedroom.

He passes Louvinia on his way outside of the trailer, her eyes glued to her stories, she doesn't even notice him leave.

Outside, Cordell stands red faced and bare chested in the ash fall. He and his wife had never been alike before they married, but he believed that they had grown alike over the years. He'd come to know her moods. Could tell when she wanted something by the nature of her silence. But losing the house changed things. Now, he couldn't tell what was on Margret Jean's mind no matter how hard he tried.

Abe walks over to his father. Cordell wipes the vinegar salt from his stomach. Flakes of ash stick to his wet skin. He looks at his son. "Never once did I put hands on your mother. But she hates me still."

"You did smack her round last year." Abe nods, remembering. "It was bout the time we lost the house."

"Hit her with an open hand, it don't count when it's with an open hand." Cordell lowers his head. "She come at me with those damn knitting needles big as ice picks. Would've kilt me if I hadn't stopped her." Cordell pulls the bottle of Cialis from his pocket, and hands it to Abe.

Abe reads the label and whistles. "Goa'll," Abe says, staring at the bottle. "Didn't know your pecker gone soft, Pa."

Cordell takes the bottle away from his son. "I always rise to satisfy that woman, even when I'm dog tired, and after twenty years together she hands me these damned pills."

"Mama spent good money on them pills."

"Course she did, but damned if I know why cause I ain't the one with the problem."

Beneath the trailer, the hounds call out. Cordell eyes Trixie set off from the group. He walks up to her and Abe follows. Trixie stands wobbly on three legs, wagging her tail at the men. The other hounds are tied to cinder block columns supporting the trailer at the opposite end. Six hounds all told, and Trixie the only bitch amongst them. Cordell runs his hands along her brown fur, sees that she's in heat and unties the chain. He leads her across the yard toward the lean-to where he keeps baled hay, three walls of unevenly spaced two-by-fours covered by a few shards of scrap sheet metal. Cordell wraps Trixie's chain around a four-by-four post then he pulls out a twenty-five pound hay bale and sets her hind end on top.

Abe eyes Trixie's stump. "Sure did a number on that poor hound."

Cordell smiles. "Dog wouldn't point." Trixie looks up at Cordell and he stares at her swollen rump. "Best thing for her is to turn her out bitch, maybe get a litter out of her before she dies."

"She ain't strong nough for that, pa."

Cordell cocks his head toward his son. "What you know bout the female of the species anyhow?"

Abe's face is sunblush from tromping the woods all summer. There's a shadow of beard growing along his cheeks, spreading down his neck and darkening his chin, but it doesn't compare to the full beard of his father. He scratches at it with his fingers, thinking. "Raised me round bitches my whole life." He pats Trixie on her head. "And I say she's had 'nough, what I say."

Cordell walks back to the trailer. "Ain't no son of mine gonna tell me he knows more bout breeding bitches than I do." He unchains two of the biggest hounds and they stick their muzzles to the hard pack clay surrounding the trailer till their noses foul in the thin ash covering the soil. They pick up Trixie's scent and drag Cordell back to the lean-to. The strongest one mounts her. Cordell hands the chain of the weaker hound over to Abe.

It takes the larger hound a moment to set the rhythm, and when he does, the hay bale slides along the lean-to's rustic floor. Cordell sticks his foot on the front of the bale to keep it from sliding. He nods to Abe. "Look at that now."

Abe pulls out a pack of menthols and raps them against his palm to settle the tobacco. "Seen it before. Need to pull that stud off her before she pops one of them there stitches." He points to the smear of blood spreading along Trixie's bandage. "She gonna bleed out."

"The hell she is." Cordell raises his foot until it rests beside Trixie on the hay bale. He takes a smoke from Abe and watches the two dogs longingly. "If ever I seen an animal built for breeding, it's Trixie. Why, she's given me four litters. Ain't never had a bitch push out five litters, and I reckon she's got one left in her."

Abe lights a menthol and shakes his head. "I don't know, Pa. Maybe if you treated her right, but with only three legs—"

"Now that there's a hell of a thing to say. I give her a meal everyday, plenty of table scraps too, a warm spot out of the wet under my trailer, and you saying I don't treat her right? Trixie is my prize bitch. It don't matter how many legs she's got. A good bitch don't even need legs. Suppose you'd want me to love on her, let her climb into bed with me nights and rub gainst me? That'd ruin a bitch for life cause the only thing a bitch understands is meanness." Cordell's face is red. "Boy, don't you know that's what love is?"

Blood drips onto the hay bale from the stump where Trixie's leg used to be, turning the light golden hay dark brown. Trixie pants, her tongue hanging from her mouth like a piece of wet leather. Abe looks down at her, his face is blank. "And if it kills her?"

Cordell raises his hands to the sky. "Only some weak-minded son-bitch treat an animal like it can't be replaced."

Abe turns his back on his father and looks at the trailer. He knows Trixie will be dead before nightfall. The stud hound finishes and Cordell switches him with the other dog. Abe looks down at the hound which just finished with Trixie. It sits at his feet panting, tail between his legs in a posture of fear.

Abe watched his mother suffer the loss of their house. Saw what it did to their marriage. Now he sees what it has done to his father. Abe looks at Cordell. "Mama's friend done told me the fire gonna be put out at the hog farm today."

Cordell flicks the spent menthol outside the lean-to where it lands on the ashes from the manure fire. "What of it?"

"Figure it's time I put in my application."

Cordell spits. "Only if they smother that goddamn fire. Till then, go dump the shit bucket. Your mother's got company."

Abe takes the hound back to the cinderblocks where the rest of the pack waits. Some of them sniff the returning hound and try and mount him. The returning hound snarls at the pack, but still they try and mount him because they can smell Trixie's scent and it drives them wild.

Inside the trailer, Louvinia lays flat in the recliner watching her stories, the volume on the television maxed out. Margret Jean sobs in the bedroom, the sound loud enough to be heard above the television. Louvinia sighs, mutes the television and rises out of the chair. She stumbles over the cracked and peeling linoleum and opens the bedroom door, finds her friend sitting on the bed, the room stinking of strawberry perfume. The drapes covering the only window are sheer, made from thin cheese cloth which hardly cut the light streaming into the room.

Louvinia sits alongside her friend and wraps her arm over Margret Jean's shoulder out of pity. "Stop this sobbing right now. Cordell's a good man."

Margret Jean stops sobbing. "I've shamed myself, Louvinia."

"You pity yourself now, you'll pity yourself forever." Louvinia smoothes back hair covering her friend's eyes. "Show Cordell your shame and let him see your hurt." Louvinia cocks her head toward the light streaming through window, and lets out a soft sigh. "The power of Jesus will let you share all things with your husband."

Margret Jean wipes her eyes. "The what?" she asks, rising to her feet and looking down on her friend. Louvinia's face has the same look of ecstasy Margret Jean saw at the Pentecostal prayer meetings.

"Christ's love gonna set you free once you let him in your heart."

Margret Jean frowns. "That's asking a whole hell of a lot."

Louvinia rises to her feet. Sensing a change in her friend, she reaches out and tries to grab her. "Why, you hasn't lost the spirit, has you child?"

Margret Jean avoids her friend's hand, straightens herself till she stands proper, shakes the wrinkles from her muumuu and looks Louvinia in the eye. "Maybe you need to look yonder at them crops to see what I lost, or take a gander at this shit box of a trailer I'm living in before you go asking a question like that."

"The bible says—"

"Says what?" Margret Jean storms out of the bedroom so fast her bare feet tear on the linoleum, leaving bloody smudges along her floor. She picks up her copy of the Pentecostal bible and holds it to Louvinia's face. "Go on and tell me what it says cause I'm fixing to know."

425

Louvinia keeps her composure. "It says true wisdom and power are found only in God's counsel and understanding of his children's plight are his own."

Margret Jean lowers the bible and slumps her shoulders and Louvinia allows a smile of triumph. The trailer is quiet. Shifting light from the moving pictures on the television casts strange shadows of the women against the fake pine wood lining the walls. Then, Margret Jean smells the ash from the outside inside her trailer. The towel she kept beneath the threshold lies away from the door. Cordell forgot to replace it when he left the trailer and ash blows through the void, covering the floor and spreading the stink of burnt hog shit through the trailer. Margret Jean sees this, and the bloody foot prints running along her floor. She begins to shake. She flips the book open. "That what the bible says?" She grabs a handful of pages and rips them from the spine and throws the book to the floor, then she wads the pages up in her hand and hikes up her muumuu and moves the pages between her thighs. "I wipe my dry cunt with it."

Louvinia grasps her mouth in shock after witnessing her friend's act of unfaithfulness. Margret Jean pushes past Louvinia and walks into the bathroom where she crushes the paper into a ball and drops it down the toilet.

Outside, Abe sees the wadded paper land on top the thin layer of lime covering the contents of the shit bucket. He one-arm lifts the five gallon bucket, the contents shift, releasing the smell of stale urine mixed with congealed bowel movements. The lime cuts the smell some, but it also drifts out of the lip of the bucket, burning his throat and making his eyes water. He takes the bucket away from the trailer up the ridge of the hollow along a path of loose shale and rain slick clay, the trees leafless in the ash. Ahead, he can see the line where the ash fall stops, a stand of cypress with rich green leaves surrounded by a copse of oak trees. A special place. Year before Abe was born, his father promised the Pentecostal church all the timber on the land. Said it was an acre set aside for God. Full of rich wood, strong and healthy. But that was before the fire at the hog farm, before the family lost the house and most of their land. The ash hadn't touched the trees set aside for the church. It choked the land the family planted in and fell directly upon the trailer, but this is where it stopped. Abe walks to the center of the green acre, the trees tower above him, their full leaves shading him. He can hear bird calls around him. Hoot of an owl. He tips the bucket and spreads the contents along the green grass and blue moss covering the floor of the woods. There's a pile next to this some two feet in height where he's dumped other buckets since the fire began almost a month ago.

Abe walks back down the ridge. He sees Louvinia's car leave as he walks back, the windshield wipers set to high, clearing the film of ash that has settled on her car since she arrived. He walks to the trailer, opens the door and finds both recliners empty. He's grown accustomed to seeing both his parents in their chairs, sitting together in front of the television. But tonight is different. Hushed sounds come from the bedroom. Abe moves to the door and hears his mother's voice whispering instructions to his father. The door is cracked open, and he sees his father lying on bed facedown between his mother's spread legs. Bedsprings creak under the weight of shifting bodies. A sighing comes from his mother. It's loud and rises in volume, but doesn't last long because Cordell lifts his head.

"Why'd you go and stop?" Margret Jean asks.

"Cause it tastes like cesspool perch."

Abe backs away from the door. His parents don't notice him. He grabs the keys to his father's truck and exits the trailer, careful to pull the old towel beneath the void of the threshold when he leaves. The pack of hounds lies restful beneath the trailer. Trixie's tied to the lean-to, and her body rests unmoving between two bales of hay. Abe likes to think she's just sleeping, but he knows different.

It's late afternoon, and soon the evening shift will be coming on at the hog farm. Abe knows the manager, a boy not much older than himself, and thinks that he can get hired today. He backs the truck to the rotting soy field. The crops only useful now as hog feed. Abe drops the tailgate, takes out a flat nosed shovel and begins loading the pickup bed with the rotten plants. He's made trips out to the hog farm with loads of soybeans before, and he's used to the wet slopping sound the leaves make when he drops shovelfuls of plants into the truckbed. It doesn't take him long to load the truck, the roots of the soybean plants are just as rotten as the leaves and they tear from the soil without much effort.

He drives the truck along the road with ease, already a year under his belt since he got his farmer's license and he's mastered the short trip to the hog farm just over the ridge in the next hollow. As the truck climbs the shifting gravel road up the ridge it leaves the ash fall and

Abe passes the old family house the bank took the year before. It escaped the ash fall, and the fields surrounding it are just as green and healthy as anything you ever saw. The trailer and dead soy fields reflect in the rearview mirror, and Abe can see the hurt in the land, feel the pain inside the trailer pinch his gut like a hornet sting.

At the hog farm, three sheds a hundred yards wide and two acres long hold over two thousand hogs. Fans the size of monster truck tires ventilate the sheds, spreading the sickly smell of warm hog shit into the air. The manager's office sits at the entrance, and Abe passes it on the way to unload the soy plants. He backs the trailer to the mouth of the nearest hog shed, steps out the truck and stares into the black entrance. There are no lights inside. The sound of squealing hogs throbs in his ears. From the mouth of the shed walks a boy, not so different from Abe. His mouth is covered with a rag and his overalls are stained brown from his waist down. He passes Abe, eyes downcast, unseeing. Abe stops him, asks him how much this load of hog feed will fetch.

The boy lowers his mask, brown mucus edges his nose, drips down the front of his face till it hangs off his upper lip. He looks at the load of rotten feed Abe brought and shrugs. "Bout twenty dollars," the boy says, then walks away.

Abe watches the boy leave, and sees his future in the way the boy moves. A vague tremor of terror runs along his spine. The sounding of the hogs calls to him from the mouth of the shed like something out of a nightmare. More men appear from the blackness of the shed pushing wheelbarrows ahead of them to unload the soy plants from the truckbed.

Behind the shed, the manure is spread out on a slab of concrete shaped like a bowl with a circumference surpassing an Olympic-sized swimming pool. One corner of the manure pile smolders, sending up the cloud of ash covering his family's land. There are stakes wrapped with chicken wire set along the edge of the burning section to keep the fire from spreading. Three bulldozers sit idle next to the fire. The machine operators lean against the treads, waiting for the order to snuff the fire.

Abe sees the manager standing with the men next to the manure fire and walks to him. The bulldozer drivers climb into their machines before Abe reaches them. Their engines crank on and they drive into the manure pit. The manager sees Abe, waves him over.

Abe shakes the man's hand. "Brung you a load of feed. Might put in for a job today if you'll have me."

The manager nods at the manure fire. "Know your family suffered cause of this here fire. If you can stand working here, I'll put you on today. Least I can do."

The bulldozers move to the fire, crushing the chicken wire and toppling the stakes separating the burning section of the manure pit. Abe turns and looks back at the shed. The rear entrance is just a large drain into the concrete slab and a constant watery mix of liquefied hog shit flows from the shed where it's left to dry on the slab. Abe thinks about the shed, one giant mouth at the front, one big asshole at the rear with a thousand stomachs in-between. Some of those stomachs will be eating the rotten soy bean plants he just sold and process out the contents into the shit pool where it will dry and add fuel to the fire spreading ash over his family.

The dozer blades dig into the smoldering fire, there are no flames, and it looks like a constant wind is blowing against the fire, causing dust to swirl in the air. The blades spread out the burning parts of the pile in hopes that they can bury the fire. But the treads of the dozers carry embers to sections of the manure pile that haven't caught fire and these embers start little fires of their own. The manager sees this, tries to stop the dozers, but it's too late. Little fires catch hold, and the whole pile now smolders, sending up a cloud of ash that blurs the evening horizon. Let night come on early. The land's used to it.

Nominated by Boulevard

WATCHFUL

by BOB HICOK

from THE GEORGIA REVIEW

A wasp had built a nest outside the back door.
Every time I went to knock it down, the wasp
was working the chambers. I waited two days,
finally turned off the water
while doing dishes, picked up a knife,
went out and cut the nest free
of the door frame, where it hung by little more
than a thread of wood the wasp had chewed
to pulp. The wasp was there, flew off,
and was back, on the fallen nest, just now,
when I checked after typing "working the chambers."
It started to walk away, the morning
too cold for flight, when I knelt
to pick up the nest. In each of the open chambers,
a grayish dot that will become a larva,
then a pupa, then a wasp who builds nests
for grayish dots. Two of the chambers were sealed.
I moved the nest to the top of a plastic box
enclosing telephone wires on the side of the house—
brightly colored wires with white stripes
running their length, wires of the human voice—
then scooped the wasp onto a long, rusted hinge
that has sat for months on the porch railing,
placed the wasp on the nest, and came back to tell you
this is the poem I've been trying to write

about the man I stood beside during the National Anthem
at a ballgame, who placed his prosthetic hand
over his heart, looking more like a boy from the outside,
where I was, and sang, in his uniform, harder
than I ever have, without a sense
of irony. Though how he would do that,
or what the inflections of irony are, I don't know,
or if it was two hands—a prosthetic, a phantom,
a grip, a ghost—over his heart, a memory
of his hand, his life, our country
as it was, whole, possible. I've wondered
every day since, like when the wasp was there, just now,
as if nothing had changed, when everything had changed.

Thinking of his hand as a phantom, just as the reasons
for the war in Iraq were phantoms. His hand a flame
as the burning of a Humvee is a torch. The sense
that we should not, who haven't been there, speak of nails,
bullets flying. Of war itself, this severing
itself. A piece of shop window, even a rib
blown free, ripping through the séance of his flesh,
the mood of his flesh to know and to hold. That
I should not, who has not been there, speak of this. But you see
how I start to. That a space is opened by his hand, absence
creating absence, and I have to fill it, it's what I do—
this isn't an *ars poetica*—it's what *we* do,
all we do, essentially, that dogs do not,
butterflies do not: see a thing and draw it
to another thing, make them clash and kiss, knit, gather.
His brain too is doing this. Fusing. Making
a kind of metaphor of sensation. His face, when he smiles,
when a breeze strokes, triggers the life of his hand,
for these encodings dwell beside each other in the cortex—
what the hand feels, what the face feels. And since his hand
is gone, and no sensations arrive to this region,
to this love, his face is taking it over, telling his mind,
This equals this.

Probably. Truth is I don't know. We didn't speak,
the man and I, of the ballgame, the weather, his hand.

Crack of the bat, blue sky, hotdogs
that smell at the ballpark like they smell
nowhere else. Perhaps he feels no haunting,
no ghost reaching for the butter knife, no itch
that isn't there being there, persistent as air.
Perhaps he would be Shiva for this war, acquire
more limbs to "lose" or "give," horrible words
that suggest misplaced keys or wrapped boxes
under tinseled trees. In an earlier version of this poem,
I used his hand as an excuse to write

>*This equals this*: I'm a phantom of the body politic
>if I don't speak, I'm required to, freedom's
>a tended dream, a public mapping of belief.
>When we're silent, government flows into the spaces
>we leave open, and remaps, acquires for itself
>the severed faculties of democracy.

An excuse, a catalyst, an image to carry these ideas.
But I kept coming back to what I didn't know, what
I couldn't say, honestly, unless I made a character
of the man, and today, finally, on the ninth attempt,
it occurred to me that the absence of his hand
speaks of his absence from my life and my absence
from his. I know no soldiers. I know no one who knows
a soldier. So this is a war on TV, a program, a dream,
The Odyssey, The Green Berets, Platoon. Proximity is required
to feel, understand. I know the wasp, have looked into . . .
its face? its life? . . . have entered some moment with it—
crack of the bat, blue sky—existed with it in time, as time,
as do beings who act in sight of each other, giving life
the motion by which it exists, as trees are required
for a copse, an edge for deer to cross between the field
and safety.
          The man's hand, possible ghost reaching
for his wife's breast, for the cloth to draw
across his son's back in the tub, under which
the lungs rise and fall, rose and fell. His son's lungs
which he felt, feels, now, with his other hand. A severing
by class? Mostly. By money? Mostly. I know no soldiers,

I write poems, we are phantoms to each other,
such that saying *no* to war is not real, saying *yes* to war
is not real. Saying—speech, the rivering of sound
to reach, enter, join, touch—is not real.
And with that loss we disappear, who are only speech,
as a cheetah is only speed, as the sun is only a burning
that does not singe the sky.

Nominated by Ed Falco, David Jauss, Rachel Loden, Richard Kostelanetz, Maxine Kumin,
Wally Lamb, Dorianne Laux, Joseph Millar, Joan Murray, Jessica Roeder

HERE, NOW: ECKHART TOLLE TAKES THE STAGE

by ADAM M. BRIGHT

from THE POINT

> *So the reality is that there is only each present moment: You are called to give a talk. You get out of a building and into a car. You look out of the window. You arrive at the venue. You sit in the chair; you wait; you step out onto the stage. Every movement is simple. There is only that.*
>
> —*Eckhart Tolle*

> *Then see to it that they accept your treasures. They are suspicious of hermits and do not believe that we come with gifts. Our steps sound too lonely through the streets. And what if at night, in their beds, they hear a man walk by long before the sun has risen—they probably ask themselves: Where is the thief going?*
>
> —*Nietzsche*

We should begin with a confession: by most metrics, I'm a New Age nut. I have a life coach. I begin my day with an hour of yoga, then proceed to my morning journal, my meditation, my visualizations and my spoken affirmations. On Sunday mornings, I wake at dawn and walk to my local Zen temple in order to sit motionless, in absolute agony, for three hours with other like-minded nuts. I am currently collaborating on a book of Eastern spirituality cartoons with my own mother (herself a yoga teacher). Yet—and here I place my brittle hand in yours—I am also, like most of you, I imagine, a cynic at heart. I am aware that I am a nut and it shames me. I despise the other nuts. I despise my own nuttiness.

* * *

For the moment, that leaves me hovering somewhere around the mid-point of the New Age spectrum, locked in a kind of dynamic equilibrium between scorn and wide-eyed wonder. But as I bear down on thirty, my recent life trajectory (increasingly marked by mental exclamations like "This stuff really works!") indicates that I am trending ever more surely toward the fringe. It's impossible for me to deny the efficacy of my spiritual pursuits, to deny that they have made me into a happier and kinder person. As a result, I'm giving over more and more of my time to yoga journals, to lecture halls crammed with other spiritual seekers, to workshops and inward-oriented activities with premises so divorced from conventional rationality that I will not confess to most of them in print. (I'll go this far: last year I took a six-week improvisational movement class in which our graduating assignment was to portray a rooster scratching in the dirt.) In short, I know that I am not long for the company of cynics like you. Soon—I think, I fear, I hope—I will be a true believer. So perhaps you should consider what follows a final transmission from a fellow traveler who once shared your doubt, a farewell report sent from the brink of the event horizon, just before I disappeared into the bright light of spiritual weirdness.

• • •

It was my life coach who first introduced me to Eckhart Tolle. We were in the cafe of the Borders bookstore over Penn Station—which is where, because my life coach has no office, and because my workday is a fiction even I no longer believe in, we meet every other Tuesday afternoon. I remember we had been talking about "accepting the present moment." All contemporary spiritual teaching boils down to the present moment: the eternal, all-encompassing, energy-releasing space of the Now. The phrase is used so often and in so many permutations—"present moment awareness," "offer no resistance to the present moment," "return to the present moment"—that it now takes me a small but appreciable philological effort to recall that it means anything at all. Anyway, in the middle of our session, my life coach, Dion, pulled out his iPod, handed me his headphones and cued up a track from Tolle's *The Power of Now*. For the first time, I understood. The present moment took me in immediately.

When I ask people what they like most about Tolle's work, they all give versions of the same response: that his words have a unique ability to transmit presence. "It's a book about transformation that transforms you while you're reading it," said Ruth, the organizer of a bi-weekly group of New Yorkers who meet to listen to recordings of Tolle's books and talks. Presence is a difficult concept to explain if you haven't spent years obsessing over it, but it's typically experienced as a combination of the following qualities: a calm, holistic intelligence; a deep sense of peace; and an intuitive appreciation of the grace uniting all things. Imagine your state of mind as an angel and you've basically got it.

Explaining how Tolle gets that presence into his writing and then back out to readers is tricky, like trying to explain the bite of pine in Hemingway or the imprint of mud-spattered boots one gets from Faulkner. "I think there is just an energetic element to this book that is almost impossible to articulate," says Munro Magruder, associate publisher of New World Library, which controls the worldwide rights to *The Power of Now.* "I don't know if you're going to figure it out. I don't try any more. I just go with the flow and the energy of it." The dominant feeling among the small circles that discuss this sort of thing is that Tolle himself is in such a profound state of presence that his words are imparted with its vector. Several people I spoke with described him as a carrier of spiritual frequencies—"tuning fork" was a term that came up more than once. The energy, the vibrations, call them what you will, are an extension of his person and they take the place of any devotional dance or mantra chanting or meditation practice. They collect readers and ferry them back to the Now.

Tolle himself emphasizes that most of his teaching takes place in "the silent space between words." The dominant quality of his many CDs, books and lectures is this enveloping silent awareness, and by his own account as well as those close to him, it's the source of his particular spiritual genius. Tami Simon, publisher of Sounds True audio books, learned this the first time she encountered Tolle. In the summer of 2001, she came across a tape of his early lectures and decided to fly up to Vancouver to interview him. At the time, little was known about Tolle's life story—basically, as Simon puts it, "he was depressed and he has this enlightenment experience and he wakes up and he hears the birds chirping." (We'll get to all that soon.) The interview was scheduled for a Tuesday in September: Tami woke up to hear that the Twin Towers had just fallen. She assumed the meeting would be postponed, but Tolle thought it was important to continue. When they met later that morning in his Vancouver apartment, Tolle asked that they start the interview by sitting quietly together. This led to 45 minutes of what Simon calls "an incredibly richly textured melting silence." Finally, she asked him one question: "So this morning, Eckhart, the World Trade Center crumbled before the eyes of the world. What is your reaction to that event?" His response ran a little over an hour and became the core of *Even the Sun Will Die*, a 2-CD set outlining the coming revolution in human consciousness.

Tolle borrows from nearly every tradition, but does not belong to any of them. (This institutional nimbleness helps him win followings in unexpected communities; I'm told he's especially popular with the MBA crowd.) His basic belief is that mind-created psychological time causes us to miss our true roots in the Now. The mind either worries over the past or anxiously rushes forward to the future; it does not know how to dwell in the present moment. But this only hints at a more fundamental error: "You believe that you are your mind. This is the delusion. The instrument has taken you over." Tolle encourages his readers to study the actual content of their minds, with the expectation that they will discover it to be an *independent* stream of continuous, repetitive, mostly negative thoughts. By learning to separate oneself from this stream, one returns naturally to the Now, the true ground of identity, a "natural state of *felt* oneness with Being," characterized by feelings of joy, ease and lightness.

The Power of Now is a unique text: partly an investigation into the nature of human suffering and its antidote (the Now), but also a catalyst, a touchstone, a pathway leading back to presence. (Tolle even employs a special symbol, ∫, to indicate a pause where the mind should go quiet, so one can "feel and experience the truth of what has just been said.") Throughout the book, Tolle avoids deliberate definitions. After introducing the concept of Being, he warns readers, "Don't seek to grasp it with your mind. Don't try to understand it. You can know it only when the mind is still. When you are present, when your attention is fully and intensely in the Now, Being can be felt, but it can never be understood mentally. To regain awareness of Being and to abide in that state of 'feeling-realization' is enlightenment." (This is immediately followed by that reflective pause symbol, ∫.) The entirety of the book is written in a question and answer format that anticipates and addresses a first time reader's likely doubts ("Isn't thinking essential to survive in this world?") and parlays them into deeper teachings ("The mind is a superb instrument if used rightly. Used wrongly, however, it becomes very destructive . . .").

Given his goal—to alert us that we must become free of our thinking minds—Tolle's writing is surprisingly precise, almost, some disappointed New Agers complain, academic. But his project isn't philosophical, in the sense that it doesn't rely on reason, the engine of Western philosophy. If anything, you'd have to say his goal is therapeutic. He aims for truth, but it is a revelatory truth, not the kind reached through careful argument. In fact, he almost always notes that his teachings offer little in the way of new ideas, that they are not designed to be intellectually interesting. Most of his lectures begin with the prediction that a few particularly mind-identified people in the room will find his talk so confoundingly boring that they will get up and leave.

Reading or listening to Tolle doesn't require much effort. That doesn't mean it's manipulative pap—you'd have to be a cynic of the palest hue to think it anything but earnest—but it's not the kind of writing that requires readers to labor after obscure conclusions. Tolle's meaning comes up on you unawares, engulfs you, and waits for an after-the-fact gesture of acquiescence. The transformation—the presence—takes hold in a moment of stillness, and, in most people, is followed by an initial shiver of resistance. It can feel too good, too much like trance. Next in those who continue reading, who allow the presence to stay, is a submission to the fact of the change. It is similar to the submission required in order to make love or undergo surgery—that inner narration, "Yes, this is happening to me, here I go . . ."

• • •

My original plan, when I took on this article, was to shadow Tolle in the manner of Tom Wolfe on Ken Kesey. I imagined us driving along highways overlooking Vancouver (in what I always pictured for some reason as an open-top Mazda Miata), quietly marveling at the collective insanity of modern society. We would pull in to rest stops where I would watch Tolle encompass the cashiers in the sphere of his present moment awareness, their eyes filling with an emerging alertness as he mindfully engaged them in small talk. We would purchase and chew our hot dogs in a state of felt oneness with Being. Later we would go down to his meditation room, where he would sit himself in the immensity of the present moment while I crouched in a corner, furiously scribbling notes.

But this is a tough time to get a hold of Tolle. His assistant, Lorine, makes this clear when I call his Vancouver office to follow up on an interview request sent weeks before. Lorine asks if I have read any of Eckhart's work and I answer that I have read everything: *The Power of Now*, *A New Earth*, *Stillness Speaks* and *Milton's Secret*, his children's book. I confide that I even have bootleg audio files from his private retreats. I compromise whatever journalistic integrity I might possess and tell her straight out that I am a huge fan.

"What are you hoping to talk with him about?" she asks.

I'm never very good at this part. "Well, Eckhart's a sort of contemporary philosopher who's not studied in philosophy departments. And he probably never will be. But he's got millions of readers. And our magazine is focused on how ideas affect everyday life, you know? So I just think that's a really interesting gap—between his impact and how little people have looked at his ideas." I want to be honest. "Plus, I want to ask him what it feels like to be a 'guru'—how he feels about the fact that his ideas enter mainstream culture with this 'New Age' stigma slapped on them."

She waits a couple seconds before responding and I can already sense the Miata pulling off without me. "What's making me uncomfortable," she says, "is that you're saying that you're an *intellectual* magazine, but Eckhart's whole philosophy is all about experience. He's all about there being no mind." I should not have said "stigma." Or "New Age." I'm told that between his scheduled talks and time allotted for private retreats, he's booked solid for the next nine months.

So two days later, I buy a last-minute ticket and fly to Toronto, where Tolle is delivering two nights of talks at Roy Thomson Hall. It's late January, and I arrive a few minutes before his first lecture ("The Power of Presence: Going Beyond the Ego") is scheduled to start. Only one ticket collector is on duty, and a bottleneck of spiritual aspirants is trying to force itself from the outer to the inner lobby. I am standing at the very back. As the house lights dim and lobby chimes chime, a voice comes over the PA to tell us to take our seats. We collectively attempt to sublimate our tension. We each work at projecting an unflustered calm. A good-looking couple nearby scolds each other *sotto voce* ("*Re-lax*, honey, there's no rush").

I take my seat just before show time. There are about 2,500 other people in the audience, which is full right up to the upper galleries. An announcement: "Just to let everyone know, we'll be starting five minutes from now." A flurry of jokes on the theme, "Oh, from *now*." Light chuckles. Then the theater goes dark and Tami Simon walks out to the podium to introduce Tolle. She calls Eckhart "a frequency holder." And what is that frequency, she asks? The frequency of Being. And what is our opportunity? "To join him in that frequency." None of this sounds spacey to me. I know exactly what she means—it actually strikes me as an incredibly accurate way to describe Eckhart's appeal. (As a test, though, I play this section of audio for one of my roommates in New York; he gets so agitated he orders me out of the room.)

Five minutes later a panel in the wall opens and Eckhart Tolle—spine kyphotically buckled, eyes cast down at his feet, hands clasped at his navel—crosses the stage in shadow. He moves with a hyper mellow domesticity, like a Trappist Mr. Rogers. He's wearing a white sweater-vest over a dress shirt, a pair of khaki pants and plain black shoes. (On the advice of a friend, I have been reading Max Weber while researching this article, and it strikes me that Tolle's sweater-vest—which he is almost always photographed wearing—functions as what Weber would call a "talisman." It's something that no normal person would wear, and reaffirms Tolle's special status as an oracular figure operating outside of social norms).

From the balcony where I sit, Tolle seems unaware that he's being observed. He's not hurrying to the microphone, not making little gestures of acknowledgment to the audience, not trying to cue us into his persona. He's *just crossing the stage*, but he's so devoted to just crossing the stage that the action appears sacred. I realize—again, nod to Weber—that Tolle's charisma, the magnetic quality of his personality, is almost an *anti*-charisma. He's made himself so boring, punched so

440

far through the back end of dullness, that we feel his simplicity must represent some incredible inner power.

The room is silent, which is also weird. It certainly fuels the feeling of the anti-charisma charisma. We're not applauding—because we've been asked not to by Simon, who informed us that Tolle preferred to be greeted by "the fullness of our silence." At first, that made me feel uncomfortable, kind of communey, but I now see that it's working. We *are* more present in this silence. I have never given a speaker so much attention. Tolle pads to the front of the stage and takes a seat in a fabric-backed office chair in the middle of a circle of light. Next to him is a table supporting a glass of water, which he will not drink, and a vase with a spray of white lilies. Tolle just sits and stares. He doesn't even move his eyes. I'm already mentally narrating the experience to my friends, and I get the feeling that everyone else in the theater is as well. What if he just looks at us for the full two hours? Could we handle it? Would people insist on refunds? Is he—"Welcome," he says, after what my voice recorder indicates (deceptively, I'm sure) has been half-a-minute, "to this moment." Awesome. I want to applaud so badly.

Throughout the talk at Roy Thomson Hall, and in all the lectures I've found online, Tolle sits stone still, essentially paraplegic, for hours. He does not cross his legs or bounce his knees or jiggle his feet. Most of the time his arms lie limp in his lap. (By way of comparison, the man seated next to me spends the full two hours of the first night's talk nervously biting the hair on his forearm and compulsively pinching his nostrils together and sniffing.) Tolle only moves when he wants to illustrate a state of mind, what he calls a "possessing entity," and he is an astoundingly gifted mime in this respect. When he's really on fire, he slips back and forth between his standard pedagogic monotone and a whimsical revue of the interior monologues that accompany pride, suspicion, worry, haste, false fellow feeling, etc. It is the only time you could say that he becomes animated. The highlight comes on the second night ("Enlightened Relationships: The Arising of the New Consciousness") when he mimes young love—showing first the googly-eyed, spellbound couple in a restaurant and then portraying the same couple, one year later, sitting at the same table with long-drawn faces, glowering at each other in silence. We laugh because we've all been there. He obviously has too, but the difference is that we will probably have to go back. It doesn't seem like he will. That's the heart of his appeal, and why we're all here: Tolle seems to have escaped from being human.

On the second day, he guides the auditorium through an experience of the present moment. He turns his face up to us like a conductor. He is still; we are still. Then the words begin. "Where is your life now? Here. Your life is here in consciousness . . . Just this. Just this . . ." His voice gets smoother—or we soften to his voice, it's hard to say. "Who you are is not your arising thoughts. Who you are is the space behind your thoughts. You are not your thoughts." I feel the mantle of my mind pulled back, but I'm okay with it. My life situation dissolves. The distant girl I'm courting, the career I haven't decided on, the perpetual litany of my discontent—it all drops away and the room starts to come alive. I become at once hypersensitive and transcendentally indifferent to my surroundings, not at all unlike being on an acid trip. The man next to me is breathing like a bear! He cracks his knuckles. Now he strokes his beard! Again the three fat ladies lean into each other to whisper! My seat squeaks! I am the alert witness to my own perceptions—disidentified with them, but at the same time sensing them more fully, enjoying them at a distance as one enjoys music.

"As presence advances, who you are deepens," says Tolle. "Suddenly there is a depth in that still alert space between thoughts and that is here, now. Very simple. A still, alert space between thoughts." There is a silent crescendo in the room that lifts all our gazes. We take our eyes from Tolle (and the live feed Jumbotrons over his shoulders), and stare across the expanse of the auditorium at ourselves. We take ourselves in for the first time. This occurs outside time. Everything opens and it hits us: he's right, there's nothing wrong with this moment. "In that clear space," he says, "you're not defining yourself anymore. In that clear space, you could say, you do not even know who you are anymore." As he fades back to silence a woman a few seats over makes warm *mmm-hmmms* of assent as if someone were making love to her in her sleep.

• • •

The story of how Tolle became a spiritual vehicle is, like many such stories, impossible to separate from the possible tarnish of its own apocrypha, but if we take him at his word, it is essentially the story of a man who stumbles upon a portal into the true nature of consciousness. Born Ulrich Tolle (he changes his name, post-portal, in honor of the thirteenth-century mystic Meister Eckhart), his life is typical in that he spends most of it in a state of profound unhappiness. His parents fight constantly and from the age of ten he begins thinking of ways to kill himself. These feelings grow more and more urgent with time. In his late twenties, he establishes himself as a research scholar in comparative literature at Cambridge. Externally, he has a successful and promising academic future. But his life is a burden and a misery.

One night not long after his 29th birthday, he bolts awake in the grip of acute despair. He is again close to suicide. He feels a "deep longing for annihilation, for nonexistence." "I cannot live with myself any longer," he thinks. Then he stops. Who is this "I" that I cannot live with? He decides there must be two selves: "the mental story of me" which he can no longer tolerate, and "a deeper sense of being, of presence," which constitutes his true Self. The realization overwhelms him. His mind goes blank, his body begins to quake and he feels himself sucked into a "vortex of energy." He blacks out.

The next morning he rises to the sound of birdsong and knows at once that an illusory sense of self has been shattered. He walks around his room in a state of wonder, marveling at life's beauty. He has been enlightened. From now on he knows himself as "the I Am." For much of the next two years, he sits on a bench in Russell Square, relishing his new state of mind and watching the world unfold in present moment bliss. His friends and family assume he has gone insane.

From time to time, Tolle ventures from his bench to visit the British Library where he leafs through the teachings of the world's great sages. He is hoping to better understand what has happened to him. At night, when the weather is nice, he sleeps under the stars in Hampstead Heath. But the bench is his true home. He sits there in silence, the knower behind the thinker. Of course his mind still expends some residual energy in worry or regret or judgment, but now he knows these thoughts are inconsequential; he need not identify with this "stream of involuntary and incessant thinking." He has gained the ability to abide simply in joy, in Being. Members of the Cambridge community whisper about the former student who dropped out of academia after having—what, a breakdown, a breakthrough, a revelation? People in the neighborhood start to notice him; not disheveled, not a drunk, smiling like a holy idiot. A few spiritually inclined individuals decide he must be a mystic. They ask him if he'll share what he knows. Yes, he says, that is a good idea. He begins leading small workshops in presence. After teaching for ten years, he knows that he has discovered a path to spiritual enlightenment. It occurs to him that he ought to move to Vancouver to begin writing a book about this discovery. Yes, he thinks, that is a good idea. He moves to Vancouver.

I always imagine the next part like this: Tolle sitting in his little Vancouver apartment (a sparse one because he has so little money at the time). He is, as usual, in a deep state of bliss. He arranges a sheet of paper on the desk. He picks up his pen. Doing all this, he is aware that he is not "Eckhart Tolle" but the I Am, Awareness Itself, and so he regards the paper and the pen and the desk and the conventional identity "Eckhart Tolle" from a place of deep and untroubled joy. He breathes in. He breathes out. He waits. Something comes, and he leans over the desk to write the words that will form the core of his teaching: "You are not your mind."

At this point the identity "Eckhart Tolle" is, again, conventionally speaking, a nobody: a guy living alone in a Vancouver apartment, working on a book that claims people should not believe their own thoughts. He supports himself by continuing to lead presence workshops, but this money never amounts to much. His popularity grows as people in Vancouver's spiritual community recommend Tolle to their friends. After a few months, a management consultant named Constance Kellough hears about Tolle from a colleague and asks him to lead weekly groups in her office's conference room. They meet every Wednesday, sometimes in groups as small as five. At the end of one session, Tolle approaches Kellough and asks if she will be the publisher of a book he is writing. Aside from having taught English literature, Kellough has no publishing experience, but she says yes anyway. "There was just a recognition of consciousness," she says. "We were in the same bandwidth."

Tolle ekes his way towards completion of the manuscript on the proceeds of a $1,000 lottery ticket. The initial run is 3,000 copies, and at first it seems *TPON* will not be very successful. Most of the books sit in cardboard boxes in Kellough's basement. Because they don't have a distributor, Kellough and Tolle walk to bookstores around Vancouver to try to tempt owners to place a few copies on their shelves. When those sell out, Tolle returns with another armful of books. He meets a lot of his first readers this way; they often linger in the store in order to see him. He's incredibly happy.

Over the next two years, the book spreads almost entirely by word of mouth: first through Vancouver, then to other large Canadian cities and eventually into the United States and England. In early 2000, a copy ends up in the hands of Steve Ross, a yoga instructor who puts the book on sale in his Los Angeles studio. Meg Ryan attends classes there; she buys the book, loves it, and contacts Tolle for teaching. She's sure he's the real thing. Meg Ryan tells Oprah, Oprah tells the world and Eckhart Tolle officially blows up.

Over the next eight years, Oprah promotes Tolle in her magazine, her lecture tours, her book club, her radio show and on TV. She tells viewers that she keeps *The Power of Now* on her bedside table. She's even more aggressive when his next book, *A New Earth*, is published, inviting Tolle to co-host a ten-session web seminar that's downloaded 38 million times. Despite the success, Tolle still seems grounded in the present moment. He does not appear caught up in what he would call "the world of form." His U.S. publisher says he never calls about his sales. "He's the only author of this magnitude that's never asked me 'How many copies have you sold and what have you done to market my book'?" says Magruder of New World Library. "It doesn't matter to him." Deepak Chopra apparently calls all the time.

• • •

Tolle's teaching is so successful because it's so carefully fitted to our contemporary world and its unique forms of pain. He takes as his primary subject not the general question of suffering, nor even its most widely recognized global brands (poverty, disease, injustice), but rather the daily distress of post-industrialized life. One of his standard routines, which he reprises during the lecture in Roy Thomson Hall, is about the uselessness of getting angry at traffic lights. "What can you add to that moment by thinking about it?" he asks. "Nothing. Only problems." His writing is filled with scenarios like these: long

445

waits, deadbeat roommates, dysfunctional marriages, irritatingly slow elevators. It's the minor battles that he coaches us through—how, for example, to keep calm when there is only one ticket collector and the bells are already dinging and the house lights dimming and the $80 talk is about to get started and who the fuck really has time to be present? We are drawn to him because he is (or was) one of us, and knows our particular forms of anguish.

This should make him acceptable, but it doesn't. In fact, I think this familiarity is precisely what makes him so suspect. Among my inner circle of miserable postcollegiate New York friends—the frontline victims of post-industrialized distress—the near unanimous opinion is that he's a charlatan. Part of what makes him especially distrusted, above and beyond the cynicism these people reserve for religious traditions generally, is precisely the fact that he is part of no *established* tradition. His movement was born in the here and now—a media phenomenon untethered to any previously unmediated institution. It has no roots in distant history, ancient civilization, or myth, but emerged out from under the aegis of our modern media apparatus. It exists for its followers as much as for its critics entirely in the unpleasantly familiar channels of mediated distribution, as a constellation of books, CDs, TV appearances, speaking tours and web groups. Because it addresses our (petty) problems directly, it doesn't seem grand enough—not even grand enough to seriously disagree with or argue against.

In other words, the fact that Tolle's story begins not in ancient Mesopotamia or a Nepalese village, but in our world, in the production offices of Harpo Studios, in a West Hollywood yoga class, under the fluorescent glare of our very own commercial distribution networks, is disappointing. Disappointing, I'd maintain, even to the hardened cynics; in them too, there's at least an adversary's nostalgia for the old traditions—the holidays rooted in the harvest, the idiosyncratic prohibitions, the creation myths and so on. Since the Enlightenment, we tacitly tolerate those belief-based institutions—the Church, the soul, fated love—that predate our turn to Reason. But we expect any new institutions to be able to explain themselves in rational terms. This is why Tolle's movement of personal revelation—like any modern appeal to mystical experience—feels so dissonant. An underlying tenet of modernity is that you can do what you like, so long as you can give reasons why you're doing it. Tolle, and the millions of people who join him in presence, refuse this stipulation. Their forays into Being are unapologetically incomprehensible. They offer not "reasons," but the example of their experience—and above all, of Tolle's experience. Their evidence is their present moment awareness.

But presence is a necessarily private affair. In the public realm, all we have is its external manifestation, an unlikely and seemingly unflappable calm. Perhaps this calmness is the modern world's version of miracle, the last thing capable of inspiring awe and dread. Awe, because it signifies an escape from the world of neurosis and anxiety. Dread, for the same reason. Tolle's composure—his ability to distance himself from the content of his thoughts, to regard them impassively as "just" thoughts—is an astounding and threatening achievement. He says that when you are enlightened, "thinking no longer gives you your sense of identity." To intellectuals, of course, nothing could be more terrifying. We revere thought as the encircling bulwark that keeps individuals whole. We think people *ought* to suffer, be deluded, yearn, regret and obsess. Since what we call *our* Enlightenment, these qualities have been taken as the quintessential, ennobling marks of humanity, the fundamental stuff of the self. To worry is our destiny and our function. Our anxious minds make us unique in the universe.

To all this—nothing less than the reigning model of the human being—Tolle says, let go. Our deep attachment to the notion of a regally troubled humanity is, he says, just the ego's strategy for staying alive. "The false, unhappy self, based on mind identification . . . knows that the present moment is its own death and so feels very threatened by it. It will do all it can to take you out of it." Tolle's most recent book, *A New Earth*, is built around the theme that we are preparing to leave this old, mind-dominated state behind, that we are already witnessing the civilization-wide flowering of a new consciousness. He believes this to be the next stage in human development. (For what it's worth, I do too.) But he won't defend it as an argument. He can't: the gulf between my experience of presence and your estimation of its worth only exposes the tautology at the heart of our respective definitions of value. Escaping thought and returning to Being is my life's purpose if I believe it is. It's a blank-faced bovine god if you believe it's not.

Tolle has created a movement that appears to have made a great number of people happier, and he seems to have done so—thus far—with-

447

out bankrupting them, seducing their women or falling into any of the other classic depravities of the spiritual demagogue. But can we say whether his movement is "good"? His teachings produce in me a state of grace and ease, and it's hard to envision a more self-sufficient guarantor of their value. At the same time, it's hard to envision one that could be any less effective in persuading a skeptic. The action of presence is mystical, its truth experiential, and its doctrine arational. Of course, this may be said of any religion, but at least the old ones offer us enshrined institutions like the papacy or the state of Israel to quibble over and evaluate. Ultimately, the adherents or detractors of presence, as evidence for either position, must return to Tolle, the inscrutable cipher. We have him, and his enigmatic example alone, to settle the question not only of what it would be like to live entirely in the moment, but whether to do so is to fulfill our potential as human beings or to forsake it.

• • •

On the last night of talks in Vancouver, after about two hours of speaking, Tolle suddenly stops and exhales. There was no penultimate buildup, no anticipation of an ending. Instead of taking another breath to speak, he just sits and stares out at us. His arms are limp, his face frozen but alert. There is a collective leaning-forward; the expectation is even greater than when he first crossed the stage the night before. I am sure that someone from the upper balcony is going to tumble forward into the silence. "Thank you," Tolle says. He stands up, gives a little bow and walks back into the darkness of stage left.

Nominated by The Point

HER CAR

by JEAN VALENTINE

from GREAT RIVER REVIEW

Her car had hit another car.
The other driver's insurance person called.

It was all going well,
a matter of time.

She lost her tongue. Her husband
thought she meant it as a metaphor.

It was her taste for life
her taste for herself, for others

She found her tongue on the floor
and paper-clipped it to

the kitchen calendar. This was back in the day
of Separation. Permanence.

Nominated by Ted Deppe, David Jauss, David Wojahn, John Allman, Great River Review

PET

fiction by DEB OLIN UNFERTH

from NOON

Somehow they have wound up with these two turtles. The woman says she saved them. Her son says all she did is move them from one place to another—from the basement of her sister's house to their apartment (also a basement)—and the turtles' lives are no better than they had been before, and her own life is significantly worse, since now she has to take care of them.

Well, the woman and her son will take care of them together.

Not him. He's not the one who took them. He doesn't even know why she did it—making off with somebody's pets? That's weird.

Those turtles would have died down there in the dark, like all the other pets in her sister's life. It was a philanthropic moment, taking them. It's called philanthropy. Does he even know what that is? she wonders.

Besides, the turtles aren't much work. She has to feed them and check their water temperature and turn the light on and off. She has to clean the tank each week. She has to take the tank's water out, cup by cup, pour it into a bowl, then carry the bowl to the tub, walk through two rooms to do it (drops of dirty water falling on the floor). She has to empty bowl after bowl. She doesn't know how many bowls fill a tank. Many. And many cups to fill a bowl. Another way to do it is by siphon. She could put the siphon in her mouth, suck, and when she sees the water coming up, pour it into the bowl.

Are you kidding me, putting that turtle shit in your mouth? says her son.

Since when does he use words like that and at his mother too.

450

Can I use words like salmonella? says her son. Can I use words like incredibly stupid?

Another question: when was the last time someone actually touched this woman, not counting the turtles? A long time.

She wound up with the turtles in the first place because that week every time she looked in the basement she saw the turtles. One of her house-sitting jobs for her sister was to feed them. Really the situation was so pathetic. You'd go down to the darkest coldest basement, make your way toward a corner that had a little light, and there would be two turtles, one sitting on top of the other because they only had one rock, and it was bad. You'd toss in a few food sticks and think, OK, this is why we will all go to hell. Or think, Well, God did put us in charge of things, right? Or think, What was God thinking? Or think, What were the owners of this house—her own sister and that God-awful husband of hers—thinking? Who are these people that they could leave these little animals down here with their long frowns? So she called her sister in Florida and said, There are two turtles in the basement, and I have to say they don't look very pleased.

Do you know how long turtles live? said the sister. Do you know what it's like to have kids who one day come home with one turtle and then another day come home with another, and you get to be either the mom who will let them have turtles or the mom who won't? And then guess who's stuck taking care of them for the next hundred years?

By all means, said the sister, I'm sure you'd do a better job. Take them. Take everything—tank, food, thermometer, rock. Get them out of my house.

Now one of the turtles is sick or something is wrong with it. It just lies on the bottom of the tank, not moving—see that? How it's lying there? It could drown.

Don't look at her son. He's just leaving, just out the door.

Was she looking at him? Would he like to report where her eyes were resting at the moment of the observation? Was it on the tank or him? And don't forget how much he always said he wanted a pet.

He wanted a pet when he was eight.

The turtle could drown.

She's responsible for it, he says. It was her philanthropic moment

451

that led her into this and he's not going to be the one to lead her out. If he were her, he would first toss the turtle out into the courtyard and vow never to have another philanthropic moment again. Then he would go out to the courtyard and find the turtle and bring it to the vet.

So she does all that and she waits her turn and then the vet says he has no idea. He's a vet for mammals, he says. He puts the turtle on a scale and says, Its weight is fine! And the nurse and the other people around there laugh. He pulls on its little legs and measures it and says, Well, it's long enough! And the nurses laugh again.

It's all a big waste of her time and embarrassing, and it costs forty bucks. Then she has to carry the turtle in a case for cassette tapes all day because she's worried it might die in the tank while she's gone. She takes the turtle to work and puts it under her desk by her feet and then she takes it to her AA meeting. She opens the case a little because she's worried it might suffocate inside.

What is that thing? someone at the AA meeting says. That is really ugly.

She looks down at it. True, it's not the nicest-looking animal, but how many creatures of the earth can honestly say that they are, including this person before her?

People gather around. What's wrong with it? they say.

It's covered in mud, they say.

The shell just looks like that, she says. It just looks that way.

You can't have that in here, they say.

It's just a turtle, a new man says. The others look at him.

It may have a disease, they say. Get that thing out of here.

She takes the case and leaves.

She sits at the kitchen table with her head in her arms. Her son comes in and says she could leave the turtle out in the street. Maybe a car would come along and hit it.

The turtle doesn't get better. She calls the pet store, calls her sister, calls other people she knows who have pets or who are generally responsible people. No one has any idea. No one knows, until finally someone says, Oh, I know. It needs those vitamin sticks and a special light so it can absorb nutrients. So she goes out and buys the special light and the vitamin sticks and it is expensive and the store is far and

452

she sees she has a ticket on her car when she comes out, but lo and behold, the turtle is better in a few days or at least swimming around like before.

No thanks to her son who couldn't help her with one little thing.

No thanks to her son who couldn't manage to get home at a decent hour. Here it is, nearly midnight. Where is he? She goes up in her robe to the entryway to see if he is lying dead in the street. The security door is propped open with a brick so anyone could come in and kill them. She stands looking out into the dark to see if her son is being held up on the corner, or being stabbed or shot. A man comes in who isn't her son.

What, of all things, are you doing? she says.

Did you prop this door open? she says. So anyone can come in here?

I'm a single woman living alone with my son, she says.

The man shrugs. So get a husband, he says.

Her son appears at two A.M. Were you drinking? she says, following him down the hall. Just tell me that.

A tall glass of shut-the-fuck-up, he says and goes into his room.

She can't do this, just can't. She's not equipped to deal with small animals, teenagers, basement apartments. She calls her sister. Do you think your kids want their turtles back?

Oh no you don't, her sister says. I don't care what you do with those turtles but don't bring them here. I'm the good guy for once. Their aunt stole them—it wasn't anything I did.

I saved them, says the woman.

I think you were looking in the wrong basement.

She hadn't been the best mom. She knows that. There were a few rough years. He used to want to be with her all the time. Now he avoids her.

Do you want to go shopping on Saturday? she says.

Do I want to sit in traffic for hours with only you to talk to? Not likely.

Go to the movies, then? Dinner?

Look, Mom, you're not my date. OK? And we're not friends. You're the parent. I'm the kid who suffers in your presence until I can get away.

* * *

She never left him chained to a radiator or locked in a closet. She did leave him with friends a couple of times, once when he had the chicken pox, once when she went into detox. Twice. Once on Halloween.

With no costume, her son says.

But it worked out all right, didn't it? You like Ron and Cici. Ron and Cici are very nice people.

At least they weren't drunk, if that's what you mean.

They liked you. They took you trick-or-treating. You got a pumpkin full of candy.

They felt sorry for me. My mother was a drunk.

They bought you a costume.

Of a superhero nobody ever heard of, he says.

And another thing, he says. You didn't leave me with them. I called them. They came and picked me up.

But now that the turtle is better it keeps fighting with the other turtle, the smaller one, hurting it, snapping at it, its friend, the only one it may ever have and some have less than that, and still the turtle keeps biting. And it is really sad because the smaller one wants to be near the bigger one all the time, can't rest unless it is next to the bigger one, who keeps biting it each time it gets close. So she calls all the same people again and they say they have no idea again and she thinks this is going to go on eternally. She'll always have a question no one can answer and a long list of people to ask. She goes to a meeting and talks about it, and they, too, look bored, wishing she'd go away. Finally the new man says, Sounds like you need a second tank. Or one less turtle. Why don't you take one to the pet store?

It has been so long since anyone gave her advice that she wanted to hear, she is tearful with gratitude.

We can't take that, the clerk at the pet store says.

Oh, please, she says. I'll pay you.

Sorry. Why don't you take it to the reptile swap?

What's that?

It turns out there's a place you go to bring your reptile if you don't want it anymore and are willing to take another one home. Maybe she could get a frog or a fish, a pet that lived less long. It's very far and it's illegal, so she takes the turtle in a hatbox, drives out on the toll road

454

on a Saturday. The reptile swap is held in a muddy field, which she hadn't understood would be the case. She is wearing high heels. Her shoes sink when she steps and she can feel water seeping through the soles. She wants a drink. It's hard to walk and she wobbles with her hatbox. People look at her strangely. She carries the hatbox from table to table. Nobody wants her turtle. They have chirping dragons, six-foot snakes. There's a single tiny monkey gripping the bars of its cage like a convict. No one looks at her turtle. She brings it back home.

Monday she finds a note on her desk: *Were you going to deposit the checks before leaving for the weekend? Never mind, I did it. P.S. I'm writing this at 9:15, did I forget you were coming in late today?*

She wonders, Why do other people have pets? Is it for the same bad reason as she? What is her bad reason? She doesn't know. They aren't even cute, the turtles, this one especially. It looks like an oven mitt. She feels nothing for these turtles. She hates them. They are ugly. They smell bad.

Now she has two tanks and she has to clean two of them and it is awful. She hates it so much that she waits and waits until the water is cloudy and polluted and stinks. Finally she begins dumping out the water, carrying both tanks' worth of water across two rooms to the bathroom and pouring it into the tub, but there is so much shit in it, it clogs. A puddle of brown water in the tub.

Oh, God, what is she going to do now? There's shit in the tub.

You put it in the tub? her son calls from his room. Shit goes in the toilet, Mom.

Oh, God, why is this happening? Why does everything she does turn out this way? There is no way out of this. This is hell. And you know what? She is supposed to have a date tonight, the only one, in what, a year? Two years?

A what? her son comes out of his room to say. What did you just say?

Yes, she has a date. With a man from a meeting.

One of those drug addicts, those drunks?

Yes, after she was forced to leave with the turtle in the cassette tape box and was crying in the parking lot holding the turtle box in one hand and her purse in the other, the new man came out and said, Let's see what you've got there? And she showed him. At the next meeting he said something nice about her remarks and at the next meeting he

455

sat next to her and asked if he could bring her a cup of coffee when he
went to get his own cup, and after that he asked after the turtles and
after her son, and at the next meeting he asked if she wanted to go to
dinner.

And you said *yes*?

And she said yes. So basically she has a date and she is trying to
hurry it up with these tanks, and dirty water keeps splashing on the
floor and now the tub is clogged. And yes, the man is a little old for
her and not as good looking as her son's father and is maybe not going
to win any awards for being dashing and rich, but anyway it is more or
less a date.

When were you going to tell me? her son says. What the fuck is go-
ing on? How old is this guy who's a little old for her, eighty?

So she goes and buys some drain cleaner, the really powerful stuff.
She pours it in and waits (You didn't mention any man, says her son,
didn't say a word. Well, she does have other concerns on her mind just
now) and the drain explodes. Turtle feces all over the tub and the wall
and the curtain and the window because that is the kind of place she
lives in with her only son, a basement apartment with cheap drains in
a bad neighborhood because her husband divorced her and left, even
though she stopped drinking, and he never calls his son, not even on
his birthday, never sends enough money, and there is turtle shit on the
wall and she has to be up early, and meanwhile years are going by, her
son growing up and she fading further from his mind.

There's turtle shit everywhere, her son is saying. And you're bring-
ing home drunks. This place has got to be unfit. Who do I call to re-
port you? I should go live with Dad.

Go ahead, she says. If you can get him on the phone.

How has she come to this? How? She can put a heroic spin on it or
a negative one. She could make herself look enlightened or close to
tramphood. She has never seen a woman make worse choices than
she. She has never known any person so transparently wrongheaded,
so obviously in need of job counseling, parenting classes, therapy, help
of any kind, any lifeboat, any raft, so obviously in need of a hard care-
ful look at herself, and so obviously not going to do it. She is that un-
aware. That full of the opposite of insight, that doomed to middling
livelihood at best, certain solitude, early illness, weakness, not-quite
poverty, strained relations with her son, relatives who don't really like
her taking care of her when she is old. The indignity of all this, the
shame. How exhausting, this life, this topic, how stupid, how difficult.

She has her face in her hands. And what is that now—turtle shit in her hair? Well, this is a lovely way to spend the afternoon. Does she feel better now, Miss Pity Party? The phone rings. That would be her date.

Don't answer that, her son says.

She reaches for the phone.

Don't you dare, her son says. You're going to go out with that drug addict and leave me here in this shit?

All right, all right, she says. She picks up the phone. I can't go, she says to the man on the phone. I'm sorry. I can't go out.

Come on, says the man on the phone. You need a night out.

She tells him about the turtle shit. She is standing in the bathroom doorway looking at it.

I'm coming over, says the man on the phone.

No, her son says. He is behind her. Tell that guy he better not show up.

I'll help you clean it up, says the man on the phone.

What? she says.

Sure, I don't mind.

Do you know what we're talking about here? she says. Have you been drinking?

He's been drinking, says her son. Tell him not to come.

I'm on my way, I'm in the car, he says. I've got all the supplies in the back.

Don't come. My son's in hysterics.

WHAT, her son screams.

We'll drive them to the turtle pond.

What turtle pond? she says.

WHAT TURTLE POND? her son says.

There's a turtle pond, hundreds of turtles. They line up on the logs like dots. Turtles that used to have owners like you. Owners who visit each spring, they bring binoculars. They ride out on the pond in canoes.

I don't have any canoe.

WE HATE CANOES, her son says.

We'll go in the spring. The turtles will walk through the grass. They'll dive bravely into the water.

They'll be the ones who get to set me free, she says.

Nominated by Kim Chinquee, Clancy Martin, Diane Williams, NOON

THE CAUL OF INSHALLAH

by MOHJA KAHF

from RIVER TEETH

My baby was born on the brink of death, with multisystem failures. One day in the eighth month, I felt him slip up in the womb, not reporting for his usual afternoon acrobatics. I reported this diminished activity, and we ended the day with an emergency C-section. Doctors were stymied by his condition—one in a million, they said, cause unknown—and nothing to do but monitor him in his little ICU crib, with all manner of wires attached, and hope his body kicked in.

Prayers poured in for him. He was prayed for by Sunni, Shia, Ahmediya, Sufi, Islamist, Salafi, Nation of Islam, and secular Muslims; by Orthodox, Reform, Reconstructionist, and secular Jews; by Catholics, Episcopalians, Lutherans, an entire congregation of Universalist-Unitarians whose minister visited me in the hospital, Mormons, Baptists, Methodists, Hindus, Buddhists, and Wiccans. Agnostic and ardently atheist friends offered good thoughts in lieu of prayers. A dark-haired, olive-skinned friend came in one morning and stood in a sort of asana and intoned over his crib. "Family only," the nurses cautioned, but let her stay when they took her for clergy (and she really was ordained—by Internet). They probably thought she was doing some sort of Islamic thing, with her arms upraised like that, but she was actually an Italian American from Long Island who believed in yoga and intoning, in conjunction with her very Christian belief in Jesus.

"God doesn't need *their* prayers," one of my orthodox Muslim visitors sniffed, dismissing the non-Muslims and heretics among them. But I and my family were not in the mood for turning away prayers—

458

from anyone. We had broken through to a place where all prayer came to One.

The neonatal doctor told me, in the early days when there was nothing really to be done about the baby's condition but stand bedside and make such conversation, that he'd read medical journal statistics saying that patients who were prayed over tended to fare better than those who didn't. Survive the baby did, thank God, rallying after seven weeks, in an unexpected recovery his doctors called "miraculous." This is not one of those "proof of the power of prayer" spiels, though. It's bad taste to talk about the ineffable so glibly. And for anyone who has prayed for the healing of a loved one who then dies, it is difficult not to hear, in those well-meant "power of prayer" talks, undertones of "You must not've prayed hard enough" or, worse, "You must not be among the deserving," as if God metes out survival from cancer or a hurricane as some sort of reward.

Yet I am going to talk about the Ineffable, breaking my own rule. When my daughter, then nine, asked me in those first uncertain days what was going to happen to her baby brother, I tented her under the sheet of my hospital bed and whispered, "He's going to be okay."

"Either he will get better and come home, or he will leave us. And both those things," I said, although here I had to take a moment, "both are good places for him. Both are sweetness and mercy for him. I mean"—I struggled to find a better way to say it for her—"Angels will hug him. Here or there. So no matter what happens, he will be *okay*. See?"

My daughter, wise child that she is, saw. Jacob, son of Isaac, also got it. When Jacob's older sons bring him news that his younger son, Joseph, has been killed by a wolf, the Quran says that he knows they are lying about what really happened—still, he knows his little Joseph is out there in some sort of terrible trouble. And there is nothing the father can do about it. "Beautiful is patience," Jacob says. He says it twice over the course of the story, that Yoda-like, grammatically inverted phrase: "Beautiful is patience." It isn't that he's a cold one; he weeps until, the Quran says, his eyes are blinded, from grieving the missing Joseph. Still his heart has assurance, in its bottom-scraping place. No matter where the boy may have gone, or how he may suffer, the father knows—knows because of some profound link he has with deeper levels of Reality—that the child will be okay. In the infinite womb of mercy that stretches beyond all possibility, nothing has been lost.

"Do not seek to be master in everything," Sophocles' Creon says in *Oedipus Rex*, "for the things you master do not follow you throughout your life." What does follow you throughout your life? Yusuf Islam, in his Cat Stevens days, called it a "moonshadow" in a song that says, if I ever lose anything precious, if I ever undergo extreme pain, an underlying resilience of heart stretches to encompass it. "Moonshadow" is a celebration of the absurdity of infinite mercy. It is a song for Kierkegaard's knight of faith, who knows that God's banquet is laid out, in the here and now. I later read somewhere that it was this surrendering type of prayer that was shown to be a factor in the well-being of patients and their families. Not prayer for a specific outcome.

My more traditionally religious visitor, who had overheard my exchange with my daughter, chided me. "How could you tell her he will be okay? Without even saying *inshallah*? You don't *know* that he will be okay!"

She missed it: my little girl and I at that moment were in the caul of inshallah, inside the womb of surrender. We were in "the thin," in Celtic terms, the moment of permeability between worlds, also called the miraculous. We were detached from all moorings but detachment. There was nothing *but* inshallah. Every breath we took under that gray-white sheet was inshallah. The visitor understood "okay" in a limited, rational, human-centered way, to mean "he will get better." She mistook it to mean a specific result. It's all right. She was not under the veil with us. She had not just experienced a childbirth, as I had, or been its witness. Though physically present, she was not in the liminal state where we were.

Surrender to all this luminous whatnot didn't mean we weren't trying to learn all that was wrong with the baby and why. I still sent friends to pull articles out of medical journal databases for me. It didn't mean I wasn't calling my doctor relatives long distance to go over what the baby's doctors were doing, asking them to tell us if we should second-guess treatment options. It didn't mean I did not scream "My baby!" in a horrific voice and lunge forward and the nurse have to hold me back when, during one of our Arkansas summer thunderstorms, the power went out and all his machines flickered—terror in my heart—before they went to emergency generator. It did mean I saw the baby's state unfolding in the hands of greater power than the doctors', however, and did not see humans or their machines as the ultimate causal agents whether the child's health succeeded or failed. And yes, this correlates to being less likely to pounce on a lawsuit as the answer if things did not go the way we wanted—which is not the same, at all, as passively accepting real malpractice. This is not the same as an embrace of irrationality or a turning away from science. Don't get that gleam in your eye, minions of Nietzsche. I didn't go all "Oriental fatalist" on you, and my ability to be an efficacious citizen of a modern democracy was not obliterated.

The afterglow of birth lasts only so long, and the heart moves from a state of grace to states as dull as Ohio. It's been four years, and the boy is a dizzying handful who needs time-out constantly, and we're back to things in their divisive, attached-to-outcomes, human meanings, the flat Midwest of the soul. The other day I flicked on a *Family Guy* episode, and Chris Griffin, the affably dim-witted teenaged son on this animated TV series, was playing with dead rats on puppet strings. How much time in a week do I spend doing that? Not playing with dead rat puppets literally, but meeting the human experience with my snarky, cynical face (I do snarky especially well).

Why am I so dim-witted most days, when there is also such beauty and joy in the things people do with each other, in the Oneness of being? I delight in the fact that my baby was prayed over by many different kinds of believers, was prayed for with joyful abandon, with sorrowful surrender, with purpose. Yes, here it comes, so get your rat puppets out if you are feeling snarky: *It was all good.*

I say this knowing the outcome was that the baby lived and has, thank God, flourished. If things had gone differently, if the insight had been gained at an even higher cost, it perhaps would be much harder to say this—but possible still and, in that case, called "letting go." It's still a letting go when the outcome is the one you want. We swam in the womb of sweetness and mercy for a small while, helplessly, and a moonshadow follows us ever since, to remind us that this state is always there, should we wish to seek the pathways to it.

Nominated by Rebecca McClanahan

461

UNDERSTANDING THE NEW GENUINE NEGRO HERO

by **THOMAS SAYERS ELLIS**

from THE KENYON REVIEW

For
never
gets a thing, ever.
Our range of high-worries, the low-joys,
every, flava-sealed

fracture, the folk
and uppity nuances of "being bla . . ."
not "happens to be . . , "

from the triflin'
to the bougie, the coon to the revolutionary,
the bama to the buppie.

A ghetto celeb might *kick it*
with a hood rat,
but a *for real for real* sistuhgirl

ain't likely to be seriously
stepped to
by Big Willie or a baller.

Without the Mountainbottom,
the Mountaintop
is just another government name.

I didn't Overcome.
This the same me I was before
skin's melanin whip,

coloring color the color
I want to color color, not the color
color colors me.

Mighty Whitey loves the cold,
so soon as I see a noose
somebody gettin' they aesthetic whooped.

Go'ne make that disrespectful paper.
More melon than water
is good
for you,
seeds too.

Nominated by David Baker, Janet Sylvester

INDOOR MUNICIPAL POOL

by ALAN SHAPIRO

from NEW OHIO REVIEW

The circulating disinfectants
make it an unearthly blue
or earth's blue seen from space,
or what pooled from the steaming
of the planet's first condensing.
In which case the pumps
and filters could be thermal
vents, and the tiny comet trail
of bubbles rising from the vents
could hold within it—if it isn't it
already—the first blind chance,
if not the promise of
the hint of the beginning
of what at long last would
emerge into the eye which
being mostly water sees
only water signaling to itself
beyond itself in accidental
wormy quiverings over
the sea floor of the ceiling.

Nominated by Dorianne Laux, Joseph Millar, New Ohio Review

FINAL DISPOSITIONS

fiction by LINDA McCULLOUGH MOORE

from THE SUN

My family is deciding what to do with me. I am the oldest sibling. Always have been. I thought the years might mute the effect of that, but nothing so far. I have been, and I remain, the reason why the siblings take each new birthday with some measure of aplomb: *Well, I'm still four, seven, fourteen years younger than her.* My age, their comfort.

They hold disposition meetings. I am not invited, but during the phone calls that follow each conclave I read the minutes of the meetings in the awkward silences and odd questions: "How do you feel about Texas?" "Do you mind the cold?" "Do you have any special friend who lives in a big house [pause] with a trained nurse?"

I don't mind this actually. I am quite pleased at their level of involvement. I think there were decades when they forgot I was alive, or, if they remembered, they forgot I was their sister—or sister-in-law, a friendlier affiliation by a mile.

"Invite me to the meetings," I say to my brother Paul. "I promise not to voice opinions or spill my drink anywhere it will show. I'd like to know just what sort of arrangement might be under consideration."

"No," he says.

I like his style. My brother Freddie would have said, *What meetings?* Paul got whatever integrity was floating in our gene pool.

"I might be able to help," I say, encouraged by his candor.

"I don't think so," Paul says.

❖ ❖ ❖

465

"Are you sure you've saved no money whatsoever?" This would be my sister Irene—I mean, Eileen—on the phone. I like it that I can never keep her name straight. It gives me hope.

"Zero money?" she says.

"Oh, no," I say. "I saved a bundle. It's. Just. That. I. Spent. It. All." Each word seems worthy of its own personal sentence.

"Tom is coming over Tuesday morning. Please write that down. I'll wait," Eileen says. She pauses. Tom is her husband.

I mime writing, "Toooosday, Doomsday," on the palm of my hand.

"Tom's taking you for a ride."

"I'll be ready," I say. "Don't tell me what time. I like to be surprised."

"Ten o'clock. Wear stockings, Margaret," she says. "Wear shoes."

"Okey-doke," I say. "Okey-dokey."

People think that *crazy* is achieved when one day the gale-force wind makes a final, violent tear, and your little craft slips its mooring. Oh, no. It is achieved by you, who, one knot at a time, untie the tethers, whimsically at first, and then with some—or sometimes no known—purpose. You write a shameless letter to a friend who has blown you off once and for all and say, with no shame, "Why don't you like me? Did you ever?" You offer up tidbits that will be the stuff of ridicule for certain, and you pass them out to members of your family on a tray like peculiar, worrisome hors d'oeuvres.

My brother-in-law Tom rings the doorbell. My siblings would have done the same. To walk right in would signify an affinity they neither feel nor seek.

"Would you like any sort of carbohydrate?" I ask. He is still standing on the porch. He never comes in unless it is a national holiday, and then it must be one celebrated across the board, not just by Jews or Christians or the tree people.

"I'm good," Tom says.

"I have no doubt," I say, "but are you hungry?"

"Oh . . ." The question catches him off guard. He clearly doesn't know the answer. It is most often decided for him by Eileen.

"Why did you marry her?" I say while he is still busy with the last question.

"Who?"

"Oh, yes," I say. "I had forgotten. You were married once before Eileen."

"I wasn't thinking about that," he says.

"No," I say. "I wasn't thinking of her either. You never talk about her."

"Well, we should be on our way."

"Maybe I could go live with her—your first wife. Let's see: I'd be the sister-in-law of her ex-husband," I say. "Stranger things happen every day. A lot of them to me."

"Do you want a coat?" Tom says.

"No," I say, "I've got a closetful of them. But thanks."

He gives me a frightened stare. The man would not know humor if it wore a name tag.

"Well," he says, clearly with no heart whatsoever for this project, "we should be on our way."

He is so dutiful it makes his skin sag.

"Why are you doing this, Tom? This is your life. You could be dead by nightfall. A lot of people will be, and you could be one of them, as easy as the next person. Let's forget about wherever Eileen wants you to take me. It will only be a waste of time. They won't admit me. It will turn out they only take retired Presbyterian clergy. Or Paul won't want to pay for it. Or they'll have a waiting list. Or at the last minute I'll kick the bucket. If this is the last day of your life, trust me when I tell you, you will want to have spent it some other way, no matter if you end up in hell or heaven."

"I don't believe in hell."

"Well, there you go."

It's the first nearly interesting thing I've heard him say since he met my sister.

"What was she like?" I say.

"Who?"

"Wife One. Eileen's predecessor."

"I don't remember," Tom says. "I've been married to Eileen for nearly thirty years."

"I'm sorry," I say. I am, too. I always thought he was born this way, never thinking what it might do to a person to be married to Eileen.

"Why did you marry her?" I say.

"Oh, I was young." He makes it sound a rather unusual thing to be. "And she was beautiful."

"Eileen?"

"Janet Moyer." His voice is just above a whisper. "Janet Helen Moyer. Look, we really need to go. Eileen has made an appointment for you."

467

My sister is forever making things for people: appointments and de-coupage; Rice Krispies treats and bright fabric snakes you're meant to keep your plastic-bag collection in.

I grab my pocketbook and slam the door behind me.

"You want to lock that?" Tom says.

"I do not," I say.

It takes me fourteen minutes to locate Janet Helen Moyer on Google. First I typed in "ex-wives." Four million, one hundred and six results. Then I tried her name, which reduced that number by about four million. Turns out she illustrates books for dyslexic children, using words as illustration. She calls them "word pictures."

It seems she draws words under the pseudonym Janelle Moy—not the most profligate use of the imagination, but I allow for the possibility that she makes the most of what she's got, a habit I refuse to despise. I send her off an e-mail through her website to say my six-year-old dyslexic son, Leroy, reads her illustrations with great pleasure, as does his auntie Eileen Ferguson (just in case Janelle Moy is a woman given to putting two and two together).

I've issued myself a poetic license: I do not have a son named Leroy, or any other name, but if I let my childlessness figure largely in every single e-mail I send off, I might as well downgrade to dial-up and be done with it.

A week later Janelle Moy (aka Wife One) sends an e-mail in return. She wishes me "every joy"—which strikes me as being a bit over the top, but I prefer it to a curse and let it be. At the bottom of the e-mail it says that she will soon be giving a reading at "a mall near you." That is to say, near me. I click on the bar that says, *Find a Mall near you*, hardly troubling to fret that Mall is capitalized, only to find the Mall (maul?) is even nearer than I thought.

I call Eileen to arrange a little rendezvous with her hubby's previous wife. Stir the pot a bit. The answering machine picks up. Eileen hasn't answered her phone since that little fiasco the day Tom and I resurrected Janet Moyer, when he took me to the perpetual-care place. How was I to know she'd paid 140 bucks for the evaluation? How was I to know she'd sent me there to take a test? A person should be told these things. Now she's terrified that no place will have me—as though I'd want to go anyplace where people are excluded on the basis of how strenuously they agree or disagree with statements like "I am not worried about the future."

I leave a message for Eileen. "There is an author reading from a book, *The Idiot's Guide to Nursing Homes*," I say. "Tuesday night at seven at the mall in Coudersport. Could you drive me? I could take the bus, but I didn't know if you wanted me appearing in public unchaperoned. Plus, if the bus crashed and I didn't get killed, but only severely maimed and injured, we'd be even worse off than we already are."

Eileen picks up just as I am finishing my final phrase.

"Hello?" she says.

"Hello," I say.

"Who is this?" she says.

"Who is *this*?" I say.

And we're off to the races.

Eileen drops me at the main entrance to the mall while she goes to park the car. I allow it. I really can't walk as well when I am with her.

There's an old man standing by the door with a collection can labeled in bright red FOR THE RETARDED, which I take as a sign he's working freelance; the organized prefer "developmentally disabled." I don't know, though. *Retarded* seems more hopeful in some way, as if it were nothing permanent or cast in stone, but more a matter of speed than anything else. Timing. "His progress is only retarded, slowed a bit, delayed, but coming—oh, yes, coming certainly. Just not today." *Retarded* gives a person something to look forward to.

"Well, I must say that was a good evening," Eileen says. When I told her I'd read the listing wrong, her sincere pleasure at my having made a mistake was enough to sweeten the whole night.

Eileen and I are shut back up inside the brand-new Japanese container that we will travel home in—or, if not, that will transport us to our long home. "Long home." I say the words out loud. They sound portentous as we drive off together into the black night. "Have you ever heard the phrase 'long home,' referring to death—or, I guess, to where death takes us to?"

"Don't talk about death," Eileen says. "It's morbid."

"Duh," I say, the word *duh* being one of the three innovations of the last half century that are really worth something, the other two being e-mail and all-day breakfast at fast-food restaurants. I don't go to fast-food restaurants, but I like knowing that, if I did, I could get a fried-egg sandwich in the middle of the afternoon.

"I don't know why you have to work death into every conversation," Eileen says. "Don't think I didn't hear you mention it to that woman tonight, the one with those oxygen tubes in her nose."

"The way she looked, it seemed to me it would have been impolite *not* to mention death. And don't say you didn't sense the general amazement that she was still alive when we went to get our coats. Trust me: death is on everybody's mind at least four times a day."

"Not mine," Eileen says. "I concentrate on happy things, like the nice books that lady was showing tonight. Her word pictures were beautiful."

I wonder would she be calling Janelle Moy, aka Janet Helen Moyer, a "lady" if she knew the author was the one woman in the universe she'd shared a husband with?

"What did you think of her?" I say.

"I thought that if she needed oxygen, perhaps she might be more comfortable at home than in a bookstore."

"I didn't mean her," I say. "I meant, what did you think of the author?"

"Someday you will appreciate what I am trying to do for you, Margaret."

"Don't hold your breath," I say. "Get it? It's an oxygen-tank joke. But what did you think of the author?"

"Why do you care?"

"Because she was Tom's wife."

Damn. I wasn't going to tell Eileen that—or, at least, not until we had invited Janet Helen Moyer to Thanksgiving. See, this is why I am no earthly good at card games. I cannot keep a secret for two minutes in a row.

"Tom who?"

She's asking for form's sake. She knows Tom who.

"Your Tom."

"But Tom's first wife's name was Janet; this woman was named Janelle."

"Uh, that's not exactly DNA evidence."

"You knew it was her. You brought me on purpose. You told me it was a book on nursing homes."

"Eileen, what person in their right mind would drive twenty-five miles on a school night to get the author to sign a book on nursing homes?"

"I'm gonna tell," Eileen says, and suddenly she is four, and I am eight, and neither one of us has even heard of Alzheimer's or hip replacements or long-term-care insurance. The only thing we know of human tragedy is what goes on inside our family.

"Who you gonna tell?" I say, but already I am warming to the prospect of our reporting all the crimes committed on the planet to the proper authorities. I want to take Eileen by her thin, clammy hand, her diamonds hurting both our fingers in the tightness of my grip. I want to pull her out of the car and drag her down the street for blocks, calling out to strangers on the way, *Police station! Where is the police station? Is that it?* and pull her with me through the heavy doors and grab the sleeve of the first policeman we see and say, *Come quick. I need you to arrest our parents. They are scaring us to death, and when we are old women, we will put each other into nursing homes and into unnatural situations in bookstores in shopping malls. Malls—places where people go so they won't have to think about death. Oh, never mind! Just come. You need to lock them up and throw away the key.*

"Remember," I say to Eileen, in a voice gone hoarse from all the yelling that I should have done a half century ago, "remember the night you started to take Freddie downtown to the police station, to show them the belt-buckle welts, the places where the tip end broke the skin?"

"Oh, Margaret. That was in another lifetime."

"No. No, it wasn't. It was this same lifetime. This one we're living in tonight. There is only just the one."

"Well," Eileen says, "I never got there. I met Grandma Chase at the corner, and I told her where I was taking him, and she told me to go back home and to never, ever tell another living soul, or God would punish me."

A different God from that one crawls into the back seat as we stop for the light.

"I was just trying to help," Eileen says. "I was trying to do the right thing with Freddie. I was just trying to save his life."

Tell her she did. It's God, in the back seat, talking.

"You tell her," I say to Him.

Nah. She's gotta hear it from you, He whispers in a raspy, smoker's voice.

"You did save Freddie's life," I say, glancing over my shoulder.

God clears His throat and makes a "Go on" motion with his hand.

"I mean, look at him," I say. "Look at Freddie's marriage. Look at

471

his kids. Look at their kids. He's had practically the best life I know."

"Yeah, well . . ."

"Yeah, well, why do you think that is?"

"Well . . ."

"Hello? Because of you."

I know she gets it. When a thing is true, you don't have to explain. I turn around to wink at God, but He's gone. Off to save some other sisters. It must take Him all night just to do one neighborhood.

"And I *am* just trying to help you," Eileen says.

"I know," I say. "And I was just trying to help you, taking you to meet old Janet Moyer tonight at the bookstore."

"No, you weren't," Eileen says as she pulls into my driveway, a little closer to the holly bushes than she might have liked.

"No, I wasn't," I say. I open the car door. "Did you forgive them?" I ask. "Our parents? For what they did?"

"Yup," Eileen says. "I did."

She gets out and walks around the car.

"And do you forgive me?" I say.

"Nope," she says, and she takes my hand and pulls just hard enough to make my standing up a thing that I can do, then lets me lean pretty hard on her arm. "Not in this or any other lifetime."

Eileen walks me to my door and leaves me there.

There's a priest in my kitchen. If I had to go to church to confess my sins, I'd spend my whole life in the car driving there and back and wouldn't need a nursing home or any other housing.

No matter that my priest is one I have concocted out of equal parts worn, shiny black cloth and blessed fathers born on the silver screen—he is just as unforgiving as the real thing. I have purged the fey Bing Crosby, long lines of priests in handcuffs on the evening news, fabled fathers that my Catholic friends have cursed after they have lost their faith or seriously misplaced it. My priest is no more efficacious than the fat man who waddles to the altar at Saint Michael's every morning, even government holidays.

Still, he is my confessor. There are agents in our lives we do not choose.

"Forgive me, Father, for I have sinned," I mumble as I open the freezer and take out a bag of frozen cherries. "It has been three hours since my last confession."

He's as silent as the night.

I wait him out.

"OK, OK," he says, "what did you do this time?"

I keep him on retainer for the reason that he has even less patience than I do.

"I took my sister to a bookstore for the express purpose of cutting her down to size—or, at the very least, of annoying the hell out of her."

"And did it work?"

"Nah. Hardly."

"So you are guilty of the sin of wasting time created by the Eternal One."

"That too."

"Are you sorry?"

"Sort of. I wish she had gotten really angry and thrown her purse at my head and forced me out of the car by the side of the road on a dark and stormy night, the avenue awash in burglars and other men in urgent need of immediate incarceration."

"*You can't always get what you want,*" he sings. He is a priest who, if he ever moved beyond the walls of my kitchen, would play guitar in church and have the Host be sourdough. "You want to be punished for your sins," he says. "There is no penance in the book for sins against the sister. And so there can be no forgiveness that way."

"Eileen just told me that tonight."

"And she's an atheist," he says, "a card-carrying member of the club that says that sin is only mental illness, mental flu, mental TB, mental appendicitis."

"But we know better."

"We know *worse*," he says. "Sin's the best hope we've got. If it's mental, all we've got is pills, and they stop working the day you stop taking them. Ah, but sin . . ." His voice softens. "Sin can be named and napalmed. You got to love a God who's up to that. Your problem is, you always want to save yourself."

It is a sermon that I've heard before. "So, what would you say to giving me a few Hail Marys here?" I say.

"All they do is keep you busy. They only sandblast sloth. What we need here is a Savior."

He turns his head, and for the first time I notice that his hair falls in gentle waves onto his shoulders.

"I always thought that you were bald," I say.

"I'm not," he says. "You never really look at me."

473

"I never really look at anyone. Could I offer you a cherry?" I hold out the bag.

"They're frozen," he says and grabs the bag of designer potato chips from the breadbox and sits down at the table to read the paper.

I don't know what the priest in your kitchen is like. Mine is a slave to carbohydrates.

I take my glasses off and place my face six inches from the mirror on the wall. My eyebrow is a composite of so many different sorts of strands. I am absorbed. Time stops for my eyebrow inspection, as time will if ever you are lost inside a moment. Time stops and waits, and then you look away, and time starts up again.

That's how I come to know there is eternity.

I awake to find I'm lying on the floor. And in this slim interval between bemusement and the stark desperation to come, the room has become all ceiling. It's wider than the floor, making the kitchen one of those odd shapes you study in geometry but rarely come across in real life. The underbelly of the antique carved desk my grandmother wrote her grocery-shopping list upon appears to be nothing more than a piece of Masonite. And exactly where have I pulled that midcentury word from? I take no small amount of comfort from its having come to me so easily. I do not think a person calls back the word *Masonite* if she has had a stroke.

I take it also as definitive proof I have not lost my mind. I give myself these periodic evaluations. A person likes to know just where she stands—or, in my case, lies. I will assume that I have not hurt my head. I find out some extent of the damage, though, when I try to drag myself, body and soul—one so thin, the other so heavy—across the kitchen floor. I left the telephone up on the counter when I immigrated to the floor, and now I find it is a one-way trip I've taken.

When I awaken again, the light has moved from the front porch to the back deck. Cold. I'm mostly cold. And I am sad and clutch the sadness like a ragged baby blanket I've uncovered in a bureau drawer. It's faded, aged by time and overuse, but it is there; that's the main thing. If I am sad, if sad is something I can still be, then it will be all right.

The next time I open my eyes, it is dark. But darkness happens, it occurs to me, once every day.

The fourth time I awaken, Eileen is beside me with a magazine. She's sitting in a chair. Her makeup isn't working for her. Any shade of orange will betray you in the end. The floor I'm lying on has gone all soft and white and warm, and I am loving lying here.

"I was sad," I tell Eileen. "I was cold, but I was sad."

"Oh, Margaret, you're awake. We were so worried. That tiny woman next door phoned us when she couldn't get you to answer the door. How do you feel?"

"Fine," I say. "Nice and warm." I don't say it, but the sadness is all gone. Now I will have to see just how I am to live with that.

"Life is so short these days."

The words are whispered by a voice I do not recognize out in the hallway, whispered by a person I don't know—although it would probably be good for me to spend some time with a person who says such things without a twisted curl, a single saffron thread, of irony.

Irony is mother's milk to me, but at the end of the day it doesn't make a twiggy twig of difference. It's not how you view your life that matters; it's what happens in it.

Right now what's happened in my life matters a great deal. I have a heart that let me down, as I have long suspected it might one day do. It actually stopped beating. Tell that to the lady in customer service when you go to get my money back.

And when that happens to your heart and you live to tell the story, people demand it be a good one. Even strangers in blue-spotted nightgowns sliding down the hallway, holding on for dear life to some rolling pole, transparent plastic bags in full sway, asses veiled from public view by loosely knotted ties—even they arrest their snail creep, stop the rolling poles, and say in voices manufactured down intubated airways, "What was it like?"

I tell them what they want to hear, once they have told me precisely what that is. They are not shy in their requests. Then it's just a matter of a spattering of *yes*es and the odd *no* and a great deal of shaking of the head.

"Did you see a great white light?" they ask.

"Why, yes, I did."

"And was it the brightest thing you ever saw or hope to see?"

"It was," I say.

"Were you amazed?"

"I still am."

"Is there hell, then?" A former Christian missionary, who has come to write her final chapter as a nurse, asks me this while standing just outside my door at the trash chute to the incinerator.

"Oh, yes," I say.

"I thought so." She upends a schoolroom metal trash basket, sending something that sounds like a bowling ball with spikes on it crashing down the chute. "I thought so," she says. "But you never know."

"No," I say, "you never do."

Actually, though, I do know. I have seen what does await us. The whole thing. There is good reason that we are not told. There is good reason why we cannot tell what we have seen and why the white light is so popular in stories resurrected people tell. White, the color of no story. Blinding light, the opposite of truth.

Everybody asks what it is like, everybody but Eileen. Her, I would tell.

My new home is a kennel. No matter that every dog in the whole place is registered and has had all its shots. I call it the "kennel club." It drives Eileen nuts.

"They give us dog food for lunch," I tell her. "In dog dishes. With dog silverware."

"Oh, Margaret, stop it. They've got paella on the menu for tonight."

"Don't let them fool you. That's code for mussel shells in red-food-coloring broth. Woof, woof," I bark.

Eileen sets about tidying up the room, which she keeps tidied up to within an inch of its life.

"Eileen," I say, "sit down. Stop fidgeting. Take a pill. Read a book. I have a copy of *Great Dog Expectations* I got from the pound library."

She doesn't take the bait. She knows me well enough to realize that in another fifteen seconds I will be so sick of dog jokes, I will never bark again.

"It is awful," I tell her. "Here," I say, in case there's any question where *awful* is.

I've not felt sad one moment since they brought me here the day I left the hospital.

Eileen comes to visit dutifully—far more often than I'd visit her, I'm pretty sure.

• • •

476

I have a dream, and in the dream I am in kindergarten, and Eileen is my grandfather. And every day she walks me to school and sits outside the schoolhouse on an old, backless wooden bench until school is over, and then she walks me home. I wake up feeling as safe as that. But sad is what I want to feel, not safe. Safe means there's harm and danger out there, just the other side of that thin windowpane. But sad—sad means there is love to be missed, or had and lost and maybe had again, or at least to be longed for, missed and reminisced about and carried in you in a place where safe has never been. Sad is the deep of feeling. Sad tells a person that good is.

And here I am, arrived at the asylum: I, who always thought that safe was everything. And only now the telegram bearing this under-standing has been forwarded to this address, carried by the last deliv-eryman on earth on the day before the world ends.

Eileen wants me to sign a power of attorney: a sheaf of papers that declare she can forge my signature on anything she wants and never spend a single night in jail.

"No," I say. That's the long answer. The short answer is the silent one. The short answer is I lift my fake-palsied hands, gone clawlike in pantomime, let one side of my mouth droop, and stare.

"It isn't funny," Eileen says.

"Are you enjoying this?" I say.

She scowls.

"I'm serious," I say. "I honestly hope that you are getting something from the roles we have been cast in here. You are well and strong and truly married, and I am enfeebled in this frightful way, and I just hope you feel the muscles of that victory. Living well, that best revenge."

"I'm not looking for revenge," she says. Her shoulders slump, and I would write a check with lots of zeros on it if she could be all spit and vinegar again; the little bony girl, all fire and spine, who told our brother Paul that he could fly if he jumped off the armoire, who said ice cream would come from the light socket if you wet your finger and stuck it in the hole; that girl I begged our father to beat one Sunday afternoon for her nefarious infractions, and when finally, near night-fall, he did, I wished her strong enough to turn on him and slay him. We had a King James childhood, with verbs that could rear up on their hind legs and scare tall men. I want Eileen to be as powerful as she seemed then. As mean.

"You do want revenge," I say.

"No, Margaret, I don't," she says. "I'm too tired for revenge. *You* want revenge."

"No, I don't," I say, telling us both a thing we didn't know. "Do you think that we will ever be friends?" I say. "You and me?"

"We're sisters," Eileen says.

We could be friends—if you would change every single thing about you, I don't say to her; she doesn't say to me.

We sit pretending it were possible, if only the wanting were there, when we both know that we will not be friends until we find ourselves on the Last Day, discovered and forgiven.

I'm pretending I am dead. It makes for a change. There are few amusements left to me. I've tired of magazines. I lie, not breathing, on the bed, mouth gaping, eyes staring. Until I blink. It's probably just as well I never took up acting.

The matron enters on her clicky shoes. I call her "the matron" in my mind, as if she were some housemistress shrew whom Dickens dissed—or would have if he'd thought of it.

"And how are we this morning?" the dragon lady says.

I don't answer. I'm pretending she is dead.

"Cat's got our tongue?"

I see this boiled tongue we were just about to slice and serve with serious mustard and a sturdy stein of Old Peculier beer, then see it being pounced on by an enormous tabby who, fierce, fat feline though she be, can do little more than gnaw one corner.

"Eeeewww," I say involuntarily.

"Do we have a problem?"

"Any number, I should think," I say. *I'm old and you're mean, for starters*, I don't say. I'm a big fan of letting the obvious speak for itself.

"Well, we will take care of you."

A threat, if I ever heard one.

Eileen pokes her head around the door frame. Have I ever been so glad of her appearance?

"May I come in?" Eileen says.

"No," the matron says, more brusquely than even she might have chosen. "No, I'll come out. If you don't mind, I'd like to have a word with you. We don't mind, do we?" she says to me.

I lie back, pretend to be dead. No one appears to notice or care.

"We will be moving her today." The matron's voice carries in from the corridor, as she must surely have known it would. Her voice is noisy, like her shoes. She must have been an irritating child.

"Moving?" Eileen says.

"Yes, dear, it's time. We must accept these things."

Who's this "we," white man? as Tonto said to the Lone Ranger when the Comanches appeared.

"Moving where?" Eileen's staying focused here. I like that.

"Upstairs, dear. To the Sunshine Unit."

Good grief, we're back to second grade, when everybody knew that "Bluebirds" was a euphemism for the kids who'd probably never learn to read. Sunshine Unit. Even the name is scary.

"But my understanding is that the upper floors are for people with bigger problems?" Eileen can sling euphemisms with the best of them. "Margaret's mind is as clear as it ever was."

"Dear, she's incontinent."

Shit! I didn't want Eileen to know. I did not want Eileen to know. I so wanted her not to know.

"A secretary I work with is incontinent." Eileen's voice is matter-of-fact. I had forgotten she looks at life with a less impassioned eye than her incontinent sister.

No matter. I hate to have her know, to have her thinking of that every time she looks at me. *She pees herself*, our mother would have said, whispering derision.

"Dear, we have to accept that there will be more changes."

"My name is Mrs. Ferguson," Eileen says.

You go, girl!

"Well, Mrs. Ferguson, dear, we need to accept little changes along the way."

Little changes. They're shipping me to hell.

"She's fine right here," Eileen says.

"And she will be fine upstairs, dear."

"Well, she won't be going upstairs," Eileen says.

"Dear, you have no choice."

"Actually," Eileen says, "I do. We have decided that my sister will be leaving Pine Brook."

"And where will you put her, dear?"

"We will not 'put her' anywhere. She will be coming home to live with me. We have been planning this for quite some time."

Hallelujah! I feel a sweet and certain sadness start at the bottom of

479

my toes and fill up all of me. Sadness everywhere. The sadness I have sought in every hiding place.

"Well, I think you will be surprised to learn just how difficult your sister can be."

"I will not be surprised at all. It's a thing I knew about before you were born."

Cue the angels. Blow the pitch pipe.

Eileen appears around the corner. She's one determined Girl Scout. "Let's pack your things, Margaret. We're getting out of here."

"Whatever you say, Sparky."

Eileen carries a small overnight bag filled with what I need tonight. "We'll be back for the rest of her things later," she tells the matron, who is standing at the front door, trying to look as though her life had meaning.

Eileen takes me by the hand and drags me past the woman, and there is no grandmother on the planet earth who will stop her this afternoon, no force in hell or heaven that would dare try.

"Well, good luck, dear," the matron says as we pass by.

"My name is Mrs. Ferguson," Eileen says, icy, stern.

"So, should I call you that too?" I say and squeeze her hand as she all but drags me across the parking lot.

When Eileen's grandson was very young, I took him to the movies, and the only movie not sold out that afternoon was *The Madness of King George*. Driving home that day, I asked the little boy if he had understood the movie. "Sure," he said. "The people said, 'God save the king,' and at the end of the movie, God did."

"Mrs. Ferguson," I say as Eileen climbs into the driver's seat and buckles in, "I like the way this ends. I like what this ending does to the whole story."

"Don't call me 'Mrs. Ferguson.'"

Eileen puts her foot down, and the car jerks forward. The whole way home she pumps the gas pedal up and down. It's how she drives; it's how she's always driven. But tonight I think she'll get us where we need to go.

Nominated by The Sun

FREEDOM OF SPEECH

by LUCIE BROCK-BROIDO

from PARNASSUS: POETRY IN REVIEW

for Liam Rector

If my own voice falters, tell them hubris was my way of adoring you.
The harrow of the hulk of you, so feverish in life, cut open,

Reveals ten thousand rags of music in your thoracic cavity.
The hands are received bagged and examination reveals no injury.

Winter then, the body is cold to the touch, unplunderable,
        Kept in its drawer of old world harrowing.

Teeth in fair repair. Will you be buried where; nowhere.

Your mouth a globe of gauze and glossolalia.
And opening, most delft of blue,
                Your heart was a mess—

A mob of hoofprints where the skittish colts first learned to stand,
Catching on to their agility, a shock of freedom, wild-maned.

The eyes have hazel irides and the conjunctivae are pale,

With hemorrhaging. One lung, smaller, congested with blue smoke.
The other, filled with a swarm of massive tenderness.

                I adore you more. I know
The wingspan of your voice, whole gorgeous flock of harriers,

Cannot be taken down. You would like it now, this snow, this hour.
        Your visitation here tonight not altogether unexpected.

The night-laborers, immigrants all, assemble here, trying
              To speak, looking for work.

Nominated by Diann Blakely

HOW WE THOUGHT
ABOUT TOYS
by NANCY EIMERS

from ZONE 3

—In 1943 Joseph Cornell spent eight months working at a defense plant, testing radio parts.

"This is no shooting gallery for children."
Deborah Soloman, on Cornell's 1943 "Habitat for a Shooting Gallery" box

Somehow out of a factory came these birds.
Out of a nobody in a radio factory
parrot, macaws, a cockatoo. Birds with numbers

on their breasts or tails. Birds in a shooting gallery
and their numbers are up.
78. 23. 43. 12.

One bird must know. The parrot is ducking,
the one behind the bullet-hole in the glass.
White bird with a splotch of red on its head.

55 cents an hour, radio parts, bits of distance and boredom
passed along, or not, if flawed.
Who knows what Cornell thought about

desire. Hands across the table were mostly women's.

✿

*Many items are manufactured to serve as toys, but items produced
for other purposes can also be used as toys. A child may pick up a
household item and 'fly' it around pretending that it is an airplane, or
an animal might play with a pinecone by batting at it, biting it, chas-
ing it, and throwing it up in the air. Some toys are produced primar-
ily as collector's items and are not intended to be played with.*

✿

To see into Cornell's *"Roses des vents"* box you must peer through
the glass of twenty-one compass dials or pry them up—pre-museum
days he would sometimes permit a guest to touch—and look through
the holes at the objects underneath: clay marbles, pushpins, spirals,
straw or string, a map of Florida, cut-out of the quarter-moon, beetle,
sequins, et cetera of all I cannot see in the color plate in my book,
and others, and so forth, and so on, all the "list of illustrations" leaves
to oblivion, all that might have been mentioned, et cetera of arrange-
ment, imagination can't help intuiting the hands, arranging for the
last time the sundries, ephemera, some long-ago muscle memory ac-
tually touching the curve of moon . . . .

✿

Gold foil, monarch wing, vermillion shell,
cutout sphinx head, paper spirals intertwined,
could such things, silver twigs, glitter, cork balls,

German maps of the Coral Sea, have begun
to seem self-enclosed? A critic had said
I remembered that there is a war and after that,

*try as I might, I just couldn't find my way back
into Mr. Cornell's world.* White parrot, red splotch
on its head, other splotches, yellow and blue

on a white interior. *How mental it all was*
he wrote to Miss Marianne Moore of a private zoo
he glimpsed each morning and night from the bus,

described its animals and birds and *a profound feeling
of consolation* but not a word about women or the war.
No word of the luckless

parrot, or if red
were the only color
that could wake it up,

no word, the room hot and his shirt wet under the arms,
those women's hands with their nerves and tendons, the 27 bones,
no word of mute temptation or the pleas

from what is merely fragment, shatter, blood.

✿

*The origin of toys is prehistoric; dolls representing infants, animals,
and soldiers, as well as representatives of tools used by adults,
are readily found at archaeological sites.*

✿

His letters to women can seem coy, a pose, like a photograph
I saw in *A Pictorial History of Radio,*
the inventor, Dr. DeForest, turning pensively in his fingers

the first three-element electron tube,
not yet "the soul of modern radio," just a clever toy.
No one knew what to do with it yet.

✿

He used to ride his bicycle to the beach—I imagine bicycle clips, I
imagine somber trousers and shirt buttoned to the neck, but the
world slips in, lawn mowers, dogs barking, the sun, the blazing sun,
though otherwise I tend to think of him as a man indoors, in base-
ment-light, kitchen-light, factory-light, or on the streets of New York
in the silvery light of engravings. He collected dried grasses, pieces
of glass, strands of Goldenrod, calling these *examples*, just one of a
number of things that together might accrue in some kind of crazy,
seamed (lines and juxtapositions of collage are essential), and barely-
held-together . . . whole? Not whole.

❖

Bright lips, repetitive motions, hands and sleeves.
A woman ahead of him in the time-card line,
gifts of nothing said each day, each night

the secret lists of her clothes in his diary.
Music at lunch, "the blatant frenzy of jitterbug."
Hands and sleeves, the hands at work

acquiring muscle memory, a kind of secret—arcane—cryptic—life—
~~so hard to get the diction right.~~
I crossed that out, I can't say why. I can.

Some old-world delicacy under glass—

❖

Diction? Hard? What is it with these puns
and hackneyed phallic symbols, spirals and balls,
inventor caressing a tube in his hands,

map of Florida, for heaven's sake, a cockatoo.
Are they mistakes? Or do I now add rockets,
staffs, torpedoes, towers, a snub-nosed warplane

I found in a vintage ad for sale on eBay,
put out by two merged companies that boasted
"A refrigerator and an automobile

GO TO WAR!
Not by ones or twos, but in fleets,
these ocean-jumping Vought-Sikorskys

will be sailing from Nash-Kelvinator assembly lines . . . ."?
Quote Oppenheimer quoting
from the *Bhagavad Gita*

as he watched the rising mushroom cloud?
Shall I?—Nevada, 1945, July 16—
I am become Death, the shatterer of worlds.

*

Who cares if there are phallic symbols in his work?

His "Penny Arcade Portrait of Lauren Bacall"—
she with her downward glance
inside of which a small red wooden ball passes

down a series of concealed glass runways
as if thus he might never have to get to the end of all this
indirection—

the boxes about women are jejune—
they hurt no one, no one, only him—
blue glass—gilt brambles—glass cubes—swan feathers

inhabiting a contraption of inner space—

*

There are sex toys, sex furniture, sex slings, toys sold
in vending machines. Adult toys. Marital aids. Unmarital
aids. Flesh-like materials. Toy boys. Inflatable dolls with orificial
  mouths.

Glass sex toys. Dildos capable of withstanding extreme temperatures.
Some, with swirls inside, or all blue glass or red,
or knobbed or pebbled beautifully,

are works of art. There's Mr. Blue.
The Studded Wand. The Indigo Intruder.
Then there are Lotus, Ivy, Proteus, Andromeda.

(O daughter of Cassiopeia and Perseus
rescued by—no—from a sea monster.)
String he would, years later, send to a girl, by which he had measured

his penis.
Where are the marbles, constellations, pearl beads, loose red and
  yellow sands?
I turn, lost items, to the asterisk

❋

it belongs
in company with all the other toys
left out or left behind

snowflake   ellipsis   candy sprinkle   little star
the tear-spoked asterisk
the Japanese rice star

the sixteen-pointed asterisk
the heavy asterisk
and loneliest of all

the heavy-teardrop-spoked pinwheel asterisk
❋

Meanwhile, the parrot is seated—perched—the parrot hunches—
stillness impaired by imaginary velocity, a permanent swerve—on an
object not listed in the "List of Illustrations." It is a twisted rose of a
cork, or it is a piece of driftwood, I can't be sure, but could driftwood
possess so many inward tunnelings—that which causes buoyancy in a
cork? Whatsoever it is, that thing is the opposite of a sundial, upon
which a bird might deposit its droppings, or safely land, or buzz, or
startle us with its veering wing, a shadow sun made mortal. What
would Keats say, whose bird was "immortal," "not meant for death,"
whose bird was metaphorical, but real, it was real . . . .
❋

*Aircraft factories near the coasts were considered prime targets for
enemy air raids; these plants were often covered with elaborate cam-
ouflage scenes intended to simulate nearby suburbs. In some cases the
camouflage was painted on, but these buildings at Lockheed's Bur-
bank plant and Douglas Aircraft's Santa Monica factory have canvas-
and-wood 'houses' erected on their roofs. Fabric strips were woven
into fake trees, shrubs, and even flower gardens, all for the benefit of
enemy aviators.*

> —online caption of two photos supplied courtesy of
> McDonnell Douglas Corporation and Lockheed
> Corporation, one photo showing a woman in a
> bathing suit clipping the "shrubs."

＊

What would you think of this, Miss Moore,
who recommended your friend Elizabeth Bishop revise
"rooster" to "cock"

as a word the more formal and elegant?
He was so polite in his letters.
What would you think of these other

Joseph Cornells? Who knows what they all thought about,
radios or beauty or the war or some woman's hands
or his cock—

do we need to know? Could we simply watch—
not just some lonely wanker, could we watch all of him
from outside a window, if there were a window—

O targets in a shooting gallery—
O dried grasses, clump of newspaper, cut-outs of birds
placed under shattered glass—

I think there was no window—

＊

The language of any war in the world is killing. I mean the language
of war is victims. I don't like to kill people. I feel sorry they been
killed—kids in 9/11. What will I do? This is the language."
                    —statement by Khalid Shaikh Mohammed at the
                    Combatant Status Review Tribunal hearings at
                    Guantanamo, March 2007

＊

You can see what look like rows of houses
in aerial photographs of the rooftops
of the bomber aircraft factories of Lockheed and Douglas

but they are toys. Each dollhouse has its life-sized
emptiness. Well, no, not really, no. For there are silver crafts inside.
And between the houses there are regular intervals

489

as any child building a dollhouse town
would by instinct or a simple mimicry allow.
Lawns and shrubs, an almost-loving

attention to detail, so if clouds did not intervene
an enemy bomber pilot, looking down, could imagine
all he couldn't exactly see. Lawn chairs,

barbeques. Bicycles. The war toys.
Courtland mechanical military gun car,
Sky Raiders game, tank bank,

tin fighter plane, a general purpose ammo carrying bag,
the German Tippco Wind-up Tin Toy Bomber Airplane Bomb.
Or maybe he just saw the passed-by look of a sad little town,

maybe he looked down as a homesick child.
Joseph Cornell,
just this once you were not making a toy.

Nominated by Susan Hahn, David Wojahn

MOT

by SARAH EINSTEIN

from NINTH LETTER

The KOA campground in Amarillo sits in a surprisingly seedy neighborhood, more urban than I had expected. A very middle-class couple with impossibly wide smiles advertises an adult video and novelty store from a billboard just before the final turn-off to the campground. Cattle graze in a pasture along the road. An unsettling mixture of the bucolic and the pornographic. Rusted trucks sit in the driveways of rusted mobile homes.

I am here to visit Mot, a new and unlikely friend who wanders from place to place, dragging a coterie of dead relatives, celebrities, Polish folktale villains, and Old Testament gods along with him in his head. He left our home in Morgantown, West Virginia a month ago, heading for Amarillo, because cars, he said, can be had more cheaply out West, and he needed a car. But more than that, although he didn't say it, he needed to move on. By his own report, he hasn't stayed in any one place for longer than three months in more than thirty years. Friends have sometimes lasted a place or two, never many, but while they are around his voices are quieter, more easily managed. Having someone real to talk with keeps him grounded, he says, and humor helps.

Our friendship is an experiment for both of us; we are trying to see if it can fend off our individual demons. His the literal sort, mine the metaphorical. Mot is dubious. "There are a lot of bad characters over here," he tells me on the phone, "And most of them don't want you around."

I originally planned to pitch my tent where he was camping. Because he had called it camping, I envisioned some uninhabited wilderness just beyond the sprawl of Amarillo. I was wrong. Mot slept behind an abandoned industrial building on a busy thoroughfare. He had few belongings: extra clothes in a small backpack, an old digital camera I'd given him, a few tools, a wooden-handled knife from Dollar Tree. Each morning, he wrapped these things in a tattered black-and-red woolen blanket he'd found in Romania. Hiding the bundle carefully under a pile of rusted scrap metal near the building, he biked into town to spend the day at the library, at Wal-Mart, or scouting around for a car to buy. In the evening, he retrieved the bundle, stashing the bike in its place. He slept on top of the old blanket, a pillow made of his extra clothes.

He'd told me all this during a rare call from the pay phone at the public library, and I immediately scoured the web to find someplace more acceptable to stay during my visit. The small one-room cabins and large communal bathrooms of the KOA seemed a workable compromise. I am comfortable with the idea of being bunkmates but not roommates. Neither Mot nor my husband would mistake bunk beds and communal bathrooms as romantic.

A few days before I left for Amarillo, Mot bought a complete wreck of a car for $400 from a kid working at an ice cream store. He broke camp behind the abandoned building and began staying overnight in the parking lots of the four Amarillo Wal-Marts. He sent me an email with a picture of his ancient sedan, gray except for one bright blue door and a bent frame that suggested a tragic past.

I pull into the KOA at noon, having promised to arrive by four. I'm a little surprised Mot isn't here. He and I share a social awkwardness; we are both always early to everything. But I am four hours early, so I'm not worried. I gather fresh clothes and head to the showers to wash away the road. I'm charmed, listening to a young mother as she tries to wrangle her toddling son through the rigors of washing his hair. I have stumbled into an oasis of civility. I had expected the campground to be full of half-drunk bikers and bedraggled women yelling at their children. I'm relieved to have been wrong, but also concerned; Mot will most certainly stand out among these vacationing families and senior citizen sunbirds. I do not want anyone to hurt his feelings, and I begin to fear these vacationing Middle Americans might. Folks stop and talk to one another, sharing vacation plans, asking about nearby attractions. I hadn't counted on that. I'm not sure how they will take his just-to-the-left-of-things answers.

The cabin is a medium-sized room with a double bed on one wall, bunk beds on the other, and three shelves. It will be closer for the two of us than I'd imagined. I am won over by the porch, which is wide and sturdy and has a swing. It looks out over a parking lot, some tent sites, and then a stockyard; it is not a lovely view. But the wind in Amarillo amazes me. It gusts with such strength that I spend a few minutes sitting on the swing, catching the breeze in my shawl and letting it pull me back, then releasing it and swinging forward again.

The afternoon sludges by, viscous and sticky inside the cabin. I'm not good at waiting—it invites worry, which I do too well. When there is no sign of Mot at four-thirty, I begin to wonder if he's all right. Finally, at a quarter till six, I cannot sit in the cabin any longer. I ask the guy behind the counter for directions to the nearest Wal-Mart, and he draws a very crude map on a napkin. I know it's a long shot. Mot has told me there are four Wal-Marts in Amarillo, and I am not certain I can find even this one with the directions I've been given. I have no idea what time he usually settles in, or if he's even still in town. I tell myself I'm not going to find him; I am going to pick up a paper and maybe grab some dinner. It sounds less ridiculous.

Only, in the end, it's not ridiculous at all. I see the old gray sedan with the tragic bent look as soon as I swing into the parking lot. I pull up several feet away and get out of my car cautiously. The very top of a man's head is visible in the driver's side window, but I can't be sure it's Mot. I'm afraid he may have abandoned the car, or given it away, and am worried about what sort of person I might startle if he has. The man in the car is slumped over something I can't see. I slam my car door loudly, but the person doesn't move. I call Mot's name, a question in it, and get no response. Left with no other choice, I walk over to the car and lean in the open window on the passenger's side.

There is Mot, pissing into an old soda bottle. He doesn't acknowledge me, and I pull my head out of the car and wait for him to finish. He looks terrible, his hair wild and his face streaked with axle grease and mud. His clothes are filthy and his shirt misbuttoned. He rarely looks his sixty-six years; today he looks that and then some. A pint of Scotch sits open on the seat beside him. When he finishes, he puts the lid on the soda bottle but does not zip his pants. He stares carefully out the windshield, unmoving, and I can't tell if he isn't aware of me or if he is ignoring me.

I have no idea what to do. I have the sick feeling that whatever I do will be the wrong thing, and if it is wrong enough I may send him screaming from the few comforts he's accumulated since he arrived here: the car, the tools to work on it, an extra few sets of clothes. But I must do something.

This is part of why I am here. I am in search of the imperative. Ambiguity erased by urgency. It's a crystalline moment, one in which I know that the only truly unforgivable response would be to fail to act. Instinct, rather than reason or experience, must guide me.

I walk around to the driver's side of the car and open the door. Mot turns his head toward me, looking more over my shoulder than at me, but he doesn't speak. "Hey you," I prod quietly, "aren't you even going to say hello?" He sits for a moment more and finally says, "No, I mean, Sarah never showed up so I figure that's that."

"What do you mean, I never showed up? I'm right here. I have been waiting for you at the campground since noon." I don't know what to say once I realize he doesn't think I'm real. "I said I would be here on Monday by four o'clock and I was. You just never came to the camp."

At the word Monday, Mot snaps his head around and finally looks at me, anger animating his face. "Yes, but you see, this is Tuesday. I went to the campground on Monday and Sarah was not there." He spits the words at me and cackles. He thinks he has outsmarted whichever of his tormentors has conjured this hallucination of me into being.

"It's not Tuesday," I say firmly. "It's Monday, and I am here exactly like I said I would be." Out of the corner of my eye, I notice a police car swing into an empty space a few yards away, watching.

Mot reaches under the passenger seat and pulls out a greasy newspaper. "No, it is not. Today is Tuesday. See, I have today's paper right here." He smacks the front page soundly with his paralyzed hand and then waves it in front of me, triumphant. I peer in, finding the date on the masthead.

"No, look, right here. It says today is Monday." I point. He looks. He looks again. Suddenly, his features seem to right themselves. He runs his hand through his hair, taming it, and then drops the paper onto his lap, hiding what he suddenly realizes is exposed. "Oh," he says, as if seeing me for the first time, "it's you!"

I move away from the car to give him time to get himself together. I turn my back a few minutes, standing between the sedan and the gaze of the policeman, and then Mot is beside me, his arms outstretched. We hug. He pokes me a few times and sniffs the air near my ear as if to make absolutely certain I am real. "Well, then, let's go to the KOA," he says merrily.

The policeman talks into his radio, his eyes meeting mine as Mot and I finish our hellos, our hugs, and our sheepish apologies. Thinking it would be best to get out of here before the cop notices the open Scotch bottle on Mot's front seat, I agree.

We pull up in front of Kabin 1. "I gotta shower," Mot says the minute we are parked, and gathers the things he needs from the trunk of his car. For half an hour I wait on the swing, rocking back and forth, trying not to decide I have to go home. In the parking lot, I saw more of Mot's illness than I had known was there, and it scares me. I think about his warning. *There are a lot of bad characters over here, and most of them don't want you around.* The reasonable thing would be to offer him the use of the cabin for the time it is already rented, and then simply drive away. But although I can't articulate why I'm here, I am sure it is not to insist that everything be reasonable.

He finally reappears, smiling broadly as if things have gone perfectly so far, and my fear vanishes. He looks younger again, his graying hair neat and just growing out of the military cut he had when he left Morgantown a month ago. His skin is wrinkled and tanned. Freshly washed, and in clean clothes, he looks more like a man with a passion for sailing than one who has been living out of doors for over thirty years. And although a close look will show his left hand is curled into itself, that he drags his left leg a tiny bit, he doesn't look frail, or old, or crazy. He is, in fact, a little handsome.

We talk about not being hungry and decide against wandering off in search of dinner. Instead, we swing. I tell him about the drive, and he reminisces about his own trips down old Route 66. He retrieves the remaining Scotch from the front seat of his car and I buy a six-pack of beer from the camp store.

We sit outside for a long time, catching up. Night never seems to fall in Amarillo; dusk stretches on well into what I would have expected to be darkness. A little into the beer, we start reciting poetry for one another. I pull up things memorized during childhood elocution lessons, mostly Emily Dickinson and a little Shakespeare, though not the best of either. Mot's repertoire is more varied. There is Wordsworth, Coleridge, and the inevitable Kipling. We struggle together through "Prufrock," only meeting up as the mermaids are singing each to each. Then Mot begins to recite from a slew of poets I

495

don't know; men who wrote verse about sailing, cattle drives, saloons, and frontiers. He finishes with Robert Service's "Dangerous Dan Mc-Grew"—a poem I would scoff at except it leaves him damp-eyed and melancholy. Mot's voice, always strong and clear, takes on a brogue that isn't his while he recites, and there is something anachronistic in the whole thing; he isn't old enough to have lived through the world of these poems, but he seems to remember it.

Once we have downed the Scotch and most of the beer, I screw up my courage and ask him what happened to make him lose a day. Asking about the goings-on in Mot's peculiar universe is always risky—speaking of the Big Guys Upstairs can sometimes summon them.

"I don't know. They can just do that. Drop me down into a dark hole so that I can't see or hear anything, and then when I wake up I'm confused and don't know what day it is or anything." His tone says this should be obvious, and I've asked a silly question.

I'm always a little startled by how matter-of-fact he is about his delusions; how he forgets I don't have a direct line into what's going on. "Who dropped you into a hole?"

"It was probably Moloch, but I don't know. Coulda been the girls. The Harpies were all excited that you were on your way. They figure they can use you to finally turn me into a girl, because I like you, and we want to be like the people we find likable, right?" He laughs. "I mean, I don't want to be a girl, but there you have it. They think it's a done deal up here." He motions upwards with his thumb.

The daedal hand of delusion paints everything that happens to Mot on an epic scale. Over the months of our friendship, I have learned enough about the characters to follow his stories; like reading *The Brother's Karamozov*, most of the trick is keeping the names straight.

"I tried to talk Kaiser Bill or Moloch into helping me out, because they don't want to be girls either, and if I'm a girl, then they'll have to be girls, too. But they said nope. Said if I'm going to be a stupid Pollack, a Jew lover, I'll just have to be a girl, then. I told you, they don't like Jews, so they don't think I should have anything to do with you." He shrugs and smiles at me. "I guess there is no hope. It's a done deal."

I don't know what to say, so I open the last two beers. Music from a nearby cabin floats by as the wind changes direction, and suddenly Mot is singing to me. Old songs, Cowboy songs, country songs, even church songs. He sings until the beer bottles are empty. I'm afraid someone might come out and complain about the noise, but his voice is good and no one does.

Once Mot and I are comfortable with each other again, we fall back into our Morgantown pattern of non-stop chatter and long drives to no place in particular. Easy conversation and a love of empty hours are part of what binds us together. He is the first friend I've had in years with the time to talk to no purpose or take a drive without a destination. We are, in our time together, aimless and free.

Mot and I had only the slimmest chance of becoming friends. We met as I was finishing up my months as the director of a drop-in center for adults with mental illness, although most of the forty or so people I saw during a day were homeless junkies coming in to sleep on the couches or use the phone to make a drug connection. Mot avoided such places, but he was already breaking with habit in staying at the local homeless shelter.

If we hadn't been the only place in town that gave out free coffee without talking about Jesus, I doubt I would have met Mot. One day he sat down in the chair next to my desk and complimented me on my shoes, shoes I was inordinately proud of because they were, in fact, very good shoes. He talked about his own shoes, which he didn't like, and a pair of boots he had loved but worn out walking across Albania. It was the best story I'd heard since I came to Friendship Room. I spent the afternoon listening to him talk about his travels: camping in a bombed-out Italian monastery; the pretty girls in Nice who gave him wine and books written in English; the students in Turkey who had been sure he was someone famous and insisted he come stay with them for a few days. After that, I couldn't stop listening to him.

Two more weeks would go by before I would decide to quit, and then only after a very frightening, very ill man cornered me in the hallway, choked me, and fondled my breasts. When he moved the arm pinning me to the wall by my throat to grab his penis, I pushed him out the door and locked it. Defeated, I wrote my resignation letter while I waited for the police.

Mot's company got me through the first of the months between my resignation and my actual leave-taking. Often, only the prospect of conversations with Mot—conversations about books, travel, art, and eventually the very literary world of his delusions—got me out the door of my house and into my car, on my way to work. At any time, his stories would have been a joy. At that time, they were all that kept me from being someone who one day walked away from her desk and, without a word, never went back.

I am on this trip, in part, to get away from there for a while and burn up the vacation time I have accumulated over the last year. But this is just an excuse. I don't know why the first real friend I have made in many years is a mentally ill, homeless man who is twenty-five years my senior. This is a question that needs an answer, and I've come to try and find it.

On my first morning in Amarillo, Mot takes me to a diner he says has wonderful waffles. This is a surprise, because it bothers Mot that I am fat much more than it bothers me. Amarillo turns out to be the perfect place for our visit. There is nothing much to do except drive out to Lake Meredith, look around, make plans to camp out one night without ever meaning to actually do it, take pictures, and talk. Most of the time, I give the keys to Mot. Behind the wheel, he is more centered; he takes on a family-man-out-for-a-drive persona, pulls up a part of himself he has imagined, but not lived, and tries to make it real. Beside him, I am also someone else; a person with hours to kill and not much that needs to be done. Relaxed. Companionable. Happy.

We don't get out of the car often, only now and then to look more closely at the desert flowers or to walk around the mostly-empty marina. He knows the names of everything. He does not like the ever-present yucca, finds its seedpod obscene, but delights in showing me my first roadrunner and explaining the dangers of camping in the arroyos. He points out cottonwood, soapberry, and sandbar willows, explains how the white limestone caprock keeps its place as the softer rock beneath erodes. He holds small spiders in his palm and talks about the different kinds of silk they use in spinning their webs. Occasionally, to turn me in the right direction to see a thing, he takes my hand or puts his arm on my shoulder. These small affections, at first awkward, soon grow natural.

Mot's knowledge is encyclopedic; perfect recall seems to be a part of his illness, a kind of compensation for the tricks his mind plays when he tries to string all the events of his life together into a narrative that makes sense. When he isn't teaching me the landscape, he tells me stories from what is left of his past. Most often, he tells the ones about how he came to be a vessel for the Others. Those stories are hard to hear, but are key to understanding the eidola that plague him now. The details in them never change, he recites them the same way he recited "Dangerous Dan McGrew." He can, if I ask him while he's in the midst of one, tell me the color of the shirt he was wearing or what smells were in the air. The skeleton of his life is there, intact, but the connective tissue is all delusion, stories his mind tells itself to explain the horrible truths in his past. It's the why of things that gives him so much trouble.

I remember when I was five; my mother took me to the movies. She took just me, not any of my brothers or sisters, and she let me pick out the kind of candy I wanted, and then what was really great was she let me hold her hand all through the movie. I was so happy; I thought she finally loved me. But then, after the movie, we went home and she told me to get into the oven. I mean, I told you, I wasn't supposed to be born. Moloch and Dubja had told her that I was supposed to be a girl. I can remember while I was in the womb, she taught me all kinds of things, like how to knit, and showed me the pretty dresses she was making for me. But I wasn't a girl, so she had to get rid of me. I mean, if I wasn't a girl, then I wasn't the promised one, so I was a mistake. She told me it wouldn't hurt, and not to be scared, so I wasn't. I remember the way the grill felt against my cheek. She must have turned on the gas, because I don't remember anything else until our house was full of people. Even my dad had come rushing home from work, and Dr. Dash was there taking care of me. It was the first time they took her away to the hospital. She didn't come back for a long time.

He tells me it's okay to cry, that he understands why someone would cry at a story like this. But I don't, at least not then. I can see The Big Guys Upstairs lurking behind Mot's words, and I don't want to give them anything they can use against him. Just as they are watching me, I've had to learn to watch them and to know their tricks. They use the tears of the women he has known to punish him—he often hears them sobbing quietly behind the other voices—and I won't add my tears to theirs. I save them until I am safely home.

I believe Mot's stories; the one about being put in an oven and another one he's told me about his aunt tying his shoelaces together and telling him to run down the stairs. In that story he falls down the steps and comes back upstairs with a Jesus inside and the ability to tell time. I don't doubt that the spirits of his dead aunts live in the moles on his body, and that the Harpies can send him back down the stairs and into a blackout whenever they want. It's the cosmological argument for

The Big Guys Upstairs: because there is a Mot, there must also be a Moloch, a Jack, Dubja, the Harpies, and the Dead Aunts—the ones who created him and control him and without whom he would be plain old Tom again, the Tom he started out to be. I accept this on faith and hope acceptance will grow into understanding. And because I believe, he can talk to me, and we can be friends. Maybe this, too, is one of the lessons I am here to learn. To listen, not to doubt or give advice, but to simply hear and accept.

These are the things we do most days: go to Wal-Mart, to the lake, swim in the pool at the campground, and cook a supper of lentils and rice on a camp stove at the cabin. We aren't eating lentils and rice for health, or to save money, but because we can't find any good alternatives. We have looked for, but not found, a decent restaurant near the campground. Amarillo seems to be a city on its way out. Every evening, we consider the Asian restaurants and taco stands near the campground, but they look too seedy to me, too much a part of the falling-apartness of the neighborhood we are in, and I am afraid to go inside. Mot doesn't understand this, but he allows it. "I'm not wanted anywhere," he says, "so it doesn't matter. I just go wherever I want."

We do eat at an obvious tourist trap towards the middle of the week, The Big Texan Steak Ranch. It's one of those places with its own gift shop and billboards fifty miles out in every direction. It has a 72-ounce steak that, if devoured completely within an hour, is free. Hostesses dressed like cowgirls and a roving string band dart between the tables of out-of-towners. We order reasonably sized steaks and a bottle of good wine. It's like being in the car, a part of Mot that never gets to show itself comes out and all signs of the Others disappear. We have a good time.

The visit is like this, mostly made up of these small moments of grace when it seems like things might be better than they have been for both of us. That perhaps Mot will be able to have and keep a friend, that maybe my faith in the dignity of those living marginal lives will be restored.

The rich steakhouse dinner doesn't sit well, and I'm up and down all night. Careful not to wake Mot, I search in the dark for my left shoe, my jacket. Under the red-and-black blanket, he sleeps on his belly like a baby in a crib—one hand by his face, the other tossed far out to the side. His breathing is soft and shallow; he doesn't snore. He looks de-

500

ceptively peaceful. Nothing suggests that he's battling demons or re-living old terrors. But he is. He's told me the Others launch their real assault against him at night and not to be frightened if he calls out in his sleep or seems to struggle. He's been told he screams and thrashes around in his sleep. But here in Amarillo, he doesn't fight at all. In-stead, he's unnaturally still.

Between bouts of intestinal distress, I curl up sleeplessly in my bed and try to imagine Mot's dreams. Watching him fills me with an aching tenderness, a little maternal and dangerously close to love.

Mot believes we all share the same dreamscape and that when I ap-pear, I am me, acting with volition, and will remember everything that happened when I awake. He holds me accountable. This terrifies and fascinates me. So far, he has only told me of two dreams that include me and in both I was helpful to him. Together, he says, we were able to hold the Others at bay. I suspect this is part of the trick—if I'm an ally now, later when the illness creates dreams in which I betray him it will be more hurtful—and so I don't take credit for whatever help he thinks I've given. "That's not me, no matter what they say, you know," I argue, but he won't listen. He tells me to reread Jung if I won't take his word for it.

When the sun finally rises, I head to the pool. After a night of lying quietly awake, I crave movement and noise. Cold water snaps the tiredness out of my bones; my head clears with the splash of each stroke. At home, I won't swim, too vain to expose my pale, middle-aged body. Here, anonymity defeats my vanity. I spend the morning gliding through the water until I am empty-headed and my muscles are loose and warm, sunning myself on a towel between sets of laps. When I can't swim any more and my skin is pink and tender, I gather my things and head back to the cabin.

Mot has made us a breakfast of coffee and papaya. He hands me a cup as I walk onto the porch.

"How did you sleep?" I ask throwing on an old denim shirt I'd stolen from my husband and a pair of shorts over my swimsuit. We sit down on the swing, balancing the plate of papaya chunks between us.

"Lousy. Of course." He rolls his eyes. "A lot going on up here. Mostly the Harpies, but also Dubja and old Willie. Something's up, but they won't clue me in on what's happening. That's how things go. I'm not supposed to know anything."

Since I've been here, the Harpies have dominated his dreams. A collective made up of all the women he has known, they speak as one

501

and don't seem to have any real power. The men in his mind give orders, make things happen. The women can only weep and beg.

"They can only manifest as animals on our plane of existence," Mot explained when he first told me about the Harpies. "That's why animals can talk to me, which is pretty scary. I mean, what does an animal have to say that I want to hear?" He also tells me they run a publishing house in the Northeast. I don't ask how the two things can both be true; he'd have to find a way to explain it, and the explanation would become another layer of the delusion. But I'm amused, imagining a publishing house run by housecats and shrews.

He sips his coffee and stares out at the cows in the nearby stockyard. "They say you're a soul sister and they are trying to warn you about the bad characters over here," he says, gesturing upwards with his thumb. "You know, that's where you'll end up if I outlive you. You'll be one of them. Only don't be like Harpies. They're not nice women. Most of them just want to get laid, that's why they are always trying to turn me into a girl." He sighs. "That's what I like about you. You're not a woman who gets a few drinks in her and says 'Let's take off all our clothes!' Kooks like that scare me." He laughs and pats me on the knee.

"What I like about you is that you're always telling me what you like about me," I say, offering him the last piece of papaya, "and you make me breakfast." I also like that sex is out of the question. Mot told me when we first met that he's been celibate for thirty years. And because sex has been off the table all along, we are able to be friends without having to guard against it.

After breakfast, we decide to drive into town. There is a tree Mot wants me to see. We drive around looking for it, circling a middle-class neighborhood near the University. While he drives, Mot tells me more about what's going on in his dreams, warning me.

"The Big Guys are trying to find a way to use this all to their advantage," he says, and I know that by "this all" he means me. "Watch out, because I don't always know what the program is. The Harpies warn me sometimes, but not all the time."

"The Big Guys Upstairs are the ones who really pull the strings," Mot says. If the Harpies are Mot's Greek chorus, these are the gods on Olympus who arbitrarily dictate the path of his days. "Jack" he says— pronouncing it "yok"—"is a likeable guy. Sometimes I think he's the one you like, really. I don't know if you've ever really seen me." I don't either, so I keep my mouth shut. "Jack is the one who learned to tell

502

time, played basketball in high school, had friends, and made people laugh. Anything likeable, that's not me. That's Jack," Mot says. "Don't get tricked into thinking that's me, because that just means you'll end up being Jack's friend instead of mine. That's what always happens. Anything good I get, anything nice, they just take it."

Mot means this literally. I'm hungry and suggest stopping at Mazzullo's Pizza, which we have passed three times in fifteen minutes, but we can't stop because Moloch, who lives in Mot's throat, is acting up and will steal the food from him as he swallows it and use it to feed the Others. There are days, maybe more than days, where Mot won't eat to try and starve Moloch out, but it never works. It only leaves Mot weak and feeling like yet another battle has been lost.

Finally, after passing the same landmarks a number of times, we go left where we had been going right and in a block or two come across a yard with an outrageous garden amid the green, watered lawns. Climbing aster grows extravagantly over a pergola on one side, morning glories over an arbor on the other. Between, hollyhocks, dinner plate dahlias, tiger lilies, and dwarf sunflowers compete for attention in the explosion of color. There are no garden gnomes, no little wheelbarrows filled with begonias, but they are implied. "There is tacky yard art in the subtext of that garden," Mot jokes. "It is way over the top. Someone retired and went nuts!" He laughs and gestures out the driver's side window. Across the street, a catalpa tree blooms with more modest pastel flowers.

"It's lovely," I say, and it is. Next to the garish, ridiculous garden it looks perfect, every bloom exactly as it should be, the subtle shades outshining the garish colors of the dahlias and lilies. "Worth the drive." As if the drive itself weren't the point.

On Friday morning, Mot wakes believing his only remaining sibling, a sister named Antoinette, has died. He knows this, he explains, because she's crying so loudly inside his head he can't hear me when I speak. Until today, she had not been one of the ones weeping in the background. Mot's angry with her sons for not notifying him. "How would they have found you?" I ask, and he doesn't know but isn't appeased. The impossible is a matter of course for him.

We decide to go out for some lunch and to see a movie. Mot is uncharacteristically adamant we see *Mr. Brooks*. I haven't heard anything about it, but he's seen the preview and insists. All I can tell from the ad is that William Hurt and Kevin Costner are in the cast and it is some sort of cop film. Not my sort of movie, really, but I'm not the one who needs to quiet the voices in my head, so I agree.

The theater is in a part of Amarillo we didn't know existed, a newer, wealthier part, where we discover all the chain restaurants and coffee houses we had thought were missing. On the drive, Mot talks about his family. He has talked about his family often enough, but its make-up is a muddle to me. I know he had four siblings. There was a brother who lived in the Pacific Northwest and seems to have done well until, in middle age, he killed himself. And, of course, the sister he believes has just died. Antoinette is the only one he ever names, so although he says "my brother did this," or "my sister did that," there's no way to know which of them he means. I believe he had two broth-ers and two sisters, but it may have been three and one. Collectively, Mot refers to the five of them as the *Five Easy Pieces*, and says they have been picked off one by one; he is the last left standing. Usually, I don't ask questions, I wait for him to tell me what he wants me to know. Today it feels possible to talk him out of believing his sister has died, so I press when I otherwise would not.

"So, why don't you and your sister speak any more?" I ask him.

"I've told you," he says, and then for five minutes a disjointed ex-planation spills out of him—a mass of words with no meaning. The trick of tracking the names doesn't work at all. He forgets to use verbs; affirmative statements become negative ones mid-sentence; only half a word gets said before he's on to the next. Oddly, he doesn't seem to notice. Finally, he looks me in the eye and says, "See, it's like I told you before. Done deal. Never gonna listen, so I can't talk to them."

Unable to follow any of what he's just told me, I pose the question in a different way, hoping for an answer I can understand. "So, if I asked your sister why you don't speak, would she tell me the same thing?"

"No," he answers. "She'd probably tell you it was because I mo-lested her when we were kids. That I was the one who ruined her life. That's what she tells everyone."

That's it; that's all he says. No denial. No explanation.

I look at the man who gentled me through my own fears after I was attacked, an incident that seems insignificant compared to what he's just confessed. It isn't that I don't know lives are complicated, or un-derstand the cycle of abuse. This grown man is not responsible for anything that poor, broken child might have done. It's just that I can't put these two halves of him together and come up with a whole. I look for the boy in the old man, but can't see him at this distance, or maybe from this angle. He's told me his mother used to try to pinch off his penis when he was little, to make him the girl he was supposed to be, and he acknowledges but won't discuss other sexual abuses. This confession changes the meaning of these stories for me; my understanding of him is more complicated now. I try to turn him back into the Mot I knew this morning. But it's impossible not to reflect and look for hints of predation in his stories, to not be afraid of what I might have let into my life. Everything I have believed about him teeters on the fulcrum of a single answer.

I work up the nerve to ask the necessary question. "Have you ever touched another child?" I can't imagine what I will do if the answer is yes.

He looks at me, his gaze clear, not even surprised. "No. I mean I've always been attracted to younger people. I'm really a kid, never was allowed to develop into a real person like the rest of you, so it makes sense that I'm attracted to kids because that's as far as I ever got in life. But I know there's a line, and I've never crossed it. Just because They hit the old erection button and try to use sex to make me be like Them, doesn't mean I have to do it." I believe him, but I'm shaken, in part by how much delusion there is in his explanation. Can I trust as truth something so entwined with madness? It's a fragile faith; I have to work to hold on to it. But I am not ready to let my own cowardice be the thing that separates us.

At the theater, I excuse myself and go to the bathroom to splash water on my face and take a few moments alone to collect myself. *Mr. Brooks*, it turns out, is a movie about a serial killer with an imaginary friend who eggs him on. Costner plays the murderer; William Hurt plays Marshall, a character only Brooks can see, who goads an unwilling Brooks into the killings. After the first gruesome scene I tell Mot I want to leave. I say I don't think I'm up for this kind of movie just now. I don't tell him how brittle my faith in him is, or that I'm afraid the movie might shatter it. He points back to the screen and barks, "Watch it!" in a demanding tone I haven't heard before. "This is just like me; this is EXACTLY what it's like." He pauses for a minute, and adds, "Did you notice I said that in Hurt's voice? Sometimes he's one of the ones over here; he wants me to go to Hollywood to make movies and be one of *them*." I have no idea what this might mean, and I'm not asking.

On the drive back to the campground, I try to pull it together, but I can't. Mot chatters excitedly about the ways in which the movie mirrors his own experience, although he makes sure to say "except for all the killing" every few minutes after I tell him he's scaring me. Once again, I feel like the reasonable thing would be to just leave, pretend I'm worn out and want to start the drive back to Morgantown a little early.

Since this drive, I've been acutely aware of how little I really know about Mot. I may never have even met Tom, the person in whose body all of these gods, demons, and regular joes reside. I believe Mot knows there are boundaries and doesn't cross them, but I don't know if he speaks for the rest of Them, or if he even knows what the Others have or haven't done. I remember that he told me once, "They don't like Jews. I mean, I can think of at least one Jew who has died because of the bad guys over here." At the time I'd thought it was more delusion, or some reference to Kaiser Wilhelm when he was a living, real person. Now I don't know.

Mot is genuinely my friend, and I know the ways in which my world is better, less lonely, because of him. I am grateful to him for getting me through a very difficult period in my life, a time made harder than it should have been because it echoed events of sexual violence in my past. I don't want to run away from him in fear and I worry about what it would mean for him if I did. But what if Mot is just this sweet, naïve guy the Others throw up to get what they need from the world, taking him back down again when they feel like it? What if someday Moloch looks me straight in the eye and says, "We warned you." For a few hours, the world feels made of spun glass, everything on the verge of shattering.

We get to the cabin surprised at how early it still is; we don't have the strength for a day so long. I swim, Mot naps. The place has filled with weekend campers. The pool roils with children wound up by long car rides and haggard parents who toss themselves onto the deck chairs and shut their eyes. I wonder if my own fragile trust is enough to make it all right that I have brought Mot among them; I'm glad he is napping rather than swimming with me. I do not want to have to watch him watching the children play, or to wonder if the longing in his eyes is for his own lost childhood or something more sinister. My fear is an ugly, alien thing. I don't know how a friendship could survive it.

It's easy to identify the events that break us, harder to name the

506

myriad tiny things that knit us back together. Saturday morning hurries by in a series of necessary tasks. We pack and load the cars so our last hours can be spent on better things. Mot sorts the camping gear and cleans the cabin while I do the laundry; together, we divide up what we've acquired over the week. He takes the coffee pot, the hotplate, and the leftover rice and lentils. I keep the straw basket and the wild alfalfa he harvested for a tea we never made. We make our last pilgrimage to Wal-Mart. Mot buys engine additives for my car that I think may do more harm than good but allow anyway. He accepts a cell phone from me, although can't go so far as to promise he'll use it.

We spend our last evening quietly, reading to one another, making a meal of the last of the fruit, bread, and cheese bought during the week. He gets out the road atlas and marks good stopping places on my route home. I sew missing buttons onto his shirts.

I am awake by five, anxious to get the goodbye over with. I shower and get the last of my things together, then wake Mot. "I'm going now," I whisper, leaning over his head on the pillow. It's the first time I've crossed the invisible barrier between his side of the cabin and mine in all the time we've been here.

He walks groggily to the porch with me, rubbing his eyes and obviously surprised to see that it's still dark, but he doesn't suggest I put off leaving.

"I left the key in the drop box by the office, but you don't have to leave until eleven. Feel free to go back to bed. I just need to get on the road."

I step off the porch and turn back to face him, car keys in my hand. He looks down at me, takes my face in his good hand, and kisses me lightly on the forehead. "Drive safely," he says, and then, looking over the top of my head at the darkened horizon, "I think I would love you if They let me feel love. This is probably the closest I'll get."

I smile and get into my car. It's a long drive home. As I pull away, Mot's still standing on the porch, staring out at the big sky.

Nominated by Sara Pritchard

LANDSCAPE WITH ARSON

by JENNIFER GROTZ

from NEW ENGLAND REVIEW

Have you ever watched a cigarette released from a driver's fingers
swim through the night air and disintegrate in tiny embers?
Invisible by day, fire's little shards, its quiet dissemination.

That's how, one hot afternoon, no one noticed when
something desperate made the boy devise the strategy
to siphon gas from the motorcycle with a discarded straw,

spitting mouthfuls into a fast food cup until there was enough
to set the apartment complex on fire.
It happened in a neighborhood at the edge of town

where the wind sifted a constant precipitation of dust
like desiccated snow and the newly-poured streets
looked like frosting spread across the desert field.

Ducks had just found the man-made pond.
At dusk, they waddled ashore
to explore the construction site like the boy.

He started with the door. Stood mesmerized
as the fire took on new colors. He fed it litter
collected from the field. It hissed and turned green,

it splintered pink, it bloomed aureoles of blue.
But there was hardly time to admire it before
remorse overtook him and he fled.

Before the howl of sirens. He was
gone before—he started with the door—whatever
he wanted to let out.

Something can stop being true in the time it takes
a cigarette to burn to its filter. It was your crime
but it's me who goes back to the scene. Now it's only me

who wants to burn something for you, but there's nothing left—how
do you set fire to the past? Only an impulse to shake free—like
    cellophane
peeled from a pack—something that clings.

Sometimes I conjure a fire for you in my mind,
the gnats swarming furiously above the water, up and down,
can you see it? How they mimic flame, hovering

at the pond's edge. Lately I find myself there all the time.

Nominated by New England Review

THREE BUDDHIST TALES

fiction by MARILYN CHIN

from BLACK RENAISSANCE NOIRE

CICADA

The Cicada is out of his shell. After seventeen years submerged in the dank earth, he is bright-eyed, horny and ready for action. He is trilling on a leafy bough, calling for a mate, but he stops to drink some droplets of dew off a waxy philodendron—so loving the dew that he doesn't hear the praying mantis lurking behind him. Intense in her focus, ready on her haunches, the praying mantis pounces, taking the cicada headfirst, crunching and relishing, so she can't feel the swift-footed sparrow behind her. The sparrow, twitter-twitters, light on the branch. She jabs her sharp beak and skewers the mantis, devouring her in three mouthfuls, so relishing this morsel that she doesn't sense the small calico cat with a spotty black nose, ready to pounce on her. So fun-loving is this calico, named Beetlejuice, that she plays with the limp carcass in her mouth for a few minutes. She rolls the sparrow around on the ground with her paws, so focused in her play that she is oblivious to the California red-tailed hawk, high on her perch, poising herself, collecting the gravity to swoop down to snatch the poor, de-clawed kitty to feed her famished chicks.

The next day Jack, my asshole neighbor, keeps tripping around in his yard, and calling kitty, kitty, kitty, finds only a bloody fur pelt on the ground. He points his rifle at the red tail hawk, shoots a few times and misses. He says, "I'll get you, bastard."

❋ ❋ ❋

I say, "Leave the poor bird alone, you loser-redneck. Or else I'll call the police; she's an endangered raptor . . ." "You, shut up, wetback bitch," he says. "Endangered raptor, my ass . . . The fucking bird ate my cat. You're lucky that I don't shoot the whole lot of you."

The next month his company sends Jack to Iraq to fix some sabotaged oil field pipes. He stops one day under an olive tree for a moment's rest and delights in a care package of Almond Joy candy bars that his mother sent him. So hungry is he that he can't eat just one but proceeds to unwrap another and another. As he is relishing each morsel of the fourth candy bar, a sniper from atop a building shoots him in the back of the head. The marksman jumps up and down, waving his rifle and shouts "God is Great, God is Great." So boastful and elated is he that he is not aware that the enemy is behind him. Scarcely has he cried out "God" a third time when he is strafed down by a UH-60A Black Hawk assault helicopter.

The pilot of the copter says "Shazaam! Got five in one!" Finally able to return home after sixteen months of combat for her reward, a brief R&R in Hemet, California, she finds that her loser husband has run off with another woman, a Lieutenant-Colonel, higher brass than hers . . . The house is emptied of furniture, save for a moldy mattress. After throwing the mattress out the backdoor, she sits on that mold-stinking perch, wearing her comfy Hello Kitty flannels, and downs a quart of Bombay Gin with Led Zeppelin blaring into her headphones. So deep is she into her despair that she tunes out the ten thousand cicadas performing an eerie birth and death song. They sing and sing. They shall finally meet their mates, make desperate love and perish satiated. Or they shall be eaten by other famished creatures, and the cycle of feeding and mating and suffering begins again . . .

The dead and the living shall bury themselves and be reborn over and over, with the same lust for life, the same fury. The egg-born, the womb-born, the moisture-born, those with form, those without form, those with consciousness, those without consciousness, those who are neither conscious nor unconscious: All singing together, in one loud hissing harmony.

PIGLETS

After their mother died, the piglets continued to suckle on her teats. The milk was still warm and tasty to them. But after a few hours, they noticed that she was stiff and cold. They nudged her with their noses, snorting and crying, trying to wake her. Finally, they no longer recognized that she was their mother and they scrambled away in fear. Except for that one piglet who refused to depart. She lingered, snorting and crying, waiting for her mother to awaken.

Suns and moons came and went. Putrescence set in. A fetid stench pervaded the world. Kites and crows descended, disemboweling her, air-lifting her limbs, and the ten thousand maggots, worms and cockroaches polished her bones. The piglet stayed, crying and squealing, still waiting for her mother to regain consciousness.

Why, Great Matriarch, shall there always be those who cannot recognize their mother when she is still whole and those who cannot detach even when she has been shattered? Why this eternal contradiction?

Meanwhile, the piglets went on with their piggy lives, carving territory, buying houses, trading up and down the margins of the stock market, losing all memory of their beginnings. Only that one piglet, crow-pecked and weakened by the vermin, kept steadfast by her mother's side and was never conquered. She couldn't keep a man and couldn't hold a job. She was arrested twice for vagrancy, hospitalized several times for hearing voices. She sometimes wrote a poem; she sometimes found a dress at the Salvation Army Thrift Store. A dress, a poem—such discoveries gave her temporary joy.

One day while she rummaged through a garbage can in the suburbs, a pretty housewife came out and chased her away: She immediately recognized that this woman was her sister and said, "Mei Ling, Mei Ling, remember, the six of us used to frolic in the woods? Remember uprooting delicious tubers in the jungle? Remember snuggling under our mother's belly in the cold? Remember the shade we shared beneath the very same belly in the heat?"

❊ ❊ ❊

The woman answered, "I am sorry. I don't know you. My name is Heather Jones and I was born in Poughkeepsie to two important professors."

But storyteller, you may ask, why introduce this paltry character to us, what is the purpose? Tousle-haired, dirty-faced, alone in this vast universe, routing through garbage and overturning stones: Her life is failure.

She survives to remember.

RYOKAN'S MOON

Mei Ling was sitting at the campsite, waiting for her boyfriend to come back from the 7 Eleven. A creepy junkie, stoned out of his mind, came trembling toward her. He said, "Take off you clothes, bitch!" She said, "No way, I'd just bought this fake Dolce & Gabbana denim camping outfit from Hong Kong, and it took me two months to find a seamstress to alter it. Go take somebody else's clothes. That lady three trailers down, she buys only couture." The creep looked dazed by her response and left.

Ten minutes later, the creep came back, still so stoned that he could barely stand up. "Bitch, take off your clothes," he said. She said, "Okay, obviously, you came a long way to do this." So she took off her clothes and gave them to him. "Okay, now, go away and sell them on Ebay. My dead grandmother would be blissed out in Nirvana that I give them to you. You know, the right intention, the right action, all that Buddhist crap. And here, take my money. All I have in my wallet is 23 dollars. I gave my boyfriend the rest of my cash to buy beer and nachos. By the way, he's coming back soon, so you better get going." The creep looked bewildered and took the clothes and went away.

Twenty minutes later, the creep came back again. "Shut up, bitch, I'm going to rape you. And don't try to fancy talk me out of it either." Mei Ling sighed but was still cool. "My grandmother, the Buddhist, would want me to be compassionate and give you what you want. But she would also want me to tell you the truth. I cannot speak falsehood. Yama, the king of hell, will boil my tongue in oil if I do. The truth is that I have a hideous infestation of the crabs. I caught them from my ex-boyfriend the punk rocker. (Notice he's an ex-boyfriend now. My new boyfriend is OK with my checkered history. He was raised by feminists.) I bought some medicine from TJ that turned my pubes blue. This stuff is so harsh that it might make your dick fall off." Indeed, he looked at her pubic hair, and her little stubbles, leftovers from her last Brazilian wax, were scintillating bright blue. He groaned in disgust and went away.

Meanwhile, Mei Ling sat naked and stared at the beautiful full moon. Ryokan would have given the creep the moon. But she was not that enlightened. Not yet. She wanted this magical moon all to herself. It was a warm and fragrant twilight, and the wild jasmine had just opened.

Nominated by Rita Dove

TALISMANIC

by DAVID WOJAHN

from THE SOUTHERN REVIEW

The boys' hair voodoos the tomato stalks.
We have swept it from the kitchen floor
after haircuts & straw colored it spirals

from the garden soil, already half-buried
like tablets etched with Linear B,
untranslatable among eggshells & soap flakes.

I kneel & watch it rain upon the diligent grubs,

beetles & the zigzag caravans of ants.
The stalks nod with unripe Big Boys,
Calypsos, green marbles of Cherries in clusters.

Human hair, marigolds, Irish Spring
I flake with a cheese grater in a talismanic
circle, charms against squirrel & raccoon.

High summer evening, high nineties & the boys run

tonsured through the sprinkler spray, the sound
as it revolves a quirky but robotic
staccato, like the voice of David Byrne

cackling "Once in a Lifetime." *You may ask*
yourself, how do I work this?
They will lay waste to the fruits of your labors,

useless are all of your spells. For now the wind

is rising. A thick, cheap scent over everything,
scent the color of Key lime pie, scent
the color of my father, eighteen years dead

& stepping from the shower stall, taking in
the steam in deep self-conscious
breaths, his own futile talisman

against emphysema, angina, Jim Beam.

Soap lather beards his face. *You may ask yourself,*
how did I get there? He is ash in a canister
in the veterans cemetery in St. Paul

& his DNA helixes up the pale outline
of Luke's spine, glinting now
in the sprinkler's jittery rainbows. *Let the water*

hold me down. Back & forth they pace

the sprinkler's cage. They squeal & turn to me
in their delight. *Same as it ever was, saamme*
as it ever wassss & the breeze pulls the spray

toward me until I am mist as well. Lord,
abide this instant back to them when I
am ash, though I kneel absurdly with

a cheese grater, kneepads, & a flint head

of soap. *Same as it e-ver was, same as it*
e-ver was. Sundown, mosquitoes
tuning up, a gilt of fireflies

slathering the Adirondack chairs.
My knees scrape eggshell, beflowered
with deadheaded marigolds & the tufts of hair

billow up from the dirt to my face.

Nominated by Philip Levine, Bruce Beasley, Ted Deppe, James Harms,
David Jauss, Tony Ardizzone

DIDO REFUSES TO SPEAK

by LINDA GREGERSON

from THE KENYON REVIEW

For Susan Botti

1.

The forestays, the sternsheet,
                    the benches,
          the yard,

                    the wooden pins to which
          the oars are
bound with strips of leather, he

                    explained this, thole
and loom, I thought the words
                    were just as lovely as the

workings. And I thought
                    I knew the principle:
          the moving forward facing where you've

                    been, the muscled
          quarrel with the muscled sea, like
love, that sweet againstness. And

                    the linen sail:
          happy the weaver whose work might bedeck
                    the chamber where we

lay us down. How strange
                    it seems from just a little distance:
          the living tree, the ax,

          the chisel, cattle
whom we kill and
skin, all so that they may live again on

          water but including us.

2.

Because she'd never not
                    been there, my Anna (I
          can feel her now, the back

          of her hand as I hold it against
my eyelid, I have always loved
to touch with eyes), because

          her voice was all the traction I'd ever
required, because
                    so long as earth contained

precisely
                    that measure of temple to eyebrow,
          eyebrow to lip, I knew

          I had a home, it was
my sister I made to
make the thing ready—the firewood in

          its lofty escarpment, the torches,
the oil—and she, of course,
                    when she asked what I meant to do,

to whom I lied. I meant
                    my bitter heart to foul
          the wind that filled his sails. I did not ask

519

what
if the wind should change direction,
who would choke.

3.
As when in early summer in the fields
of silver thyme, the bees
are thick with happy industry . . .

As when the workmen trust
their overseer to be just . . .
As when the world was tuned to us and we

the world, my city
on its quarried footing rose and rang with
purpose and

the water loved its channels and the
terraces their civic flight
of stairs. Reluctant

evening, loathe
to lose the sight of them, would finger
the vertical facings until they

blushed. I know
a better mind would not require
the elements to

be like us, we smear
our sorry longings on
the rocks and trees, but then

the very daylight
seemed to say we'd built to scale.

4.
Once in a narrow garden I
encountered a thing I'd known
before. A scent. I had

no words for it. Not citron,
though it bore that solvent
aptitude. Not anise, though it harbored

a touch of clay. A fragrance I
had known as in another life,
or this life, but before

the daily watering down. Which left me
half transported on an un-
distinguished plot of ground. So think

what it meant when he began to
speak. The story we'd stowed
as ballast on the fleeing ships, had painted

on our temple walls, the very lights
and darks we had depended on to make
the place less strange, and on

a stranger's lips. To whom
the story properly belonged. Or he
to it, is there a difference? And

poor Dido mere excursus for them both.

5.

If I burn the oars he won't be able to use them
to leave if I
lock up the winds in my cellar

if I shred the rigging or just
that pair of tendons at his inner
thigh not

so he suffers no but so he isn't able to
walk without help
and as for the eyes

he's already seen how I love him what need
            for the eyes I was
    —wasn't I?—young when the

            other one came to me dressed
        in his wounds which
wounds my brother gave him I

        have ever . . . in faithfulness since but
mistaken the . . . yes or lost
            the thread and now

these swarming . . . whom I
            welcomed as more of our own as
    on a carcass their indecent haste

            their blackened . . . when I ought . . .
the tar-slicked hulls . . . And now
        these trails of filthy mucus in the sand.

6.

The child.
            I might
        except for the child have been

            content.
    But he in all his careless beauty—
cheekbone still untrammeled and the tidemark

        of hair at his nape—he sat
beside me where we ate,
            he laughed, his every un-

self-conscious bit of lassitude or
            fervor was
        a manifest that pled the father's case.

        There is no
    outside to such arguments.
And surely I took precautions? What

was true for me ought doubly to
have been the case for one whose
                    future he

secured. So hostage both.
                    All three. And now
I'm told he wasn't a

                    child at all but a
          god in the shape of a child.
Redundant.

                              7.
Wasn't it nearly too sweet to be borne,
                    that motherwit
          bought me a kingdom. *Every inch*

               that will fit in the oxhide.
          Which I shaved so fine,
in strips of such exquisite near-

          transparency, we thought the whole
of Africa might fall within our
                    grasp. So dredged

the ports and felled the woodlands in the
                    heady tide
          of heaven's bright approval . . .

               I am glad to find
          they haven't cut the woodland here.
Give me a margin of shadow, I'll tell you

               no lies. The myrtle
suits me, understory to
                    the last, and mutes those sounds of

sorrow from the river. Not a single
                    pine, no
          striving toward the masthead or the

        roofbeam, just
    these little purple blossoms, which
I do not take ironically.

    And best: the plates of silver
bark, which must be
        what happens to words.

Nominated by David Baker, Susan Hahn, Mark Irwin

SPECIAL MENTION

(The editors also wish to mention the following important works published by small presses last year. Listings are in no particular order.)

POETRY

Job Site, 1967—Lucia Perillo (*Inseminating the Elephant*, Copper Canyon)
Combine—Adam Day (Agni)
Folio—Mary Privett Leader (Cimarron Review)
Field—Margaret Reges (Shenandoah)
Encounter With John Malkovich—Jeffrey Harrison (Yale Review)
Mark Morris at Jacob's Pillow—Philip Dacey (Hanging Loose)
In Praise of Big Men—Edward Field (Live Mag!)
Florescence on 4th Avenue—Rebecca Seiferle (Ploughshares)
Shine—Cecilia Woloch (*Carpathia*, BOA)
Catheter—Janice Harrington (specs)
After Virgil—Stephen Burt (InDigest)
A Custom of Mourning—Mary Ruefle (Kenyon Review)
Politics—Susan Holahan (New Haven 005)
Canticle of More Wishes—Jennifer Atkinson (Field)
Paternoster—Beth Bachman (*Temper*, University of Pittsburgh Press)
To The Ice Cream Man—Gary Dop (Blue Earth)
What Isn't Mine—Jill A. Essbaum (Poetry)
The House Rhapsody—John Gallagher (Crazyhorse)
Good Place for a Handout—Patrick Moran (Nimrod)
Alwaies Autumne—Philip Murray (Hampton-Sydney Poetry Review)
Famous Song—Paisley Rekdal (Willow Springs)
Deliver Us From Evil—Dana Roeser (Michigan Quarterly Review)
Neighbor—Catie Rosemurgy (Crazyhorse)

FICTION

White Fire—Stephen O'Connor (TriQuarterly)
Green Street Incidents—Jon Boilard (The Sun)
Unaddressed—Olufunke G. Bankole (Antioch Review)
Man of Steel—Bryan Furuness (Ninth Letter)
Prayer—Adam Levin (Dossier Journal)
Spring Leapers—David L. Morse (Alaska Quarterly Review)
Noddles—Kuangyan Huang (Glimmer Train)
Pi Day—James Wyatt (Republic of Letters)
Lucky Abbott—Chris Bachelder (Cincinnati Review)
The Strange Genius of American Men—Jung H. Yun (Massachusetts
    Review)
Dyads—Jacob M. Appel (Jabberwock Review)
Protect and Serve—Elizabeth Oness (Crazyhorse)
The Wreckers—George M. Clark (Ecotone)
Apparition—Liza Wieland (Sou'wester)
Last Song of Saravat—Sharon May (Mānoa)
Us Kids—Melinda Moustakis (Alaska Quarterly Review)
SPQR—Brian D. Mooney (Cincinnati Review)
We Are The Animals Here—Anna Solomon (Brooklyn Review)
History Lesson—Micah Riecker (Mid-American Review)
Byobu—Lynn Ahrens (Calyx)
Much Peace—Clare Beams (Ink Well)
As God Made Us—A.L. Kennedy (Zoetrope)
Read The Snow—Terese Svoboda (Brooklyn Rail)
Susan and the Zunis—Beth Alvarado (Third Coast)
Bukharin's Fox—Michael Hinken (West Branch)
Dead Letter Days—Thomas Cooper (Blue Earth Review)
The Philosopher of Paper—Honoree F. Jeffers (Mythium)
A Splendid Life—Carrie Brown (One Story)
The Ballad of Ailin' Alan Smithee—Andrew Farkas (Copper Nickel)
How Someone Can Not Recognize You—Aja Gabel (New Ohio Re-
    view)
RPM—Michael Martone (Hopkins Review)
Cousin Julia's Visit—Janet Kirk (Kelsey Review)
The End of the Mayan Calendar—Steven Ramirez (Blue Mesa)
The Summer of Cancer—Erin Flanagan (Florida Review)
A Lesser Sonata—Marjorie Sandor (Georgia Review)
Rivers to Gilead—Steve Davenport (Gulf Coast)
A Street Guide to Providence—Samuel Ligon (New England Review)
Alice Elm's Blue Gown—Tom Filer (Chariton Review)

NONFICTION

A History of My Befuddlement—Philip Levine (Five Points)
Cinema É Luxo—Emily Witt (N+1)
Saunter—Tom Montgomery—Fate (Iowa Review)
A Crack In Everything—David Jauss (Haystack Mountain)
Growth Rings—Benjamin Busch (Michigan Quarterly)
The End of Something—Hilary Masters (Sewanee Review)
Me vs. Animals—Benjamin Percy (Paris Review)
From The Adventures of Cancer Bitch—S.L. Wisenberg (Colorado Review)
The Terribly Lonely & Deadly Serious Business—Stuart Dybek (TriQuarterly)
In The Frame—Dinah Lenney (Water-Stone)
Headquarters—Annie Lampman (Idaho Magazine)
Imagining Influence—Robert Boyers (Yale Review)
Black Holes—Bill Capossere (Colorado Review)
Silence and Storytelling—Alice Mattison (Writer's Chronicle)
The Guinea Pig—Clancy Martin (New Letters)
The Facts About John Cheever—Brock Clarke (Rumpus)
The Country I Came From—Lili Wright (Wag's Revue)
I Love You In Twelve Languages—Wendy Brenner (Oxford American)
Fourteen—Jaquira Diaz (Passages North)
To Famous Cases of Syphilis—Re'Lynn Hansen (PMS)
Fear of A Terrible Wife—Elizabeth Crane (Bat City Review)
2007–2003—Francisco Goldman (Brick)
The Dead Dog Essay—Marcia Aldrich (Florida Review)
The Wilhelm Scream—Elena Passarello (Gulf Coast)
Buying Time—Deborah Thompson (Florida Review)
Mac—Debra Gwartney (TriQuarterly)
In Transit—Kathryn Rhett (Harvard Review)
On Rape—Rebecca Curtis (Noon)
Fatigue—Heather Frese (Michigan Quarterly)
In The Midst of Death—John Crowley (Lapham's Quarterly)
When History Gets Personal—Mimi Schwartz (Agni)
Glass Fibers—Robert L. Foreman (Under the Sun)
Soup Kitchen, Mishna, Yoga, Kavannah—Efrem Sigel (The Journal)
The Boy Murderers—Andrew Levy (Missouri Review)
Senior Speech—Floyd Skloot (Southwest Review)
The Literary Scene Changes—Ted Solotaroff (New England Review)
Family Feet—Peggy Shinner (Southern Review)

Middle Man—Loren Glass (Minnesota Review)
Nowhere Need Be Foreign—Pico Iyer (Lapham's Quarterly)
Sail On, My Little Honey Bee—Amy Leach (A Public Space)
Hi-Ho, Hi-Ho, Off To The Gun Show We Go—Paul Ruffin (The Literary Review)
The Heartless Immensity—Jason Anthony (Virginia Quarterly)
The Bigamists—Lee Upton (Southwest Review)
On Our Skin—Kelly Blikre (Gulf Coast)

PRESSES FEATURED IN THE PUSHCART PRIZE EDITIONS SINCE 1976

Acts
Agni
Ahsahta Press
Ailanthus Press
Alaska Quarterly Review
Alcheringa/Ethnopoetics
Alice James Books
Ambergris
Amelia
American Letters and Commentary
American Literature
American PEN
American Poetry Review
American Scholar
American Short Fiction
The American Voice
Amicus Journal
Amnesty International
Anaesthesia Review
Anhinga Press
Another Chicago Magazine
Antaeus
Antietam Review
Antioch Review
Apalachee Quarterly
Aphra
Aralia Press

The Ark
Art and Understanding
Arts and Letters
Artword Quarterly
Ascensius Press
Ascent
Aspen Leaves
Aspen Poetry Anthology
Assembling
Atlanta Review
Autonomedia
Avocet Press
The Baffler
Bakunin
Bamboo Ridge
Barlenmir House
Barnwood Press
Barrow Street
Bellevue Literary Review
The Bellingham Review
Bellowing Ark
Beloit Poetry Journal
Bennington Review
Bilingual Review
Black American Literature Forum
Blackbird
Black Renaissance Noire

Black Rooster
Black Scholar
Black Sparrow
Black Warrior Review
Blackwells Press
Bloom
Bloomsbury Review
Blue Cloud Quarterly
Blueline
Blue Unicorn
Blue Wind Press
Bluefish
BOA Editions
Bomb
Bookslinger Editions
Boston Review
Boulevard
Boxspring
Bridge
Bridges
Brown Journal of Arts
Burning Deck Press
Caliban
California Quarterly
Callaloo
Calliope
Calliopea Press
Calyx
The Canary
Canto
Capra Press
Caribbean Writer
Carolina Quarterly
Cedar Rock
Center
Chariton Review
Charnel House
Chattahoochee Review
Chautauqua Literary Journal
Chelsea
Chicago Review
Chouteau Review
Chowder Review

Cimarron Review
Cincinnati Poetry Review
City Lights Books
Cleveland State Univ. Poetry Ctr.
Clown War
CoEvolution Quarterly
Cold Mountain Press
Colorado Review
Columbia: A Magazine of Poetry and Prose
Confluence Press
Confrontation
Conjunctions
Connecticut Review
Copper Canyon Press
Cosmic Information Agency
Countermeasures
Counterpoint
Crawl Out Your Window
Crazyhorse
Crescent Review
Cross Cultural Communications
Cross Currents
Crosstown Books
Crowd
Cue
Cumberland Poetry Review
Curbstone Press
Cutbank
Dacotah Territory
Daedalus
Dalkey Archive Press
Decatur House
December
Denver Quarterly
Desperation Press
Dogwood
Domestic Crude
Doubletake
Dragon Gate Inc.
Dreamworks
Dryad Press
Duck Down Press
Durak

East River Anthology
Eastern Washington University Press
Ecotone
Eleven Eleven
Ellis Press
Empty Bowl
Epiphany
Epoch
Ergo!
Evansville Review
Exquisite Corpse
Faultline
Fence
Fiction
Fiction Collective
Fiction International
Field
Fine Madness
Firebrand Books
Firelands Art Review
First Intensity
Five A.M.
Five Fingers Review
Five Points Press
Five Trees Press
The Formalist
Fourth Genre
Frontiers: A Journal of Women
    Studies
Fugue
Gallimaufry
Genre
The Georgia Review
Gettysburg Review
Ghost Dance
Gibbs-Smith
Glimmer Train
Goddard Journal
David Godine, Publisher
Graham House Press
Grand Street
Granta
Graywolf Press

Great River Review
Green Mountains Review
Greenfield Review
Greensboro Review
Guardian Press
Gulf Coast
Hanging Loose
Hard Pressed
Harvard Review
Hayden's Ferry Review
Hermitage Press
Heyday
Hills
Hollyridge Press
Holmgangers Press
Holy Cow!
Home Planet News
Hudson Review
Hungry Mind Review
Icarus
Icon
Idaho Review
Iguana Press
Image
In Character
Indiana Review
Indiana Writes
Intermedia
Intro
Invisible City
Inwood Press
Iowa Review
Ironwood
Jam To-day
The Journal
Jubilat
The Kanchenjuga Press
Kansas Quarterly
Kayak
Kelsey Street Press
Kenyon Review
Kestrel
Lake Effect

Latitudes Press
Laughing Waters Press
Laurel Poetry Collective
Laurel Review
L'Epervier Press
Liberation
Linquis
Literal Latté
Literary Imagination
The Literary Review
The Little Magazine
Living Hand Press
Living Poets Press
Logbridge-Rhodes
Louisville Review
Lowlands Review
Lucille
Lynx House Press
Lyric
The MacGuffin
Magic Circle Press
Malahat Review
Mānoa
Manroot
Many Mountains Moving
Marlboro Review
Massachusetts Review
McSweeney's
Meridian
Mho & Mho Works
Micah Publications
Michigan Quarterly
Mid-American Review
Milkweed Editions
Milkweed Quarterly
The Minnesota Review
Mississippi Review
Mississippi Valley Review
Missouri Review
Montana Gothic
Montana Review
Montemora
Moon Pony Press

Mount Voices
Mr. Cogito Press
MSS
Mudfish
Mulch Press
Nada Press
Narrative
National Poetry Review
Nebraska Review
New America
New American Review
New American Writing
The New Criterion
New Delta Review
New Directions
New England Review
New England Review and Bread Loaf
    Quarterly
New Issues
New Letters
New Ohio Review
New Orleans Review
New Virginia Review
New York Quarterly
New York University Press
Nimrod
9 × 9 Industries
Ninth Letter
Noon
North American Review
North Atlantic Books
North Dakota Quarterly
North Point Press
Northeastern University Press
Northern Lights
Northwest Review
Notre Dame Review
O. ARS
O. Blēk
Obsidian
Obsidian II
Ocho
Oconee Review

October
Ohio Review
Old Crow Review
Ontario Review
Open City
Open Places
Orca Press
Orchises Press
Oregon Humanities
Orion
Other Voices
Oxford American
Oxford Press
Oyez Press
Oyster Boy Review
Painted Bride Quarterly
Painted Hills Review
Palo Alto Review
Paris Press
Paris Review
Parkett
Parnassus: Poetry in Review
Partisan Review
Passages North
Pebble Lake Review
Penca Books
Pentagram
Penumbra Press
Pequod
Persea: An International Review
Perugia Press
Per Contra
Pipedream Press
Pitcairn Press
Pitt Magazine
Pleiades
Ploughshares
Poet and Critic
Poet Lore
Poetry
Poetry Atlanta Press
Poetry East
Poetry Ireland Review

Poetry Northwest
Poetry Now
The Point
Post Road
Prairie Schooner
Prescott Street Press
Press
Promise of Learnings
Provincetown Arts
A Public Space
Puerto Del Sol
Quaderni Di Yip
Quarry West
The Quarterly
Quarterly West
Raccoon
Rainbow Press
Raritan: A Quarterly Review
Rattle
Red Cedar Review
Red Clay Books
Red Dust Press
Red Earth Press
Red Hen Press
Release Press
Republic of Letters
Review of Contemporary Fiction
Revista Chicano-Riquena
Rhetoric Review
Rivendell
River Styx
River Teeth
Rowan Tree Press
Runes
Russian *Samizdat*
Salmagundi
San Marcos Press
Sarabande Books
Sea Pen Press and Paper Mill
Seal Press
Seamark Press
Seattle Review
Second Coming Press

Semiotext(e)
Seneca Review
Seven Days
The Seventies Press
Sewanee Review
Shankpainter
Shantih
Shearsman
Sheep Meadow Press
Shenandoah
A Shout In the Street
Sibyl-Child Press
Side Show
Sixth Finch
Small Moon
Smartish Pace
The Smith
Snake Nation Review
Solo
Solo 2
Some
The Sonora Review
Southern Poetry Review
Southern Review
Southwest Review
Speakeasy
Spectrum
Spillway
The Spirit That Moves Us
St. Andrews Press
Story
Story Quarterly
Streetfare Journal
Stuart Wright, Publisher
Sugar House Review
Sulfur
The Sun
Sun & Moon Press
Sun Press
Sunstone
Sycamore Review
Tamagwa
Tar River Poetry

Teal Press
Telephone Books
Telescope
Temblor
The Temple
Tendril
Texas Slough
Third Coast
13th Moon
THIS
Thorp Springs Press
Three Rivers Press
Threepenny Review
Thunder City Press
Thunder's Mouth Press
Tia Chucha Press
Tikkun
Tin House
Tombouctou Books
Toothpaste Press
Transatlantic Review
Triplopia
TriQuarterly
Truck Press
Tupelo Press
Turnrow
Undine
Unicorn Press
University of Chicago Press
University of Georgia Press
University of Illinois Press
University of Iowa Press
University of Massachusetts Press
University of North Texas Press
University of Pittsburgh Press
University of Wisconsin Press
University Press of New England
Unmuzzled Ox
Unspeakable Visions of the Individual
Vagabond
Vallum
Verse
Vignette

Virginia Quarterly Review
Volt
Wampeter Press
Washington Writers Workshop
Water-Stone
Water Table
Wave Books
West Branch
Western Humanities Review
Westigan Review
White Pine Press
Wickwire Press
Willow Springs
Wilmore City
Witness

Word Beat Press
Word-Smith
World Literature Today
Wormwood Review
Writers Forum
Xanadu
Yale Review
Yardbird Reader
Yarrow
Y'Bird
Zeitgeist Press
Zoetrope: All-Story
Zone 3
ZYZZYVA

CONTRIBUTING SMALL PRESSES FOR PUSHCART PRIZE XXXV

A

A Cappella Zoo, 105 Harvard Ave., E., #A-1, Seattle, WA 98102
A Golden Place, 3714 Sunset Trace Circle, Palm City, FL 34990
A River & Sound Review, 17317 136th Ave. Ct. E., Puyallup, WA 98374
Able Muse Review, 467 Saratoga Ave., #602, San Jose, CA 95129
ABZ Press, PO Box 2746, Huntington, WV 25757-2746
Academic Press and Publishers Library, Prantik, Apt, #D2, House #70/1, Road 6/A, Dhanmondi, Dhaka-1209, Bangladesh
The Acentos Review, CMR 459 Box 06112, APO, AE 09139
Agni Magazine, Boston University, 236 Bay State Rd., Boston, MA 02215
Alabama, Unversity of Alabama Press, Box 870380, Tuscaloosa, AL 35487-0380
Alaska Quarterly Review, Univ. of Alaska, 3211 Providence Dr., ESH 208, Anchorage, AK 99508
Alice James Books, 238 Main St., Farmington, ME 04938
Alimentum, PO BOX 210028, Nashville, TN 37221
Allbook Books, PO Box 562, Selden, NY 11784
Alligator Juniper, 220 Grove Ave., Prescott, AZ 86301
Amaranth Review, 30 Greenhill Rd., Hamburg, NJ 07419
American Arts Quarterly, 915 Boardway, Ste. 1104, New York, NY 10010
American Literary Review, PO Box 311307, Univ. No. Texas, Denton, TX 76203-1307
The American Poetry Review, 117 South 17th St., Ste. 910, Philadelphia, PA 19103
The American Scholar, 1606 New Hampshire Ave. NW, Washington, DC 20009
American Short Fiction, PO Box 301209, Austin, TX 78703
Amoskeag, So. New Hampshire Univ., 2500 No. River Rd., Manchester, NH 03106-1045
Anderbo, 270 Lafayette St., New York, NY 10012
Anhinga Press, P. O. Box 10595, Tallahassee, FL 32302
Annalemma Magazine, 3300 University Blvd., Ste. 218, Winter Park, FL 32792
Anti-, 4237 Beethoven Ave., St. Louis, MO 63116-2503
The Antioch Review, PO Box 148, Yellow Springs, OH 45387-0148
Antrim House Books, PO Box 111, Tariffville, CT 06081
Another Chicago Magazine, 2608 W. Diversey Ave., #202, Chicago IL 60647
Appalachian Heritage, CPO 2166, Berea, KY 40404
Apparatus Magazine, 2013 W. Farragut Ave., #2, Chicago, IL 60625
Apple Valley Review, Queen's Postal Outlet, Box 12, Kingston, ON K7L 3R9, Canada
Aquarius Press, PO Box 23096, Detroit, MI 48223
Arava Review, c/o Gardner, Kibbutz Ketura, D.N Elot 88840, Israel
Arizona Authors, 6145 West Echo Lane, Glendale, AZ 85302

Arroyo Literary Review, MB 2579, CSU, 25800 Carlos Bee Blvd., Hayward, CA 94542
Arsenic Lobster Poetry Journal, 1830 W. 18th St., Chicago, IL 60608
Artful Dodge, English Dept., College of Wooster, Wooster, OH 44691
Arts & Letters, Campus Box 89, Milledgeville, GA 31061
Asheville Poetry Review, PO Box 7086, Asheville, NC 28802
Ashland Poetry Press, Ashland University, Ashland, OH 44805
Askew, P.O. Box 559, Ventura, CA 93002
Atlanta Review, PO Box 8248, Atlanta, GA 31106
The Aurorean, PO Box 187, Farmington, ME 04938
Autumn House Press, 87½ Westwood St., Pittsburgh, PA 15211
Axe Factory, PO Box 40691, Philadelphia, PA 19107

B

Bamboo Ridge Press, PO Box 61781, Honolulu, HI 96839-1781
Barbaric Yawp, 3700 County Route 24, Russell, NY 13684
The Barefoot Muse, PO Box 115, Hainesport, NJ 08036
Barn Owl Review, Dept. of English, Univ. of Akron, Akron, OH 44325-1906
Barrelhouse, PO Box 17598, Baltimore, MD 21297-1598
Barrow Street, PO Box 1831, New York, NY 10156
Bartleby Snopes, 625 Norton Ave., St. Louis, MO 63122
Bat City Review, Univ. of Texas, 1 University Station B 5000, Austin, TX 78712
Bayou Magazine, Univ. of New Orleans, 2000 Lake Shore Dr., New Orleans, LA 70148
bear creek haiku, PO Box 3787, Boulder, CO 80307
Bear Star Press, 185 Hollow Oak Dr., Cohasset, CA 95973
Beloit Fiction Journal, 700 College St., Beloit, W 53511-5595
BelleBooks, 1092 Ridgeway Rd., Dahlonega, GA 30533
Bellevue Literary Review, NYU School of Medicine, 550 First Ave, New York, NY 10016
Bellingham Review, MS-9053, WWU, Bellingham, WA 98225
Bellowing Ark Press, PO Box 55564, Shoreline, WA 98155
Beloit Poetry Journal, PO Box 151, Farmington, ME 04938
Berkeley Fiction Review, 10 B Eshleman Hall, UCB, Berkeley, CA 94720
Big Valley Press, 5551 W. Bluff Ave., Fresno, CA 93722
The Binnacle, 9 O'Brien Ave., Machias, ME 04654
Birmingham Poetry Review, University of Alabama, Birmingham, AL 35294
BkMk Press, UMKC, 5101 Rockhill Rd., Kansas City, MO 64110-2499
The Black Boot, 1742 N. Edgemont St., #201, Los Angeles, CA 90027
Black Clock, California Institute of the Arts, 24700 McBean Pkwy, Valencia, CA 91355
Black Renaissance Noire, NYU, 269 Mercer St., New York, NY 10003
Black Warrior Review, PO Box 870170, Tuscaloosa, AL 35487-0170
Blackbird, VCU Dept. of English, PO Box 843082, Richmond, VA 23284
Blood Lotus, 2732 N. Bremen, Unit A, Milwaukee, WI 53212
Blood Orange Review, 1495 Evergreen Ave. NE, Salem, OR 97301
Bloodroot Literary Magazine, PO Box 322, Thetford Center, VT 05075
Blue Earth Review, 220 Centennial Student Union, Minnesota State University, Mankato, MN 56001
Blue Fifth Review, 267 Lark Meadow Circle, Bluff City, TN 37618
Blue Guitar Magazine, 1616 N. Alta Mesa Dr., #33, Mesa, AZ 85205
Blue Mesa Review, UNM, Humanities Bldg, #217, Albuquerque, NM 87131-1106
Blue Unicorn, 22 Avon Rd., Kensington, CA 94707
Blueline, 44 Pierrepont Ave., Potsdam, NY 13676-2294
BluePrint Review, 1103 NW 11th Ave., Gainesville, FL 32601
BOA Editions, 250 North Goodman St., Ste 306, Rochester, NY 14607
Bomb, 80 Hanson Place, Ste. 703, Brooklyn, NY 11217
Bone World Publishing, 3700 County Route 24, Russell, NY 13684
Boston Review, Building E-53, Room 407, MIT, Cambridge, MA 02139
Bottom Dog Press, PO Box 425, Huron, OH 44839
Boulevard, 7507 Byron Place, 1st Floor, St. Louis, MO 63105
Bowery Books, 310 Bowery, New York, NY 10012
Boxcar Poetry Review, 510 S. Ardmore Ave., #307, Los Angeles, CA 90020

Brain, Child, PO Box 714, Lexington, VA 24450
The Briar Cliff Review, 3303 Rebecca St., PO Box 2100, Sioux City, IA 51104-2100
Brick, 50 Baldwin St., Toronto, ON M5T 1L4, Canada
Brilliant Corners, Lycoming College, Williamsport, PA 17701
The Brooklyn Rail, 99 Commercial St., #15, Brooklyn, NY 11222
The Brooklyn Review, Brooklyn College, 2900 Bedford Ave., Brooklyn, NY 11210

C

Caketrain Journal, PO Box 82588, Pittsburgh, PA 15218-0588
Callaloo, 4212 TAMU, Texas A&M Univ., College Station, TX 77843-4212
Calyx Inc., Box B. Corvallis, OR 97339
Carve Magazne, PO Box 701510, Dallas, TX 75370
Cave Wall Press, PO Box 29546, Greensboro, NC 27429-9546
Center, 202 Tate Hall, University of Missouri, Columbia, MO 65211-1500
Central Avenue Press, 5390 Fallriver Row Court, Columbia, MD 21044
Cerise Press, PO Box 241187, Omaha, NE 68114
Cervena Barva Press, PO Box 440357, W. Somerville, MA 02144-3222
Cha, 10 A Langdale Rd., Greenwich SE10 8UA, London, UK
Chandelle Press, 12106 Red Oak Crt. So., Burnsville, MN 55337
Chaparral, 7352 Sylvia Ave., Reseda, CA 91335
Chautauqua, UNC Wilmington, 601 South College Rd., Wilmington, NC 28403-5938
Chelsea Green Publishing, 85 North Main St., PO Box 428, White River Jt., VT 05001
Cherry Pie Press, 28 Glen Ridge Dr., Glen Carbon, IL 62034-2905
Chicago Quarterly Review, 517 Sherman Ave., Evanston IL 60202
Chiron Books, 9902 Crystal Ct., #107, Laredo, TX 78045
The Chrysalis Reader, 1745 Gravel Hill Rd., Dillwyn, VA 23936
Cider Press Review, 777 Braddock Lane, Halifax, PA 17032
Cimarron Review, Oklahoma State University, Stillwater, OK 74078
Cincinnati Review, Univ. of Cincinnati, PO Box 210069, Cincinnati, OH 45221-0069
Clockroot Books, 46 Crosby St., Northampton, MA 01060
Coal City Review, English Dept., University of Kansas, Lawrence, KS 66045
Cold Mountain Review, ASU Box 32052, Boone, NC 28608-2052
The Collagist, 2779 Page Ave., Ann Arbor, MI 48104
Colorado Review, 9105 Campus Delivery, Colorado State Univ., Fort Collins, CO 80523-9105
Columbia, 415 Dodge Hall, 2960 Broadway, New York, NY 10027
Columbia Poetry Review, 600 South Michigan Ave., Chicago, IL 60605-1996
Coming Together, PO Box 1273, Dellslow, WV 26531
Common Ground Review, 40 Prospect St., #C-1, Westfield, MA 01085-1559
The Comstock Review, 214 E. First St., E. Syracuse, NY 13057
Concrete Wolf, PO Box 1808, Kingston, WA 98346-1808
Conduit, 788 Osceola Ave., Saint Paul, MN 55105
Confrontation, Long Island Univ., 720 Northern Boulevard, Brookville, NY 11548-1300
Conjunctions, Bard College, Annandale-on-Hudson, NY 12504
Connecticut Review (CT Review), 501 Crescent St., New Haven, CT 06105
Convergence Review, 611 Courtland St., Apt. A, Greensboro, NC 27401-6231
Copper Canyon Press, PO Box 271, Port Townsend, WA 89368
Copper Nickel, Campus Box 175, POB 173364, Denver, Co 80217
Country Dog Review, 215 Karen Dr., Oxford, MS 38655
Court Green, Columbia College, 600 South Michigan Ave., Chicago, IL 60605-1996
Crab Creek Review, PO Box 1524, Kingston, WA 98346
Crab Orchard Review, Mail Code 4503, So. Illinois Univ., Carbondale, IL 62901
Crazyhorse, College of Charleston, 66 George St., Charleston, SC 29424
Creative Nonfiction, 5501 Walnut St., Ste. 202, Pittsburgh, PA 15232
Cross-Cultural Communications, 239 Wynsum Ave., Merrick, NY 11566-4725
Crucible, Barton College, PO Box 5000, Wilson, NC 27893
Curbstone Press, 321 Jackson St., Willimantic, CT 06226-1738
Cutthroat, A Journal of the Arts, PO Box 2414, Durango, CO 81302

D

Danse Macabre, 7413 Winter Garden Ct., Las Vegas, NV 89145
Dappled Things Magazine, 2876 S. Abingdon St., #C-2, Arlington, VA 22206
decomP, 3002 Grey Wolf Cove, New Albany, IN 47150
The Delmarva Review, PO Box 544, St. Michaels, MD 21663
Denver Quarterly, University of Denver, 2000 E Asbury, Denver, CO 80208
Deuce Coupe, 327 Kathy Lane, Poplar Bluff, MO 63901
Dislocate, 1 Lind Hall, 207 Church St., SE., Minneapolis, MN 55455
The DMQ Review, 16393 Bonnie Lane, Los Gatos, CA 95032
Dogwood, Fairfield Univ., 1073 North Benson Rd., Fairfield, CT 06824-5195
Dossier, 244 DeKalb Ave., Brooklyn, NY 11205
Dragonfly Press, 23685 Marble Quarry Rd., Unit #14, Columbia, CA 95310
Drash, Temple Beth Am, 2632 NE 80th St., Seattle, WA 98115-4622
Dreams & Nightmares, 1300 Kicker, Tuscaloosa, AL 35404
Durable Goods, PO Box 282, Painted Post, NY 14870

E

Ecotone, UNC Wilmington, 601 South College Rd., Wilmington, NC 28403-5938
Eden Waters Press, 16 Harcourt St., #2B, Boston, MA 02116
Ekphrasis, PO Box 161236, Sacramento, CA 95816-1236
Electric Literature, 325 Gold St., Ste. 303, Brooklyn, NY 11201
Electrik Mik Bath Press, PO Box 833223, Richardson, TX 75083
Eleven Eleven Journal, 1111 Eighth St., S.F., CA 94107
Elkhound, PO Box 1453, Gracie Sta., New York, NY 10028
Emprise Review, 197 W. Lafayette #2, Fayetteville, AR 72701
The Enigmatist, 104 Bronco Dr., Georgetown, TX 78633
Entelechy International, New England College, 98 Bridge St., Henniker, NH 03242
epic rites press, 240-222 Baseline Rd., Ste. 206, Sherwood Park, AB T8A 1SB, Canada
Epicenter: A Literary Magazine, PO Box 367, Riverside, CA 92502
Epiphany, 71 Bedford St., New York, NY 10014
Epoch, 251 Goldwin Smith Hall, Cornell University, Ithaca NY 14853-3201
Esopus, 64 West 3rd St., Room 210, New York, NY 10012-1021
Ethos Books, 160 Paya Lebar Rd., #06-01, Orion@Paya Lebar, Singapore 409022
Europa Editions, 116 East 16th St., 6th Floor, New York, NY 10003
The Evansville Review, Univ. of Evansville, 1800 Lincoln Ave, Evansville, IN 47722
The Evening Street Review, 7652 Sawmill Rd., #335, Dublin, OH 43016
Event, PO Box 2503, New Westminister, BC, V3L 5B2, Canada
Excaliber Press, 3950 Old Shell Rd., Mobile, AL 36608-1334
Exit 13 Magazine—PO Box 423, Fanwood, NJ 07023

F

Failbetter, 2022 Grove Ave., Richmond, VA 23220
Fantasist Enterprises, PO Box 9381, Wilmington, DE 19809
Faultline, 5305 Palo Verde Rd., Irvine, CA 92617
Fiction Fix, 370 Thornycroft Ave., Staten Island, NY 10312
Fiction International, SDSU, 5500 Campanile Dr., San Diego, CA 92182-6020
Field, 50 North Professor St., Oberlin, OH 44074
Fifth Wednesday Journal, PO Box 4033, Lisle, IL 60532-9033
Final Thursday Press, 815 State St., Cedar Falls, IA 50613
Finishing Line Press, PO Box 1626, Georgetown, KY 40324
First City Review, 941 N. Orianna St., 3rd Floor, Philadelphia, PA 19123
The First Line, PO Box 250382, Plano, TX 75025-0382
Fithian Press, PO Box 2790, McKinleyville, CA 95519
5 AM, Box 205, Spring Church, PA 15686

Five Chapters, 1401 Highland Ave., Louisville, KY 40204-2028
Five Points, Georgia State University, PO Box 3999, Atlanta, GA 30302-3999
Five Star Publications, 4696 West Tyson St., Chandler, AZ 85226-2903
Flash Me Magazine, PO Box 803, O'Fallon, IL 62269
The Flea, 99 Faunce St., Gosford, NS W 2250, Australia
Fleur-de-lis Press, Spalding University, 851 South Fourt St., Louisville, KY 40203
The Florida Review, 855 S. Pennsylvania Ave., Winter Park, FL 32789
Fogged Clarity, PO Box 1016, Muskegon, MI 49443
Foliate Oak Literary Magazine, UAM, Monticello, MCB 113, Monticello, AR 71656
Forge Journal, 1610 S. 22nd St., Lincoln, NE 68502
Four Way Books, P.O. Box 535, Village Station, New York, NY 10014
Fourteen Hills, SF State Univ., 1600 Halloway Ave., San Francisco, CA 94132
Fourth Genre, Michigan State University, Morrill Hall, East Lansing, MI 48824-1036
Fox Chase Review, 7930 Barnes St., Apt. A-7, Philadelphia, PA 19111
Free Lunch, PO Box 717, Glenview, IL 60025-0717
Free Verse, M233 Marsh Rd., Marshfield, WI 54449-9292
Freedom Fiction, Nirli Villa, Flat No. 7, Village Rd., Bhandup (west), Mmbai 400078, India
Freight Stories, PO Box 44167, Indianapolis, IN 46244
Fringe Magazine, 93 Fox Rd., Apt. 5A, Edison, NJ 08817
From East to West, 12 Jonathan Dr., Brunswick, ME 04011
Fugue, English Dept., University of Idaho, Moscow, ID 83844
Full of Crow, PO Box 1082, Beacon, NY 12508
Future Earth Magazine, 500 N. Santa Maria, #21, Santa Paula, CA 93060

G

Gargoyle Magazine, 3819 13th St. N., Arlington, VA 22201-4922
Gemini Magazine, PO Box 1485, Onset, MA 02558
The Georgia Review, 285 Jackson St., Univ. of Georgia, Athens, GA 30602
The Gettysburg Review, Gettysburg College, Gettysburg, PA 17325-1491
Gigantic, 337 Bedford Ave., #3R, Brooklyn, NY 11211
Gilbert Magazine, 3460 N. Hackett Ave., Milwaukee, WI 53211-2945
Glimmer Train Press, 1211 NW Glisan St., Ste. 207, Portland, OR 97209-3054
Gold Wake Press, 5 Barry St., Randolph, MA 02368
Goose River Press, 3400 Friendship Rd., Waldoboro, ME 04572-6337
Grace Notes Books, 10254 Alexandria St., Ventura, CA 93004
Grateful Steps, 1091 Hendersonville Rd., Asheville, NC 28803
Graywolf Press, 2402 University Ave., Ste. 203, Saint Paul, MN 55114
Great River Review, Anderson Center, PO Box 406, Red Wing, MN 55066
Green Fuse Poetic Arts, 400 Vortex St., Bellvue, CO 80512
Green Mountains Review, Johnson State College, Johnson, VT 05656
The Greensboro Review, PO Box 26170, Greensboro, NC 27402-6170
The Greensilk Journal, 1459 Redland Rd., Cross Junction, VA 22625
Grevious Jones Press, 53 Romilly Rd., Canton, Cardiff CF5 1FJ, UK
Grist: The Journal for Writers, Dept. of English, Univ. of Tennessee, Knoxville, TN 37996-0430
Groundwaters, PO Box 50, Lorane, OR 97451
Guernica Magazine, 395 Fort Washington Ave., #57, New York, NY 10033
Gulf Coast, University of Houston, Houston, TX 77204-3013

H

Hamilton Stone Editions, PO Box 43, Maplewood, NJ 07040
Hampden-Sydney Poetry Review, Hampden-Sydney College, Box 66, Hampden-Sydney, VA 23943
Harbour Publishing Co., 4437 Rondeview Rd., Madeira Park, BC V0N 2H0 Canada
Harpur Palate, PO Box 6000, Binghamton University, Binghamton, NY 13902
Harvard Review, Lamont Library, Harvard University, Cambridge, MA 02138
Hawai'i Pacific Review, 1060 Bishop St., LB7, Honolulu, HI 96813-4210

Hawai'i Review, Univ. Hawaii, Manoa, 1733 Donaghho Rd., Honolulu, HI 96822
Hayden's Ferry Review, Arizona State Univ., PO Box 875002, Tempe, AZ 85287-5002
The Healing Muse, Center for Bioethics & Humanities, 750 East Adams St., Syracuse, NY 13210
The Hedgehog Review, UVA, PO Box 400816, Charlottesville, VA 22904-4816
The Hell Gate Review, 24–29 19th St., Astoria, NY 11102
High Country News, PO Box 1090, Paonia, CO 81428
Hobart, PO Box 1658, Ann Arbor, MI 48106
Hobble Creek Review, PO Box 3511, West Wendover, NV 89883
The Hobkins Reviews, 135 Gilman Hall, 3400 N. Charles St., Baltimore, MD 21218-6828
The Hollins Critic, PO Box 9538, Hollins University, Roanoke, VA 24020
Holly Rose Review, 12 Townsend Blvd., Poughkeepsie, NY 12603
Home Planet News, PO Box 455, High Falls, NY 12440
Hopewell Publications, PO Box 11, Titusville, NJ 08560
Hotel Amerika, English Dept., 600 S. Michigan Ave., Chicago, IL 60605-1996
How Journal, 12 Desbrosses St., New York, NY 10013
HILR Review, 21 Grozier Rd., Cambridge, MA 02138
The Hudson Review, 684 Park Ave., New York, NY 10065
Hudson View Poetry Digest, PO Box 295, Stormville, NY 12582-0295
Hummingbird Review, 122 Chestnut Ave., Narberth, PA 19072
Hunger Mountain, Vermont College, 36 College St., Montpelier, VT 05602

I

Ibbetson Street Press, 25 School Street, Somerville, MA 02143
The Idaho Review, Boise State Univ., 1910 University Dr., Boise, ID 83725
Ideomancer, 2889 Neil Ave., Apt. 411C, Columbus, OH 43202
Illogical Muse, 115 Liberty St., Apt. 1, Buchanan, MI 49107
Illya's Honey, PO Box 700865, Dallas, TX 75370
Image, 3307 Third Avenue West, Seattle, WA 98119
In Digest Magazine, 3285 33rd St., #F8, Astoria, NY 11106
In Posse Review, 2360 43rd Ave. E., #201, Seattle, WA 98112
In the Write Mind, CFCC-Citrus, 3800 S. Lecanto Hwy., Lecanto, FL 34461-9026
Indiana Review, 1020 E. Kirkwood Ave., Bloomington, IN 47405-7103
Indigo Editing, PO Box 1355, Beaverton, OR 97075
Inglis House Poetry, 2600 Belmont Ave., Philadelphia, PA 19131
Ink-Filled Page, PO Box 1355, Beaverton, OR 97075
Inkwell, Manhattanville College, 2900 Purchase St., Purchase, NY 10577-2132
The Iowa Review, 308 EPB, University of Iowa, Iowa City, IA 52242
Iron Horse Literary Review, English Dept., Texas Tech Univ., Lubbock, TX 79409-3091
Irreantum Magazine, PO Box 970874, Orem, UT 84097-0874
Iris G. Press, 2848 Nolt Rd., Lancaster, PA 17601
Isaiah Publishing, 52 Bliss Rd., New Britain, CT 06053
Isotope, Utah State University, 3200 Old Main Hill, Logan, UT 84322-3200

J

J Journal, John Jay College of Criminal Justice, 619 West 54th St., 7th Fl, NY, NY 10019
Jabberwock Review, Mississippi State University, Mississippi State, MS 39762
Jack Magazine, 214-4451 Albert St., Burnaby, BC V5C 2G4, BC, Canada
Jane Street Press, 1 Jane Street, New York, NY 10014
Jewish Currents, PO Box 111, Accord, NY 12404
The Journal, English Dept., Ohio State Univ., 164 West 17th Ave., Columbus, OH 43210
Journal of New Jersey Poets, 214 Center Grove Rd., Randolph, NJ 07869-2086
Journal of Truth and Consequences, 110 Scenic Dr., Hattiesburg, MS 39401
joyful!, PO Box 80054, Springfield, MA 01138
Juked, 110 Westridge Dr., Tallahassee, FL 32304

K

Karamu, Eastern Illinois University, 600 Lincoln Ave., Charleston, IL 61920
Kartika Review, 14447 Griffith St., San Leandro, CA 94577
Kelsey Review, Mercer County Community College, PO Box B, Trenton, NJ 08690
Kenyon Review, Neff Cottage, 102 W. Wiggin St., Gambier, OH 43022
The Kerf, College of the Redwoods, 883 W. Washington Blvd., Crescent City, CA 95531
Keyhole, 1307-B 15th Ave. So., Nashville, TN 37212
The King's English, 3114 NE 47th Ave., Portland, OR 97213
Kitsune Books, PO Box 1154, Crawfordville, FL 32326-1154
Knee-Jerk Magazine, 3140 W. Sunnyside, Apt. 1, Chicago, IL 60625
Knockout, 9 Nina Court, Isanti, MN 55040
Kore Press, PO Box 42315, Tucson, AZ 95733-2315
Kudzu, Hazard, 1 Community College Dr., Hazard, KY 41701-2402

L

The L Magazine, 20 Jay St., Ste. 207, Brooklyn, NY 11201
Lake Effect, 4951 College Drive, Erie, PA 16563-1501
Lamplighter Review, PO Box 92, Overton, TX 75684
Lapham's Quarterly, 33 Iriving Place, New York, NY 10003
Lalitamba, 110 West 86th St., #5D, New York, NY 10024
Leaf Garden Press, 20610 Denford Ct., Katy, TX 77450
The Ledge, 40 Maple Ave., Bellport, NY 11713
The Legendary, 710 W. 9th St., Clifton, TX 76634
Limbertwig Press, 15048 Draper Rd., Fayetteville, AR 72704
Linebreak, 1716 N. Garland Ave., Fayatteville, AR 72703
Lips, 7002 Blvd. East #2-26G. Guttenberg, NJ 07093
Lit, The New School, Room 514, 66 West 12th St., New York, NY 10011
Literal Latte, 200 e. 10th St., Ste. 240, New York, NY 10003
Literary House Review, PO Box 295, Stormville, NY 12582-0295
The Literary Review, Fairleigh Dickinson Univ., 285 Madison Ave., Madison, NJ 07940
Litterbox, 305 Fiddlers Knoll Court, Kernersville, NC 27284
Little Balkans Review, 909 S. Olive, Pittsburg, KS 66762
Lorimer Press, PO Box 1013, Davidson, NC 28036
Los Angeles Review, PO Box 1829, Lake Oswego, OR 97035
Lost Horse Press, 105 Lost Horse Lane, Sandpoint, ID 83864
The Louisville Review, Spalding University, 851 S. Fourth St., Louisville, KY 40203
The Lowbrow Reader, PO Box 65, Cooper Station, New York, NY 10276
Lumina, Sarah Lawrence College, Slonim House, 1 Mead Way, Bronxville, NY 10708-5999
Luna, University of Minnesota, 207 Church Street SE, Minneapolis, MN 55455
Lyric, PO Box 2494, Bloomington, IN 47402

M

The MacGuffin, Schoolcraft College, 18600 Haggerty Rd., Livonia, MI 48152
Magrapoets, 13300 Tecumseh Rd. E., #226, Tecumseh, Ontario N8N 4R8, Canada
Main Street Rag, PO Box 690100, Charlotte, NC 28227
MAKE Literary Productions, 2229 W. Iowa, Chicago, IL 60622
make/shift, PO Box 2697, Venice, CA 90294
The Malahat Review, PO Box 1700 STN CSC, Victoria BC V8W 2Y2 Canada
Mammoth Books, 7 Juniata St., DuBois, PA 15801
Mandorla, Illinois State Unviersity, #4240, Normal, IL 61790-4240
Manhattan Media, 79 Madison Ave., New York, NY 10016
The Manhattan Review, 440 Riverside Dr., #38, New York, NY 10027
Manoa, English Dept., Unversity of Hawaii, Honolulu, HI 96822
Manorborn, 2121 Cox Rd., Jarreettsville, MD 21084

Many Mountains Moving, 1705 Lombard St., Philadelphia, PA 19146
Mardel Books, 6145 West Echo Lane, Glendale, AZ 85302
MARGIE, The American Journal of Poetry, PO Box 250, Chesterfield, MO 63006-0250
Marginalia, PO Box 258, Pitkin, CO 81241
The Massachusetts Review, South College 126047, Amherst, MA 01003-7140
Matchbook, 14 W. 85th St., #5B, New York, NY 10024
May Fair Publishing, 3514 Mapleton Rd., Sanborn, NY 14132
Mayapple Press, 408 N. Lincoln St., Bay City, MI 48708-6653
McSweeney's Publishing, 849 Valencia, San Francisco, CA 94110
Measure: A Review of Formal Poetry, University of Evansville, 1800 Lincoln Ave., Evansville, IN 47722
Melusine, 12302 Skylark Lane, Bowie, MD 20715
Memoir, PO Box 1398, Sausalito, CA 94966-1398
Memorious, 3424 Brookline Ave., #16, Cincinnati, OH 45220
Meridian, University of Virginia, PO Box 400145, Charlottesville, VA 22904-4145
Michigan Quarterly Review, Univ. of Michigan, 915 E. Washington St., Ann Arbor, MI 48109-2420
Mid-American Review, Bowling Green State University, Bowling Green, OH 43403
Milkweed Editions, 1011 Washington Ave. So., Ste. 300, Minneapolis, MN 55415
Milspeak Foundation, 33 Winding Way, Beaufort, SC 29907
The Minnesota Review, Carnegie Mellon University, Pittsburgh, PA 15213
Minnetonka Review, P.O. Box 386, Spring Park, MN 55384
Mississippi Review, 118 College Dr. #5144, Hattiesburg, MS 39406-0001
The Missouri Review, 357 McReynolds Hall, Univ. of Missouri, Columbia, MO 65211
Mobius, the Poetry Magazine, PO Box 671058, Flushing, NY 11367-1058
Modern English Tanka Press, PO Box 43717, Baltimore, MD 21236
Modern Haiku, PO Box 33077, Santa Fe, NM 87594-9998
Monkey Puzzle Press, 3116 47th St., Boulder, CO 80301
Monkeybicycle, 16 Netcong Heights, #2, Netcong, NJ 07857
Moon City Press, MSU Dept of English, 901 S. National, Springfield, MO 65897
Moosemeat Writer's Group, 15 Lebos Rd., Toronto, ON M2H2L8, Canada
The Morning News, 6206 Wynona Ave., Austin, TX 78757
Mud Luscious, 2115 Sandstone Dr., Fort Collins, CO 80524
Mudfish, 184 Franklin St., New York, NY 10013
MungBeing Magainze, 1319 Maywood Ave., Upland, CA 91786
Muse-Pie Press, 73 Pennington Ave., Passaic, NJ 07055
Muumuu House, 352 Graham Ave., Brooklyn, NY 11211
Mythium, 1428 N. Forbes Rd., Lexington, KY 40511

N

N + 1 Magazine, 68 Jay St., #405, Brooklyn, NY 11201
Nano Fiction, PO Box 667445, Houston, TX 77266-7445
Narrative Magazine, 2130 Fillmore St., #233, San Francisco, CA 94115
Naugatuck River Review, PO Box 368, Westfield, MA 01085
Necessary Fiction, Emerson College, 120 Boylston St., Boston, MA 02116-4624
neoNuma Arts, POB 460248, Houston, TX 77056
New American Writing, Oink! Press, 369 Molino Ave., Mill Valley, CA 94941
The New Criterion, 900 Broadway, New York, NY 10003
New England Review, Middlebury College, Middlebury, VT 05753
New Haven Review, 352 West Rock Ave., New Haven, CT 06515
New Issues Poetry & Prose, WMU, 1903 W. Michigan Ave., Kalamazoo, MI 49008-5463
New Letters, Univ. of Missouri, 5100 Rockhill Rd., Kansas City, MO 64110-2499
New Madrid, Murray State University, 7C Faculty Hall, Murray, KY 42071-3341
New Ohio Review, Ohio University, 360 Ellis Hall, Athens, OH 45701
New Orleans Review, Box 195, Loyola University, New Orleans, CA 70118
The New Orphic Review, 706 Mill St., Nelson, B.C. V1L 4S5 Canada
New Rivers Press, PO Box 38, Moorhead, MN 56563
New Southerner Magazine, 375 Wood Valley Lane, Louisville, KY 40299
New Verse News, Les Belles Maisons H-11, Jl. Serpong Raya, Serpong Utara, Tangerang-Baten 15310, Indonesia

New York Press, 79 Madison Ave., New York, NY 10016
New York Quarterly, P.O. Box 2015, Old Chelsea Station, New York, NY 10113
New York Skyline Review, PO Box 295, Stormville, NY 12582-0295
New York Tyrant, 676 A Ninth Ave., #153, New York, NY 10036
Nimrod International Journal, 800 South Tucker Dr., Tulsa OK 74104-3189
Ninth Letter, University of Illinois, 608 S. Wright St., Urbana, IL 61801
Niteblade Magazine, 11323 126th St., Edmonton, AB T5M 0R5, Canada
No Tell Books, 11436 Fairway Dr., Reston, VA 20190
Nodin Press, 530 North Third St., Ste. 120, Minneapolis, MN 55401
Noon, 1324 Lexington Ave., PMB 298, New York, NY 10128
The Normal School, 5245 N. Backer Ave., M/S PB 98, Fresno, CA 93740-8001
North American Review, Univ. of No. Iowa, 1222 West 27th St., Cedar Falls, IA 50614-0516
The North Carolina Literary Review, East Carolina Univ., Greenville, NC 27858-4353
North Dakota Quarterly (NDQ), 276 Centennial Drive, Grand Forks, ND 58202-7209
Northwest Review, 5243 University of Oregon, Eugene, OR 97403-5243
Not One Of Us, 12 Curtis Rd., Natick, MA 01760
The Notre Dame Review, 840 Flanner Hall, Notre Dame, IN 46556-5639
Noun Vs. Verb, Burning River, 169 S. Main St., #4, Rittman, OH 44270
The November 3rd Club, 65 Paine St., #2, Worcester, MA 01605

O

Oak Bend Review, 2901 Oak Bend Ct., Flower Mound, TX 75028
OCHO, 604 Vale St., Bloomington, IL 61701
Off the Coast, PO Box 14, Robbinston, ME 04671
Old Crow Review, 66 West St., #3, Northampton, MA 01060
Old Mountain Press, 2542 S. Edgewater Dr., Fayetteville, NC 28303
Old Red Kimino, 3175 Cedartown Hwy. SE, Rome, GA 30161
One Story, Old American Can Factory, 230 3rd St., #A111, Brooklyn, NY 11215
Open City, 270 Lafayette St., Ste. 1412, New York, NY 10012
Open Thread, 138 Stratford Ave., Pittsburgh, PA 15206
Opium, 144A Diamond St., Brooklyn, NY 11222
Orange Alert, PO Box 3897, St. Charles, IL 60174
Orbis, 17 Greenhow Ave., West Kirby, Wirral, CH48 5EL, UK
Orchises Press, PO Box 320533, Alexandria, VA 22320-4533
Oregon East, Hoke 304, Eastern Oregon University, La Grande, OR 97850
Original Plus, 17 High St., Maryport, Cumbria CA15 6BQ, UK
The Orion Society, 187 Main St., Great Barrington, MA 01230
Osiris, PO Box 297, Deerfield, MA 01342
Other Press, 2 Park Ave., 24th Floor, New York, NY 10016
Out of Nothing, 2639 Sharpview Lane, Dallas, TX 75228
Out of Our, 1288 Columbus Ave., #216, San Francisco, CA 94133
Overtime, PO Box 250382, Plano, TX 75025-0382
Oxford American, 201 Donaghey Ave., Main 107, Conway, AR 72035-5001

P

P.R.A. Publishing, PO Box 211701, Martinez, CA 30917
Palabra, PO Box 86146, Los Angeles, CA 90086-0146
Palo Alto Review, 1400 W. Villaret Blvd., San Antonio, TX 78224
Pank, Michigan Tech. Univ., 1400 Townsend Dr., Houghton, MI 49931-1295
The Paris Review, 62 White St., New York, NY 10013
Parnassus, 205 W. 89th St. (8F), New York, NY 10024
Parthenon West Review, 738 Minor Ave., Kalamazoo, MI 49008
Passages North, English Dept., 1401 Presque Isle Ave., Marquette, MI 49855-5363
Paterson Literary Review, 1 College Blvd., Paterson, NJ 07505-1179
PAX Americana, 91 Kingsland, #3, Brooklyn, NY 11222

Pearl, 3030 E. Second St., Long Beach, CA 90803

Pecan Grove Press, 1 Camino Santa Maria, San Antonio, TX 78228

PEN America, PEN American Center, 588 Broadway, Ste. 303, New York, NY 10012

Performance Poets Association, 2176 Third St., East Meadow, NY 11554

Perugia Pres, PO Box 60364, Florence, MA 01062

Petigru Review, SCWW, PO Box 7104, Columbia, SC 29202

Phoebe, GMU, 4400 University Ave., Fairifax, VA 22030

Phrygian Press, 58–59 205th St., Bayside, NY 11364

Pirene's Fountain, 3616 Glenlake Dr., Glenview IL 60026

The Pinch, English Dept., 467 Patterson Hall, Memphis, TN 38152-3510

Pine Hill Press, 343 W. 4th St., Chadron, NE 69337-2321

Pitt Poetry Series, University of Pittsburgh, Pittsburgh, PA 15260

Platte Valley Review, University of Nebraska, Kearney, NE 68849-1320

Pleiades Press, Dept. of English and Philosophy, University of Central Missouri, Warrensburg, MO 64093-5046

Plexus Publishing, 143 Old Mariton Pike, Medford. NJ 08055

Ploughshares, Emerson College, 120 Boylston St., Boston, MA 02116-4624

PMS, University of Alabama, 1530 3rd Ave. So., Birmingham, AL 35294-1260

Poemeleon: A Journal of Poetry, 5755 Durango Rd., Riverside, CA 92506

Poems and Play, MTSU, Box 70, Murfreesboro, TN 37132

Poet Lore, The Writer's Center, 4508 Walsh St., Bethesda, MD 20815

Poetry, 444 N. Michigan Ave., Ste. 1850, Chicago, IL 60611-4043

Poetry Atlanta Press, 701 Highland Ave., NE, #1212, Atlanta, GA 30312

Poetry Bay, PO Box 114, Northport, NY 11768

Poetry Center, Cleveland State Univ., 2121 Euclid Ave., Cleveland, OH 44115-2214

Poetry In the Arts Press, 5110 Avenue H, Austin, TX 78751

Poetry Internal, English Dept., SDSU, 5500 Campanile Dr., San Diego, CA 92182-6020

Poetry Kanto, 959 Yamanouchi, Kamakura, Kanagawa, 247-0062, Japan

Poetry Northwest, 4232 SE Hawthorne Boulevard, Portland, Oregon 97215

Poetry Review, 22 Betterson St., London WC2H 9BX, United Kingdom

Poetry South, Mississippi Valley State Univ., 14000 Hwy 82 W., Box 7242, Itta Bena, MS 38941-1400

Poets and Artists, 604 S. Vale St., Bloomington, IL 61701

Poets Wear Prada, 533 Bloomfield St., 2nd Floor, Hoboken, NJ 07030

The Point, 732 S. Financial Pl., Apt. 704, Chicago, IL 60605

Polymer Grove, PO Box 3, Roseville, CA 95661

Poor Souls Press, PO Box 236, Millbrae, CA 94030

Porchlight: A Literary Magazine, 25 Magaw Place, #5E, New York, NY 10033

Possibilities, 23 Willabay Dr., Unit D, Williams Bay, WI 53191

Potomac Review, Montgomery College, 51 Mannakee St., Rockville, MD 20850

Prairie Schooner, UNL, 201 Andrews Hall, PO Box 880334, Lincoln, NE 68588-0334

Presa :S: Press, PO Box 792, Rockford, MI 49341

Press 53, PO Box 30314, Winston-Salem, NC 27130

Pretend Genius Press, PO Box 6502, Silver Spring, MD 20906

Prick of the Spindle, PO Box 12784, Pensacola, FL 32591

Prism Review, 1950 Third St., La Verne, CA 91750

Project Muse, c/o Rachelle Winkle-Wagner, UNL, PO Box 880630, Lincoln, NE 68588-0630

Provincetown Arts, 650 Commercial St., Provincetown, MA 02657

Provincetown Journal, PO Box 1535, South Dennis, MA 02660

A Public Space, 323 Dean St., Brooklyn, NY 11217

Puerto Del Sol, New Mexico State University, MSC 3E, Box 30001, Las Cruces, NM 88003

Puffin Circus, 442 S. Columbia Ave., Somerset, PA 15501

Puna Press, PO Box 7790, San Diego, CA 92167

Q

Qarrtsiluni, 1397 rue Rachel E., #102, Montreal, H2J 2K2 QC, Canada

The Quarterly Conversation, 5872 Chabot Rd., Oakland, CA 94618

Quarterly West, 255 S. Central Campus Dr., Rm. 3500, Salt Lake City, UT 84112-0109

Quick Fiction 13, www.quickfiction.org, PO Box 4445, Salem, MA 01970

Quiddity, Benedictine University, 1500 N. Fifth St., Springfield, IL 62702
Quill and Parchment Press, 2357 Merrywood Dr., Los Angeles, CA 90046

R

R. L. Crow Publications, PO Box 262, Penn Valley, CA 95946
Ragged Sky Press, 41 William St., Princeton, NJ 08540-5237
Raritan: A Quarterly Review, Rutgers, 31 Mine St., New Brunswick, NJ 08903
Rattle, 12411 Ventura Blvd., Studio City, CA 91604
The Raven Chronicles, 12346 Sand Point Way N.E., Seattle, WA 98125
Raving Dove, PO Box 28, West Linn, OR 97068
Real, Box 13007-SFA Station, Nacogdoches, TX 75962
Red Bone Press, PO Box 15571, Washington, DC 20003
Red Hen Press, PO Box 3537, Granada Hils, CA 91394
Redactions: Poetry & Poetics, 58 South Main St., Brockport, NY 14420
Redheaded Stepchild, 62 Kilbride Dr., Pinehurst, NC 28374
Redivider, Emerson College, 120 Boylston St., Boston, MA 02116
Reed Magazine, SJSU, English Dept., 1 Washington Sq., San Jose, CA 95192-0090
relief, 2216 Thorne St., Newberg, OR 97132
The Republic of Letters, Apartado 29, Cahuita, 7032, Costa Rica
Rhino, 630 Clinton Place, Evanston, IL 60201-1768
The Right Eyed Deer Press, POB 236, 119 Pine St., Haliburton, ON, Canada K0M 1S0
River Styx, 3547 Olive St., Ste. 107, St. Louis, MO 63103-1014
River Teeth, Ashland University, 401 College Ave., Ashland, OH 44805
Roanoke Review, Roanoke College, 221 College Lane, Salem, VA 24153-3794
roger, Roger Williams University, One Old Ferry Rd., Bristol, RI 02809
The Rome Review, Georgetown Design Group, 1920 N St., NW, Washington, DC 20036
Rougarou, Dept. of English, PO Box 44691, Lafayette, LA 70504-4691
rough copy, 8 Jornada Loop, Santa Fe. NM 87508
Ruminate, 140 N. Roosevelt Ave., Ft. Collins, CO 80521
Rusty Truck, 327 Kathy Lane, Poplar Bluff, MO 63901
Ryga, 7000 College Way, Vernon, BC V1B 2N5 Canada

S

Salamander, Suffolk University, English Dept., 41 Temple St., Boston, MA 02114-4280
Santa Monica Review, 29051 Hilltop Drive, Silverado, CA 92676
The Saranac Review, Plattsburgh State Univ., 101 Broad St., Plattsburgh, NY 12901-2681
Scapegoat Review, 85-101 N. 3rd St., #508, Brooklyn, NY 11211
Scarab, 1212 Eastern Drive, Urbana IL 61801
Schuylkill Valley Journal, 240 Gold Hills Rd., Havertown, PA 19083
Scopcraft Press, PO Box 1091, Portales, NM 88130-1091
Scribendi, 1 University of New Mexico, Albuquerque, NM 87131-0001
Seems, Lakeland College, PO Box 359, Sheboygan, WI 53082-0359
Seven Circle Press, 6047 NE 61st St., Seattle, WA 98115
Seven Corners, 206 W. Shelbourne Dr., Apt. B, Normal, IL 61761
Sewanee Review, University of the South, 735 University Ave., Sewanee, TN 37383
Shadow Archer Press, 15 Brookdale Ave., Greenville, SC 29607
Shenandoah, Mattingly House, Washington and Lee Univ., Lexington, VA 24450-2116
The Shine Journal, PO Box 80054, Springfield, MA 01138
The Shop, Skeagh, Schull, Co. Cork, Ireland
Silenced Press, 449 Vermont Place, Columbus, OH 43201
Silver Boomer Books, 3301 South 14th St., Ste. 16—PMB 134, Abilene, TX 79605
Silverfish Review Press, PO Box 3541, Eugene, OR 97403
Siren Song Publishing, 2331 Avenue Beaconsfield, Montreal, Quebec H4A 2G9, Canada
Sixers Review, 86-13 Eldert Lane, Woodhaven, NY 11421
Sixth Finch, 95 Carolina Ave., #2, Jamaica Plain, MA 02130

Skyline Publications, PO Box 295, Stormville, NY 12582
Sleet Magazine, 1846 Bohland Ave., St. Paul, MN 55116
Slice, PO Box 150029, Brooklyn, NY 11215
Slipstream, Box 2071, Niagara Falls, NY 14301
Slow Trains, PO Box 4741, Englewood, CO 80155
Small Beer Press, 150 Pleasant St., Ste. 306, Easthampton, MA 010127-1264
Smartish Pace, PO Box 22161, Baltimore, MD 21203
So to Speak, 4400 University Dr., MS2C5, Fairfax, VA 22030-4444
Song of the San Joaquin Quarterly, PO Box 1161, Modesto, CA 95353-1161
Sonora Review, English Dept., University of Arizona, Tucson AZ 85721
Soundings Review, PO Box 639, Freeland, WA 98249
South Loop Review, Columbia College, 600 South Michigan Ave., Chicago, IL 60605
Southeast Missouri State University Press, MS 2650, 1 University Place, Cape Giradeau, MO 63701
The Southeast Review, English Dept., Florida State Univ., Tallahassee, FL 32306
Southern Humanities Review, 9088 Haley Center, Auburn University, Auburn, AL 36849-5052
Southern Indiana Review, 8600 University Blvd., Evansville, IN 47712
Southern Illinois University Press, 1915 University Press Dr., Carbondale, IL 62902
Southern Poetry Review, 11935 Abercorn St., Savannah, Georgia 31419-1997
The Southern Review, Louisiana State University, Baton Rouge, LA 70803
Southern Women's Review, 1125 22nd St., So., Ste. 5, Birmingham, AL 35205
Southwest Review, So. Methodist University, PO Box 750374, Dallas, TX 75275-0374
Sou'wester, Southern Illinois University, Box 1438, Edwardsville, IL 62026-1438
Specs, Rollins College, English Dept., 1000 Holt Ave., Winter Park, FL 32789-4499
Spoon River Poetry Review, Illinois State Univ., Campus Box 4241, Normal, IL 61790
Squid Quarterly, 810 Myrtle St., Hattiesburg, MS 39401
St. Petersburg Review, Box 2888, Concord, NH 03302
Star Cloud Press, 6137 East Mescal St., Scottsdale, AZ 85254-5418
Stone Canoe Journal, 700 University Ave., Ste. 326, Syracuse, NY 13244-2530
Storyglossia, 1004 Commercial Ave., #1110, Anacortes, WA 98221
The Storyteller, 2441 Washington Rd., Maynard, AR 72444
Stymie, 1965 Briarfield Dr., Lake St. Louis, MO 63367
Sugar House Review, PO Box 17091, Salt Lake City, UT 84117
The Summerset Review, 25 Summerset Dr., Smithtown, NY 11787
The Sun, 107 North Roberson St., Chapel Hill, NC 27516
sunnyoutside, PO Box 911, Buffalo, NY 14207
Sustone Magazine, 343 No. 300 West, Salt Lake City, UT 84103
Swarthmore Literary Review, c/o diFeliciantonio, 500 College Ave., Swarthmore, PA 19081
Sweet: A Literary Confection, 110 Holly Tree Lane, Brandon, FL 33511
Sycamore Review, Purdue University, 500 Oval Dr., West Lafayette, IN 47907

T

Tampa Review, 401 W. Kennedy Blvd., Tampa, FL 33606
The Taylor Trust, PO Box 903456, Palmdale, CA 93550-3456
10 X 3 Plus, 1077 Windsor Ave., Morgantown, WV 26505
Terrain.org: A Journal of the Built & Natural Environments, 10367 East Sixto Lane, Tucson, AZ 85747
Thieves Jargon, 23-11 41st St., #2R, Astoria, NY 11105
Think Journal, PO Box 454, Downingtown, PA 19335
Third Coast, Western Michigan University, Kalamazoo, MI 49008
13 Miles from Cleveland, 6846 Chaffee Court, Brecksville, OH 44141
Threepenny Review, PO Box 9131, Berkeley, CA 94709
Tiferet, 211 Dyrden Rd., Bernardsville, NJ 07924
Tightrope Books, 602 Markham St., Toronto, ON M6G 2L8, Canada
Tikkun Magazine, 2342 Shattuck Ave., Ste. 1200, Berkeley, CA 94704
Timber Creek Review, 8969 UNCG Sta., Greensboro, NC 27413
Tin House, PMB 280, 320 7th Ave., Brooklyn, NY 11215
Tipton Poetry Journal, PO Box 804, Zionsville, IN 46077
Toasted Cheese Literary Journal, 44 East 13th Ave., #402, Vancouver V5T 4K7, BC
Toadlily Press, PO Box 2, Chappaqua, NY 10514

Tonopah Review, 340 Redwood Ave., Corte Madera, CA 94425
Top Pen Press, PO Box 223436, Hollywood, FL 33022
TotalRecall Publications, 1103 Middlecreek, Friendswood, TX 77546
Traprock Books, 1330 E. 25th Ave., Eugene, OR 97403
Trinacria, 220 Ninth St., Brooklyn, NY 11215-3902
TriQuarterly, Northwestern Univ. Press, 629 Noyes St., Evanston, IL 60208-4210
Tupelo Press, PO 1767, North Adams, MA 01247
Turtle Ink Press, 5807 Germantown Ave., 1R, Philadelphia, PA 19144
The Tusculum Review, PO Box 5113, 60 Shiloh Rd., Greenville, TN 37743

U

U.S. 1 Poets' Cooperative, U.S. 1 Worksheets, PO Box 127, Kingston, NY 08528-0127
Umbrella, 102 Wesst 75th St., Ste. 54, New York, NY 10023-1907
Underground Voices, PO Box 931671, Los Angeles, CA 90093
The University of Georgia Press, 330 Research Dr., Athens, GA 30602-4901
University of Massachusetts Press, PO Box 429, Amherst, MA 01004
University of Pittsburgh Press, 3400 Forbes Ave., Pittsburgh, PA 15260
University Press of New England, 1 Court St., Lebanon, NH 03766
UNO Press, 2700 Lakeshore Dr., Educ. Bldg. #210, New Orleans. LA 70148
upstreet, PO Box 105, Richmond MA 01254

V

Vacteam, 5710 S. Kimbark Ave., #3, Chicago, IL 60637
Valley Voices, State University, Itta Bena, MS 38941
Vallum, PO Box 598 Victoria Stn, Montreal, Quebec, H3Z 2Y6 Canada
Valparaiso Poetry Review, English Dept., Valparaiso Univ., Valparaiso, IN 46383
Vanilla Heart Publishing, 10121 Evergreen Way, Bldg. 25, Ste. 156, Everett, WA 98204
Verna Press, 3828 Dryades St., New Orleans, LA 70115
Versal, Postbus 3865, 1001 AR Amsterdam, The Netherlands
Vestal Review, 2609 Dartmouth Dr., Vestal, NY 13850
Virgogray Press, 2103 Nogales Trail, Austin TX 78744
The Virginia Quarterly Review, 1 West Range, PO Box 400223, Charlottesville, VA 22904
vis a tergo, 24413 Madison St., Torrance, CA 90505
VoiceCatcher, PO Box 6064, Portland, OR 97228
vox poetica, 160 Summit St., Englewood, NJ 07631

W

Waccamaw, PO Box 261954, Conway, SC 29528-6054
Wag's Revue, 2865 W. Lyndale St., Chicago, IL 60647
Water~Stone Review, MS A1730, 1536 Hewitt Ave., St. Paul, MN 55104-1284
Wave Books, 1938 Fairview Avenue East, St. 201, Seattle, WA 98102
Wayne State University Press, 4809 Woodward Ave., Detroit, MI 48201-1309
West Branch, Stadler Center for Poetry, Bucknell University, Lewisburg, PA 17837
West End Press, PO Box 27334, Albuquerque, NM 87125
West Virginia University Press, PO Box 6295, Morgantown, WV 26506-6295
The Westchester Review,, Box 246H, Scarsdale, NY 10583
The Weston Magazine Group, 21 Jesup Rd., Westport, CT 06880
What Books Press, 23371 Mulholland Dr., #118, Los Angeles, CA 91364
Wheat Field Press, PO Box 20237, Keizer, OR 97307
Whiskey Island Magazine, 2121 Euclid Ave., Cleveland, OH 44115-2214
Whispering Angel Books, 2416 W. Victory Blvd., #234, Burbank, CA 91506
White Pine Press, PO Box 236, Buffalo, NY 14201

Wild Apples, PO Box 171, Harvard, MA 01451
Wilderness House Literary Review, 145 Foster St., Littleton, MA 01460
Willow Springs, 501 N. Riverpoint Blvd., Ste 425, Spokane, WA 99202
Wings Press, 627 E. Guenther, San Antonio, TX 78210
Wisdom Publications, 199 Elm St., Somerville, MA 02144
Wising Up Press, PO Box 2122, Decatur, GA 30031-2122
Witness, Black Mountain Institute, Box 455085, Las Vegas, NV 89154-5085
The Worcester Review, Keene State College, 229 Main St., Keene, NH 03435-4000
Word Catalyst Magazine, 57 Waldron Rd., Lempster, NH 03605
Word Walker Press, 1125½ E. California Ave., Glendale, CA 91206
WordHustler, PO Box 27338, Los Angeles, CA 90027-0338
Workers Write!, PO Box 250382, Plano, TX 75025-0382
World Audience Publishers, 303 Park Ave. So., #1440, New York, NY 10010-3657
World Literature Today, 630 Parrington Oval, Ste. 110, Norman, OK 73019-4033
Write Bloody Publishing, #609, 235 East Broadway, Long Beach, CA 90802
Writecorner Press, PO Box 140310, Gainesville, FL 32614-0310
The Writers Studio, 78 Charles St., #2r, New York, NY 10014

Y

The Yale Review, Yale University, PO Box 208243, New Haven, CT 06520

Z

Zahir Publishing, 315 S. Coast Highway 101, Ste. U8, Encinitas, CA 92024
Zero Ducats Collective, 409 E. Pine, #3, Missoula, MT 59802
Zoetrope: All Story, 916 Kearny St., San Francisco, CA 94133
Zone 3, APSU Box 4565, Clarksville, TN 37044
ZYZZYVA, PO Box 590069, San Francisco, CA 94159-0069

THE PUSHCART PRIZE FELLOWSHIPS

The Pushcart Prize Fellowships Inc., a 501 (c) (3) nonprofit corporation, is the endowment for The Pushcart Prize. "Members" donated up to $249 each. "Sponsors" gave between $250 and $999. "Benefactors" donated from $1000 to $4,999. "Patrons" donated $5,000 and more. We are very grateful for these donations. Gifts of any amount are welcome. For information write to the Fellowships at PO Box 380, Wainscott, NY 11975.

Siv Cedering
Dan Chaon & Sheila Schwartz
James Charlton
Andrei Codrescu
Tracy Crow
Dana Literary Society
Carol de Gramont
Karl Elder
Donald Finkel
Ben and Sharon Fountain
Alan and Karen Furst
John Gill
Robert Giron
Doris Grumbach & Sybil Pike
Gwen Head
The Healing Muse
Robin Hemley
Jane Hirshfield
Helen H. Houghton

Joseph Hurka
Janklow & Nesbit Asso.
Edmund Keeley
Thomas E. Kennedy
Sydney Lea
Gerald Locklin
Thomas Lux
Markowitz, Fenelon and Bank
Elizabeth McKenzie
McSweeney's
Joan Murray
Barbara and Warren Phillips
Hilda Raz
Mary Carlton Swope
Julia Wendell
Philip White
Eleanor Wilner
David Wittman
Richard Wyatt & Irene Eilers

MEMBERS

Anonymous (3)
Betty Adcock
Agni
Carolyn Alessio
Dick Allen
Russell Allen
Henry H. Alley
Lisa Alvarez
Jan Lee Ande
Ralph Angel
Antietam Review
Ruth Appelhof
Philip and Marjorie Appleman
Linda Aschbrenner
Renee Ashley
Ausable Press
David Baker
Catherine Barnett
Dorothy Barresi
Barrow Street Press
Jill Bart
Ellen Bass
Judith Baumel
Ann Beattie
Madison Smartt Bell
Beloit Poetry Journal
Pinckney Benedict
Karen Bender
Andre Bernard
Christopher Bernard
Wendell Berry
Linda Bierds
Stacy Bierlein
Bitter Oleander Press
Mark Blaeuer

Blue Lights Press
Carol Bly
BOA Editions
Deborah Bogen
Susan Bono
Anthony Brandt
James Breeden
Rosellen Brown
Jane Brox
Andrea Hollander Budy
E. S. Bumas
Richard Burgin
Skylar H. Burris
David Caliguiuri
Kathy Callaway
Janine Canan
Henry Carlile
Fran Castan
Chelsea Associates
Marianne Cherry
Phillis M. Choyke
Suzanne Cleary
Martha Collins
Ted Conklin
Joan Connor
John Copenhaven
Dan Corrie
Tricia Currans-Sheehan
Jim Daniels
Thadious Davis
Maija Devine
Sharon Dilworth
Edward J. DiMaio
Kent Dixon
John Duncklee

Elaine Edelman
Renee Edison & Don Kaplan
Nancy Edwards
M.D. Elevitch
Failbetter.com
Irvin Faust
Tom Filer
Susan Firer
Nick Flynn
Stakey Flythe Jr.
Peter Fogo
Linda N. Foster
Fugue
Alice Fulton
Eugene K. Garber
Frank X. Gaspar
A Gathering of the Tribes
Reginald Gibbons
Emily Fox Gordon
Philip Graham
Eamon Grennan
Lee Meitzen Grue
Habit of Rainy Nights
Rachel Hadas
Susan Hahn
Meredith Hall
Harp Strings
Jeffrey Harrison
Lois Marie Harrod
Healing Muse
Alex Henderson
Lily Henderson
Daniel Henry
Neva Herington
Lou Hertz
William Heyen
Bob Hicok
R. C. Hildebrandt
Kathleen Hill
Jane Hirshfield
Edward Hoagland
Daniel Hoffman
Doug Holder
Richard Holinger
Rochelle L. Holt
Richard M. Huber
Brigid Hughes
Lynne Hugo
Illya's Honey
Susan Indigo
Mark Irwin
Beverly A. Jackson
Richard Jackson
Christian Jara
David Jauss
Marilyn Johnston
Alice Jones

Journal of New Jersey Poets
Robert Kalich
Julia Kasdorf
Miriam Poli Katsikis
Meg Kearney
Celine Keating
Brigit Kelly
John Kistner
Judith Kitchen
Stephen Kopel
Peter Krass
David Kresh
Maxine Kumin
Valerie Laken
Babs Lakey
Maxine Landis
Lane Larson
Dorianne Laux & Joseph Millar
Sydney Lea
Donald Lev
Dana Levin
Gerald Locklin
Rachel Loden
Radomir Luza, Jr.
William Lychack
Annette Lynch
Elzabeth MacKierman
Elizabeth Macklin
Leah Maines
Mark Manalang
Norma Marder
Jack Marshall
Michael Martone
Tara L. Masih
Dan Masterson
Peter Matthiessen
Alice Mattison
Tracy Mayor
Robert McBrearty
Jane McCafferty
Rebecca McClanahan
Bob McCrane
Jo McDougall
Sandy McIntosh
James McKean
Roberta Mendel
Didi Menendez
Barbara Milton
Alexander Mindt
Mississippi Review
Martin Mitchell
Roger Mitchell
Jewell Mogan
Patricia Monaghan
Rick Moody
Jim Moore
James Morse

William Mulvihill
Nami Mun
Carol Muske-Dukes
Edward Mycue
Deirdre Neilen
W. Dale Nelson
Jean Nordhaus
Ontario Review Foundation
Daniel Orozco
Other Voices
Pamela Painter
Paris Review
Alan Michael Parker
Ellen Parker
Veronica Patterson
David Pearce, M.D.
Robert Phillips
Donald Platt
Valerie Polichar
Pool
Jeffrey & Priscilla Potter
Marcia Preston
Eric Puchner
Tony Quagliano
Barbara Quinn
Belle Randall
Martha Rhodes
Nancy Richard
Stacey Richter
James Reiss
Katrina Roberts
Judith R. Robinson
Jessica Roeder
Martin Rosner
Kay Ryan
Sy Safransky
Brian Salchert
James Salter
Sherod Santos
R.A. Sasaki
Valerie Sayers
Maxine Scates
Alice Schell
Dennis & Loretta Schmitz
Helen Schulman
Philip Schultz
Shenandoah
Peggy Shinner
Vivian Shipley
Joan Silver
Skyline

John E. Smelcer
Raymond J. Smith
Philip St. Clair
Lorraine Standish
Maureen Stanton
Michael Steinberg
Sybil Steinberg
Jody Stewart
Barbara Stone
Storyteller Magazine
Bill & Pat Strachan
Julie Suk
Sun Publishing
Sweet Annie Press
Katherine Taylor
Pamela Taylor
Susan Terris
Marcelle Thiébaux
Robert Thomas
Andrew Tonkovich
Juanita Torrence-Thompson
William Trowbridge
Martin Tucker
Victoria Valentine
Tino Villanueva
William & Jeanne Wagner
BJ Ward
Susan Oard Warner
Rosanna Warren
Margareta Waterman
Michael Waters
Sandi Weinberg
Andrew Weinstein
Jason Wesco
West Meadow Press
Susan Wheeler
Dara Wier
Ellen Wilbur
Galen Williams
Marie Sheppard Williams
Eleanor Wilner
Irene K. Wilson
Steven Wingate
Sandra Wisenberg
Wings Press
Robert W. Witt
Margo Wizansky
Matt Yurdana
Christina Zawadiwsky
Sander Zulauf
ZYZZYVA

CONTRIBUTORS' NOTES

L.S. ASEKOFF's fourth poetry collection, *Freedom Hill*, is due soon from TriQuarterly Books. Other books are available from North Star and Orchises.

CHARLES BAXTER is the author of five novels and four books of stories. His new and selected stories will be published in 2011.

ADAM BRIGHT lives in Boulder, Colorado. He is working on an essay about actors who appear in TV commercials.

LUCIE BROCK-BROIDO has published three books of poetry with Knopf. She directs the Poetry MFA Program at Columbia University.

COLIN CHENEY's debut collection, *Here Be Monsters*, a winner of the 2009 National Poetry Series Open Competition, was published in 2010 by the University of Georgia Press.

MARILYN CHIN was born in Hong Kong and raised in Portland, Oregon. Her poetry collections include *Rhapsody In Plain Yellow* (W.W. Norton, 2002). Her novel, *Revenge of the Mooncake Vixen*, is just out.

MICHAEL COLLIER is director of The Bread Loaf Writers' Conference. His most recent book is *Dark Wild Realm* (Houghton Mifflin, 2006).

ANTHONY DOERR's work has been translated into eleven languages and won awards including the Rome Prize, the Barnes & Noble Discover Prize, a Guggenheim, an O'Henry and Pushcart Prizes. He lives in Boise, Idaho.

SHARON DOLIN's *Burn and Dodge* won the 2007 Donald Hall Prize in Poetry (University of Pittsburgh Press). She lives in New York.

STEPHEN DUNN is the author of the forthcoming *Here and Now* (Norton, 2011). In 2001 he was awarded the Pulitzer Prize for his *Different Hours*.

TONY EARLEY is the author of four books, including the novels *Jim The Boy* and *The Blue Star*. He is a winner of the National Magazine Award for Fiction and lives in Nashville where he teaches at Vanderbilt University.

NANCY EIMERS's fourth poetry collection, *OZ*, is due out soon from Carnegie Mellon. She lives in Kalamazoo.

THOMAS SAYERS ELLIS is both a photographer and a poet. His *Skin Inc.* is just out from Graywolf Press.

SARAH EINSTEIN is an MFA candidate at West Virginia University whose work has appeared previously in *Whitefish Review*, *Fringe* and *Pank*.

SETH FRIED's stories have appeared in *McSweeney's*, *The Missouri Review*, *Tin House* and elsewhere. He lives in Toledo, Ohio.

JOANNA FUHRMAN's most recent poetry collection, *Pageant*, was published by Alice James Books. She teaches at Rutgers and is reading series curator for the Saint Mark's Poetry Project in New York.

WILLIAM GIRALDI's first book, *Busy Monsters*, is forthcoming from W.W. Norton Co. He teaches at Boston University and is a senior editor at *Agni*.

LOUISE GLÜCK's most recent collection, *A Village Life*, was published in 2009 by Farrar, Straus & Giroux. She lives in Cambridge, Massachusetts.

LINDA GREGERSON's *Magnetic North* was a finalist for the 2007 National Book Award. She has received many honors and teaches at the University of Michigan.

JENNIFER GROTZ's *The Needle* is forthcoming from Houghton Mifflin. She teaches at the University of Rochester and is assistant director of the Bread Loaf Writer's Conference.

JEFFREY HAMMOND teaches at St. Mary's College of Maryland. He is the author of three previous non-fiction books and won a Pushcart Prize, the Carter Prize from *Shenandoah* and the *Editor's Prize* from *The Missouri Review*.

TERRANCE HAYES is the author of *Lighthead* (Penguin, 2010). He lives in Pittsburgh.

BOB HICOK's *This Clumsy Living* (University of Pittsburgh Press) won the 2008 Bobbitt Prize from the Library of Congress. He lives in Blacksburg, Virginia.

JEN HIRT is the author of the memoir *Under Glass: The Girl With A Thousand Christmas Trees*. She holds an MFA from the University of Idaho.

TONY HOAGLAND teaches at the University of Houston. He is the author of a book of essays and four poetry collections.

ELLIOTT HOLT's stories have appeared in *Guernica*, *Bellevue Literary Review* and elsewhere. She has an MFA from Brooklyn College and lives in Brooklyn, New York.

CAITLIN HORROCKS lives in Grand Rapids, Michigan. Her first short story collection, *This Is Not Your City*, is forthcoming from Sarabande.

MARY-BETH HUGHES is the author of the story collection *Double Happiness*, just out from Grove/Atlantic.

RODNEY JONES won the 2007 Kingsley Tufts Prize and the 1990 National Book Critics Circle Poetry award. He teaches at Southern Illinois State University in Carbondale.

LAURA KASISCHKE's new collection of poetry is due out soon from Copper Canyon Press. She won a Guggenheim Fellowship in 2009.

MOHJA KAHF was born in Damascus, Syria and teaches comparative literature at the University of Arkansas. Her novel *The Girl In The Tangerine Scarf* was a *Booklist* Reading Group favorite in 2007.

BRIGIT PEGEEN KELLY's *The Orchard* was just published by BOA Editions. She teaches at the University of Illinois.

HARI KUNZRU is the author of three novels and was included in *Granta*'s Best of Young British Novelists. He lives in New York City.

AMY LEACH lives in Chicago. She is writing a book about plants, animals and stars.

PHILIP LEVINE won the 1995 Pulitzer Prize in poetry for *The Simple Truth*. His latest book is *News of The World* (Knopf, 2009).

TIMOTHY LIU's *Bending the Mind Around The Dream's Blown Fuse*, was recently published. He lives in New York City.

ANTHONY MARRA is in the MFA program at the Iowa Writer's Workshop. "Chechnya" is his first published story.

GAIL MAZUR is the author, most recently, of *Zeppo's First Wife: New & Selected Poems* (2006). She has been a finalist for the National Book Award and The *Los Angeles Times* Book Prize.

SUSAN McCALLUM-SMITH was born in Glasgow, Scotland and worked in the international fashion industry before becoming a freelance editor and reviewer. Her short story collection, *Slipping the Moorings*, was published by Entasis Press in 2009.

LINDA McCULLOUGH MOORE is the author of *The Distance Between* (Soho Press). A short story collection is ready for publication.

JOE MENO is the author of five novels and two short story collections. He is the winner of the Nelson Algren Award and a Pushcart Prize.

MARTIN MORAN lives in New York, where he works as an actor. His memoir, *The Tricky Part* (Beacon, 2005), won a Lambda Literary Award. His solo play of the same title won an Obie.

PAUL MULDOON's eleventh collection of poems, *Maggot*, was published in 2010. He is Chair of the Lewis Center for the Arts at Princeton University.

SIGRID NUNEZ's novel, *Salvation City*, is just out from Riverhead Books. Her memoir about Susan Sontag will be published soon.

WILLIAM OLSEN has published three collections from TriQuarterly Books, most recently *Avenue of Vanishing* (2007). He teaches at Western Michigan University and Vermont College.

SUSAN PERABO is writer-in-residence at Dickinson College. She is the author of the story collection *Who I Was Supposed to Be*, and a novel, *The Broken Places*.

LIA PURPURA's essay collection, *On Looking*, was a finalist for the National Book Critics Circle Award. Her poetry collection, *King Baby*, won the Beatrice Hawley Award from Alice James Press.

AMANDA REA lives in Colorado where she is at work on a novel. She has appeared in *The Kenyon Review*, *Iowa Review*, *Indiana Review*, *Green Mountains Review* and elsewhere. This is her first published essay.

JAY ROGOFF has authored three books of poetry. His next, *The Code Of The Terpsichore*, is due out soon from LSU Press.

BARNEY ROSSET is the legendary founder of Grove Press. He lives in New York.

JESS ROW's new story collection is *Nobody Ever Gets Lost* (2011). He won a previous Pushcart Prize and an O'Henry. He lives in Princeton, New Jersey.

PHILIP SCHULTZ won the 2008 Pulitzer Prize in poetry. His charming dog is named "Penelope" and he runs The Writer's Studio.

PATTY SEYBURN's most recent poetry collection is *Hilarity*. She is on the English faculty of California State University, Long Beach.

RAVI SHANKAR is associate professor and poet-in-residence at Central Connecticut State University. He is founding editor of *Drunken Boat* and author of *Instrumentality* (Cherry Grove) and two chapbooks.

ALAN SHAPIRO's *Old War* was published in 2008 by Houghton Mifflin. He lives in Chapel Hill, North Carolina.

CHERYL STRAYED's memoir *Wild* is just out from Knopf. "Munro Country" appears in *Mentors, Muses and Monsters: 30 Writers On the People Who Changed Their Lives*, edited by Elizabeth Benedict (Free Press).

JENNIFER K. SWEENEY is the author of two poetry collections—most recently, *How To Live On Bread and Music* (Perugia Press, 2009), winner of the James Laughlin Award and the Perugia Press Prize. She lives in Kalamazoo with her husuband, poet Chad Sweeney.

ARTHUR SZE's lastest book of poetry, *The Ginkgo Light*, was selected for the PEN Southwest Book Award for Poetry. He lives in Santa Fe, New Mexico.

EMILY TODER is a translator, letterpress printer and native New Yorker residing in Northampton, Massachusetts. Work is due out soon from Tarpaulin Sky Press and Minutes Books.

CHASE TWICHELL's *Horses Where the Answers Should Have Been: New & Selected Poems* was published in 2001 by Copper Canyon Press.

DEB OLIN UNFERTH is the author of the novel, *Vacation*, and the story collection *Minor Robberies*, both from McSweeney's. Her memoir, *Revolution*, is due soon from Holt.

JEAN VALENTINE is the current State Poet of New York. She is the author of nine poetry collections and won the 2004 National Book Award for Poetry.

VALERIE VOGRIN is prose editor of *Sou'wester* and author of the novel *Shebang* (University Press of Mississippi, 2004). Her stories have appeared in *Natural Bridge*, *Black Warrior Review* and elsewhere.

ROSANNA WARREN is University Professor at Boston University and the author of four books of poetry. She is a past co-editor of poetry for the Pushcart Prize.

MARC WATKINS is the winner of the 2008 *Boulevard* magazine short fiction contest for emerging writers. He teaches at Texas State University, San Marcos.

C.K. WILLIAMS won the National Book Critics Circle award, the National Book Award and the Pulitzer Prize. He lives in Paris, and Princeton, New Jersey.

DAVID WOJAHN's *Interrogation Palace: New and Selected Poems, 1982–2004* was published by the University of Pittsburgh Press in 2006. He lives in Henrico, Virginia.

INDEX

The following is a listing in alphabetical order by author's last name of works reprinted in the *Pushcart Prize* editions since 1976.

567

568

572

575

576

578

582

583

586

587

594